John Augustus Spalding

Illustrated Popular Biography of Connecticut

John Augustus Spalding

Illustrated Popular Biography of Connecticut

ISBN/EAN: 9783337098315

Printed in Europe, USA, Canada, Australia, Japan

Cover: Foto ©Raphael Reischuk / pixelio.de

More available books at **www.hansebooks.com**

POPULAR BIOGRAPHY

OF

CONNECTICUT

COMPILED AND PUBLISHED BY J. A. SPALDING

HARTFORD, CONN.
PRESS OF THE CASE, LOCKWOOD & BRAINARD COMPANY
1891

A SECTION OF BUSHNELL PARK, HARTFORD, WITH THE STATE CAPITOL AND MEMORIAL ARCH.

INTRODUCTION.

IN presenting to the public this new contribution to the State literature of Connecticut, the author appreciates the fact that various and differing standards will be adopted by both its casual and its careful readers in forming their opinions of its merits; hence he desires in the outset to offer a few thoughts which appear to him to be essential to a correct understanding of the work, and particularly of its success as an accomplishment of a purpose. The critic who views it solely from a literary and artistic standpoint, and reaches his conclusions from such an observation, will be likely not only to do its author an injustice, but to lose sight altogether of some of the best and it is believed the most praiseworthy features of the book. It may be said, too, that whoever has made up his mind in advance that a biographical work which includes but six or seven hundred subjects must exhaust the field and probably embraces everybody of any note whatever within the borders of the State, is doomed to a large disappointment. And the few — perhaps it may prove the many — who expect here, as in most other biographical works, to find simply a collection of governors, and United States senators, and college professors, and gentlemen distinguished for very rare and profound attainments of one sort or another, will find that this is not the work they have expected it to be. In a word, whatever reader forgets or overlooks the Popular feature of this volume will need to be set right in that respect before he can enjoy or even understand, much less pass intelligent judgment upon, its contents.

The inception of this work is indirectly attributable to the annoyance which its author has experienced in his previous daily newspaper work, through the poverty of biographical information obtainable from public sources concerning most of the fairly prominent citizens of our State. His recent complete release from journalism afforded him an opportunity for undertaking to supply in some degree the deficiency referred to; and with that end in view this work was begun. It is due to the reader, and to all who have been successfully or unsuccessfully solicited to appear as subjects of this biography, to know something of the methods which have governed its preparation.

During the month of December, 1890, one or two leading citizens of every town and city in Connecticut were interviewed by the writer, and an arrangement was made in conformity with which these gentlemen subsequently submitted a list of names of nearly two thousand persons in all portions of the State, prominent in business or professional life, or who were holding public positions and properly entitled to be included in a popular biography of the Commonwealth. The list thus furnished included State, county, town, and municipal officials, representatives of the judiciary, the clergy, the military, the bar, physicians, merchants, manufacturers, artizans, business men, and whoever else among the inhabitants of the State could be regarded as commendably conspicuous in local or general affairs. To each of the individuals thus designated a personal invitation was extended to appear in the proposed volume, the scope and character of which were fully described and explained. Each recipient of the invitation was requested to furnish data from which an accurate biography of himself might be prepared, and to provide a photograph from which a vignette portrait might be made, for publication in the book. The invitation was a cordial one, but no effort was made to induce anybody to accept it against his wishes. Of the two thousand persons thus invited, about seven hundred accepted unconditionally and furnished the information sought. These seven hundred are included in the present volume. Others desired to appear in the book, but imposed conditions which could not be complied with,—such as that the portrait should be a full-page steel plate; or that the sketch should carry an advertisement of the subject's business; and in one case a gentleman who has a local reputation for writing poetry insisted that sundry specimens of his verse must accompany the sketch. Others declined the invitation for various reasons, principally on the score of "modesty"; and still others would have nothing to do with the matter because they had the impression that somehow they were going to be swindled. Of the entire list fully one-half never responded to the invitation. As will be observed, however, the favorable responses were enough to render the volume sufficiently formidable in size, thoroughly comprehensive in character, and representative of every section of the State. It is a good beginning of an effort the principal object of which has been to familiarize the people of Connecticut with the qualities, the characteristics, the accomplishments, and the features of their fellow-citizens who are or have been leaders and chief burden-bearers in all the active duties of life. To fully accomplish the work thus begun, and similarly present the numerous subjects yet remaining, would require and perhaps may occasion the issue of succeeding volumes.

Reference has already been made incidentally to the Popular feature of this compilation; wherein it differs, as it was intended to differ, essentially, from all other compilations of State biography that have heretofore been made in this country. The term Popular in this connection is intended in its best sense — as opposed to Exclusive. This is not the biography of a class, or a sect, or a party, but of the People. Its subjects are selected from all walks of life; and while the list includes some names of world-wide celebrity, and many of great distinction in the State, it embraces also others unknown to fame beyond perhaps the limits of their own neighborhood, yet among the most honorable and in their sphere the most useful citizens of the Commonwealth. It may be safely stated that there is absolutely no other published collection that includes fifty, even, of the seven hundred sketches which are spread upon these pages; yet for the purposes of a reference book of the citizens of Connecticut, to be consulted for information concerning people who are prominent in their respective spheres of activity, the least of all these could not have been omitted from this volume without abridging its usefulness and impairing its value. The careful reader will doubtless be surprised to discover how many citizens on lower pinnacles of fame than those whose deeds embellish the pages of familiar history or biography, are proven by this record to be the peers of their more celebrated contemporaries. It is believed that this publication will be the means of pleasantly introducing to their fellow-citizens a great many gentlemen of distinguished ability and accomplishments, whose lines of action have been circumscribed by local limits,—whose works are universally recognized, but whose personality has heretofore been comparatively obscure.

Inasmuch as the publication of these sketches was to be made with the authority and approval of their subjects, it has been the intention of the author in every instance to consult individual wishes in their preparation. In some cases only the briefest data were furnished; and the sketches of this class of subjects will be found to be correspondingly brief. Others entered enthusiastically and extensively into the work of supplying information, affording opportunity in many instances for complete and quite elaborate biographies. The results in every case furnish a fair indication of the extent to which facilities have been supplied or withheld by the subjects themselves. The author is under obligation to many gentlemen, whose names and faces appear on the following pages, for their active co-operation with him in his efforts to make this work in the highest possible degree interesting to the reader as well as valuable for reference.

The political entanglements resulting from the State election (or non-election) in November, 1890, have involved many of these biographies, contributing an element of uncertainty as to the political status of some of the subjects which has rendered all reference thereto a matter of considerable delicacy. Wherever allusion has of necessity been made to the political career of members of either the legislative or executive branch of the present State government, or of unsuccessful candidates for such honors, all expression of opinion has been avoided and the record intentionally confined to a statement of facts.

In the production of this volume it has been the aim of the compiler to exhaust every resource for securing absolute accuracy of detail in the matter of biography, and to make its illustrations faithful and creditable. He is conscious of having exerted himself earnestly and honestly to prepare for and place before the public a work of thorough reliability and sterling value. He trusts that the effort will meet popular appreciation and approval.

J. A. SPALDING.

HARTFORD, July, 1891.

INDEX.

BIOGRAPHY OF CONNECTICUT.

HON. MORGAN G. BULKELEY, HARTFORD:
Governor of Connecticut.

Morgan G. Bulkeley was born in East Haddam, in this state, December 26, 1837, and removed to Hartford in 1846, where he obtained his education

M. G. BULKELEY.

at the Center District and High schools. His American ancestor, Rev. Peter Bulkeley, emigrated from England in 1634, settled in Massachusetts, and after a life of much usefulness died in 1659. His son, the Rev. Gershom Bulkeley, prominent in Connecticut colonial history, married the daughter of President Chauncey of Harvard College ; and their son, the Rev. John Bulkeley, became the first minister of Colchester in this state. His grandson Eliphalet was father of John Charles of Colchester, and grandfather of Eliphalet A., whose career is too well known to the older residents of Connecticut to require much presentation here. He became a lawyer, interested himself in politics and finance, was the first president of the Ætna Life Insurance Company of Hartford, assisted in the organization of the republican party of this state, and was its first speaker of the house of representatives. Among his sons was Morgan G., the subject of this biography.

Governor Bulkeley began his business career as bundle-boy in a mercantile house in Brooklyn, N. Y., in 1852. He quickly advanced by merit to be salesman, confidential clerk, and finally partner. Upon the breaking out of the rebellion he went to the front as a private in the Thirteenth New York Regiment, and served during the McClellan Peninsula campaign under General Mansfield, at Suffolk, Va. After his father's death in 1872, he located permanently in Hartford, the better to supervise his enlarged financial interests. He was the prime factor in the organization of the United States

Bank, and became its first president. When the presidency of the Ætna Life Insurance Company became vacant by the retirement of Thomas O. Enders, he transferred his abilities to that position; and the unexampled success which has followed his management of that company's affairs is another tribute to his rare perception and managerial skill.

Mr. Bulkeley inherited his father's love of politics, and naturally became a participant as well as an interested observer in local political affairs. Having made municipal problems a matter of conscientious study, he became councilman, alderman, and finally for eight years mayor of Hartford. During his incumbency of this office he exercised a watchful care over income and expenditure, advocating such measures, irrespectively of partizan considerations, as would advance the interests of the municipality. He was liberal with his private means for the amelioration of the distressed and the comfort and pleasure of the working classes within the city; and it is probable that he distributed in this way every year more than his salary as mayor.

Developing as he did while mayor of Hartford such rare executive ability in civil affairs, it was not singular that Mr. Bulkeley's friends should urge his availability as a candidate for gubernatorial honors. Following this conviction his name was presented before the republican state convention in the fall of 1886; but the movement in favor of Mr. Lounsbury had acquired such momentum that in the interest of harmony Mr. Bulkeley authorized the withdrawal of his name as a candidate, and ardently joined in support of his rival through the succeeding campaign. In August, 1888, at the next state convention of the party, Mr. Bulkeley was nominated for governor by acclamation, and on the following January, 1889, he was inaugurated and took his seat at the capitol. The vigorous administration which followed was characteristic of the man, and will long be remembered as among the most notable within the history of the commonwealth.

At the state election in November, 1890, the first gubernatorial election under the new secret ballot law, results were declared which were not accepted as conclusive by the State officials to whom the election statistics are returnable under the statute, or by the house of representatives. The legislature failing to settle the question of gubernatorial succession by the recognition of a claimant or otherwise as provided by law, it became Governor Bulkeley's duty, under the constitution, to continue to exercise the functions of that office, which he has done and will doubtless continue to do until his successor " shall be duly qualified."

AMOS W. PRENTICE, Norwich: Merchant.

Amos W. Prentice of Norwich was born in Griswold, Dec. 20, 1816, and received a common school education, preparing him for a successful business

and public career. Most of his life has been spent in the city of Norwich, where he has conducted a mercantile business in one place for fifty-seven years. He now holds the presidency of the Norwich Savings Society, with one exception the largest savings institution in Connecticut. He has also been a director in a number of corporations and for half a century has been a prominent manager of financial and industrial interests in the community where he resides. In 1854 he represented the old eighth senatorial district in the senate, his colleagues including James Dixon of Hartford, subsequently United States Senator, Gov. Henry B. Harrison of New Haven, Colonel William H. H. Comstock of New London, the late Gov. Wm. T. Minor of Stamford, and John Boyd of Winsted. In 1859 he was elected mayor of Norwich and in 1877 he represented that town in the legislature. The associates of Mr. Prentice in the house that year included the late Lieut.-Gov. Gallup of Plainfield, H. R. Hayden of East Hartford, Eugene S. Boss of Willimantic, Internal Revenue Collector John I. Hutchinson, Ex-Mayor Wallace A. Miles of Meriden, Lucius G. Goodrich of Simsbury, brother of the bank commissioner, Lynde Harrison of New Haven, and Winthrop M. Wadsworth of Farmington. Ex-Comptroller Chauncey Howard and Henry M. Cleveland were also members that year. Mr. Prentice was on the republican side and exerted an important influence during the session. May 18, 1840, he married Miss Hannah E. Parker, whose death occurred Dec. 24, 1887. Two daughters, Mrs. John Willard and Mrs. A. H. Chase, are

living. Mr. Prentice is a deacon of the Broadway Congregational Church and is regarded with the utmost esteem in the city where he resides.

JAMES GOODWIN BATTERSON, Hartford: President Travelers Insurance Company, and a leading builder and building-stone contractor.

Hon. Jas. G. Batterson was born in Bloomfield Feb. 23, 1823, of stocks which have furnished some of the ablest and most versatile business and professional men of Connecticut. His mother was sister to Major James Goodwin, long president of the Connecticut Mutual Life Insurance Company. His father having established a building-stone business in Litchfield, Conn., he lived there through his boyhood, and was given the ordinary education of the academy, where he fitted for college, but did not enter.

He gained from his father's business a living interest in and knowledge of geology and the qualities of different stones and minerals, which has been a large element in his business success. After leaving school, he went as an apprentice into the publishing and printing house of Mack, Andrus & Woodruff, in Ithaca, N. Y., and served out his time; then returned home and studied law in the office of the noted Judge Seymour. His health, however, rendered a life of confined study impracticable, and he went into business — first with his father, and subsequently (in 1845) independently in the same line, as importer of and dealer in granite and marble, and later removing the headquarters of the business to Hartford. His business has grown into one of the largest in the United States, owning large granite quarries in Westerly, R. I., and using their products in carrying out important contracts for public and private building; among others the magnificent Connecticut Capitol building, the Connecticut Mutual building at Hartford, and the Mutual Life and Equitable Life Insurance Companies' buildings and the Vanderbilt residence, New York. He was the first in this country to use machinery for polishing granite, and has devised many other improvements in his business. He is master of every subsidiary detail of his business and a practical architect and builder of fine taste, as well as expert in mechanical details.

Mr. Batterson in 1863 had been on one of his various tours through Europe and the East, which have made him one of the best informed men of the generation on oriental geography, history, politics, and social life; and returning from Italy, where he had given acute attention to marbles and architecture, passed through England, where the success of the Railway Passengers' Assurance Company, founded a few years before, had demonstrated that accident insurance was practicable — a fact much shadowed by the failures of previous petty attempts in England. Grasping at once the possibilities of the new business, and as a Hartford man feeling the instinctive local capacity for success in the insurance field, he induced a number of other capitalists and active business men to join with him in starting an accident company; $300,000 was paid in as capital, and a charter obtained the same year for insuring against accidents of travel alone. But it was not till the next year, when the charter was amended to allow it to insure against accidents of all kinds, that much business was done. Very few but the promoters expected it to live any length of time, and when in a year or so it became evident that it was to be one of the great business successes of the age, this sudden growth and prosperity came near being more ruinous than its first difficulties; for it inspired such a belief that the accident business was the sure road to wealth that, in the " boom " which followed, a swarm of new companies were organized, and most of the great railroads ejected the Travelers and started accident organizations of their own. A new corporation, the Railway Passengers' Assurance Company, composed of representatives from all the leading accident companies, was formed in the winter of 1866 to consolidate the railway " ticket " business under one management; five years later every one of the others was dead, and the Travelers, as the sole legatee, turned the company into the ticket department of its own organization. Its superiority of brains, money, and incredibly hard work and economy, had enabled it to remain the solitary survivor. Meanwhile, in 1866, it had added a regular life-insurance department, which in the last few years has taken sudden and enormous strides that have placed it among the foremost of New England companies.

Mr. Batterson is a man whom a robust physical frame, and a still more robust, assimilative, and flexible intellect, enable to accomplish an amount and variety of work which fills the ordinary man with wonder and despair. One of his most valuable intellectual qualities is the faculty of instant adjustment to any new piece of work — one of the rarest and most precious of faculties; to him, five minutes' time are good for five minutes' accomplishment whenever taken. He is a formidable debater, a capable actuary, a thorough student of economics, and even a poet.

The amount of solid reading he does would alone tax severely the energies of most men; he keeps abreast of the highest thought of the age, and knows what its leaders are thinking and saying on every subject. He has a large library, of the highest quality in selection. His judgment in art is delicate and just, and his fine collection of pictures covers a remarkable range of schools and subjects. Altogether, few men live a more symmetrical life of business and thought, assimilation and production; and in his combination of vigor and delicacy of mind, of solid judgment and nice taste of appreciation alike of the profoundest thought and the subtlest graces of style, he has few equals.

He might easily have attained high political honors, but he has never coveted them, though his help and advice are eagerly sought and valued. He is, of course, an influential member of several societies for the advancement of learning; holds the degree of M.A. both from Yale and from Williams Colleges (the former given at the suggestion of the late Dr. Bushnell); and the educational interests of Hartford (whose noted High School he built) are indebted to him for powerful service and upbuilding.

JEREMIAH M. ALLEN, HARTFORD: President Hartford Steam Boiler Inspection and Insurance Company.

Jeremiah M. Allen was born in the town of Enfield, May 12, 1833, and was educated at the Westfield Academy in Massachusetts, preparing him for the profession of a mechanical engineer. After finishing his studies, he devoted himself to teaching for four years, spending what time he was able to win from that pursuit in special lines of research and investigation. In 1865, when only 32 years of age, he became the general agent and adjuster of the Merchants Insurance Company of Hartford. Sub-

J. M. ALLEN.

sequently he was appointed to a similar position by the Security Fire Insurance Company of New York and engaged in the business with characteristic earnestness and energy. But the insurance field in which Mr. Allen was to become a pioneer and the most successful of managers, had not at that time commanded more than a cursory examination from American underwriters. The work of personal preparation in his case, however, had been continued with the utmost fidelity, and when the time arrived for him to engage in the enterprise that has occupied his maturest thought and energy, he was amply fitted for the task. Mr. Allen was an accomplished scientist when he became the president of the Hartford Steam Boiler Inspection and Insurance Company in 1867. This company, which has become one of the prominent insurance organizations in New England, was incorporated June 30, 1866, the cash capital being $100,000. The late Enoch C. Roberts of this city was its first president, and retained the position until the beginning of 1867, when Mr. Allen was elected to the presidency, and the company commenced the career of prosperity that has won the admiration of underwriters everywhere. When he first entered the field there might have been reasonable doubts concerning the success of the enterprise. It was new and untried in this country. The ablest talent in special lines was needed for the inauguration even of the first business of the company. In President Allen the man needed most of all for originality and leadership was found, and the work of his life has been one of gratifying success. The history of the great organization of which he is the president is the history of his own business career. Mr. Allen is the president also of the Hartford Board of Trade—an organization that has exercised important influence in business and manufacturing centers in the capital city. He is a member of the board of trustees of the Society for Savings, director in the Security Company, the Connecticut River Banking Company, and the Orient Insurance Company, and one of the trustees of the Hartford Theological Seminary. He is also associate executor and trustee of the large estates left by Messrs. John S. Welles and Newton Case, the two estates aggregating upwards of $1,500,000. These facts indicate more successfully than columns of writing would the position which President Allen holds in a community in which fiduciary trusts are bestowed only upon men of the highest personal integrity and honor. To be thus honored in the city of Hartford is the proudest attainment to be reached in a business life. President Allen was one of the organizers of the Asylum Hill Congregational Church, and is a member of the Connecticut Congregational Club. In personal thought, aim, and life he is one of the most admirable exponents of New England Congregationalism. His scientific attainments have been already indicated in this sketch. The concrete proofs of his scientific knowledge will appear from the fact that he has been for a number of years one of the non-resident lecturers at Sibley College, Cornell University, member of the American Association of Mechanical Engineers, and of the American Association for the Advancement of Science. He is also a member of the American Historical Association at Washington, D. C., the American Academy of Political and Social Science at Philadelphia, and a life member of the Connecticut Historical Society at Hartford. In politics President Allen is a Republican. He has been a member of the court of common council in Hartford, and of the board of water commissioners. For ten years he was actively identified with the management of the American Asylum for the Deaf and Dumb in this city, and is a gentleman of the broadest public spirit. The wife of President Allen was Miss Griswold, daughter of Hermon C. Griswold of Ellington, and the family includes two children.

HON. JAMES NICHOLS, HARTFORD: President National Fire Insurance Company.

President James Nichols was born in Newtown, Dec. 25, 1830, and was educated for the bar. In 1854 he commenced the practice of his profession in

Thompsonville, but removed to Hartford within a few months, and was appointed assistant clerk of the Hartford county superior court. In 1861 he was elected judge of probate in the Hartford district, which embraced the towns of Hartford, Wethersfield, Rocky Hill, West Hartford, Windsor Locks, East Hartford, and Glastonbury. The office was one of great importance and required exceptional ability for the discharge of its duties. Judge Nichols won the admiration of all parties on account of the successful way in which the judicial work of the office was performed. In 1867 he became the adjuster and special agent of the Merchants' Insurance Company of Hartford, and was rapidly promoted by the board of directors. From the outset he manifested especial adaptability for the insurance business. At the time of the great Chicago fire in 1871 Judge Nichols was the secretary of the Merchants and a manager of recognized standing in the insurance community. The Merchants company was not able to recover from the unprecedented disaster at Chicago, and surrendered its charter. The National Fire Insurance Company, which had been incorporated in May, 1869, organized in 1871 with the late Mark Howard as president and Judge Nichols as secretary. When President Howard died four years ago, he was succeeded by the Judge, the latter's ability as an insurance manager entitling him to that promotion. The National has made decided progress under President Nichols, and is one of the ablest and most carefully conducted insurance companies in New England. President Nichols is the vice-president of the Charter Oak National Bank, a director in the Phœnix Life Insurance Company and a trustee in the State Savings Bank. In politics he is a republican. He is a prominent member of the Park church in this city. The wife of Judge Nichols, who is still living, was Miss Isabella M. Starkweather, daughter of Mr. Nathan Starkweather of this city. There is one daughter, Mrs. H. A. Smith of Rochester, N. Y. The life of Judge Nichols has been one of thorough success and honor. He is held in the highest esteem in the city of Hartford, of which he has been a resident since the summer of 1854.

HON. WILLIAM W. BACKUS, NORWICH.

William W. Backus, the son of James and Dorothy Church Chandler Backus of Woodstock, was the sixth of a family of eight children, and at the time of his father's death was but thirteen years of age, — having been born October 22, 1803. His mother was the daughter of Charles Church Chandler, a member of the Windham county bar, and one of the leading lawyers at the bar of the state. His whole life has been spent in Norwich, except part of the year 1819 spent in Marietta, Ohio, in the

W. W. BACKUS.

mercantile establishment of Dudley Woodbridge, Jr. Ill health necessitated his return to Norwich, where, since 1819, he has resided at the home of his ancestors, completing seven generations. His time has been spent mainly in farm operations, causing the old farm, with large additions, to bud and blossom, raising large crops of corn, rye, potatoes, grass, etc.; keeping a large amount of stock — annually fattening one hundred head and buying and selling many more. His losses have been many and his gains considerable — some losses and some gains all the time. An eager student, he worked days and studied nights after going to bed — sometimes into the small hours. His genealogical researches have been tireless, and he has recently published an exhaustive record of the Backus family in a book of about 400 pages, including memoirs, poems, and many other papers of general interest beyond the limits of the family involved. Mr. Backus is a gentleman of large means, and his private charities and public benefactions

illustrate his wisely philanthropic disposition. His recent gift of $75,000 toward the founding of the W. W. Backus hospital in Norwich is an example of his practical sympathy for the unfortunate and distressed. He is now living quietly at his home in Norwich in fairly comfortable health, though bent under the burden of nearly ninety years.

HENRY C. ROBINSON, HARTFORD: Attorney at Law.

Among the members of the legal profession in the city and county of Hartford, there is, perhaps, none who occupies a position nearer the head of the list, in point of personal attainment or the esteem of his contemporaries, than Henry C. Robinson, the subject of this sketch. Mr. Robinson is a native of Hartford, born August 28, 1832, descended on the paternal side from Thomas Robinson, who emigrated from England and settled in Guilford in 1667, and tracing his maternal ancestry in a direct line to

HENRY C. ROBINSON.

William Brewster, the devout elder of the Pilgrim colony which landed at Plymouth in 1620. Mr. Robinson's early education was obtained at the Hartford Grammar School, and in the High School after its union with the Grammar School. From the preparatory course here he entered Yale College in 1849, graduating with honors in the distinguished class of 1853. He at once commenced the study of law in the office of his brother, Lucius F. Robinson, with whom, after his admission to the bar in 1855, he became associated in practice and maintained the relation of partner until the death of L. F. Robinson in 1861. From that time he practiced alone until recently, though taking care of a volume of business scarcely exceeded by any law firm in the state, and maintaining connections as leading counsel for corporations with such vast interests as the Connecticut Mutual Life Insurance Company, the New York, New Haven & Hartford Railroad Company, and others. His son is now in partnership with him, the firm being H. C. & L. F. Robinson. He has also, in the midst of his exacting professional duties, found time to serve his city and the state in various capacities. For two years, 1872–74, he was mayor of Hartford, in 1878 he represented the town of Hartford in the general assembly, and has twice been the candidate of the republican party for gubernatorial honors. In 1866 he accepted from Governor Hawley an appointment as fish commissioner, and through his instrumentality laws were placed on the statute book providing for the condemnation of the pound fishery at the mouth of the Connecticut River, and the discontinuance of that horrible style of fishing. Before these wholesome laws could become fairly operative, under partisan influences they were repealed and others substituted which were of no practical use, as has been proved, in preventing or arresting the destruction of the shad fishery in these waters, in spite of artificial propagation. The first artificial hatch of American shad was made under Mr. Robinson's direction as commissioner, before the Connecticut Legislature, and in presence of the late Professor Agassiz, who was a deeply interested spectator in the experiments and in the legislative contest upon the subject, then in progress. Mr. Robinson also was the commissioner for Connecticut in the Constitutional centennial celebration at Philadelphia in 1889.

Mr. Robinson's connections with the various institutions of his native city are numerous and honorable. Beside being a director in the New York, New Haven & Hartford Railroad and the Hartford & Connecticut Valley Railroad, he sustains the same relation to the Pratt & Whitney Company, the Connecticut Fire Insurance Company, and the Hartford Steam Boiler Inspection and Insurance Company, is a trustee of the Connecticut Trust and Safe Deposit Company, and of the Wadsworth Atheneum, a member of the Hartford Tract Society, vice-president of the Connecticut and the Hartford County Bar Associations, has been president of the Yale Alumni Association of Hartford, is a member of the Hartford Board of Trade, Sons of the Revolution, and of various social organizations. He is an active member of the Second Congregational Church of Hartford, and an officer of the corporation. He is esteemed an important factor in the management of all business, educational, and charitable enterprises, and his counsel is widely sought in affairs thus beyond the range of professional practice. He is a trustee of the Hartford Public High School, for which institution he feels the tender regard of an alumnus and the common pride shared by every resident of the city.

Mr. Robinson has been a republican since the formation of that party. The political offices which he has held have been conferred by the Republicans, though his support has always come in greater or less degree from the best element of all political parties. He was a member of the Chicago convention of 1880. But he is more a patriot than a politician; and his eloquent addresses, whether in the heat of a political campaign or over the graves of the nation's dead at the celebration of

" Memorial Day," savor most of loyalty and devotion to country, subordinating always persons and parties to the commonwealth, and the eternal principles on which the Republic was founded. His admirable oration, delivered in Brooklyn on the occasion of the unveiling of the Putnam equestrian statue in 1887, excited universal commendation as worthy to be classed with the best efforts of Stuart and Deming. Mr. Robinson is an accomplished orator and scholar, and worthily bears the honors successively conferred upon him by his Alma Mater.

In 1862 he married Miss Eliza Niles Trumbull, daughter of John F. Trumbull of Stonington. They have five children: Lucius F., the oldest son, and now his professional associate; Lucy T. (Mrs. Sidney Trowbridge Miller of Detroit), Henry S., John T., and Mary S. It may be mentioned that no less than three matrimonial alliances have connected the Robinson and Trumbull families; H. C. Robinson's brother, the late Lucius F., having married a daughter of Governor Joseph Trumbull, while Dr. J. Hammond Trumbull's wife is a sister of the subject of this sketch.

ISAAC W. BROOKS, Torrington: Banker.

Isaac W. Brooks was born in Goshen, Litchfield County, Nov. 8, 1838, and was educated at the Goshen Academy and Brown University. He was

a member of the legislature from Torrington in 1884, occupying the house chairmanship of the committee on finance. For ten years prior to his removal from Goshen to Torrington he held the townclerkship of the former, being regularly elected by the republicans. He has been the town treasurer of Torrington, treasurer of the savings bank there, and president of the Torrington Water Company. For the past nineteen years he has been engaged in the banking business, being at the head of the banking firm of Brooks Brothers. He was appointed one of the receivers of the Charter Oak Life Insurance Company of Hartford, by Judge Pardee of the supreme court, and has devoted a large amount of time during the past five years to settling the affairs of that institution. Mr. Brooks is a gentleman of superior business capacity and has been eminently successful in his management of financial interests. He is without family.

HON. JOHN TURNER WAIT, Norwich: Advocate, Jurist, Politician, Statesman.

The subject of this sketch presents so marked a character in contemporary state biography, that the author of these papers is reluctant to attempt to give, in the brief space to which he is confined, so condensed a history as these limits require. A full half century in the state's service, with active intellect, earnest purpose, and constant application, has accomplished what can be scarcely more than hinted at in this brief résumé. We must be content, therefore, to refer chronologically to some of the important events in

J. T. WAIT.

the life of this distinguished son of Connecticut, and leave their more elaborate record to the future historian of the commonwealth.

John Turner Wait was born at New London, Conn., August 27, 1811. He received a mercantile training in early life, and, leaving that, passed a year at Bacon Academy, Colchester, and two years at Washington, now Trinity, College, Hartford, pursuing such studies as would benefit him in the profession he proposed to enter. He studied law with Hon. L. F. S. Foster and Hon. Jabez W. Huntington, was admitted to the bar in 1836, and commenced to practice at Norwich, where he has since remained. He was states' attorney for the county of New London in 1842-44 and 1846-54, and has been president of the Bar Association of that county from its organization in 1874 to the present time. He was candidate on the democratic ticket for lieutenant-governor in 1854, 1855, 1856, and 1857, and with his associates on the ticket failed of an election. He was the first elector-at-large as a war democrat in 1864, on the Lincoln and Johnson ticket, the republican state convention nominating him for that position by acclamation. He was a member of the state senate in 1865 and 1866, being chairman of the committee on the judiciary both sessions, also serving the last year as president *pro tempore*. He was a member of the state house of representatives in 1867, 1871, and 1873, serving as speaker the first year, his party nominating him for the place by acclamation, and subsequently declining that position, but acting as chairman of the committee on the judiciary on the part of the house, and serving on other house committees. He was candidate for lieutenant-governor on the republican ticket in 1874, but with his associates on the ticket failed of an election. He received the degree of A.M. from Trinity College in 1851 and

from Yale in 1871, and the degree of LL.D. from Howard University in 1883, and from Trinity College in 1886. In 1876 he was elected to the forty-fourth congress (to fill the vacancy caused by the death of the Hon. H. H. Starkweather), and re-elected to the forty-fifth, forty-sixth, forty-seventh, forty-eighth, and forty-ninth congresses. Subsequently he declined a further renomination. While a member of congress Mr. Wait served on the committee on commerce, on elections, on foreign affairs, and on several subordinate committees; and was also one of the three members of the house associated with three members of the senate, as a joint commission to consider the existing organizations of the signal service, geological survey, coast and geodetic survey, and the hydrographic office of the navy department, with a view to secure greater efficiency in those bureaus.

It may also be stated here, that while a member of the house of representatives in 1883 the compliment was bestowed upon him of an appointment as chairman of the select committee of the house to attend the unveiling of the statue of Professor Joseph Henry at Washington, his associates on that committee being among the most distinguished and prominent members of the congressional body thus represented.

As a member of congress Mr. Wait cared for the interests of his constituents with untiring vigilance and zeal. The extensive industries which give employment to thousand of citizens in the two eastern counties of the state had in him an intelligent and watchful guardian. As the advocate and friend of home industries he steadily opposed in Congress every attempt to impair or weaken the laws under which Connecticut manufacturing and mechanical interests have sprung up and prospered, and gave his support to every measure calculated to advance the commercial and agricultural prospects of the State.

During his ten years of service at Washington he was invariably attentive to the demands made upon his time and consideration by his constituents in matters affecting their private interests. Courteous and frank toward all who approached him, he allied men to him by the strongest personal ties, and became universally popular as a consistent representative and champion of his district and state.

The speeches as well as deeds which marked the congressional career of Mr. Wait, were admirable and effective. Among those best remembered, perhaps, have been his very elaborate and able tariff speech delivered in April, 1884, his speech on the Chinese indemnity fund in 1885, and his earlier effort in 1882, when the South Carolina contested election case of Smalls vs. Tillman was under consideration in the house; also, earlier than either of the preceding, his speech in the election case from

Colorado of Patterson and Belford, delivered December 12, 1877; and that in a similar case from California, of Wigginton and Pacheco, July 6, 1878 — three clear and forcible presentations of evidence; and his effectual effort in 1880 for an appropriation for the New London Navy Yard, finally carrying a bill through giving $20,000 for a building. His address of welcome delivered at Roseland Park in Woodstock on July 4, 1879, has been characterized as "a gem of oratorical expression and patriotic sentiment;" and his published eulogy of the late Hon. LaFayette S. Foster, delivered September 28, 1880, before the superior court at New London on presenting the resolutions adopted by the bar of New London county, bears testimony to the versatility of his genius, and the depth and sincerity of his friendships.

Before entering upon legislative and congressional duties, in the interim between sessions, and since retiring from public service, Mr. Wait's law practice has been extensive and profitable, his commanding influence at the bar insuring him all the business that could possibly be attended to. For forty years he was engaged in nearly all the important cases, civil and criminal, that have come before the New London county courts. His practice has included scores of important cases, not only in his own county and the state, but before the United States courts, all of which he conducted in a masterly manner, and was generally able to bring to a successful and satisfactory termination for his clients. He is still in active practice, in his eightieth year, at his office every day, enjoying good health, with faculties practically unimpaired. During the past year Mr. Wait has made several public addresses, all of which were spoken of in very complimentary terms by the press of Norwich. It is believed that there is, at the time of writing this sketch, not another lawyer in this state still in practice who was contemporary with him in admission to the bar.

It should be mentioned that Mr. Wait is one of the corporators of the "W. W. Backus Hospital" of Norwich, incorporated under the general laws of this state, and organized April 8, 1891, to make available the munificent gift of W. W. Backus and W. A. Slater for the charitable purpose indicated. He is also president of "The Eliza Huntington Memorial Home" for aged and infirm ladies in Norwich, a most worthy institution which was created by the benefactions of the late Jedediah Huntington and wife — the latter having been a sister of Mr. Wait. By his will, of which Mr. Wait was one of the executors, Mr. Huntington provided buildings and grounds for the Home, and $35,000 cash to insure the proper maintenance of the charity. Mr. Wait is and has been connected, officially and otherwise, with many financial institutions and trusts in New London county, to refer in detail to which would require more space than can be given here. Among these may be mentioned his connection, as trustee, with the Norwich Savings Society, as vice-president with the Chelsea Savings Bank, and his directorship of the Uncas National Bank of that city.

From his youth up Mr. Wait has been a liberal contributor to the public press. He was a writer for Greeley's *New Yorker* in 1839, and when in 1840 C. W. Everest (not then Rev.) prepared a beautiful gift volume and engaged John Williams (not then Bishop), Mrs. Sigourney, Wm. Jas. Hamersley, Park Benjamin, James Dixon, Willis Gaylord Clark, Robert Turnbull, Melzar Gardner, and others of the brightest writers of the day to contribute to it, Mr. Wait's contribution was one of the best of the collection. And now, when a special historical event is to be written up or an obituary notice of some prominent citizen furnished, his ready pen is the first one thought of to be called into service.

Mr. Wait is connected by blood with many of the oldest and leading families in eastern Connecticut. On his father's side he is associated with the Griswolds and Marvins of Lyme, while on his mother's side he is a lineal descendant of William Hyde and Thomas Tracy, two of the thirty-five colonists who settled at Norwich in 1659. His family has given many prominent members to the legal profession. His father was long one of the leading lawyers at the bar of New London county, and for several years a judge of the old county court. He was a presidential elector in 1793, and cast his vote for Washington. He represented the town of New London for nineteen sessions in the general assembly of Connecticut. Before the war of the rebellion Mr. Wait was a democrat. The outbreak of the war, however, found him a strong union man, and from that time his political sympathies and efforts have been with and for the republican party. His son, lieutenant Marvin Wait, of the Eighth Connecticut Regiment, served with distinguished courage on the field, and in the gallant charge of that command at Antietam he fell mortally wounded. Enlisting as a private soldier when but eighteen, the story of his heroic fortitude amid the battle will be preserved upon Connecticut's historic page along with that of Nathan Hale, the youthful martyr spy. Though severely wounded in his right arm Lieutenant Wait refused to go to the rear, and seizing his sword with his left hand, encouraged his men to press on, until he fell, riddled by bullets.

In the history of the part Connecticut took in the war of the rebellion, as written by Rev. John M. Morris and W. A. Crofut, and published by Ledyard Bill, a very high compliment was paid to Mr. Wait by the formal dedication of the work to him.

This history contains about nine hundred pages, and gives a record of the splendid services of our state regiments, and the leading officers in the same, with portraits of a large number of the officers. The following is the text of the dedication:

TO
JOHN TURNER WAIT,
LATE SPEAKER
OF THE CONNECTICUT HOUSE OF REPRESENTATIVES;
A PATRIOT
WHOSE ONLY SON FELL IN DEFENCE OF HIS COUNTRY,
AND WHOSE MANY ACTS OF KINDNESS HAVE
ENDEARED HIM TO THE SOLDIERS OF CONNECTICUT:
THIS VOLUME,
THE RECORD OF THEIR SERVICES AND SUFFERINGS,
IS CORDIALLY DEDICATED.

Mr. Wait married, in 1842, Mrs. Elizabeth Harris, who died in 1868. He has not married again. Two daughters are now living; the elder the wife of Col. H. W. R. Hoyt of Greenwich, the younger the wife of Mr. James H. Welles. Those who have known Mr. Wait most intimately in the social relations of life, bear ready testimony to his exceptional worth as a neighbor and friend. He is a gentleman of the old school, courteous, hospitable, and generous to a fault. It is the sincere hope of his fellow-citizens that he may yet survive many years to enjoy the honors which he has earned and which are cheerfully accorded to him by his contemporaries of all political parties throughout his district and the state.

CHARLES S. LANDERS, NEW BRITAIN: Cutlery Manufacturer.

Mr. Landers was born in New Britain June 8, 1846, where he has since continuously resided. He graduated from the New Britain High School in 1860, and entered Williston Seminary, Easthampton, Mass., in December, 1861, preparatory to a college course at Yale, but left in 1862 to engage in the manufacturing business. He has always taken an active interest in politics. Being the son of the Hon. George M. Landers, ex-member of Congress from the First district, he may be said to have been reared for a

C. S. LANDERS.

democrat, but he has always been an enthusiastic republican. He was a member of the republican state central committee for the campaign of 1884, but beyond this he has always declined to accept any public office whatsoever. Mr. Landers is at present manager of the extensive cutlery manufacturing business of Landers, Frary & Clark; also a director in the New Britain National Bank, the Savings Bank of New Britain, and the North & Judd Manufacturing Company. He married in 1869 the only daughter of Mr. Loren F. Judd of New Britain, and has one son, who was a member of the class of '91 at Yale.

HENRY ELMORE RUSSEGUE, M.D., HARTFORD: Physician.

The subject of this sketch was born in Franklin, Norfolk County, Mass., August 11, 1850. He passed his early years in his native town, attending the common schools and afterward Dean Academy.

H. E. RUSSEGUE.

In 1867, he left Franklin to enter mercantile pursuits in Boston, which held his attention until Boston's "big fire," November 9, 1872, when he was thrown out of his business situation. A year subsequent to this, after occupying a position in a wholesale dry-goods house, he was prevailed upon, through the influence of zealous medical friends, to enter the profession of medicine. March 4, 1874, he matriculated at the Boston University School of Medicine, where he took a full graded course of three years' study. At the end of the three years, after a competitive examination, he was appointed to the position of resident physician and surgeon in the Massachusetts Homœopathic Hospital, receiving the diploma of the hospital in March, 1878, and afterwards the diploma of M.D. from Boston University. He married Caroline, the youngest daughter of Hon. Jos. S. Wheelwright of Bangor, Maine, and in November, 1878, settled in South Framingham, Mass. During his residence in this place, he built for himself a large practice, remaining there until 1884, when, upon the death of the celebrated Dr. Taft, he removed to Hartford, where he has since practiced his profession most successfully.

Throughout his professional career Dr. Russegue has taken a high rank, both with his fellow physicians and the public, filling many positions of trust and responsibility. He is a member of the Masonic fraternity and has, for several years, held the position of medical examiner for numerous beneficial insurance associations, among which are the Knights of Honor and the Royal Arcanum.

LEONARD A. DICKINSON, Hartford: Insurance Agent.

General Dickinson, as the subject of this sketch is familiarly known, was born in New Haven, November 5, 1826. Both his parents died when he was

L. A. DICKINSON.

quite young, and he was obliged to earn his living from the early age of nine years, being thus deprived of the means of obtaining a more liberal education than a few months each year as the district school afforded. He has always evinced a great fondness for military affairs, and for fifteen years following 1846 he was a member or officer in various military organizations in his native city, and in Hartford after taking up his residence here. In October, 1861, he enlisted as private in the 12th regiment, Connecticut Volunteers, for active service in the war of the rebellion. He was commissioned captain of Company C November 20, was mustered into service the first of the following January, and participated in all the engagements in which his regiment took a part. In 1864 he was assigned to duty as assistant acting adjutant-general of the second brigade, first division, of the 19th army corps, and in that capacity took part in Sheridan's Shenandoah Valley campaign, until mustered out of service November 21, 1864. He was then commissioned as major of the Twelfth regiment, but declined the appointment. Since his discharge from service in the army he has made Hartford his home, and has been honored with many positions of trust. He was quartermaster three years on Governor Jewell's staff; postmaster of Hartford four years under President Garfield; has been a member of the Connecticut Soldiers' Hospital Board since 1886; and is a trustee of "Fitch's Home for the Soldier." He has held the local agency of the Ætna Insurance Company of Hartford since 1869, in discharge of the duties of which position he is now principally engaged. He was made a free mason in New Haven in 1856. His affiliations in Hartford are with St. John's Lodge, No. 4, in which he has held various offices; with Pythagoras Chapter, No. 17, Royal Arch Masons, of which he was for five years the secretary; with Wolcott Council, No. 1, Royal and Select Masters; and with Washington Commandery, No. 1, Knights Templars. He has received from the Grand Lodge the appointments of grand junior steward and grand marshal, and the electoral offices of grand senior deacon and grand junior warden. He is an active member of St.

Thomas' Episcopal Church of Hartford, and for several years has been the senior warden of that parish.

General Dickinson traces his genealogical descent in an unbroken line from the time of Edward the First of England, in 1272, and in American from Josiah Dickinson, who landed in Boston in 1630. Several of his later ancestors were officers in the revolutionary war, it thus appearing that the military tastes of the subject of this sketch are clearly a matter of inheritance. He is a gentleman of the highest honor and probity, a firm friend, a kind neighbor, and an upright and useful citizen.

HON. JAMES A. HOVEY, Norwich: Ex-Judge Superior Court.

Ex-Judge James A. Hovey of Norwich, who was on the superior court bench in this state from November 13, 1876, until April 29, 1885, and chair-

J. A. HOVEY.

man of the commission appointed to revise the public statutes in 1885, holding the latter position from June 1, 1885, until January, 1888, is one of the ablest jurists which Connecticut has had, and the numerous public honors which have been extended to him have been deserved on account of the character of his public services. The work of Judge Hovey on the revised statutes of 1887 was invaluable. His was the mature mind and experience of the commission and his advice and counsel were in constant demand while the revision was in progress. He was assignee in bankruptcy for New London county under the act of 1841, executive secretary 1842 and 1843 under Governor Chauncey F. Cleveland of Hampton, member of the board of aldermen in Norwich from 1849 until 1853, judge of the New London county court from 1850 until 1854, member of the general assembly in 1859 and in 1886, and mayor of Norwich from 1870 until 1871. His colleagues in the house in 1859 included the Hon. Augustus Brandegee of New London, the Hon. Jeremiah Halsey of Norwich, Colonel W. H. H. Comstock of New London, the late Colonel Henry C. Deming of Hartford, Judge Edward W. Seymour, now of the supreme court, the late O. H. Perry of Fairfield, speaker of the house, A. H. Byington of Norwalk, who attained high distinction as a war correspondent, and the late Daniel Chadwick of Lyme. In the senate were the Hons. Dwight W. Pardee of Hartford and James Phelps of Essex, who have occupied high positions on the bench and in public life. Judge Hovey has been a democrat from the outset and is one of the most honored members of his party in Connecticut. He has been vice-president and trustee of the Chelsea Savings Bank, and trustee of the Norwich Savings Society. He was president of the Uncas bank and the Uncas National Bank of Norwich from 1852 until 1872. The wife of Judge Hovey, who was Miss Lavinia J. Barber, is dead and the only son is also dead. The judge was born at Hampton April 20, 1815, and was educated in the common and private schools of his time. He chose the law as a profession and has met with eminent success. From 1830 until 1842 he was connected with the state militia. His life has been spent in the towns of Hampton, Windham, and Norwich.

- - - - -

HON. A. P. HYDE, HARTFORD: Attorney-at-Law.

Hon. Alvan Pinney Hyde was born in Stafford, March 10, 1825, being the son of Alvan and Sarah Pinney Hyde. His grandfather, Nathaniel Hyde, and father, were success-
ful iron manufacturers at Stafford. The subject of this sketch was prepared for college at Munson Academy and graduated from Yale with honor in 1845. He studied law in the office of the late Hon. Loren P. Waldo of this city, but at that time a distinguished lawyer in Tolland, and at the Yale Law School, being ad- mitted to the bar at Tol-

A. P. HYDE.

land in 1847. He remained in Stafford until 1849, when he married Miss Frances Elizabeth Waldo, daughter of Judge Waldo, with whom he had studied his profession, and removed to Tolland. He remained there until 1864, being associated in practice with his father-in-law, who was one of the leading lawyers of the state. Judge Waldo came to this city with Mr. Hyde. In 1867 the firm was changed, becoming Waldo, Hubbard & Hyde, the late Governor R. D. Hubbard joining as a mem- ber. Mr. Charles E. Gross was admitted to the firm in 1877. Four years afterwards Judge Waldo died here and the firm assumed the name of Hub- bard, Hyde & Gross. William Waldo Hyde and Frank Eldridge Hyde, sons of Mr. Hyde, were ad- mitted to the copartnership. Both of the new partners were Yale graduates. In fact all the members of the firm at that time and since were distinguished Yalensians. In 1884 the death of Gov. Hubbard involved a new change in the firm

name which was then made and has since remained Hyde, Gross & Hyde. The senior member is one of the ablest lawyers in Connecticut, his standing at the bar being one of marked distinction and honor. His forensic ability is not less brilliant than his legal, and his eloquence is universally admired. Mr. Hyde was a member of the general assembly in 1854, 1858, and 1862, representing the town of Tolland in the house. He is a democrat in politics and one of the ablest representatives of his party in the state. He is a past grand master of the Connecticut Grand Lodge of Masons, occupy- ing the position of grand master for two terms from May 15, 1862. He was made a Mason in 1858, becoming a member of Uriel Lodge No. 24, which is located at Merrow Station in Tolland county. His administration was eminently suc- cessful. Mr. Hyde is one of the most prominent members of the Yale Alumni Association in this city. He has traveled extensively in Europe and has visited all sections of the United States, in- cluding a trip to Alaska. He is a gentleman of broad culture and intelligence and one of the most gifted men in Connecticut. His home is on Charter Oak Place, the grounds including the spot where the famous Charter Oak stood for centuries. The historic associations of the place are reverently pre- served, Mr. Hyde being one of the most ardent of patriots as well as the most fascinating of orators.

B. R. ALLEN, HARTFORD: Insurance Agent, Stock and Bond Broker.

Bennet Rowland Allen was born in Enfield, May 17, 1838, and was educated at E. Hall's classical school in Ellington, Wm. C. Goldthwait's in Long-
meadow, Mass., and at the Connecticut State Normal School in New Britain. He became a teacher in the Ellington school, which was one of the leading classical schools in Hartford coun- ty in its day. Subsequently he engaged in manufac- turing business at Wind- sor Locks, remaining there from 1861 until 1868. A portion of the time he was the manager of the Med-

B. R. ALLEN.

licott mill, which was occupied through the war in making knit goods for the soldiers' use. Afterwards he became a member of the firm of C. H. Dexter & Sons, Mr. Dexter, the founder of the company, being Mr. Allen's father-in-law, and engaged in the manufacture of manilla papers. In 1868 he re- moved to Hartford and became the local manager of the Hartford Fire Insurance Company, the Royal Insurance Company of England, and of the Pennsylvania Insurance Company of Philadelphia. In addition to the management of the local transactions of these companies, Mr. Allen is engaged in the business of a stock and bond broker. He is held in the highest esteem in business centres in this city, and is deserving in every way of the universal confidence felt in his ability. He is prominently associated with Masonic interests, being a knight templar; is a member, also, of the Connecticut Society Sons of the American Revolution. Mr. Allen is a republican, politically, but has paid no attention to public office, having resolutely refrained through life from seeking public position. During the war he voluntarily sent a substitute into the service, and was thoroughly interested in the success of the Union cause. The business in which he was engaged at the time as manager of the Medlicott company made it of great importance that his services should be retained here. Mr. Allen is an active and influential member of the Asylum Hill Congregational church. His family consists of a wife and son. The former was Miss Annie Pierson Dexter of Windsor Locks prior to her marriage. The son occupies a responsible position in the Society for Savings on Pratt street.

HENRY S. MARLOR, Brooklyn: Banker.

Mr. Marlor was born in England in 1835, and came to this country in 1840 with his parents, settling in New York city. After spending six years in attendance at public school No. 11 in that city, at the age of eleven years he began to learn the trade of gold watch-case making with E. L. Preston of Brooklyn, Conn. In 1862 he spent three months in active military service as a member of the Twenty-second New York Regiment. Later he entered the Metropolitan National Bank of New York city, remaining in

H. S. MARLOR.

that institution for ten years. He afterward became a member of the New York Stock Exchange, and was elected its vice-president. He retired from active business in 1868, but has retained his membership in the Exchange. Since 1869 he has resided chiefly in Brooklyn, Conn., but is accustomed to spend his winters, with his family, in New York city, where he owns and maintains a handsome residence on Lenox Hill, at No. 18 East Seventy-eighth Street. He is a gentleman of

means and culture, who from humble beginnings has risen by the force of his own exertions to a position which he has a right to enjoy, and of which he may well be proud.

Mr. Marlor is a democrat in politics, a member of the Baptist Church, of the Grand Army of the Republic, and of the Metropolitan Museum of Art of New York. His wife's maiden name was Harriet J. Van Brunt, and she is a descendant of one of the old Long Island families.

FREDERICK ST. JOHN LOCKWOOD, Norwalk: President Fairfield County National Bank.

Frederick St. John Lockwood of Norwalk was born in that city Aug. 23, 1825, and graduated from Yale College in 1849, his classmates including

F. ST. J. LOCKWOOD.

President Timothy Dwight of the university, ex-Congressman Augustus Brandegee of New London, and ex-President W. D. Bishop of the Consolidated road. During the war he was on the staffs of Major-Generals King and Russell, and discharged his official duties with marked competency and gallantry. At the close of the war he returned to Norwalk, and represented that city as a republican in the legislatures of 1865 and 1866. In 1872 he was also a member of the house, the legislature of that year containing many of the ablest men in the state. Prominent on the list were ex-Governor James E. English, T. M. Waller, Judge V. B. Chamberlain of New Britain, ex-Speaker William C. Case, Judges Torrance of the Supreme and John M. Hall of the Superior Courts, Colonel John A. Tibbits, and Railroad Commissioner George M. Woodruff. Mr. Lockwood acquitted himself with decided credit during the session. From 1859 until 1862 he was bank commissioner. He is at present at the head of the Danbury & Norwalk Railroad Company, and is also engaged in banking and manufacturing interests. He has been the president of the Fairfield County National Bank, the office extending from 1868 to January, 1891. He has been the president of the railroad company since 1882. He is a past worshipful master of St. John's Lodge, No. 6, of Norwalk, and is a member of the Norwalk Club. His family consists of a wife and three children, the former being Miss Carrie Ayres at the time of her marriage. The children are Elizabeth, born July 30, 1868; Frederick Ayres, born

November 18, 1870; and Julia Belden, born June 30, 1881. Mr. Lockwood is a member of the Congregational church, and is held in high esteem in the city of Norwalk.

PROF. W. A. ANTHONY, MANCHESTER: Electrician.

The subject of this sketch was born November 17, 1835, at Coventry, Rhode Island. He attended the village school, where he began at an early age the study of algebra and geometry. He also read all the books on science to be found in the school library, and obtained considerable experience with machinery and tools in his father's mill. At the age of 15 he went to the Friends' Boarding School in Providence, where he pursued his favorite studies in mathematics and science, and for a time assisted in the preparation

W. A. ANTHONY.

of experiments for the lectures on chemistry and physics. Completing his preparations for college at the academy at East Greenwich, he entered Brown University in 1854, but under the compulsion of his deepening interest in mathematical and scientific studies he left Brown to enter the Scientific School at Yale, where he graduated in 1856.

After graduating, Prof. Anthony became the principal of a graded school. He then taught science in an academy, then physics and chemistry at Antioch College, then physics at the Iowa State Agricultural College, and in 1872 he was called to Cornell University to take charge of the department of physics. He remained there till 1887, and left behind him an imprint that the work of Cornell in his special field will long bear. His interest was specially strong in electricity and optics, and he devised a great number of experiments to illustrate his instruction. Even in the academy, in 1863–66, his students in physics were required to perform experiments for themselves. This was the beginning of his physical laboratory instruction, which he tried to improve upon and extend as long as he had to do with students, and to prepare for their careers the physicists and engineers of the next generation.

It is interesting to note that in 1874, after trying in vain to procure a Gramme machine from Europe, as a piece of laboratory apparatus, he designed and constructed one for the university laboratory himself. This machine was exhibited at the Philadelphia centennial exhibition in 1876. It is still in use

and doing good service in the physical laboratory at Cornell.

In 1881, appreciating with clear foresight the important place that electrical applications were to take in the near future, Professor Anthony set on foot a movement looking to the establishment at Cornell of a special course of study for the training of electrical engineers. This plan met with great opposition at first, but was finally successful, and the course is now one of the best attended in the university.

In 1887, desiring relief in a change of occupation, Prof. Anthony resigned the appointment he had held with so much credit to himself and so much honor to Cornell, and assumed the duties of electrician for the Mather Electric Company of Manchester, in this State, in which capacity he has since continued, devoting himself to the improvement of the apparatus and the extension of the affairs of the company.

WILLIAM EDGAR SIMONDS, HARTFORD: Attorney-at-Law.

William Edgar Simonds was born at Collinsville, in the town of Canton, Hartford county, Connecticut, November 24, 1842. He was educated at the graded and high schools in Collinsville, graduated at the State Normal School in New Britain in 1860, and taught school until 1862. August 14, 1862, he enlisted in Company A of the Twenty-fifth Connecticut Volunteers, as a private, and was soon promoted to be sergeant-major. At the battle of Irish Bend, Louisiana, April 14, 1863, he was promoted to be

W. E. SIMONDS.

lieutenant of Company I for gallantry in the field, and was discharged from the service, August 26, 1863, by reason of the expiration of his term. He then entered Yale Law School and there graduated in 1865. Since that date he has practiced law in Hartford. He is the author of books on patent law as follows: "Design Patents," "Digest of Patent Office Decisions," "Summary of Patent Law," and "Digest of Patent Cases." Since 1884 he has filled the lectureship on patent law at Yale Law School. In 1890 Yale University gave him the honorary degree of A.M. Mr. Simonds was a member of the Connecticut house of representatives in 1883 and chairman of the committee on railroads. He was speaker of the Connecticut house in 1885. He has been a trustee of the Storrs Agricultural School of Connecticut since 1886. In

1848 he was elected to congress from the first district of Connecticut. He signalized his service in the fifty-first congress by his successful efforts in connection with international copyright. A bill looking to that end had been decisively defeated in the house when Mr. Simonds drew and introduced another bill and secured for it, after repeated contests, a victory quite as decisive as its former defeat, which bill subsequently became a law, it being the first international copyright act of the United States, a measure which had been contended for ever since Henry Clay began the agitation of the subject a half century before.

His record in congress has been one of great activity and intense loyalty to the interests of his constituents and the state. The services which he has been able to render will be borne in mind by his party, who, no less than the entire district, have been placed under lasting obligation to him for the conscientious and honorable work he has performed while an incumbent of this important office.

HON. DAVID GREENSLIT, Hampton.

David Greenslit was born at Hampton, June 2, 1817. After graduating from the public schools of his native town, he spent a year or two in teaching

DAVID GREENSLIT.

and in mercantile business in the city of Norwich, after which he paid his attention exclusively to farming until 1844, since which date his time has been occupied almost continuously in official duties. May 26, 1840, he was united in marriage to Miss Elizabeth Searls, daughter of John Searls of Brooklyn, settling in Hampton, where he has since principally resided. He held the offices of sheriff and deputy sheriff for Windham county for sixteen years. In 1866 he was elected state senator, serving as chairman of the State Prison committee. During his term in the senate he lost his only child, a beautiful young lady of twenty-two years, by which sad blow he was almost completely prostrated. In 1873 he represented Hampton in the lower house, where he was again appointed chairman of the State Prison committee. Mr. Greenslit has held the office of president of the Windham County Mutual Fire Insurance Company for about twelve years, and is the adjuster of all the company's losses. He is a director in the Windham County National Bank, also in the Dime Savings Bank of Willimantic. He

has held various town offices, having been acting school visitor, agent of the town deposit fund, and first selectman, for terms varying from ten to forty years. He was in the provost-marshal's office in Norwich during two years of the war of the rebellion, and acted for the government as general recruiting officer for Windham county. During the last thirty years he has been extensively engaged in the settlement of estates, many of which have involved large responsibilities and required the exercise of soundest judgment. Mr. Greenslit has given much attention to the law, not professionally, but in order to prepare himself for the requirements of his duties and to enable him to act promptly and intelligently on the many occasions when legal counsel might not be at ready command. His advice in business is thus often sought and highly valued. Politically Mr. Greenslit is an ardent republican, and has been more or less active in state and local politics ever since the formation of that party. He served on the state central committee for a long succession of years. Whatever the welfare of his town or the state has called for, politically, socially, educationally, or morally, he has heartily and earnestly undertaken; and very rarely has he enlisted in an undertaking which was not carried to a triumphant success. Mr. Greenslit's life has been one of great activity and usefulness, and his circle of intimate acquaintances and friends extends to all borders of the state.

REV. LEWELLYN PRATT, D.D., Norwich: Pastor Broadway Congregational Church.

The subject of this sketch was born in Saybrook (now Essex), in this state, August 8, 1832. In his youth he was a pupil at Essex and Durham Academies, and was afterward

LEWELLYN PRATT.

graduated at Williams College. He was ordained to the ministry by the Philadelphia Presbytery in 1864. For several years he was professor in the National Deaf-Mute College of Washington, D.C., and of Knox College, Galesburg, Ill., preaching more or less while serving as professor; for some time at the New York Avenue Presbyterian Church of Washington, and for two years at the second Presbyterian Church of Galesburg. In 1870 the Congregational Church of North Adams called him to its pastorate, where he labored with marked success, until Williams College, his *alma mater*, invited him to the professorship of rhetoric. Thence, in 1880, he was called to the chair of practical theology in the Hartford Theological Seminary, where he remained until the spring of 1888, resigning to accept the pastorate of the Broadway Congregational Church of Norwich, Conn., where he continues to labor with great acceptance. Not inappropriately he might still carry the title of "Professor of Practical Theology," for in all departments of church work he is eminently practical, not only finding time to attend to the many duties of his own church and various calls for occasional sermons and addresses, but also coöperates, or rather leads, in many movements of reform, being identified with the charities and reforms of his own city and state, rendering valuable service by his wisdom and tact, and exercising in them all a thorough catholicity of spirit. The church over which he is pastor, through its commanding influence, contributes to his strength; it being not only the largest Protestant church of Norwich, but in a sense the representative church of that half of Connecticut lying east of the river.

The secret of Professor Pratt's success as an educator and preacher lies not in the predominance of one talent, but rather in a rare and happy combination of gifts. A commanding presence, genial disposition, thoroughness and tact, yet withal a becoming modesty, unite to form in him a well-rounded man. As an educator, his broad and accurate knowledge led the students to have confidence in him, while his genial bearing gave them confidence in themselves. If possible, he was even more to the students outside than within the classroom, a friend and counsellor to whom they naturally came with their troubles. Not unnaturally many of these former pupils continue to turn to him for counsel, while the institutions with which he has been connected have shown their appreciation of his talents — Williams College, by conferring upon him the degree of D.D. in 1877, and later by electing him a trustee; and Hartford Theological Seminary, by electing him to the same office. The latter of these he continues to fill. As a preacher, he masters his subject, covers thoroughly all the ground, gets at and gives the kernel. The analysis is correct, delivery easy and forceful, the voice clear and resonant, and the manner full of earnestness. His delightful social accomplishments, too, are an important auxiliary to his professional success; as the influences which attend companionship with the cultured and refined are conceded to be among the most fascinating and powerful that can be exerted.

Professor Pratt was married early in life to Miss Sarah Putnam Gulliver. They have one son, Waldo S. Pratt, A.M., professor of music and hymnology in the Hartford Theological Seminary.

DR. P. W. ELLSWORTH, HARTFORD.

Dr. Pinckney Webster Ellsworth was born in that city, December 5, 1814, being the grandson of Chief Justice Oliver Ellsworth of the United States Supreme Court and the son of Governor W. W. Ellsworth of Connecticut. His mother, Emily Webster Ellsworth, was the eldest daughter of Noah Webster, the noted lexicographer. He is a descendant of Governor Bradford of the *Mayflower*, and also of John Webster, one of the first governors of the Connecticut colony. Governor Webster was one of the

P. W. ELLSWORTH.

leading members of the First Church of Christ, now known as the Center Church, in Hartford, but owing to differences of opinion concerning baptism he removed to Massachusetts, establishing his home in Haverhill. This Governor Webster was one of Noah Webster's ancestors, and it is supposed that the text of the original Unabridged Webster was prepared in the old Massachusetts home of the governor. John Steele, who came to Hartford about six months prior to Thomas Hooker's arrival here was also an ancestor of Dr. Ellsworth. Chief Justice Ellsworth, who represented Connecticut in the national constitutional convention in Philadelphia, was the originator of the plan giving each of the states two senators in the national congress. Dr. Ellsworth graduated from Yale College in the class of 1836 and pursued the most exacting medical course then required in the noted medical schools in Philadelphia and New York, graduating from the College of Physicians and Surgeons in the latter city in 1839. His medical studies were afterwards continued in Paris, London, and Dublin. He settled in Hartford as a practitioner in 1843 and in a few years became one of the foremost surgeons in the state. He was the partner of Amariah Brigham, who became, subsequently, the superintendent of the Retreat for the Insane in this city. From this city Dr. Brigham removed to Utica and became the superintendent of the Insane Asylum there. Dr. Ellsworth, in conjunction with his father, Governor Ellsworth, was mainly instrumental in procuring these promotions for Dr. Brigham. Dr. Ellsworth was himself one of the visiting physicians for a considerable period at the Retreat. He was one of the organizers of the City Medical Society, and is among the leading members of the Hartford county and the state medical societies, and honorary member of the New York State Medical Society. During the war his distinction as a surgeon led to his appointment to a brigade-surgeonship, receiving his commission from Governor Buckingham. He served on the staff of General Isaac I. Stevens of the Army of the Potomac, who was shot and killed at the head of his command in the second battle of Bull Run. General Stevens was the governor of California and one of the bravest men in the field. Dr. Ellsworth was an examiner of recruits for the service and probably made the personal examination of 9,000 men for the service. He has also held the office of pension examiner in this state for nine years, serving in that capacity under Presidents Johnson, Grant, and Cleveland. He is a member of the Center Church, where he was baptised in infancy by the Rev. Dr. Strong, one of the most noted divines of his day. He became a member of the church soon after his graduation. His father, Governor Ellsworth, was a deacon in the Center Church for fifty years. The only brother of Dr. Ellsworth, Oliver Ellsworth, was interested for several years with John F. Trumbull of Stonington in the manufacture of cotton gins. Afterwards he became a successful publisher of school books in Boston. Losing his fortune in the end, he went to Montana and died there some years ago. There were four sisters in the family, only one of whom is now living. One died in infancy; one was the wife of President Jackson of Trinity College; and one the wife of Russell S. Cook, who was secretary of the American Tract Society. The youngest sister, Elizabeth Ellsworth, married the late Waldo Hutchins of New York, a distinguished lawyer and member of congress from the metropolis. She is still living. Dr. Ellsworth has been married twice. His first wife was Julia M. Sterling, daughter of Jesse Sterling of Bridgeport, who was one of the first treasurers of the Housatonic Railroad Company. She died at the age of twenty-nine years. The second wife, who is now living, was Julia Townsend Dow, daughter of Lucius K. Dow of New Haven. There are six children by this marriage now living. The three elder are Mrs. Augustus Julian Lyman of Asheville, N. C., son of Bishop Lyman of North Carolina; Wolcott Webster Ellsworth, who is now pursuing a post-graduate course at Yale University, a brilliant linguist and a student of great promise; and Emily Webster Ellsworth. The three remaining children of the family are under age. The son of Dr. Ellsworth by his first marriage died in the old home on Main street near St. John's Church, when only two and a half years old. From that day until now it has been impossible for Dr. Ellsworth to speak of the loss without the deepest emotion. The busiest part of the doctor's life was spent in the home which he occupied for years, where the Phœnix Insurance Company's office now stands on Pearl street. Dr. Ellsworth is an independent in

politics and has invariably abstained from public office. Even in the church, where his father was a deacon for half a century, he has maintained the same position with regard to the holding of office. Dr. Ellsworth has long been a thorough and conscientious student of the Scriptures, the Greek Testament especially attracting his attention and interest. He is the author of a number of valuable contributions to the science of theology, including a work of more than ordinary research entitled " Immanuel, God with us." His life has been a notable one in this city.

C. W. HUNTINGTON, HARTFORD: Professor of Music.

Prof. Charles Wesley Huntington was born in New London, March 13, 1829, and received a common school education. He adopted the profession of music and was organist and teacher from 1846 until 1856. He located in Hartford in 1856 and occupied for years the professorship of music in the State Normal School in New Britain, and in the Hartford High School, and Hartford Female Seminary. Prof. Huntington was the first to discover the merits of the great singer, Signor Foli, and introduced him to

C. W. HUNTINGTON.

the brilliant experience he has had in Europe and the United States. When the Professor first observed the talents of the distinguished vocalist, he was a carpenter in this city. The first systematic musical training which he received was from Prof. Huntington. As a musician, the Professor has attained an enviable reputation, and his efforts in behalf of the higher musical instruction and training have placed the public under permanent obligations to him.

It should be stated that the subject of this sketch is of the eighth generation from Christopher Huntington, who as a child sailed from England with his father (Simon) and mother in 1633, the father dying on shipboard and being buried at sea. Christopher and his mother settled in Windsor, Conn., after their arrival in America, and since that generation all the American ancestors of C. W. Huntington have been natives of Connecticut.

There are many pleasant memories of Mr. Huntington's early professional career. Away back in 1852 he organized the " Continental Vocalists," and with them made a complete and most successful tour of the United States. After four years thus occupied he came to Hartford just before the opening of the presidential campaign of 1856. During this year the republican party in Hartford effected its original organization, and Mr. Huntington entered ardently into the work. He formed a patriotic glee-club of one hundred and twenty-five members, whose singing he personally conducted, which became one of the most effective features of the public demonstrations of that enthusiastic campaign. Later he organized the old " South Church quartette," by means of which the devotional exercises at that church acquired new interest and effectiveness. The musical accomplishments of this quartette and its leader made for them a reputation beyond the limits of the city, and they were induced to make frequent excursions into neighboring towns and cities, giving popular concerts and receiving a most royal welcome. All the members of the old quartette are still living. Since 1886 Mr. Huntington has discontinued active professional work, and devoted his time to various business enterprises. He is connected with the masonic fraternity, being one of the charter members of LaFayette Lodge, No. 100, of Hartford. His wife was Miss Martha Eddy of New Britain before her marriage. She has been for years one of Hartford's most noted singers. Professor and Mrs. Huntington have but one child, who is the wife of Mr. Charles E. Newton of this city.

SHERMAN WOLCOTT ADAMS, LL.B., Hartford: Attorney-at-Law; President Board of Park Commissioners.

Sherman W. Adams was born in Wethersfield, Conn., May 6, 1836, and is a son of the late Welles Adams of that place. The latter was descended from Benjamin Adams, an early, but not one of the earliest, settlers of the township. The subject of this sketch is also descended from Ens. William Goodrich, Ens. John Nott, John Robbins, " Gentleman," Michael Griswold, Gov. Thomas Welles, and other pioneer settlers of Wethersfield; and from Henry Wolcott, the Windsor settler. His education was obtained

S. W. ADAMS.

in a common school (in the section now known as South Wethersfield), in the academy of the town, and in a select school or " institute " at Cornwall, Conn. His early life was partly spent upon his father's farm, and partly in a general " store " in Wethersfield belonging to his father. It was while in the latter occupation that he turned his attention to the study of law. His legal studies were pursued in the offices of the late Thomas C. Perkins and Heman H. Barbour; after which he studied at, and was graduated from, the Law School of Harvard University, taking the degree of LL.B. in the class of 1861. In March, 1862, he received from Secretary Welles a commission as acting assistant paymaster in the Navy; reported at once to Com. Hiram Paulding at the navy yard, Brooklyn, for duty on board the gunboat Somerset. The vessel proceeded to the gulf and was attached to the eastern gulf squadron. Here Paymaster Adams remained until June, 1864, on the same gunboat. At that date, being much worn down, he was relieved, and came north to settle accounts, and also to regain his impaired health. In October, 1864, he called upon Secretary Welles and tendered his resignation, which was accepted.

Returning to his profession in 1865, Mr. Adams has continued in practice ever since in Hartford, with the exception of one year, 1868-9, spent in Europe. While there, he devoted special attention to the study of the French and German languages, and translated and published Eugène Ténot's narrative of the *coup d'état* of 1851. He has also made occasional translations from the German, Spanish, and Italian languages, and has paid some attention to the Dutch, Portuguese, and Danish. He is also fond of studying the natural sciences, more especially botany.

Mr. Adams has been much of a delver in matters of local history, having written many articles in that line. He is the author of several chapters in the Memorial History of Hartford County. He is a member of the National Historical Association, and of the Connecticut Historical Society, having been one of the officers of the latter institution for some years, and compiled the pamphlet recently issued by its authority.

While republican in politics, Mr. Adams has never been an active politician. Nevertheless, he represented his native town in the legislature of 1866, when he introduced a proposed constitutional amendment, providing for a sole capitol for this state. It passed, but barely failed to receive the requisite two-thirds majority in the following year. He is the author of some of the laws of this state, of which, perhaps, the most important is the " judgment-lien " law. He is also author of the resolution providing for a topographical survey of the state, passed in 1889. Beginning in 1877, he was for six years associate judge of the Hartford police court. Since 1884 he has been president of Hartford's park commissioners, and was the active member of the commission for the erection of the Memorial Arch. While not robust in health, he has never ceased to be active in some useful labor. He is unmarried.

FRANCIS A. PRATT, HARTFORD: President the
Pratt & Whitney Company, Manufacturers of
Machine Tools, Gun Machinery, etc.

The name of Pratt occurs among the earliest of
English sirnames, and the family, in many of its
branches, held stations of influence and power in
the British Empire. The
first American ancestor
of Francis A. Pratt was
John Pratt, who came to
America from the south-
ern part of England, and
settled in Dorchester,
Mass., where he was made
a freeman May 4, 1632.
His grandson, John Pratt,
3d, and subsequent de-
scendants for several generations, were natives or
citizens of Reading,
Mass., from which place
the family ultimately removed to Reading, Vt.

F. A. PRATT.

The subject of this sketch is of the ninth generation from the original John Pratt above mentioned. The later ancestors of Francis A. Pratt,
for several generations, have been natives and
residents of Vermont, in which state, in the town
of Woodstock, he was born Feb. 15, 1827. His
father, Nathaniel M. Pratt, a leather merchant, and
a noted temperance agitator, was a native of Reading, Vt., where he was born in the year 1800. His
grandfather, Charles Pratt, also a native of Reading, died at the advanced age of ninety-four, in
Michigan, to which state he removed from Reading in 1834. They were both men of great mental
and physical strength, of the true New England
type of that period.

From his childhood Francis A. Pratt possessed
mechanical inclinations which indicated genius.
Whether inherited or not, they were manifested at
a very early age, when the boy was found repeatedly stealing away from his companions to con-
struct and put in operation a water-wheel, or a
turning lathe, or a steam engine. The time after
school or on holidays, which other lads devoted to
play, he employed with his jackknife and such
rude tools as he could command, in giving shape
and form to mechanical designs which had been
evolved from his busy brain during school hours or
while lying awake in bed at night; mechanical
schemes even then, as later in life, often effectually
banishing sleep. It is related of him that when he
was ten or twelve years old he would set up a train
of simple machinery, including perhaps a wood
lathe, to be driven by a belt from the grindstone;
and by some inducement would tempt his younger
brother Rufus to turn the grindstone while he
fashioned a top or a ball-club with his rude turn-

ing-lathe, keeping poor Rufus at the fountain of
power till his back seemed breaking, by his special
pleading or by the tender of some favorite toy.

Mr. Pratt's parents moved from Woodstock to
Lowell, Mass., when he was but eight years old.
His schooling, begun in his native town, was continued in Lowell, and here at an early age he was
apprenticed to the machinist trade with Warren
Aldrich, a machinist of good reputation at that
time as to his products, and a kind master, who is
now living at an advanced age. The indifferent
facilities which the machine-shops of that day were
supplied with, furnished just the incentive which the
mind of this young apprentice needed to bring into
exercise his expanding inventive genius; and the
lack of an appropriate tool was often the father (as
necessity is said to be the mother) in his case of an
invention which eventually supplied it. In 1848,
when twenty years of age, he went to Gloucester,
N. J., where he was employed in the Gloucester
Machine Works, first as a journeyman and afterwards as a contractor. The leading partners in
the concern, Messrs. Melchor and Ranlett, were
both New England men. Associated with him in
his contract work for the Gloucester concern, was
a Mr. Samuel Batchelder, who, leaving New Jersey soon afterwards and coming to Hartford,
Conn., became connected with the pistol factory of
Samuel Colt. Through his influence, in 1852, Mr.
Pratt followed him to Hartford and took a position
in the same establishment, where he found and became acquainted with Amos Whitney. While he
was there an application came from Lincoln's Phœnix Iron Works for a good foreman, and Mr. Pratt
was selected and recommended for the position.
He accepted the situation, and afterwards became
superintendent of the works. Later on, when another important opening was to be filled under his
direction, he selected Mr. Whitney for the place,
and the two worked together in this establishment
until 1861. The year before closing their connection with the Phœnix Iron Works, the young men
resolved to unite their fortunes and open a shop
of their own, and accordingly hired a room on
Potter street, doing some of their first work for the
Willimantic Linen Company. The next February
their shop was destroyed by fire, but a month later
they were settled in new quarters, where they continued to grow until all the available space in the
building was occupied by them. In 1862, Pratt &
Whitney took into the partnership Monroe Stan-
nard of New Britain, each contributing $1,200. In
1865, the firm erected the first of the present group
of buildings, and from time to time others have
been added till the plant now occupies about four
acres. In 1869, under a charter from the state,
the Pratt & Whitney Company was incorporated
with a capital of $350,000, afterwards increased

from earnings to $500,000. The story of the financial and other struggles of the early partners, Messrs. Pratt and Whitney, in laying the foundations of the present great corporation, sounds almost like a romance. Nobody but the parties themselves can ever understand or appreciate the nature or the magnitude of the obstacles they encountered, the sacrifices involved, and the unceasing and gigantic efforts employed, in surmounting them one after another as they presented themselves. The end sought, and finally obtained, would never have been successfully pursued if the two young men had not possessed a reserve-fund of determination, pluck, and endurance, which gave them a sublime faith in themselves and a confidence which cannot suffer defeat.

Of the present company F. A. Pratt is president, and has been from the outset the leading spirit. He has made no less than eight trips to Europe, principally in the interests of the company, traveling in England, Germany, France, Austria, and Italy, and has first and last secured foreign business for the company amounting to between two and three millions of dollars. The European features of the company's business is entirely the result of Mr. Pratt's suggestion and efforts ; and the value of the connection thus formed, and of the reputation thus made for the Pratt & Whitney company all over the civilized world is beyond computation in dollars and cents. Mr. Pratt entertains a broad and comprehensive view of business, believing that for his company the world is the field, and that it is only necessary to seek business in a liberal and intelligent way to command it in the open market every time.

Mr. Pratt has been a prominent and leading representative of the industrial enterprises of Hartford for thirty years. He has also acquired a high reputation among scientific men at home and abroad, and is regarded as an expert in pretty much all branches of mechanical art. He has recently been appointed by the secretary of the treasury of the United States as one of the board of commissioners for the expert examination of the treasury vaults ; the other members of the commission being Theodore N. Ely, superintendent of motive power of the Pennsylvania railroad, and Professor R. H. Thurston of Cornell University. He has served the city of Hartford four years as member of the board of water commissioners, and four years as alderman. He is a director of the Hartford board of trade, the Pratt & Cady Company, president and director of the Electric Generator Company, and is officially connected with various industrial corporations. He is a member of the American Society of Mechanical Engineers, and of the Masonic fraternity a master mason and member of St. John's Lodge of Hartford.

Mr. Pratt was married, Oct. 31, 1850, to Miss Harriet E. Cole of Lowell, ex-Alderman Asa S. Cook of Hartford marrying an older sister at the same time and place. There have been eight children, five of whom died in infancy ; and one son, Melvin D., dying in 1883, at the age of twenty-six years. Of the two surviving children, the elder, Carrie Louise, was married, in 1885, to J. E. Spalding of Hartford, and they have one son. The younger, Francis C. Pratt, recently graduated from the Sheffield Scientific School of Yale University, is in business with his father.

—

REV. WILLIAM DELOSS LOVE, JR., HARTFORD : Pastor of the Pearl Street Congregational Church.

Rev. William DeLoss Love, Jr., was born in New Haven, Nov. 29, 1851, being the second son of Rev. Dr. Wm. DeLoss Love. He was prepared for college in the Milwaukee Academy at Milwaukee, Wis., and graduated from Hamilton College at Clinton, N. Y., in the class of 1873. His theological studies were pursued at Andover Seminary, his graduation from that institution occurring in 1878. He was ordained at Lancaster, Mass., Sept. 18, 1878, and remained there for three years. He then spent one year in 

foreign travel, visiting important centers of interest in the East. After returning home he resided at Keene, N. H., for two years, occupying the position of private secretary to Gov. S. W. Hale during his administration. In 1884, on account of an obstinate throat trouble, he engaged in commercial enterprises. On the first of January, 1885, he resumed the work of the pastorate and was settled over the Pearl Street church, May 6, in that year. Mr. Love has been married twice. His first wife was Miss Ada M. Warren of Leicester, Mass., the marriage taking place July 6, 1878. Her death occurred May 31, 1881. His present wife was Miss Mary Louise Hale, daughter of ex-Gov. Hale of Keene, N. H., the marriage with her occurring Oct. 30, 1884. There are two daughters by this marriage. Mr. Love is the chaplain of the Connecticut Society of the Sons of the American Revolution, and an interested member of the Connecticut Historical Society. His preaching and pastoral work in Hartford have been eminently successful, and the church, under his leadership, has made decided progress. Mr. Love is a man of superior culture and training, and his pulpit ministrations have entitled him to much recognition in Connecticut.

HON. FRANKLIN CHAMBERLIN, HARTFORD: Attorney-at-Law.

Franklin Chamberlin was born in the town of Dalton, Mass., April 14, 1821, and was educated in the best public schools in Berkshire county and at the Harvard Law School in Cambridge, being a member of the class of 1844 in that institution. His classmates in the Harvard Law School included Anson Burlingame, subsequently the champion of Charles Sumner in congress and Minister to China under the administration of President Lincoln. Henry Stevens, the celebrated antiquarian, was also a member of

FRANKLIN CHAMBERLIN.

the class of '44. Mr. Chamberlin has spent a portion of his life in Springfield, Mass., and in New York city. He removed to Hartford prior to the war and immediately established himself in a large and prosperous legal business. For years the late Ezra Hall was associated in the partnership, which became one of the best known in this community, its standing in legal circles being of the highest character. In 1865 Mr. Chamberlin was elected a member of the house of representatives from this city, his colleagues on the floor including Governor Henry B. Harrison and the late E. K. Foster of New Haven, speaker of the house that year, the Hon. Frederick J. Kingsbury of Waterbury, ex-State Treasurer V. B. Chamberlain of New Britain, the late David Gallup of Plainfield and David P. Nichols of Danbury, the former subsequently lieutenant-governor and the latter state treasurer, Railroad Commissioner George M. Woodruff of Litchfield, ex-Bank Commissioner A. B. Mygatt of New Milford, P. T. Barnum of Bridgeport, Judge Henry S. Barbour of this city, then a member of the house from Torrington, the late Edward L. Cundall of Brooklyn, Edwin A. Buck of Ashford, the late John W. Thayer of Ellington, and John M. Douglas of Middletown. Mr. Chamberlin was one of the ablest representatives that Hartford has had in the general assembly during the past thirty years and his work as a legislator was recognized as being of a high order. His legal attainment and standing placed him among the most prominent representatives in the house. Mr. Chamberlin was a member of the state capitol commission,

succeeding Commissioner Barber of this city, whose death occurred while the erection of the capitol was in progress. He brought to the commission the taste and culture of a man who had devoted his life to intellectual pursuits, and became one of its most valued members. Mr. Chamberlin is one of the most honored citizens of Hartford. He is at the head of the law firm of Chamberlin, White & Mills, and is connected with the Park Congregational church. His wife, who was Miss Mary W. Porter prior to her marriage, is still living. The home occupied by them is one of the most charming and cultivated centers in the city.

HON. A. HEATON ROBERTSON, NEW HAVEN: Judge of Probate.

Judge Robertson comes of one of the old families of New Haven, where he was born September 25, 1850. He prepared for college at the Hopkins Grammar School, graduated from Yale College in 1872, and in 1874 from the Columbia Law School. He was an aide upon Governor Ingersoll's staff with rank of colonel in 1873, '74, '75, and '76. From 1877 to 1881 he was an alderman from the Sixth Ward of New Haven. For a time he was at the head of the important lamp department.

A. H. ROBERTSON.

In 1880 he was the junior, and in 1882 the senior, representative from New Haven in the legislature. In 1880 he was a member of the committee on railroads and on contested elections, and in 1882 of the committee on the judiciary and the Governor Buckingham statue. He was senator from the Eighth District in 1885 and 1886, serving both years on the committees on roads and bridges and contingent expenses. He was elected judge of probate of the New Haven district in 1886, re-elected in 1888, and again in 1890—the last time receiving the nomination from both the great political parties. His business connections are as director with the New Haven & Northampton Railroad Company, Southern New England Telephone Company, Co-operative Loan and Trust Association, and Young Men's Institute. He is a member and vestryman of Trinity Protestant Episcopal Church of New Haven; a democrat; and belongs to the Knights of Honor.

Judge Robertson is the eldest son of Hon. John B. Robertson, ex-mayor of New Haven, who is the grandson of Alexander Robertson, an officer of Marion's Brigade of South Carolina. He is a grandson of Abram Heaton of New Haven on his mother's side, who was a descendant of a brother of Theophilus Eaton. Judge Robertson married Miss Graziella Ridgeway of Philadelphia, Penn., and they have two children: Heaton Ridgeway and Mabel Harriet Joy Robertson.

Judge Robertson has been constant and successful in the practice of his profession, and has a high standing before the bar of New Haven county and the state.

DR. CHARLES J. FOX, WILLIMANTIC: Physician and Surgeon.

Ex-Surgeon-General Charles James Fox was born in Wethersfield, Dec. 21, 1854, and was educated in the Hartford High school and the New York University of Physicians and Surgeons. In April, 1877, he became a resident of Willimantic, where he is engaged in the practice of his profession. Governor Lounsbury appointed him surgeon-general on his staff, and he is known throughout the National Guard as a popular and efficient officer. Since 1883 he has held the place of United States examining surgeon for pensions, and is one of the medical examiners for Windham county. Dr. Fox is ex-president of the Windham County Medical society, chairman of the committee on matters of professional interest in the Connecticut State Medical society, member from Windham County of the centennial committee for 1892, for the coming centennial of the State Medical Society at New Haven, a frequent contributor to state, national, and international medical journals, and was elected in 1881 and 1882 to represent the American Medical Association before the medical organization in Europe. In December, 1890, he was appointed on a committee of fifteen to draft Willimantic's city charter and present it to the General Assembly of 1891.

C. J. FOX.

Dr. Fox is a member of the Putnam Phalanx of Hartford; an officer of Eastern Star Lodge, F. and A. M., of Willimantic; member of the Knights Templar Commandery; Grand Junior Warden of the Grand Commandery Knights Templars of the state of Connecticut; charter member of the Odd Fellows Lodge in Willimantic; and charter member of the Willimantic board of trade. He is a republican in politics. Dr. Fox is a widower without children, and a member of the Congregational church. He is a gentleman of extensive and influential acquaintance throughout the state.

HON. JOSEPH R. HAWLEY, HARTFORD: United States Senator; Associate Publisher Hartford *Courant*.

Joseph Russell Hawley was the son of a Congregationalist minister who in 1826, being engaged in some missionary work in North Carolina, was temporarily residing there with his family. J. R. Hawley was born on the 31st of October of that year, and is thus a native of North Carolina, from which state, however, his father shortly removed his family, to settle at Peterboro in central New York. Here the lad grew up, gaining his education at the public schools of the district, and closing it at Hamilton College, from

J. R. HAWLEY.

which he graduated in 1847. In 1850, at the suggestion of his Uncle David, who was the well-known city missionary of Hartford, he removed to this city and began the practice of law, having previously spent three years in preparation therefor. He prospered in his profession, and in five years after his settlement in Hartford he married Miss Harriet Foote, daughter of General Foote of Guilford, on Christmas day, 1855.

Gen. Hawley early distinguished himself as one of the leaders of the Free Soil party, became active in politics, and soon decided to abandon the law and devote himself to journalism. He was connected and thoroughly identified first with the *Hartford Evening Press*, and subsequently with the *Hartford Morning Courant*, of which latter journal he is still the leading proprietor. At the breaking out of the rebellion Hawley was one of the very first to enlist for active service, and was made first lieutenant of Company A, First Regiment, which was mustered into service for three months on the 22d of April, 1861. He served until his term of service expired, again enlisted, and was in active service entirely through the war, being honorably mustered out on the 15th of January, 1866. He enlisted as a private, was advanced through all the grades of promotion, and when finally discharged held the rank of major-general of volunteers. Returning home he was nominated by the republican party as its candidate for governor, to which office he was enthusiastically elected. In 1872 he was chosen president of the United States Centennial Commission. The same year he was elected to the forty-second congress to fill the vacancy occasioned by the death of Congressman Julius L. Strong, and was re-elected for the full term in April, 1873. He was defeated in 1875 and

1876, but elected to the forty-sixth congress in 1878, taking his seat March 4, 1879. Thence, March 4, 1881, he was transferred to the senate, and was re-elected for a second term in 1887. His record in congress is one of loyalty to his state, of fidelity to his party, and of patriotic devotion to the welfare of the republic.

General Hawley is a vigorous campaign speaker, and is always in demand when important elections are pending. He rarely prepares his speeches in detail, but relies upon the inspiration of the moment, and in purely extemporaneous effort has few superiors. He has strong and earnest convictions, and possesses the courage to avow them on all proper occasions.

HON. ALEXANDER WARNER, Woodstock: Ex-Treasurer of Connecticut.

Colonel Alexander Warner was born January 10, 1827, at Smithville, R. I. In 1834 the family moved to Woodstock, Conn., where the son received an academical education. After leaving school he engaged in business. The year 1861 found him part owner and manager of a prosperous twine manufactory in Woodstock. An aptitude for military matters had already drawn him into the state militia, and he was then lieut.-colonel of the Seventh Regiment.

ALEXANDER WARNER.

A spirit like his could not move on in the routine of ordinary life, however attractive the surroundings, when a great crisis was calling the brave to arms. Among the earliest to enlist, he was appointed by Governor Buckingham major of the Third regiment, Connecticut Volunteers, and took part in the battle of Bull Run. After the disbandment of the three months' troops he was made lieut.-colonel of the 13th Connecticut regiment, and served in that capacity till near the close of 1863, when a severe attack of sickness compelled him to withdraw from active service.

In the autumn of 1865, Colonel Warner purchased one of the finest plantations in Mississippi, located in Madison county, near the center of the state. Without preconcert about twenty families from the north simultaneously bought homes in the same neighborhood. They brought with them wealth and intelligence. Curiously enough the new comers made the acquaintance of each other in an attempt to recover a large number of horses and mules which had been stolen from them with absolute im-

partiality by a gang of desperate villains. In the pursuit, which was swift and successful, the brilliant talents of Colonel Warner gave him at once the position of leadership, which thenceforth continued undisputed.

Colonel Warner pursued the most exact and scrupulous methods in dealing with the large number of freedmen whom he employed. This kind of education aroused the somewhat dormant minds of other freedmen to a perception of the injustice they were in many cases suffering at the hands of their old masters. Among the whites the new and exact way of treating the negro provoked deep resentment. A little later, as agent of the freedmen's bureau, he stirred up more violent antagonisms by compelling the planters to fulfill their contracts with emancipated slaves. During this period his life was in constant danger, but he never faltered in throwing around the blacks the full protection of the law.

The home of Colonel Warner was a center of profuse and elegant hospitality. He was unavoidably drawn into politics and played a stirring part in the stormy drama of reconstruction. He was secretary of state, trustee and treasurer of the state university, six years a member of the state senate, four years chairman of the republican state committee, and a delegate to three national conventions.

Long before leaving Mississippi Colonel Warner had taught the old *régime* to respect and admire him. In fact he was importuned to enter into the closest business relations by several prominent native capitalists. He decided, however, to return to Connecticut, and in 1877 purchased a farm in Pomfret. In the fall of 1886 he was elected state treasurer, and his administration of the office marked an epoch in its history, as by modernizing the methods of conducting the business he brought it into harmony with present requirements.

While still a resident of Pomfret, Colonel Warner has extensive interests in Baxter Springs, Kansas, being president of the Baxter Bank, the local Light and Power Company, the Baxter Springs Milling Company, and the Baxter Springs Manufacturing Company. His son, Benj. S. Warner, now a permanent resident of Baxter Springs, is associated with him in these various enterprises.

Colonel Warner married, Sept. 27, 1855, Mary Trumbull Mathewson, a woman of great sweetness and force of character, whose ancestors in different lines have been among the foremost people of New England. Her great-grandfather, General Samuel McClellan, of Woodstock, married, 2d, March 4, 1766, Rachel Abbe of Windham, one of the social queens of the period. Their eldest child, John McClellan, married, Nov. 22, 1796, Faith Williams, daughter of Wm. Williams, a signer of the Declaration of Independence, and granddaughter of Gov-

ernor Jonathan Trumbull. The wife of Governor
Trumbull was a daughter of Rev. John Robinson
of Duxbury, Mass., and a direct descendant of John
Alden and Priscilla Mollines of the *Mayflower*.

CHARLES M. JOSLYN, HARTFORD: Attorney-at-Law.

Mr. Joslyn was born in Tolland, Conn., March
26, 1849, his ancestors being prominent citizens of
that town. He was educated at the Tolland High
School and at Monson
Academy, at which insti-
tutions he took a high
rank as writer and speak-
er. He fitted for and ex-
pected to enter Yale Col-
lege, but entered the Law
office of Waldo, Hubbard
& Hyde instead. He was
admitted to the bar in
May, 1873, and for two
years was associated pro-
fessionally with Hon. Wm.
Hamersley and Hon.
George G. Sumner. On

C. M. JOSLYN.

the first of April, 1875, with E. H. Hyde, Jr., he
formed the law firm of Hyde & Joslyn, which has
ever since continued. The firm has steadily won
its way to the confidence of the public, and stands
second to none in the State for ability and integrity and in the volume and character of the business entrusted to its care.

Mr. Joslyn has always been a democrat in politics, believing in cleanliness and good morals therein, and of much influence in the councils of his
party. By reason of his ability as a parliamenta-
rian and speaker he has frequently been called to
preside over its state conventions. In 1874, he
was a member of the legislature from his native
town, receiving the unanimous vote of both parties. In 1877-8, he was on Gov. Hubbard's staff.
In 1884, he was the senior representative from
Hartford, and the candidate of his party for speaker. He was also the democratic candidate for
mayor of Hartford, but was defeated. He has
been chairman of the Hartford High School committee for the past eight years; is president of the
Hartford Library Association, vice-president of the
Hartford Trust Company, and a director in various other corporations. Has always been in demand as a speaker on public occasions, and some of
his addresses have been models worthy of study
and imitation. Among his best known orations
may be mentioned his address on the life and character of Nathan Hale at South Coventry in 1878,
his Memorial Day address at Hartford in 1884, his
address at Storrs Agricultural School in 1888, and

his oration at the dedication of the statue of Governor Hubbard in 1890. He has been president
of the Hubbard Escort since its organization in
1880, when it participated in the Hancock campaign.

Mr. Joslyn was married, in 1878, to Miss Minnie
L. Brown, of Providence, R. I. They have one
child. His religious connections are with the South
Congregational church of Hartford, of which Rev.
Dr. Parker is the pastor.

THEODORE SEDGWICK GOLD, WEST CORN-WALL: Secretary State Board of Agriculture.

The subject of this sketch was born at Madison,
N. Y., March 2, 1818, and is a son of Dr. Samuel
Wadsworth and Phebe (Cleveland) Gold. During
that year his father re-
turned to Cornwall,
Conn., which was his na-
tive place. In 1824 he
removed to Goshen,
where he remained in the
practice of his profession
fifteen years. He then
returned to Cornwall to
till his ancestral acres.
Theodore S. Gold gradu-
ated at Yale in 1838. He
spent three years after
graduation as teacher of
Goshen and Waterbury

T. S. GOLD.

academies, and as a student of medicine, botany,
and mineralogy at New Haven. In 1842 he began
farming with his father on Cream Hill, Cornwall,
with no resources but their much-neglected farm.
In 1845 they established on their farm the Cream
Hill Agricultural School, which was successfully
conducted till 1869. The advancement of the general agricultural interests of the state has been his
favorite work. He originated the movement in
1850 which resulted in the formation in 1852 of the
Connecticut State Agricultural Society, and from
the beginning has held some official position in its
control. In 1866, at the establishment of the Connecticut Board of Agriculture, he was chosen its
secretary, which office he still holds. In 1864, he,
with the aid of the names of the other corporators,
obtained from the general assembly a charter for
the " Connecticut Soldiers' Orphans' Home." This
was located at Mansfield, and during its maintenance, or until 1874, he was secretary of the corporation. He was one of the editors of *The Homestead*, an agricultural paper published in Hartford
from 1856 to 1861; and in 1878 published a history
of Cornwall, Conn. He is a member of the board
of control of the Connecticut Agricultural Experi-

ment Station, and one of the trustees and secretary of the Storrs Agricultural School at Mansfield.

He was twice married: first, at Bridgeport, September 13, 1843, to Caroline E., daughter of Charles and Eunice Lockwood, who died April 25, 1857; and second, on the 4th of April, 1859, to Mrs. Emma (Tracy) Baldwin, daughter of A. W. Tracy of Rockville. He has had nine children, of whom six are living. The oldest son, Charles Lockwood, a graduate of the Sheffield School at Yale in 1883, is a farmer on Cream Hill; the youngest, James Douglas, a graduate of the same institution in 1888, is a student of medicine.

PROF. J. M. HOPPIN, New Haven: Art Professor Yale University.

Professor James Mason Hoppin was born in Providence, R. I., Jan. 17, 1820, and graduated from Yale College in the class of 1840. This class contained some able thinkers and leaders of the present generation, including the Rev. Dr. John P. Gulliver, who occupied the presidency of Knox College, at Galesburg, Ill., for a number of years, ex-Governor Charles R. Ingersoll, the late Rev. Drs. Henry M. Dexter of Boston, and Lavalette Perrin of this city, and the Connecticut historian, the late Gideon

J. M. HOPPIN.

H. Hollister of Litchfield. Professor Hoppin pursued a thorough course of theology and was settled as a minister in Salem, Mass., for nine years. He was appointed to a professorship in the Yale Theological Seminary thirty-two years ago, and was an instructor in that institution until 1879. For the past twelve years he has been connected with the Yale School of Fine Arts as professor of the history of art. He has studied in Germany, and has traveled extensively through Europe, being one of the most scholarly and polished representatives of the university. In 1870, the degree of S.T.D. was conferred upon him by Knox College on account of his exceptional attainments as a theological writer. He has written several books, among them being "Old England, its Art, Scenery, and People," which passed through eleven editions, "Homiletics," "Pastoral Theology," and "Sermons upon Faith, Hope, and Love." He is also the author of the "Life of Rear-Admiral Andrew Hull Foote," one of Connecticut's naval heroes during the war. This varied list was dealt with in the ablest and most attractive manner, the theological writings being not less enjoyable than the volumes of biography and travel from his pen. He is also a magazine writer of noted ability. Professor Hoppin is a good preacher, and his pulpit ministrations during the time that he occupied one of the most important professorships in the Yale Theological Seminary were of an exceptional order of merit. His sermons as well as his writings are models of English. The treatise on "Pastoral Theology" is one of the ablest productions of New England scholarship, and will ensure Professor Hoppin permanent renown as a theological thinker and scholar. He has the *entree* to the most distinguished literary societies throughout the country, while his career as the professor of the history of art in the great university at New Haven has made him an authority in that field. During his early years the professor was in the military service of Rhode Island for six weeks on the side of the state in the Dorr insurrection. His wife, who is living, was Miss Mary Deming Perkins prior to her marriage. There are two sons, one of whom, Benjamin Hoppin, graduated from Yale in 1872 and afterwards became an instructor in the university. Professor Hoppin is a member of the Yale College church. In politics he is a republican, with a leaning towards the independent party.

GEORGE LEWIS CHASE, Hartford: President of the Hartford Fire Insurance Company.

George L. Chase was born in Millbury, Worcester County, Mass., January 13, 1828, and was educated at Millbury Academy, receiving a thorough English course of studies. At the age of nineteen years he engaged in the insurance business as the agent of the Farmers' Mutual Fire Insurance Company of Georgetown, Mass., and was subsequently elected a member of the board of directors. He became an efficient canvasser, operating at first through southern Massachusetts and eastern Connecticut, and within a

G. L. CHASE.

short time his agency included four companies, transacting business on the mutual plan. One of the number, the Holyoke Mutual of Salem, is still engaged in successful operations. In 1848 Mr. Chase was appointed traveling agent for the People's Insurance Company of Worcester and retained the position until 1852, when he was appointed assistant superintendent of the Central Ohio Railroad Company and removed to Ohio. Soon afterwards he was advanced to the office of general superintendent of the road. He was one of the first representatives who organized the first association of railroad superintendents in the United States, the meeting for the purpose being held at Columbus, Ohio, in 1853. President Chase resumed the fire insurance business in 1860, accepting the western general agency of the New England Fire Insurance Company of this city. This position was held until 1863, when he received the appointment of assistant western general agent of the Hartford Fire Insurance Company. In this position, as in all others which he had occupied, Mr. Chase displayed ability of the highest order, attracting from the outset the attention and approval of the board of directors. In 1867 the presidency of the company was placed at his acceptance. After thorough deliberation Mr. Chase consented to assume the duties and responsibilities of the position, and in June of that year he succeeded Timothy C. Allyn as president. From that time until now he has been at the head of the Hartford Fire, one of the oldest and most successful insurance institutions in the United States. His management of the company's business and interests has been matchless in character, placing him in the foremost rank of fire insurance representatives.

The standing of President Chase as an insurance manager was recognized from the outset by his associates and competitors in the business. In 1876 he was elected president of the National Board of Fire Underwriters and is at present the board chairman of the committee on legislation and taxation, in all respects the most important committeeship in the organization. President Chase's connection with the national board has been one of commanding influence and leadership. He is a member of the board of trustees of the Society for Savings in this city, which is the largest savings bank in Connecticut, and is also a trustee of the Connecticut Trust and Safe Deposit Company and a director in the American National Bank. He is a leading member of the Hartford Board of Trade and is thoroughly interested in the industrial development and prosperity of the city of which he is so prominent and influential a citizen. President Chase is a member of the Asylum Hill Congregational Church in Hartford, and was elected president of the Connecticut Congregational Club for the fourth annual term in March. This club is the most important lay organization connected with the congregational churches in the state and wields the most extended influence. The late United States Senator Lafayette S. Foster of Norwich was its first president. The wife of President Chase, who was Miss Calista M. Taft prior to her marriage, is still living. There are two children, one son and one daughter. The former, Mr. Charles E. Chase, is assistant secretary in the company of which his father has been the president for so many years. The most of President Chase's life has been passed in this city. He has also resided in Chicago, Ill., and Dubuque, Ia.

WOOSTER A. ENSIGN, New Haven: Iron and Steel Merchant.

The subject of this sketch was born in New Haven, June 14, 1823, being the son of Thomas and Esther Ensign, and of a family which is identified with the early history of his native city and of the commercial industry there which he now represents. He was educated in the common schools and at the famous Lancasterian school then under the charge of John E. Lovell of educational fame. At the age of fifteen he left school and engaged in business as a clerk in the employ of English & Mix, then in

the hardware trade. At the end of an engagement with this firm covering nine years, he began business on his own account as a dealer in iron and steel goods, which business has prospered and increased, requiring in 1876 the erection of the spacious store which is now occupied by himself and his eldest son, who constitute the enterprising and solid firm of Wooster A. Ensign & Son. Mr. Ensign was married June 24, 1846, to Miss Charlotte A. Prescott, daughter of Roger Sherman Prescott of New Haven. They have three children. He holds or has held many important connections with the financial institutions of New Haven, having been for twenty-five years a director in the City Bank, vice-president and director in the New Haven Watch company until the removal of their factory to New Jersey, and a director in the Maryland steamboat company of Baltimore, Md. He has been prominent among the business men and interests of New Haven for nearly half a century, outliving many of his early contemporaries. From small beginnings he passed uninterruptedly through the various grades of success to the honorable position which he occupies to-day among the most prosperous and wealthy establishments in his line in New England. Mr. Ensign is a member of St. Paul Episcopal church of New Haven, and is still active in religious work as he is in the secular duties of life. In politics he is connected with the democratic party, in whose honors he has repeatedly been called to share.

HON. DANIEL NASH MORGAN, Bridgeport: Banker.

Daniel N. Morgan, one of the most widely-known citizens of Fairfield county, was born in Newtown, August 18, 1844, and educated at the Newtown

D. N. MORGAN.

Academy, Bethel Institute, and in the common schools. He was thoroughly educated to the mercantile pursuit, during the last five years of his minority in his father's store, when he succeeded to the control of the business for one year; subsequently for three years he was of the flourishing firm of Morgan & Booth, retiring in 1869, and removing to Bridgeport, where for more than ten years he was of the firm of Birdsey & Morgan, transacting a large and profitable business in dry goods and carpets, having also during that period probably the largest dressmaking establishment in the state, enjoying a choice southern trade. During the year 1877 he was connected with the firm of Morgan, Hopson & Co., wholesale grocers. He was a member of the common council of Bridgeport in 1873-4; mayor of Bridgeport in 1880 and 1884; on the board of education in the same town in 1877-78, and for many years parish clerk, and is senior warden of Trinity Church. He is vice-president and member of the board of directors of the Bridgeport Hospital; vice-president of the Consolidated Rolling Stock Company; sinking fund commissioner of the city; vice-president of the state democratic club; president of the City National Bank since 1870,—during which time $125,000 has been added to its surplus; president of the Mechanics' and Farmers' Savings Bank,—whose deposits have increased half a million during the past five years, with assets now of $1,100,000. Mr. Morgan was state senator from the fourteenth district in 1885 and 1886, having been previously, in 1883, elected to the lower house by a majority of 940—the largest ever given a member since the organization of the town. For two years he was Worshipful Master of Corinthian Lodge, No. 104, F. and A. M. He is now a member of Hamilton Commandery, No. 5, K. T., and also of Pequonnock Lodge, No. 4, I. O. O. F. He married, in 1867, Medora H. Judson, daughter of the late Hon. Wm. A. Judson, formerly of Huntington, a lifelong democrat, and senator from the tenth district in 1852, and a member of the house in 1844, 1848, 1850, and 1854. Mr. Morgan's maternal grandfather was Daniel Nash, late of Westport, who was well-known locally as an eminent financier, living into his 99th

year. Mr. Morgan's father, Ezra Morgan, represented Newtown in the legislature in 1842, 1862, and 1868. He was of one of the oldest families of the state; was for many years a merchant, and for a long time president of the Hatter's National Bank of Bethel.

The subject of this sketch has two children, a son and a daughter.

—

PELEG S. BARBER, Stonington: President People's Savings Bank of Pawcatuck.

Mr. Barber was born in North Kingston, R. I., April 29, 1823. He received the advantages of a good common school education, and has been

P. S. BARBER.

largely engaged in mercantile and manufacturing business, though at present confining his attention chiefly to transactions in real estate. He was for sixteen years in cotton manufacturing, and from 1850 to 1853 was in the gold mines of California. He married, early in life, Miss Sarah Gardner, who is still living. Mr. Barber is largely interested in the Pawcatuck National Bank, of which he is, and for sixteen years has been, a director. He is president of the People's Savings Bank of Pawcatuck; also treasurer of the Pawcatuck Fire District since its organization in 1887, for sixteen years treasurer of his school district, fifteen years a member of the town board of relief, and a notary public. He was on the board of assessors for several years, and has held various other local offices in the town in which he resides, where he has led an active and useful life for thirty-four years, and is highly respected and esteemed by all his townsmen. Mr. Barber comes from an ancestry which have been prominently identified with the whig and republican parties ever since their formation. In the fall of 1884 he became the candidate of the republicans for representative from Stonington in the general assembly, to which position he was elected by a large majority. He served in the house on the committee on appropriations. As an ardent supporter of republican principles and a consistent advocate of temperance, he did good work for his constituency and the state during the session of 1885, and made an honorable record as a legislator. Mr. Barber is a member of the Baptist church and takes an active interest in all moral and religious enterprises in the town, which he is always ready to aid whenever called upon to do so.

JOHN A. CONANT, WILLIMANTIC: President New England Christian Association.

John A. Conant is a descendant in the seventh generation from Roger Conant, who came from England in 1623, and finally settled in what is now Salem, Mass. He was born at Mansfield, Conn., August 16, 1829, being the oldest son of Lucius and Marietta (Eaton) Conant, who were unable to give him anything more than a common school education. At ten years of age he went to live on a farm with his mother's brother, George Eaton, and remained there until nearly fifteen, when he returned home,

J. A. CONANT.

and soon after went to work in a silk mill of which the Hon. Augustus Storrs was agent. In 1849, because of the depressed condition of the silk manufacturing business, he was thrown out of work, but secured employment at the American mills in Rockville, where he became acquainted with Miss Caroline A. Chapman of Ellington, to whom he was married in 1852. In 1854 he engaged with Messrs. Cheney Brothers to take charge of the winding department of their mills in Hartford. There he remained two years, during which time he took a letter from the Wesleyan Methodist Church of Tolland, and, with his wife, united with the Fourth Congregational Church of that city, Rev. William W. Patton pastor. In 1856, being weary of mill life, he bought a small farm in West Hartford, but only a year elapsed before he yielded to the earnest solicitations of the Watertown Manufacturing Company to superintend their silk mill at Watertown, in this state. Having lost the companion of his youth, who died in 1863, leaving one son, he was married the following year to his second wife, Mrs. Marietta (French) Brown of Mansfield, by whom he had two sons, but only one is now living. In 1866 he engaged with Messrs. J. H. & G. Holland to superintend the throwing department of their silk works in Willimantic, where he still resides.

When Mr. Conant became an elector he commenced voting with the free soil party, with which he acted until it was merged into the newly-organized republican party, in which he was a zealous worker until after the war of the rebellion, when, seeing the successful influence of the liquor traffic over its leading men, he left it in 1872 to act with the prohibitionists. Meanwhile the anti-secret reform began to engage his attention. Mr. Conant has been a member of three secret societies, two of which are now extinct, and the other he abandoned many years since because of the clannish spirit and idolatrous tendency he discovered in such societies. He has come to look upon all secret organizations as dangerous to the state, and a hindrance to the work of the Christian church; and he now holds the position of president of the New England Christian Association, formed for the purpose of opposing and exposing the evils of the lodge system. In 1884 he was nominated on the anti-secret ticket by the American party for vice-president, but with the other candidate, Dr. J. Blanchard, withdrew in favor of St. John and Daniel; since which time he has generally acted with the prohibitionists, except when such action would conflict with his anti-secret principles.

IRVING EMERSON, HARTFORD: Professor of Music.

Professor Irving Emerson is one of the most widely-known and successful musical directors in the state and the author of leading musical publications and works now used in the public schools. These works include "Song Land," "Song Tablet", "Morning Hour," "Public School Hymnal," "First Steps in Song Reading," and "Song Readers," Nos. 1 & 2, and also a large number of compositions for church choirs. He organized and directed for four years a large choral society in Hartford called "The Emerson Chorus,"

IRVING EMERSON.

of two hundred voices, giving three or more concerts each season, with Theodore Thomas' and the Germania orchestras and celebrated vocal soloists, and presenting at each entertainment some new work. Afterwards he formed the Hartford Opera Company, drilling and directing the performances of "Patience," "Pirates of Penzance," "Iolanthe," "Maritana," "Pinafore," "Chimes of Normandy," "Betsy Baker," "The Sleeping Queen," and "Priscilla," not only here, but in the neighboring cities of Springfield, New Britain, Middletown, and Rockville. He also directed several public school festivals, where over a thousand children took part. He has been busy in the same kind of work all through this part of the state. Professor Emerson became a resident of Hartford in 1869 and has been the director of music and organist in the leading churches in this city, including the South Congregational, the Asylum Hill and Pearl Street churches, Christ church and the First Methodist, this service covering a period of twenty-two years. But his most important work has been accomplished in the public schools of the city, in which he has been the musical instructor for years. Prior to his removal to Hartford he resided in Boston, Belfast, Me., and Montpelier, Vt. During the war he served in the forty-third Massachusetts; he is now a member of the Army and Navy Club of Connecticut. He is a 32° Mason and occupies official positions in Wolcott Council and Pythagoras Chapter in this city. He is also a member of the Improved Order of Red Men. In politics he is a republican and in religious belief a Unitarian. His wife was a Miss Mary E. Young, a prominent teacher in the public schools here prior to her marriage, and the family consists of two sons. Professor Emerson and wife were married in June, 1888.

DR. N. W. HOLCOMBE, West Simsbury: Postmaster.

Dr. Noah Webster Holcombe was born in Granby in 1831, and was educated in the University Medical College of New York city. He has devoted his life to the practice of medicine. He has served in both branches of the general assembly, being a member of the senate in 1869, and of the house in 1876. Prior to the war, he was connected with the democratic party, but for the last thirty years he has been a republican. He was in the service as a volunteer surgeon during the rebellion. He has held numerous offices of trust and responsibility in the town

N. W. HOLCOMBE.

where he resides, serving on the board of selectmen and as postmaster at West Simsbury. The latter is one of the positions that he still retains. He is also post surgeon at Simsbury. Dr. Holcombe is a member of Hartford Lodge, F. and A. M., Washington Commandery, Knights Templar, surgeon of the Putnam Phalanx, and is connected with Trumbull Council of the National Providence Union, and the Order of Red Men. He is president of the Simsbury Agricultural Society, president of the Tunxis Rogue Detective Society, president of the Connecticut Detective Association, and also president of the Simsbury Creamery Company. He is a director in the National Life Association of this city, and vice-president and treasurer of the Connecticut Association for the protection of game and fish. Dr. Holcombe is one of the busiest of men, but always has time to be the most companionable of gentlemen. He has been a resident of Connecticut during the whole of his active life with the exception of three years spent in Wilmington, Del.

He is a member of the Baptist church. His wife, who was Elizabeth B. Moses prior to marriage, is still living, but there are no children in the family.

E. M. HUNTSINGER, Hartford: Principal Huntsinger's Business College.

Mr. Huntsinger is what the world calls a self-made man. Most men are self-made, and especially those who are well-made. The subject of this

E. M. HUNTSINGER.

sketch is worthy of mention, not only for his natural gifts but for the quality which New Englanders appreciate, energy, persistence, and directness. He is a positive man both in his convictions and in his actions. Whatever he conceives to be right, that he does, even if it should require him to do differently when guided by a different light.

He was born at Valley View, Pa., February, 1855. His early educational advantages were good, and he improved them, finishing his school education in the English course of the State Normal School at Shippensburg, Pa. In accomplishing this he did as so many brave and self-respecting American boys have been proud to do—defrayed his own expenses through his own labor. He taught in the public schools for three years, and then, with the view of entering upon a business life, he took a course of training in bookkeeping and penmanship under Mr. A. H. Hinman at Pottsville. He soon showed such a liking for commercial studies and such aptness in receiving and imparting instruction therein, that he was induced to enter the business college field. In pursuance of this purpose he began his professional work at the Bryant & Stratton College of Providence, R. I., where he taught from 1877 to 1884; following this with four years of instruction in the Packard Business College of New York. In 1888 he opened Huntsinger's Business College in Hartford, which proved a success at the start, and which is now in the full tide of prosperity and usefulness. Mr. Huntsinger is a progressive man in all good directions. He has an assured standing among the teachers in his line, and is everywhere known as a conscientious, thorough worker. He is a zealous upholder of organized religious work, a member of the Methodist church and of the Y. M. C. A. He is, besides, a thirty-second degree Mason, and an influential member of that mystic body. He is a natural "boomer," and to whatever he deems worthy of his attention he gives his whole heart, soul, might, mind, and strength. In his college work he has the valuable assistance of his wife, who is a lady of rare intellectual attainments, and an excellent equipoise to his ardent outreachings. Together, they make an uncommonly strong educational combination, the results of which the city of Hartford and the state of Connecticut will feel in the coming years.   S. S. PACKARD.

STILES JUDSON, JR., Stratford: Attorney-at-Law.

The subject of this sketch was born in Stratford, Fairfield county, Conn., February 13, 1862. He received his early education in the public schools of the town and at the Strat-
ford Academy. At the age of twenty-one he entered the Law School of Yale University where he was graduated in June, 1885, with the degree of LL.B., and was awarded the prize for the best examination in his studies. He was admitted to the bar of Connecticut the same year, and entered the office of the well-known

STILES JUDSON, JR.

law firm of Townsend & Watrous in New Haven, where he remained until September, 1886. He then removed to Bridgeport, where he has since continued the practice of his profession, and is a member of the law firm of Canfield & Judson. He is an active practitioner in the courts, and has been identified with some of the most important cases that have arisen in Fairfield county. He is of good presence before a jury, a fluent and earnest pleader, quick to grasp the important points in a case, and has been remarkably successful in his practice.

Mr. Judson has been connected with the Connecticut National Guard for ten years, and is now captain of Company K, Fourth Regiment, located at Stratford. He makes a popular and efficient officer. He was married in 1889 to Miss Minnie L. Miles of Milford, and has since made Stratford his residence, where he has always taken an active part in town affairs, and has acceptably filled various offices in the town. He is at present chairman of the republican town committee and an active party worker. In the presidential campaign of 1888 Mr. Judson went upon the stump and won a reputation as an eloquent and convincing speaker upon public issues. He is a member of St. John's Lodge of Masons in Stratford. At the celebration

of the 250th anniversary of the settlement of the town of Stratford he was chosen as the president of the day, and was at the time the youngest male representative of the oldest family in the town. Mr. Judson was elected to the legislature from Stratford in the fall of 1890, and was at once recognized as one of the leaders on the republican side of the house in the memorable gubernatorial contest in the winter of 1891. He was also appointed to the important position of chairman of the judiciary committee of the house, a position for which his talents peculiarly fitted him. The position he has attained in the professions of law and politics gives promise of a very successful future career.

FRANCIS H. RICHARDS, Hartford: Mechanical Engineer.

One of the early settlers of Hartford was William Whiting, a merchant, whose name is mentioned in the histories of this country as early as
1632. He was chosen treasurer of the colony of Connecticut in 1641, which office he retained until his death. His son, Joseph Whiting, was elected to the same office, holding it thirty-nine years until his death, when Joseph's son, John Whiting, succeeded to the treasuryship and continued in the office for thirty-two years. Thro' this line, in the sixth generation from William,

F. H. RICHARDS.

came Maria S. Whiting, who married Henry Richards and became the mother of the subject of this sketch. Francis H. Richards' paternal ancestor in America was Thomas Richards, who came to Connecticut in 1637, and settled in Hartford, in which vicinity his immediate descendants were prominent in planting of new settlements, one of them being of the party which settled at Waterbury. Those in the direct line of the present subject lived in Hartford for nearly a century after its first settlement. F. H. Richards was born at New Hartford, Litchfield county, October 20, 1850, and in his early years lived a part of the time at the home of his grandfather, Marquis Richards, on the ancestral estate which was founded by his great-grandfather, Aaron Richards, during the war of the revolution, and is in part still held in the family. His school life began at New Haven, whither his father, Henry Richards, removed with his family in 1856, where he attended the then celebrated "Eaton" graded school. The years from 1857 to 1865 were spent on his father's farm, near Bakersville, in New Hartford, working summers at farming, and during the winter months attending first the village school and later the academy, which ordinary advantages were supplemented by private instructors. In 1865, the family removed to New Britain, where for a few months he attended the high school. The following year, being offered the alternative of attending a technical college or of learning the machinist's trade, he chose the shop and began his mechanical and inventive career in the factories of the Stanley Rule and Level Company, under the supervision of his father, an ingenious mechanic and inventor, in charge of the machinery department of this extensive establishment. Here, by persistent work and systematic study extending over a period of eight years, he acquired both a practical and theoretical knowledge of the machine-building trades, including, besides the trade of machinist, the arts of wood-working, forging, and the allied branches. During this time, he made frequent tours for the critical observation of machinery and manufactures, began the study of patent law, and made numerous inventions of labor-saving machines, several of which are still in successful operation.

Mr. Richards' business connections have been in Hartford since 1882; principally with the Pratt & Whitney Company from 1883 to 1886, at which latter date he established his office in that city. In October, 1887, he was married to Mrs. Clara V. Dole (née Blasdale) of Springfield, Mass., who is of English birth, her father having been a prominent expert and designer in the lace manufacture until his emigration to this country about 1852. Since his marriage, he has resided in Hartford. In 1889, in company with his wife he visited Paris as a member of a touring party of American engineers, including scientific gentlemen representing all the leading industries of America. Mr. Richards is a member of the American Society of Mechanical Engineers, a national organization with headquarters at New York; of the Civil Engineers' Club of Cleveland, Ohio; and of the New York Engineers' Club. In the Masonic fraternity he is identified with Washington Commandery, No. 1, Knights Templar; also with the several Scottish Rite bodies, up to the 32d degree. His religious associations are with the Church of the Redeemer (Universalist), of Hartford; his political affiliations with the republican party.

Mr. Richards is the author of many important inventions, among which is the "Richards Envelope Machine," patented in the United States and foreign countries — the American patents being now owned and controlled by the White, Corbin & Co., of Rockville. This machine prints, folds, gums, counts, and bands, automatically, 80,000 letter envelopes per day, greatly exceeding any other envelope machine in its capacity and in its economy in the consumption of paper. He is also the inventor and patentee of the fundamental features of the "Norton Door Check," a device for automatically closing light or heavy doors by an air-cushion arrangement, which is now in quite general use. He has taken out, first and last, 225 United States patents, a larger number, probably, than any other person in western Connecticut. Mr. Richards has practically elevated the matter of inventing machinery to an art. Whatever is sought to be done through the medium of mechanical appliances, he simply finds a way and invents a machine to do it.

WILLIAM HAMERSLEY, Hartford: Attorney-at-Law.

Mr. Hamersley was born in Hartford, September 9, 1838, being a son of the late Hon. William James Hamersley, who was for many years a distinguished

WILLIAM HAMERSLEY.

resident of the city. He was a scholar at the old Hartford grammar school, afterwards at the High school, and entered Trinity college in 1854, but left during his senior year, beginning his legal studies in the office of Welch & Shipman. He was admitted to the bar in 1859, in 1863 was elected a member of the court of common council, later was vice-president of the board, and president during 1867 and 1868. He also held the position of city attorney, resigning in the end to accept the appointment of state's attorney for Hartford county in 1868, a position which he held for twenty years. He represented Hartford in the legislature of 1886, serving on the judiciary and federal relations committees. He was one of the founders of the Connecticut State Bar Association, and, with Richard D. Hubbard and Simeon E. Baldwin, constituted the committee of that association, through whose initiatory efforts the American Bar Association was founded. He was one of the original promoters of the civil procedure reform, and a member of the commission that drafted the practice act, and the rules and forms of procedure adopted by the court for giving due effect to the provisions of that act; he was also an early and active promoter of the reform in the jury system in Connecticut. His time has been mainly given to the practice of his profession and to work relating to law reform.

JOHN H. LEEDS, NEW HAVEN : Superintendent of the Stamford Manufacturing Company.

The Leeds ancestry is identified in history with the city of Leeds, England, in which the family, centuries since, was an important one. In 1680 three brothers, Leeds, emigrated to New England, one of whom settled in Stamford, in this state. A descendant of the last was Joseph H. Leeds, a farmer, resident at the Leeds' place in Darien, where his son, the subject of this sketch, John Harris Leeds, was born March 4, 1836. It was not, as is said of many, an accident that deter-

J. H. LEEDS.

mined the course of his life, but the prevention of an accident. The New York & New Haven Railroad had been opened but a few months, and had but a single track. Just at dusk, June 24, 1849, John H. Leeds, then thirteen years of age, chanced to be on its line at a crossroad halfway between Darien and Stamford, when he heard a train coming from the east. He knew there was also a train coming from the west, although it was hidden from sight by a deep cut and a sharp curve. All the horrors of a collision were inevitable unless he could prevent it. He would try. In an instant he sprang on to the track, and, facing the New York bound train, waved his hat to attract the attention of the engineer, and then bounded to one side, barely escaping being crushed as it went thundering by. As it passed him in its lightning speed he pointed to the west, and shouted to the engineer, "Another train is coming this way." The engineer at once reversed his engine, and whistled "down brakes," and then blew a long and loud alarm. The other train was still unseen, but its engineer was on the alert, and, hearing the signal, in turn reversed his engine and whistled the same signal. But such was the speed of both trains and the feebleness of the brakes then in use that when the trains stopped they were only an engine's length apart. When the boy gave the warning they were rushing for each other at full speed. On board the two trains were five hundred people,— men, women, and children. It is fearful to contemplate the horrors that were inevitable had not the lad been at the crossroad and done exactly the right thing. He certainly had not been born in vain, and the passengers thought so as they shuddered at their narrow escape. The railroad company, acting upon their sense of obligation, gave him a free pass over their road, good for life, and

also presented him with an elegant silver goblet, with this inscription:

PRESENTED BY THE PRESIDENT AND DIRECTORS

of

THE NEW YORK & NEW HAVEN RAILROAD COMPANY

to

JOHN H. LEEDS.

" Just as the twig is bent the tree's inclined."

Annexed is a copy of the letter from the company accompanying the present, together with young Leeds' reply:

STAMFORD, August 11, 1849.

My Dear Young Friend :

The president and directors of the New York & New Haven Railroad Company, by a unanimous resolution, have assigned to me the pleasing task of presenting to you the accompanying cup, as a slight testimonial of their approbation of your manly conduct in preventing a collision of their trains.

May the impulse which prompted you then continue to animate you, cheered with the pleasant recollection of having done unto others as you would they should do unto you. Your Friend,

H. J. SANFORD, Director.

To MASTER JOHN H. LEEDS.

[REPLY.]

DARIEN, August 17, 1849.

Mr. H. J. Sanford :

SIR,—I acknowledge with feelings of gratitude and pleasure the receipt of the very handsome present from the New York & New Haven Railroad Company through your hands, but beg to disclaim any merit for an act which the impulse of the moment prompted and duty urged me to do.

Probably the lives of some of my fellow creatures were saved through my humble endeavors, and the consciousness of that is sufficient reward.

Yours very respectfully,

JOHN HARRIS LEEDS.

The railroad company did not lose sight of the lad, for three years after he removed to New Haven and went into their service to learn to be a mechanical and constructing engineer, beginning as an apprentice and going up through all departments. At one period he ran an engine on the road. He remained in their employ until 1860. At that date he engaged with the Stamford Manufacturing Company as their superintendent and consulting engineer, taking charge of the mineral branch of their business, they being the oldest and largest manufacturers of chemical and dyeing extracts in the United States. He has continued with them to the present time.

Mr. Leeds ever has been, and now is, an exceedingly busy man. He has largely served the public in many and varied capacities, and how worthily is shown by the testimonials bestowed upon him by his associates. The positions he has held have been such that, while of invaluable service to the community, they have been generally with no recompense save in the consciousness of well-doing. He was alderman in 1863–64, and was assistant judge of the city court for two years, this office being then selected by law from the board of aldermen. During the construction of the Derby railroad, which occupied two years, he was its city director. He was for many years a member of the volunteer fire department. In 1862, when the department was reorganized, he was one of the first fire commissioners under the new régime, and was president of that board for about fifteen years. Steam fire-engines, fire-alarm telegraphs, and paid firemen were introduced under his presidency. One of the new steam fire-engines, by order of the board, was named in his honor " John H. Leeds." When the imposing firemen's monument in Evergreen cemetery was dedicated he was appointed orator of the day. He was for several years president of the board of steam engines and boilers; chairman of the fire and water departments of the city for two years; and represented the city in making contracts for water supply. In 1875, owing to increased business duties and the claims of the Stamford Manufacturing Company which required his services abroad, he withdrew from all public offices. Upon this the city passed and presented highly complimentary resolutions signifying their sense of his eminent services. These were ordered to be engrossed and presented in a permanent framed memorial. The fire department also presented a magnificent and costly badge, a miniature steam fire-engine, and fire apparatus, with the city coat-of-arms highly embellished with diamonds and rubies. Rarely has any citizen on his withdrawal from public service been so honored. In 1879-80 he was sent to the legislature as the city's first representative. His colleague, Colonel Dexter R. Wright, was chosen speaker of the house. It was the first legislature that met in the new state house. He was one of the committee on railroads, and one of the peculiarly important committee on the construction of the dome of the state house. Mr. Leeds was state director of the Wethersfield penitentiary for six years, from 1879 to 1885. He is now a director of the Yale National Bank, the New Haven Savings Bank, the New Haven Water Company, and a managing director of the Stamford Manufacturing Company, in whose business he has passed most of his time for years in Europe and the Orient. Mr. Leeds' first trip to Europe was in 1876, when he opened a barytes mine on the south coast of Ireland. Since then his time has been mostly spent in matters of a commercial and productive nature that are found only in the Orient, where he obtained many of the supplies of crude materials, such as dyes, drugs, and chemicals that are used by the Stamford Manufacturing Company. He is a most extensive traveler, the nature of his business requiring him to go to rarely visited places and among half-civilized and rude people. Besides every country of Europe, he has visited Asia Minor, Syria, Northern Egypt, nearly every island of the Grecian Archipelago, all the cities of the seven churches of Asia, as well as Tarsus, Antioch, Aleppo, and the whole of Palestine. In the two years, 1884-85, he traveled over 80,000 miles by steamship, railway, horse, canal, and on foot. His business transactions have been with all the tribes of the Orient, Turks, Greeks, Armenians, Bulgarians, Koords, Bedouins, Arabs, and Egyptians. His experiences have impressed him with the conviction that, as a body, they are commercially and politically dishonest, and morally corrupt; while religious fanaticism is the controlling element of their lives. Mr. Leeds was married January 27, 1858, to Miss Frances A. Hine of Milford.

Physically, he is one of the largest and most powerful of men. He stands 6 ft. 1½ in., has heavy broad shoulders, a chest measurement of 46 inches, and weighs 250 pounds, but not accompanied with extraneous flesh. His health is vigorous, and his constitution is one capable of long-sustained and continuous labor. He is of a serious turn of mind, and, being full of business, has little time for the lighter conversation and frivolities of life. This record shows that he has had a wide acquaintance with men, and a useful and honorable career, working with and upon those material forces that move civilization on its ascending pathway.

S. T. HOLBROOK, Norwich: Judge of Probate.
Judge Supply T. Holbrook of the probate court, Norwich district, is a gentleman of superior legal attainments and has held numerous offices of trust and responsibility. He has been the judge of the court of common pleas, and is regarded with marked esteem by the New London county bar. In politics Judge Holbrook is a republican. He is connected with the Second Congregational church at Norwich and is thoroughly interested in the religious and educational standing of the community. Judge Holbrook has been married twice. His first wife was Sarah E. Shepard. The surviving one was Miss Carrie Stark before marriage. There are five children in the family, two sons and three daughters. The subject of this sketch was born at Roxbury, Mass., Sept. 7, 1822, and received a common school education in that state. His classical training was from private tutors. His life has been spent in Massachusetts and Connecticut. In this state he has resided in Hartford, New London, and Norwich. He was formerly a professor of music.

S. T. HOLBROOK.

HON. PHINEAS C. LOUNSBURY, Ridgefield: Ex-Governor of Connecticut; President Merchants' Exchange National Bank of New York city.

P. C. Lounsbury is a native of the town where he still resides; he was born in 1840. His father was a farmer, and like most farmers' sons he worked on the farm during the years of boyhood and early manhood. He found time, however, to acquire a thorough academic education in the schools of learning in his native state. He then went to New York city where he secured a position as clerk in a shoe store, and in time familiarized himself with all departments of the business. Having laid the foundations for a

P. C. LOUNSBURY.

successful commercial career he began, upon attaining his majority, the manufacture of shoes with his brother in New Haven under the firm name of Lounsbury Brothers. The business was afterward removed to South Norwalk, and carried on under the firm name of Lounsbury, Matthewson & Co. When the civil war broke out he enlisted as a private in the Seventeenth Connecticut Regiment, but after four months' active service was compelled by severe sickness to return, being honorably discharged and recommended for a pension, which he would not accept.

Mr. Lounsbury represented Ridgefield in the Connecticut house of representatives in 1874, and occupied a leading position throughout the session. He was a prominent factor in state politics for the succeeding decade, and his name was before the republican state convention in 1884, unsuccessfully, however, as a candidate for the chief executive office. In 1886 he was the only prominent candidate for that position before the convention, and received the nomination for governor by an overwhelming majority on the first ballot. His incumbency of the office of chief magistrate during the succeeding two years gave signal satisfaction to his constituents and the state. He maintained the position with becoming dignity, performed its duties ably and well, and achieved distinction among the many conspicuous citizens who have administered the affairs of the commonwealth.

Ex-Governor Lounsbury is a life-long and consistent member of the Methodist Episcopal church, in which his liberal views and enlightened sentiments have always been duly recognized; and he now occupies an honored relation to her foremost schools,— notably to Wesleyan University at Mid-

dletown in this state, of which institution he has long been a trustee. His business connections are largely in New York, and he has for some years been president of the Merchants Exchange National Bank of that city, which under his control has become one of the most solid and prosperous of the banking houses of the metropolis.

HON. ORVILLE H. PLATT, Meriden: United States Senator.

Orville H. Platt was born in the town of Washington, Litchfield county, in this state, on July 19, 1827. He was a son of Daniel G. Platt, a farmer, and worked upon his father's farm until he was twenty years of age. His education was received in the common schools and in the academy of Frederick W. Gunn, of wide reputation in later years as the principal of " The Gunnery," so called, in the town of Washington, an institution of learning which became justly celebrated. Mr. Platt studied law in the office of

O. H. PLATT.

Hon. Gideon H. Hollister, Litchfield, the well known historian of Connecticut, now deceased, and was admitted to the bar in Litchfield in 1849. Subsequently he secured admission to the Pennsylvania bar in Towanda, Bradford county, and spent six months in the office of Hon. Ulysses Mercur, now judge of the supreme court of Pennsylvania. He returned to Connecticut in 1851, and located in Meriden as a practitioner of law, and has since made that city his home. In 1855-6, he was clerk of the Connecticut senate and was elected secretary of state in 1857. In 1861-2, he was a member of the senate, and in 1864 and 1869 was elected to the house,— the last year serving as its speaker. In all these positions he displayed exceptional qualifications and showed a special aptitude for legislative business. In 1877, he was chosen state attorney for New Haven county, and held that place till elected in 1879 to the United States senate to succeed Hon. William H. Barnum. He was unanimously re-elected at the expiration of his first term, in 1885, and again at the close of his second term in 1891.

Senator Platt is a pleasant speaker and a good debater — always clear and concise, wasting very few words for the sake of oratorical effect. As a lawyer he has had for many years a high standing at the bar, and has made a specialty of patent cases, though doing a general law practice. All his life he has been a promoter of Christian and philanthropic enterprises, actively working for the best good of society through the organized channels of religion and temperance, while by his own example assisting every good cause. His career has been in all respects useful and honorable.

AARON C. GOODMAN, HARTFORD.

Mr. Goodman is a native of West Hartford, where he was born April 23, 1822. After the usual custom of New England village boys, he had his

experience of wrestling with the district school, and at the age of thirteen years left that institution to try his hand at clerking in a Hartford bookstore. After some years of such employment he went to Philadelphia, in 1841, to enter the service of A. S. Barnes & Co., the noted publishers,— who had established themselves in the Quaker City, under the impression that

A. C. GOODMAN.

Philadelphia, and not New York, was destined to become the mercantile metropolis of this country. Mr. Goodman engaged with this firm for two years; but before the expiration of the first year, he received an advantageous proposal from his former employer in Hartford to return and become associated with him in the capacity of partner. Looking upon the proposition with favor, he obtained a release from Messrs. Barnes & Co., at the expiration of his first year, and on the first of April, 1842, he came back to Hartford and completed the proposed connection with his old employer, taking an equal interest with him in the business, which was thereafter conducted under the firm name of Sumner & Goodman. After being together six years, Mr. Goodman bought his partner's interest in the store, which he continued to manage alone until 1852, when he in turn sold out and went to New York to engage in the paper trade. He was in business in New York twenty-one years. At the organization of the Phoenix Mutual Life Insurance Company, in Hartford, in 1851, Mr. Goodman became a stockholder, and subsequently a director in the company. He closed his business in New York and returned permanently to Hartford in 1873. Two years later, in June, 1875, he was made president of the Phoenix Life, succeeding in that office the Hon. Edson Fessenden. He held the presidency of this company a little more than fourteen years, resigning in 1889. Since retiring from his official con-

nection with the Phoenix Mutual Life Insurance Company, Mr. Goodman has embarked in no other active enterprises, feeling that his health had been somewhat impaired by long and close application to business, and that he needed rest. He is not inclined to make any changes which will increase his business cares or anxieties, and feels that he has probably performed his full share of the active duties of an ordinary lifetime.

Mr. Goodman is a member of Trinity church, Hartford, and has long been connected with the masonic fraternity.

GEORGE W. DAINS, EAST LITCHFIELD: Paper Manufacturer.

Mr. Dains was born in Litchfield, February 11, 1844. He attended the common schools of the town, and in 1861, at age of seventeen, enlisted in

the New York Fourth Cavalry regiment, from which he was discharged in the spring of 1862 on account of disability from sickness. In the fall of 1862 he enlisted in Company K, Twenty-Third regiment, Connecticut Volunteers, and served until the expiration of his term of enlistment; afterwards enlisting in the Third Connecticut Light Battery, and serving until

G. W. DAINS.

the close of the war. He worked at farming two years or more, then entered and graduated from Eastman's National Business College at Poughkeepsie, N. Y., after which he was cashier for the mercantile house of Benedict, Merriman & Co. of Waterbury, during which time he was married to Miss Mary A. Page, daughter of John D. Page, of the firm of Page & Keeney, paper manufacturers of East Litchfield. October 1, 1871, he bought Mr. Keeney's interest in the mill, and commenced the business in company with Mr. Page, under the firm name of Page & Dains, which firm is still carrying on the business at the old stand.

Mr. Dains has had three children, two of whom — one son and one daughter — are living. He has held the offices of justice of the peace, school visitor, town auditor, and registrar of voters. At present he holds the office of county auditor for Litchfield county and also that of commissioner of the superior court. He was brought up a democrat, and went into the army as a democrat, but came out an uncompromising republican. While his post-office address is East Litchfield, his residence is on the Harwinton side of the Naugatuck river, which divides the two towns of Harwinton and Litchfield. He has twice represented the town of Harwinton in the legislature, first in 1877 and again 1889, when he served as house chairman of the joint standing committee on claims. At the November election in 1890 he was elected to the state senate from the eighteenth district, and was with the minority in that body during the peculiar proceedings which characterized the remarkable session of 1891. He has been engaged in local politics for many years and chairman of the republican town committee for the past thirteen years. He is a member and past commander of L. W. Steele Post, G. A. R., of Torrington; also belongs to the orders of Royal Arcanum and Knights of Honor, in which last-named order he is grand assistant dictator. In his religious faith and connections Mr. Dains is a Congregationalist.

HON. SAMUEL E. MERWIN, NEW HAVEN: Lieutenant-Governor of Connecticut.

Samuel E. Merwin was born in the town of Brookfield, Fairfield county, Conn., August 31, 1831. His education was that afforded by the district school of that day, supplemented by a year's instruction in a school of higher grade in the adjoining town of Newtown. In his sixteenth year he removed to New Haven with his father, where he spent one year in school before beginning his business life. After serving as clerk for two or three years he associated himself with his father, whose name he bears, under the

firm name of S. E. Merwin & Son, and continued in this relation until 1889. Outside of his very active and successful business life General Merwin has been identified with a variety of important public and private trusts. For two years he served his city as commissioner of police, and for nine years was an active and efficient member of the board of education. In 1872 he represented the fourth senatorial district in the legislature, being elected by a majority of 500 in a district heavily democratic. He has also been a candidate of the republicans for mayor of his city, and member of congress from the second district, his great popularity in both cases nearly resulting in overcoming large democratic majorities. His great admiration and friendship for the soldiers led to his appointment as chairman of the committee to build the soldiers' monument erected by the town of New

Haven, and it is largely due to his untiring zeal and energy that a most beautiful tribute has been dedicated to their memory.

General Merwin is at present the president of the Connecticut Hospital Society, trustee of the Orphan Asylum, and president of the New Haven Savings Bank — the largest savings institution in New Haven. The various positions show the esteem in which he is held by his associates, and show also his charitable nature, as they are all a drain upon his time and pocket, without any pecuniary compensation. He is almost daily the counsellor and advisor of widows and orphans, and has been called frequently during the past twenty years by the business men of his city to settle various estates, including those of insurance companies, banks, manufacturers, and merchants; and in these important trusts, often complicated, he has ever won the esteem and thanks of the creditors for faithful and energetic settlements.

In military circles General Merwin has been more conspicuous even than in civil life. During the war he was in command of the New Haven Grays, subsequently he became lieutenant-colonel, and colonel of the second regiment, and later was adjutant-general under Governor Jewell for three years. Probably no man in Connecticut, not in actual service, was more efficient during the civil war than General Merwin. In response to a call from Governor Buckingham, the Grays under his command volunteered to go to Gettysburg. During the draft riots in New York his company remained under arms for thirty days, in hourly expectation of being called upon to aid in averting that appalling danger. Guarding conscripts, burying with appropriate honors many officers and soldiers who had fallen in battle or died in hospitals, and receiving with proper military display the returning veterans of the war, became a part of his official duties while in command of the regiment. His last military service was to direct in the capture of a party of prize fighters and their associates at Charles Island opposite Milford. By his judicious management the whole party were taken to New Haven and turned over to the civil authorities. The prompt and efficient action at that time has since saved our state from scenes of such brutal character.

General Merwin was chosen lieutenant-governor of Connecticut for two years, on the state ticket with Hon. Morgan G. Bulkeley at its head, by the legislature of 1889. In the fall of 1890 he was nominated by the republicans for governor, but failed of an election by the people at the polls in November. On the assembling of the legislature in January, 1891, a series of entanglements arose and no legal election or inauguration of state officers was accomplished by that body — except in

the case of the comptroller, who was declared to
have been elected by the people. Lieut.-Governor
Merwin is therefore, at the present writing, acting
lieutenant-governor of the commonwealth, and,
under the constitution will remain such until his
successor shall be duly chosen and qualified.

General Merwin's name, in all the various walks
of life, whether civil or military, public or private,
has been synonymous with honor, integrity, and
energy. He has done his duty at all times to the
satisfaction of his fellow-citizens.

CHAUNCEY G. JOHNSON, Meriden: Real Estate.

Chauncey G. Johnson, who is engaged in the
real estate business in Meriden, with a large and
successful patronage, was born at Johnstown, Ohio,

C. G. JOHNSON.

Aug. 15, 1843, and at four
years of age removed with
his parents to Durham,
Conn., where he was ed-
ucated in the common
schools. Both of his pa-
rents died before he was
thirteen years of age. In
1861 at the age of sixteen
he removed from Durham
to Meriden and has grown
up with the city, being
identified with its best
interests. He is an ac-
tive member of the Con-
gregational church and the Young Men's Christian
Association. In 1884 he commenced the building
up of a successful fire insurance business, but in
1889 disposed of his interest to the Meriden Fire Insurance Co. Since then he has devoted his time
entirely to real estate interests. During the winter of 1888 he took a three months' trip through the
principal cities of the south and to California, and
on the return trip visited the principal western
cities with a view of gaining a thorough knowledge
of real estate. Flattering offers were made him
while in California and also in Denver to locate
there in real estate interests, but having built up a
successful business in Meriden he concluded to remain there where he was well known and possessed
the confidence and patronage of the people. He
also has the management of several large estates,
giving his personal attention to the business in all
its details. Mr. Johnson is a republican in politics. He was one of the first letter carriers in
Meriden. He is connected with a number of clubs
and associations and is a popular gentleman. His
wife, who was Miss Lucy M. Lee prior to her marriage, died in October, 1889. Only one daughter
remains in the family.

SAMUEL SIMPSON, Wallingford: President the Simpson, Hall & Miller Company, and the Simpson Nickel Silver Company.

Samuel Simpson, one of the best-known manufacturers in the state, was born in Wallingford,
April 7, 1814, and received a thorough common-

SAMUEL SIMPSON.

school education. In Jan-
uary, 1835, he engaged in
the manufacturing busi-
ness, and has since con-
tinued in that line of activity, building up an extensive industry in bri-
tannia, nickel, silver, and
electro silver-plated ware.
He is the president of the
Simpson, Hall & Miller
Company, and of the
Simpson Nickel Silver
Company. He is also the
president of the National
and Savings banks, occupying this position in each
since its establishment. Mr. Simpson is a prominent democrat and has held important positions
within the gift of his party. In 1856 he was a delegate to the national democratic convention at Cincinnati, and has represented the town of Wallingford in the legislature during the sessions of 1846,
1859, 1863, and 1870. He has been the nominee of
his party on various occasions for the state senate,
and has held the offices of justice of the peace,
selectman, assessor, member of the board of relief,
and warden of the borough. When he first ran for
state senator, he was on the ticket with Samuel
Ingraham for governor, and Samuel Arnold for congress. As the New Haven *Register* of that day
expressed it: " We have three Sams on our ticket."
Only one Sam, however, was elected — Arnold of
Haddam. In the legislature Mr. Simpson exercised a wide influence and was invariably instrumental in promoting the best interests of the state.
His business interests and associations have extended beyond Wallingford. From 1840 until 1850
he was engaged in mercantile pursuits in New York
city under the firm name of Simpson & Benham,
his place of business being on Pearl street. He
was one of the original stockholders of the First
National Bank in Meriden in 1863, subscribing to
one-tenth of the stock. He has been a director
since the organization of the bank, Joel H. Guy
being the president. Mr. Simpson married Miss
Martha DeEtte Benham of Cheshire, July 6, 1835.
She is still living. Of a family of six children only
one survives. Mr. Simpson is a member of St.
Paul's church in Wallingford, and holds the office
of senior warden, having been the incumbent of the
position since 1857. He began his career as a citizen of the state by sustaining the administration of

President Jackson, and has voted for every democratic candidate for the presidency since he became of age.

EDWARD C. LEWIS, WATERBURY: President Waterbury Farrel Foundry and Machine Company.

E. C. Lewis, who is one of Waterbury's most substantial citizens, and interested in some of the largest enterprises of that prosperous city, is a native of North Wales, born September 23, 1826. At the early age of four years he came to this country with his father and mother, locating at Bridgeport. His parents being possessed of but little money, they could only give him a common-school education, and early in life he was compelled to go to work in cotton and woolen mills, where he was engaged

E. C. LEWIS.

for eight years. He then sought other occupation and entered, as an apprentice, the Bridgeport Iron Works, a concern which he, with others, in later life, owned and managed. In 1847 he removed to Birmingham and worked for Colburn & Bassett, who were then prominent iron founders in that vicinity. In 1849 he became foreman for the Farrel Foundry & Machine Company of Ansonia, and it was here that Mr. Lewis demonstrated his thorough knowledge of the business, and also his executive ability, which soon resulted in his being transferred to Waterbury as foreman for the same concern, which had a branch foundry and machine shop at that locality. Mr. Lewis rapidly rose in the estimation of those by whom he was employed, and by the simple force of his ability and character soon secured an interest in the business, and in a short time became the active manager and head of the concern at Waterbury. The Farrel Foundry & Machine Company have long been known throughout the Naugatuck valley as successful iron founders and builders of machinery, and no one concern in that section has done more to build up its material interests than they. In this work Mr. Lewis has done much by giving it his best thought and untiring effort. Politically, he has always been a pronounced republican, and as such has held several offices under the city government, having been elected twice as a member of the common council, and also served one term as police commissioner. In the fall of 1883 he reluctantly accepted a nomination for representative in the legislature, from Waterbury and was handsomely elected

against an able political opponent, and that in a town which usually gives a democratic majority — a sufficient tribute to his popularity and ability.

Mr. Lewis is a member of Trinity Episcopal church of Waterbury; a member of the order of Odd Fellows, and of the Waterbury club. Additionally to his connection with the Farrel company, he is a director and one of the original projectors of the Manufacturers' National Bank of Waterbury, an owner in several manufacturing concerns, and has a large real estate interest in Waterbury. He is thus thoroughly identified with the material prosperity and welfare of his section, and is also in hearty and active sympathy with all efforts for the public good in its higher and broadest sense.

EDWIN A. BUCK, WILLIMANTIC: Wholesale and Retail Merchant.

The subject of this sketch was born in Ashford, Conn., February 11, 1832, and received in addition to a common school education one term at the Ashford Academy. At the age of eighteen he commenced teaching and for six years followed the business of teaching in winter and working on a farm in summer. In 1855 he married Delia Lincoln, also a native of Ashford. In 1856 he commenced business in sawed lumber, which soon grew into a large trade in car timber, plow beams and handles, and also chestnut

E. A. BUCK.

finishing lumber, large quantities of which were shipped to New York. In this business he used several water-power sawmills and employed a large number of men. In the year 1865 he purchased at bankrupt sale the property of the Westford Glass Company, and associating with him the late Capt. John S. Dean and Charles L. Dean, also residents of Ashford, commenced the manufacture of glass under the firm name of E. A. Buck & Co. This firm employed in various capacities about one hundred and fifty men, and made a large addition to the business interest of the town; and so successfully was the business carried on that it became necessary to establish houses in both New York and Boston, not only for the sale of the firm's goods but other lines of goods not manufactured by them. In 1874 he sold out his glass business. For several years he was a director in the Stafford National Bank and one of the original corporators of the Stafford Savings Bank, and also became president of that institution. In 1873 he became interested in real estate in Willimantic and removed to that place in the autumn of that year, resigning his offices in the Stafford banks. In the year 1877 he formed a partnership with the late Allen Lincoln of Willimantic and Everett M. Durkee of Ashford for carrying on a grain business, and soon after purchased the hardware business of Crawford & Banford at Stafford Springs and located his oldest son at that place to take care of the business. This business is still in the same firm name of E. A. Buck & Co., and he has also two other firms of E. A. Buck & Co., one in oil the other in hardware, in Palmer, Mass. In addition to the Willimantic firms of E. A. Buck & Co., dealers in hard wood lumber, of which firm Col. Marvin Knowlton is a member, he is also the head of the firm of E. A. Buck & Co., wholesale and retail dealers in flour and grain, of which firm W. A. Buck, the son, is junior partner. In 1885 he was elected a director and the following year president of the Willimantic Savings Institute, holding the position two years through a very critical time in its history caused by the irregularities of its treasurer, but finally placing it on a sound financial basis. He was elected to his first political office, that of constable of the town, soon after his admission as an elector, and in 1856, at the age of twenty-four, was elected by the republican party a member of the legislature, being the youngest member in the house. In 1862 he was again elected to the legislature by a coalition of union democrats and republicans by a very large majority. He was also appointed by the town to fill its quota of soldiers, and was a firm friend of the union cause, furnishing money to pay for enlisted men which was afterwards paid by the town. He has always been a firm friend of the soldiers, assisting many of them in obtaining pensions from the government. In 1864 he joined his fortunes with the democratic party, and the town having previously been republican, was carried by the democrats, and in 1865 he was again elected a member of the legislature. He has held nearly all of the town offices, — selectman, assessor, town clerk, and judge of probate. In 1874 and again in 1875 he was re-elected to the legislature, and during both sessions served on the judiciary committee. In the spring of 1876, after his removal to Willimantic, he was elected to the senate, it being the last session in the old state house. In the autumn of that year he was nominated and elected treasurer of the state, which office he filled for two years. He was renominated for the same position in 1878, but shared the fate of the rest of the democratic ticket. He has always been active in politics, filling the position of town committee and state central committee of the democratic party, and also a member of the finance committee for the last two years.

THOMAS W. RUSSELL, HARTFORD: President Connecticut General Life Insurance Company.

Mr. Russell is a native of Greenfield, Mass., where he was born May 22, 1824. Educated in the district schools of his native town and the adjoining

T. W. RUSSELL.

town of Coleraine, with a supplementary academic course, he engaged in teaching for a single winter. This calling, however, he forsook for mercantile business, following the latter for about six years, or until 1852, when he entered upon what has proved his life work by soliciting insurance for the Charter Oak Life Insurance Company of Hartford. After four years service as a local agent, incidental to his mercantile business, he was made the general traveling agent for the same company, and in 1857 was chosen its vice-president. In 1864, Mr. Russell was induced to leave the Charter Oak Life Insurance Company and become nominally the actuary of the Connecticut Mutual Life Insurance Company. In 1865, the legislature of Connecticut chartered the Connecticut General Life Insurance Company, and Mr. Russell was induced to become its secretary. He subsequently became president and active manager, having held the latter relations now for nearly a score of years. Under his control and advice the original scope and plans of the company were radically changed, and it was long ago placed on an equal footing with the best life companies of the country. One of the most competent insurance critics of the present day says of President Russell that " he is perhaps as fine an example as there is in this country of the man who seeks his contentment in the daily round of duty, satisfied if the end of the year finds the cause of his company advanced, its business increasing and the death-rate normal. He is one of the old workers in life insurance, who has a steady faith in his business, an earnest desire to benefit all with whom he comes in contact, and who keeps about him the clean and pure atmosphere of business honor." The healthy and prosperous condition of this company is sufficient evidence of the ability and integrity of its management, of which the subject of this sketch is the head and front.

Outside his business relations Mr. Russell is called upon to aid in social, civil, and religious work. He has been a member of the general assembly of this state, was for a number of years connected with the Hartford city government, is a director in several of the city corporations, an officer and active worker in Park Congregational Church, and a director in the city missionary society. He is interested in and often called to assist in the administration of the educational affairs of his city.

LEVERETT M. LEACH, Durham: Investment Securities.

Mr. Leach was born in Madison, Conn., in 1822, a lineal " son of the Revolution," his grandfather on his mother's side having been a soldier in the revolutionary army, who enlisted at the age of sixteen, served throughout the war, was in the line and witnessed the surrender of General Cornwallis at Yorktown. In 1833 he removed with his parents to Durham, where his father, Leverett W. Leach, established an extensive country store, and where he has ever since resided. He was educated at the public and select schools of his native and adopted town, until about eighteen years of age. He was then employed as clerk in his father's store until he reached his majority. In 1843 he became a partner in the business, under the firm name of L. W. Leach & Son, and continued as such until the death of his father in 1866. In 1855 his only brother, Oscar Leach, was admitted a partner, and since the decease of his father and until the year 1882, has been the senior partner in the business, thereafter conducted under the name of L. M. & O. Leach; thus having been for forty-three years in active mercantile life, as clerk or principal. In 1844 he married Lydia M. Thayer, who, with one daughter, the wife of Charles E. Bacon of Middletown, is now living. He was a representative in the somewhat memorable legislature of 1849, when Joseph Trumbull, the last of the famous governors of that name, was chosen governor by the general assembly, the " free soilers" holding the balance of power in the house of representatives. He was also a representative in the legislature of 1860 and the special session called by Governor Buckingham in December of that year. He was elected senator from the " old " 18th senatorial district in 1862. Was postmaster from 1849 to '53. He has held various town offices and was for ten or twelve years first selectman, justice of the peace, etc. He has been a director in the First National Bank of Middletown for a number of years, and a trustee of the Middletown Savings Bank since 1864. He is a member of the Methodist Episcopal Church. In

L. M. LEACH.

politics is connected with the republican party, with a large reserve of independence. He is not at present engaged in any active business enterprise, but generally occupied in such business of a public or private character as a large and extensive acquaintance with his townsmen and the surrounding community brings to him, besides being the local agent of several of the largest and soundest investment companies of this and other states.

HON. ARTHUR B. CALEF, Middletown: Judge Middletown City Court.

Arthur B. Calef was born at Sanbornton, N. H., June 30, 1825. He worked on a farm and taught school winters until twenty-one years of age, prepared for college in a year at the New Hampshire Conference Seminary at Tilton, N. H.; entered Wesleyan University in 1847 and graduated therefrom in 1851. During his college course he taught district schools three winters and was principal of Woodman Sanbornton Academy at Sanbornton, N. H., one term. He studied law at Middletown with Judge

A. B. CALEF.

Charles Whittlesey and was admitted to the bar of Middlesex county in 1852. He was soon after appointed clerk of the courts in Middlesex county and held the office for about eight years. Judge Calef has been councilman, alderman, recorder, and city attorney of the city of Middletown, school visitor, and treasurer of the state of Connecticut. Elected to the latter office at twenty-nine years of age, he has survived the distinction for a longer period than any other living state treasurer. He has been Grand Junior Warden of the Grand Lodge of A. F. and A. Masons of the state; was trustee of Wesleyan University about twenty years, and for some years its secretary, and has been lecturer on constitutional law in the university. He was a delegate to the national republican convention in 1860 and 1864; was postmaster at Middletown from 1861 to 1869; was for several years president of the Xi Chapter of Psi Upsilon at Wesleyan University, and also president of the Alumni Association. He is president of the Middletown Gas Light Company, director in several financial institutions, and is now and has been for seven years past, judge of the city court of Middletown. He has had an extensive practice in the state and United States courts. Judge Calef married, March 21, 1853, Miss Hannah F. Woodman, granddaughter of Col. Asa Foster of the revolutionary army. They have four sons, all living, among whom are Dr. J. F. Calef of Cromwell, and Arthur B. Calef of Middletown, an attorney-at-law. Judge Calef is a direct descendant of Robert Calef of Boston, who wrote and published a book in opposition to witchcraft in 1700 and in reply to Cotton Mather.

CHARLES H. PINE, ANSONIA : President Ansonia National Bank.

Charles H. Pine was born at Riverton, in the town of Barkhamsted, September 20, 1845. He left the public schools at the age of sixteen years to enlist in Company E, Nineteenth Regiment, afterwards the Second Heavy Artillery, and served as musician for three years, or until the close of the war. At its termination he engaged in mercantile business with N. B. Lathrop in Wolcottville, now Torrington, remaining two years. In 1867 he entered the Ansonia National Bank as clerk, and was subsequently appointed bookkeeper, then teller, elected cashier in 1873, and president in 1880, a position he now holds. He has held various offices of trust and responsibility during his residence in Ansonia, such as treasurer of the borough of Ansonia, treasurer of the Pine Grove Cemetery Association, and treasurer of the Fourth School District of Derby. He represented the town of Derby in the general assembly of 1882, and served as house chairman of the committee on military affairs; was re-elected a member of the house of 1883, and chosen speaker. He was paymaster-general on the staff of Governor Lounsbury in 1887-8. He is an ardent republican, believing in the principles of the republican party most thoroughly, and has always been an earnest, faithful worker in the cause of republicanism. He is a member of the Grand Army of the Republic, of the Society of the Sixth Corps, of the Society of the Army of the Potomac, and the Army and Navy Club of Connecticut. He is actively engaged in business pursuits, for, besides holding the position of president of the Ansonia National Bank, he is president of the Sperry Manufacturing Company of Ansonia, of the Seymour Manufacturing Company of Seymour, and of the Bridgeport Forge Company of Bridgeport, treasurer of the Bridgeport Copper Company of Bridgeport, and of the Parrot Silver and Copper Company of Butte City, Montana. He is also a special partner

in a commission house in New York City doing business with the West Indies.

Mr. Pine has been, literally, the architect of his own fortune. Starting a poor boy, without influential friends, he has made his own way in life, and has reached a degree of success, financially and socially, rarely attained by much older men than he. He is regarded with high esteem in political and business circles throughout the state, and particularly in Ansonia, with whose interests he is closely identified.

SAMUEL R. CRAMPTON, MADISON :

Mr. Crampton was born at East Guilford, now Madison, July 11, 1816. He received a common school education. Circumstances over which he had no control kept him with his father until his majority. Like many young men without means, he engaged in several kinds of business which gave him only a bare living. At the age of twenty-one he was chosen town constable. His father being the trial-justice of the town gave him most of his business in this line. During the administration of Leander Parmelee, sheriff of New Haven county, he held the position of deputy for about six years. After the retirement of Sheriff Parmelee he was the candidate of the republican party for sheriff at two different elections, but was defeated each time, the county being strongly democratic. In 1854, he was elected to the legislature, of which body he was one of the youngest members. In 1856, he was at the convention which organized the republican party, and has been in every state convention of the party since,— a republican who looks back upon the achievements of the party with great satisfaction. In business he has been connected with New York houses about twenty years, first as commercial traveler for nine years, and afterwards with Messrs. E. & H. T. Anthony for a like period, holding a prominent position in their extensive establishment, then at 591 Broadway. In all these years of New York life he held his residence in Madison. Later, under the administration of Prof. Cyrus Northrup, as collector of the port of New Haven, he held the position of weigher and gauger for twelve years. He has been a member of the Congregational church of Madison for more than fifty years, and has been active there as in all local matters pertaining to the

S. R. CRAMPTON.

interest of the town. He is now living with his second wife, by whom he has had four children, among whom he is now enjoying his old age.

DELOS D. BROWN, CHATHAM: Hotel Proprietor.

Mr. Brown was born at Orleans, Barnstable County, Mass., in 1838. His education was acquired at Chase's Institute in Middletown, and at Wesleyan Academy in Wilbraham, Mass. During active life he has been engaged in manufacturing and mercantile business, and in the promotion of these interests has traveled extensively through the southern and western states. He was at one time house reporter of the legislature for the New Haven *Morning News.*

D. D. BROWN.

At the outbreak of the war Mr. Brown enlisted in the federal service, raised a company for the Twenty-first regiment, C. V., going out as first lieutenant. He was promoted to the rank of captain, and commended in special orders for gallant conduct at the battle of Drewry's Bluff. He participated in nearly all the battles in which the Twenty-first was engaged, including among others, Fredericksburg, the siege of Suffolk, the siege of Petersburg, Va., Cold Harbor, and Drewry's Bluff. When the rebel general, Fitz-Hugh Lee, was captured at White House Landing, Va., Captain Brown was detailed with his company to conduct him to Fortress Monroe, and deliver him up as a prisoner of war. His regiment belonged to Burnside's famous Ninth Army corps, and was commanded by Colonel Arthur H. Dutton of the regular army, and later by Colonel Thomas F. Burpee of Rockville, Conn., both of whom were killed in the service.

The father of Captain Brown enlisted in the war of 1812, but saw no active service. His grandfather served in the war of the revolution. All the male members of his father's family were in the army or navy during the war of the rebellion, his older brother as paymaster and his younger brother as paymaster's assistant in the navy, and his brother-in-law, Lieutenant F. W. H. Buell, was with him in the Twenty-first regiment and died in the service. His father, the Rev. Thomas G. Brown, when sixty-three years of age, anxious to take part in the conflict, was appointed chaplain of the Twenty-first regiment, and by gallant conduct under fire, at the battle of Drewry's Bluff, where he

was wounded in the arm, became known as the "Fighting Chaplain." Captain Brown was a member of the house of representatives in 1882; was county commissioner for Middlesex county for two terms; is chairman of the republican town committee; a member of the Army and Navy Club of Connecticut; also of Mansfield Post, No. 53, G. A. R.; a prominent member of the masonic fraternity, and of the order of American Mechanics. At the present time he is proprietor of the Lake View House, a beautiful summer resort on Lake Pocotopaug at East Hampton, in this state.

REV. WILLIAM W. McLANE, NEW HAVEN: Pastor College Street Congregational Church.

Rev. William W. McLane was born in Indiana Co., Pa., Nov. 13, 1846. His father was of Scotch ancestry and his mother of English descent, the original members of her family having come to Philadelphia with Wm. Penn or his immediate followers. Mr. McLane grew up in the country and was trained in the Presbyterian faith. He was graduated Bachelor and Master of Arts from Blackburn University, graduated in theology from the Western Theological Seminary in Allegheny, and subsequently

W. W. McLANE.

took the degree of Doctor of Philosophy from Yale University for special studies in biology and philosophy. He received the degree of D.D. from his alma mater in 1882. He taught one year in an academy and two years in college before entering the seminary, and stood at the head of a large class numbering almost fifty when he graduated in theology. He was ordained a Presbyterian minister in May, 1874, and continued in that denomination nine years, spending the last five as pastor of the Second Presbyterian church, Steubenville, O., then the largest Presbyterian church in that part of the state. He then left the Presbyterian denomination and has been pastor of College Street Congregational church, New Haven, since January, 1884. Dr. McLane has been twice married, his last wife, *nee* Miss Fanny Robinson, being a descendant of the family of John Robinson the Pilgrim pastor. She is also descended on her mother's side from Governor Bradford and on the father's from Governor Carver. Her ancestors have formed almost an unbroken line of ministers. There are in the family five children, all boys, two being sons of the first wife and three sons of the second. Dr. McLane is the author of a book on theology, and has contributed articles to the leading religious newspapers and to different magazines. Several sermons and addresses of his have also been published.

JOSHUA PERKINS, D.D.S., DANIELSONVILLE.

Dr. Joshua Perkins is a descendant of the sixth generation of John Perkins, who came from Newent, Gloucester County, England, in 1631, and settled in Ipswich, Mass., and some of whose descendants settled in Lisbon, Conn., then included in the town of Norwich, Conn. He was born in Lisbon, Conn., April 16, 1818, attended the common district school until twelve years of age, and at fifteen taught a district school, and, as most all teachers did at that time, " boarded around in the district."

JOSHUA PERKINS.

At seventeen years of age he was fitted for college at Plainfield Academy, under the instruction of that excellent and respected teacher, John Witter, and in the same class that included Dr. Lowell Holbrook of Thompson, Dr. Elijah Baldwin of Canterbury, and Hon. Albert H. Almy of Norwich, now of New York, and other classmates from this and other states. He did not enter college, as did many of his classmates.

At nineteen he was chosen captain of the Sixth infantry company, Eighteenth regiment of Connecticut militia. After serving three years and having no taste or ambition for military matters he resigned the captaincy of the company.

Having followed mercantile business in the then " far west " for a number of years, he returned to Lisbon, then, after a few years, he came to Danielsonville, where he has followed a successful and remunerative practice of dentistry for more than thirty years.

In religion he is a Unitarian, and in politics he can say of himself, " I am a democrat." He has taken an active interest in local matters and political questions. He was clerk and treasurer of the borough of Danielsonville six years ('57 to '63); was warden of the borough three years ('53 to '56); was registrar of voters in the town of Killingly three years ('69 to '72); was a member of the board of education three years ('77 to '80; and is now and has been for many years past a town auditor. He was a delegate to the Union National Convention in Philadelphia in 1866, and a delegate to the Democratic National Convention at Chicago in 1884, which nominated President Cleveland, and was by his fellow delegates chosen a vice-president of that convention. Dr. Perkins has long been a recognized and trusted leader of the democratic party in his town, and is well known in Windham county as an efficient organizer and worker in the democratic ranks. He has twice ('83 and '88) received the nomination for state senator in the Sixteenth senatorial district. Unfortunately for him and the democratic party he is in a town and a senatorial district dominated by adverse political conditions, otherwise his well-known abilities would have done his party able service in a broader field than his town limits. As a writer and speaker Dr. Perkins is direct and effective and is worthy of and has the confidence of his party.

HON. JOHN WHITTLESEY MARVIN, SAYBROOK: Insurance and Investments.

John W. Marvin was born, the youngest son of Deacon John Marvin, in Lyme, January 13, 1824. He came of excellent stock, being a lineal descendant of Captain Reynold Marvin, justly renowned in the history of the town. Up to his thirteenth year the family lived in Lyme; then it removed to Deep River (Saybrook). There the subject of this sketch has since lived. The town has found him a capable and efficient officer. He has been town clerk, a member of the board of relief, justice of the peace,

J. W. MARVIN.

and has held various other elective offices. In 1871 and 1872 he represented Saybrook in the legislature, and both years served upon the leading committee — the judiciary. Among his associates were some of the ablest minds that have found their way recently to membership in the house — Messrs. Waite, Ingersoll, Treat, Eaton, and Seymour. In 1871 he was also a member of the committee on constitutional amendments. During the past several years he has been engaged in the general insurance business, and latterly has added to it a western loan and farm mortgage agency. His excellent judgment and sterling integrity have raised him to financial positions of prominence. He is now a director in a national bank and savings bank and in an insurance company. In the fall of 1885 he was elected by his party — the republicans — as senator from the twenty-first district. As a legislator, his practical knowledge of public and general affairs greatly facilitated the discharge of senatorial duties, and he easily took rank among the ablest and most active of his colleagues.

RUFUS STARR PICKETT, New Haven: Attorney-at-Law, Judge of the City Court.

Judge Pickett, a resident of New Haven since 1854, is a descendant of the sixth generation of an English ancestor who emigrated from Dover, England, and settled at Milford, in this state. He was born at Ridgefield, Feb. 28, 1829, studied in the common schools, and prepared for college at Hugh Banks' academy, in his native town.

RUFUS S. PICKETT.

On account of the failing health of his father, Rufus H. Pickett, Rufus S. was, when eighteen years of age, compelled to relinquish study, and devote himself to the management of his father's business, which he continued for six years, when he removed to New Haven, and for seven and a half years worked at building and repairing locomotives for the New York & New Haven Railroad, when it was a single track road, doing its business with twenty-four engines only.

In the Lincoln campaign of 1860 Mr. Pickett, then, as now, an ardent republican, was encouraged to take an active part, by his friend and former schoolmate, Cyrus Northrop, then a professor in Yale college, now president of the University of Minnesota. He answered some of the numerous calls for speakers in New Haven and adjoining towns, speaking in company with Professor Northrop, Hon. N. D. Sperry, John Woodruff, M.C., and others. After the Lincoln administration came into power, and the late James F. Babcock was appointed collector of the port of New Haven, he appointed Mr. Pickett an inspector of customs, which office, and that of weigher and gauger, he held for several years; and while in these offices, and performing his duties faithfully, resumed study, entered the Yale Law School, took the Jewell prize as essayist at the close of the first year, graduated with fair honors in 1873, and entered upon the general practice of law. In 1877 he was appointed city attorney, being continued in that office six years; in 1885 was appointed assistant judge, and in 1887 judge of the city court of New Haven. Judge Pickett heard some of the early boycott cases, and prepared opinions on them, which had a

wide circulation in the country, and which have been substantially confirmed by the higher courts of several states.

Judge Pickett is married, and has four children. His religious connections are with the Congregationalists, and he is a "Son of the Revolution" through his maternal ancestry.

WATSON J. MILLER, Shelton: President and General Manager Derby Silver Company.

Watson J. Miller was born in Middletown, Conn., November 23, 1849. His early education was acquired in the public schools, including the Middletown high school and Chase's institute of that city. This was supplemented by a business course at a commercial college in New Haven, from which he went into business in Middletown, in March, 1868, engaging in the manufacture of silver plated ware. He remained there until 1873, when he removed to New York, where he continued in the same branch of

W. J. MILLER.

business for six years. From New York he went to Shelton, Conn., in 1878, and when the Derby Silver Company was re-organized, Mr. Miller was made its secretary and treasurer, and general manager, having been already on the board of directors. Ten years later he was elected president of the company, still being continued in the general management, both which positions he continues to occupy at the present time. He is also president of the South End Land Company, and of the Shelton Loan and Savings Institution, and is largely interested in real estate in the borough of Shelton. He is recognized as one of the ablest business men in the Naugatuck valley; is thoroughly public-spirited, a wise and discreet counsellor, and actively interested in the welfare and progress of the community of which he is so important a factor.

Mr. Miller was married October 13, 1874, to Miss Susie J. Waite, only daughter of Alonzo Waite, Esq., of Chicopee, Mass. He is an attendant at the Protestant Episcopal church, but not a member; and cheerfully aids in the material support of all religious organizations and charities. He is also a member of several mutual benefit societies. He was one of the first promoters of the enterprise which resulted in the organization of the Shelton board of trade, of which he is now a member and director. He has always kept out of politics, though often urged to become the candidate of his party for both borough and town offices, preferring to devote his attention to business and accomplish what he could for the benefit of his townsmen in the capacity of a private citizen, rather than as a public office-holder.

Mr. Miller is a practical philanthropist. He has helped many of the workingmen of his borough to build houses of their own, and to save something for a rainy day. He is strongly in favor of the savings system among laboring men, and was second in the state to get a special charter for a savings and loan institution to furnish aid to workingmen and mechanics in providing homes for their families. He also favors the co-operative principle in business, to the extent of admitting as stockholders in his own company those who have been faithful as workmen and have accumulated something for investment, even though the amount be small. It is a settled principle with him to promote those who are deserving, and give every man a chance to rise in the world. As a consequence, the Derby Silver Company is a prosperous institution, the management is popular, and Mr. Miller has the satisfaction of seeing his faithful workmen share in the general prosperity.

JULIUS A. HART, Beacon Falls: Station agent N. Y., N. H. & H. R. R.

Julius A. Hart was born at Hubbardton, Vt., April 4, 1846, being the son of a farmer of moderate means, and was educated in the common school.

He remained on the farm until he reached the age of nineteen, when he removed to Nashua, N. H., and engaged in mercantile pursuits. July 1, 1867, he accepted the position of head clerk in the country store of C. W. Elkins & Co. at Beacon Falls. He was appointed station agent in that place, Dec. 21, 1868, and has since retained the position. He is also the agent for the Adams Express Co. and the manager of the Western Union Telegraph Co. at Beacon Falls. Mr. Hart has held the offices of town clerk, treasurer, and collector. He is a republican in politics, a member of the Methodist church, an influential Christian worker, and a member of Centennial Lodge, No. 100, I. O. O. F. of Naugatuck. His wife was Miss Sarah A. Mitchell prior to marriage. The family includes three children.

REV. THOMAS K. NOBLE, Norwalk: Pastor First Congregational Church.

Rev. Thomas Kimball Noble was born in Norway, Me., Jan. 19, 1832, and was educated at Bowdoin College and Bangor Theological Seminary.

After the completion of his studies he was elected master of the High School in Augusta and remained there for five years, preparing students for Yale, Harvard, and other New England colleges. During the war he was in charge for seven months of the Christian Commission at the Army of the Potomac headquarters, the hospital in connection with the work being designed for the accommodation of 15,000 patients. Subsequently he accepted the chaplaincy of Gen. Charles Howard's old regiment. By order of the Secretary of War he was detached from this position and assigned to duty on the staff of Gen. Scott, Department of the South, occupying the position for eighteen months. He was then transferred to the staff of Gen. Jeff. C. Davis with headquarters at Louisville, Ky., where he remained for two years, when he was again transferred to the staff of Gen. Burbank, who was Gen. Davis's successor. This position he retained for one year, when he accepted a call to the Jennings Avenue Congregational church in Cleveland, O. The pastorate of this church was occupied for three years and a half. During that period an embarrassing debt on the church was extinguished and the membership trebled. In 1872, having declined a call to the Winthrop church in Boston, which possessed a membership in excess of 600, Mr. Noble accepted the pastorate of Plymouth church in San Francisco, where he remained for fourteen years. During this time a beautiful church edifice was constructed and the church membership increased by 700 or more. Impaired health compelled him to resign the pastorate in San Francisco in 1886, and he traveled extensively through England and the Continent, visiting France, Belgium, Holland, Switzerland, Germany, and Italy, during the succeeding months. On his return he supplied the pulpit of the Eastern Presbyterian church in Washington, D. C., for more than two years. The membership of the church was doubled and the congregation trebled during this period. Declining a call to the pastorate of the church permanently, he removed north and accepted the pastoral office of the First Congregational church in Norwalk, one of the oldest organizations in the state and the mother of eight surrounding churches. During his pastorate of the San Francisco church he was one of the lecturers in the Pacific Theological Seminary, and for seven years was the department chaplain of the Grand Army in California and Nevada. He is still a member of Lincoln Post of San Francisco. He is also a member of the Clerical Union Club and of the Aldine Club, both of New York city. His wife, who is still living, is a sister of Professor Bradbury of Cambridge, Mass. He has two daughters, both of whom are residing in San Francisco. In politics Mr. Noble is a republican.

DAVID BENJAMIN LOCKWOOD, Bridgeport. Attorney-at-Law.

David B. Lockwood was born in Weston, Conn., January 7, 1827. He prepared for college at Staples' Academy in Easton, and graduated from Wesleyan University in 1849. He studied law with the late Judge Sidney B. Beardsley, and was admitted to practice in 1851. After practicing in Bridgeport for several years, he removed to New York city, where he continued his profession until the breaking out of the war of the rebellion, when he returned to Bridgeport and enlisted in the Second Connecticut Light Battery, where he served for three years. At the close of the war he returned to Bridgeport, and resumed the practice of his profession. He has held the office of city clerk of Bridgeport, was for three years judge of the city court, and was elected a member of the house of representatives in 1875 and in 1883. He held the office of city attorney in 1880 and 1885. From 1882 to 1887 he was one of the trustees of Wesleyan University. He is one of the original incorporators of the Mechanics and Farmers' Savings Bank. He is one of the original board of directors of the Bridgeport Public Library, and was largely instrumental in changing it from a private to a public institution. He drew the public act providing for county law library associations, and gave the initial movement to the Fairfield county law library, which is now by far the most important county law library in the state. He has closely followed the practice of the law, and is senior member of the firm of Lockwood & Beers, which has been in existence for twenty years, and has a large and successful practice. Mr. Lockwood first married Caroline A. Redfield in 1856, who died in 1868, leaving a daughter and son.

D. B. LOCKWOOD.

In 1869 he married Lydia Ellen Nelson, who is still living, and by whom he had two daughters and a son. Politically, Mr. Lockwood is a democrat. His religious connections are with the Methodist Episcopal church. He is a member of the Grand Army of the Republic, and of the Seaside Club of Bridgeport.

CHARLES EDWARD PRIOR, Jewett City. Secretary and Treasurer Jewett City Savings Bank.

Mr. Prior was born at Moosup, Conn., Jan. 24, 1856. When he was four years old his parents moved to Jewett City, where he has since resided. He received his education in the common schools of the town of Griswold. At the age of seventeen he secured a situation in the office of the N. & W. R. R. Co., in Norwich, where he remained one year. In 1875 he entered the employ of the Ashland Cotton Company, and soon became bookkeeper and paymaster for that flourishing corporation. In 1883 he was elected

CHAS. EDW. PRIOR.

secretary and treasurer of the Jewett City Savings Bank. Two years later he became a member of the corporation, and after four years of service he was elected a director. The bank under his care has become a widely-known institution, and its greatly increased usefulness is owing in no small degree to his acknowledged ability in the management of its affairs. During his administration a large premium account has been nearly annihilated, and the surplus account has been quadrupled.

Mr. Prior has taken a lively interest in musical matters for many years. He became organist of the Congregational church in Jewett City when but fourteen years of age, and resigned eight years later to serve the Baptist church in the same capacity. In 1883 he brought out his first volume of Sunday-school songs, entitled " Spicy Breezes," and in 1890 his second book, " Sparkling and Bright," was given to the public. His compositions are now in great demand, as their appearance in nearly all of our Sunday-school and Gospel praise books testifies. Mr. Prior is an honorary member of the Worcester County Musical Association of Worcester, Mass., and takes an active interest in its affairs. He is a member of the Jewett City Baptist church, which body he serves as choir-leader and organist, and has been president of the Young People's Society of Christian Endeavor since its organization. He is past master of Mount

Vernon Lodge, No. 75, A. F. and A. M., and has advanced in masonry to the degree of Knight Templar, being a member of Columbian Commandery, No. 4, K. T., of Norwich, Conn. Mr. Prior married Miss Mary E. Campbell, and has one son, Charles Edwin Prior.

MARVIN KNOWLTON, Willimantic: Lumber Manufacturer.

Marvin Knowlton is to-day best known in Connecticut as the leader of the prohibition party, and he is gratefully remembered in Canada as among the foremost in Good Templar work and in efforts for temperance legislation during the decade of 1870-80. The best years and best efforts of his life have been devoted to the temperance and prohibition cause.

MARVIN KNOWLTON.

Born in Ashford, in old Windham county, in 1837, he came of a heroic line, in whose veins the fires of patriotism and self-sacrifice had burned since colonial days. His father, of the same name, fought in the war of 1812. Lieutenant Daniel Knowlton, the famous scout of French and Indian war, was his grandfather. He is a grand-nephew, also, of Col. Thomas Knowlton of revolutionary fame, the close friend and adviser of Washington, who fell at Harlem Heights; and a cousin of General Nathaniel Lyon, the beloved son of Connecticut who fell at Wilson's Creek in 1861.

The obligations of home kept young Marvin in Ashford until his thirtieth year, and when he was only nineteen the management of the farm devolved upon him. In 1866, just after his father's death, he removed to the city of London, Ontario, in Canada, and engaged in the wholesale lumber business with a brother-in-law. Two years later he purchased the whole business and developed it to large proportions.

In 1870 he began to take an active interest in the temperance work. He joined the Good Templars, and at once became prominent in the order. He entered the field as lecturer and organizer, was largely instrumental in increasing the membership from 12,000 to 35,000, and was successively elected to the positions of grand counsellor and grand chief of the order for Ontario and Quebec; his grand lodge at that time being the largest on the continent, and the third largest in the world. He was delegate to the international grand lodge in the conventions of 1873 and 1876, at Bloomington, Ill., and Louisville, Ky., respectively, being chairman of the Canada delegation in the latter body. During these years he developed great power as a temperance orator. His experience led him to appreciate the insufficiency of moral suasion work alone. Hence he became one of the foremost advocates of the so-called Duncan bill, a county local-option measure which was championed by the temperance men of all parties, under the auspices of the Canada Temperance Alliance, in 1875. This agitation culminated in 1878 in what is known as the Canada Temperance Act or the Scott Act; and Mr. Knowlton was among the foremost of those who were active and influential in securing the passage of this measure. Mr. Knowlton thus became a tower of strength to the temperance cause in Canada. He was identified with the reform wing of the liberal party and was strongly urged to accept various public positions, but he preferred to attend to his own business and to pursue the temperance work in his own way. In 1883 he decided to return to his native state and county, and in 1884 he engaged in the lumber business with the firm of E. A. Buck & Co. of Willimantic (where he is now), as manufacturers and wholesale jobbers in native hard woods for railway and domestic uses. Firmly convinced by his Canadian experience that moral suasion and legal suasion must be supplemented by public officers and organization in sympathy therewith, Mr. Knowlton promptly identified himself with the national prohibition party in this country, and he has, with characteristic self-sacrifice, given to the movement an abundance of his substance, energy, and political wisdom, to the signal advantage of the cause. As a prominent lecturer and political adviser in the Forbes campaign in 1886; as the chosen representative sent by Connecticut friends of prohibition to assist in the campaign for the amendment in Michigan in 1887; as field manager in the Fisk and Camp campaign in 1888; as chairman of the special amendment committee in 1889; and as state organizer in 1890, he has been generally recognized as the leader of the prohibition movement in Connecticut; while the party has risen from a spasmodic agitation to a steady, permanent place, with a growing political issue.

Mr. Knowlton is a single man and a member of the Masonic order. He also retains connection with the order of Good Templars in this country. He is a man of strong personal popularity, of marked power and magnetism as a public speaker, a sagacious politician in the best sense, and always keenly alive to the whole political situation. He is a thorough and determined champion of the cause of "the home against the saloon," and believes in the speedy coming of a new party of the people, which shall faithfully preserve the democratic principle of equality in the public regulation and administration of wholesome industries, while bringing the full power of government to bear against the forces of rum, monopoly, and corruption.

GEORGE N. MORSE, MERIDEN: Ex-State Senator.

George Newton Morse was born in Meriden, Oct. 16, 1853. He is a descendant of John Morse, born 1604, who was one of the seven Puritans of that name who emigrated from England to America in 1635, settled at New Haven, and was one of the founders of Wallingford in 1670, and was a deputy and commissioner to the general court for fourteen years, dying in 1707 at the age of 103. On his maternal side Mr. Morse is a descendant of Rev. Samuel Hall of Cheshire, born 1695, died 1776, who married Annie

G. N. MORSE.

Law, daughter of Gov. Jonathan Law and granddaughter of Gov. Wm. Brenton of Rhode Island.

After the usual training in the common schools, Mr. Morse attended, when sixteen years of age, the Connecticut Literary Institute at Suffield in 1869–70. For several years he was correspondent of the *New York Mirror* and the *Turf, Field, and Farm*. He has been at one time or another in various mercantile pursuits. In 1872 he was a member of Charter Oak Hose Company in the old volunteer fire department. In 1882 he moved to Kansas City but returned to Meriden the following year. Was married in 1877 to Mary A., daughter of John C. Byxbee, by whom he has had two children: John B., born 1880, and Ida L., born 1882. He has been a prominent figure in local and state politics. At the state convention held in Hartford in May, 1888, to choose delegates to the democratic national convention, he was chairman of his town's delegation. He was a delegate to the state convention held in September of the same year at New Haven, presenting the name of Hon. Carlos French for governor in the county caucus, and Hon. E. B. Manning to the convention for electoral delegate. The latter was nominated and elected. Mr. Morse was nominated for state senator in 1888 and was elected by a plurality of 353. In the presidential campaign of 1888, he organized and was president of the Cleveland democratic club of Meriden. In the state senate he was chairman of the manufactures and woman's suffrage committees; introduced and advocated the passage of the cigarette bill, which is now the law. The most notable speeches which he delivered in

that body were those on ballot reform, the Westport ballot box contest, oleomargarine, and the Storrs School appropriation. He was the author of the famous Parnell resolutions, which were finally passed by the general assembly after a bitter contest. He organized and is the secretary of the Senate Club of 1889–90. He was chairman of the town delegation to the state convention held in Hartford in September, 1890, and at this convention was a candidate for the office of secretary of state. He is a member of St. Andrews Episcopal Church, an officer in the state Democratic Club, trustee of the Royal Arcanum, a member of the I. O. Odd Fellows, O. U. American Mechanics, Golden Eagles, I. O. Red Men, Political Equality Club, and Sons of the American Revolution.

JOHN S. KIRKHAM, NEWINGTON: Farmer.

Mr. Kirkham is a native of Newington. He was born April 6, 1826, and reared on his father's farm, working hard and attending the common schools during such portions of the year as might be conveniently spared from farm work for that purpose. His education was finished in the Springfield High School and Newington Academy. In 1849 he went to California, being one of the pioneer band of Argonauts organized in Hartford by Major Horace Goodwin, C. G. Smith, Joseph Pratt, and others. He was chosen

J. S. KIRKHAM.

on the board of managers, and also clerk of elections in El Dorado county in 1850. After a valuable experience in the gold regions he returned to Newington, where, since 1855, he has been justice of the peace. When the town was incorporated in 1871, he was chosen town clerk, and has remained such since, save for three years. From 1866 he has been school visitor, and is now chairman of the board. In addition to these places of trust he is treasurer of the State Board of Agriculture. He was a leader in the farmers' organization a few years ago to contest the claims of the "Granite Agricultural Works" of Lebanon, N. H., growing out of fraudulent notes. Always a staunch defender of farmers' rights and a leading spirit in the local and state Grange, he is more active in the support of agricultural interests than even the interests of the democratic party. In 1878 he represented Newington in the lower house of the general assembly, and ten years later served as state senator from the second district. Mr.

Kirkham has been twice married; first to Miss Harriet P. Atwood, who died in 1882; his second wife being Miss Mary K. Atwood, to whom he was married in 1885. He has four children. He is a member and clerk of the Congregational church in Newington, and occupies an influential position in all local religious affairs.

HERBERT C. BALDWIN, BEACON FALLS: Farmer.

Herbert C. Baldwin was born in Oxford, in this state, Sept. 3, 1840. He was one of four sons of Lucian Baldwin, and grandson of Matthew Baldwin, of what was formerly called Salem, now Naugatuck. His educational accomplishments were derived mainly from the district school. At the age of fifteen his father died, throwing the young man upon his own resources. He hired out upon a farm and for several years was occupied in working summers and attending school winters.

H. C. BALDWIN.

At the outbreak of the civil war he enlisted in Company K, Thirteenth regiment, Connecticut Volunteers, commanded by Colonel Henry W. Birge. This regiment was included in the great New England division for the extreme south, under Major-General B. F. Butler, and was sent by sea to Ship Island in the Gulf, where the expedition was fitted out against New Orleans. He served in the department of the Gulf until July, 1864, participating in the Bayou Lafourche campaign, Teche, siege of Port Hudson, and Red River campaigns. He was one of those who volunteered under general order No. 49, dated before Port Hudson, La., June 15, 1863, the day after the general advance had been made, to carry the rebel works, in which the Union forces suffered defeat. The language of the order, after congratulating the troops upon the steady advance made upon the enemy's works, conveyed the " commanding general's summons to the bold men of the corps, to the organization of a storming column of a thousand men, to vindicate the flag of the Union and the memory of its defenders who have fallen," and promised a just recognition of their services by a medal of honor " fit to commemorate the first grand success for the freedom of the Mississippi." This promise has never been fulfilled by the government. In 1864 that portion of the army, the 19th corps, was transferred north into Virginia, under General P. H. Sheridan, and took part in the general clearing-out of the Shenandoah Valley. Mr.

Baldwin was wounded in the battle of Cedar Creek, Va., Oct. 19, 1864; the following December his regiment was transferred with his division to Savannah, Ga., where they met Sherman's army and remained with them through the Carolinas until the final surrender. Mr. Baldwin was in active service for four years and six months, being present with his command in every battle and skirmish in which the regiment took part, serving as private and through the succeeding grades to that of second lieutenant, and being brevetted for gallant and meritorious services. After the war closed Mr. Baldwin bought the farm in Beacon Falls, on which he still resides. He married Josephine H. Jones of Central New York, and settled down to farming. They have five children, four sons and one daughter. He has been called to fill most of the local offices of his town, has been elected selectman seventeen years, during sixteen of which he was chairman of the board. At present he is first selectman and town agent, justice of the peace, secretary of the board of education, and representative of his town in the general court. He has previously represented the town in the house during the sessions of 1876, 1880, 1883, and 1884. He has always been a republican, and a zealous worker for the principles which that party represents. His health is greatly impaired, and he feels that he should be relieved from any further public service.

HORACE E. KELSEY, WESTBROOK: Farmer and Fisherman.

Horace E. Kelsey was born in Old Saybrook, September 17, 1862, and received a common school and academic education, graduating from the Westbrook Academy.

H. E. KELSEY.

He was formerly master of a coasting craft, but gave up that avocation in December, 1887. Since that time he has been engaged in farming and fishing pursuits. He is the chairman of the board of selectmen and has the charge of the town's business. Mr. Kelsey is a democrat politically. He is a member of the Westbrook Grange and of the United Order of American Mechanics. He has a wife and three children, two sons and one daughter. His marriage occurred January 25, 1877, the bride being Miss Nancy M. Burdick. Mr. Kelsey has been a resident of Westbrook since the first year of his life, and is thoroughly honored in the town where he resides.

DOLPHIN SAMUEL FLETCHER, Hartford:
General Manager National Life Association.

D. S. Fletcher is a native of Buffalo, N. Y., where he was born April 9, 1847, his father removing with his family to Shelburne, Vt., when the lad was nine years old. He was brought up on a farm, and by personal experience became entirely familiar with all the duties and pleasures of a farmer's life. He laid the foundation of an education at the district schools, graduating at Hinesburg (Vermont) academy in 1865. Shortly thereafter he removed to Brandon in that state, and entered the insurance business,

D. S. FLETCHER.

receiving the appointment of special agent and adjuster for several companies. This position he retained for several years, performing its duties with success and to the satisfaction of his principals, and gaining by experience a knowledge of the details of underwriting which has proved of immense advantage to him in the broader field in which he has since been engaged. After a long and faithful service in Vermont he resigned his connection with the companies alluded to, desiring to extend the scope and area of his activities, and in 1882 came to Hartford, the home and center of the insurance interest. Here, in January, 1883, he organized the National Life Association of Hartford, and was elected its general manager, still holding the position. Mr. Fletcher is an efficient organizer and a tireless worker. He has labored hard and persistently in bringing the peculiar and original system of the National Life before the people, and in establishing it in the public confidence. The success which has been achieved is very largely attributable to his personal exertions, and to the enthusiasm with which he inspires those who are associated with him as well as his subordinates in the company's service. Mr. Fletcher is a member of the republican party, and while in Vermont was a participant in the activities of local and state politics. Since his residence in Connecticut he has confined himself to business and eschewed active politics. He is a member of Wangank Tribe, No. 11, of the Improved Order of Red Men, of Hartford, but has no further connection with clubs or fraternities. Mr. Fletcher has been twice married; first, in 1871 to Miss Mary Tagert, daughter of Hugh Tagert, M. D., of Shelburne, Vt.; who died in 1872, leaving one son; second, in 1875 to Miss Clara L. Smith, daughter of the late Rev. Eben Smith of Hartford, by whom he has two children.

HON. HENRY BILL, Norwich: Book Publisher,
State Senator, Bank President.

Henry Bill, son of Gurdon and Lucy Yerrington Bill, was born in the north parish of Groton, now Ledyard, on the 18th day of May, 1824. Up to the age of fifteen he was occupied by the ordinary life of a farmer's boy, attending the public school during the winter months. Then he was for a short time an apprentice in the printing office of the New London *Gazette*, but, not being satisfied with the profession, he abandoned it and engaged in school keeping in the neighboring town of Preston. He then engaged in school

HENRY BILL.

teaching in Plainfield and Groton during the winter months and assisting his father on his farm in the summer, till he was twenty years of age. Then he entered the field as a book agent, and for three years traveled through the Western States in this business. In 1847, having acquired a practical knowledge of the book business, he returned to Norwich and established the subscription book publishing business, on his own account. For more than twenty-five years he followed this business with great success, employing hundreds of agents, in all parts of the country, distributing some of the most useful and popular books of the day. His business outgrowing his strength, he turned it into a joint stock company, put it in charge of younger men, and nominally retired from active life, to recuperate his failing health.

In 1853 he represented the 8th senatorial district in the state senate, as a free soil democrat, and was the youngest member of that body, but in 1856 he zealously espoused the free soil cause and cast his lot with the republican party, with which he has since been affiliated. In 1868 he was one of the presidential electors on the Gen. Grant ticket. With these exceptions, he has held no public office.

During the civil war he was one of the strong men upon whom Governor Buckingham relied at all times for advice and assistance, and after the war was deeply interested in the work of educating the colored people of the South, and gave freely of his time and means in this cause. He has manifested his interest in his native town by presenting the homestead of his family to the Congregational society for a parsonage, and by endowing a free library in connection with the same, the good influence of which will endure forever.

Mr. Bill was married on the 16th of February, 1847, to Miss Julia O. Chapman of Groton, and has three living children, two daughters and a son. For more than thirty years he was a vice-president of the Chelsea Savings Bank, and for two years was its president, and only resigned that office on account of declining health. From his youth up he has been a member of the Congregational church, and since his residence in Norwich has been a member of the Broadway church. A fact worthy of mention in connection with his business life, because worthy of imitation, is this, that he has invested the proceeds of his enterprises almost wholly in the city of his residence, by laying out and building up the most beautiful of its suburbs, Laurel Hill, and by holding and improving some of the most valuable of its business property. This has proved to him not only good citizenship but sound financial foresight.

Mr. Bill is one of the best products of our old Connecticut institutions, — self-made, self-reliant, strong to execute whatever he plans, a good citizen, a good neighbor and friend, and one who will leave a lasting mark for good upon the community where he has passed the active period of his life.

CHARLES A. MILLER, MERIDEN: Machinist.

Charles A. Miller, who occupies the position of master mechanic at the works of the Wilcox Silver Plate Company in Meriden, was born in Peter-

C. A. MILLER.

borough, Hillsborough county, N. H., June 2, 1836, and was educated in the Peterborough academy. He learned the trade of a machinist and remained in Peterborough until 1862, when he removed to Meriden and was employed there as a toolmaker and contractor in the works of Parker, Snow, Brooks & Co., in the manufacture of Springfield rifles for the government, and in making the Scott & Triplet rifle for the state of Kentucky. At the close of the war he became master mechanic of J. Wilcox & Co.'s woolen mill and remained there for eight years. He was then employed for a short time as a toolmaker for the Parker shot gun. The present position he has held for a number of years. Mr. Miller was married June 7, 1854, to Miss Sarah M. Ames, daughter of Alvah and Betsey Ames, and has two sons and one daughter. He is a republican in politics and was a member of the Meriden city council in 1870, 1871, and 1875. He is a member of the Center Congregational church and belongs to Meriden Lodge, No. 77, F. and A. M., of Meriden, and to the Order of the Iron Hall.

J. DWIGHT CHAFFEE, MANSFIELD: President the Natchaug Silk Company.

J. D. Chaffee was born in Mansfield, Conn., August 9, 1846. After finishing his education at Fitch's boarding school at South Windham, he en-

J. D. CHAFFEE.

tered business with his father in manufacturing sewing silk and machine twist at Mansfield Center and Willimantic, Conn., under the firm name of O. S. Chaffee & Son, which business was established by the senior Chaffee in 1838. This connection was maintained with uninterrupted success for a long period of years. In the spring of 1884, Colonel Chaffee became interested in the manufacture of silk and mohair braids for coat bindings, the plant being at Willimantic. He has been a director of the Morrison Machine Company of Willimantic, which was incorporated July, 1882, and is doing a flourishing business in the manufacture of silk machinery of all kinds. He was also one of the incorporators of the Dime Savings Bank of Willimantic. He is now the president of the Natchaug Silk Company of Willimantic, whose New York office is at 546 Broadway. Colonel Chaffee is a breeder of thoroughbred Jersey cattle, and has upon his farm at Mansfield some of the best strains of Jersey blood to be found upon the American Jersey cattle club book.

As a politician he has never entered into any scheme or device to put himself forward, as his strict attention to business would not permit it. He represented his native town in the legislature in 1874, and acquitted himself with credit as clerk on the committee of cities and boroughs. He was called upon to represent the twenty-fourth district in the senate of 1885, and responded with a majority larger than was ever given a candidate, republican or otherwise, in his own town, and for the first time in the history of the party carried every town in the district. He served the first year upon the committee of fisheries, and had the satisfaction of seeing all the bills reported favorably by himself pass both houses. The last year in the senate he served upon the labor committee, which had before it every conceivable bill that might seem to benefit laborers. The press gave him great credit for his deliberations and as being fair and conscientious in his reports.

As a military man, Colonel Chaffee has had no training whatever, but his selection by Governor Lounsbury to a position upon his staff as aid-de-camp, with rank of colonel, in 1887, gave great satisfaction to all people with whom he is associated.

GEN. LUCIUS A. BARBOUR, HARTFORD: President Willimantic Linen Company.

General Barbour was born at Madison, Ind., January 26, 1846, and was educated at the Hartford High School, graduating from that institution in 1864. He was appointed teller of the Charter Oak Bank, and held the position until 1870, when he resigned for the purpose of spending two years in European travel. He is a man of wide culture, and his civic and business career has been exceptionally brilliant and successful. His military advancements, however, have the widest notice in the state. Sep-

L. A. BARBOUR.

tember 9, 1865, he enlisted as a private in the Hartford City Guard, then attached to the First regiment as Battery D. Rapid promotion awaited him, his instincts and tastes entitling him to the place of a military leadership from the outset. In 1871 he resigned from the company and was out of service until Feb. 1, 1875, when he was elected major of the First regiment. Dec. 29, 1876, he was elected lieutenant-colonel and was advanced to the command of the regiment June 26, 1878. He was in command of the First at the Yorktown Centennial in 1881, and won a national reputation by the splendid efficiency and discipline which his organization displayed. The memorable visit to Charleston, S. C., was made in connection with the Yorktown anniversary, and resulted in the attainment of the highest military praise. The tribute paid to Colonel Barbour's command by the celebrated London war correspondent, Archibald Forbes, was deserved by the superb *esprit de corps* which prevailed in the First. Colonel Barbour resigned the command of the regiment Nov. 12, 1884. He was one of the most popular officers connected with the National Guard, and his selection as adjutant-general met with universal satisfaction throughout the state. General Barbour was a member of the house of representatives in 1879, being the colleague of Hon. Henry C. Robinson. His legislative career was in keeping with the course which he had followed in other callings of life, and added to his reputation and popularity. He was prominently identified with Battle Flag Day, being a member of the legislative committee which had the arrangements in charge. He is honored throughout the state as a distinguished representative of the national guard.

General Barbour is at the head of the Willimantic Linen Company, of which he has been the president and treasurer since 1884, and is regarded as one of the ablest business managers in Hartford. He is also a director of the Charter Oak National Bank, and a member of the firm of H. C. Judd & Root. In politics he is a republican, and his religious connections are with the First Congregational church of Hartford. General Barbour married Miss Harriet E. Barnes of Brooklyn, N. Y., a daughter of A. S. Barnes, the head of the well-known New York publishing house of A. S. Barnes & Co. They have two children.

GEORGE P. McLEAN, SIMSBURY: Attorney-at-Law.

George P. McLean was born in Simsbury, October 7, 1857. He was educated at the public schools of his native town and at the Hartford High School, from which latter institution he graduated in 1877. After leaving school he became connected with the *Hartford Evening Post*, on the reportorial staff of which journal he did excellent service, but soon abandoned journalism for the law, for which he has special taste and ability. After a thorough course of legal study in the office of Hon. Henry C. Robinson, he was ad-

G. P. McLEAN.

mitted to the Hartford county bar in 1881, and has remained in practice in the city of Hartford to the present time, retaining his residence in Simsbury. Mr. McLean represented his town with honor and distinction in the general assembly during the sessions of 1883 and 1884, his facility in debate and argumentative powers making him one of the most influential members on the republican side. As chairman of the State Prison committee in 1883 he reported the bill establishing the board of pardons and delivered a strong and successful speech in support of the measure. On the organization of the board in November of the same year, he was unanimously elected clerk, and still retains the position. In 1885 Governor Harrison appointed him a member of the commission on revising the public statutes, and, on its organization, he was elected secretary. In the fall of 1885 he was elected state senator from the third district, and was naturally accorded in the upper house the same influential position which his ability and usefulness had secured

for him in the lower branch of the legislature two
years before. During the presidential canvass in
1884 he stumped the state in support of Blaine and
Logan, and performed considerable similar service
in the campaign of 1888. The versatility of his
gifts as an orator has been often illustrated before
critical audiences, and on more than one occasion
he has received distinguished compliments from
eminent sources, of which he would be justified in
feeling proud.

**HON. THOMAS S. MARLOR, BROOKLYN:
Banker.**

Hon. Thomas S. Marlor of Brooklyn is an Eng-
lishman by birth, though an almost lifelong resident of this country. He was born in England on
the 10th of December,
1839, but at the early age
of two years came to
America, his parents set-
tling in New York, in
which city, as a boy, he
received his education at
the public schools. He
early engaged in mercan-
tile business in the me-
tropolis, but his tastes inclined him decidedly
toward financial pursuits,
and at length he became
a banker, a member of

T. S. MARLOR.

the New York Stock Exchange, and a prominent
and successful operator among the active financiers
of that great money center. Although having
scarcely reached his majority at the breaking out
of the war of the rebellion, Mr. Marlor was intensely loyal to the government of his adoption;
and, unable himself to take up arms in its defense,
he not only contributed liberally and freely through
the ordinary channels, but at his own personal expense procured a recruit and sent him into the field,
thus performing by proxy a duty which he felt to
be upon him, but which was not proper or wise for
him to undertake to perform in person. In 1869,
having met with very gratifying success in business,
and being desirous of disengaging himself to some
extent from its burdens, Mr. Marlor purchased a
tract of land in the village of Brooklyn, in this state,
and erected upon it a handsome country residence,
to which he retired with his family. He soon afterwards acquired considerable other real estate in the
neighborhood of his home, and at once identified
himself with the town of his adoption in the most
thorough and liberal manner. He has in many
ways manifested his public spirit and practical
generosity, by the bestowment of various gifts and

privileges upon the town, village, and religious
society with which he is connected. The handsome
soldiers' monument which stands on a public square
in the village was wholly the gift of Mr. Marlor, as
was the site of the state monument to the memory
of General Israel Putnam, which occupies a commanding position in the vicinity of the memorial
referred to. The Putnam equestrian statue was
erected by the state, but the site and all improvements thereon, including the grading, the heavy
granite coping, and the granite roadway, were provided by Mr. Marlor at his own personal expense,
to the acceptance of the state monument commission. Probably no individual citizen of Brooklyn
ever gave so liberally and voluntarily of his time
and money for the benefit of his fellow-citizens and
the improvement and beautifying of their village as
the subject of this sketch has done since he first
made that delightful town his permanent abode.
Mr. Marlor has several times been called to accept
positions of public service and trust, but he has
been disinclined to office-holding and has refused
more importunities of this kind than he has
accepted. Although claimed by the democrats, he
is an independent in the best political sense, and
his elections to office have almost invariably been
by such majorities as to show the voice of the people rather than of any particular party. Mr. Marlor has twice represented Brooklyn in the general
assembly, and once the sixteenth senatorial district
in the upper house. He has repeatedly declined
re-nominations for both branches of the legislature,
and in 1886 received the nomination of the democratic congressional convention, but refused to accept. In addition to his political services Mr. Marlor has rendered important aid in civil affairs of
local concern. He is one of the corporators of the
Prisoner's Friend Society, and also of the Brooklyn
Savings Bank. He is an active member of the
Episcopal Society of Brooklyn, and is always ready
to perform his part in every movement which has
in view the welfare and proper entertainment of
the people and particularly the education and refinement of the rising generation. He is not now
in active business, though retaining his membership in the New York Stock Exchange. He therefore has the leisure as well as the inclination
and the means to gratify his laudable ambition
to make the world better and happier while he is
on the stage of action. Mr. Marlor married, early
in life, Miss Mary F. Loper, and there have been
three children, two of whom, both adult sons, are
living and residing in their native town. The
homestead is on the Pomfret road, just on the edge
of Brooklyn village, a delightful spot where many
a guest has tasted and enjoyed the abounding
hospitality of Mr. Marlor and his accomplished
wife.

JOHN C. COLLINS, New Haven: Secretary and Treasurer International Christian Workers' Association.

Mr. Collins was born in Albion, N. Y., September 19, 1850. He prepared for college at the State Normal school at Brockport, N. Y., graduated at Yale in the class of 1873, and from Yale Theological Seminary in 1878. He spent two years with his brother in the Sixteenth New York Cavalry, as a sort of " Boy of the regiment," in the neighborhood of Washington, D. C. This regiment was the one that captured John Wilkes Booth, the assassin of President Lincoln. Young Collins was present at the hanging of

JOHN C. COLLINS.

the four " Lincoln conspirators," as they were called — probably the only person under fifteen years of age who saw the conspirators hung — gaining access to the execution on account of his familiar acquaintance with the guard.

After graduating from college Mr. Collins considered several lines of Christian work before reaching a decision as to the particular branch to which he ought to devote his energies. He finally decided to undertake mission work in the city of New Haven, in which he at once engaged in the capacity of general superintendent of the Gospel Union, a mission society in New Haven, the members of which were prominent Christian people of different denominations, the Christian work of which consisted in holding gospel services in the center of the city, carrying on a Sunday-school, working among prisoners in police courts, doing auxiliary work such as penny savings bank, temperance work, and the like. In 1886, in connection with Col. Geo. R. Clarke of Chicago, Ill., he was privileged to take the initiatory steps which resulted in the holding for eight days (June, 1886), in Chicago, the first convention of Christian Workers in the United States and Canada. In this year also he was ordained by the Congregationalists to the work of the ministry as an evangelist,— an unusual proceeding, as Congregationalists do not as a rule ordain ministers unless they become settled pastors or are going abroad as foreign missionaries. It was to some extent prophetic of a new order of things in which the church would recognize the need of ordained ministers among the masses. During the work in New Haven, in one way and another, he gathered in over two thousand children to Sunday-school who had not been habitual attendants, and reduced the number of Protestant non-Sunday-school children

from nearly three thousand to about three hundred. The penny savings bank which the society organized was a pioneer in juvenile savings, and the poor children of New Haven put into the bank about $2,000; and perhaps five thousand more in the larger savings banks, as a direct result of the influence of saving in the small bank. Mr. Collins was appointed secretary of the committee which was formed after the first Christian Workers' convention, called the committee for Christian Workers in the United States and Canada. Out of the work of this committee has grown the International Christian Workers' Association, which now numbers nearly eight hundred of the most prominent Christians-at-work from all the different evangelical denominations in the United States and Canada, and whose yearly conventions for the consideration of Christian work and methods are considered the most influential religious gatherings of the year. He was continued as secretary and executive of the association, which has been incorporated under the laws of the state of Connecticut. In 1887 the Christian Workers' Association authorized him to organize a work for street boys under their authority and subject to such rules as he might think advisable, and in three years the work has extended into four states, being chiefly confined, however, to Massachusetts and Connecticut. It consists, in a word, of opening rooms in the different cities during the evenings of the colder months of the year, supplied with instructive books and interesting games, to which free access is given to the boys who are accustomed to spend their evenings in the streets. A Christian young man is placed in charge of the room as superintendent. During the day and summer months when the club is not open the superintendent visits the homes of the boys, goes to police court, and watches over those who get into the hands of the police, having their cases continued and doing what he can to help them. He secures employment for them, and in every way acts as a helpful friend. Every superintendent is in constant communication with the secretary, sending him a report every week of the visits made, the boys found in police court, what action has been taken, etc. Mr. Collins's long experience and the " facility " which he has acquired in this kind of work enables him to give important advice to his subordinates, and to aid in the disposition of individual cases thus brought to his attention by the superintendent. The total number of boys brought under the supervision of the work has reached perhaps about thirteen thousand during the less than four years it has been in operation. The Boys' Brigade in Scotland, which has the same object in view, namely, that of saving street boys, has been in operation since 1882, and they have gotten in about eighteen thousand boys of this class. So it would seem that this society's plan of work is reaching an even larger number than that of the Scottish philanthropists. The boys have penny savings banks, manual training classes, bath-rooms, and light gymnastics in their club room, as a means of attracting and helping them. A work among the students in colleges has also grown out of the International Christian Workers' Association, which consists of the appointment of a secretary who obtains young men from the colleges and puts them into missions for two months during their summer vacations, in order that they may come into contact with the great needs of humanity and be better fitted to sympathize with the sufferings of men when they become ministers later on. Besides this, the association has resulted in the starting of a number of very flourishing missions, and imparting new life to many churches of different denominations.

Mr. Collins was married in 1878 to Miss Fannie M. Smith of Brockport, N. Y. They have seven children, five boys and two girls. He is a member of the Church of the Redeemer, New Haven; in politics a prohibitionist. His chief ability is in the line of an executive, and he has thus been intrusted with most of the executive work connected with the International Christian Workers' Association, although having done a great deal of public speaking in mission work, and for a number of years made a thorough study of various forms and methods of aggressive Christian effort through Christian, evangelical, and mission agencies both in this country and abroad.

GEORGE P. FIELD, TOLLAND: Farmer.

George P. Field is the secretary of the Tolland Grange and a prominent farmer in his section of the county. He has resided in Massachusetts, Vermont, New Hampshire, New York and California. He was born at South Hadley, Mass., Dec. 3, 1826, and received a common school education. Most of his life has been spent in mercantile pursuits and farming. He has held the office of justice of the peace and is a republican. He is a member of the Baptist church and is connected with the F. and A. M.

G. P. FIELD.

fraternity. His wife was Miss Emily L. Phelps of Simsbury prior to marriage, and is still living. There are also three children living, and one is deceased. While in California Mr. Field was in the militia service of the state.

ALBERT MILLER CARD, SHARON: Attorney-at-Law.

Mr. Card has been engaged in active legal practice since 1866, with offices at Sharon and on Nassau street, in New York city. He was born in

A. M. CARD.

Ancram, Columbia county, N. Y., July 21, 1845, and is related to the Hon. Theodore Miller of Columbia county, a judge of the New York court of appeals. He removed to Sharon when quite young and was educated at Sharon high school, Amenia seminary, and at Eastman's college at Poughkeepsie, N. Y., graduating from the two latter. In 1861, he enlisted for the war, and soon thereafter was injured in a Harlem railroad accident while going from Sharon to Amenia, and was obliged to walk on crutches for nine years. In 1865, he married Miss Mary L. Morey, an intelligent and refined lady of English origin, a descendant of the Livingston, Lewis, Ryder, and Northrop families, who assisted in settling Columbia and Dutchess counties, N. Y., and especially the Hudson River valley. They have one son, Clayton M. Card, now twenty-two years of age, and all are members of the Methodist Episcopal church.

Mr. Card was United States District revenue assessor under President Johnson, with headquarters at Poughkeepsie, a school commissioner of Dutchess county, N. Y., ran for assembly from Dutchess county against Hon. A. A. Brush, now warden of Sing Sing prison. He was elected a delegate to the general M. E. Conference of 1888, and with ex-Governor Lounsbury constituted the only two lay delegates to that conference from the state of Connecticut. As a member of the general assembly of 1886 he championed the child's labor and other labor bills, and assisted materially in the legislation that resulted in their becoming laws. He is a justice of the peace, commissioner of the superior court of Connecticut, a director and trustee in the Sharon Water Company, president of the fire district of Sharon, is serving his second term as probate judge of the district of Sharon, and is now a member of the general assembly. Speaker Page having appointed him one of the three minority democratic members of the house on the canvass of votes for governor and other state officers. He is a member of Hamilton Lodge of F. and A. M., belongs to the Harlem Democratic club, the Sagamore club, the Tammany Society of Columbian Order of New York city, and is a member of the

N. Y. state Bar Association. He is a democrat, and has always taken an active part in politics, speaking for McClellan in the campaign of 1864, and in each successive campaign for the democratic nominees down to and including President Cleveland in the last campaign of 1888; and his portrait and biographical sketch appear in the book entitled "The Leading Orators of Twenty-five Presidential Campaigns," written by Wm. Roberts and published by Strouse & Co. of New York, in 1884.

Mr. Card possesses an intelligent comprehension of legislative duties, has filled all offices with fidelity, integrity, ability, and honor, and in a manner satisfactory to his constituents. He makes a valuable member of the general assembly, is a thoroughly useful citizen, and commands the respect and esteem of all who know him.

FRANCIS ALEXANDER MARDEN, Stamford: Attorney-at-Law.

Francis A. Marden is a native of West Windham, New Hampshire, where he was born January 19, 1840, and in which place he spent his early years at the public schools. He was fitted for college at Phillips, Exeter, and Andover Academies, after which he entered Harvard University, and was graduated in 1863, taking the degree of M.A. in 1865. He taught school at Stamford, Conn., from 1863 to 1864, and studied law at Harvard Law School 1864 to 1865, and in October, 1865, was admitted to

F. A. MARDEN.

the bar in New York city. In 1866 he was married in Stamford to Miss Lillie B. Skiddy, which union has been blessed with four children. Since his marriage he has been a resident of Stamford, practicing his profession in New York city, and latterly, with his family, spending his winters in New York, his residence there being at No. 640 Madison Avenue. A democrat in politics, he has occupied various positions of trust within the gift of his party, such as delegate to state and national conventions, judge of probate for the district of Stamford, burgess of the borough, nine years member of the school committee, and a representative from Stamford in the general assembly for two terms — 1876 and 1878 — when he served on the judiciary and insurance committees. He was commissary-general on the staff of Governor Waller in 1883–4. At college he was a member of the Phi Beta Kappa and President of the Harvard Society of Natural His-

tory. He is a member of Union Lodge, No. 5, F. and A. M., Rittenhouse Chapter, No. 11, Royal Arch Masons, Washington Council, and Clinton Commandery. Mr. Marden has recently devoted himself almost exclusively to his legal practice, which is very large and of such a character as to demand the most intelligent and careful attention.

CHARLES NORTHEND, New Britain: Author and Educator.

Charles Northend was born in Newbury, Mass., April 2, 1814. His preparatory education was under the charge of that accomplished and efficient instructor, N. Cleaveland, Esq., who for about twenty years was principal of Dummer Academy, located in the immediate vicinity of Mr. Northend's paternal home. At the age of sixteen Mr. Northend entered Amherst College, where he spent two years, and from which he received the honorary degree of A.M. On leaving college he engaged in

CHAS. NORTHEND.

teaching, first as assistant at Dummer Academy, and subsequently in Danvers and Salem, Mass. After nearly twenty years of experience in the work of the school-room in these two places, he was called to the superintendency of the schools of the former place, a position he held for three years, when he accepted a position as assistant to the state superintendent of schools of Connecticut. In this situation he spent about eleven years, during which time he had principal charge of the state teachers' institutes, and for nearly ten years the chief editorial charge of the *Connecticut Common School Journal*. For two successive years he was called to assist in conducting institutes in the state of Maine, working in nine different counties. He has also assisted at institutes in New Hampshire, Massachusetts, Rhode Island, New York, Pennsylvania, and Vermont.

In a historical address on Dummer Academy, printed in 1865, in speaking of Mr. Northend, the author says: "During these busy years he has found time, not only for the editing of an educational journal and the preparing and publishing of several school books, but also to attend about a hundred and fifty teachers' institutes, lasting generally four or five days, and fifty or more of them under his direction. For eight years he was superintendent of schools of New Britain and for twenty years a member of its school committee, making in all nearly forty-five consecutive years in the work of education.

Mr. Northend was for many years an active member of the two oldest educational associations of our country — the American Institute of Instruction and the Essex County Teachers' Association. Of both of these institutions he was elected president. His works on education, "The Teacher and Parent" and "The Teachers' Assistant," have passed through several editions, and have had an extensive sale. Of the former the *North American Review* said: "There probably lives not the teacher or parent to whom this book might not furnish suggestions worthy his diligent heed and profound gratitude."

Mr. Northend is a member of the First Congregational church of New Britain. Politically he is a republican. Early in life he was married to Miss Lucy A. Moody, who died some years ago. He remains a widower. Two sons have survived the mother.

ABNER S. HART, Unionville (Farmington) Merchant.

Abner S. Hart was a member of the general assembly in 1887, representing the town of Farmington in the house. Mr. Hart cast his first vote

A. S. HART.

for Henry Clay for president in 1844 and has since been a member of the whig and republican parties. He was born in Barkhamsted, July 15, 1823, and received a thorough education, preparing him for the avocation of teaching in the public schools. He pursued that calling for fourteen years, teaching winters and farming through the summer. In 1866 he established himself in the drug business at Riverton and became postmaster there in 1869. The latter position was retained for twelve years. He has held various local offices, including that of acting school visitor for fourteen years and chairman of the board of relief. Since 1881 he has resided at Unionville, where he is engaged in mercantile pursuits. Mr. Hart is a member of Evening Star Lodge, No. 101, F. and A. M., of Unionville. He is descended from revolutionary stock, both of his grandfathers having served in the war for independence. He has in his possession a sword that was carried in the service by one of them. Mr. Hart is a prominent citizen of Unionville, and is held in thorough esteem in that community as well as in his old home in Barkhamsted.

HON. HENRY C. DWIGHT, Hartford: Mayor.

Henry C. Dwight was born at Northampton, Mass., January 19, 1841. His father, Henry A. Dwight, was for a number of years at the head

H. C. DWIGHT.

of an educational institute at Norfolk, Va., and Henry C. was there with him during 1853 and 1854. Returning north, he engaged early in life in the dry goods trade at Northampton, and was living there at the outbreak of the war. He enlisted in the three-months service, but the Northampton quota being filled, he was not able to go to the front with the first troops from the state. He again enlisted in September, 1861, and was instrumental in organizing Company A of the Twenty-seventh Massachusetts regiment. September 20, 1861, he was appointed Sergeant-Major of the command, and was with it through the Burnside Expedition in North Carolina. In December, 1861, he was appointed Second Lieutenant of Company H, and April 1, 1862, he was promoted to the First Lieutenancy of Company A. In August of that year he received his captain's commission. Mr. W. P. Derby, in his admirable history of the Twenty-seventh Massachusetts, speaks in the highest terms of Captain Dwight. "Fortunately for Company A," he says, "there was one in the regiment, by birth and association allied with them, who was a natural leader, of courage and ability, and to him the command fell." Captain Dwight's advancement was won through earnest and valiant services at the front. He remained with his regiment in North Carolina until the fall of 1863, when he was assigned to provost duty at Norfolk, where he had passed a couple of years — 1853 and 1854 — as a student under his father's direction and tutorship. He remained there until the spring of 1864, when he accompanied his regiment in the James River campaign under General Butler. March 1, 1864, he was appointed recruiting officer of the Twenty-seventh, and under his leadership 343 members re-enlisted. He served with the Twenty-seventh until May 16, 1864, when, under special order from headquarters, Eighteenth Army Corps, he was assigned to staff service as assistant-commissary of subsistence, and remained with the second division of the corps until the close of his term of service, September 28, 1864. Throughout his army career of three years, "Captain Dwight's intelligent, courageous, patriotic service," says Mr. Derby, "with his genial, self-forgetful spirit, inspired universal confidence and regard." He is still one of the regiment's most popular representatives, and is president of the regimental association.

General Dwight removed from Northampton to Hartford in January, 1863, and has since resided here. He engaged in business with E. N. Kellogg & Co., wool dealers, and afterwards with Austin Dunham & Sons. In 1879, with Drayton Hillyer of this city, he organized the firm of H. C. Dwight & Co., at present Dwight, Skinner & Co., conducting an extensive wool trade throughout the West, Southwest, and New England. General Dwight has served in the court of common council from the fourth ward, both as alderman and councilman, several years, and was a member of the board of street commissioners about ten years. He is a director in the American National Bank and the Phœnix Insurance Company, vice-president and trustee of the Mechanics Savings Bank, a member of the south district school committee, and sustains other minor official relations with the institutions of the city. In April, 1890, he was elected mayor of Hartford, the duties of which office he discharges with ability and dignity.

Mayor Dwight was one of the charter members of Robert O. Tyler Post, G. A. R., of Hartford, and was commander of the Union Veteran Battalion on Battle-Flag Day, and also on Buckingham Day. As an old soldier and citizen, as well as in his official capacity, he enjoys the fullest confidence of the public, and is a man whom all delight in honoring.

ALONZO GRANNISS, WATERBURY : Sheet Brass and Steel Worker.

Alonzo Granniss was born in Waterbury, March 27, 1820, and received a public school education. He has followed the avocation of a sheet brass and silver roller at Benedict & Burnham's Manufacturing Company. He entered the employ of the company when twelve years old, and at sixteen was entrusted with the charge of the department. This position he has held since his original appointment, and is a man deserving in every way of the trust that has been reposed in him. Mr. Granniss is a member of the

ALONZO GRANNISS.

Episcopal church and a republican in politics. His wife, who was Miss Esther D. Payne before marriage, is still living. There is also one son. The only office that Mr. Granniss has held is that of member of the council board of Waterbury for six years.

REV. ALEXANDER HAMILTON, M.A., WESTON : Rector of Emanuel Parish, Minister in charge of Christ Parish, Redding, and Missionary in Fairfield County.

The subject of this sketch is third in descent from Alexander Hamilton of Revolutionary days, and son of General Alexander Hamilton of Tarrytown, New York; and on the maternal side a descendant of Richard Nicoll, the famous English governor of New York. He was born at Setauket, Long Island, where he spent his youth until eleven years of age, when, his father owning large estates in Northern New Jersey in the Ramapo Valley, he removed there in 1858 — remaining till the close of 1861, when

REV. ALEX. HAMILTON.

his family became residents of New York city. He was educated at the public school and by tutors; took a special course in the General Theological Seminary of New York; and in 1870 was ordained by Bishop Potter. Having a special aptitude for missionary work, he became engaged in such effort successively at Armonck, Newcastle, and Pleasantville, and at Lewisboro, Westchester county, New York.

Resigning the work at Lewisboro, he purchased, in 1884, the historical Smith residence on Newtown avenue, Norwalk, Conn. While residing there, he prosecuted missionary work; and, taking a deep interest in the cause of education, was elected a member of the school board annually. In 1889 the rectorship of Emanuel Parish became vacant, and a call therefrom being extended to Mr. Hamilton, he moved to the rectory, and is now rector of that parish and missionary of two of the oldest parishes in Connecticut, — that at Redding being organized in 1727, and at Weston in 1744. Belonging to these churches are many old and valuable books and an ancient communion set; at Redding a Bible and prayer book, bound in one cover, under date 1726; while the communion set dates from 1735. Again elected as school visitor and committee in Weston, he renders valuable and appreciated service. He inherits the financial ability of Hamilton, and possesses the keenness and aptitude of one who has trained himself in the practical duties of life. He is fully alive to the responsibility that rests upon him, and earnestly desires and endeavors to advance by personal effort every good cause. Blessed with robust health, he is enabled to perform laborious work without fatigue; on Sunday holding three services and two Sunday-schools, preaching three sermons, and driving seventeen miles. These, with calls upon the sick, fill up each of the fifty-two Sundays of every year. Taking an interest in local improvements, he aids all enterprises for promoting the welfare of the community in which he lives. In politics he is a republican, though recognizing the principle of equal rights among all men in the exercise of the elective franchise. Mr. Hamilton has traveled throughout the British Isles and on the Continent, where he was received with consideration, preaching in the American churches there, and attending many public receptions. In 1872 he married Miss Adele Walton, daughter of William W. Livermore, banker, of New York city, and a grand-niece of Charles Floyd, a signer of the declaration of independence. He has four children living, the youngest a son. He is a member of the Cincinnati Society, Sons of the Revolution, Sons of Veterans, and the Historical Society of Westchester County, New York. He is also a frequent contributor of articles to the press.

ERASTUS GEER, LEBANON: Farmer.

The Geer family, or the branch of it which is now so numerous in New London county, traces its origin directly to George Geer, who was born in Hevitree, England, in 1621,

and his brother Thomas in 1623. The biography of the ancestor and his descendants, to and including the subject of this sketch, is given in the history of New London county substantially as follows:

"They (George and Thomas) were bereaved of their parents while young, and were put in charge of an uncle. They

came to America and settled in Boston in 1635, without friends or money. George Geer became an early settler in New London, Conn., about 1651, and Thomas 1652.

On the 17th of February, 1658, George Geer married Sarah, daughter of Robert Allyn, one of the earliest settlers in New London, Conn. Immediately after his marriage he settled on a tract of land adjoining or near said Allyn's land, on the grant of fifty acres made to him by the town of New London, now called Ledyard. He was one of the first officers of the town. He died towards the close of the year 1726 at the age of one hundred and five years. He had a family of eleven children, the eighth of whom was Robert, born Jan. 2, 1675, and died in 1742. Robert married Martha Tyler

and had five children, the second of whom was Ebenezer, born April 1, 1709, and died August 25, 1763. Ebenezer Geer married Prudence Wheeler, Jan. 2, 1735. She was born Sept. 25, 1712, and died June 2, 1797. They had ten children, the youngest of whom was David, born June 18, 1755, and died Aug. 31, 1835.

David Geer married Mary Stanton, May 17, 1781. She was born Aug. 28, 1756, and died December, 1837. Their children were Dorothy, David (2) born Jan. 20, 1784, William S., Prudence, Joseph, Cyrus, Anna, Robert, Isaac W., and Charles, all born in Groton, now Ledyard, Conn.

David Geer (2) married Anna Gallup, Jan. 11, 1810. She was born Sept. 3, 1787, and died Feb. 12, 1862. He died May 19, 1867. Their children were Cyrus G., William F., Thankful S., an infant son, Sarah A., David, and Erastus, the immediate subject of this sketch, born Oct. 9, 1823. David Geer settled in Lebanon, Conn., 1817, on the farm now (1891) owned and occupied by his son Erastus. His farms, now comprising nearly eight hundred acres, are in a good state of cultivation. Among Lebanon's substantial men and representative farmers, none, perhaps, have accomplished more than the Geer family, and much credit is due to the indefatigable energy and perseverance of David Geer. He was a whig and republican in politics.

His brothers and sisters settled in New London county, excepting Wm. S., Robert, and Charles, who settled near Syracuse, New York. His children settled in Lebanon, with the exception of Wm. F., who settled at Syracuse, New York.

Erastus Geer was reared on the farm, and early learned the cardinal principles of success — industry and frugality. His advantages for an education were such as the common schools of the day afforded, supplemented with a few terms at Bacon Academy, at Colchester, Conn. At the age of nineteen he commenced teaching school, and taught ten terms during the winters, working on the farm summers. Being the youngest of the family, he very naturally continued the occupancy of the homestead. He is energetic, prudent, and practical alike in public and private affairs. As a man he is respected at home and abroad; as a farmer he ranks among the most enterprising of the town. In addition to his farming interests, he manufactures the patent iron stall window frame, a device the result of his own invention. In politics a life-long whig and republican, and as such has held important offices of the town.

In 1877 he was a member of the state legislature, serving on the committee of claims. In 1878 he was appointed one of the county commissioners of New London county, and served two terms, retiring in 1884. He has been twice married, — first to Almira

H. Saxton, May 12, 1852. She died May 30, 1853, leaving one son, Wm. H.; second, to Frances A., daughter of Joseph and Lura (Witter) Geer of Ledyard, Conn., Nov. 21, 1860. Mr. and Mrs. Geer are members of Goshen Congregational church in Lebanon, Conn.

EDWARD LUDLOW COOKE, Hartford: Manufacturer of Burial Caskets, Handles, and Undertakers' Supplies.

E. Ludlow Cooke was born in North Haven, April 5, 1840, and was the youngest of six children. When he was but six months old the family moved to New Haven, where they resided many years. Mr. Cooke's ancestors, who were Puritans, came from Kent, England, to Plymouth, Mass., sometime before 1640. One of them was a celebrated admiral in the English navy, whose remains are entombed in Westminster Abbey. Samuel Cooke was one of the first settlers of Wallingford, Conn., and among his descendants were Commodore Foote and the wife of Ex-President Hayes. Stephen Cooke, the father of Ludlow, was a man of sterling qualities. He was one of the original members of the Free Congregational church of New Haven, and its building on Church street was erected under his supervision. Its pastor at this time was the Rev. Mr. Ludlow, and after him Edward Ludlow Cooke was named. Stephen Cooke was the publisher of the *Christian Spectator* and the *Religious Intelligencer*. Beside being interested in the growth of Congregationalism he worked earnestly in the anti-slavery movement, but died before his hopes in that direction were realized, and when his youngest child was but six months old, leaving his widow dependent on her own exertions for the support of her family. She, however, was a woman of the true New England type, and her strong Christian character, unfailing courage, and indomitable will, enabled her to overcome obstacles that a weaker nature would have deemed insurmountable. She supported and educated her children, and lived to see them settled in homes of their own.

Ludlow inherited his father's strong anti-slavery principles, and very early in life his sympathies were aroused for the colored people fleeing from slavery. His home was near that of Amos Townsend, who for many years was the agent of the " Underground Railroad," and being so well known

in that capacity, feared to shelter the runaways himself, and used to send them to the home of Mrs. Cooke, who would keep them for days at a time when they were sick and foot-sore and unable to continue their journey; and her youngest son — though a lad of not more than twelve years — was often called up at three o'clock in the morning to act as guide to slaves who were fleeing to Canada. Very often there were slaveholders in the city offering rewards of five hundred, eight hundred, and a thousand dollars for the capture of the fugitives, and they would have the streets near Mr. Townsend's house patrolled to prevent their escape. Mr. Cooke was present at the famous meeting held in the North Church of New Haven one Sunday evening in 1857, to bid farewell to a company of men who were being sent to help make Kansas a free state. Rev. S. W. S. Dutton presided and called for donations of the necessary equipments for the company. Few meetings have equaled that since the days of the Revolution. The excitement was intense as man after man arose offering rifles, Bibles, blankets, and money, but the climax was reached when Miss Mary Dutton stood up and contributed a rifle, and the applause was so great as to fairly shake the building. The next day the New Haven *Register*, a democratic paper, in its account of the meeting printed a doggerel, beginning:

> "Shoulder arms, Miss Mary Dutton,
> Your knapsack buckle tight,
> Put on your soldier breeches
> And show them how to fight.
> Quick! march upon the foe,
> And now your rifle, cock it
> And send a slaveholder to H——
> With every whistling bullet."

Mr. Cooke was a great admirer of Wendell Phillips and never failed to hear him when he delivered his lectures in New Haven. In 1860, soon after the execution of John Brown, Mr. Cooke and a young friend invited Mr. Phillips to deliver his celebrated lecture on that subject. One of the Yale professors promised to introduce the speaker to his audience, but at the last moment withdrew, saying that he feared the act would injure his political prospects. The result was that Mr. Cooke, though a very young man, was obliged himself to present the lecturer. At this time there were many southern students in Yale, and they were persistent in their attempts to prevent Mr. Phillips from speaking, and at one time during the lecture the orator stood twenty minutes before he could make himself heard.

Mr. Cooke attended the public schools of New Haven until his fourteenth year, when he entered a dry goods store, where he remained eight years. At this time, his health being impaired, he spent a winter on the island of Porto Rico. At this period the oil excitement was running very high, and

Mr. Cooke, after his return from the West Indies, went as agent for a company to West Virginia, where he sunk two wells, one eight hundred and the other twelve hundred feet deep, but found no oil. Another winter was spent in prospecting, when he traveled over six hundred miles on mule-back in Alabama.

In 1864 Mr. Cooke married Ella E., the youngest daughter of Oliver Parish of Hartford. In 1865 he associated himself with Mr. Herman Glafcke in the manufacture of burial caskets. Three years later the firm was changed to Cooke & Whitmore, and is, perhaps, the oldest partnership in Hartford, it having remained unchanged for twenty-three years. For twenty years Mr. Cooke was the traveling man of the business and probably journeyed more miles than any other person in the city at that time. This being the pioneer concern in this line of goods, the territory covered was a large one, extending from Bangor to St. Louis. In 1872 Mr. Cooke built his fine residence on Woodland street, where he still resides. The summer of 1888 he spent in Europe, traveling through Belgium, Germany, Switzerland, France, England, and Scotland.

All strong characters have their weak points and Mr. Cooke's appears to be a passion for antiquities. He has the largest collection of ancient clocks in Hartford and also possesses many other unique and valuable pieces of antique furniture. Mr. Cooke has been a prominent member of the Fourth Congregational church for twenty years, and for thirteen years was superintendent of the Sabbath-school.

DAVID M. MITCHELL, South Britain (Southbury): Farmer.

David Merwin Mitchell is a well-known resident of the town of Southbury, where he was born October 16, 1841, in that part of the town known as

South Britain, where he still resides. He was born and bred on the farm, but took time enough at the district school to lay the foundation for a good education, which was subsequently acquired at Hinman's well-known academy. He married Miss Hattie I. Lemmon, who with their three children is still living. He is a republican in politics, and as such has served his party and his town as selectman, and has held other minor offices. He belongs to the Congregational church of South Britain.

HON. LEVERETT MARSDEN HUBBARD,
WALLINGFORD: Attorney-at-Law.

Leverett M. Hubbard was born at Durham, April 23, 1849. He was educated at the Wilbraham Academy and Wesleyan University, at which latter

institution was also educated his father, Rev. Eli Hubbard, who, for many years before his death, in 1868, had been a clergyman of distinction in Mississippi. His mother was the daughter of Mr. L. W. Leach, for many years a prominent merchant and honored citizen of Durham, and the only sister of Hon. L. M. Leach and Hon. Oscar Leach, both of whom are well known as among the most substantial and influential men in Middlesex county. Mr. Hubbard's mother died when he was three years of age, and from that time until he went from home to attend school he lived with his grandparents at Durham. After leaving college he studied law at the Albany Law School, graduating in 1870. In August of that year he located in Wallingford, and soon became marked at the bar of his county, and by the community generally, as a young man of fine spirit and rare intellectual endowments. From that time he has steadily grown in the confidence and esteem of the community, until now, no lawyer of his age in New Haven county has a more remunerative practice, or is more widely known and respected. From the beginning of his practice he has maintained an office connection in New Haven. For a year he pursued his studies with the late Charles Ives. From 1874 to 1877 he was a law partner of Morris F. Tyler, and since that time he has been associated with John W. Alling, one of the leading lawyers in the state. Mr. Hubbard was appointed postmaster of Wallingford by President Grant in 1872, which office he held by successive re-appointments until the inauguration of President Cleveland in 1885, when he resigned with an unexpired commission for three years. He administered that office with great intelligence and fidelity, and to the universal acceptance of its patrons, who, without respect of party, tendered him, upon his retirement, a complimentary banquet, which was widely remarked at the time for its elaborateness and the enthusiasm which attended it.

Mr. Hubbard has been borough attorney since 1870, and counsel for the town during most of the same period. He has been a director in the First National Bank of Wallingford since its organization in 1881, and a director in the Dime Savings Bank since 1884. He has also been a trustee of the Wesleyan Academy at Wilbraham, Mass., since 1881. Upon the establishment of a borough court for Wallingford by the legislature of 1886 he accepted the position of its first judge, and is now discharging the duties of that office to the eminent satisfaction of the community. In 1886 he was elected Secretary of State on the republican ticket, which had Governor Lounsbury at its head, and during the term of his office performed its duties with signal ability.

Mr. Hubbard is esteemed throughout the community as an honorable and upright citizen, enjoying great popularity among all classes and in both political parties.

HEZEKIAH L. READE, Jewett City: President Jewett City Savings Bank.

Hezekiah L. Reade was born in Lisbon, Oct. 1, 1827. He is the only child of Silas and Sarah (Meech) Reade. His ancestors emigrated from England to this country in 1640; settled at Ipswich, Mass., and subsequently came to Norwich, Conn., where they bought a tract of land one mile long by half a mile wide, of Owaneco, the brother of Uncas, on which the family has since continuously resided. The deed of this land bears date 1686. He was educated in the common schools of his town; in select schools in a

H. L. READE.

near village — Jewett City — and in Plainfield academy. Spending his summers at work on the farm, he commenced teaching school winters at the age of seventeen, continuing this occupation with success for many years. In 1864, he added to his farm and other occupations that of manufacturer of paper. The business was successfully conducted, and at length grew into the "Reade Paper Company," which owned and profitably operated three paper mills. Of this company he was for a considerable time the business manager. Disposing of his interest in this business, he was called to the city of New York to take charge of the agricultural department of "The Hearth and Home" — an illustrated paper published by Pettingill & Bates, and of which both Donald G. Mitchell and Harriet Beecher Stowe were editors. He continued with this paper until it was sold to another leading New York journal. In 1873, he was one of the projectors of the "Jewett City Savings Bank," and

upon its organization was elected its president, and has been reëlected at each annual meeting of the corporation since. The institution is one of the most prosperous in the state. At the age of twenty-two he united with a Congregational church. He immediately began public speaking on temperance, Sunday-schools, and on specially religious topics, and in 1874 began the work of an evangelist. His labors since that time have been in five of the New England states, and more or less elsewhere, beside stated ministrations for indefinite times to a large number of churches.

In 1880, he conceived the idea of "compulsory temperance teaching in public schools." He introduced the first bill into the legislature of Connecticut for a public act to this end that was ever presented before any legislative body. He procured letters commendatory of the idea from Noah Porter, D.D., LL.D., president of Yale College; Hon. Chief-Justice John D. Park, D.D., LL.D., of this state; Leander T. Chamberlain, D.D., at that time pastor of Broadway church, Norwich, and others, which he published in leaflet form, and whose wide circulation prepared the way for the subsequent adoption of the idea in this state and elsewhere. In 1883, he traveled extensively in the west and south in advocacy of this measure; had personal interviews with the governors of Illinois, Wisconsin, Kansas, Missouri, Arkansas, and other states; presented the matter to legislative committees, and through the columns of western papers to the people, sowing the seed that afterwards yielded a harvest. Subsequently, the Woman's Christian Temperance Union took up the matter, and he withdrew for work in other fields.

Mr. Reade has written a number of books: "Money, and How to Make it and Use it," 600 pages: "Boys' and Girls' Temperance Text Book"; "Reade's Business Reader"; "Story of a Heathen and his Transformation," and others, all of which have had and are having a wide sale. He has been a large contributor to the secular and religious press, and some of his sketches have, with others from kindred pens, taken permanent forms. His editorial connection with Connecticut journalism covers many years.

Mr. Reade was married to Faith B. Partridge in 1847. Having no children of their own, they educated a girl who subsequently became a missionary in Japan; and recently have helped to educate a Japanese who already fills a high place in his government, and whose future is one of great promise, both in secular and sacred lines in the "Sunrise Empire."

Mr. Reade is a republican in politics. Was assistant United States assessor during the last years of the war, and until the office was abolished.

CHARLES STORRS HAMILTON, New Haven: Attorney-at-Law.

Charles S. Hamilton was born Jan. 3, 1846. He is descended on his father's side from the famous family of which Alexander Hamilton was a member.

C. S. HAMILTON.

The family, which is of Scotch-Irish extraction, came to Rhode Island in 1640, and went from there to Norwich, Conn. The Storrs family, from which Mr. Hamilton takes his middle name, is connected with the Hamilton family by marriage. On his mother's side, Mr. Hamilton's ancestors were of German descent, who came to New York about the year 1600, his maternal grandfather being a direct lineal descendant of Conrad Gesner, the Zurich scholar and philosopher. The early years of Mr. Hamilton's life were spent entirely in study, and in 1869 he graduated from college with high honors. He has never failed in his love for the classics, and still reads Greek and Latin as a pastime, and speaks both French and German fluently. After graduating, Mr. Hamilton went to Boston and commenced the study of law with Congressman Clarke, and entered the Yale Law School in 1872, graduating one year later on account of advanced standing. He also took a special course in the Yale Medical School, to the more thoroughly fit himself for the extensive practice in technical cases in which he has since been so successful. The following winter was spent in traveling in the southern states, and in May, 1874, he opened an office in the Yale Bank building, which he still occupies. As a jury lawyer he has been peculiarly successful, and an inspection of the different court dockets shows that he appears in a large percentage of jury cases. He has always from the first fought his cases single-handed and alone, except where he has been called in to act as senior counsel in closely contested cases. Mr. Hamilton's success at the bar is due to his superb generalship and thorough preparation. He is never surprised by an adversary, and never fails to detect the weak point in the enemy's line, and take advantage of it. He frequently wins his case before the actual trial, by outgeneraling the other party in the preliminary manoeuvering. He is a "master of English," and his jury addresses are fine specimens of the use of wit, pathos, and sarcasm. An announcement that Mr. Hamilton is to speak in an important case never fails to crowd the court room with students and fellow members of the bar. In poli-

ties, Mr. Hamilton has always been a republican, but has seldom accepted office. In 1888, in response to the urgent request of the residents of the western part of the city, he was nominated for councilman of the second ward, and was elected by a handsome majority, although the ward is naturally democratic. In 1889 he was nominated for alderman, and received a majority of 110. In 1890 he received the unanimous nomination of the convention for state senator, and succeeded in reducing the usual democratic majority by several hundred. In the year 1890 he was chairman of the commission to compile the charter and revise the city ordinances of the city of New Haven, and earned the perpetual gratitude of the members of the bar and city officials by the thorough and discriminating manner in which that task was accomplished. He takes a deep interest in legislative matters, and has drafted many of our important statutes.

Mr. Hamilton has a charming family, consisting of an accomplished wife and two young children. He is an Episcopalian in religion, and is a member of St. Paul's church. He has been for many years a vestryman of that church. Mr. Hamilton is a Freemason, and a member of Hiram Lodge, No. 1.

DANIEL KELEHER, Pawcatuck (Stonington): Granite Cutter.

Daniel Keleher holds the position of captain in Company B of the Third regiment, C. N. G., and is a popular officer. He enlisted as a private March

DANIEL KELEHER.

4, 1875, and became second lieutenant March 23, 1876. He resigned August 9, 1876, but re-enlisted as a private in December, 1877. He was commissioned second lieutenant August 18, 1879; first lieutenant May 16, 1882, and captain July 28, 1886. He was a charter member of the company. He was born in the County of Cork, Ireland, August 20, 1851, and received a public school education. Captain Keleher is a granite cutter by avocation. His work has led him to different parts of the country, and he has resided in Rhode Island, New Jersey, and Pennsylvania. November 28, 1877, he married Ellen Tuite of Leeds, Greene County, N. Y., and has a family of five children. He is a member of St. Michael's Roman Catholic church of Stonington. In politics Captain Keleher is a democrat. He held the office of assessor in 1887 in the town. He is an officer of the Pawcatuck fire district, assessor of the eighteenth school district, and is in other ways connected with the interests of the community. He is a charter member of Narragansett Council, Knights of Columbus, and is past grand knight. He was chairman of the Stonington delegation to the democratic state convention September 16, 1890.

WILLIAM E. MOSES. WATERBURY: Publisher "The Connecticut Guardsman."

First Lieutenant William E. Moses is a commissioned officer in the Connecticut National Guard. He first saw the light of day in the "Hub," having been born in Boston, Mass., March 12, 1861, in which city he received his education. Upon leaving the public schools, he took a thorough course in theoretical bookkeeping for the purpose of becoming an expert and consulting accountant. Since graduating from commercial college, he has performed expert work for corporations and large firms engaged in nearly every

W. E. MOSES.

kind of business, and located in the cities of Boston, New York, Providence, Washington, and Baltimore. In addition to this work he has found time to design and copyright several books and devices, used in accounting, which are meeting with a sale that is highly gratifying. He is at present cashier of the Connecticut Indemnity Association, a well-known life insurance corporation of Waterbury, with which he has been connected for the last five years. Lieutenant Moses comes of a military family — one proud of its records made in all the wars, from Indian to Rebellion — and has served eleven years in the National Guard of three states. He is the proprietor of a publication, entitled *The Connecticut Guardsman,* devoted to the interests of the national guard of the United States and enjoying a national circulation. The following is his military record: Entered the service as private in Company C, First regiment, Mass. V. M., March 19, 1880; discharged November, 1882, to engage in business in Washington, D. C. Joining Company A, Washington Continentals, as a private, in 1883, he held the several appointments of commissary-sergeant and sergeant-major, and in May, 1884, was elected first lieutenant and adjutant, which commission was resigned August, 1885. Enlisting as a private in Company A, Second regiment, C. N. G., March 2, 1887, he was appointed corporal, August 12, 1887; commissioned second lieutenant, January 30, 1888, and commissioned first lieutenant, February 26, 1890.

WILLIAM HENRY POST, HARTFORD: Merchant.

William H. Post is a descendant in the seventh generation from Stephen Post, one of the first settlers of Hartford, who came to America from Chelmsford, England, in 1633, and was a member of the congregation which Rev. Mr. Hooker led through the wilderness in 1636 to found the new colony of Connecticut. His name is inscribed on the monument in the ancient cemetery of the Center church, erected by the citizens of Hartford in memory of the founders of that city. The subject of this sketch was

W. H. POST.

born in Andover, Tolland county, April 1, 1833. He received his education at the "little red schoolhouse" in Columbia, and divided his attention between study and filial duties at his father's homestead until his sixteenth year, when he went to the neighboring village of Hebron to assume the duties of clerk in a country store. After six months' service in that capacity he was called to Hartford to a more responsible position in the dry goods establishment of Talcott & Post, — his brother Amos being junior partner in the firm. Upon the death of his brother, three years later, he took the vacant place as partner, January 1, 1853, and was connected with the firm twenty-eight years, or until its dissolution in 1881. In April of the year last named he opened a carpet house in Hartford, under the firm name of William H. Post & Company, E. S. Yergason being the junior partner. This establishment is one of the most extensive of its kind in the state, and stands at the head of the carpet houses of Hartford, embracing all lines of interior decorations, and enjoying a reputation of national extent. Mr. Post's business ability has been well evidenced in the success of the two firms of which he has been the financial and managerial head. It is further illustrated in the positions of trust which he has been called by his fellow-citizens to occupy since his residence in Hartford. He is a director in the Hartford National Bank and the Society of Savings — two of the strongest and best managed financial institutions in the state; and is on the boards of management of many other enterprises of which Hartford is the home. He takes an active interest in social, educational, and religious affairs. Under the pastorate of Dr. Horace Bushnell he united with the old North church — now the Park church — in 1852, and has been greatly privileged in having that distinguished divine, and his suc-

cessor, the late Dr. Burton, not only as pastors,
but as intimate personal friends. Mr. Post married
in September, 1858, Miss Helen Maria Denslow,
daughter of the late William Judd Denslow of
Hartford, and they have four children — one son
and three daughters. Two of the latter are married: Helen Louise is Mrs. Thomas Brownell Chapman of Hartford, and Alice Maria is the wife of
Frederick Everest Haight of Brooklyn, N. Y. The
only son, William Strong Post, is engaged in the
New York house of W. & J. Sloane, and the juvenile
member of the family, Miss Anne Wilson Post,
a young lady of twelve, is attending school in
Hartford.

ANTHONY AMES, Danielsonville: Retired Merchant and Banker.

Anthony Ames of Danielsonville was a member
of the general assembly in 1889 and served with
credit on the republican side of the house. On account of his connection
with the state board of
education, his influence
was of great importance
in the lines of public
school improvement. Mr.
Ames was born at Ster-
ling, Jan. 15, 1826, and
was educated in the West
Killingly academy at Dan-
ielsonville. At the age of
18 he commenced teach-
ing school and followed
that pursuit for six years.
When he was 28 years of

ANTHONY AMES.

age, he engaged in the dry goods business at Danielsonville in partnership with George Leavens.
Subsequently, he disposed of his interest and established himself in the business of a merchant tailor.
In 1858 he was elected town clerk, treasurer, and
registrar of births, deaths, and marriages, retaining
the position for twenty years. In 1878 he was appointed treasurer of the Windham County Savings
Bank. Ten years afterwards he was compelled
to give up this place on account of impaired
health. In 1889 he represented Killingly in the
legislature, serving on the railroad committee
and the committee on education. He has
been a member of the school board at Killingly
for 30 years, and is at present the acting
school visitor. Mr. Ames will complete his third
term as a member of the state board of education
in July, 1892. He is a member of Moriah Lodge,
F. and A. M., of Danielsonville, occupying the position of secretary. The lodge is one of the largest
and most influential in eastern Connecticut. The
wife of Mr. Ames, who is still living, was Miss
Abby M. Wheaton prior to marriage. There are

no children. The subject of this sketch is most favorably known throughout the State in which he
has represented the best interests of education and
citizenship.

COL. WILLIAM H. STEVENSON, Bridgeport:
Vice-President and General Manager of the
Housatonic Railway System.

Colonel Stevenson was born in Bridgeport in
1847, and, after receiving a thorough literary training and education, graduated early in life from

W. H. STEVENSON.

Eastman's National Busi-
ness College with the de-
gree of Master of Ac-
counts. In 1864 he entered
the offices of the Housa-
tonic railway in Bridge-
port and remained there
for several years. In 1872
he was appointed special
agent of the New York
& New Haven railroad,
an office which he filled
for two years, when he
was appointed paymaster
of the New York Central
& Hudson River railroad, and in the same year
was made superintendent of the Shore Line road.
This line he brought to a high state of efficiency,
placing it in a better position and condition than it
had ever before attained, and as a consequence
he became in demand by several lines, and in 1882
accepted the office of superintendent of the New
York division of the New York, New Haven &
Hartford railroad. In this position, as in all the
offices he had filled, he displayed so much energy,
ability and capacity for managing and controlling
large interests, that he became one of the acknowledged railway experts of the east, and in 1885 was
elected president of the association of American
railroad superintendents, in 1887 was brought back
to the railroad in which he received his first lessons
in railroading and was made vice-president and
general manager of the Housatonic railway. It
would scarcely be expected that a man who gave
so much attention to so vast a subject as railroading, and who had by great application and ability
risen rapidly to the head of a prominent system in
so short a time, could have given much thought to
anything else; yet Col. Stevenson has found time
to do a great many other things and to rise to
prominence in other ways as well as in the great
business of his life. In 1875 he was elected councilman in Bridgeport and served on the finance
committee, and in 1876 he was returned as alderman, and in 1877 was re-elected, and served on the
most important committees of the board. During
this year he was honored with the democratic

nomination for the legislature, against Hon. P. T. Barnum. In 1878 he was again elected alderman and was chairman of the finance committee and also the committee on ways and means. In this year he passed the required examination as a lawyer and was admitted to the bar of Fairfield county. In 1881 he was nominated by the democratic party for mayor, and in 1884 was elected president of the young men's democratic Cleveland and Hendricks club and took an active part in the campaign which resulted so favorably for his party. He served on the democratic state committee during the campaign of 1888. But he gave attention to and attained prominence in yet another field, and was appointed aid-de-camp with the rank of captain on the staff of Brigadier-General S. R. Smith of the Connecticut National Guard in 1879. He served as captain until 1884, when he was promoted to the office of brigade commissary, with the rank of major, on the staff of General Smith. In the same year he was again promoted, acting as aid-de-camp with the rank of colonel on the staff of Governor Thomas M. Waller. He was the third president of the old Eclectic Club of Bridgeport, which was for ten years one of the most popular social institutions in the city. In 1884 he was elected grand master of the grand lodge of Independent Order of Odd Fellows for the state of Connecticut, and in the following year was sent as representative to the sovereign grand lodge I. O. O. F. by the grand lodge of Connecticut, at which time he was elected grand marshal of the sovereign grand lodge. In 1886 he was appointed general aid, with the rank of colonel, on the staff of Lieut.-General Underwood of the military branch of patriarchs militant of the order of Odd Fellows. He is also a member of the Masonic order, and in 1883 was chosen exalted ruler of the Bridgeport order of Elks. In 1887 he was elected director and president of the New York, Rutland & Montreal railroad, and also a director in the New York & New England railroad. In the following year he was made president of the New Haven & Derby railroad. He is also a director in the Danbury & Norwalk railroad and a director in the West Stockbridge railroad. One of his projects, which has been successfully carried through, was the extension of the New Haven & Derby railroad to the Housatonic railroad, the latter road building a branch to meet it, which was completed in November, 1888, and opened with great enthusiasm on the part of the general public, because of its making a new and independent route from New Haven to the west. Under the able management of Col. Stevenson the Housatonic railroad is fast becoming one of the leading railway systems of New England. Recently Col. Stevenson was elected one of the directors and vice-president of the Shepaug,

Litchfield & Northern railroad. In 1890 he was a leading figure in the political campaign and was the choice of a large portion of the democratic party for governor, but he declined to be considered a candidate, his business interests demanding all his attention.

GENERAL EDWARD E. BRADLEY, New Haven: President New Haven Wheel Company and Boston Buckboard and Carriage Company.

General Edward E. Bradley occupies a foremost place among the business men of New Haven, being at the head of one of the largest and most important industries in that city. His standing as a public representative is equally notable. The General was born in New Haven January 5, 1845, and received a thorough public school education. At the age of sixteen he engaged in the employ of the New Haven Wheel Company, beginning as shipping clerk. He is now the president of the corporation, which has

business relations throughout the world, its trade extending to most European and South American countries. General Bradley is also the president of the Boston Buckboard and Carriage Company. He has but few superiors in his section of the state as a business manager, and the rapid promotions which he has met with in life have been deserved. In 1861 he became a member of the New Haven Grays, one of the celebrated military companies of the state at that time. The soldierly traits and instincts which he manifested at the outset attracted attention, opening the way for the brilliant series of advancements in the service that awaited him. He was placed at the head of the company and became a field officer in the Second Regiment within a dozen years from the date of his enlistment as a private in the Grays. Under the administration of Governor R. D. Hubbard he was made paymaster-general with the rank of brigadier in the service. General Bradley represented the town of Orange in the general assembly during the years of 1883 and 1884, his career in the house proving him to be a legislator of decided capability and leadership. The constitutional amendment providing for biennial sessions was introduced in the house by General Bradley during the session of 1883 and was ordered published in the laws of that year. The amendment that had been submitted to the people in 1879 had been overwhelmingly rejected and it was feared at the beginning that General Bradley's renewal of the idea would prove ineffective. But the General's influence was an important factor in getting the proposed amendment incorporated in the session laws. In 1884 the legislature ordered the submission to the people for ratification and it was adopted at the October election in that year. General Bradley was elected a member of the senate from the seventh district in 1885 and ably served in that body through the session of 1886. The democratic state convention of 1886 was held in New Haven and resulted in the selection of General Bradley for the second place on the state ticket, the Hon. Edward S. Cleveland of Hartford being the candidate for the governorship. The superb enthusiasm with which the general's nomination was received in the convention was the most complimentary of tributes to his popularity. His total vote at the polls was larger than that of his chief and exceeded by 1,979 the total received by the republican candidate for the governorship. General Bradley is a member of the New Haven Park Commission and of the New Haven Chamber of Commerce. He is also a director in the New Haven County National Bank, and president of the New Haven Grays Veteran Association. He is a communicant of St. Paul's Church in that city and is a gentleman of the most exemplary personal character. His family consists of a wife and three daughters. The former was Miss Mary E. Kimberly prior to her marriage with General Bradley.

EDWARD DEACON, Bridgeport: Secretary Consolidated Rolling Stock Company.

Edward Deacon was born in England in 1846, descended from an old Bedfordshire family of that name. He completed his education at Liverpool 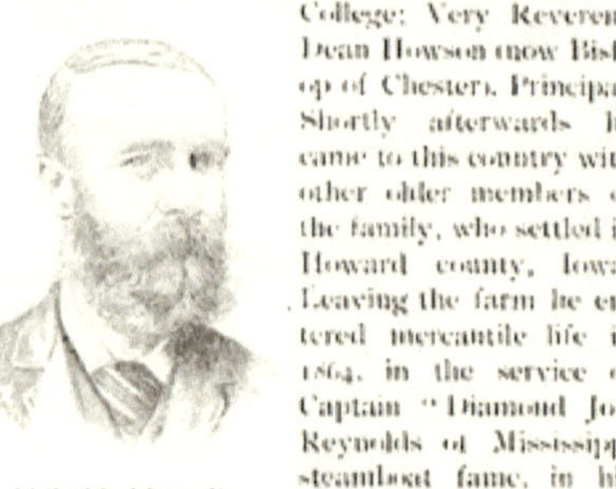 College; Very Reverend Dean Howson (now Bishop of Chester), Principal. Shortly afterwards he came to this country with other older members of the family, who settled in Howard county, Iowa. Leaving the farm he entered mercantile life in 1864, in the service of Captain "Diamond Jo" Reynolds of Mississippi steamboat fame, in his then immense grain and

EDWARD DEACON.

pork business at McGregor, Iowa, and soon proved himself so capable that large financial interests were entrusted to his care. Subsequently he assisted in the construction of the Milwaukee & St. Paul Railroad in 1866-7, being paymaster for

the contractors, Judge Greene of Iowa, Alexander Mitchell of Milwaukee, and Russell Sage of New York. In this capacity it became his duty to purchase and pay for large supplies for the army of men and horses, which was strung along the unbroken prairie, at that time almost entirely unsettled and unknown. With one attendant and well armed, he would drive over the prairies from section to section between Austin, Minn., and Ossian, Iowa, carrying forty to fifty thousand dollars, paying the men by day upon the estimates of the engineers, and sleeping at night in the tents and shanties of the workmen with his cash box under his head.

In 1868 he started for himself in the wholesale agricultural implement business, with headquarters at McGregor, Iowa, and established agencies for the sale of threshers and reapers in nearly every county of southern Minnesota, northern Iowa, and western Wisconsin. In this he was fairly successful, but the hard times in the West antecedent to the panic of 1873 compelled him to close up his business and remove to Detroit, Mich., where he married and accepted a position in the First National Bank of that city. A few years later he engaged with the great seed house of D. M. Ferry & Co., in which he became a stockholder, and remained with them several years.

Having had some previous knowledge of the rolling stock business, upon the organization of the Consolidated Rolling Stock Company of Bridgeport Mr. Deacon was tendered the office of secretary of the company, which he accepted and removed with his family to that city in 1886. This company, whose capital stock is $4,000,000 (four millions), owns many thousand freight cars, and maintains three shops, located in the west, for the building and repair of its rolling stock. These shops are under the management of Mr. Deacon, who acts as purchasing agent and superintendent for the company. Mr. Deacon is a director of the Detroit Rolling Stock and other similar companies. He married, in Detroit, Miss Eliza Stoddard, daughter of Rodman Stoddard of Connecticut, the fifth in descent from Rev. Solomon Stoddard, the first librarian of Harvard College, who was grandfather of the celebrated Jonathan Edwards, and was also the ancestor of Aaron Burr and General W. T. Sherman. The result of this union is a son and daughter, who are both living.

Mr. Deacon has neither sought nor held public office, his tastes rather inclining to a literary turn. He is the possessor of a fairly well filled library, and enjoys the privileges which membership in the Fairfield County Historical Society and the Bridgeport Scientific Society brings to him. He is a member of the Presbyterian church and a republican.

JOHN N. NEAR, Bridgeport; Mercantile Printer and Publisher.

John N. Near was born in Rhinebeck, N. Y., June 15, 1837, of Dutch ancestry, the name being originally spelled Neher. At fourteen years of age he entered the office of the *American Mechanic* in that place as an apprentice. In 1855 he left there to accept a position on the *Berkshire County Eagle* at Pittsfield, leaving there in 1856 to accept the foremanship of the *Daily Farmer* at Bridgeport, Conn. In 1857 he left this position on a trip to better his fortunes, but after an absence of several weeks he returned to Bridge-

J. N. NEAR.

port, and took the foremanship of the City Steam Printing House. At this time he engaged in active politics, and was elected town and city treasurer. The printing house soon after went into a joint stock concern, and after a few years the owners sold the business to young Near, without the payment of a dollar down.

From this time forth he withdrew from all active participation in politics, refusing to accept any office, though often tendered, preferring to devote his entire time to the business, having a laudable desire to pay off his obligations, and become in fact, as well as in name, the owner of the property. After several years of hard work and personal supervision of the business he has the satisfaction of seeing his hopes realized and himself in possession of the largest job printing business in Bridgeport. The office now no longer requiring all his attention, being in charge of his sons, and being again drawn into politics, he was elected a member of the council, and president of the board in 1885-6. In 1886, and again in 1887, he was the candidate of his party for mayor. Each time he was defeated, owing to the active opposition of the saloon element in his party. They had been allowed to keep their places open, not only after 12 o'clock at night, but also on Sundays, and it was published that if he were elected the laws would be enforced. Although defeated for mayor, yet when he came before the people as a candidate for representative in 1888, he was elected by over five hundred majority.

Mr. Near married Miss Sarah F. Barnum of Bridgeport, and has two children. He is a democrat, and as such has held the offices of town and city treasurer, city councilman, and president of the board, representative in the general assembly, and is now chairman of the board of fire commission-

ers. He is a member of the Universalist church, and of the order of Knights of Pythias. He is emphatically a " self-made man," having by dint of strict business methods and unswerving integrity won an honorable position in the business and social world, and a competence at the same time. It is a pardonable boast of the subject of this sketch, that, starting with nothing, he has never seen the time when he was absolutely in want of a dollar. His credit has always been unlimited, for the reason that he never has failed to pay when promised. To-day, the business which he has established ranks as the second largest in this line in the state.

SELLECK Y. ST. JOHN, New Canaan; Banker.

S. Y. St. John was born at South Salem, in the state of New York, February 10, 1819. His education was obtained in district schools and academies, where was laid the solid foundation upon which his successes in business pursuits have since been constructed. He was engaged in mercantile affairs for many years, but his connections have been chiefly with banking and other financial institutions. He was treasurer of the New Canaan Savings Bank for seventeen years from its organization in 1859, and has been

S. Y. ST. JOHN.

cashier of the First National Bank of that place since it was organized under the national banking law in 1865. He has been director of the New Canaan Railroad for a number of years, and was president of the company from 1876 to 1878. He is also president of the New Canaan Cemetery Association, and has held a number of local offices in that town, including that of town clerk for nine years, and justice of the peace for even a much longer term. Mr. St. John is a republican in politics, and as such was elected, successively in 1879, 1881, and 1882, to represent New Canaan in the general assembly of the state, where he rendered important service to his constituents and the state. The subject of this sketch is a prominent citizen of his town, deeply and actively interested in all public affairs, and highly esteemed by all who know him. He married December 1, 1840, Miss Mary A. Seymour, daughter of Holly Seymour of New Canaan, and they have had two children, neither of whom is now living. A granddaughter, who is unmarried and resides with them, is their only representative.

ANER SPERRY, Hartford. Trustee in Settlement of Estates.

The subject of this sketch was born in the town of Russia, Herkimer County, New York, February 5, 1812. For a great many years he was in active

ANER SPERRY.

business in Hartford, and well-known throughout the city and county. He practically retired years ago, and has since devoted his attention to the settlement of estates. His erect form is still a familiar one on the streets of Hartford; and, although nearly eighty years of age, his step is firm and his eye bright. He has personally prepared a sketch of his life, which is printed verbatim below, and will be read by his acquaintances with greater relish than anything which the editor could offer in its place.

Mr. Sperry writes: " My father and mother went from New Haven to Russia, N. Y., in the year 1800, and settled on a farm in the wilderness. They had then one daughter, Laura; they constructed a log house in which they lived several years, but the family increased and a larger house was required. It was built at the foot of a small hill, of logs, and in this house I was born. I take great pleasure in visiting the spot where the old log house stood, and looking at the little babbling brook near by where I have taken so much comfort in wading in the water, building dams, and after school filling my fish basket with speckled trout, or picking twelve quarts of blackberries and carrying them to ' the corners,' one and a half miles away. I could generally get two cents per quart, but if the market was dull Esq. Frink would take them and give me a yard of cotton cloth that was worth one York shilling. Mother could always find use for it, as I had five sisters and two brothers. The school-house was one and a half miles away, and I did not spend much time there. Father was a tailor and spent most of the winters in ' whipping the cat,' and that left the chores and wood-chopping for me to do. The old bay mare ' Cub ' was a great help to me in getting up the wood; she also carried us to mill and to meeting. We had about three acres of orchard and I remember the names of nearly every tree. Father built a frame barn and one of our neighbors had a frame house; he died one day and father bought the house for fifty dollars, and the neighbors that had oxen came and moved the house to our place and we dug a cellar under it and that made us a very good home. It was a hard struggle for our parents to clear up the land and

raise so large a family. We were all brought up in the Methodist faith and the fear of hell was before our eyes; but I ' did not see it.' Our advantages for knowing what was in the future were very limited. The answer to any and all questions was ' faith.' Our farm was very hilly and it made lots of hard work. The soil was good. A brook ran through the south part of it, and a spring supplied the north part; we had a good sugar bush. Our neighbors were kind and agreeable. I took lots of comfort attending singing school.

" At the age of sixteen I left home and went to live with John Graves in the fall, and did chores for my board and went to school. Perhaps some of the sixteen-year-old boys of the present day would like to know what chores I had to do. Well, the first was to get out of bed at four o'clock A. M., dress and go to the barn and milk six cows, feed forty cows, two oxen, and five horses, then go to another barn and feed twenty calves and forty sheep; then go to a haystack half a mile away and feed five colts, shovel away the snow and cut a hole in the ice for them to drink, feed six hogs,— all of which must be done before daylight. Who can guess how much hay has been handled? Now breakfast is ready. After eating in a hurry the cows are all turned out to water, and put back if stormy, horses led out to water, and all of the stables cleaned out; now comes wood-sawing and filling the woodbox in the kitchen, and then I am now ready for school. At twelve I must hurry home and feed all the cattle, and get back to school for the afternoon. As soon as it is closed I am seen running home to do the chores, which are not finished until about eight o'clock; then when supper is over I am soon between the sheets. This is repeated every day until spring arrives. I then go to work for seven dollars per month. This is followed up for five years; the last summer the wages reach ten dollars per month. My father takes all of my wages for the five years. I then arrive at the age of twenty-one. During my boyhood, when at home, my father gave me a small patch of ground on which I raised watermelons and sold them at general trainings and picked up a little money of my own. I enlisted into the artillery company, Twenty-sixth regiment, N. Y. S. artillery under David Joy. Dr. Walter Booth commanded the company afterward, and our general trainings were held at Herkimer. F. E. Spinner was colonel, he who was afterwards United States treasurer. On the 26th of July, 1830, I was appointed corporal of the company and received my warrant from Colonel Spinner on that day. Our uniform was blue, trimmed with gilt braid, bell-crowned caps made of patent leather and brass trimmed, with tall red feather, sword, and belt. I enlisted when I was seventeen. When I became twenty-one I was sick of farming and decided to look for some other business. Father said ' If you will stay here and take care of me and mother, when we get through you shall have all that is left.' I thanked him for his very kind and generous offer, and said to him, ' You have worked all of your life so far and got together a farm of fifty acres, and it is well-stocked and worth about $1,500. Now I shall decline the offer for two reasons: first, I have brothers and sisters, and would not take it all; second, I think I can do better.' I was then twenty-one and had thirty dollars in my pocket. I left Russia about the 4th of April, 1833, for New Haven, by stage; could not get work, and my thirty dollars was reduced to one dollar and seventy-five cents. Left New Haven at eight A.M., arrived in Hartford at four P.M., having walked thirty-six miles; applied at the Retreat for work without success; went to Mr. Johnson's house near by and staid over night; told him my situation, and he gave me my supper, lodging, and breakfast, and it was valued higher than any gift that I ever received. Next morning went over to the Retreat and obtained a situation. Was employed in the house for six months; then went outside and drove the team seven and one-half years. My stay there was very pleasant and agreeable. I had fifteen dollars per month for two years and twenty dollars per month for six years. The managers made me a present of fifty dollars when I left. Dr. Todd was superintendent and Phineas Talcott steward when I went there, and Dr. Brigham was superintendent and Virgil Cornish steward when I left. The boys there wanted to use their money faster than they earned it, and I lent them money every month at a large interest. I saved my money and the big interest helped me out. I spent but very little. I attended dancing school two winters. The first thousand dollars that I earned I put into the grocery trade with a partner, who managed the business two years and then left with all of the funds. I left the Retreat in the spring of 1841, and manufactured root beer for five months; cleared $875. Then I formed a copartnership with Frederick F. Taylor. We bought out Solomon Smith's livery stable, price $2,500. I had $2,200, and Mr. Taylor had $300. We were located on Front street. Mr. Smith still owned the office, which we afterwards bought for $700. Then we bought of Christopher Colt a barn for $1,200; then bought of Griffin Stedman a house on Talcott street for $1,500; then sold the whole to Daniel Buck for an advance of $500. We then bought of Wm. Kellogg a barn corner of Front and Talcott streets for $4,000. On this ground I built my first house; it was a neat little house of four rooms. August 18, 1844, I was married to Nancy B. Miller; she was from East Hampton, N. Y.; she was six years younger than myself.

We were married at the Methodist Church. I played the bass viol there five years. I think Nancy was the best housekeeper in the wide world. We lived together thirty-nine years; she died August 31, 1883. Mr. Taylor and myself bought, in the spring of 1847, the old Goodwin livery stable in rear of the Exchange Bank, State street, for $13,200. Mr. Taylor's health failed in 1850 and I bought him out and paid him $8,000. I continued the business until 1859. I had ten hacks and twenty-five single teams, and generally kept fifty horses and attended to most of the funerals. I employed fifteen men and had a large run of business. Kept my own books. My hacks cost generally from $1,200 to $1,500; I had one that cost $2,000, and Mrs. Sigourney had the first ride in it. I lost over fifty horses, the value of which was at least $10,000, and bad debts on my books $40,000. My barn was burned and the loss, over the insurance, was $8,000. I gave Geo. K. Reed $5,000, Mrs. Sharp's family $2,500, Geo. W. Loveland $3,100, Frederick S. Sperry $300, Philena Fithian $250, Polla Osborn $250, and many other smaller gifts, also S. A. L. $2,200. Lost by endorsements and otherwise over $20,000. The aggregate amount of losses and gifts $70,000. The interest added, this amount would, at this time, make the whole amount considerably over $100,000.

" I bought ten hacks here, three in New Haven, thirty-five in Bridgeport. My livery property would generally inventory about $30,000. When I commenced the business, our capital being but $2,500, I was obliged to have some credits. I got Robert Buell to endorse for me. He was on my paper most of the time. I gave him what riding he wanted, which amounted to about one hundred dollars per year. I have been interested in the hack business outside of my own business with James Givin, Mr. Boyington, Mr. Briggs, John White, E. P. Cottrell, James Tehan, C. B. Boardman, Geo. Goyt, I. A. Chamberlain, and Merrick Freeman. I finally wound up by selling out to Freeman. I took a house of him on Pleasant street and lived there one year; changed that for a farm on Windsor avenue. In the spring of 1860 I bought my house on Ann street. During 1859 and 1860 I was out of business, and it was the two hardest years' work that I have ever done. At that time Hewett & Rogers failed in the livery business, and theirs was the first estate that I ever settled; but I have followed the business ever since, and my list numbers now 175. My fees will amount to about $17,000.

" When I first started out to take care of myself the main object was to provide for myself a good home. I have denied myself many things in my youth that would have been pleasant to enjoy, but by so doing I have accomplished my object. I have got my long-desired good home, although in getting it I have passed through many storms; but the storms are over and the sun shines bright."

Since the above sketch was prepared, Mr. Sperry has married, May 6, 1891, Mrs. Emily J. House of Hartford.

FREDERICK S. STEVENS, BRIDGEPORT; Wholesale and Retail Druggist.

Frederick S. Stevens comes of a long and illustrious line of Connecticut ancestry, being of the seventh generation from Thomas Stevens, who died in

F. S. STEVENS.

Stamford in 1658; a great-grandson of Lieutenant Ezra Stevens of Revolutionary fame; and grandson of Zadoc Stevens, an honored representative of his native town of Danbury in the legislature of 1824-5. Oliver Wolcott was then governor and Ralph I. Ingersoll speaker of the House. The men who were sought for legislative honors in those days were the leading men of Connecticut; and of the gentlemen who served with Zadoc Stevens one became a United States senator, six became governors of Connecticut, six members of congress, one United States minister to the court of Russia, and thirty-four others obtained high places in the administration of state affairs. Israel Coe of Waterbury is to-day the only surviving member of the distinguished legislature of 1824-5.

F. S. Stevens was born in Danbury, 1848, and removed to Knoxville, Illinois, when quite young. The public schools of Knoxville and two years in Knox College, Galesburg, Ill., completed his educational advantages. For about twenty years he has been engaged in the drug trade in Bridgeport, which city has honored him with various positions of trust. He was one of the twenty-five originators of the Connecticut State Pharmaceutical association. He was five years on Colonel Watson's staff, C. N. G. 4th Regt. He was elected last fall to represent Bridgeport in the general assembly, as a democrat. He is secretary and a director of the Masonic Temple Association of Bridgeport, a past master of Corinthian Lodge, No. 104, F. & A. M., a prominent member of the board of trade, the Seaside Club, and of Christ Protestant Episcopal church. He was married in 1876 to Anna May, only daughter of Edward L. Gaylord, ex-president of the Eagle Lock Company of Terryville. His family consists of four children. Mr. Stevens is a quiet, genial gentleman, and a thorough business

man, whose sound sense, sterling integrity, and good judgment, have always forced him into the front rank of his fellow-citizens and his party.

WILLIAM I. LEWIS, GROVE BEACH, WESTBROOK.

Mr. Lewis was born at New Canaan, in this state, in 1840, the son of Isaac Hayes Lewis, and nephew of John Lewis, for whom the town of Lewisboro,

W. I. LEWIS.

Westchester county, N. Y., is named. He is descended from the old French Huguenot family of Hayes, who settled New Rochelle, N. Y., and from the old Connecticut family of Lewis. He was solidly educated at the New York public schools and free academy. He studied law three years in the office of Lawyer Sherman in New York city, and two years at the Columbian University, Washington, D. C. His life has been a varied and busy one: in the army, in manufacturing and mercantile pursuits, and at times holding several important offices of trust under the government. In the early part of the war he enlisted as a private in the 20th Connecticut volunteers, and being a rapid and fine penman, he was soon placed on detailed service with Captain John P. Green, now vice-president of the Pennsylvania railroad, and in the field with the fearless General Thomas L. Kane, brother of the famous Arctic explorer, and while on this duty was with the general day and night, of whom it was said "He never slept." Mr. Lewis was captured by the famous guerilla chief Mosby and incarcerated in Castle Thunder and Libby prisons. Before the close of the war he was made the general accountant of the military railroads, U. S., which was organized by Thomas A. Scott, the great president of the Pennsylvania railroad, and he undertook and successfully accomplished the work of classifying, arranging, and tabulating the multifarious reports of the thirty-five railroads operated by the government throughout the rebellious states into one volume or tabulated statement, comprising over 200 folios, which is on file in the archives of the state department at Washington, D. C., and it is said to be the finest and most elaborate and complete statistical report of its kind in existence. He was for three years in the office of the secretary of the treasury, and while there originated and established the system of accounting and rules now in use, governing the expenses of collecting the revenue from customs throughout the United States, whereby the secretary of the treasury controls these expenditures, and which has resulted in saving millions of dollars to the government. His knowledge of public men is large, having been connected with the treasury and for the past seven years associated with the sergeant-at-arms of the U. S. senate at Washington. Mr. Lewis has always risen in the estimation of those with whom he has been associated by simple force of his ability and character. Shortly after the war he married Isadora, daughter of Mr. William D. Winship of Georgetown, D. C. Three sons and three daughters are the fruit of this union. He is a member of the Presbyterian church and with his good wife founded a mission church of that denomination, while sojourning in Washington. He is also a free mason and in politics has always been a pronounced republican. He believes in progression and takes great interest in everything pertaining to the welfare of Connecticut; especially is he interested in all improvements in his own locality. He is an enterprising citizen of the town of Westbrook. He has resided at Grove Beach, between the villages of Clinton and Westbrook, with his family since 1872. He is a very nervy, tireless worker at whatever he undertakes, as shown by his energy in causing the opening of the new and beautiful shore highway running through Grove Beach and connecting the towns of Clinton and Westbrook, and in his untiring and persistent work for the breakwater improvement at Duck Island Harbor on the sea front of these towns. He is the founder of Grove Beach, and the improvements and wonderful growth of this place in the past few years is due to him more than to any other person for his enterprise and push in developing this charming summer resort.

JOSEPH PIERPONT, North Haven, Merchant.

Joseph Pierpont was born in North Haven March 11, 1853, and was educated in the common schools and at Cheshire academy, providing him with a thorough equipment for business. He is engaged in mercantile pursuits and is a careful and judicious manager. Mr. Pierpont is a member of St. John's Episcopal church at North Haven, occupying the position of junior warden. In politics he is a republican. He is a member of the board of school visitors, his present term expiring in 1892. Mr. Pierpont has a wife and three children. The former was Miss Hattie B. Brockett prior to her marriage.

JOSEPH PIERPONT.

HON. W. W. EATON, Hartford: Ex-Congressman.

William W. Eaton was born at Tolland, October 11, 1816, and received a public school education there, preparing him for business life. His father, Hon. Luther Eaton, was a man of notable honesty and integrity, possessing the fullest confidence and respect of the community in which he resided. He was also a man of political influence and control, at one time representing the old twentieth district in the state senate. Mr. Eaton inherited the strict probity and independence of conviction of his father, and from the earliest period of his life his course has been one of fearless adherence to what he has believed to be right. On arriving at his majority he engaged in mercantile pursuits at Columbia, S. C., and spent three or four years there in business. The strong individual views which characterized his subsequent course in public affairs were established in part at least by his residence at the South. At the conclusion of his commercial career, which lasted upwards of four years, he returned North and commenced the study of law at his old home in Tolland, and was admitted to the bar in Tolland county. In 1847 he was elected a member of the Connecticut house of representatives from Tolland, and was returned the following year from that town. From that time until now he has been a prominent figure in Connecticut politics. In 1850 he was elected to the state senate from the old twentieth district. At the end of the session of the general assembly that year Mr. Eaton removed to Hartford, and has since been a resident here. He received the appointment of clerk of the Hartford county court, and proved himself a thoroughly competent official. In 1853 he was elected a member of the house from Hartford and was chosen speaker, a position for which he was amply qualified both by reason of ability and experience. Mr. Eaton was also a member of the house from Hartford during the sessions of 1863, '68, '70, '71, '73, and '74. In 1873 he was elected speaker for the second time, and discharged the duties of the position with characteristic efficiency and success. Mr. Eaton possesses special adaptation for the legislative function, and his career in the general assembly was marked by the highest personal integrity and uprightness. During the session of 1874 he was elected United States senator from Connecticut, succeeding Hon. William A. Buckingham, whose term expired March 4, 1875.

W. W. EATON.

Upon the death of Senator Buckingham in February, 1875, Mr. Eaton was appointed United States senator, filling the vacancy caused by Mr. Buckingham's death, and assumed the duties of the office February 13, 1875. Commencing his full term on the 4th of March following, he remained in Washington during the succeeding six years, establishing for himself a record in which the state might experience a just sense of pride. During the concluding years of his senatorial life he was senate chairman of the committee on foreign relations, one of the most important in congress. He was opposed to the appointment of the electoral commission by which, in 1876, the election of President Hayes was ratified, and was the only democrat in the senate who voted against the measure. Mr. Eaton was one of the strongest advocates of tariff reform during his term in congress, and was the author of an important measure providing for the appointment of a tariff commission. His term expired March 3, 1881, before his bill could be made a law, but the subsequent congress enacted a measure covering the main provisions of Mr. Eaton's act. He was a hard-money democrat, and held positive views with regard to the greenback controversy which agitated the country a few years ago. In the fall of 1882 he received the democratic nomination for congress from the first district, and was elected by a handsome majority. At the close of his term he retired from active political life, though his voice is still heard and his influence felt in the councils of his party.

HARVY GODARD, North Granby: Farmer and Miller.

Harvy Godard was born in North Granby, March 15, 1823, and was educated in the common schools, preparing him for a useful and successful life. In 1873 he was a member of the general assembly from the town of Granby, and was master of the state grange from 1875 until 1879. He has held most of the offices within the gift of his town, and is an active and influential citizen of Granby. He is a democrat in politics. Mr. Godard has devoted his life to agricultural pursuits. He is a member of St. Mark's

HARVY GODARD.

Lodge, No. 36, F. and A. M., of Tariffville. He has always lived in North Granby, where, in addition to his farming occupations, he has carried on a sawmill and gristmill. One of his yearly pastimes is to distill a small quantity of cider brandy in the old-fashioned way. Mr. Godard has a wife and five sons. The former was Miss Sabra L. Beach prior to her marriage. His only daughter, Grace M., died in 1878, aged three years.

NORMAN C. STILES, Middletown: Manufacturer of Machinery.

The subject of this sketch, like very many other persons who have risen to prominence, and who have been largely instrumental in building up great

N. C. STILES.

enterprises, was a poor boy, but possessed with energy and push, and succeeded in establishing one of the most important industries in the country, from which he retired in December last, leaving his son, E. S. Stiles, in his place. He was born at Feeding Hills, a village of Agawam, Mass., June 18, 1834. Through misfortunes to the father, the subject of this sketch was deprived of the educational advantages enjoyed by most boys of his age. He early developed inventive genius and remarkable mechanical ability, and various devices were constructed by him, previous to the age of sixteen, when he removed to Meriden and engaged with his brother, Doras A. Stiles, in the manufacture of tinware; but this gave him no opportunity to develop his mechanical tastes, and he soon after became connected with the American Machine Works, at Springfield, Mass., where he remained until he attained his majority. Soon after he returned to Meriden, Conn., and entered the employ of Messrs. Snow, Brooks & Co., now known as Messrs. Parker Brothers. He was employed in making dies and other small work, requiring great skill and ingenuity. He subsequently entered the employ of Messrs. Edward Miller & Co., of Meriden, where he remained until 1857, when he concluded to "paddle his own canoe," and began the manufacture of presses and dies. His business increased at a rapid rate and required additional facilities, and Mr. Stiles selected Middletown as a good place for wider operations, removed there, and has remained there ever since. Previous to removing to Middletown, Mr. Stiles made several improvements in his punching press, among others an eccentric adjustment, which was a great improvement on other punching presses then in use, and far superior to what was known as the Fowler press. This device he patented in 1864. Parker Bros. of Meriden, who were engaged in manufacturing the Fowler press, adopted Mr.

Stiles' eccentric adjustment, which involved a long and expensive litigation, resulting finally in a compromise and the organization of the Stiles & Parker Press Co., in which Mr. Stiles held the controlling interest. In 1873 Mr. Stiles attended the Vienna exposition, through which he obtained a foreign market for his goods. His presses are used in the armories and navy yards of the United States, as well as those of Germany, Austria, Prussia, Sweden, Turkey, Egypt, France, and Mexico. He has interested himself in the public affairs of Middletown, and served several years as a member of the boards of councilmen and aldermen. He married, March 23, 1864, Sarah M., daughter of Henry Smith of Middletown. They have three children, Doctor Henry R., Edmund S., secretary and superintendent of the Stiles & Parker Press Company, and Milly B. Mr. Stiles is a member of the church of the Holy Trinity (Episcopal), of Middletown; of the society of Mechanical Engineers and Engineer's Club of New York, and of the Knights Templar of Middletown. In politics he is a republican.

GEORGE E. JONES, Litchfield: Cashier First National Bank.

George Eaton Jones was born in Litchfield, March 31, 1849, and received a thorough common school and business education. He is engaged in banking and farming, being the cashier of the First National Bank of Litchfield for sixteen years and one of the best-known breeders and importers of Jersey stock in the state. He is the vice-president and one of the directors of the Connecticut Jersey cattle breeders association, treasurer of the Litchfield county agricultural society, treasurer of Litchfield county,

G. E. JONES.

founder and director of the Litchfield Water Co., and the treasurer of Darius Chapter, No. 16, R. A. M. He is also past master of St. Paul's Lodge of Litchfield and member of Buell Council, M. E. M. Mr. Jones is a member of the Reform Club of New York city and a staunch democrat in politics. He has held the positions of burgess and warden of the borough of Litchfield. He belongs to St. Michael's Episcopal church in Litchfield. The wife of Mr. Jones, who was Eva Freelon Colver, countess prior to her marriage, died in 1873. There is one daughter, the fruit of this union. Mr. Jones formerly resided in Hartford, spending six years in this city.

WILLIAM HENRY WATROUS, Hartford: President, Treasurer, and General Manager of the Wm. Rogers Manufacturing Company.

William H. Watrous was born July 18, 1841, in Hartford; received his education under Mrs. M. M. Perry in the Arsenal school; attended the Hartford Public High school one year; and in 1855, at the age of 14 years, began to learn the trade of electro-plating in the factory of his uncles, Rogers Brothers, who built the shop foot of Trumbull street, now occupied by Jewell Belting Company. In 1859 he was engaged with Rogers, Smith & Co. on Mechanics street. In 1861 he was among the first to enlist in Rifle Company

W. H. WATROUS.

A, First Regiment, Connecticut Volunteers, and served under Captain Joseph R. Hawley, now United States senator. In 1862 he re-entered the United States service as first sergeant of Company B, Twenty-fourth Regiment, C. V., being afterwards promoted to second lieutenant of the same company. In 1865 he was with William Rogers when the latter organized the Wm. Rogers Manufacturing Company at the corner of Front and Grove streets. In 1868 he removed to Waterbury, where he had charge of the plating department of Rogers & Brother. In 1870 he returned to Hartford, and founded the Rogers Cutlery Company with his uncle, Asa H. Rogers. They commenced business on Asylum street with only two employes. Soon after Mr. Rogers withdrew, and the business was moved into a factory in rear of the Fourth church on North Main street. In 1879 he purchased one-half of the stock of the Wm. Rogers Manufacturing Company, and moved the Rogers Cutlery Company into their factory, corner of Front and Grove streets, when he became president, treasurer, and general manager of both companies, in which positions he has since continued. In 1887 he bought the Kohn silk mill property on Market street, and moved the Rogers companies into the buildings which they now occupy. They employ 150 hands, and sell over $600,000 worth of goods per year. In 1889 he made a contract with a factory in Taunton, Mass., to make hollow-ware, and over 100 hands are kept busy in making blanks for the Rogers companies. In 1890 he bought the Wickersham property in Norwich, in this state, and commenced the manufacture of solid steel handle knives, carvers, fruit knives, etc. One hundred hands are employed, and 2,000 dozens of knives are made each week. The secret of the transition of Mr.

Watrous from the condition of a poor boy to a successful business man, worth many thousands of dollars and employing hundreds of hands, has been his strict business integrity and the undeviating quality of goods manufactured, — always selling a better quality of goods than his competitors for the same money, — his thorough, practical mechanical knowledge, and his daily personal supervision of every detail connected with the business, and his interest in employes, many of whom have been constantly in his employ for from ten to fifteen years. He is a strong republican, a member of Robert O. Tyler Post, G. A. R., a member of Hartford Lodge of Free Masons, and a member of Washington Commandery, Knights Templar.

WILLIAM ROGERS, Hartford: Manufacturer of electro-plated ware.

William Rogers was born in Hartford, Nov. 14, 1833, and was educated in the Hartford grammar school, at the same time with Senator Joseph R. Hawley, Hon. Henry C. Robinson, Hon. Charles J. Hoadly, LL.D., of the state library, Charles E. Perkins, and ex-Mayor Charles R. Chapman. His wife, who is still living, was Miss Lucy J. Ramsey, the soprano of the famous Christ Church choir. One son, a lad of ten years, is the fruit of this marriage. Mr. Rogers is a republican in politics, but has not held public office of any kind. He is engaged in the manufacture of electro-plated ware, and is at present connected with Simpson, Hall, Miller & Co., at Wallingford, in this state, under a contract that gives him absolute control of the manufacture and quality of the goods that bear his name, being made by the original Rogers plan, as taught him, and as practiced by his father. The subject of this sketch was connected from boyhood with the original Rogers Brothers in Hartford, his father being the senior member. He was afterwards connected with the Rogers Brothers, in a contract for 120 months with the Meriden Britannia Company at Meriden, supervising and controlling the quality of goods then stamped Rogers Brothers. He is the only survivor of the four Rogers of the original Rogers family, who established, upheld, and retained the reputation of the Rogers name upon electro-plated goods. The Rogers were the first successful electro-platers. This involved the first successful electro battery, and preceded by many years the great electrical

WILLIAM ROGERS.

improvements of late years. In fact, it was the first step in these wonderful developments. Mr. Rogers resides on Ann street in this city, and is widely known throughout the country.

JAMES SHEPARD, New Britain: Solicitor of Patents and Expert in Patent Causes.

Mr. Shepard is a descendant of the eighth generation of Edward Shepard, who came from England, and was settled at Cambridge, Mass., in 1639; and of the seventh generation of John Shepard of Cambridge, who settled in Hartford, Conn., about 1666. On his mother's side he is a descendant of the eighth generation of Thomas Alcott, who came from England in 1630, and settled at Charlestown, Mass. He was born at Southington, Conn., May 16, 1838, and received a common school and academic education.

JAMES SHEPARD.

On September 22, 1859, he married Celia A. Curtis of Bristol, and their only child is a daughter. In 1862, they removed to Bristol, where they resided for twelve years. In 1866 he began the business of soliciting patents and has followed it ever since. Prior to that time he had been employed as a machinist. He opened an office in New Britain in 1868, dividing his time between that place and Bristol until 1876, when he abandoned his Bristol office and changed his residence to New Britain. About 1873 he began to testify as an expert before the United States circuit courts, in causes appertaining to patents. He has now had a successful experience of twenty-five years in soliciting patents, and ranks among the best and most skillful patent solicitors in the country. As an expert in mechanics, he is widely known among manufacturers and patent lawyers, having testified in several hundred causes, and his testimony having been used in all parts of the United States, from California and Oregon on the west, to Pennsylvania and Maine on the east, and from Wisconsin on the north to Louisiana on the south.

In religion he is a Congregationalist, and in politics a republican. When in Bristol, he was one of the leaders of his party, but made his change of residence to New Britain the occasion to withdraw from all such outside matters as would be liable to interfere with his regular business. For recreation he frequents the fields and woods, "hunting without a gun" and "fishing without a hook," for he and his family are all great admirers of nature, with no desire to kill or catch. He is president of the New Britain Scientific Association, and an occasional writer on scientific subjects, botany, mineralogy, archaeology, and conchology being the branches to which he has paid most attention. Valuable contributions have been made by him to the Peabody Museum of Yale College, and to the National Museum of the Smithsonian Institution, for which he has received special public acknowledgment. He is also an enthusiastic amateur photographer, and within the last six years has carried a camera over twenty thousand miles.

HON. DAVID M. READ, Bridgeport: Manufacturer and Merchant.

Hon. David M. Read of Bridgeport, at present democratic state senator from the fourteenth district, is one of the leading manufacturers and merchants of New England. He was born in Hoosic Falls, N. Y., October 12, 1832. After the ordinary educational advantages of the district school, he attended Drury academy at North Adams, Mass. In 1855, he married Helen Augusta Barnum, daughter of Philo F. Barnum of Bridgeport. They have two sons and one daughter. Mr. Read was chosen a representative

D. M. READ.

from Bridgeport to the general assembly of 1881, and served upon the committee on military affairs. He was a delegate to the National convention in Chicago in 1884. He has been councilman and first alderman of Bridgeport, and is vice-president of the Savings Bank and a director of the National Bank. He is a prominent member of the board of trade and was for fifteen years its president. His superior business training is shown in the success he has achieved. He is president of the D. M. Read Company, and treasurer and selling agent of the Read Carpet Company, the New York office of which is at 934 Broadway. He served for several years as commissary of our Connecticut brigade of the National Guard, and under Governor Ingersoll, in 1876, the centennial year, he was induced to accept the position of acting commissary-general. Senator Read has always exercised great influence in matters legislative. He was elected to the senate of 1889, returned to that body in 1891; was president *pro tempore* of the senate of 1891, and performed with signal ability the difficult duties devolving upon him

during that remarkable session. Has been prominently mentioned as an available candidate for governor.

HON. ALLAN WALLACE PAIGE, Huntington: Attorney-at-Law.

Allan W. Paige was born in the town of Sherman, February 28, 1854; graduated from the Yale Law School in 1881; and subsequently became the partner of the late David B. Booth of Danbury. His classmates in the law school included Messrs. Frank E. Hyde of Hartford, John C. Gallagher of New Haven, ex-senate clerks Charles P. Woodbury and Clinton Spencer, and Sidney E. Clarke of Hartford. Mr. Paige pursued a preparatory college course at General Russell's Military School and the Hopkins Grammar

A. W. PAIGE.

School in New Haven, being a student at the former institution with Mr. John Addison Porter of the *Hartford Post*. In 1882, Mr. Paige was elected a member of the house from Sherman, and was assigned to the chairmanship of the state prison committee by Speaker John M. Hall. In that position he performed excellent service for the state. In 1883, he was elected assistant clerk of the house, clerk in 1884, and senate clerk in 1885. For several years Mr. Paige was a member of the republican state committee, and in 1884 was its secretary. In addition to his law practice in Connecticut, Mr. Paige is associated with the firm of Duncan & Paige of 120 Broadway, New York. At the November election in 1896, Mr. Paige was elected a member of the house from the town of Huntington, receiving a majority of 228, the largest majority ever given to any candidate in the town, and on the assembling of the legislature in January received the unanimous nomination for the speakership from the republicans. He was elected January 7, receiving the total vote of his party in the house. With one exception, that of Hon. Augustus Brandegee of New London, he is the youngest speaker the house has ever had, and the third republican speaker in continuous succession from Fairfield county.—Col. H. W. R. Hoyt of Greenwich being speaker in 1887, and Judge John H. Perry of Fairfield in 1889. His unanimous selection, in spite of geographical objection, was due to his large legislative experience, and knowledge of parliamentary law, both essential accomplishments for the speakership. And it is generally conceded that at no time within the history of the state, not even during the war, have party lines been so closely drawn, and the duties of the speaker so difficult of successful execution as during the session of the house for the winter of 1891. Mr. Paige proved himself fully equal to the occasion, fertile in parliamentary knowledge and resources, quick in execution and firm in decisions. His position was a most difficult and trying one, but his administration of the office was such as to win for him the unwavering and enthusiastic support of every member of his party in the house, and the admiration and plaudits of the republican press and his party in the state. Speaker Paige is a gentleman of interesting and attractive personal qualities, and has met with marked success in Connecticut politics. His career has been the result of his own efforts and energy, and shows what a man of spirit and perseverance can accomplish.

The wife of Speaker Paige is the daughter of the late Nelson Downs, who previous to his death was a prominent manufacturer in Birmingham, and one of the leading citizens of the Naugatuck valley.

CHARLES E. OSBORNE, Stepney (Monroe): Merchant.

Charles Edward Osborne represented the town of Monroe in the general assembly of 1887, and was appointed a member of the special committee, of

which Senator Coffin was the chairman, to erect a memorial tablet in the main hall of the capitol in honor of John Fitch of Connecticut, the first to apply steam power in navigation. Representatives Higgins and Wood were associate members of the committee from the house. Mr. Osborne has been a member of the board of relief, collector of taxes, and is at present a justice of the peace, secretary of the board of school visitors, and acting school visitor. He is a member of the democratic party, and is an active participant in its management locally. He was born in Brooklyn, N. Y., June 5, 1849, and was educated at the Connecticut Literary Institute in Suffield, and Wesleyan University, entering but not continuing the college course. He has resided at Southport, Bridgeport, Bethel, Watertown, and Southbury. In 1876 he was married to Miss Martha C. Burritt. There are three children, all daughters. Mr. Osborne is engaged in mercantile pursuits, being a dealer in pianos, organs, and sewing-machines at Stepney, which is located in the town of Monroe.

REV. FREDERICK DELLMAR CHANDLER, Eastford: Congregational Clergyman.

The subject of this sketch was born in Pawlet, Rutland County, Vermont, June 21, 1842. His father, Thomas Jefferson Chandler, of English

lineage, was a stalwart abolitionist, and a man highly respected for his sterling Christian character. Noted for his attitude toward slavery, he was thoroughly identified with the noble band of men whose lives formed a part of that thrillingly interesting historic period, and to whose conscientious efforts are indirectly attributable the fate which American negro slavery met at the hands of this government through the emancipation proclamation of President Lincoln in 1863. The son inherited largely the traits of character which distinguished the father. Himself a strong anti-slavery man, it is related of him that the first money he ever possessed (forty-nine cents) was invested by him when he was nine years of age in a pocket Bible; the next money, earned and owned by him, was expended for a copy of "Helper's Impending Crisis." Mr. Chandler inherited from his mother,— a noble Christian woman,—a strong character and an intensely religious nature, his religious convictions, manifested at a very early age, showing the trend of his mind toward the calling which in after years he chose for his life work. Like many another ambitious son of a kind but poor father, he had to fight a very unequal battle with poverty in his attempt to gain an education in the common and select schools of his native town. In early life he was noted for his studious habits and unconquerable energy, always standing at the head of his class; and never,— but once, and then unjustly,— losing a prize, if one was offered, in any competition in which he had the opportunity to join. He attended several terms at Castleton Seminary, then under the wise management of Dr. S. N. Knowlton. Finally he established a high school in the town of Middletown, but was induced to go to another seemingly more advantageous opening at Poultney. From thence, under the auspices of the M. E. Church, he went to one of their theological seminaries, which was then located at Concord, N. H., but about that time became a part of Boston University. It should be stated here that before entering the university, and while engaged in teaching, Mr. Chandler began the study of law, thinking it would be his life avocation; but under other and stronger influences his mind was turned toward the ministry. After leaving the Methodist institution above specified, finding that he was not in all points in accord with that denomination, he united with the Congregationalists, and served acceptably and with good success the churches in Hampton, N. H., Kensington, Alton, and East Hardwick, Vt., city of Frankfort, Mich., and Eastford and West Woodstock, in this state. Mr. Chandler is an earnest and effective speaker, an easy and fluent writer, and has rendered good service in the cause of temperance wherever he has resided, always being found in the front ranks of earnest workers for that most important of moral reforms. He is in politics a republican of the stalwart type, believing that whatever of lasting good has been accomplished for the temperance cause has been through the influence and agency of the republican party. He is the friend of the poor man, and in sympathy closely allied to their interests, which he makes his own. He has held several important local offices, including that of justice of the peace of Grafton county, N. H., under the administration of Governor Walter Harriman, and a state justice under Governor Cheney.

Mr. Chandler was married October 25, 1868, to Miss Julia E. Howe, daughter of Samuel Howe of Haverhill, N. H., a graduate of old Newbury (Vermont) Seminary. He has no children living. Mrs. Chandler is an excellent musician and teacher, and has been an able and successful worker in her husband's calling.

HENRY A. WARNER, New Haven: Iron Manufacturer and Sewer Pipe Dealer.

Henry A. Warner was born in Waterville, town of Waterbury, March 10, 1842, and was educated in the private and public schools of New Haven, where he has lived since he was six years of age. He was formerly an iron manufacturer and is now a dealer in drain and sewer pipe. He resides on Orange street in New Haven and is also the proprietor of Warner Hall on Chapel street. Mr. Warner has served in the second company of Governor's Horse Guard and is a member of the New Haven

Republican League. He is a member of the College Street Congregational church in New Haven. He has not held public office. Mr. Warner is married, his wife being Miss Gertrude E. Morton. They have no children.

HON. EDWARD SPICER CLEVELAND, Hartford: State Senator.

Edward S. Cleveland was born at Hampton, in this state, May 22, 1825, and received a common school education. At the age of sixteen he left home to engage in mercantile life in Hartford. In 1848 he was chosen assistant clerk of the Connecticut house of representatives, and two years later he was appointed engrossing clerk of the lower house of congress at Washington, being associated with John Galpin of New Haven. In 1854 he was a delegate to the democratic state convention and secured the

adoption of resolutions averse to the repeal of the Missouri Compromise, then pending in the celebrated Kansas-Nebraska bill before congress. Mr. Cleveland continued to act with the democratic party until the attempt was made to force upon Kansas the Lecompton pro-slavery constitution. He was instinctively opposed to slavery, and would not go a step with any political organization which proposed its extension. In 1860, he entered the field for Lincoln on the anti-slavery extension issue, and stumped a number of the states in support of the republican ticket. Soon after the inauguration of President Lincoln he was appointed postmaster at Hartford, and occupied the office for eight years, proving himself one of the ablest officials of the government in the state. Under his administration the highest business principles were enforced, and it is due to Mr. Cleveland that the post-office in Hartford was made one of model efficiency and excellence. He was a firm friend of the Union cause, and gave without stint of his time and means for the support of the government. Toward the union soldiers he has always been a true friend. After the war Mr. Cleveland found himself in harmony with the democratic party on the restoration of the union and the rehabilitation of the states which had participated in the rebellion. In 1875 and also in 1876, he was elected representative from Hampton on an independent ticket, carrying the town each year by a large majority. For a number of years back he has taken an active interest in Hartford affairs, having resumed his residence there in 1876.

Mr. Cleveland has been prominently connected with Connecticut politics during the past twenty-five years, and is one of the best-known citizens of the state. In 1880 he was one of the leading members of the senate from the first district, having the chairmanship of the committee on insurance, before which were many important measures. In the fall of the same year he had the honor of being nominated for governor by the democrats. He was returned to the senate in 1888, retaining the unquestioned leadership of his party in that body throughout the session. He was again returned to the senate for its succeeding term, and in the memorable transactions of that body occupied a conspicuous position not entirely in harmony with the majority of his political associates, though highly commended and approved by his constituents and personal friends.

Mr. Cleveland's social and domestic relations have always been exceedingly pleasant, and his hospitality is proverbial. He has a large circle of acquaintances and friends, while his amiable and cordial ways give him added popularity with the people, among whom rather than with any class or party he always prefers to be assigned, and for whose welfare it is his highest ambition to labor effectively in whatever official position he is called to occupy.

REV. REUBEN E. BARTLETT, Lebanon: Pastor of the First Baptist Church.

Reuben E. Bartlett was born at Shutesbury, Mass., May 25, 1843, and was educated at Madison University. During the war he served as a member of the Thirty-seventh Massachusetts Volunteers, belonging to Company F of that command, from July, 1862, until the conclusion of hostilities in 1865. His pastorates have been in the states of Delaware, Kansas, New Hampshire, and North Dakota. Prior to his settlement in Lebanon he was engaged under the auspices of the Home Mission Society, in North Dakota

R. E. BARTLETT.

and Montana. He became the pastor of the Lebanon Church in October, 1891. In politics he is a republican. The courage and heroism exhibited by the subject of this sketch on the battlefield has entitled him to membership in the Grand Army of the Republic, in which he is an honored representative. He was distinguished for gallantry at the battle of Winchester, Sept. 19, 1864. Mr. Bartlett has been twice married. His first wife, Josephine Moore, died in 1882; the second, Lydia M. Dyer, was the daughter of the late C. H. Dyer of Boston, Mass. The latter marriage occurred April 4, 1884. There are seven children by the first wife, all of whom are now living.

HON. EZRA BREWSTER BAILEY, Windsor Locks: Secretary and Treasurer and Manager of the E. Horton & Son Company; Collector of Customs for the Port of Hartford.

Hon. E. B. Bailey is a native of the town of Franklin, in New London county, where he was born March 20, 1841. He is of the sturdiest New

E. B. BAILEY.

England stock, his early ancestry through both branches representing prominent families of both the revolutionary and puritanic periods in our country's history, who, with their descendants, have been distinguished for physical vigor and intellectual attainments, as well as for inflexible integrity and patriotism. He is a son of Aaron and Eliza (Brewster) Bailey of Franklin, and through the maternal line is ninth in direct descent from Elder William Brewster of the *Mayflower* through the eldest son, Jonathan Brewster, who joined the Connecticut colonists in his early manhood and settled below Norwich. Mr. Bailey's paternal ancestors were the Baileys of Groton, whose lineage through the Puritans establishes theirs as among the most ancient of English families. It may be mentioned here, although out of chronological order, that Miss Katie E. Horton, who became the wife of Mr. E. B. Bailey in 1871, is a descendant in the eighth generation from John Alden and Priscilla (Mullens) Alden, prominent characters in Puritanic history; thus in the present generation mingling several strains of ancient English blood which have separately quickened the best subjects of American history. The Hortons of Windsor Locks represent one of the oldest and best of New England families which, since colonial times, has contributed numerous and distinguished names to the country's service and history.

Mr. Bailey's early life in Franklin was spent on the ancestral farm (of which the subject of this sketch is now the proprietor), where he was nurtured in habits of industry, and acquired at the district school the elementary education which is the basis of all literary accomplishments. His daily toil in the hayfield or cornfield, in the woods and meadows, or at the old mill where his father made the shingles which supplied the covering for the roofs of all the houses in the neighborhood, gave the boy a rich experience of the hardships and the pleasures of farm life, and sharpened his appetite for the healthy farmer's fare on which he throve and grew to the stature of vigorous manhood. Here he laid the foundation of his future success, while he imbibed inspiration from the precept and example of his God-fearing parents and deported himself in a way to secure the respect and esteem of his associates and neighbors.

The breaking out of the rebellion in 1861 found Mr. Bailey still in his minority, but his patriotic impulses impelled him to enlist for the defense of his country, and he joined Company B of the Twenty-sixth Connecticut regiment, going into camp September 5, 1862. While in camp, however, he was prostrated by a severe attack of typhoid fever, and was taken home, still in a critical condition, on the fifth of the following November. Although he was for a long time unable to rally from this attack, his health gradually returned, but at no time thereafter during the progress of the war was he in a condition for active service, and his patriotic designs were of necessity abandoned. As soon as able to perform any laborious work he again engaged in farm duties with his father, and remained at the old homestead until 1867, when he removed to Windsor Locks, and for one year carried on a farm there, devoting considerable attention to the raising of tobacco. He then was made assistant postmaster at Windsor Locks, and in connection therewith had charge of a store for two or three years, and held a general agency for various publications sold on subscription by canvassers. He afterwards made an engagement with W. J. Holland & Co., a large subscription book publishing firm of Springfield, Mass., and exercised the prerogative of a supervisor of agencies. In the discharge of the duties of this position he traveled extensively, visiting nearly every town and village in the Northern States, Canada, and the provinces, having charge of most of the company's outdoor work for four years, and building up a very large and profitable business. In 1873, upon the organization of the firm of E. Horton & Son of Windsor Locks as a joint stock company, under the corporate name of The E. Horton & Son Company, manufacturers of The Horton Lathe Chuck, he became its secretary and treasurer, continuing in the position for three years. In 1876 he severed the connection, and removed to his farm in Franklin, — a delightful country place, whose attractions include some of the most romantic spots to be found in the state, the shady vales and hillsides of which have become of late favorite resorts for picnic and excursion parties. Here he devoted his time to agricultural pursuits and the raising of Jersey stock until 1880, when he was called to assume control of The E. Horton & Son Company at Windsor Locks; since which time he has remained its secretary, treasurer, and general manager. He is also connected with other important business enterprises, being president and director, as well as an incorporator, of The

Windsor Locks Electric Lighting Company, in the establishment of which he was intimately concerned; a director in The Windsor Locks Savings Bank; also in The Connecticut River Company, an important corporation which owns the Enfield and Windsor Locks water power, and furnishes water power for all the mills in Windsor Locks; a director in The Dwight Slate Machine Company of Hartford, manufacturers of fine tools and special machinery; director and one of the original incorporators and a prominent promoter of The Windsor Locks Water Company, which furnishes the village with water for domestic purposes; and a director in The J. R. Montgomery Company, manufacturers of warps and fancy yarns, recently re-organized as a joint stock corporation, with a large capital, doing a large and profitable business, and at the head of all enterprises of its class in the country.

Mr. Bailey is an ardent and active republican, and as such has been elected to various positions of public trust. He has held the office of selectman, and is now a member of the school board and acting school visitor. He was elected to the legislature from Franklin in 1879 and from Windsor Locks in 1882, carrying the former town by the largest majority any candidate ever received, and carrying Windsor Locks by a majority of thirteen, although it is naturally heavily democratic. During the session of 1883 he was on the committee on incorporations, and did essential service for the incorporation of The Windsor Locks and Warehouse Point Bridge Company. He was elected state senator in 1887, running ahead of his ticket in seven towns of his district, and as chairman of the fisheries committee and of the committee on education carried through a number of important measures. He was active and prominent in support of the measure, in the senate, giving to towns the control and management of school district affairs, his efforts in this reform giving him favorable notoriety among the friends of education all over the state. He was appointed United States Collector of Customs for the port of Hartford in 1890, for which position he was warmly endorsed by both Senator Hawley and Congressman Simonds, the duties of which office he performs with characteristic ability and fidelity.

Mr. Bailey's social connections include membership with the American Society of Mechanical Engineers, an "organization for promoting acquisition of that knowledge which is necessary to the mechanical engineer to enable him most effectively to adapt the achievements of science and art to the use of mankind," with whose high reputation all are familiar; the Law and Order League, of Windsor Locks, whose object is the enforcement of laws relative to the sale of intoxicants; the Connecticut Society of the Sons of the American Revolution; and, in the Masonic fraternity, with Euclid Lodge, No. 109, F. A. M. of Windsor Locks, Washington Chapter, No. 30, R. A. M., of Suffield, Washington Commandery, No. 1, K. T., stationed at Hartford, and Pyramid Temple, A. A. O. N. M. S., at Bridgeport. His social instincts and tastes are strong; he engages with enthusiasm in all the activities of the various organizations with which he is connected. He is a member of the Congregational Ecclesiastical Society of Windsor Locks, and a liberal supporter of its institutions and charities. He is an excellent representative Connecticut citizen, and always equal to his opportunity whenever it comes. He has been successful in whatever he has undertaken, and occupies an important and influential position in business, politics, and social affairs.

As already mentioned, Mr. Bailey was married, December 14, 1871, to Miss Katie E. Horton of Windsor Locks, daughter of Eli Horton, celebrated as the inventor of the Horton Lathe Chuck. They have two children, a son and a daughter; the former, Philip Horton Bailey, in his eighteenth year, is a member of the senior class at the Hartford Public High School; the latter, Helena Ellsworth Bailey, in her fifteenth year, is at school in Windsor Locks.

DAVID A. ROOD, HARTFORD: Retired; formerly Proprietor United States Hotel.

Col. D. A. Rood is one of Hartford's best-known citizens, whose name has been familiar with the public as the long-time proprietor of one of Hartford's best-esteemed and ancient hostelries. Colonel Rood was born in Sheffield, Berkshire county, Mass., Sept. 28, 1817. His education was liberal for the times, being gained at the excellent public schools of Massachusetts. His life has been spent in Sheffield, Mass., Winsted and New Hartford in this state, but largely in the city of Hartford, where he was pro-

D. A. ROOD.

prietor of the United States Hotel for about thirty-eight years. He has been twice married; first to Miss Maria W. Woodford, who died Jan. 25, 1883; and afterwards to his present wife, who was Abbie F. Carroll prior to their union. There are two sons and a daughter by the first marriage. Colonel Rood is a consistent republican in politics, having been identified with that party since 1856, and often honored by offices within its gift. He was on the Hartford board of police commissioners for ten years; treasurer of the Brown School for fourteen

years; and long a director in the Dime Savings Bank of Hartford. He is a member of the Pearl Street Congregational church. His military connection was formerly with the Connecticut National Guard, as Lieutenant-Colonel of the First regiment.

JOHN FRANCIS GAFFEY, NEW HAVEN: Proprietor Gaffey's Business School.

John F. Gaffey was born in Hartford, Feb. 15, 1862, and was educated in the public schools of the University City. He was employed at the Winchester

JOHN F. GAFFEY.

Repeating Arms Company's establishment for six years, and saved money enough to educate himself for the special line of work that has engaged his attention for several years past. While at Winchester's he patented a combination rifle sight; sporting, military, and wind-gauge combined.

During the Blaine campaign he was private secretary to the republican state central committee, of which Hon. Lynde Harrison was the chairman. In the campaign of 1888, he was secretary of the Connecticut republican state league; managed the headquarters at New Haven, and also the document bureau for the state central committee, and organized 123 clubs in the state. He was in the city council for one term, and refused a second in order to become deputy collector of internal revenue under Col. John I. Hutchinson, which office he held for one year, and resigned last November to give his whole time to his business. While deputy collector, he had charge of eighteen towns, and made many arrests for violation of the internal revenue laws.

He has been running his school of shorthand and typewriting for nearly ten years, and has recently added penmanship and book-keeping; also has a stenographic and copying department and furnishes supplies for typewriters of all makes, and stenographers' supplies, all over the country. He is the author of "Gaffey's Helps to Cogswell's Compendium," and has made many improvements in the shorthand and typewriting business, especially in teaching. For two years he had nine schools in as many different cities, and in four different states, but he is now giving his whole time and attention to the New Haven business (having sold out all the other schools), pupils coming to him to New Haven from almost every state in the Union.

Prof. Gaffey has resided in Trenton, N. J., Philadelphia (Frankford), Pa., and Bridgeport, being at present a resident of New Haven. His wife, who is still living, was Miss Elizabeth Martin prior to her marriage. There are no children living in the family.

HEUSTED W. R. HOYT, GREENWICH: Attorney-at-Law.

H. W. R. Hoyt, who won marked distinction in legislative circles and throughout the state by his admirable discharge of the important duties of speaker of the house of representatives during the session of that body in 1887, was born in Ridgefield, in this state, on the 1st of November, 1842. He studied in the common school and the academy, and entered Columbia College, New York city, but about the middle of his first term was seized with a severe and protracted illness, and could not continue. Upon his

H. W. R. HOYT.

recovery he immediately began the study of the law in New York city, and for the period of about two years was secretary of the United States prize commissioners for the district of New York. He was admitted to practice in 1865. He is an attorney and counselor-at-law, and has served the town as its counsel, and the borough as attorney. Among other important litigation in which he has been engaged, he was sole counsel for the late William M. Tweed in a suit brought against him by James H. Ingersoll in the Connecticut superior court, in which over $160,000 was claimed by plaintiff, and successfully defended his client. He is trustee and attorney for the Greenwich Savings Bank, and a director in The Byram Land Improvement Company. He is also attorney for the Belle Haven Land Company and other large corporations. His public life has been quite marked. In 1869 and 1873 he was in the state senate; in the former year chairman of the committees on military affairs and engrossed bills; in the latter chairman of the committee on incorporations. In 1886 he was a representative from Greenwich, and occupied the leading position upon the floor and in the committee-room, being house chairman of the committee on the judiciary. He was returned to the house in 1887, and, as before intimated, was called to preside over the deliberations of that body as its speaker, discharging the duties of the office with signal ability and to the entire satisfaction of all parties. Mr. Hoyt is a staunch republican, an able debater, quick and effective at repartee, and an affable man. In every measure presented or dis-

7

cussed he manifested a lively interest, and, whether in the chair or on the floor, always commanded respect and wielded an important influence in legislative affairs. His nomination for speaker by the republican party was by acclamation, and his election by the house was by more than the republican majority.

Mr. Hoyt's legal practice is extensive, his standing before the bar and the public being such as to secure for him a numerous and profitable clientage. He is judge of the borough court of Greenwich, and in addition to his professional duties is often called by his fellow-citizens of Greenwich to fill local positions of public trust.

JAMES HOYLE, WILLINGTON. Woolen Manufacturer.

James Hoyle was born in Bradford, Yorkshire, England, April 3, 1830. His early education was received from the common schools of his native town. In 1856, then a young man of twenty-six, he emigrated to America. On arriving in this country, he went to Paterson, N. J., where he spent a year engaged in his trade of wool-sorting. He afterwards went to Norwich, Conn., and worked a year at the same trade, and subsequently to Webster, Mass., where he engaged with Nelson Slater. He followed his

JAMES HOYLE.

chosen avocation in several places in the Bay State until 1863, when he settled in Worcester, where for ten years he was engaged as foreman of the wool-sorting department of the Adriatic Mills, then run by Jordan, Marsh & Co. of Boston. In 1873 he removed to Willington, Conn., and bought a half interest in the Daleville Woolen Mills, then owned and run by James J. Reagan. The business was carried on two years under the firm-name of Reagan & Hoyle, when the latter purchased the property and continued the business with two partners, under the name of Hoyle, Smith & Co. He shortly after bought out his partners' interests, since which time he has carried on the manufacturing business alone and quite successfully. During his fifteen years' proprietorship of the Daleville Mills, improvements in the little hamlet and in the mills have been steadily going on. He is a man of sterling integrity and good business qualities, and is held in high esteem by his fellow-townsmen for his enterprise and moral worth. He has never sought for office, but allowed the use of his name as a candidate of the republicans of his town for representative, at the fall election of 1884, to which position he was chosen by a good majority, and where he performed valuable service for his constituents and the state.

Mr. Hoyle is married and has one child.

AUGUSTUS C. WILCOX, New Haven: Dry Goods.

Augustus C. Wilcox was born in East Guilford, now the town of Madison, Aug. 22, 1812, and received an academic education. He is the founder of the firm of Wilcox & Co., of New Haven and has been engaged in the dry goods business since March 1, 1836. Through his long business career his financial liabilities have been promptly met and discharged. The record is deserving of mention as it covers three of the most disastrous financial eras in the history of the country.

A. C. WILCOX.

Mr. Wilcox is one of the clearest-headed business managers in New Haven. He was formerly connected with the state militia and held a first lieutenant's commission in the Madison Light Artillery at the time of his removal from that town to New Haven. He was honorably discharged from the service by Gov. Henry W. Edwards. In 1871 Mr. Wilcox was a member of the general assembly from Madison, representing that town on the democratic side of the house. Two years afterwards he was elected to the senate from the old sixth district, his colleagues including Hons. Geo. M. Landers of New Britain, Allen Tenny of Norwich and Wm. T. Elmer of Middletown, ex-Judge Stoddard of New Haven and ex-Speaker Hoyt of Greenwich. Mr. Wilcox has also taken an active part in New Haven politics and has served as a member of the common council and of the board of selectmen. In all of these public positions his judgment and thorough knowledge of affairs have been of great value, enabling him to render the city and state the best of service. Mr. Wilcox is a member of the Congregational church in Madison and is a most exemplary representative of religious thought and principle. He has been married twice. His first wife was Catherine Amelia Cruttenden of Madison. The second was Miss Bertha C. Payne of West Haven. In business, political, and social life Mr. Wilcox has exerted an important influence from the outset, and is regarded with the sincerest esteem and honor by all who know him.

ARTHUR F. EGGLESTON, Hartford: Attorney-at-Law.

Judge Eggleston was born at Enfield, Conn., October 23, 1844. He graduated from Williams College in the class of 1868, and after preparation by legal study was admitted to the bar of Hartford county and opened an office for legal practice in this city in 1872. During the war he enlisted as a private in the Forty-sixth Massachusetts regiment, and served until honorably discharged. During his residence in Hartford he has been a member of the court of common council and president of the board; has held the

A. F. EGGLESTON.

office of judge of the police court for several terms; and is now treasurer of Hartford county, and state's attorney. He is a republican in politics, a member of the Masonic fraternity, and of the Army and Navy Club. He is associated professionally with Hon. John R. Buck, the law firm being Buck & Eggleston. Judge Eggleston's standing before the bar and the public is that of an able and conscientious lawyer, and his career has been one of great usefulness and honorable distinction.

ROBERT R. SMITH, New Hartford: Agent Greenwoods Company.

Robert R. Smith was born in New Hartford, April 15, 1843, and received a thorough business education. At the age of sixteen he became a clerk in a Chicago hardware establishment, where he remained until sufficient experience had been acquired to prepare him for travel through the western states as the representative of the house. Returning home for a visit in 1865 he became engaged in the building of the Greenwoods Scythe Company's works, and was afterwards persuaded to remain as manager of

ROBERT R. SMITH.

the concern. He continued in that position until 1870, when, upon the death of his father, he found himself in charge of Greenwoods Company, Greenwoods Scythe Company, the New Hartford Carriage Company, and an interest in what was known as "the brick store." From that time to the present his occupation has been in connection with these different concerns, two of which have become extinct.

Mr. Smith is a director in a number of corporations, and is a gentleman of superior business qualifications. He was married in 1867, his wife being Miss Minnie M. Simmons of Canaan. She died in 1890, leaving three children. The subject of this sketch has strenuously opposed the acceptance of public office. The only place he has ever accepted has been that of pound keeper, his reëlection having taken place annually for the past twenty years, and there have been a good many jovial occasions over the fact. He is a member of the North Congregational Ecclesiastical society, and also of Amos Beecher Lodge, F. and A. M., of New Hartford, together with two or three other secret organizations. Mr. Smith is held in thorough regard and esteem in the community where he lives.

HON. WILLIAM COTHREN, Woodbury: Attorney-at-Law.

William Cothren, son of William and Hannah Cothren, was born at Farmington, Me., Nov. 28, 1819. In his ancestral lines he is the descendant of a soldier in King Philip's war, 1676; a soldier in the war between England and France, 1744-5; a lieutenant in the war of the revolution; and a sergeant in the war of 1812. He prepared for college at Farmington academy, and graduated at Bowdoin College in 1843. He received his second degree, in course, at the same college, in 1846, and the degree of Master of

WILLIAM COTHREN.

Arts, *ad eundem*, at Yale University, in 1847. He studied law under the direction of Hon. Robert Goodenough of Farmington, Me., and Hon. Charles B. Phelps of Woodbury, in this state. He settled in Woodbury in 1844, and was admitted to the bar of Litchfield county in October, 1845. He entered upon a large and successful practice at Woodbury, and has continued in practice there ever since. He ranks among the leading lawyers of the state. As a citizen he has ever been public spirited and generous. He has lent his voice and pecuniary aid to every monument or other public improvement during his time. He was elected a county commissioner for Litchfield county in 1851. In 1855 he was elected senator for the old sixteenth district, by the face of the returns, received his certificate, and took his seat in the senate. During the session his seat was successfully contested by his opponent, on a ground which ever since has been held universally untenable, both in Congress and in the several states where the question has been raised. He served as a member of the lower house in 1882. In April, 1856, he was admitted an attorney and counselor of the United States circuit court, and on the 8th of March, 1865, he was admitted an attorney and counselor of the supreme court of the United States. He was elected corresponding member of the New England Historic-Genealogical Society, at Boston, Mass., May 5, 1847, and a member of the Connecticut Historical Society, Nov. 23, 1852, of which for many years he was a vice-president; an honorary member of the Old Colony Historical Society, at Plymouth, Mass., April 24, 1854; a corresponding member of the Wisconsin Historical Society, Jan. 17, 1855; a corresponding member of the Vermont Historical Society, Feb. 3, 1860; a corresponding member of the Maine Historical Society, Sept. 18, 1861; elected worshipful master of King Solomon's Lodge, No. 7, of F. and A. M., in December, 1852, which office he held two years; a member of the Phi Beta Kappa Society, Alpha of Maine, Sept. 20, 1873; a member of the Sons of the American Revolution in 1889; and a member of the First Congregational church in Woodbury, July 7, 1850. He has held the offices of justice of the peace and notary public during all his professional life. On the 3d of September, 1849, he was married to Mary Jane Steele, a descendant of Hon. John Steele, first secretary of the colony of Connecticut, and of Rev. Benjamin Colton of West Hartford, a descendant of George Colton, the first of the name in Connecticut. They have had one child, who died young. He was one of the organizers of the republican party, and has been somewhat active in its interests, but has never been a chronic office-seeker. During the civil war he was a zealous and active supporter of the Union cause, giving a large share of his time, and more of his means than he could well afford. He was, during the whole contest, a member of the committees for the enlistment of men, and the care of their families, and was eminently the soldier's friend, and has so continued ever since. From the twentieth year of his age he has been a contributor, in prose and verse, to the press and magazines of the day. A short time after his settlement in Woodbury he turned his attention to the collection of the historical data of the town, the result of which has been the publication of an elaborate history of the town, in three volumes of twenty-five hundred pages. The first volume was issued in 1854, and was the pioneer work, in its scope and completeness, as a full history of a New England town, that had been issued. He has also published numerous legal and historical pamphlets.

HENRY N. WALES, Willimantic: Judge of Probate.

Judge Wales is a native of the town of Windham. He was born August 10, 1837. He lived and was employed on a farm with his father until he became

H. N. WALES.

twenty-one years of age, availing himself in his childhood of such educational advantages as the public schools of Windham offered. He was in the employ of William C. Osgood in Norwich in the meat business from November, 1858, till the early part of 1862. From 1862 to 1867 was engaged in mercantile business at South Windham and Willimantic, being a member of the firm of Webb & Wales. From 1867 to 1873 was in the employ of George H. Norman, contractor, of Newport, R. I., in superintending the construction of public water-works in Waterbury, Conn., New Bedford, Medford, Charlestown, and Lowell, Mass. In 1873 and 1874 was employed by the city of Manchester, N. H., as superintendent of the construction of their water-works. In 1875 and 1876 was employed by Frye & Kitridge, contractors, of Lowell, Mass., to superintend the construction of a portion of the Boston water-works. In 1887 he returned to Willimantic, and engaged in the pork-packing business two years; then entered the employ of Hyde Kingsley of Willimantic, dealer in lumber, coal, and building supplies, as bookkeeper and manager; continued in that capacity until 1882; from March, 1883, acted as his business agent by power of attorney till his death in February, 1886. Mr. Wales occupied the position of town clerk and treasurer in 1880, 1882, 1883, and 1884. Was elected clerk and treasurer of the Natchaug school in 1883, and has continued to hold the office since. He was elected in borough meeting chairman of a committee to ascertain the best method of introducing water in the borough of Willimantic in July, 1882; also chairman of a committee to draft a charter for the introduction of water and petition the general assembly for such charter. In 1883 he was elected water commissioner for three years from January 1, 1884. Was appointed postmaster by President Cleveland December 19, 1885; took possession of the office January 1, 1886, and served four years and two months, to March 1, 1890. He was elected judge of probate for the district of Windham November 4, 1890, and still holds the office. In these numerous and varied positions of public trust Mr. Wales has made a record of honorable, faithful, and able service, to

which his fellow-citizens bear ready testimony. His important services to the borough of Willimantic, in connection with the introduction of the system of water-works there in 1885, is a matter of history, and has placed the citizens of that thriving community under lasting obligation to him.

Mr. Wales was married October 31, 1871, to Miss Euphemia A. Tanner, daughter of Warren Tanner of Willimantic. She died August 18, 1889, leaving no children.

APOLLOS FENN, Plainville: Deputy Jailer Hartford County Jail.

Apollos Fenn was born in the town of Plymouth January 12, 1820, and was educated in the common school of Litchfield county. His early years were

APOLLOS FENN.

spent in the clock industry. In 1864 he represented the town of Farmington in the general assembly, being elected by the republicans by one of the largest majorities ever given a representative from that town. Through the war period he held the office of provost-marshal under Marshal L. G. Goodrich, and was brought into contact in numerous ways with the troops at that time. After the war he removed to Hartford and was a member of the board of police commissioners in 1874. He was also a member of the council from the second ward. He has been deputy sheriff in Hartford county for thirty years and has held the position of jailer for twenty, being the senior officer in the state in that line of service. During this period he has had upwards of 1,700 prisoners under his charge. His experience as a detective extends over a period of thirty-five years, commencing with the arrest of the notorious horse thief, Herring, who was sentenced and died in State Prison. He was the successor of Colonel Henry Kennedy in the office of jailer, and retained the position until the new jail on Seyms street was completed. During the term of Sheriff O. D. Seymour he was displaced. The accession of Sheriff Spaulding to the shrievalty resulted in the restoration of Jailer Fenn to his old place, which he has since held for ten years. As a detective deputy sheriff Fenn has been entrusted with important business, being commissioned for special service by Governors Buckingham and Hubbard, Sheriffs Westell Russell and O. D. Seymour, and by L. G. Goodrich of Simsbury and Wm. Hamersley of Hartford. He was commissioned by the late Governor Chauncey F. Cleveland as the captain of an independent rifle company in Litchfield when a young man. Deputy Sheriff Fenn has had a family of fourteen children, six of whom are living. Among the latter is General Wallace T. Fenn of Governor Bulkeley's staff. His wife was Amelia C. Clark of Plainville. He is connected with the Congregational society at Plainville and has also been associated with the Park church in this city. At one time he resided in New Haven, but the most of his life has been spent in Farmington, Plainville, and Hartford. In each of these towns he is held in the highest esteem. A quarter of a million dollars has passed through his hands during the period in which he has been in active life and not one cent has been lost or misappropriated. Absolute personal integrity has been the watchword of his career.

LEWIS WORDEN, Danielsonville: Hotel Proprietor.

Lewis Worden, the veteran proprietor of the Attawaugan hotel in the borough of Danielsonville, was born in Charlestown, R. I., September 3, 1818, where he spent his boyhood and attended school until fifteen years of age. Since leaving Charlestown he has resided temporarily in several places, being fourteen years in Brooklyn, two years in Plainfield, and one year in Providence, R. I. He removed to Danielsonville forty years ago, engaging in the livery business; and it is said that he has owned some of the finest 

LEWIS WORDEN.

teams in eastern Connecticut. In 1859 he became proprietor of the Attawaugan house, the principal hotel in the borough, which he has owned and managed uninterruptedly up to the present time, a period of more than thirty-two years. He is also the owner of a fine farm a short distance outside the borough limits, to which he devotes his personal attention. Mr. Worden has been twice married; first to Miss Olive S. Cox, who died nearly forty-five years ago; second to Miss Sarah Darby, whose death occurred in 1889. One son, the fruit of his first marriage, died in the military service during the late war. Mr. Worden is a member of the Westfield Congregational church of Danielsonville, and of the republican party. He has been identified with the business and social affairs of the borough for more than a generation, and is generally esteemed as an upright and honorable citizen.

CURTIS THOMPSON, Bridgeport. Attorney-at-Law.

The ancestors of Curtis Thompson were of Puritan stock, and among the early settlers and planters of the old town of Stratford, Conn. He was born in Trumbull, Oct. 30, 1835, where his parents, George Thompson and Lucy A. Curtis, were temporarily residing. He was educated at the Stratford school and academy, and Harvard University; admitted to the bar in Fairfield County in 1864. He has since practiced law at Bridgeport, residing, most of the time, in Stratford or Bridgeport. Stratford honored him by 

CURTIS THOMPSON.

an election to the general assembly during the years 1865, '66, and '67, where he served on the judiciary, incorporation, and other committees. In 1868 and '69, and '72, he was deputy judge of the city court of Bridgeport. In 1874, '75, and '76, he was councilman and alderman. In 1879, '82, '86, and '87, he was city attorney, and, in 1883, town attorney. Since 1872 he has been an active trustee of the Bridgeport Savings Bank, and he is an officer or attorney of many other corporations. He is a member of the South Congregational church and society, is connected with the Seaside club, and with the masonic fraternity. He received the degree of M.A. from Yale College in 1871.

He married in 1867 M. Louise Willcox, daughter of James Willcox, then president of the Willcox & Gibbs Sewing Machine Company, and Katharine Barry of New York city; is of English, Irish, and Dutch stock. They have two living children, James Willcox Thompson, a graduate of Yale, '90, and now a member of the bar at Knoxville, Tenn., and Katharine Barry Thompson.

An early experience of four years in the probate court laid the foundation of a large and extensive practice in the settlement of estates and litigation growing out thereof. His general practice in all branches has, however, been wide, and especially in real estate, corporation, and banking law. He possesses the confidence and esteem of the best citizens, and for many years was the trusted counsellor of Hon. P. T. Barnum. He has tried many very important criminal and civil cases. Believing it to be the duty of every citizen to actively participate in the management of public affairs he has always voted, and promoted the success of the republican party. He is the friend of temperance, and is often found contending against the establishment of new saloons. In municipal affairs he has

had much to do as attorney for many towns and
communities. In 1888-89 he was the mover, and
the chairman of the committee, in procuring the
consolidation of the city and town government of
Bridgeport; which great measure has resulted in
giving to Bridgeport not only the most economical
but also the most efficient local government in the
state. It is his purpose to be always found on the
right side of every moral, civil, and religious question, and to be ready to help and advance it with
such means as he can command.

NATHAN DOUGLAS SEVIN, Norwich: Phar-
macist.

N. Douglas Sevin, senior member of one of the
best known drug firms in New London county,
was born at Bozrah, June 1, 1842. His education was obtained at
public schools, with eighteen months in a private
school at Norwich. He
became identified with the
drug trade as early as
1859, having in that year
begun a clerkship in one
of the oldest Norwich
houses, with which he re-
mained until the estab-
lishment of the firm of
Lanman & Sevin in 1864.
The business was thus
conducted until 1870,

N. D. SEVIN.

when Mr. Sevin bought his partner's interest and
became sole proprietor. Later his son was taken
into the business and the firm name changed to N.
D. Sevin & Son. During the civil war Mr. Sevin
served in the Twenty-sixth Connecticut Volunteer
Infantry as hospital steward, and was with Banks's
expedition to Port Hudson. He is now a prominent
member of Sedgwick Post, No. 1, G. A. R., the first
grand army post established in this state. He has
long been identified with the masonic order, and is
past commander of Columbian Commandery,
Knights Templar; past high priest Franklin Chapter, No. 4, and has reached the thirty-third degree,
Scottish rite. He is a member of and also has held
the office of president of the state board of pharmacy, and for many years has been a vestryman in
Trinity Church. In 1882 he was elected on the
democratic ticket to represent Norwich in the state
legislature, and his eminent popularity is clearly
demonstrated by the fact that he was the first democratic legislator elected in Norwich since 1859.

Mr. Sevin united in marriage with Miss Anna M.
Jennings of Norwich, by whom he has had one son,
the young man who is now associated with him in
business as a partner.

JOHN C. WEBSTER, Hartford: Vice-Presi-
dent Ætna Life Insurance Company.

John C. Webster was born at Kingfield, Me.,
May 24, 1839, and received a thorough English
education, completing the course at the High School

J. C. WEBSTER.

in Concord, N. H. He
acquired the printer's
trade at Concord, and
was at the head of one of
the largest offices in that
city before he was twen-
ty-two years of age. In
1864 he became the gen-
eral agent of the Ætna
Life in New Hampshire,
and made rapid advance-
ment in that capacity,
displaying from the out-
set marked adaptation for
the life insurance busi-
ness. In 1873 he was appointed superintendent of
agencies for the company, and removed from Concord to Hartford. He was elected vice-president
in July, 1879, and has since retained that position,
discharging the duties of the office with exceptional ability and success. During the past twelve
years Mr. Webster has been the editor of *The
Ætna*, a quarterly publication devoted exclusively
to the interests of the Ætna Life. His writings
have commanded wide attention in insurance
circles, giving the paper a standing that could have
been attained in no other way. Mr. Webster is
also a member of the board of trustees of the
Hartford Trust Company, one of the largest institutions of the kind in the state. He was one of the
founders of the Hartford Horticultural Society,
which was organized in April, 1887, and incorporated by the legislature in May, 1889, Mr. Webster
being the president of the society at that time.
The Horticultural Society has been an organization
of great influence in Hartford county, and its exhibitions have not been surpassed in Connecticut
for years. The work that it has accomplished is
due largely to the leadership of Mr. Webster. The
Gentlemen's Driving club of Hartford, an organization that comprises the names of many of Hartford's worthiest citizens, has borne the name of
Mr. Webster on its roll of membership and list of
directors for a number of years. In politics he is a
republican. He is connected with the First Unitarian Congregational Society of Hartford, and is
a member of the executive committee. With the
exception of one year, 1856, which was spent at
Lawrence, Mass., the active business life of Mr.
Webster has been passed in Concord, N. H., and in
Hartford, Conn. His home, however, is in West
Hartford, being within a short distance of the city
boundary. His public spirit has done a great deal

towards the development and prosperity of that town. Mr. Webster has been twice married. His first wife, who was Miss Sarah B. Norton of Kingfield, Me., died in 1868. The second wife, Mary E. L. Abbott, was of Concord, N. H. She is still living. There are no children. While Vice-President Webster has steadily declined public office and position, he regards public affairs with great interest, and is one of the most patriotic and public-spirited of citizens.

DAVID GINAND, BRIDGEPORT: Cutler.

Mr. Ginand was born in Spire, Germany, October 18, 1837, where he received a public school education. For the past thirty years he has resided at Bridgeport and is one of the leading German citizens of that city. In 1875 he was president of the German School Corporation, a society organized in Bridgeport for the promotion of the study of German and took an active part in the agitation in that city for school district consolidation. In 1876 he was elected a member of the first board of education there on a non-partisan ticket, and has been re-elected regularly to

DAVID GINAND.

the office since. He is a republican in politics. Mr. Ginand is a member of the leading German societies in Bridgeport, including the Concordia and the Turner organizations. He has represented the latter in the North American Turnerbund at its biennial assemblies in Indianapolis, Newark, Davenport, Boston, Chicago, and New York. For the last ten years he has represented the Connecticut societies in these national gatherings of the Germans. He removed to the United States in 1851 and lived in Waterville and Naugatuck until the war broke out, when he removed to Bridgeport and engaged in the manufacture of arms. From 1864 until 1868 he was employed in the Wheeler & Wilson works. He then established himself in business and has since carried on a cutlery business. Mr. Ginand is a member of St. John's Lodge, No. 3, F. and A. M. of Bridgeport, and formerly belonged to the German Reformed Church, but resigned his membership on account of differences with the society. He is a man of marked independence of thought and action and thoroughly believes in the right of personal judgment. His wife, who is still living, was Miss Christiane Landschulz prior to her marriage. There are five children in the family, two of whom are sons.

CORNELIUS S. BUSHNELL, MADISON: Merchant, Ship Builder, Railroad Builder and Manager.

Cornelius S. Bushnell, vice-president of the Ericsson Coast Defense Company of New York, was born in Madison, July 18, 1828, and received a public school education. Mr. Bushnell resides in Madison through the winter, spending the summer in New York. He was formerly a resident of New Haven, and represented that city in the legislature of 1862, being a member of the house. It is necessary in delineating the public services of Mr. Bushnell to speak at some length of the general assembly of 1862, in which

C. S. BUSHNELL.

he was a leading and distinguished figure. It contained many of the prominent men of the state, including Josiah M. Carter of Norwalk (who was elected speaker), John S. Rice of Farmington, Abijah Catlin of Harwinton, Thomas Clark of North Stonington, Abner L. Train of Milford, John P. Elton of Waterbury, Erastus S. Day of Colchester, Amos S. Treat of Bridgeport, Henry G. Taintor of Hampton, Bartlett Bent, Jr., of Middletown, Charles Chapman of Hartford, and Alvan P. Hyde of Tolland. Mr. Bushnell was one of the strongest supporters of the war, and when the capture of the national capital was threatened in 1862 he was identified with the best measures presented in the legislature providing for the organization and equipment of troops for the front. He was the heartiest of co-operators with Governor Buckingham, one of the foremost and most patriotic of the New England war governors, and sustained his hands in every effort that was made to furnish the government with troops. The legislature of 1862 held two sessions, the exigencies of the period demanding a session in December. The demand that the soldiers in the field should be allowed to vote for state and national officers became a memorable issue of the legislative year. Mr. Bushnell took an active interest in all the questions that the war forced upon public attention, and was a trusted leader on the republican side. His most important service in connection with the war, however, related to the adoption of the *Monitor* that was designed by Ericsson, Mr. Bushnell being one of the principal colaborers with the great inventor in the effective presentation of the new and marvelous enginery that was to revolutionize naval warfare. He is the vice-president of the noted Ericsson Coast Defense Company, and his name will be permanently associated with the war period. He was with C. M. Clay's battalion for the defense of Washington during the conflict, and is a member of Admiral Foote Post, G. A. R., in New Haven. Mr. Bushnell has been a prominent railroad builder and manager, and at one period was the controlling power in the Shore Line road. He has also been extensively interested in commerce, merchandise, and ship-building. He has spent most of his life in New Haven and New York. His church relations are with the Dwight Place Congregational church in New Haven, and his family consists of a wife and eight children. He has been married three times, his present wife, Elizabeth Maxwell, being the widow of E. C. Ford, of Cleveland, O., at the time of her marriage. Mr. Bushnell is an honored citizen of Connecticut, deserving in every way the place which he holds in the respect and admiration of the republic.

A. WELLS CASE, MANCHESTER : Paper Manufacturer.

A. Wells Case and A. Willard Case are twin brothers and constitute the well-known firm of Case Brothers, manufacturers of papers at Highland Park, in the town of Man-

chester. They operate the Highland Mills, the Chaplin Mills, and the Unionville Mills. They are also proprietors of the famous mineral springs at Highland Park, where are bottled the Rock and Tonica waters, the latter of which has acquired a deserved reputation by its successful employment for the relief and cure of many diseases of the blood. A.

A. W. CASE.

Wells Case, the subject of this sketch, was born in Manchester, October 30, 1840, and received his education in the public schools of that town; his vacations being passed on his father's farm. At the age of seventeen he entered the employ of the then well-known firm of Messrs. W. & E. Bunce, paper manufacturers. At the age of twenty-one he left home and engaged in mercantile pursuits with success. Later on he associated himself with his brother in business, as above stated. Mr. Case is an inventor of some note, which talent he has turned to good account in his manufactories. He is a republican and represented Manchester in the legislature in 1889. He has been an influential temperance man for years, and is held in high esteem by his townsmen as an honorable and useful citizen.

CHARLES E. PERKINS, HARTFORD : Attorney-at-Law.

Charles E. Perkins is descended from a noted line of jurists, his father, Thomas C. Perkins, and grandfather, Enoch Perkins, being in their time

among the foremost lawyers of the state. Enoch Perkins graduated from Yale College in 1781 and was afterwards a tutor in that institution. He became a leader of the bar in Hartford county. His death occurred in 1828. Thomas C. Perkins, the father of Charles E. Perkins, graduated from Yale in 1818, the late Governor Henry Dutton of New Haven being one of his

C. E. PERKINS.

classmates. Mr. Perkins became the successor of his father, Enoch Perkins, as a leading lawyer in this city, being the foremost practitioner here for years. He died in 1870, half a century after his graduation from Yale, honored and revered by the entire community. The subject of this sketch was born in this city, March 24, 1832, and was educated at the Hartford high school and Williams College, graduating from the latter in 1853. He adopted the legal profession and has been for twenty years one of the most prominent lawyers in Northern Connecticut. He has devoted his attention principally to civil and patent suits and is an influential counsel, not only in the courts of Connecticut, but also in the United States supreme court at Washington. One of his two sons, Mr. Arthur Perkins, who is a graduate of Yale, is associated with him in business. The remaining son, Mr. Thomas C. Perkins, is an electrical engineer. Mr. Perkins is a republican in politics, but is not in the least sense of the word a politician. The only public offices which he has held have been the city attorneyship and the position of water commissioner. At no time in the city's history has the municipality received abler service than during Mr. Perkins's term as legal adviser and counsel concerning its interests. He is a member of the Asylum Hill Congregational church, and is held in the utmost respect and regard throughout the community. The family of Mr. Perkins consists of a wife and five children — two sons and three daughters. Mrs. Perkins, who was Miss Lucy M. Adams of Boston prior to her marriage, is a descendant of Presidents John Adams and John Quincy Adams. Mr. Perkins is a gentleman of exceptional modesty and reticence, both in his home and among business associates. His professional career from the outset has been characterized by the highest personal honor and integrity.

EDGAR SMITH YERGASON, HARTFORD: Merchant.

E. S. Yergason was born in the town of Windham on the 10th day of September, 1840. He remained in his native town in attendance upon the district school and at the Pine Grove Seminary in South Windham, until he had fully completed his education, and in 1859 went to Hartford and engaged in service as a clerk with the dry goods firm of Talcott & Post. His connection with the house continued twenty-two years, during which period he acquired a most thorough and practical knowledge of the business in all its

E. S. YERGASON.

branches. During the presidential campaign of 1860, Mr. Yergason was one of the thirty-six young republicans of Hartford who on the evening of March 7th, organized the original "Wide Awake" club, an organization which spread over the whole country, and undoubtedly elected Abraham Lincoln President of the United States. Mr. Yergason as a young man was an ardent republican and patriot, and at the breaking out of the war of the rebellion he early enlisted and served as a private in Company B, of the Twenty-second regiment, Connecticut Volunteers. At the expiration of his term of service he returned to the store and remained in the employ of Talcott & Post until the two partners separated in 1880, when he joined the last named gentleman in the formation of the firm of William H. Post & Company, whose extensive establishment in the line of carpets and interior house decorations, in the city of Hartford, has a reputation co-extensive with the country itself. As a professional decorator Mr. Yergason is a gentleman of excellent taste and executive ability, and he personally superintends this entire department of the firm's extensive business. He has made and executed contracts for the most elaborate decorations in the private residences of the wealthiest citizens of Washington, New York, Brooklyn, Albany, Providence, and other metropolitan cities,—competing for the business with the most noted decorators of New York and Philadelphia. The recent decoration of the White House at Washington by the firm of Wm. H. Post & Co., under the exclusive management of Mr. Yergason, has been commended by connoisseurs at the capitol as the finest example of artistic taste in the line of interior decoration to be found on the continent. Referring to the effect produced in the "Blue Room" of the executive mansion by Mr. Yergason's treatment of it, one of the government officials publicly states his belief that "it is to-day the most beautiful room in the world." It is no small compliment to the house of Wm. H. Post & Co. when it is selected to produce the finest possible effects in the dwellings of the wealthiest citizens of the land, and the home of the chief magistrate himself.

Mr. Yergason is an attendant at the Asylum Avenue Congregational church, is a member of Robert O. Tyler Post, G. A. R., and of the Army and Navy Club of Connecticut. He married in Hartford Miss Emeline B. Moseley, third daughter of the late D. B. Moseley, who was editor, as well as proprietor and founder, of the *Religious Herald*, the organ of Connecticut Congregationalists. They have three children.

PATRICK H. PEARL, HAMPTON: Farmer.

Patrick Henry Pearl is a descendant of the fourth generation from Timothy Pearl, who came from Dorchester, Mass., early in the last century, and settled in Hampton, where he lived until his death in 1773. Many of his descendants are living in various parts of the country. Patrick H. Pearl was the son of Philip and Clarissa Pearl, and was born in Hampton June 8, 1819, and has resided in that town during his life-time. He was educated at the common schools of his native town, and at the Connec-

P. H. PEARL.

ticut Literary Institution at Suffield. Soon after attaining his majority he was engaged in mercantile pursuits for a few years in partnership with the late Hon. Mason Cleveland, but most of his life has been spent in farming until within a few years past. He was married Oct. 25, 1853, to Deborah Williams of Pomfret, who died May 18, 1861, leaving a son, Philip Pearl, who is now a member of the firm of D. Wood & Co., merchants, of Webster, Mass. On March 15, 1866, he contracted a second marriage with Mary L. Cowles, daughter of William C. Cowles of East Hartford, who is still living, having no children. He has held various offices in the gift of his townsmen, representing his town in the legislature of 1861, and held the office of justice of the peace for more than thirty years, acting as trial justice in a majority of cases brought in his town during his term of office. At the election held on the first Monday of April, 1863, he was elected to the office of judge of probate for Hampton district, took possession of the office July 4, 1863, and held it continuously by reëlection until January, 1889, extending over a period of twenty-five years and six months, and then retired from the office on account of constitutional limitation, having arrived at the age of seventy years. He was formerly a whig, and has been identified with the republican party since its formation, but never allowed himself to be swerved from the right by love of party. He is not connected with any church or religious society, but is a regular attendant at the Congregational church in his town. He is a member of the masonic fraternity, and a staunch supporter of its principles and tenets. He is now spending his days quietly at his pleasant home in his native village and attending to the various calls upon him for advice in legal and business affairs.

COL. SELAH G. BLAKEMAN, HUNTINGTON: Farmer.

Colonel Blakeman is a native of the town of Stratford in this state, where he was born May 23, 1841. He attended the district school in that town,

S. G. BLAKEMAN.

and later the high school in Milford. He enlisted as a private in the Seventeenth regiment, Connecticut volunteer infantry, July 29, 1862, and was in every engagement, and on every march that the command took part in as a regiment, until he was discharged as a sergeant at the close of the war. In 1866 he married and bought a farm in Huntington, where he now resides. He has been first selectman of the town, has held the office of deputy sheriff for three years, and other minor offices in the town. In 1879 he was elected to represent the town in the legislature. He served as aid-de-camp on Governor Lounsbury's staff in 1887–8 with the rank of colonel. He is a past post commander of Kellogg Post, G. A. R.; was a delegate to the national encampment, G. A. R., held at Denver, Col., in 1883; was an aid-de-camp on Commander-in-Chief Burdette's staff, in 1886, at the encampment at San Francisco, California, and on Commander-in-Chief Alger's staff, in 1890, at the encampment in Boston. He has served between four and five years as foreman of the Echo hose and hook and ladder company of Shelton. He is a prominent member of the I. O. O. F., and has the reputation of being one of the best drill masters in the order. His business is farming, but for the past few years he has spent most of his time in building roads and grading. In politics he has always been a strong republican.

JOHN E. HIGGINS, HARTFORD: City and Town Clerk and Registrar.

John E. Higgins has held the position of city clerk in the state capital since 1874, with the exception of one year, and the office of town clerk and

J. E. HIGGINS.

registrar of births, marriages, and deaths without interval during the same period. His career in these offices has been one of marked success and satisfaction. While Mr. Higgins is a pronounced democrat in politics, his course as a public official has been so characterized by devotion to the interests of the community, without regard to partisan lines, that men of all parties politically have given him an enthusiastic support at the polls, ensuring his retention in office, no matter how popular a competitor might be in the field against him. The plan of placing his name on both tickets has prevailed for a number of years. Of course, it is impossible to consider majorities under such circumstances. A gentleman whose public career attracts all classes of citizens to his support, irrespective of political affiliations, deserves the heartiest of commendations. It would be a mistake, however, to presume that City Clerk Higgins owes his success simply to good fellowship and affable manners. While he possesses these traits beyond even most public favorites, his reception of the popular suffrage has depended, in the main, on the character and value of his services. There is not a town clerk's office in the state that is more intelligently conducted than the Hartford office. The systematic classification of town records, the order and precision with which the work of the office is managed, and the uniform courtesy with which the public has been treated have made the office the model one in Connecticut. This is not saying a word beyond what the place merits. As city clerk, Mr. Higgins is *ex officio* clerk of the board of aldermen in Hartford. It is in this capacity that much of his best public work has been accomplished. The journal of the board, which is prepared and printed under the city clerk's hand, is far superior as an official production to the journals of the state legislature. The Year Book, which is also arranged and edited by Mr. Higgins, is sought for far and wide by the municipal governments. Great improvements have been made in both the town and city clerkships during Mr. Higgins's incumbency of these offices. The subject of this sketch was born in New London, June 19, 1844, and received a public school education. At the outbreak of the war he was a teacher in the Portland public schools. This position was resigned for the military service of that period. Mr. Higgins became a member of the Third United States Artillery, and was in the army for three years. He is a prominent member of Robert O. Tyler Post of the Grand Army in Hartford, and has taken an active part in the noted veteran assemblages and demonstrations that have occurred in this city since the war. He is also a member of Green Cross Council, Knights of Columbus, and of the Hartford Lodge of Elks. City Clerk Higgins is a member of the Roman Catholic church in this city, being connected at present with the cathedral parish; but for, twenty-five years he was a member and attendant at St. Peter's. The wife of Mr. Higgins, who is held in the most thorough esteem in the community, was Miss Adella E. Collins prior to marriage. There are no children in the family. Mr. Higgins removed to Hartford from New London after the war, and was employed for eight years at the Colt works. He was first elected city clerk in 1874, and from that time until now he has been an occupant of public office and position.

RUFUS B. SAGE, Cromwell. Farmer.

Rufus B. Sage, the son of Deacon Rufus Sage, was born March 17, 1817, in that part of Middletown since known as the town of Cromwell. The

youngest of a family of seven children, he was left fatherless at the age of nine and thrown upon his own resources to make his unaided way in the world; hence his boyhood was a scene of struggling toil, quite unfavorable to educational attainments However, by his energy in making use of the common school and academy at winter terms, he was enabled to lay the founda-

R. B. SAGE.

tion for after efforts in the slow progress of self-tuition. He thus became the student of opportunity, impelled by a strong desire to learn. This induced young Sage to choose the occupation of printer, and he became initiated to the mysteries of that art at a newspaper office in the city of Middletown. In the fall of 1836 he went to Washington county, Ohio, serving as school teacher for a term and then laboring as compositor upon the *Marietta Gazette*. A favorable opening presenting itself at Parkersburg, W. Va., he engaged in the capacity of foreman upon the only paper published in that

place. While there, in the spring of 1838, he embarked in an enterprise which took him southward with a cargo of ice. This transaction resulted in a money loss, but proved rich in experience and observation, for that which he then saw and heard in Louisiana and Mississippi transformed him into the future unrelenting foe of the slave institution. Upon his return north he accepted a situation at Circleville, O., where he became well known as a writer, speaker, and participator in public affairs. His stay here was signalized by the organization of a debating club, through his influence, which became very popular, and his connection with the press also brought him in contact with the most prominent citizens of the country. His next engagement was at Columbus, late in 1839, a busy compositor upon the *Ohio State Bulletin*, carefully improving any leisure at his disposal in attendance at the state library or upon the legislative sessions. Early in 1840 commenced the ever memorable political struggle, known as the "log cabin campaign," in support of Gen. W. H. Harrison for the presidency. With this Mr. Sage was identified and bore a conspicuous part from the very first. A weekly campaign paper, and later on a daily, was edited and published by him, that did most effective service in bringing about the grand result of electing the whig national ticket by an overwhelming majority. One incident among the many that are noteworthy, wherein Mr. Sage performed the part of detective, is worthy of special mention. The democratic leaders, in their desperation, sought to stem the popular current by setting adrift an ingenious forgery, purporting to come from the whig state central committee, Alfred Kelly, chairman, which unexposed would have proved very damaging to the whig interest. Mr. Sage, by his shrewdness, most thoroughly penetrated the secret, exposing the infamous act and those concerned in it, thus springing upon their own necks the noose they had so cunningly looped for others. The day following Gen. Harrison was in Columbus, and meeting our detective said, extending his hand, "Well, Mr. Sage, you outgeneraled their generals this time! I congratulate you." The turmoil of party strife being closed, public attention began to be directed to other things. The great west, from Missouri to the Pacific ocean, then so little known, became a theme of much interest. Sharing largely in that interest, and incited by a strong desire to know more of the vast region beyond the Missouri frontier, Mr. Sage set about organizing a party of enterprising young men to visit and explore those countries. His efforts were successful, so far as talk was concerned; but at starting, May 1, 1841, only five came to time, and only one besides himself reached Independence, Mo., at which point that one also left him. Undaunted by the gloomy outlook, after a delay of several weeks, Mr. Sage joined a party of Indian traders and pushed his onward way toward the setting sun. Now began a series of adventures, explorations, and extensive travels, among Indians and wild beasts, alone or with such company as chance presented, for an interval of three years, the details of which the reader can find in a book entitled "Scenes in the Rocky Mountains," etc., by Rufus B. Sage, Carey & Hart publishers, Philadelphia, Pa., 1846. In July, 1844, he returned to Columbus, O., and immediately issued a campaign weekly in support of Henry Clay for U. S. president, protesting with all earnestness against the annexation of Texas and the consequent extension of the slave power. The result was a grand triumph in Ohio, which however was neutralized in New York by the abolition vote, cast for Barney, thus giving the national election to James K. Polk, and setting in train the tremendous evils that followed. Mr. Sage next appeared in the editorial chair of the Chillicothe, O., *Gazette*, with which paper he severed his connection in 1845, and returned to visit his old home after an absence of ten years. In this quiet retreat he prepared his book of travels, which had a successful run through several editions. And at this point came a change of long-cherished plans. An aged invalid mother required of him the care he could not find heart to deny. Yielding to her wishes, he married and set himself faithfully to solve the puzzling question so often discussed, " Will farming pay ?" Mr. Sage says it will. Satisfied with home comforts and busied with home interests, he has kept aloof from public office, having never held one, either town, state, or national. His estimate of merit does not count any one the more worthy because of popular favor, office, money, fine clothing, or proud display. He remarks that it is not often the richest ore crops out upon the surface, neither is the mere place-seeker the best deserving of popular confidence. At the age of fourteen, Mr. Sage joined the Congregational church in Cromwell, and amid all the vicissitudes of his eventful life he has been more or less active in support of religion and good morals. His name was upon the pledge-roll of the first temperance society of Connecticut, and he has been a prohibitionist from the first genesis of the idea, ever prompt to strike in its favor whenever such blow would tell, but " not as one who beateth the air." Uniformly a studious and laborious man, he is now over seventy-four years old, hale and robust, with good prospect for several years to come. He seldom drinks coffee, tea never, has been a lifelong abstainer from spirituous drinks of all kinds, nor has he used tobacco in any form. In brief, the grand result is, he has never been laid by from sickness for a single day during his whole life.

HON. SAMUEL FESSENDEN, Stamford. Attorney-at-Law.

The Hon. Samuel Fessenden, one of the ablest and foremost leaders of the republican party in Connecticut, was born in Rockland, Me., April 12, 1847, and prepared for college at Lewiston Academy. At the age of 16, however, he sacrificed his college pursuits for the army, and enlisted as a private in the Seventh Maine Battery. December 14, 1864, he was appointed to a second lieutenancy in the Second United States Infantry by President Lincoln, the promotion being recommended by General Grant.

SAMUEL FESSENDEN.

One week afterwards he was advanced to the rank of captain in that command. But having been recommended for promotion in the artillery service, he declined the captaincy in the Second regulars, and January 13, 1865, was commissioned second lieutenant in the First Maine Battery. At that time he was less than 18 years of age. He was appointed on the staff of Major-General A. P. Howe May 1, 1865, and remained in that position until the conclusion of the war. He participated in the battles of the Wilderness, Spottsylvania, Cold Harbor, and Petersburg, and won honorable recognition from his superiors. At the time when under normal circumstances he would have been a brilliant student at college, he was serving with the heroism of a veteran in the field. Returning from the war, he entered the Harvard Law School, where he completed his legal course. March 4, 1869, he was admitted to the Fairfield county bar in this state, and has since resided in Stamford. In 1874, when he was but 26 years of age, he was elected a member of the general assembly from Stamford, and was appointed on the judiciary committee. He made one of the ablest speeches of the session on the parallel railroad project, carrying the house by the eloquence and force of his presentation of the case. In 1876 he was one of the delegates from Connecticut in the national republican convention at Cincinnati, which nominated President Hayes. In 1879 he was re-elected to the general assembly, and was the foremost republican in that body. The nomination of the Hon. O. H. Platt for the United States senatorship was due mainly to the leadership displayed by Mr. Fessenden. In 1884 Mr. Fessenden was elected secretary of the national republican committee, and manifested in that capacity executive training of the highest order. He is still a member of the national committee and a member of the executive committee, and one of its most trusted advisers. For fifteen years he has been a prominent figure in republican conventions in this state, being the recognized leader by the delegates. His eminent qualities as a lawyer led to his appointment as state's attorney in Fairfield county, a position which he has held with marked success for a number of years. Mr. Fessenden prepares his cases with great thoroughness, and in the courts where he appears his knowledge of law and eloquence in addressing courts and juries makes him a formidable opponent. He was one of the founders and original members of the Army and Navy Club of Connecticut, and the universal favorite with veterans of the war throughout the state. His personal traits have endeared him to thousands of men in the country, who know of no honor too important to be conferred upon him. His future is full of promise and inspiration, whether considered from a professional or political point of view.

JOHN CHAPIN BRINSMADE, WASHINGTON.

John Chapin Brinsmade, principal of the Gunnery School, was born in Springfield, Mass., April 24, 1852. His father, William B. Brinsmade (Yale 1840) was for a long time superintendent of the Connecticut River Railroad. His mother is the daughter of the late Colonel Harvey Chapin, a descendant in the sixth generation of Deacon Samuel Chapin, who settled in Springfield in 1642. On his father's side he is descended from Rev. Daniel Brinsmade (Yale, 1745), who came to Washington (then a part of

J. C. BRINSMADE.

Woodbury) in the latter half of the eighteenth century, and was for some time the minister of the Judea Congregational Society. His son, Daniel N. Brinsmade (Yale, 1772), was a member of the state convention for the ratification of the constitution of the United States.

The subject of this sketch attended private schools in Springfield and the Gunnery in Washington, and graduated at Harvard University in the class of 1874. In the fall of that year he became assistant teacher at the Gunnery. In October, 1876, he was married to Mary Gold Gunn (his cousin), daughter of F. W. Gunn, principal of the school. Since Mr. Gunn's death in 1881 he has been principal of the Gunnery. He has five children, three sons and two daughters.

HENRY GILDERSLEEVE, PORTLAND: Shipbuilder.

Henry Gildersleeve was born in Portland, in that part of the town now known as Gildersleeve, on the 7th of April, 1817; was educated at the district school, and at the age of seventeen commenced in his father's yard to learn the business of shipbuilding. He soon acquired a thorough knowledge of the details of the business, and at the age of twenty-five he was taken into partnership with his father under the firm-name of S. Gildersleeve & Son, which firm, up to the present time, have built 142 vessels of all classes, both

HENRY GILDERSLEEVE.

sail and steam. In December, 1872, he associated himself with the house of Bentley, Gildersleeve & Co., shipping and commission merchants on South street, New York. He retained his connection with the Gildersleeve ship-building firm, and at the end of ten years he retired from the New York firm, resigning in favor of his son, Sylvester, who continued the business in connection with his brother Oliver, under the firm name of S. Gildersleeve & Co. Henry Gildersleeve, since retiring from his New York business, has devoted his whole time and attention to the ship-building and other interests with which he is connected in his native town.

On the 29th of March, 1839, he married Nancy, daughter of Samuel Buckingham of Milford, by whom he had one child, Philip, born February 1, 1842. His first wife died on the 14th of March, 1842, and on the 25th of May, 1843, he married Emily F., daughter of Oliver Northam of Marlborough, by whom he had seven children: Oliver, born March 6, 1844; Emily Shepard, born September 8, 1846; Mary Smith, born March 8, 1848, died October 18, 1851; Anna Sophia, born February 26, 1850, died August 27, 1854; Sylvester, born November 24, 1852; Louisa Rebecca, born May 9, 1857; and Henry, born September 4, 1858. The death of the second wife of Henry Gildersleeve occurred on the 11th of November, 1873; and on the 12th of June, 1875, he married Amelia, daughter of Colonel Orren Warner of East Haddam, by whom he had one child, Orren Warner, born November 26, 1878.

Mr. Gildersleeve has been identified with many public enterprises outside of his ship-building interests. He was for a number of years a director in the New York & Hartford Steamboat Company, and president of the Middletown Ferry Company, and is now president of the Middlesex Quarry Company, also president of the First National Bank of

Portland, and trustee and one of the original incorporators of the Freestone Savings Bank, also a director of the Middlesex Mutual Assurance Company of Middletown. He has been for many years an active member and liberal supporter of the Trinity Episcopal church at Portland, was a large contributor to the funds for the erection of their elegant new church edifice, and a member of the building committee. In 1861, as the nominee of the democratic party, he represented Portland in the state legislature, and sustained every measure for the vigorous prosecution of the war.

JOHN SAMUEL GRAVES, NEW HAVEN.

Mr. Graves was born in Hebron, Tolland county, Connecticut, September 2, 1807. He was educated at the district school. Books were few, but the Bible and catechism were thoroughly taught. Governor Peters of colonial times, after whom he was named, took especial interest in his education and welfare. His mother was a Peters, the family being at that time one of the largest and most respectable in the state. At fourteen years of age he left home and served four years as a clerk with Joseph Goodspeed of East

J. S. GRAVES.

Haddam. At the age of eighteen he was taken to Hartford to begin the study of medicine. His health failed him, and he went to New Haven, his present residence, intending to lead a mercantile life. From 1828 to 1830 he conducted a brokerage business, after which he undertook the dry goods trade, in which he became highly successful. Besides having the largest store in the state he carried on a heavy southern trade until 1847, when he sold out to Wilcox & Crampton, having in view the starting of a gas company. He married, in July, 1837, Polly Merwin, the daughter of Dr. Philo Merwin of Brookfield, in this state. Eight children live to mourn a lovely and devoted mother. His elevation to many official stations of responsibility and trust shows him to have been a man of great ability and honor, as well as of broad and progressive views. He has held the offices of notary public, justice of the peace, city councilman, and of vestryman in Trinity Episcopal Church. He was the prime mover and founder of the New Haven Gas Light Company, holding the offices of vicepresident, secretary, and treasurer, and variously in active official service for twenty-three years. He still continues in the company of which he has been

a member for forty-three years. Politically he is a Jeffersonian democrat, and although he was nominated as a candidate of that party for mayor, he declined the honor, preferring a quiet life outside of all political entanglements.

JAMES WALKER BEARDSLEY, BRIDGEPORT: A Retired Farmer and Stock Dealer.

Mr. Beardsley is a son of Elisha H. Beardsley, and has been a farmer all his life. He is a native of the town of Monroe, where he was born May 8,

J. W. BEARDSLEY.

1820, and where his father pursued the same occupation. He is descended in regular line from William Beardsley, one of the first settlers of Stratford; and on his mother's side, through a distinguished ancestry, from Robert Walker, one of the founders of the Old South Church of Boston in 1669. Mr. Beardsley was educated at the common schools and at the preparatory institute of Samuel B. Beardsley. As before stated, his life has been spent entirely on the farm, and he long ago became the holder of much landed property, including a large and valuable stock farm in the state of Illinois. His residence has been in Monroe and in Bridgeport, to both of which localities he has contributed much in the way of material adornment and of personal influence. In 1878 he gave to the city of Bridgeport one hundred acres of land for a public park, on condition that the city should expend a certain comparatively small amount of money yearly, for a number of years, in its care and management. At first the city doubted the propriety of accepting the gift on the conditions which the donor imposed, but it was finally accepted, and the conditions have been fulfilled. This park is now regarded as one of the great features of the city. For the original property Mr. Beardsley had been offered $20,000; it would be worth for city lots today hundreds of thousands. It cannot be doubted that he takes great satisfaction in seeing the improvements which the city is making from year to year in "Beardsley Park," many of which were of his own suggesting. He bestows yearly upon it much time, attention, and money, and his efforts in its behalf are highly appreciated by the citizens of Bridgeport, as is the original magnificent gift.

Mr. Beardsley's fine residence was originally the homestead of James Walker, Jr., which descended to the former through his mother, Betsey (Walker)

Beardsley, the daughter of James Walker, Jr. It is kept very choicely, and regarded sacredly as the home of his ancestors for three generations, or since 1730. Mr. Beardsley was a member of the Connecticut legislature in 1848, representing the town of Monroe, and being elected to the office by the democratic party. He is an influential member of the Protestant Episcopal Church, and a liberal contributor to its charities.

EDWARD V. PRESTON, HARTFORD: Superintendent of Agencies of the Travelers Insurance Company.

Major Edward V. Preston was born in Willington, Conn., June 1, 1837, being the second son of Joshua and Caroline Eldredge Preston. The family consisted of seven children, three of whom reside in Hartford. The major's grandfather, Amos Preston, and great-grandfather, Darius Preston, were born in the same house in Willington in which his father and himself first saw the light. This ancient structure, which has been the birth-place of four generations in the family, is still standing. The Prestons

in this country are descendants of William Preston, who emigrated from England in 1635, reaching Boston on the *True Love*, the last of the seventeen ships from London to Boston in that year. The genealogy of the family, however, is traced back to the time of Malcolm, King of the Scots. The name of Preston was assumed on account of the territorial possessions of the family in Mid-Lothian, Scotland. The first of the name on record is Leolphus De Preston, living in the time of William the Lion, about 1040. His grandson, Sir William Preston, was one of the Scotch nobles summoned to Berwick by Edward I. in the competition for the Crown of Scotland between Bruce and Baliol, the decision having been submitted to Edward. Subsequently, Westmoreland county, England, was represented in Parliament by members of the family, Edward III. being king at the time. John Preston, also a member of the family, retired from the bench in 1427 on account of his great age. William Preston, from whom the American branch is descended, originally located in Dorchester, but afterwards removed to New Haven, where he died in 1647. Some of his children remained in Dorchester. The Eastern Connecticut Prestons are traced from John Preston of Andover, Mass., who married

Mary Haynes of Newbury in that state in 1706 and removed to Windham county, where he died in 1730. The Connecticut branch of the family figured conspicuously in the Revolutionary war, the Lexington alarm, April 19, 1775, calling them to the front. The list of Revolutionary soldiers published by this state shows twenty-five representatives of the Connecticut Prestons in the service. The family has been equally active and prominent in church interests. The history of Windham county is rich with narratives concerning their work in this direction.

At the outbreak of the war in 1861, the subject of this sketch was engaged in business in this city, being a member of the firm of Griswold, Griffin & Co., which was located at the southeast corner of Asylum and Trumbull streets. April 22, 1861, he volunteered temporary assistance as a clerk in the adjutant-general's office under General J. D. Williams. In July, Col. Orris S. Ferry of the Fifth Connecticut, which was then organizing, requested the appointment of Major Preston as quartermaster of the command. July 17th he received the appointment, being given the rank of first lieutenant, and was mustered into the service July 23d. In September, 1861, he was detailed by Col. Dudley Donnelly and afterwards by Gens. G. H. Gordon and A. S. Williams to be acting assistant quartermaster of the First Brigade, Gen. Banks's division, and retained the position until Jan. 1, 1862, when he returned to his old place in the Fifth Connecticut. In March, 1862, Lieutenant Preston was detailed as an aid-de-camp on the staff of Gen. Ferry, who had received a brigadier's commission. During a part of the time until Feb. 19, 1863, he was acting assistant quartermaster of the division. On that date he was commissioned by President Lincoln as "additional paymaster U. S. Volunteers, with the rank of major," and held this position until July 31, 1865, when he was honorably discharged by the secretary of war. Millions of dollars passed through his hands during the war and his accounts squared to a cent in the final settlement with the government. Major Preston is a member of the veteran association of the Fifth regiment; also of the Army and Navy Club of Connecticut, and of Robert O. Tyler Post, G. A. R. He is one of the trustees of the $10,000 fund owned by the Post. He is also a member of the board of trustees of the Connecticut Literary Institution at Suffield, of the Baptist state convention, and president of the Baptist Social Union of the state. For the past twenty years he has been the treasurer of the Asylum Avenue Baptist society in this city. He is at present a member of the board of aldermen from the second ward, and has also served from that precinct two years in the council board. In politics he is a republican. His business life since the war has been connected with the Travelers Insurance Company, where he has held the position of superintendent of agents for a quarter of a century. The duties of the office require executive ability of the highest order. In the discharge of these duties he has visited every section of the United States, Canada, and Mexico. The family of Major Preston consists of a wife and two children, one son and a daughter. Mrs. Preston, prior to her marriage, was Miss Clara M. Litchfield, daughter of the late John G. Litchfield of this city. The son, Mr. Harry E. Preston, is also connected with the Travelers. Major Preston's career from the outset has been one of honor and integrity, and he is regarded throughout the country with the utmost esteem and respect.

AVERY A. STANTON, Sterling: Farmer and Lumberman.

The subject of this sketch was born in Preston in 1837, and is the great-great-grandson of General Thomas Stanton, who came from England and settled in Stonington. He is brother of Captain John L. Stanton who fell at the seige of Port Hudson, and of Rev. William E. Stanton who was for several years pastor of the First Baptist church at Lowell. In 1848 Mr. Stanton and his mother (his father having died one year previous), removed to Voluntown in this state. He received his education at the

A. A. STANTON.

schools of Voluntown, East Greenwich, R. I., and at the Connecticut Literary Institution of Suffield. He taught school about eight years in eastern Connecticut and Rhode Island, and in 1862 settled in the town of Sterling, where he has since resided, engaged in farming and lumber business.

In 1864 he was elected one of the school visitors of Sterling, which position he held for twenty-four years. In 1873 he was elected first selectman, and has held other important town offices, being town agent and auditor for a number of years. In 1874 he represented the town of Sterling in the state legislature. In 1884 he was chosen to fill the unexpired term of R. H. Ward, county commissioner, and by the same legislature was chosen county commissioner for the term of three years. He still holds this position, having been appointed for a second term of four years. Mr. Stanton married the daughter of Benjamin Gallup of Voluntown — has five sons and three daughters. He belongs to a family that is able to trace 6,000 relatives. He is a Baptist, and in politics a zealous republican.

SAXTON B. LITTLE, Meriden: School Teacher.

Saxton Bailey Little, a descendant of the seventh generation from Thomas Little, who came to Plymouth, Mass., from near London, England, in 1630, was born in Columbia, Conn., April 19, 1813. His ancestral mother was Ann Warren, whose father, Richard Warren, was one of the company who came over in the Mayflower in 1620. His education was in the common schools, supplemented by some instruction in Tolland, East Hartford, and Bacon academies. Beginning to

S. B. LITTLE.

teach school at the age of sixteen, he taught fifteen winters, "boarding 'round," as was the custom sixty years ago. He taught in Bacon Academy in 1836, one year; six winters in Goshen Hill, Lebanon, Conn.; two and a half years in Willimantic; and in Greeneville three years. In 1850 he removed to Rockville, in the town of Vernon, Tolland County, and remained there nearly four years, which completed his service in the public schools. In April, 1854, he was appointed assistant superintendent and teacher in the Connecticut State Reform School at Meriden, and upon the death of the lamented Dr. E. W. Hatch, Feb. 7, 1874, he was appointed acting superintendent. He closed his connection with the institution July 31, 1875, after a continuous service there of twenty-one years and four months. The trustees of the school, in their report to the general assembly in 1874, speaking of Mr. Little said: "We should fail in our duty if we did not signify to you our high appreciation of the well-applied and faithful services of this officer during these many years, and to testify that his labors in the position of assistant superintendent and teacher have contributed largely to the marked success of the school." Since he left this school he has made the tour of Europe, going as far as Naples and Pompeii. He has traveled quite extensively in the United States and Canada, visiting Central and Southern California, Florida, the New Orleans exposition, Yosemite Valley, Luray and Mammoth Caves, etc. He was married Aug. 19, 1836, to Sarah Maria Tracy. She died Dec. 31, 1844, leaving two sons, Charles L. and Frank Eugene, the former a well-known contractor and builder in Meriden; the latter is post-office inspector. Both were in the Union army. Frank served four years and was breveted major in the One Hundred and Seventh colored regiment.

Mr. Little has filled many public offices in Meriden. He has been a member of the common council, of the high school committee, and is now, and has been for many years school district committee. He is a republican and a member of the First Congregational church in Meriden. He is a great lover of books, and has been an efficient helper in establishing a free library in Columbia, his old home. He gave to it $1,500 as a permanent fund, the interest only to be used for the purchase of books; and he has also given the library more than a thousand volumes. He is one who believes that it is wise to give to public objects of charity while living, leaving no chance for one's heirs to practically question his sanity or thwart his wishes. It may be added that Mr. Little has throughout his life been very strict in his habits. He never used tobacco in any form, and has been a total abstainer from all alcoholic drinks for sixty-one years. Has personally employed a physician but once for over fifty years, and that solitary exception was a case of measles.

HORACE WHITE, MANCHESTER: Farmer.

Horace White, honored, respected, and called "Uncle Horace" by all classes, and whose name is a familiar one in Manchester and adjoining towns, was born at the old pine tree homestead of his father (Henry White) in East Windsor, Conn., in the year 1801; was given by his parents a good common school education, which was the best thing possible for a farmer to do for his children in those days and times. He remained in the service of his father during his minority and continued in the care of the farm until

HORACE WHITE.

the death of his father, some few years later, and in company with his brother Willard (long ago deceased) had the full care and control of the old Tolland turnpike until it was abandoned or discontinued as a turnpike. In 1842 the part of East Windsor where the old homestead was located, together with the village of Oakland, was set off to and became a part of Manchester; some three years later a goodly portion of said East Windsor was set off to what is now known and called South Windsor.

Mr. White was married to his first wife, Asenath Fuller, in 1827, and soon after erected for himself, on the eastern portion of the old homestead, a new and model farmhouse and buildings, where he continued to live a sturdy, prosperous, and thrifty New England farmer until 1875. Then finding himself at the age of seventy-four years, and in comfortable financial circumstances, he decided to abandon farming and retire to more pleasant and social surroundings. He therefore sold his farm and stock complete and purchased a residence property in North Manchester, near the depot, and fitted it up with all the requisite improvements and luxuries of the present time, and now lives there, an old gentleman in his ninetieth year of age, in comfortable health, with his daughter, Wealthy A., as housekeeper, who keeps a watchful and careful eye to his every comfort, enjoying the fruits and means of his well-spent life. His first wife died in 1866 while at the farm, leaving, as the fruits of their union, two children, H. Tudor White, now a prominent citizen of Windsor, and Wealthy A. White, now having care of her father in his declining years.

Mr. White married for his second wife (in March, 1869) the widow of the late Warren Fuller of Monson, Mass., and they lived nearly twenty-one years in happy companionship of one another (she dying January, 1890), a venerable old couple.

Mr. White, in his early years, and especially after becoming a resident of Manchester, has been honorably and prominently connected with all, or nearly all, of the town's industries, enterprises, and progress. He was for many years connected with the manufacture of stockinet at Manchester Green, and with the concern known as the "New Pacific" at the extreme eastern part of Manchester, now Lydallville. During his almost lifelong residence in Manchester he has occupied every position of prominence within the gift or suffrage of his townsmen. He was elected a member of the legislature in 1857; was appointed and elected a county commissioner of Hartford county in 1862, and served with eminence and credit to his county and constituency for the term of three years; was appointed by the honorable superior court one of the commission of three (his colleagues being the Hon. Wm. Hamersley of Hartford and Civil Engineer Rice of New Britain) to establish the disputed boundary line between the towns of Suffield, East Granby, and the Massachusetts border, Governor Hubbard acting as counselor for Granby and Buck & Eggleston for Suffield,—a contest lasting sixteen days, in which Mr. White proved himself a competent and effectual arbitrator for the towns directly interested.

Mr. White has been in politics a lifelong republican, always standing prominent and firm in what he believed to be just and fair, never recognizing the tricks of cheap politicians further than to stamp upon and spurn them. He has been connected with the Second Congregational church of Manchester from its organization to the present time, and always an honorable, consistent member thereof.

C. W. C.

FRANCIS GRANGER ANTHONY, New Haven: Deputy Collector.

Francis G. Anthony was born in Lima, Livingston county, New York, October 6, 1830. He is the son of William Miles Anthony, who was a native

F. G. ANTHONY.

of Harwinton, in this state, where he was born in August, 1804. Mr. Anthony's education was acquired in the public schools of Lima and the neighboring town of West Avon, with part of a year at a select school in Batavia, N. Y. The death of his father when the lad was but thirteen years of age terminated his attendance at school, as the family were left without means, and thus were unable to incur the expense of a liberal education. During the year of his father's death Mr. Anthony came to New Haven, — part of the trip, from Rochester to Albany, being made on a canal boat, — to live with his uncle, Willis M. Anthony, who proved to be better, if possible, than a father to him. Here he spent nearly four years as clerk, first in Washington Yale's dry-goods store, and then with Fairman & Johnson. He is one of the original " Forty-niners," having taken the California gold fever on its first outbreak. On the 6th of February, 1849, he sailed from New York with a party of gold-seekers for California on the bark *Clarissa Perkins*, going around Cape Horn, the trip occupying two hundred and seventeen days. Arriving in San Francisco, the party disbanded, and Mr. Anthony went to the mines. He was a practical gold miner for two years, meeting with varying success, making some days $200 a day, other days nothing. Was a baker in Nevada, California, for about one year, at which business he did better than at mining — the income being more certain, and not so much up and down as in " prospecting for diggings." He returned east in 1852; lived in Michigan two years, operating a foundry; went to Kentucky in 1854, where he was in general merchandizing eleven years at Athens, in Fayette county, seven or eight years of which time he was postmaster. The succeeding five years he spent in New York city, and in 1870 he returned to New Haven, where he has since been employed in the tax collector's office; at the present time is the deputy tax collector, and for the last thirteen years has been the rate-book maker. He has been a director in the Masonic Mutual Benefit Association of New Haven for fourteen years, and is at present executor of several estates. He is also a commissioner of the superior court for New Haven county.

His acquaintance with New Haven people is very extensive, his business giving him familiarity with nearly every tax-payer in the city. He has been a lifelong democrat, though not an active politician; is a prominent member of the Masonic fraternity, in which he has taken all the degrees up to and including the thirty-second. He has held the office of recorder of New Haven Commandery, Knights Templar, since 1880; belongs to the Arabic order of the Mystic Shrine.

Mr. Anthony was married July 31, 1854, to Miss Electa Hulbert of Ann Arbor, Michigan, by whom he has had three children. Mrs. Anthony died February 29, 1888, and but one of the children, the youngest, has survived her.

HON. DUDLEY P. ELY, South Norwalk: Banker.

Dudley P. Ely is a native of Connecticut, having been born in the town of Simsbury, Hartford county, on the 16th of November, 1817. Thirty

D. P. ELY.

years of his business life were spent in New York city, where he secured a competency. In 1861, he returned to his native state, becoming a resident of South Norwalk, where for many years he was one of the most active and prominent citizens of that place, and until increasing years required him to lay aside some of the burdens and responsibilities which his numerous and varied interests had laid upon him. He was the youngest child of Benjamin Ely, who was a graduate of Yale College of the year 1786, and a prominent citizen of this state. The Ely family are of French descent, the first of the name in England having come there from France. John Ely, a great uncle of Dudley P. Ely, was colonel of the Third Connecticut regiment in the revolutionary war, and carried the French coat-of-arms engraved on his sword hilt. The first American ancestor of Dudley P. Ely was Richard Ely, who arrived in America about the year 1660, and settled in Lyme in this state. Mr. Ely's maternal ancestry was English, and his grandfather was an officer in the revolutionary war. Mr. Ely was educated at the public schools of Simsbury until the age of fourteen years, when he was sent to Hartford and took a two years' course at Mr. Olney's school, a noted institution of that day. He then started to make his own career. His first employment was at a store in his native town. His aptitude and activity were such that at the age of eighteen years he had placed in his entire charge and management a store in West Hartland. After remaining there a year, his ambition led him to seek his fortune in New York city. He first became a bookkeeper there for his brother, with whom he subsequently became a partner, and whom he afterwards succeeded in the business. His ability and energy found full scope here and brought him a substantial fortune. After going to South Norwalk, he identified himself with many of the business and public interests of that place. He invested largely in real estate, and is to-day the largest owner of real estate property in that prosperous city. He built the Hotel Mahackemo block on the corner of Washington and Main streets, the largest business block in South Norwalk. In April, 1865, Mr. Ely was elected president of the First National Bank of that place, which position he still retains. When South Norwalk was incorporated as a city in 1870, Mr. Ely was chosen its first mayor, and was re-elected to that office four subsequent terms. He was president of the Norwalk Gas Light Company for more than twenty years, but recently resigned that office to relieve himself of the burden of its duties. He was also president of the South Norwalk Savings Bank for more than ten years, but retired from that office to free himself from its cares. He was the first president of the Norwalk Iron Works Company, and the first president of the South Norwalk Printing Company. In addition to these positions, he was a director of the Danbury & Norwalk Railroad Company, the Norwalk Horse Railroad Company, the Fairfield County Fire Insurance Company, the Norwalk Fire Insurance Company, the Relief Fire Insurance Company of New York, and the Peter Cooper Fire Insurance Company of New York, which latter position he still retains. In agricultural matters Mr. Ely has taken a lively interest, and for many years was president of the Fairfield County Agricultural Society, which had an exceptionally prosperous career under his administration. More for the purpose of recreation than of profit, he has carried on a farm owned by him in the suburbs of the city, and has been an enthusiast on the subject of poultry and pigeons, having raised many varieties of the best species. In his business career, Mr. Ely has furnished an example of honor, integrity, and reliability worthy to be imitated by the younger generation, who can see in him and his career what can be accomplished by industry, thrift, and good character. Mr. Ely is of social disposition, a good story teller, and an entertaining talker upon topics that have come under his personal observation and experience, or within the range of his reading, always having intelligent and often original ideas of value upon both public and private matters. He has been a valued and a valuable adviser of many people, and in many good causes, which he has aided both by his counsels and his means. He has been a large, though modest, contributor to charitable causes, and particularly interested in charities like the Children's Aid Society and such institutions, which seek to protect and make better the children and youth of the land. He is a member of the Congregational church of South Norwalk.

HENRY E. TAINTOR, Hartford: Attorney-at-Law.

Henry Ellsworth Taintor was born at Hampton, Windham county, Conn., Aug. 29, 1844. He is a son of the late Hon. Henry G. Taintor of Hampton, who was for many years a prominent citizen of that town, and at one time the state treasurer of Connecticut. On his mother's side Mr. H. E. Taintor is a great-grandson of Oliver Ellsworth, formerly chief justice of the United States supreme court. Mr. Taintor prepared for college at Monson, Mass., and entered the class of 1865 at Yale University, con-

H. E. TAINTOR.

tinuing a member until he left in January, 1864, to enter the army. After leaving the United States service he did not return to college, but received a degree in regular form as if he had completed his course there. His military record covers nearly two years: he enlisted Jan. 14, 1864, as private in Company A, First Connecticut Heavy Artillery, served with his regiment till the close of the war, and was discharged as second lieutenant Sept. 25, 1865. In 1866 he established his residence in Hartford, and soon afterwards began the practice of law here, which he has since continued uninterruptedly. He was married May 13, 1869, to Miss Jane G. Bennett, daughter of Lyman Bennett of Amsterdam, N. Y., who is a descendant of an old Hampton family. They have one child. Mr. Taintor was executive secretary to Governor Jewell in 1872-73, and associate judge of the Hartford city court at the same time. He has been a member of the court of common council several terms, and of the board of aldermen two years; was clerk of the Hartford city court for thirteen years. He is now assistant judge of the Hartford police court and coroner for Hartford county. He is also one of the trustees of the State Savings Bank, as well as one of its attorneys, and attorney for the Society for Savings on Pratt street. He is a member of the Grand Army of the Republic, and has held several offices therein including those of commander of the department of Connecticut and judge-advocate-general on the staff of the commander-in-chief. His religious connections are with the First Congregational church of Hartford, and in politics he is a republican. There is not a lawyer in the state who has a more honorable standing before the bar or the public.

JAMES W. HYATT, Norwalk: President Fairfield County National Bank.

The subject of this sketch is among the citizens of Connecticut who are distinguished for their services both to the commonwealth and the republic,

JAMES W. HYATT.

and for the wide range of public honors which have been conferred upon them. Mr. Hyatt was born in Norwalk in 1837. He studied in the common schools until he was thirteen years of age, when he commenced an active business life. Step by step he rapidly and steadily advanced, and we find him from 1860 to 1872 a trusted clerk with the banking firm of Le Grand Lockwood & Co. of New York. Since his return to Norwalk, Conn., in 1873, he has had positions of trust placed in his charge. In 1873 he was elected justice of the peace, and also vice-president of the Danbury & Norwalk Railroad Company, which office he held until 1881, when he was elected its president. In 1874 he was elected president of the Norwalk Horse Railroad Company, and has been re-elected each year since. In 1875 and 1876 he represented the town of Norwalk in the state legislature, and was appointed on the house committee on finance, a position of considerable importance, and in 1876 did much excellent work for the commonwealth. In 1876 Governor Ingersoll appointed him bank commissioner to fill the vacancy caused by the resignation of the Hon. George M. Landers, who was returned to congress. This position he held almost continuously until the spring of 1887, when he was appointed United States treasurer by President Cleveland. He was warden of the borough of Norwalk for six years; a selectman of the town; has held the offices both of vice-president and president of the Danbury & Norwalk Railroad; vice-president and director of the National Bank of Norwalk; and president of the Norwalk Club. He was elected to represent the Thirteenth senatorial district of Connecticut in the legislature of 1884, but resigned his seat on February 26 of that year to accept a re-appointment to the bank com-

missionership by Governor Waller. At the close of his term in the service of the state he was appointed United States bank examiner for Connecticut and Rhode Island; and subsequently, as above stated, to the treasuryship of the United States. His present active official connections are with the Fairfield County National Bank and the Norwalk Horse Railroad Company, of both which corporations he is the president.

Mr. Hyatt is a member of the Episcopal church of Norwalk, of the Masonic fraternity, and the Independent Order of Odd Fellows. He married Miss Jane M. Hoyt of Stamford, and has a family of four children. He is a straightforward democrat of the old school, to the principles of which political faith he consistently adheres. He is of a nervous temperament and positive character, quick to decide and prompt to act, a discriminating student of human nature, strong and loyal in his personal friendships, a useful and honored citizen, and a true patriot.

THOMAS DUNCAN, Poquonock (Windsor): Paper Manufacturer.

Thomas Duncan was born in Scotland, August 13, 1832, and was educated in the Scottish parochial schools. He remained in Scotland until he was

THOMAS DUNCAN.

twenty years of age, when he removed to this country, where he has since resided. He spent nine months in New Jersey after his arrival from Scotland. For thirty-eight years he has been a resident of Connecticut and has been prominently associated with business, political, and religious interests during that time. He has been twice a member of the legislature from Windsor, serving on the republican side of the house. He is identified with the Congregational church and is an influential representative of that denomination in the state, being a member of the Connecticut Congregational Club. He is connected with the Hartford Paper Company, the Globe Sulphite Boiler Company, and is treasurer and general manager of the Hudson River Water Power and Paper Company at Mechanicsville, N. Y. At present he is engaged in the erection of a large paper mill in connection with the pulp works there, which will be one of the largest in the country when finished. Mr. Duncan has been married twice. His first wife, who died in 1867, was Miss Grace Yule prior to her marriage. The second wife, who is still living, was Janet Gillies. There were five children by his first marriage, four of whom are living. Mr. Duncan is one of the leading manufacturers in Hartford county, and is widely known as a business manager. He is a gentleman of the most enjoyable personal character, and has hosts of friends in Hartford county. Mr. Duncan's home is at Poquonock.

SOLOMON LUCAS, NORWICH: Attorney-at-Law.

Solomon Lucas, one of the most successful practitioners at the bar of New London county, was born at Norwich, April 1, 1836. His early educational advantages were somewhat limited, but he acquired a solid education in the public schools, and proceeded to a preparation for his life work with a determination and spirit which made the undertaking almost an accomplishment from the outset. He was a diligent and earnest law student in the office of Hon. John T. Wait of Norwich, and in

SOLOMON LUCAS.

1862 was admitted to the bar, since which time he has been in active and continuous practice in that city. He was married in 1864 to Miss Elizabeth A. Crosby, daughter of Hiram Crosby, a prominent woolen manufacturer and dealer of Lyme, Conn., who removed to Norwich and there spent the last years of his life. Mrs. Lucas died in October, 1874, leaving two daughters. Mr. Lucas is a democrat in politics, and as such represented Preston in the legislature of 1863, of which body he was one of the youngest members. He has since declined to run for any political office, being entirely devoted to his profession. He is, however, state's attorney for New London county, to which position he was called on account of his professional fitness rather than for political reasons. His religious connections are with the Second Congregational church and society, and he has been first committeeman of that society for many years. He holds a directorship in the Norwich Street Railway Company, and sustains semi-official relations with various minor local enterprises. He is an active and useful citizen, always ready to perform any public service which lies clearly within the line of duty, not incompatible with his professional obligations.

Mr. Lucas enjoys an enviable reputation among his legal contemporaries and with the public. His standing as a lawyer is high, and he is accorded universal credit for the great success which he has conquered. He has been absolutely untiring in working his way upward in his profession, until at the present time he ranks among the leading practitioners of the state. As state's attorney he has discharged his duties ably and faithfully. A distinguished member of the New London county bar says of Mr. Lucas: "He is a bright, keen, successful lawyer, earnestly devoted to his profession; one who takes good care of his clients, and is not dismayed by any opposition. He has been the architect of his own fortune, and deserves great credit for winning the high position which he occupies as an attorney and advocate."

WILLIAM WALDO HYDE, HARTFORD: Attorney-at-Law.

William Waldo Hyde, acting school visitor and president of the street board, was born in Tolland, March 25, 1854, and was educated at Yale College, graduating with honor in the class of 1876. His classmates in the university included Prof. Arthur T. Hadley, John J. Jennings of Bristol, and the late Walker Blaine of Washington. Mr. Hyde is a member of the distinguished law firm of Hyde, Gross & Hyde of this city, and is a lawyer of superior attainments. He has been a member of the board of school visitors

W. W. HYDE.

and the acting school visitor for a number of years, winning especial distinction in that position. The public schools of the city, which must be affected in an important manner by his administration and influence, have not been noted for more thorough or conscientious work during their history than at present. Mr. Hyde is the president of the board of street commissioners, a position of more than ordinary responsibility in the municipal government, and has discharged the duties of the place with uninterrupted success. He is a member of the South Congregational church, the University Club of New York, the Hartford Club, St. John's Lodge, No. 4, F. and A. M., of this city, and of Washington Commandery, Knights Templar. He is also a member of the Improved Order of Red Men. He is one of the ablest and most influential representatives of the democratic party in Hartford, and is widely known as a leader throughout the state. His father, Hon. A. P. Hyde of this city, and his grandfather, the late Judge Loren P. Waldo, have conveyed to him through training and education the purest principles of democracy. Mr. Hyde has a family, consisting of a wife and two children. The former was Miss Helen E. Watson, daughter of the late George W. Watson.

JOHN HENRY WOOD, THOMASTON: Superintendent Seth Thomas Clock Company; President Thomaston Knife Company.

J. H. Wood is the oldest son of Henry and Julia (Ford) Wood, and grandson of James and Susan (Elmer) Wood of East Windsor, his mother being a  direct descendant of Barnabas Ford, one of the oldest settlers of Northbury (now Thomaston), then part of the town of Waterbury. Mr. Wood was born June 30, 1828, and began early in life to earn his own living, working at farming summers and attending school during the winter months. At the age of fifteen he received from his father his time as a heritage,

J. H. WOOD.

and immediately contracted with Morse & Blakeslee (both cousins of his), to serve a three years' apprenticeship in learning the trade of making clock movements, remaining in the employ of the firm one year after the expiration of the term. Since 1848, with the exception of about nine months, he has been connected with the Seth Thomas Clock Company as contractor and foreman, and for the past thirty-four years, as superintendent of the clock movement factory of the company. He was married at the age of twenty-one to Mary Ostrom of Torrington, by whom he has had two children, a daughter and son. The daughter, Eliza, married Lieutenant O. B. Sawyer of Company A, Fourteenth regiment, Connecticut Volunteers, and died Feb. 17, 1872, leaving two sons, Frederick H. and Wilbur J., and one daughter, who died in infancy. Lieutenant Sawyer died Nov. 16, 1874, leaving his two orphaned boys in the care of their grandparents, John H. and Mary Wood; both of them are at present pursuing a collegiate course at Wesleyan University in Middletown. The son, Henry O., is married to Bell Mallory, resides in Thomaston, and is assisting his father by keeping the books of the department under his charge.

Mr. Wood is a public-spirited, kind-hearted, affable gentleman, and a man of thorough temperance principles and habits. In politics he is a republican, having been connected with that party since its formation. He has been grand juror, school committee, trustee for thirty years (and at present) of the Methodist Episcopal Church, chairman of the building committee which erected the present church in 1866, one of the corporators, and at present a director, vice-president, and one of the loaning committee of the Thomaston Savings Bank, and president of the Thomaston Knife Company.

He was a member of the general assembly of Connecticut from Thomaston in 1887, having in the election a clear majority, over three other candidates for the same office; he was assigned by Speaker Hoyt to the committee on banks.

JONATHAN B. BUNCE, HARTFORD: President Phœnix Mutual Life Insurance Company.

Mr. Bunce is a native and has remained during most of his life a resident of Hartford, where he was born April 4, 1832. His father was a merchant,  and the boy's early educational experience in the district and public high school was sandwiched with mercantile apprenticeship in the paternal establishment. A year and a half in the scientific department of Yale University effectually and permanently disturbed his connection with the home store, and, at the age of twenty-two, the young man embarked in the

J. B. BUNCE.

commission business in New York city, as a member of the firm of Dibble & Bunce, which he followed for nine years, or until called back to Hartford by the death of his father in 1860. Here he became a partner—which relation his father had sustained until his death—with Drayton Hillyer, in the wool business, the firm being Hillyer & Bunce. This partnership and business was maintained for fifteen years, at the expiration of which period he accepted the vice-presidency of the Phœnix Mutual Life Insurance Company. From 1874 to 1889 he occupied that position, and on the reorganization of the company in 1889 was advanced to the presidency, in which latter position he has remained to the present time. At the breaking out of the war he was appointed quartermaster-general of Connecticut, holding the office through the unexpired term of his predecessor, to complete which he was appointed. He was married May 9, 1860, to Miss Laura Dibble, daughter of Calvin B. Dibble of Granby. They have had eight children, of whom six are now living—three sons and three daughters. Mr. Bunce is a member of the Pearl Street Congregational church and society, of which institution he was one of the original incorporators. In politics he is a republican, and has been such since the birth of the party. He has been and still is connected with several of the financial and charitable organizations of the city, among which may be mentioned his relations as director with the Phœnix National Bank, Hartford Fire Insurance Company, the Society for Savings, Connecticut

Trust and Safe Deposit Company, the American Deaf and Dumb Asylum, and the Hartford Hospital. He has been for thirty years secretary of the Hartford Retreat for the Insane, and has sustained various official positions of minor importance not here enumerated.

The Bunce family is one of the ancient and representative families of Hartford, going back in a direct line to John Bunce, one of the early settlers of the town. The father of the subject of this sketch, James M. Bunce, and his grandfather, Russell Bunce, will be well remembered, either personally or by reputation, by many of the older inhabitants of Hartford of the present day. They were, as are all their descendants, men of stalwart integrity, and of great sagacity in civil and commercial affairs, and strict observants of external courtesies in their intercourse with men; conscientiously fulfilling to the best of their ability all the duties and obligations of life.

CHARLES E. GROSS, HARTFORD: Attorney-at-Law.

Charles E. Gross, of the Hartford law firm of Hyde, Gross & Hyde, was born in this city August 1st, 1847, and educated at the Hartford High School and Yale College, graduating with honor from the university in 1869. After graduating he taught for a time in Ellington. He then studied with Waldo, Hubbard & Hyde, and was afterward admitted to partnership. At the death of the senior member, Judge Loren P. Waldo, his name was incorporated in that of the firm, which was known as Hubbard, Hyde & Gross,

C. E. GROSS.

until the demise of Governor Hubbard. Mr. Gross is a prominent member of the Hartford county bar and one of the most successful practitioners in the city. He is a democrat in politics. The only office that he has held is that of school visitor. But he has declined numerous nominations, preferring to give his entire attention to business. He is a member of the Asylum Hill Congregational church and a gentleman of the most exemplary character. He has a wife and two children. The former was Miss Nellie C. Spencer, daughter of the late Calvin Spencer of Hartford, and is a lady of high social prominence. Mr. Gross is a member of the Yale Alumni Association and is one of the ablest representatives of Yale training and culture in this city. As a lawyer and citizen he is held in the highest personal regard.

GEORGE MAXWELL, ROCKVILLE: President and Treasurer Hockanum Company, Woolen Manufacturers.

The Maxwell family are of Scotch-Irish descent, and for many years resided in the north of Ireland, Hugh Maxwell, the grandfather of the subject of this biography, having been a native of Minterburn, county Tyrone, where he was born in 1733. His father, who bore the same name, being a Calvinist, and disliking the established church of Ireland, determined to remove to America with his family. The younger Hugh ardently espoused the cause of the colonists during the war of the revolution, attained

GEORGE MAXWELL.

the rank of colonel, and was well known as a brave officer and Christian patriot. He died in 1799, at the age of sixty-seven. His son Sylvester, the father of George Maxwell, was born in 1775, graduated from Yale in 1797, married Tirzah Taylor, by whom he had four sons and four daughters, settled in Charlemont, Mass., as a lawyer, and died in 1855.

George Maxwell, the only surviving brother among Sylvester's eight children, was born July 30, 1817, in Charlemont, where he remained until seventeen years of age, varying the time with such employments as the farm requires, when not engaged in his school duties. He then removed to Greenfield, Mass., and for ten years filled the position of a clerk, making Rockville his residence in 1843. Here he began a mercantile course, which extended over a period of four years, when he became identified with the New England Company, manufacturers of woolen goods. He remained ten years with this company, and then transferred his relations to the Hockanum Company, first holding the office of treasurer and subsequently that of president, both of which he now fills. On the re-organization of the New England Company he was made its president. He speedily became an influential factor in the leading financial enterprises of Rockville, where his executive genius and sound business qualities placed him in many positions of trust. He is treasurer of the Springville Company, president of the Rockville National Bank, president of the Rockville Gas Light Company and of the Rockville Railroad Company, treasurer of the Rockville Water Power Company, president of the Rockville Aqueduct Company, and director of various other enterprises, including the Society of Savings of Hartford, the Hartford Trust Company, and the National Fire Insurance Company of the same city. Mr. Maxwell's political affiliations are with the republican party, by whom he was elected to represent the town of Vernon in the general assembly of 1871, and his district in the state senate in 1872. He was an active and influential member, and for many years a deacon in the Second Congregational church of Rockville, and now sustains the same relations in the Union Congregational church, in which the First and Second churches were recently merged. He is also a trustee of Hartford Theological Seminary. In benevolent enterprises, and all efforts to advance the cause of Christianity, he has been a leading spirit and a tireless worker. He has during his long residence in Rockville ever been actively enlisted, by personal effort and generous pecuniary aid, in the advancement of all public improvements, and in the widest possible dissemination of intelligence through the medium of the public schools.

Mr. Maxwell was married, November 3, 1846, to Harriet, daughter of the late Hon. George Kellogg, the founder of Rockville and a gentleman whose memory is revered by all who ever knew him. They have five children, three sons and two daughters.

[Mr. Maxwell died at his home in Rockville, April 2, 1891, after the above sketch had been prepared. — ED.]

AMOS WHITNEY, HARTFORD: Superintendent The Pratt & Whitney Co.

Amos Whitney, one of the founders of The Pratt & Whitney Co., the largest concern of the kind in the state, was born at Biddeford, Me., Oct. 8, 1833,

and was educated in the common schools at Saccarappa in that state. At the age of twelve he removed to Exeter, N. H., where he remained until he was fourteen years of age. He then entered the employ of the Essex Machine Co. in Lawrence, Mass., and learned the machinist trade. He is one of the most competent mechanical workers in New England and has attained an enviable reputation not only in this country, but abroad. Mr. Whitney came to Hartford forty years ago. In connection with Mr. Francis A. Pratt, who has been for years at the head of the Pratt & Whitney Company, he organized the business, which was begun in the most unassuming manner. The most extravagant dreams

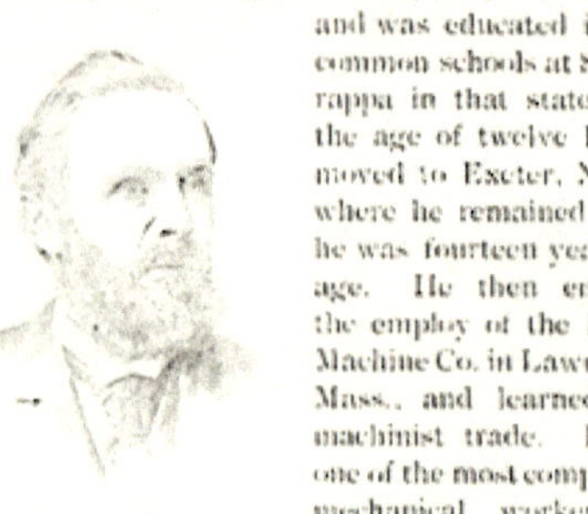

AMOS WHITNEY.

of the founders could not have foreshadowed the success that has attended their work and management. The company is known in every European capital of importance, its productions of machinery and ordnance giving it a world-wide distinction. Mr. Whitney is a gentleman of the most retiring disposition and has declined active participation in public affairs. He is a republican in politics. His religious associations are with the Universalist church. The family of this noted business manager consists of a wife and two children, one son and one daughter. Mrs. Whitney, prior to her marriage, was Miss Laura Johnson. His home is one of delightful social attractions and domestic felicity.

JOSEPH B. PIERCE, HARTFORD: Secretary and Treasurer of the Hartford Steam Boiler Inspection and Insurance Company.

Mr. Pierce was born in that part of Plymouth which is now known as the town of Thomaston, Oct. 13, 1835, and received a common school educa-

tion, preparing him for a business career that has proved exceptionally successful. Prior to his removal to this city he was connected with the Seth Thomas Clock Company. Most of his business life, however, has been associated with insurance interests. He was in the fire insurance business from 1861 until 1873. In March of the latter year

J. B. PIERCE.

he accepted a responsible position with the company which he now represents, and has sustained his share in advancing and promoting its interests. He is a gentleman of exceptional ability in the insurance field, and has had an invaluable experience in the special line of insurance which his company has developed. He is a prominent member of the Fourth Congregational church in this city, chairman of the society's committee, member of the board of deacons, treasurer of the evangelistic fund, secretary of the Hartford Tract Society, and member of the board of trustees of Warburton chapel. He is also the president of the Hartford Manufacturing Company. In politics Secretary Pierce is a republican. His wife, who is still living, was Miss Sophia A. Boardman, daughter of the late Elizur Boardman, and a descendant of one of Hartford's oldest families. The only daughter, Mrs. Arthur H. Merry, is now residing at Augusta, Ga. Mr. Pierce has been a resident of Hartford since 1854, and is thoroughly esteemed and honored in the community.

MILES B. PRESTON, HARTFORD: Sheriff of Hartford County.

Miles Barber Preston was born in Simsbury in May, 1850, his parents being Truman W. and Mary Etta Preston of that town, the latter, whose maiden name was Mary E. Brong, was a native of Addison. N. Y. Her death occurred a few years ago at Culpeper, Va. The father of Sheriff Preston is still living at Hartford, having returned north after the death of his wife in Virginia. The subject of this sketch was educated in the public schools, completing his studies in the private school of the late Rev.

M. B. PRESTON.

O. S. Taylor in Simsbury. Mr. Preston's father was, during this period, the town clerk of Simsbury, this fact in itself opening to him the best opportunities for obtaining a satisfactory education. At an early age Mr. Preston exhibited a decided taste for ornamental painting, and his business career has been shaped in the main by that fact. His father was the proprietor and manager of a carriage shop, and the ornamental work in painting offered special attraction to the son. He learned the trade and at the age of nineteen removed to Hartford, engaging in the railroad shops of the New York & Hartford road. In 1870 he accepted a position of responsibility in the works of John Markham at Pleasant Valley, in Barkhamsted, being placed in charge of the painting department and remaining there three years. In 1873 he returned to Hartford and entered the employ of the H., P. & F. road as an ornamental painter. After spending five years in the company's shops, he decided to engage in business for himself, and bought out the place owned by Theodore Thorpe, Jr., at the corner of Pearl and Trumbull streets. Benjamin W. Kenyon was admitted to partnership with him, the firm being Preston & Kenyon. The business was commenced in 1878 and has developed into one of large proportions. Messrs. Preston & Kenyon unquestionably have the largest amount of sign work of any house in New England outside of Boston. The presidential campaign of 1880 opened an interesting and profitable field of work, the net campaign banner becoming an indispensable adjunct of the canvass. Mr. Preston caught the idea and developed an admirable specialty in connection with it. In 1884 house painting was added to the firm's business, employing a considerable corps of workmen. The firm of Bonner, Preston & Co., which conducts one of the finest trades in the city in its line, was estab-

lished February 4, 1889, its place of business being in the Hills block, opposite Exchange corner. The house carries the largest stock of artists' materials in the state; also extensive lines of photographer's supplies. The firm devotes special attention to wall papers and decorations and altogether employs a force of fifty hands. Mr. Preston is an active participant in both of these firms, being one of the busiest managers in the city.

He was one of the founders and vice-president of the Hubbard Escort, the best political organization in this locality. He has been a member of the Putnam Phalanx for twelve years, and at present occupies the position of quartermaster on the staff of Major O. H. Blanchard. He is a member of Amos Beecher Lodge, F. and A. M., of New Hartford, and belongs to the higher orders of Masonry in this city, being a member of Wolcott Council, Pythagoras Chapter, and Washington Commandery, Knights Templar. He is a past chancellor of Washington Lodge, Knights of Pythias, and is a member of Hartford Lodge of Elks and of Trumbull Council, National Provident Union. His political career has been as honorable as it has been successful. For a number of years he was the chairman of the democratic committee in the first ward in this city. Although the precinct is a republican stronghold it gave Mr. Preston a majority of forty-one for sheriff in November. He was not a resident of the ward at the time and had not been for a considerable period. The tribute was in recognition of his manliness and integrity of character and was the more gratifying as it was spontaneous and unsought. Mr. Preston was one of the East Hartford bridge commissioners at the time it was transferred to the towns of Hartford, East Hartford, Manchester, Glastonbury, and East Windsor. During the administration of President Cleveland he held the responsible position of Deputy United States Marshal in this state, receiving the appointment from Marshal N. D. Bates of Norwich, who made him chief deputy. It was in this office that Sheriff Preston's best official work was executed. He showed marked adaptability for the duties and performed them with exceptional success. When he retired from the deputy's office in 1890 it was with the knowledge that he had won and received the fullest approval from the public. His nomination for sheriff added strength to the democratic ticket from the outset, and his election was by the largest majority of any candidate on the general ticket. Mr. Preston is a member of the First Methodist church in this city and is connected with the Young Men's Christian Association. He has been married twice. His first wife was Miss Hattie H. Seymour, daughter of ex-Sheriff O. D. Seymour of this city. Her death occurred five years ago. The two children, the fruit of this

marriage, died in infancy. The second wife, who
was recently married to Mr. Preston, was Miss
Nellie F. Dole of Springfield, Mass., stepdaughter
of Francis H. Richards of this city, the patent expert and mechanical engineer. The rapid progress
which Sheriff Preston has attained during the past
twelve years, both in business and politics, has
been the result of personal merit. He is profound-
ly interested in the measures and reforms that have
been instituted for the advancement of workingmen, and his sympathies and counsel will invariably be in favor of improving their condition.

JOHN PALMER, BROOKLYN: President Windham County National Bank.

   John Palmer, the son of James B. Palmer, was
born in Ashford, Windham county, Conn., April
24, 1820. His education was acquired in the common schools of his native
town and in Wilbraham
academy. During his mi-
nority he was employed
as a clerk in a country
store in Eastford, and in
1839 removed to Brooklyn,
where he conducted a
mercantile business for
fifteen years, disposing of
his interest in 1854 to a
successor. He was dur-
ing a part of this time
postmaster at Brooklyn,
under the administration

JOHN PALMER.

of Postmaster-General Collamer. Mr. Palmer was
town clerk and treasurer of Brooklyn for five years.
He has held since 1857, and now holds, the office of
secretary and treasurer of the Windham County
Mutual Fire Insurance Company; and is president
of the Windham County National Bank, which position he has occupied since 1880. He is also at
present a trustee of the Brooklyn Savings Bank.
Mr. Palmer has resided in Brooklyn uninterruptedly
for fifty-one years, and his whole life has been one
of distinguished honor and usefulness; while his
name has been closely identified with the successes
of the staunch financial and fiduciary institutions of
which he has been so long the chief or associate
manager. He is a member of the Episcopal church
of Brooklyn, one of the ancient religious societies of
the commonwealth, whose roll of membership has
included some of the most distinguished citizens of
the state in former generations. He is a republican
in politics, having been identified with that party
since its original organization in 1856. Mr. Palmer
was married in 1850 to Miss Frances M. Davison,
daughter of Septimus Davison, Esq., of Brooklyn.
She is still living, with three daughters, Frances L.,
Charlotte H., and Helen M.

HON. PHILIP CORBIN, NEW BRITAIN: Hardware Manufacturer.

   Philip Corbin was born in Willington, October
26, 1824, the son of a farmer with a large family,
whose genealogical tree goes back to the Puritans.

PHILIP CORBIN.

From earliest school age
to nine years he received,
the year through, such
educational advantages as
the common schools af-
forded. From the age of
nine to sixteen he could
attend only the winter
terms, being busy on the
farm at other seasons.
Six full weeks at the
academy completed what
may be technically called
his schooling, but his later
travels, observation, and
wide reading have given him a liberal education.
Two years afterward, or in 1844, he went to New
Britain, where he was apprenticed to North &
Stanley, hardware manufacturers in a small way,
in what was then a village. So thoroughly did he
apply himself to the principles of the business that
when he came of age he applied for and secured a
large contract for some of the best work given out.
For five years he went from success to success, and
then, in 1849, having an ambition not for wealth,
but to become a larger employer of labor, he and
his brother, Mr. Frank Corbin, founded what has
grown into the present extensive hardware manufactory of P. & F. Corbin. It is one of the leading
firms in the country, and employs 1,200 persons in
its various departments. Mr. Corbin has always
been at its head, carrying it through the most dis-
couraging circumstances, with a sagacity that
places him in the front rank of our captains of industry. Ever an active member of the whig party
first, and then of its successor, the republican, he
has never cared for office, content to see, from a
private station, the best interests of the country
conserved. In 1849 he was induced to accept the
position of warden of the borough, and when New
Britain was incorporated became a member of the
common council. The establishment of the water
works was largely his work, and he has served
many years upon the board of water commissioners.
He is also a trustee of the New Britain Savings
Bank. In 1884 he was chosen to the house, and
served as house chairman of the exceedingly important committee on insurance. It was characteristic of him to spend a great deal of time in examining the technical merits of the measures submitted.
His nomination for state senator in the fall of 1888
was wholly unsolicited, but was demanded by the
interests of the district. His election which followed

proved the wisdom of the convention's choice, and gave to the district an able senator and a loyal worker. As in all other fields of service, his experience in the senate chamber was one of great usefulness to his constituents and the state, and of lasting credit to himself.

GEORGE W. FOWLER, HARTFORD: President The Fowler & Miller Company, Commercial Job Printers.

George W. Fowler, who has been at the head of town affairs in Hartford as selectman since 1883, was born in Westfield, Mass., October 15, 1844. He received a public school education, and learned the printer's trade in the office of *The Westfield News Letter.* During the war he was with *The Springfield Republican.* In 1864 he removed to Hartford, and entered the employ of *The Hartford Times.* Eight years were spent in the composing-rooms of that paper. In 1873 Mr. Fowler organized the

G. W. FOWLER.

printing firm of Smith, Fowler & Miller. Afterwards the organization was incorporated under the name of The Fowler & Miller Company. Mr. Fowler became the president, and has since retained that office in the company. He is a man of exceptional business ability, and the company under his management has become one of the leading printing houses in the city. Mr. Fowler entered political life as a member of the council board from the Sixth ward. He represented that precinct in the board of aldermen for eight years, and was one of the best informed members of the city government. He was appointed a member of the special committee on revision of ordinances, serving with Messrs. John H. Brocklesby and Henry E. Taintor. He has been a member of the board of selectmen for eleven years. He was elected to the first place on the board in October, 1882, and has served continuously in that office since 1883. During the past three years he has been nominated by both political parties for the position. During his administration the new almshouse has been erected, and the old town property that was formerly used for the purpose has been transformed into one of the most delightful and attractive sections of the city, increasing the grand list by $200,000. The committee in charge of the sale of the old town property has been composed of First Selectman Fowler, A. E. Burr, E. W.

Parsons, J. W. Dimock, and E. C. Frisbie. Mr. Fowler is also the chairman of the free bridge commission. He is a member of St. John's Lodge, No. 4, F. and A. M., of this city, Hartford Lodge of Elks, Wangunk Tribe of the Improved Order of Red Men, the National Provident Union, and the Gentleman's Driving Club. Mr. Fowler has a wife and one daughter. Mrs. Fowler prior to her marriage was Miss M. Louise Rowles, daughter of Judge Rowles of Tennessee. In politics Mr. Fowler is an out-and-out democrat, and is one of the sincerest leaders of that party in the city. It is an interesting fact that the first selectman and ex-Mayor John G. Root were born in the same town. During Captain Root's administration as mayor the town and municipal departments were under the control of two honored citizens who made their way here from Westfield.

REV. H. MARTIN KELLOGG, LEBANON: Pastor First Congregational Church.

Rev. Henry Martin Kellogg was born at New Boston, N. H., April 2, 1851, and received a collegiate education. He graduated from the Manchester High School in 1868 and from Dartmouth College in the class of 1873. He studied theology at Princeton and in Union Theological Seminary, New York, graduating from the latter in 1876. His pastorates have been First Presbyterian church, Atlantic City, N. J., Congregational church at Francestown, N. H., First Congregational church,

H. M. KELLOGG.

Greenwich, Conn., and the First Congregational church at Lebanon. Mr. Kellogg has been married twice, his first wife being Miss Cora O. Alton, the marriage occurring October 16, 1879. This lady's death took place March 5, 1882. The second wife, who is still living, was Mrs. Stella G. West, the marriage with her being solemnized May 5, 1885. The family includes three daughters. In politics Mr. Kellogg is a prohibitionist. During his college career Mr. Kellogg was a member of the Delta Kappa and the Theta Delta Chi societies. He has been a somewhat extensive writer for the secular and religious press. He is the author of "Twelve Hours with Young People," and "The Genealogy of the Billerica French Family." Mr. Kellogg is an earnest preacher and pastor in the church and is regarded with marked favor in eastern Connecticut.

THOMAS S. WEAVER. HARTFORD: Journalist.

Thomas Snell Weaver was born in Willimantic Feb. 5, 1845. He received a common school education and was one of the graduates of the old stone

school-house, a historical educational institution of Windham county. At fourteen years of age he entered the office of the Willimantic *Journal* to learn the printer's trade, and was engaged there for eight years during a greater part of the time, his father, the late William L. Weaver, being the editor, and for a short time he was editor of that paper himself. He went

T. S. WEAVER.

to Worcester, Mass., in 1867, and after several years connection with the job printing business became attached to the Worcester *Daily Press*, to which daily newspaper he contributed local and paragraphic work. In 1878 he assumed the position of telegraph editor and paragraph writer on the New Haven *Register*, and was connected with that paper for four years, during which time he made a national reputation for writing sentimental and humorous paragraphs, being more widely quoted by the newspaper press of the country than any one in the business, with the exception of "Bob" Burdette. He also did a large share of the editorial work for the *Register*. He assumed a position as a special writer on the Boston *Globe* in 1882, but remained there only a few months. He was then offered the chair of editorial writer on the Hartford *Evening Post*, which position he held for eight years, adding considerably to the reputation of that paper by his sharp political work and brief paragraphs under the head of "Postings." The duties of the position becoming onerous and his health being in danger of breaking down he consented, after repeated urging, to return to Willimantic and assume the editorship of the *Journal*, his alma mater. He is now with that weekly, attending to all the multifarious duties which fall to the lot of the editor of a weekly newspaper, doing his own reporting and editorial work. He resides in Hartford, where he has important newspaper connections with out-of-town dailies. He is regarded as a newspaper man of untiring industry and capacity, covering a wider range in his work than almost any other newspaper man in the state. He married Delia A. Chipman of Willimantic in 1870, and has five children, his oldest son being connected with the New Haven *Register* as general reporter. He is prominent in Royal Arcanum circles, and a member of the Grand Council. He is a republican

"from the word go," having cast his first vote for Joseph R. Hawley for governor of Connecticut, and voted the straight republican ticket at each election since. He is a member of the Windsor Avenue Congregational church of Hartford, and has taken a lively interest in its affairs.

WILLIAM HENRY PRESCOTT, ROCKVILLE, Secretary and Treasurer of The White, Corbin & Company.

William H. Prescott is a native of Loudon, New Hampshire, where he was born Aug. 12, 1840. At the age of four years his parents removed to Man-

chester, in the same state, three years later to North Chelmsford, Mass., and again, after two years, to Holyoke, in which latter city his education was chiefly acquired. After ten years in Holyoke, at the age of nineteen, the young man went to Rockville and entered the employ of Messrs. White & Corbin, as accountant in the office of the firm, which had recently com-

W. H. PRESCOTT.

menced the then comparatively new industry of envelope manufacturing by machinery. Mr. Prescott developed at once a very marked ability for business management, and from being frequently consulted by the firm on important issues, he came in a few years to be considered as an indispensable factor in the company's affairs, though not pecuniarily interested therein. In 1866 he was admitted into the firm as a partner, which then became White, Corbin & Company, with the office business entirely in his charge. As time passed, Mr. White, the senior partner, became interested in manufacturing enterprises outside, and the whole burden of management came upon Mr. Prescott. Since the incorporation of "The White, Corbin & Company" in 1881, although Mr. White has occupied the position of president of the corporation, Mr. Prescott has been its secretary, treasurer, and general manager, as well as a director, and has discharged the duties of his position with such masterly ability as to place the company at the head of envelope manufacturers of the country, if not of the world, in point of enterprise, financial strength, and capacity for production. His judgment in all business affairs is rated as of the highest order, in recognition of which every considerable financial concern in the city of Rockville has first or last called him to a place in its management or control. Additionally to the position he occupies in his own company, Mr. Prescott is a director in the American Mills Company, in the First National Bank, in the People's Saving Bank, and in the Rockville Water Power Company; president of the Rockville Mutual Insurance Company, and of the Standard Envelope Company; trustee and director in the Rockville Building and Loan Association; auditor of town accounts; and sustains various minor official relations among the institutions of the town and city. He is an active and influential member of the Union Congregational society, is thoroughly interested in educational affairs, and in all matters appertaining to public improvements. He is a stockholder in nearly or quite every prosperous corporation in Rockville, and owner of much real estate in the city and its vicinity, all acquired by his own individual exertions, and by the careful application of business principles which he had learned by close study and observation to be wisest and best.

Mr. Prescott married Miss Celia E. Keeney, daughter of the late Francis Keeney, who for many years was proprietor of the Rockville hotel, and a highly-esteemed gentleman. They have two children.

COLONEL JACOB L. GREENE, Hartford: President Connecticut Mutual Life Insurance Company.

Jacob L. Greene was born at Waterford, Maine, August 9, 1837. His father, Captain Jacob H. Greene, was a man of staunch character, distinguished for physical vigor, intellectual force, positive convictions, and strong religious views. His mother was a lady of most affable character, winning and graceful in manner, thoroughly intelligent, and earnestly devoted to the welfare and advancement of her children. At an early age the subject of this sketch manifested a strong disposition for study, and

J. L. GREENE.

sought every opportunity within his reach for intellectual attainment. The Michigan University at that time opened its doors without cost, so far as tuition was concerned, and the young student turned his steps thitherward. There he completed his course of studies, and engaged in the practice of law at Lapeer. Hardly had he begun his profession when the war broke out, and he enlisted as a private in the Seventh Michigan infantry, being soon afterward made a commissioned officer. His regiment was ordered to the School of Instruction at Fort Wayne, where it was filled up, and in August was sent to the front. Colonel Greene served until the spring of 1862, advancing to the first lieutenancy of his company. In 1862 he suffered a long and exhaustive illness, prostrating him for an entire year. He recovered, however, during the summer of 1863, and returned to the field; accepted an appointment as assistant adjutant-general on Custer's staff, and served with him until the battle of Trevellyan Station, where he was captured, June 11, 1864. He was in Libby, Macon, and Charleston prisons. While at Charleston he was one of the Union officers placed under the Union fire by the rebel authorities. He was afterward removed to Columbia, where he was paroled and transferred to the Union lines. He was not able, however, to secure an exchange until April 8, 1865. Immediately after his exchange he returned to the front, joining General Custer at Burksville Junction, April 10. After the grand review of the Army of the Potomac at Washington, General Custer was ordered to New Orleans. Colonel Greene accompanied him, and went with him up the Red River to Alexandria, where a division of cavalry was organized. Thence Custer advanced into Texas, having been made commander of the central division of Texas, and of the cavalry in the department, with headquarters at Austin. Colonel Greene was made chief of staff in both commands; meanwhile he had been promoted to the full rank of major, and was brevetted lieutenant-colonel for distinguished gallantry. When Custer was mustered out as a major-general of volunteers, Colonel Greene applied for his muster out, and finally received it in April, 1866, one year after the close of the war. He spent the next four years at Pittsfield, Mass., where he became assistant secretary of the Berkshire Life Insurance Company. He began his insurance career as an agent of that company, but his executive ability soon manifesting itself, he was asked to take a position on the office staff. He was called to Hartford June 1, 1870, as assistant secretary of the Connecticut Mutual Life Insurance Company, was made secretary in April, 1871, and president of the company in March, 1878, succeeding the late President Goodwin. He is at the head of one of the largest insurance organizations in the United States, to which honorable position he brings the qualifications of undoubted ability, the most absolute fidelity, a clear conception of duty, and a loyalty to principle which under no circumstances either surrenders or compromises.

As a citizen, Colonel Greene's abilities and habits of industry lead him into various useful activities. He is a frequent and popular speaker at meetings of religious and scholastic bodies, and has been selected as the orator of the day on several important state occasions. He is senior warden of Trinity church, a leading member of the Church Temperance society, and trustee of the Bishop's fund. He is a director of the Connecticut Trust and Safe Deposit Company, and of the Society for Savings; a director also of the Hartford Fire Insurance Company, and the Phœnix National Bank. His social connections include membership in the Connecticut Society of the Sons of the Revolution, trusteeships in the Watkinson Library, Church Home, and other local organizations; and he is a man of superior intellectual endowments, which render him not only an able business manager, but a thoroughly useful and greatly-valued citizen.

FRANK F. WEBB, WINDHAM: Merchant and Banker.

Frank F. Webb was born in Scotland, November 6, 1852. He is the son of Paschal and Rhoda (Kingsley) Webb, and his father, now some years deceased, is remembered as a man of the highest respectability, who enjoyed the confidence of his townsmen, and was by them frequently during his lifetime called to occupy positions of honor and trust. F. F. Webb lived at home on his father's farm in Scotland during his youth, and had the advantages of the public school there, which were later supplemented

F. F. WEBB.

by a finishing course at the High school in Willimantic. After the death of his father in 1870, the old homestead was sold, and the family moved to Willimantic. Here, after attaining his majority, he embarked in trade with Jerome B. Baldwin, under the firm name of Baldwin & Webb; and for several years conducted a successful business in clothing and furnishing goods. In 1878 he was married to Miss Janette Lincoln of Willimantic. He was elected clerk and treasurer of the borough of Willimantic, and last fall was elected to represent the town of Windham in the state legislature, being the candidate of the democratic party. He is a director in the Windham National Bank and the Willimantic Savings Institute, of which latter he was treasurer for two or three years. He is a member of the Congregational Society of Willimantic.

Mr. Webb is a gentleman of quiet habits, careful and conscientious in his expressions of opinion, of undeviating honor and integrity, and is regarded as an excellent judge of men and affairs from a business standpoint. His mercantile career and brief public service have been alike honorable and successful.

SILAS PALMER ABELL, LEBANON: Farmer.

Silas P. Abell was born in Lebanon, August 10, 1822, the youngest of seven children. His father dying in 1825, and the family not being blessed

S. P. ABELL.

with much of this world's good, the subject of this sketch when nine years of age was put out to work for his board and clothes, and was to attend school in the winter months until sixteen years of age. At the age of sixteen he made another bargain with his employer, in which he was to stay with him until he was twenty-one years of age, and was to receive in addition to his board and clothes, one hundred and twenty-five dollars. Young Abell, by improving time at school and his evenings at home, was able to teach school two winter terms before he was of age, for which his employer received ninety dollars. During all these years there was no written agreement between the parties. The young man was faithful to his employer, and the latter was as kind as a father to his ward. He attended a select school for one term after his "time was out," and continued to work for his old friend during the summers and to teach school during the winters, until he was married. Mr. Abell and his wife live on the same farm still, which they have owned since the death of their old friend. The old gentleman (Col. Julius Clark) died in 1865. Mr. Abell married Miss Sophronia Robinson of Lebanon, March 22, 1846. They have had six children, of whom three are still living, viz.: Mrs. C. A. Brown, Mrs. Elisha P. Spafard, and Myron R. Abell. Mr. Abell has been an assessor, a member of the board of relief, selectman, town agent, notary public, justice of the peace, — appointed to the latter office for the first time in 1850 by the legislature. He has probably written more wills than any other person now living in his part of the town, and has settled, either as executor or administrator, nineteen estates of deceased persons in his district and those adjoining. He was a member of the legislature during the sessions of 1869 and 1880. In his early manhood Mr. Abell was a democrat and voted with that party. He has subsequently been identified with the free soil party, the republican, and the prohibitionists; being led to change his political affiliations first because of his abhorrence of slavery, to which he believed the democratic party to be wedded, and last, for the reason that he held the temperance reform to be paramount in importance to any political party whose platform is not soundly constructed on prohibition principles. Mr. Abell is an independent thinker, and makes it a point to vote as he thinks. He holds no office at present, except that he is clerk of the Congregational church in Lebanon, of which church he was one of the deacons for eighteen years, until he resigned in 1887.

F. W. BRUGGERHOF, NOROTON: Seedsman.

Frederick W. Bruggerhof was born in Prussia, October 15, 1830, and received a thorough public school education. His early life was spent at St. Louis, Mo., but for the past forty-two years he has been a resident of New York city and Connecticut. He is a member of the firm of James M. Thorburn & Co., New York city, being one of the oldest establishments of the kind in the metropolis. It has been in business since 1802, being engaged in the seed trade. Mr. Bruggerhof is the active partner in the concern.

F. W. BRUGGERHOF.

But it is not in business alone that he has attained eminent success. He has also won wide attention in the state of his adoption as a public representative. Mr. Bruggerhof was elected to the house of representatives from Darien on the democratic ticket in 1874, his colleagues from Fairfield county at that time including the Hon. Samuel Fessenden of Stamford, ex-Governor P. C. Lounsbury of Ridgefield, and that old and popular legislator, Cornelius Mead of Greenwich. In 1875 Mr. Bruggerhof was elected to the senate from the Twelfth district, and was chairman of the committee on finance. His associate members in the senate included the Hon. Thomas S. Marlor of Brooklyn, ex-State Comptroller Chauncey Howard of Coventry, the Hon. Caleb B. Bowers of New Haven, and the Hon. Washington F. Willcox, now member of congress from the Second district. In 1876 he was returned from the Twelfth district, his colleagues that year including General S. E. Merwin of New Haven, Edwin A. Buck of Windham, Charles C. Hubbard of Middletown, collector of internal revenue under President Cleveland for the Connecticut district, Congressman Willcox, and ex-Lieutenant-Governor Ephraim H. Hyde of Stafford. Senator Bruggerhof was on the state democratic electoral ticket in 1884, being one of the electors-at-large, and had the satisfaction of casting his electoral vote for Grover Cleveland, who was elected to the presidency. Politically, as well as from a business point of view, the ex-senator from

the Twelfth has won gratifying distinction and success. He is connected with the Presbyterian church. The wife of Senator Bruggerhof, who was Miss Cordelia E. Andreas of New York city, is living. The family includes one son and four daughters. The oldest daughter is the wife of W. N. Capen, Esq., of New York city. The second is the wife of E. C. Hoyt, son of the late Senator Oliver Hoyt of Stamford. The third is the wife of A. H. Smith, son of Commodore James D. Smith of Stamford, ex-treasurer of the state under Governor Bigelow. The fourth daughter is the wife of Franklin M. Jones, a member of the banking house of J. D. Smith & Co. of New York city. The son, Edward Everett Bruggerhof, was lately married to Miss Lucy F. Otis of Yonkers, N. Y.

FRANCIS B. ALLEN, HARTFORD: Second Vice-President Hartford Steam Boiler Inspection and Insurance Company.

Francis Burke Allen was born in Baltimore, Md., in 1841, and received a thorough education, preparing him for the avocation of a mechanical engineer. In February, 1862, he was appointed in the engineer corps, United States navy, from Illinois, remaining in active service until 1868. He was with various ships and squadrons, and on special duty in New York during the entire period. His service through the war was exceptionally creditable. In 1868 he resigned his commission in the navy to enter the service

F. B. ALLEN.

of the Novelty Iron works in New York. Afterwards he was assistant to the superintendent of motive power on the Northern Pacific R.R. In 1872 he became the special agent of the Hartford Steam Boiler Inspection and Insurance Company in the New York department. In 1882 he was promoted to the position of supervising general agent in the home office, and in 1888 was made second vice-president of the company. His department involves a general supervision of the company's business in the field and the superintendency of agents. Mr. Allen is exceptionally adapted to this work by training and experience. He is connected with the American Society of Mechanical Engineers of New York, the American Society of Naval Engineers, Washington, D. C., the Marine Engineers' Society of New York, the National Association of Stationary Engineers; and is lieutenant commander of the National Association of Naval Veterans, vice-president of the Naval Veteran Association of Connccticut, member of the Army and Navy Club of Connecticut, and of Robert O. Tyler Post, G. A. R. He is the senior aid on the staff of Commander Wells, N. A. of N. V., and is one of the most popular of the naval veterans of this state. He has resided in Portland, Me., Philadelphia, Chicago, and New York, and is widely known by reason of his business and naval associations. Mr. Allen is a member of the Congregational church, and a gentleman of the most enjoyable personality. He has a family, consisting of a wife and five children. The name of Mrs. Allen prior to marriage was Miss Margaret Louise Williams. In politics Mr. Allen is a republican.

EDGAR D. WHITE, ANDOVER: Farmer.

Edgar D. White was born at Andover in this state February 20, 1848. He was educated at the public schools of Andover and the select schools of

E. D. WHITE.

that town and of Willimantic. He began teaching at the age of seventeen, an occupation which he followed most of the time winters and part of the time throughout the year, until he arrived at the age of thirty-nine. During this time the larger part of his summers have been spent on the farm, and a portion of the time he has been employed in bookkeeping and as railroad station agent. For the past few years a large part of his time has been and is now being spent in settling estates of deceased persons and in various positions of trust. He has been elected to office by his school district, town, and church, having been almost constantly in office from the age of twenty-one to the present time. He has served his town as school visitor, assessor, grand juror, and auditor, and is at present a member of the school board. He is a member, as well as deacon, clerk, treasurer, and Sabbath-school superintendent, of the Andover Baptist church.

Mr. White married, at the age of twenty-one, Miss Lydia A., daughter of Norman Sprague of Andover. They have one daughter, an only child. Politically he has been a lifelong democrat. His home has always been in Andover, although his labors have temporarily located him in New Britain, Coventry, and Columbia. He has served as clerk of the probate court for four years, ending in January of the present year. He is guardian of two boys, aged respectively thirteen and fifteen years — the sons of a cousin.

JAMES MONROE GILLMORE, ROCKVILLE: Photographic Artist.

The subject of this sketch was born at Gillmore's Hill, in Stafford, Tolland county, in this state, December 31, 1838, being of the second generation

J. M. GILLMORE.

from Captain Nathaniel Gillmore, who settled at that place in the early history of the town. His father, William Gillmore, was a man of strong character and occupied prominent places of public trust in civil and military affairs during his lifetime as well as conducting important manufacturing enterprises on his own account. It may be mentioned that Nathaniel Gillmore, in his day, held a commission as commander of a "troop of cavalry," the original of which document is in the hands of James M. Gillmore, signed by Governor Jonathan Trumbull — who was a son of the famed war governor of Connecticut, and a tried and trusted friend of General George Washington — and by Samuel Wyllis as secretary. Also that the first military commission of William Gillmore was signed by Governor Henry Edwards; while his appointment "to be colonel of the Nineteenth regiment" bears the signature of Governor William W. Ellsworth, and is dated May 28, 1838, being less than a year prior to the birth of the subject of this sketch. The elder Gillmores, not unlike many of their New England contemporaries, were hardy, self-reliant, and resolute people, accustomed to the hardships of long journeys on foot, and to personal undertakings which would appall the present generation. Young Gillmore was nurtured and trained in the same sturdy line of moral, religious, and business economics that characterized his ancestors, and thus received a thorough preparation for all the active duties of his later life. His education was such as could be obtained in the common schools of his time, and was of the practical, rather than the ornamental, type. It proved to be sufficient, however, with the advantages he has taken of observation and experience, to enable him to occupy and adorn the many social and civil positions he has been called upon to fill. His first start in business was made at the age of eighteen years, when his father sent him to Hinsdale, Mass., to establish a branch of his foundry and iron works in that place. He executed the trust in a successful and satisfactory manner. Two years later he went to Springfield, Mass., and turned his attention to art works, and subsequently adopted photography as a profession; since which time he has had art rooms in various places in New York and the New England states. His studios have invariably been the resort of patrons of æsthetic taste and culture, and his productions have borne favorable comparison with those of the best artists in this or any other country. He has for some years conducted a flourishing business in the city of Rockville, where he is now permanently located.

Mr. Gillmore married, in July, 1864, Abbie M., daughter of Silas Batchelder of Canterbury, N. H. She is a direct descendant on her father's side from a branch of the Kimball family, which was distinguished in central and southern New England for its probity, sound sense, and general thrift. They have two daughters, Jennie and Josie, bright and interesting girls, who are the pride and light of their domestic circle.

Mr. Gillmore's connection with social and fraternal organizations are numerous and honorable. He has been a member of the Masonic fraternity for thirty-two years, and is now senior warden of the Blue Lodge, King of the Chapter and Captain of the Guard in the Council. He is a charter member and vice chancellor of Damon Lodge, K. of P., a member of the organization of American Mechanics, and of the Rockville republican club, with which political party he has been identified all his life. In all masonic organizations and gatherings he bears an intelligent and active part, and is held to be a master workman and authority in the ritualistic ceremonies, fundamental laws, and constitutional spirit of the order. The circle of his official and personal friendships is thus wide and still extending, including the best social element of his city and the state.

JOHN HENRY GATES, North Branford; Farmer.

Mr. Gates was born, and has always lived, in North Branford. The date of his birth is recorded as April 29, 1831. He was married January 3, 1858, to Miss Sara Louisa Todd, who, with two sons and one daughter, is still living. He was a tax collector in 1870, and in 1889 represented the town of North Branford in the state legislature. He attends the Congregational church of his place, and for twenty-six years has been the librarian of its Sunday-school. In politics Mr. Gates is a republican. He cast his first

J. H. GATES.

vote in 1856 for John C. Fremont, and has voted at every presidential election since, save one.

JOHN K. BUCKLYN, Mystic; President and Principal Mystic Valley Institute.

John Knight Bucklyn is a native of Rhode Island, in which state he was born March 15, 1834. He was educated at Smithville Seminary and Brown University. Most of his life has been spent as a teacher, preacher, and lecturer. A part of early manhood was passed in the machinist business. Principal Bucklyn graduated from Brown University in 1861. He was a member of the Phi Beta Kappa society while in college. Immediately after graduation, he enlisted in Battery E, First Rhode Island Light Artillery,

J. K. BUCKLYN.

and was mustered Sept. 1, 1861, and won an honorable record in the war. He was commissioned second lieutenant March 1, 1862, and first lieutenant in December of the same year. Oct. 19, 1864, he was made captain by brevet "for gallant, meritorious, and often distinguished services before Richmond and in the Shenandoah Valley," and received a full commission as captain in 1865. He participated in forty-five battles and was wounded at Fredericksburg. He was also shot while commanding his battery at Gettysburg. In 1864–65 he was on staff duty at the headquarters of the Sixth Corps, Army of the Potomac, which was commanded by Connecticut's most distinguished soldier, Gen. Sedgwick. After returning from the war he became the principal of the public school in Mystic, and remained in that position until 1868. He founded the Mystic Valley Institute in 1868, and has since been the principal of the school, which has attained decided success in its field. The institute was chartered in 1880. During that year Principal Bucklyn traveled in Europe extensively. He has also spent considerable time in visiting the states of the Union east of the Rocky Mountains, acquiring material for his profession and work. He is the commander of Williams Post, G. A. R., member of the New London County Historical Society, also of the Rhode Island Historical Society of Soldiers and Sailors, and of the Loyal Legion. He is a member of the Baptist church and has been a superintendent of Sunday-school work for twenty years. He has held the office of school visitor and is a notary public. In politics he is a republican. Principal Bucklyn was married by the Rev. Dr. Swaine in the Central Congregational church at Providence, Jan. 9, 1864, his bride being Miss Mary McKee Young, daughter of Edward R. Young. He has two sons, John K., Jr., and Frank A. Bucklyn, both of whom are graduates of the Mystic Valley Institute and the New York Medical College. Both are practicing. Mrs. Bucklyn, wife of the principal, is living, and has been an earnest and efficient participant in the work of the institute. The present faculty of the school consists of John K. Bucklyn, A.M., LL.D., John K. Bucklyn, Jr., M.D., Frank A. Bucklyn, M.D., Miss Ella M. Addis, A.B.

HON. LEVERETT BRAINARD, HARTFORD: President of The Case, Lockwood & Brainard Company.

Mr. Brainard is one of the most prominent and successful business men in the state. He was born in Westchester Society, Colchester, Feb. 13, 1828,

LEVERETT BRAINARD.

and was educated in the public schools and Bacon Academy in that town. From the age of thirteen years, when he was left in charge of the old homestead in Westchester on account of the death of his father, he has been the architect of his own success in life. The standing which he has won as a business manager in Connecticut will show the character of his work. He is at the head of the largest printing establishment in the state, a director in the Ætna Life Insurance Company, the New York, New Haven & Hartford Railroad, the Ætna National and State Savings Banks, the Orient Fire Insurance Company, the Connecticut General Life, and in the Hartford Silver Plate Company, and is the president of the Hartford Paper Company. A portion of his early life was spent in the state of Pennsylvania. In 1853 he became a resident of Hartford, coming here as the first secretary of the City Fire Insurance Company. He remained with this institution until he became one of the active partners of the firm of Case, Lockwood & Co. When the present company was incorporated by the legislature, he became the secretary and treasurer, retaining the position until 1891, when he succeeded the late Newton Case in the presidency. Mr. Brainard has been a member of the court of common council of the city of Hartford, and represented the town in the legislature in 1884. He was appointed house chairman of the committee on railroads, and rendered in that capacity invaluable service in the legislature. In 1890 he was appointed at the head of the world's fair commission from this state, his principal associate being ex-Governor T. M. Waller. Mr. Brainard was appointed by the joint members of the commission at Chicago as chairman of the committee on manufactures, in all respects the most important of the working committees of the commission. The selection of a citizen from Connecticut for this responsible place was a high compliment to the state, not less than to the gentleman upon whom the honor was conferred. In politics he is a republican, and has been a distinguished representative of that party's interests from the outset of his public career. He is a member of the Pearl Street Congregational Society in Hartford. His wife, who was Miss Mary J. Bulkeley prior to her marriage, was a daughter of the late Hon. E. A. Bulkeley of Hartford, the founder of the Ætna Life Insurance Company. Mrs. Brainard is a sister of Governor Morgan G. Bulkeley, and of ex-Lieutenant-Governor William H. Bulkeley. There are seven children in Mr. Brainard's family, the home being on Washington street.

JOSEPH DANA BARTLEY, BRIDGEPORT: Educator and Author.

Joseph Dana Bartley was born in Hampstead, N. H., September 17, 1838. His father was Rev. John M. C. Bartley, who was pastor of the Con-

J. D. BARTLEY.

gregational church of that town for over twenty years. His paternal grandfather was Dr. Robert Bartley, who was educated in Edinburgh University, Scotland. His mother, Susan Dana, was the daughter of Rev. Daniel Dana, D.D., who was a pastor in Newburyport for over fifty years, and was for one year president of Dartmouth College. His great-grandfather, Joseph Dana, was pastor of the South church of Ipswich, Mass., for sixty-two years. Mr. Bartley was fitted for college at the academy in Atkinson, N. H., and took the regular course at Williams, graduating in 1859. We quote the following from the quarter-centennial report of his class.

"After graduation, he spent one year of theological study at Princeton, and then became assistant in the academy at Blairstown, N. J., and afterwards, principal of the Susquehanna Institute at Duncannon, Pa. In 1863 he was called to the charge of Skaneateles Academy, where he remained till April, 1866, when he became principal of the Female High School at Newburyport, Mass. In 1868 he was elected to the head of the High School of Concord, N. H., and in 1873, in response to a second call, accepted the principalship of the High School at Burlington, Vt., where he remained until 1882, when he took charge of the High School at Bridgeport, Conn., in one of the finest school buildings of the state. He has compiled several school books, made his gift of song useful, and entered generously into all good citizenship. He has had active membership in the Teachers' Associations of the several states of his service, has been vice-president and director of the American Institute of Instruction, member of the New Hampshire Historical Society and of the Philharmonic Society of Burlington, trustee of the Concord Public Library, and examiner of Dartmouth College, had part in the Peace Jubilee at Boston, and has contributed to various educational journals, notably *The New England Journal of Education*, and in all methods, old and new, has kept well at the head of his profession."

In Bridgeport, Mr. Bartley has been a director of the Y. M. C. A. from its foundation, and is vice-president of the Choral Society. He has recently resigned his position in the High School after ten years of service.

SYLVESTER W. TURNER, M.D., CHESTER: Physician.

Sylvester W. Turner, son of Rufus Turner, M.D., and Sarah (Wooster) Turner, was born at Killingworth, Conn., March 12, 1822. At the age of sixteen he entered Yale College, and graduated in 1842. Taught school at Norwalk, Conn., and Newbern, Ala., for a year; then commenced the study of medicine, and in 1846 received the degree of M.D. from Yale. In 1847 he married Gertrude, daughter of the Rev. Sylvester and Lucy Swift Selden of Hebron, Conn. His wife was a descendant of Governor Griswold

S. W. TURNER.

of Connecticut, and also of John Eliot, "The Indian Apostle." She died in May, 1890, leaving a son and two daughters. Since graduation Dr. Turner has been a practicing physician for forty-one years at Chester. He was for seven years clerk and treasurer of the Middlesex County Medical Society, and for three years member of the state board of examiners for the Yale Medical College. He was a delegate to the meetings of the American Medical Association at New Haven, New York, Philadelphia, Washington, and Newport, and since 1880 has been a permanent member

of the association; is also a member of the American Academy of Medicine. He has been for more than thirty years active in educational matters, being during that time secretary of the board and acting school visitor. Was a member of the Connecticut legislature in 1865, at the close of the rebellion. Politically he is an earnest republican. He has been a trustee and director of the Chester Savings Bank since its incorporation in 1871. Is a member of the Congregational church, and president of the Chester Library Association.

JOHN GRAY, M.D., MYSTIC: Physician and Surgeon.

John Gray, M.D., the second eldest of five sons and four daughters of Robert and Sarah Sherman Gray, was born in the town of Plainfield, Windham county, Connecticut, Sep-

JOHN GRAY, M.D.

tember 7, 1824, where he received his early and preliminary education at district, select, and academic schools, and where, at the age of eighteen years, he commenced the study of medicine and surgery under William H. Cogswell, M.D., a highly-esteemed and successful practitioner in that town. From July, 1842, to November, 1844, he was under the able instruction of Fordyce Barker, M.D., at Norwich, Conn., a young physician who had rapidly acquired an enviable reputation for his professional skill, and subsequently occupied the professor's chair of obstetrics in Bellevue Hospital Medical College, New York.

While in Norwich he learned practical pharmacy in the drug store of R. W. Mathewson, M.D. For a brief time after leaving Norwich he was with E. F. Coates, M.D., at Mystic, to assist him in practice. In 1845-6 he attended lectures at the University Medical College, New York. In March, 1846, he permanently located in practice at Mystic, by request of its citizens and the first-settled and oldest physician in the place, Benj. F. Stoddard, M.D., whose esteem, confidence, and professional favors he eminently and gratefully enjoyed up to his death in February, 1848. In connection with his practice he established the first drug store in the place, and has continued it with his son. He has two professional degrees, M.B. and M.D., from Yale College, and is a member of the New London county and state medical societies. He has never published or written any medical work or papers of importance, nor occupied or desired any more prominent position in the profession and general public than to be held in their esteem as strictly honorable, courteous, and a skillful physician. He has filled some town positions of trust, and for eleven years prior to 1869 was acting and commissioned postmaster at Mystic.

He was married July 14, 1847, to Miss Emma Packer, the daughter of M. R. and P. Packer, at Mystic, and has one child only (a son), Mason P. Gray, born April 2, 1850, who is a prosperous pharmacist in the place.

JOSEPH OLCOTT GOODWIN, East Hartford: Town Clerk and Notary Public.

Mr. Goodwin is a descendant in the seventh generation of Ozias Goodwin, one of the first settlers of Hartford. He was born in East Hartford, April 16, 1843, and has always resided in that town, upon land that has been in his family for over two hundred years. He attended the common schools, and afterwards a private school under the veteran teacher, Mr. Salmon Phelps, in East Hartford. His first knowledge of business was obtained in the general store and post-office kept by his father, Edward S. Goodwin, Esq., who was for many years justice of the peace and town clerk, besides holding many other positions which showed the confidence and esteem of his townsmen.

J. O. GOODWIN.

Mr. Goodwin left his father's store in 1862, and learned the printing business in all its details in the office of the Calhoun Brothers of Hartford. With the assistance of two other young men he began in 1863 the publication of a little paper, *The Elm Leaf*, the first newspaper issued for East Hartford readers. In this work he tasted a brief experience of the sweets, and the incidental discipline and fatigues, of the editorial career. He left the printing office in 1871. His evenings and vacations had been devoted to reading and study, and in 1870 a sketch from his pen appeared in *Harpers' Magazine*. He has since contributed occasional articles to Harpers' publications and other periodicals, and has been a frequent contributor to the local press. His leisure time for a number of years was given to the work of gathering material for a history of his native town, and he read a paper on that subject in the lecture course of 1877-8. During the following year he published, "East Hartford: Its History and Traditions." Later he prepared a shorter sketch of the town's history for the Memorial History of Hartford County. In politics, a democrat, he was, in 1874, appointed deputy-registrar for East Hartford, and was, in October of that year, chosen town clerk. He has since been annually re-elected to that office, often by the cordial assent and nomination of both the leading political parties. Chosen a member of the board of school visitors in 1876, he was for a number of years its chairman, — has been acting visitor since 1877, and is secretary and auditor of the board. To his active interest in schools is mainly due the establishment of the high school in East Hartford. In 1878 he was chosen representative by an unusual majority.

Besides the settlement of numerous estates, many minor offices and trusts have been committed to Mr. Goodwin's care. Associated with the Raymond Library Company as one of the original trustees, he is at present one of its directors and its secretary. As town clerk and notary public, Mr. Goodwin has been brought into close intimacy with the public and private business interests of East Hartford. He was married, October 26, 1876, to Hattie J., daughter of Ralph G. Spencer, whose ancestors were among the first settlers of the colony of Connecticut. They have three children. He attends the First Congregational church.

B. G. NORTHROP, LL.D., Clinton: Clergyman, Educator, Author, Lecturer.

Dr. Northrop, the apostle of "Village Improvement," whose name will ever be associated in this land with that important work, is a native of Litchfield county, a section of Connecticut which has been prolific in great men. He was born in the town of Kent, July 18, 1817. Born and bred on a farm, he has carried through his whole life a keen appreciation of the privileges and privations of the farmer's lot. Early in life he experienced difficulties in acquiring a collegiate education,

B. G. NORTHROP.

which inspired him with the lofty resolve of making the public schools in Connecticut free to all. In his youth he manifested a fondness for trees and tree-planting, which has grown with his growth, till he has become their foremost advocate. His life, both in Yale College and the Yale Theological Seminary, was characterized by the same faithful energy which enabled him to surmount all difficulties in preparing for college. Before and after graduating he taught, in all, two years. During his ten years' pastorate of a Congregational church in Framingham, Mass., his intelligent and efficient interest in the schools of his town soon attracted attention, and introduced him to a wider sphere of usefulness. For nearly eleven years he was agent of the Massachusetts board of education, when his services were required by his native state, and he was made secretary of the Connecticut board of education. This responsible position he held for sixteen years, during which, in the face of an opposition which would have daunted any less determined advocate, he was the leading agent in making the schools of Connecticut by law free to all. This period of over twenty-six years' service in state supervision of schools is believed to be longer than the similar service of any other person in this country. In 1867 the Massachusetts board of education expressed " much regret at his resignation of the office he has filled with great ability and acceptance, and their high appreciation of his fidelity and devotion to his duties, and the good he has accomplished for the schools of Massachusetts." Similarly, the report of the Connecticut board of education, issued in January, 1883, contains a very complimentary review of his labors during the sixteen years of his administration, " which produced lasting and important results of great benefit to the entire state."

The nation is especially indebted to Dr. Northrop for what is known as " Arbor Day in schools," an idea suggested by him eight years ago, and since then so efficiently urged and supported by him that thirty-eight states have adopted the day. The number of trees planted by school children under the stimulus of Arbor-day observance in these different states, within the period included, already reaches into the millions — a result whose present and prospective importance and value can hardly be estimated. He has given a great deal of voluntary, unpaid labor to the general cause of village improvement in the past sixteen years, and villages on both sides of the Connecticut river, and beyond the borders of New England, across the continent and in California, eloquently attest his success in interesting not only the boys and girls in the schools, but also the grown folks, in the good work of making the home and the town beautiful.

Dr. Northrop has twice visited Europe, and has found time, in his busy life, to write a number of valuable and timely books and pamphlets. He has lectured widely over the country, on the lyceum platform, in normal schools, academies, colleges, and educational conventions, including a course of twelve lectures before the Lowell Institute of Boston, and two courses before the Peabody Institute of Baltimore. His tall, commanding figure, earnest,

nervous manner, readiness of apt illustration, suiting specific advice to special needs, forces home his views far more vividly than is possible to the printed page.

Dr. Northrop was married early in life to Miss Harriette E. Chichester, and they have two children. His political affiliations are with the republican party.

CAPTAIN LEVI FRISBE SCOTT, BETHLEHEM: Farmer.

Levi F. Scott was born in Bethlehem, Conn., Nov. 11, 1818. He had only a common school education; has always been a farmer, and always lived, and now lives, on the same farm on which his father, grandfather, and great-grandfather lived. He had, in his youth, only limited means; but by his energy and perseverance, he has worked himself up to the top of a farmer's calling. At the age of eighteen he was enrolled in an infantry company in his own town, was chosen corporal, and went up, step by step, to be

captain of the company, which office he held for several years. He had the best drilled company in his regiment, and, at a meeting of the officers, he was chosen colonel, but declined the office. He was, however, strongly urged by his superior officers to accept, as he owed the honor to the regiment and the regiment owed the same to him, but he still declined.

At the age of twenty-one he joined the Congregational society, and has been a faithful worker in it over fifty years, and has held many of its offices of trust. Soon after joining the society he also united with the church, and has always maintained an exemplary Christian life. On Nov. 11, 1850, he married Miss Emiline Young, a near relative of the late Governor Young of New York. Mrs. Scott died Jan. 21, 1890, deeply mourned by all who knew her. She left one son and one daughter, both of whom are still living. In 1880 Mr. Scott was invited by Secretary T. S. Gold to deliver a lecture on " Farm Life " before the state board of agriculture, held at Newtown. He gave another lecture before the same board in 1883, held at Waterbury. He has also delivered lectures upon different subjects in all the towns around him, and in some of them he has appeared several times; his knowledge, wit, and sound logic drawing a full house. He has also written for different agricultural papers all over the country. His treatment of his theme has always been reasonable and persuasive, taken from experience and observation. He has spoken before farmers' clubs and granges many times, but never till 1891 did he unite with the grange, when one was formed in his own town. Previous to this he had been president of a farmers' club. He has held offices of honor and trust in the town of which he has always been a citizen, and has been a leading temperance advocate in Bethlehem, and several places where liquor was sold were broken up through his influence and writings. He was director in a fire insurance company fifteen years.

BARNEY BARZILLAI GIBBS, BLOOMFIELD: Pastor Baptist Church.

The subject of this sketch was born Jan. 13, 1822. Early in the seventeenth century three brothers Gibbs, from Scotland on the English border, settled on Long Island, N. Y. The son of one of them, Samuel Gibbs, moved into New Jersey about 1750. Leaving there, he settled in Genoa, Cayuga County, now Lansing in Tompkins County, N. Y., on a farm four miles north of the present beautiful city of Ithaca. Mr. Gibbs' father lived on that farm sixty-six years. He died there March 5, 1857. The

F. B. GIBBS.

maternal grandparents, Oliver Bigelow and Esther Harding, born in Colchester, Conn., in 1759, belonged to most worthy and patriotic families, well known in the early history of the commonwealth of Connecticut. Having finished a course of academic study, Oliver Bigelow enlisted as a soldier in the army of the revolution. After the war he graduated from a medical course. For a short time he practiced medicine in Goshen, N. Y., to which place the Hardings and others went, in consequence of the desolation of the Wyoming Valley, where they had settled before the war. They afterward left Goshen and returned to the valley. At the time of the memorable "Wyoming Massacre" in 1778, when the fort was about to fall into the hands of Indians, two brothers of Esther Harding were slain. The lead in the fort was buried. Esther, then eighteen years old, assisted by a colored girl, took the powder in a leather sack to the river and sunk it. Though seen by the savages, they reached the fort in safety. For six months Esther was a captive among the Indians. Dr. Oliver Bigelow and Esther Harding were married in 1786. To them were born five daughters and

one son. The eldest of these, Nancy, married Gerritt Goodwin Gibbs (son of Samuel above mentioned). They had four sons and four daughters. Of these children, Barney Barzillai, the subject of this notice, was the fifth, and the third son. As to health, he was never strong. His grandmother Bigelow used to tell him that God had spared his life in answer to her prayer, and that he would have to preach. His eldest sister was the special instrument, through grace, in awakening him to a sense of his need of God's mercy. While in his academic course he professed faith in Christ. Dr. John S. Maginis, president of "The Hamilton Literary and Theological Institution," baptized him into the fellowship of the Baptist church of Hamilton, N. Y., Nov. 18, 1839. His father designed him for the legal profession; but he chose the ministry of the gospel. Graduating from "Madison," now "Colgate University," in 1846, and from the Theological Seminary in 1848, he was ordained to the work of the gospel ministry at Ithaca, N. Y., a few weeks after. He went south that fall, into the Mississippi Valley. He spent a few months in Southwest Louisiana, in the "Attackapa Country," seeing slavery there on the sugar plantations, in, perhaps, its severest forms. The next year was spent in middle Mississippi, preaching to three churches, and to several congregations of slaves, in the four counties of Yazoo, Warren, Hinds, and Madison. He rode 3,000 miles on horseback and 2,000 by steam that year. In 1851 he took the pastorate of the Wall Street Baptist Church in Natchez, Miss. He was married that year to Miss Eliza E. Poyer of North Norwich, N. Y. His labors in Natchez were greatly prospered. Beginning with a new church of eighteen members, he left it, after three years and six months, with one hundred and seventy-seven communicants. The sickness of his wife called him north. In a few weeks she passed away. He did not return south, but supplied various pulpits and labored as evangelist. In 1855 he became pastor of the Baptist church in Geneva, N. Y. In 1857 he was married to the daughter of Colonel Samuel Hartwell of Chenango County, N. Y. He has three sons. Dr. Charles B., of New York, Herbert H., attorney and counsellor in the city of New York, and Clesson F. Gibbs, D.D.S., of Bridgeport, Conn.

Mr. Gibbs has said: "Had I given myself especially to evangelistic work I should have accomplished more." Possibly, yet his pastorates have been successful. The condition at Geneva was low, house sadly out of repair, and congregation small. But stimulus came; the attendance increased, and additions gave strength and courage. The work with the church in Jordan, N. Y., was one of correction and earnest labor to lead the membership to deeper spirituality. Returning to

Geneva, in a second pastorate there he succeeded in inspiring the people with a better apprehension of Christian life and to higher motives in gospel work. Prosperity followed, and the impulse then given lingers there to this day.

In 1865 his mother (widowed and alone) urged him to come home. He thought change for a time would be advantageous. He went; but the cares of the farm and the wear and tear of much travel in supplying neighboring churches caused him to accept, after two years, the pastorate of the church at Union Springs, N. Y. Four years of ordinary prosperity were had there. He went to Spencer, N. Y., in 1871 — a country field, ten miles across it, with many outposts for service. Additions strengthened the church; expensive repairs greatly improved the house; but the pastor's health failed. He was called to New York city, where he worked with varying success nearly five years. He suffered much there from malaria. Going to Catskill on the Hudson, his health began immediately to improve. Five years there, beginning with conditions of disorder and discouragement, were favored with much success. Two years were spent in Wales, Mass., with the Baptist church.

Mr. Gibbs considers that the gospel supplies the true grounds of culture and advancement for all people. His six years in the south were a most interesting and valuable experience. They supplied him with more intelligent thought on the great national issues of the day; assured him of the need of sounder ethical principles in our civil government; showed him that the people, north and south, should have more intimate acquaintance in social, political, and commercial matters; that such acquaintance would check the growing strife, and modify the bitterness of discussion. The late Jefferson Davis was then rising to the acme of southern popularity. In the senate chamber of Mississippi, he heard Mr. Davis in his famous and eloquent eulogy of Calhoun, and felt that a crisis was near at hand. But his southern life supplied him neither with feeling nor argument for slavery. As a gospel minister he had to do with the highest interests of both master and slave. He has, therefore, always held it both as privilege and duty to notice the fact that he was never hindered, but often encouraged, in his labors for the slave; and he felt himself respected and trusted by the southern people. Ten miles from Jackson, the state capital, in the little town of Raymond, rumor said one morning that a slave had been killed. Mr. Gibbs was assisting the pastor there as evangelist. The excitement called a meeting of planters, at once, over which he presided as chairman. He, with a committee of planters, investigated the case, and reported the next day that the slave had been cruelly beaten *with a hand-saw*, but that he

would recover. The meeting censured the master, and required of him a promise of humane treatment for the future.

Mr. Gibbs has given forty-three years to his chosen work — the highest of earthly callings. Loyalty to truth has marked his course. He is now in Bloomfield, Conn. His work there will appear more fully in the future. Extreme conservatism is tenacious, and also persistent; not to be changed in a day. Connecticut was the home of some of his ancestors. The interests of the state and people he cherishes with special regard, confiding in the appointed instrumentalities of truth. Another says, " The garment of praise must be the outgrowth of the inner life;" and it is wise to remember that —

> " Across the fields of toil there fall
> The notes of yonder sunset bell."

HON. WASHINGTON F. WILLCOX, Chester: Congressman, Second District.

Washington F. Willcox was born in Killingworth August 22, 1834. He remained at home with his father, who was a farmer, until sixteen years of age. He attended the common district schools, and subsequently a select school conducted by Rev. Mr. Bell, pastor of the Congregational church of Killingworth, from whom he also received private instruction for several years in the higher English branches and in Latin. Subsequently he entered the Hopkins Grammar School at New Haven, where he prepared

W. F. WILLCOX.

for college, but entered the Yale Law School, from which he graduated in 1861. The same year he was admitted to the bar in Middlesex county, and opened a law office in Deep River, where he has since continued the practice of law. During the years 1862 and 1863 he represented his native town in the lower house of the legislature; was elected to the state senate in 1875–6, serving as chairman of the judiciary committee during two terms. In 1875 he was appointed state attorney for Middlesex county, which office he held for eight years. He was elected to the fifty-first congress as a democrat, receiving 24,959 votes, against 24,161 for the republican candidate and 1,165 scattering.

Mr. Willcox was married January 1, 1868, to Salome C. Denison, who is now living, a daughter of the late Judge Socrates Denison of Chester. They have four children, the issue of their said marriage, two daughters and two sons.

FREEMAN M. BROWN, HARTFORD.

Mr. Brown comes of revolutionary stock, his maternal grandfather having enlisted from Rhode Island and served through the war as a private.

F. M. BROWN.

He was born in the town of Union, February 26, 1817, but soon afterwards his father removed with his family to the neighboring town of Stafford, where his boyhood was chiefly spent upon the farm. He attended the district schools until he became fifteen years of age, when he entered a store at Southbridge, Mass., as clerk and learned the business which he followed through much of his later life. He commenced mercantile business for himself in Stafford in 1838, and while there held the office of deputy sheriff for Tolland county. In 1843 associated with Dwight Slate (now of Hartford) under the firm name of Slate & Brown, he removed to Windsor Locks and was engaged in mercantile pursuits and the manufacture of general machinery, putting up a building therefor, which was the first movement in the growth of that village. This firm made the first one thousand pistol barrels and cylinders for Colt's revolvers, which were ordered by the United States government before Colonel Colt had any facilities whatever for the manufacture of fire arms. During his residence at Windsor Locks, covering a period of nearly twenty-five years, he was largely engaged in building, completing more private residences and tenement-houses than any other single individual in the place. While at the Locks, he was also a part owner in and agent for a woolen manufacturing establishment known as the Sequassen Woolen Company, located at Windsor. He held the office of postmaster there for several years, was also selectman, town clerk, a member of the board of education, and represented the town of Windsor in the legislature during the sessions of 1847 and 1853, and Windsor Locks in 1864 and 1868. He afterwards removed to Hartford, and since his residence in this city has been deputy internal revenue collector for four years and selectman during one year. He also acted as census enumerator in 1890. His business connections are now with the Beach Manufacturing Company of Hartford. Major Brown has been for twenty years a member of the Putnam Phalanx, and was for nearly eight years major of the command. He was also a member of the Odd Fellows' fraternity, and was grand master of the grand lodge of Connecticut in 1855-56. He is a member of the First Universalist society of Hartford; in politics he is a democrat. The major is living with his second wife and has three surviving children, two by his first wife and one by the second. He has traveled very extensively in all parts of the country and for twenty-five years was among the farmers of the west and northwest, buying wool. His life has been one of great activity and usefulness, and he has performed his share of public service, always discharging with fidelity and a good conscience the trusts that have been committed to his charge.

ANDREW YALE BEACH, SEYMOUR: Merchant.

Andrew Y. Beach was born in Derby, Conn., in that part of the town which is now Seymour, October 27, 1836. His father is Sharon Y. Beach of the same town, and his mother's maiden name was Adeline Sperry. Mr.

A. Y. BEACH.

Beach lived at Seymour until he was 20 years old, attending the public schools in his native town, and being for a while a student at the West Rock Seminary at New Haven. Previous to leaving home he was employed in his father's paper mill at Seymour. In 1856 he went to Springfield, Mass., and was clerk in the freight office of the Hartford & New Haven Railroad Company, which position he held for nearly two years, resigning to accept the agency of the Naugatuck Railroad at Naugatuck. Later Mr. Beach was appointed agent for the same road at Seymour, holding that position till 1867, when he was appointed general ticket agent of the road, with headquarters at Bridgeport. He held this position five years, making thirteen years in the employ of the Naugatuck Railroad Company. Mr. Beach resigned his position with the Naugatuck Railroad and removed to Springfield, Mass., in 1872, to become agent of the New York, New Haven & Hartford Railroad, having entire charge of the company's business in Springfield, excepting the ticket department. This position he held until June, 1887, when, owing to a much-needed rest, he resigned and removed to Seymour, where, after a few months of rest, he engaged in the coal and grocery business, in which occupation he is still engaged.

Mr. Beach's political record has always been that of a republican. He was a member of the Springfield board of aldermen in 1884, 1885, and 1886, the latter year being honored with the presidency of the board. During the years in Springfield he made his church home with the State street Baptist people, by whom he was highly esteemed, and was frequently called on to assist in mission work in different parts of the city. He is a director of the S. Y. Beach Paper Company of Seymour, holding one-fifth of the stock.

Mr. Beach has been twice married. His first wife was Mary C. Woodford, daughter of B. B. Woodford, formerly of Winsted. This union was blessed with one daughter, who is now married and resides in Seymour. His present wife's maiden name was Alice M. Hilton, also born in Seymour, where they now reside.

BENEZET H. BILL, Rockville: Attorney-at-Law.

Benezet Hough Bill, who has held the office of state's attorney in Tolland County since 1869, was born at New Milford, Penn., Feb. 26, 1829, and was educated in the Suffield Literary Institute, the academies at Worcester and Wilbraham, and in the Yale Law School at New Haven, graduating from the latter institution in 1854. Prior to engaging in his profession at Rockville, Mr. Bill resided in Lebanon. He has held a number of town offices and is a useful and valued citizen. In politics he is a re-

B. H. BILL.

publican. He is connected with the Union Congregational society at Rockville. Mr. Bill commenced his professional practice in Rockville when quite a young man, and was for many years a partner with Judge Dwight Loomis of the Superior Court. He established, in a very brief period, not only a remunerative business, but a most excellent reputation as a citizen. He proved himself to be an honorable and public-spirited gentleman, as well as an able attorney, and his townsmen were not slow to recognize his abilities and signify the confidence which they have ever since continued to repose in him. He has for many years occupied a leading position among the lawyers of Rockville, and indeed of all Tolland county; and no citizen of his section has won more honorable distinction in all the walks of public or private life. He is now, and has been for many years, president of the Rockville Savings Bank, one of the old and prosperous institutions of that city.

Mr. Bill has twice married, his first wife being Miss Kate Griggs, daughter of Rev. Dr. Griggs of Bristol. The second wife, who is living, was Miss

Lucinda R., daughter of Mr. Charles Bronson of Waterbury, before her marriage with Mr. Bill. One daughter, Lelia L., married Mr. Charles Phelps of Rockville, but is now deceased. The remaining daughter, Kate E., is the wife of Dr. Thomas F. Rockwell of Rockville.

JOSEPH ANDREWS, West Haven (Orange): Carpenter and Builder.

Joseph Andrews was born in Meriden, February 14, 1832, and was educated in the common schools. He is at present first selectman and town agent in Orange, where he is engaged in the building business. He has held the position of warden of the borough. In politics he is a republican. Mr. Andrews is a past master of Annawan Lodge, F. and A. M. in West Haven, and has been a representative in the Grand Lodge. He has resided in the towns of Wallingford and New Haven, and is prominently known in his sec-

JOSEPH ANDREWS.

tion of the state. His wife, who was Miss Eliza Jane Peck prior to her marriage, is still living. One son is a physician in Buffalo. Mr. Andrews is a member of the Congregational church.

JOHN H. LEAVENWORTH, Roxbury: Farmer.

John H. Leavenworth was born in Roxbury, Aug. 13, 1830, and received a common school and academic education, completing the course in the Woodbury Academy. He has devoted his life to farming and teaching. He commenced the latter pursuit in the public schools of Roxbury and Woodbury when he was seventeen years old, and taught for twenty-nine terms. In 1880 he was a member of the general assembly from Roxbury, serving on the democratic side of the house. He has held all of the impor-

J. H. LEAVENWORTH.

tant town offices, serving as selectman for eight years, member of the board of assessors six, member of the board of relief, juror, and grand juror. For twelve years he was the superintendent of the North Congregational church Sunday-school, which he attended in Woodbury, and is at present a member of the church committee, having declined the chairmanship of the society's committee. Mr. Leavenworth lives in the same home in which he was born sixty years ago. He was married April 12, 1852, to Miss Mary Ann Peck, daughter of Marquis D. Peck. She is still living. The family also includes one son and one daughter. Mr. Leavenworth is a member of King Solomon's Lodge, No. 7, F. and A. M., of Woodbury, and is one of the most honored citizens in the community where he resides.

R. N. FITZGERALD, HARTFORD: Wholesale Merchant.

Ransom N. Fitzgerald was born in Manchester, May 3, 1848, being the youngest son of the well-known paper manufacturer of that town, who was

R. N. FITZGERALD.

engaged in the business upwards of forty years, the firm name being Keney & Fitzgerald. The subject of this sketch was educated in the common schools of Manchester, and at the age of sixteen he commenced learning the business of paper-making in his father's mill. Eventually he was admitted to partnership in the establishment. At the death of his father in 1872 he purchased the mill and formed a partnership with Messrs. George W. Cheney and Edwin Bunce, under the firm name of R. N. Fitzgerald & Co. This partnership existed until 1874, when the mill property was destroyed by fire. Mr. Fitzgerald then removed to Hartford, and purchased the boot and shoe business at No. 201 Main street, conducting it successfully for a number of years. In 1880 he became a partner in the wholesale grocery house of Bronson & Fitzgerald, No. 142 State street, where he is still engaged in business. The firm is widely known through the Connecticut Valley, conducting a large and successful business. Mr. Fitzgerald is a member of the court of common council from the Fourth ward, and represents the council board on the city hall committee. He is a democrat in politics. The councilman was one of the founders, and has been for two years the president, of the Gentleman's Driving Club in this city, and is a prominent member of the Hartford order of Elks. He is a member of LaFayette Lodge, F. A. M., of this city, an officer in Washington Commandery, Knights Templar, and has held various offices in the Scottish Rite bodies. He is also a member of the Mystic Shrine, and has attained to the thirty-second degree in Masonry. Councilman Fitzgerald was married in 1876 to Miss Alice C. Bunce of Manchester, only daughter of the late Edwin Bunce of that town. Mr. and Mrs. Fitzgerald reside at 36 Main street in this city, owning one of the pleasantest residences in that section of the municipality.

CHARLES DENNIS BARNES, SOUTHINGTON: Merchant, and President Southington National Bank.

Charles D. Barnes, senior member of the boot and shoe firm of Charles D. Barnes & Son, was born in Southington, December 12, 1841. He en-

C. D. BARNES.

joyed the ordinary advantages of the district schools, with a finishing experience at the Meriden High School; and became an apprentice at the carpenter's and joiner's trade, which he followed until 1872, and then took charge for two years of the shipping department in the bolt works of the Peck, Stow & Wilcox Company. In 1874 he established the boot and shoe business in Southington now conducted under the firm name of C. D. Barnes & Son. Mr. Barnes sustains official relations with several of the business institutions and corporations of his native town, being secretary, treasurer, and general manager of the Southington Lumber and Feed Company, which position he has occupied since 1881; one of the directors and on the loan committee of the Southington Savings Bank; a director, and elected vice-president, of the Southington National Bank in January, 1889, and appointed president of the institution in January, 1890; also president of the Oak Hill Cemetery Association. He was a selectman and grand juror in 1873; town clerk, treasurer, and registrar of births, marriages, and deaths in 1874, and continuously since with the exception of a single year; also treasurer of the school fund. When the borough of Southington was formed, he was nominated for warden on the only ticket in the field, but declined and was finally persuaded to accept a position as one of the burgesses; and is now on the committee on highways and sidewalks, and chairman of the sewer committee. He is representing the town of Southington in the general assembly the present year, being a member and clerk of the appropriations committee. Among his society connections it may be mentioned that he is vice-president of the Merchants Club of Southington; was one of the charter members of Trumbull

Post, No. 16, Grand Army of the Republic, and its first post commander, holding the office for some years. Mr. Barnes was in active military service during the war of the rebellion. He enlisted in Infantry Company B, Fifteenth Connecticut Volunteers, June 22, 1862, and was with that regiment every time it left camp, until wounded and captured at the battle of Kinston, N. C., March 8, 1865. He spent the remaining time, until Richmond was surrendered, in " Hotel Libby," and was discharged as sergeant, June 9, 1865.

Mr. Barnes has been twice married; first to Sarah E. Hamlin of Southington, in September, 1863, the issue of which marriage was two children, one dying in infancy, the other, a son, Frank H., now living and in business with his father. Mr. Barnes' second marriage was with Sarah H. Gridley, widow of Lieut. Henry Lewis of the Twentieth Connecticut Volunteer Infantry.

Mr. Barnes has always been a staunch republican, as may be inferred from the many positions of trust to which he has been called as the candidate of that party. He is a member of the First Congregational church of Southington, active in church and society work, and in harmony always with whatever is undertaken to elevate and improve the moral and religious status of the community.

JOHN H. LEE, Norwalk: Warden of the Borough.

John Hawley Lee was born in Redding, August 9, 1850, and was educated in the public schools and under Albert B. Hill, tutor at the Sheffield Scientific School in New Haven. Since 1871 he has resided at Norwalk, and is prominently associated with public affairs, as warden or mayor, member of the board of education, school committee, and vice-president of the board of trade. He is a member of St. Paul's Episcopal church, and has been master for three years of St. John's Lodge, No. 6, F. and A.

J. H. LEE.

M., of Norwalk. He was one of the founders of the Masonic Temple, and is third vice-president of the Coöperative Building Bank, located in the World building, N. Y. city. He is a member of the Norwalk Club, its first president for two years, and chairman of the local democratic committee. He is the manager of the Cleveland Baking Powder Company, Boston, Mass. The wife of Mr. Lee was Miss Annie B. Heins prior to her marriage.

KARL GERHARDT, Hartford: Sculptor.

Karl Gerhardt, the artist, whose country house is at Cottage Grove, in Bloomfield, was born in Boston, January 7, 1853, and was educated in Phillips school in that city. He is of German parentage, and is a fluent linguist, speaking English, German, and French gracefully. Mr. Gerhardt, who has attained noted eminence as a sculptor, spent a year and a half in the regular army. He began his business life as a designer of machinery, and first worked with the Ames Manufacturing Company of Chicopee, Mass. In

KARL GERHARDT.

1874 he visited California, and on his return was employed by the Pratt & Whitney Company of Hartford, as a designer in their extensive machine works. While thus engaged he made a bust of his wife in his leisure hours, and subsequently a life-size statue of a " Startled Bather." These two works not only attracted the attention of the Hartford press, but so greatly interested Charles Dudley Warner and Samuel L. Clemens that they requested J. Q. A. Ward, the eminent sculptor, to pay them a visit and examine them. The object of this invitation was to ascertain whether Mr. Gerhardt gave such proofs of talent as would warrant the attempt to raise a sum of money large enough to pay his expenses to Europe, and to educate him under the best masters of the art in Paris. Mr. Ward's opinion was emphatically in favor of the idea. After several efforts to enlist the coöperation of wealthy citizens had failed, Mr. Clemens (" Mark Twain ") and his wife determined to assume the expense themselves, both of travel and maintenance — a pledge which they nobly redeemed, although the fact is known to few persons outside of the sculptor's personal friends. On his arrival at Paris, he successfully passed the preliminary examination. Among sixty competitors, most of them having been favorably circumstanced to study the art, the self-taught Hartford sculptor was recorded as the twenty-eighth. At the end of the first year, Mr. Gerhardt received, in the annual examination, an honorable mention; at the end of the second year he was received at the annual Salon; and in 1884, the last year of his study abroad, *two* pieces were received — " Echo," a marble statuette now in the possession of Mark Twain, and " Eve's Lullaby," a life-size group, which received a diploma of honor at the World's Exposition at New Orleans.

The statue of Nathan Hale, which is stationed in the east corridor of the state capitol, and the bronze statue of Governor R. D. Hubbard on the capitol grounds, were designed by Mr. Gerhardt. Both of these statues have received the highest praise from competent sculptors. The home of Mr. Gerhardt in Bloomfield is a delightful one. Besides the wife who was the inspiration of his first attempts in sculpture, there are two children, daily adding joy and delight to his domestic surroundings. He is connected with the Congregational church and is independent in politics.

CHARLES PHILIP BRADWAY, West Stafford: Inventor, and Manufacturer of Turbine Water Wheels and Motors.

C. P. Bradway was born in South Glastonbury, May 23, 1843. Having completed his education at Monson Academy, he served the Monson firm of

C. P. BRADWAY.

Merrick, Fay & Co., straw hat manufacturers, as boiler tender the following winter. His health becoming delicate, he joined a fishing party, coasting along the New England shore, Sable Island banks, etc., taking the position of cook when at every landing the steward invariably became disabled. Evidence of his early inventive genius may still be seen on the chamber-floor, the pentagonal checker-board, and the old bedstead head-boards of his boyhood's home in Monson, where designs of water-wheels formerly covered every available surface. His knowledge of machinery seemed intuitive. His first water-wheel that came into actual service was used for running the home shop. In its manufacture he obtained permission to use a lathe in a factory, seven miles away, just as the hands were going out to dinner. On their return the superintendent was astonished to find the lad busily at work. "Where did you learn to turn iron?" inquired the superintendent. "Right here," was the reply. In this home shop he spent his spare moments, repairing an infinite variety of articles for the neighboring boys, manufacturing pistols, powder, etc., grinding the latter in a coffee mill and surviving an explosion that singed his eyebrows, and imprinted the form of the dish in his forehead. In the intervals of helping about the farm he also built a saw-mill on the home place, using one of his wheels as motive power. The first wheels for which he received a remuneration were sold to a Mr. Finlay of East Glastonbury and a Mr. Jones of Woodbury, for which he received $150 and $200 re-

spectively. On this wheel he neglected to take out a patent, and the design was appropriated by another. Thus he was obliged to abandon the manufacture of his own invention. He then tried his fortune as a book agent with marked success, in Vermont and Pennsylvania. He afterward fitted up a store in Danville, Pa., from which he equipped scores of agents. It was in Danville that he found his wife, Sarah J. Houghawout. They were married in 1873. Eight children have been born to them, seven of whom are living. Mr. Bradway has been a prominent member of the Y. M. C. A. and is connected with the Congregational church. In politics his principles are republican. Since his return to the east he has purchased a pleasant home in West Stafford, including a large machine shop where he has been engaged in producing cultivators and other agricultural implements in their season, water-motors, and especially the giant turbine wheel, which from the fact of its having twelve gates, it has been suggested should be called the " New Jerusalem."

JESSE MILTON COBURN, M.D., Brooklyn: Physician and Surgeon.

Dr. Jesse Milton Coburn was born in Pittsfield, N. H., March 27, 1853, being a descendant of William Colborne, Esq., herald under Queen Elizabeth

DR. J. M. COBURN.

of Dudley Castle, near Dudley, Worcestershire, Eng. His father was Rev. J. Milton Coburn of Manchester, N. H. Dr. Coburn was educated in the public schools of that city, Pembroke academy, and the Boston University. He pursued his medical studies under Prof. J. H. Woodbury of Boston and received the degree of M.D. at the university in 1874. He commenced the practice of medicine at South Framingham, Mass., but subsequently removed to Shrewsbury, where he married Miss Abbie M. Cutler, daughter of Aaron G. and Lucy Nourse Cutler. In 1880 he settled in Brooklyn, Conn., succeeding to the practice of the late Dr. James B. Whitcomb of that town, where he has since resided. He has an extensive practice and is regarded as one of the most successful physicians in Eastern Connecticut. Dr. Coburn has two sons. He is a member of the Baptist church in Brooklyn and is a prohibitionist in politics. He belongs to the order of Odd Fellows, and is a gentleman of decided popularity in the town where he resides.

JOSEPH SELDEN, NORFOLK: Manufacturer.

Joseph Selden was a member of the general assembly in 1885, serving on the republican side of the house. He is connected with the Ætna Silk Company, and is one of the leading business men in this section of the state. He was born in West Hartford, October 17, 1823, and was educated in the common schools and the Westfield Academy. In the military service he attained the rank of lieutenant-colonel. Prior to his election to the legislature he was honored with political position and had served on the board of

JOSEPH SELDEN.

selectmen. The business life of Colonel Selden has been spent in the town of Norfolk for the most part. A part of his career, however, was passed in Rockville. He has been married twice; his first wife, Lavinia Fuller, died in 1857. The present wife was Miss Emma Fuller. One child is living. Colonel Selden is a member of the Norfolk Congregational church, and is held in high esteem in the community where he resides.

STEPHEN BALL, HARTFORD: Secretary Hartford Life and Annuity Insurance Company.

The accompanying vignette fairly presents the familiar features of Stephen Ball, who for twenty-four years has been officially connected with one of the most popular and progressive life insurance corporations of Connecticut. Mr. Ball is a native of New Haven, where he was born in 1839. Most of his life has been spent in this state, and a large part of his active business experience has been in Hartford with the company in whose service he is still engaged. He was in the employ of the government at New Orleans

STEPHEN BALL.

before coming from that city to Hartford in April, 1867. In the following August he formed a connection with the Hartford Life and Annuity Company as its assistant secretary. In 1874 he became its secretary, and has since been its chief manager. Mr. Ball has a thorough knowledge of the science and practice of life insurance, and in the management of that company he has been instrumental in giving it a reputation and standing which few

kindred corporations have achieved. He is so thoroughly identified with the company that its history is practically his biography. Mr. Ball, at fifty-two years of age, is still in the prime of life, and devoting his undivided energies to the maintenance of the high standard of excellence in life insurance which, under his management, this company long ago reached.

REV. EUGENE MELNOTTE GRANT, STAMFORD: Universalist Clergyman, Editor, and Correspondent.

Mr. Grant was born at Auburn, N. Y., August 29, 1847. His father, Franklin W., was born at Nashua, N. H. The family is descended from a Scotch clan of Grants in the same line with the late General U. S. Grant, but which separated some four generations back. His mother, Miss Sarah Ann Dias, was born of English parents in the city of London, but came to this country when only seven years old, and never returned. The Grant family of the last generation were all educated machinists and successful

E. M. GRANT.

railroad men, Franklin holding various positions, including master machinist, assistant superintendent, and contractor. This made the child life of the subject of this sketch a roving one. Auburn, Syracuse, Corning, Rome, Sackett's Harbor, Cape Vincent, and Buffalo, in New York state, and Toronto, Ontario, were successively places of residence until the family returned to Auburn to settle down. Here the young man was early put to learn the trade of his father, machinist, soon after which the latter died, leaving him the eldest of five children at seventeen years of age, with the responsibility of their maintenance. His trade completed, he accepted a business offer, which he pursued for somewhat more than two years, when his attention was attracted to the ministry. He at once began preparations for study, which ended with the Theological school of St. Lawrence University. His first pastoral settlement was at Madrid, N. Y., in the spring of 1870, some months before leaving school. A year later he removed to Churchville, N. Y., where he was elected standing clerk of the Niagara Association of Universalists, and again to Tidioute, Penn., then a thriving oil town. While there he married Miss Emma E. Pepper, of Little Falls, N. Y. Four children have been born to them, one son and three daughters. A call to a double pastorate at Waterville and West Waterville (now Oakland) took him to Maine, where he held his only public office — that of chairman of the school committee, to which he was elected by a large majority for the purpose of reorganizing and properly grading the public schools, according to his expressed ideas, which was afterwards accomplished to the satisfaction of the town. In the fall of 1876 he accepted a call to the church at Portsmouth, N. H., one of the oldest in the denomination, having had for pastors some of the most noted of her preachers. During a harmonious and successful pastorate of more than five years he held the office of standing clerk of the Rockingham Association of Universalists, and successively trustee and president of the New Hampshire Universalist convention. Late in 1881 he removed to Stamford, Conn., to take charge of the Second Universalist church (the First church being at Long Ridge, in the northern part of the town), where he still continues. Unity and prosperity have accompanied his ten years' pastorate. He has established a promising mission at Mianus, under the care of his church. He and his church are greatly respected, and their works highly commended by the people of the town. Every department of church activity is carefully superintended by the pastor.

Mr. Grant has been active in every effort to promote the welfare of his church in the state, as will appear from the number of offices he holds in her interest. He has been several times elected delegate to the general convention of Universalists, has twice been elected assistant secretary, and by virtue of holding the office of state secretary he becomes a permanent member of that body. He is secretary of the state convention, the executive committee thereof, and the missionary board; is standing clerk of the Southern Association, and secretary of the Connecticut Universalist Club, of which he was one of the founders. He is editor of the Connecticut department of the *Gospel Banner* of Augusta, Me.; Connecticut correspondent of the *Christian Leader* of Boston, Mass., the leading denominational organ in America; and he also edits and publishes *The Message*, a small weekly paper, having the local importance of being the recognized organ and advocate of his own church, the Long Ridge church, and the Mianus mission. He is the author of a vesper service book, and contributor to various publications. He is a Free and Accepted Mason, with the rank of Knight Templar, and an Odd Fellow. He has achieved considerable success during the last half dozen years as the organizer and conductor of summer excursion parties throughout New England, the St. Lawrence, and the Province of Quebec. In politics he has uniformly voted the republican ticket, casting his first vote for his distant relative, General Grant, for president of the United States.

WILBERT N. AUSTIN, Plymouth.

Wilbert N. Austin was born in the town of Goshen, June 23, 1859, and was educated in the Torrington high school. He is the proprietor of

the stage line between Thomaston and Terryville and carries the United States mail. He is a vestryman of St. Peter's church in Plymouth and is thoroughly interested in the work of the church. In politics Mr. Austin is a democrat. He lived in the town of Goshen until he was thirteen years of age, when he removed to Torrington, residing there for five years. Most of

W. N. AUSTIN.

his business life has been spent in Plymouth. He was married in 1882 to Miss Minnie I. Mattoon of Plymouth. They have one son, Ellsworth Wells Austin, born May 23, 1891.

NORRIS BENNET MIX, Hamden: Ice Merchant.

Norris B. Mix is a native of the town of Hamden, and one of a family of ten children. He was born February 3, 1826. His parents being in moderate

circumstances, at the age of ten years the boy was put out to work for his board and clothes with Judge Dyer White in New Haven. While there he had the opportunity of attending John E. Lovell's school, and thus during the four years that he remained with the judge he acquired considerable literary culture. At fourteen he went to Westport to learn the tailor's

N. B. MIX.

trade, but the length of his legs rendered the favorite posture of a tailor uncomfortable, and he abandoned this design and turned his attention to the cabinet-maker's trade, at which he worked until the confinement of indoor-life affected his health. He then for two or three years worked at house-carpentering, and in the open air succeeded in fully regaining his health. Subsequently he was employed in the shops of the New York & New Haven railroad, and in 1864 moved back to Hamden, his native town, where he engaged in and has since followed the ice business. While in New Haven he was elected to the common council and to a place on the board of street commissioners. Afterwards he represented Hamden in the state legislature during the sessions of 1878-79, and for six years served as first selectman of the town, to which position he was chosen as the candidate of the democratic party. Mr. Mix has been many years married, his wife's maiden name being Maria N. Hendrick. They have three children, one of his sons being associated with him in business. He is a member of the Methodist church, of the Odd Fellows, and of the Masonic fraternity.

LUZERNE I. MUNSON, WATERBURY: Druggist.

L. I. Munson was born in Wallingford (Northford Society), in March, 1838. He received a common school education, and also attended for two years the Durham Academy. In 1854, at the age of sixteen, he came to Waterbury and engaged as a boy in the service of Apothecaries' Hall Company, where he remained until 1861, when he went as bookkeeper and shipping clerk with the City Manufacturing Company, since merged with the Benedict & Burnham Manufacturing Company, occupying the position for

L. I. MUNSON.

a year and a half. In 1862 he moved to Meriden to take the offices of secretary and treasurer of Julius Pratt & Co., and later was secretary and treasurer of Pratt, Read & Co., when the three firms, of which that firm was constituted, were consolidated. In 1863, at the age of twenty-five, he returned to Waterbury and re-entered, as secretary and treasurer, the establishment where he had previously been employed as a boy, the Apothecaries' Hall Company, of which he has since been the active manager. Aside from his large political acquaintance, Mr. Munson is widely and popularly known throughout the state as one of the original members of the Connecticut Pharmaceutical Association, for several years the chairman of its executive committee, and for one year its president. He is also a member of the American Pharmaceutical Association. Mr. Munson's political record is that of a party leader and worker rather than that of an office-holder. He has served for years as a member of the board of fire commissioners, assessor, and member of the board of sewer commissioners. Twice he has been the candidate of his party for mayor of the city of Waterbury, and in 1885 and 1886 was state comptroller, having been elected on the republican state ticket with Hon. H. B. Harrison at its head. His administration of the affairs

of that important position was conspicuously successful.

As a business man Mr. Munson exhibits industry, honesty, and ability, and has achieved a substantial success. As a political leader he possesses similar qualities, with corresponding results. The openness of his political methods and the frankness of his manners makes him popular alike with supporters and opponents, and he has escaped, in a large degree, the personal bitterness and hostility which political activity often entails. He belongs to the Waterbury Club and the Republican League of New Haven. He has a wife and two daughters. He is active in all public affairs relating to the community in which he lives.

GEORGE H. BURDICK, HARTFORD: Secretary Phoenix Insurance Company.

Mr. Burdick is a native of Granville, Washington county, New York, where he was born in December, 1841. He is descended from Connecticut stock, his grandfather, David Burdick, being a native and long a resident of Stonington. He removed to Granville, New York, where his son, A. S. Burdick, the father of the subject of this sketch, was born and resided the most of his life, engaged in the practice of the law. His standing as a lawyer was very high, and his legal practice extended over Washington and Saratoga

G. H. BURDICK.

counties, in which last-named county the closing years of his life were spent.

As a boy, Mr. Burdick attended the public schools of his native town, and at about the age of fifteen came to Hartford and entered the dry-goods store of C. S. Weatherby, then located on the corner of Main and Morgan streets. The dry-goods trade did not, however, seem to be well suited to his tastes, and after remaining in the store a few months he returned to Granville, and soon after entered the academy at Poultney, Vt., where he prepared for and afterwards entered the University at Troy, N. Y. It was the hope of his father that the young man would take a theological course and enter the ministry, but this plan did not harmonize with his own ambitions; and after a year at the university he fully decided to abandon all thoughts of a profession, and to engage at once in active business. Having relatives in Hartford, and having made some pleasant acquaintances during his brief residence here, as before noted, he came to this city in search of business, and almost immediately entered the office of the Phoenix Insurance Company as a clerk. He was advanced through succeeding grades of promotion, and in 1867 was made assistant secretary of the company, retaining that position until September, 1888, when he was elected secretary. This latter office he now holds.

Mr. Burdick was married in 1865, and three children have been born to him, only two of whom — a son and a daughter — are now living. He is an active member of the Asylum Avenue Baptist church, and has been the clerk of the church since its organization in 1872. In politics he is always to be found acting with the republican party.

HON. CHARLES ADDISON RUSSELL, Killingly: Manufacturer; Congressman from the Third District.

Charles A. Russell was born at Worcester, Mass., March 2, 1852. He received his primary education in the common schools of that city, and prepared for college under the tuition of Rev. Harris R. Greene. He graduated at Yale in the class of 1873, taking high rank as a student, as well as winning popularity in his class by his genial manner and his enthusiasm in college sports. After his graduation, he immediately devoted himself to newspaper work, and was, up to 1878, actively engaged on the Worcester

C. A. RUSSELL.

Press as city editor, and was for a short time thereafter connected with the Worcester *Spy*. Since that time Mr. Russell has been engaged in the business of manufacturing at Dayville, in the town of Killingly, as treasurer of the Sabin L. Sayles Company, woolen mills, incorporated. In 1884 he was appointed aid-de-camp on the staff of Governor Bigelow, and was a very popular member of the official gubernatorial family. He served the town of Killingly in the house of representatives in 1883, and was chairman of the committee on cities and boroughs on the part of the house. While in the legislature he distinguished himself by his readiness in debate and skill in disposing of public business. He was secretary of the state in 1885-86, having been elected on the republican state ticket with Hon. H. B. Harrison at its head. Thus the stages were very natural that in the fall of 1886 led to his elevation as candidate for congress in the third district; and, as before whenever a candidate for public office, he received a victorious support at

the polls. The honor thus bestowed has since been twice repeated, Mr. Russell now serving his third term in the house. The record shows that the interests of the third district were wisely entrusted and have been safely guarded at the national capitol during Mr. Russell's incumbency of the high and honorable office.

Of Congressman Russell's genealogy, it may be mentioned that his paternal ancestors settled near Cambridge, Mass., and lived there long enough to take a hand in the celebrated Lexington fight before they migrated to New Hampshire, where the father of the subject of this sketch was born in 1820. The mother — a Wentworth — traces her lineage directly to the old colonial Governor Wentworth of New Hampshire. The well-remembered Henry Dunster, first president of Harvard College, was also of kin with the ancestry alluded to.

Mr. Russell was married in 1880 to Miss Ella Frances Sayles, daughter of Hon. Sabin L. Sayles of Killingly, and they have two children.

HON. WILBUR B. FOSTER, Rockville: President "The Boston Clothing Company."

Wilbur B. Foster was born in Monson, Mass., March 31, 1853, and educated at the Monson Academy. At twenty years of age he went to Rockville and established himself in the ready-made clothing trade, which business he has continuously followed until the present time, being now the senior member of his firm, and representing the largest clothing establishment in the city. In 1874 he married Miss Edna Winchell, only daughter of Cyrus Winchell, Esq., one of the leading manufacturers of Rockville.

W. B. FOSTER.

In 1886 he was appointed postmaster of Rockville, holding the office four years. He was secretary of the local board of education for a number of years, and is at present acting school visitor. He has held many important town and city offices, and last fall was elected state senator from the twenty-third district, being the candidate of the democratic party. He is a prominent member of several secret organizations; is past Chief Ranger Court "Hearts of Oak," Ancient Order of Foresters of America; and has twice been selected by Foresters as their representative to national conventions, at Chicago and Minneapolis. He has recently been appointed a trustee of the Connecticut Hospital for the Insane, at Middletown.

HENRY A. BAKER, Oakdale (Montville): Postmaster.

Henry Augustus Baker occupied the offices of judge of probate and town clerk for twenty-five years, and has been a notary public for thirty. Since 1875 he has been engaged in the fire insurance business, but was formerly a carpenter and farmer. He is also the postmaster at Oakdale, receiving the appointment in 1889 as a republican. For the past sixteen years Judge Baker has been engaged in compiling a history of Montville and a genealogy of the first settlers there. The work is now nearly ready for

H. A. BAKER.

publication. From 1853 until 1857 he resided in Norwich. The judge is a native of Montville, the date of his birth being October 29, 1823. He received a common school education. May 18, 1846, he was married to Miss Hannah Fox Scholfield, who is still living. There are also two children living, three having died. Judge Baker is a deacon in the First Congregational church at Montville, and clerk and treasurer of the church. He is also a member of Oxoboxo Lodge, F. and A. M., at Montville, and has held the position of chaplain of the organization.

JAMES W. BRASIE, Washington: Town Clerk.

James W. Brasie was born at Norfolk, February 1, 1868, and was educated at Winsted. He was elected town clerk of Washington by the democrats the first year of his majority, and is now serving for the second term. He is also clerk of the probate court for the district of Washington. He is the station agent of the Shepaug, Litchfield & Northern road at Washington depot, and is an active business man. Mr. Brasie is a member of the First Congregational church at Winsted. His wife, who is still living, was Miss

J. W. BRASIE.

Minnie G. Cook prior to her marriage. The subject of this sketch is thoroughly popular in his community. His election as town clerk was carried by a majority of 47 votes.

C. W. BARKER, North Branford: Printer.

Clarence W. Barker was born in the town of Branford, Oct. 6, 1856, and was educated in the common schools. He has been engaged in the card and novelty business for twelve years, his avocation being that of a card printer and novelty dealer. Most of his life has been spent in Branford. Eight years ago he removed to North Branford, where he has since resided. During President Cleveland's administration he held the office of postmaster. He is a member of the grange at North Branford and of the

C. W. BARKER.

Knights of Pythias lodge in Branford. He is also actively connected with the Congregational church, and the Young People's Society of Christian Endeavor work and is an influential member of the society. Mr. Barker has a wife and four children. The former was Miss Minnie G. Bartholomew of Northford prior to her marriage.

ANDREW JACKSON BOWEN, Willimantic: Attorney.

Andrew J. Bowen was born in 1845 at Eastford, and educated on his father's farm and in the schools of his native town. A desire at one time to enlist was not approved by his parents, and consequently his military record did not materialize. After teaching school a few terms he engaged in trade in one of the village stores of Eastford, doing a good business, amounting one year to $20,000. While living in his native town he held the offices of school visitor, school district committee, bank director, constable, board

A. J. BOWEN.

of relief, justice of the peace, postmaster, and representative in the state legislature. The latter position was occupied in 1880, when he served on the committee on incorporations. He introduced several bills and resolutions, part of which were passed and became law. He studied law four years, some of the time with Judge Richmond of Ashford; after which, in 1881, he moved to Willimantic, where he has since resided and practiced law. He has become identified with the moral and business interests of Willimantic, and at one time was president of the Morrison Machine Company of that place, and is now the treasurer of said company. In politics he was reared a democrat, but always votes republican, and uses pen and voice in advocacy of the principles of the latter party. Since 1865 he has been a member of the Congregational church. He married Hannah R. Rindge at the age of twenty-two, and has three children, namely, Bessie, Clarence, and Ernest.

S. A. GRANGER, Winsted: Secretary and Treasurer The Morgan Silver Plate Company.

Salmon Algernon Granger was an officer in Litchfield county's favorite regiment, the Second Heavy Artillery, during the war, and possesses a record that commands admiration wherever it is mentioned. He enlisted April 25, 1861, as a private in the Second Connecticut under the late General Alfred H. Terry, and was at the first battle of Bull Run. He re-enlisted in the nineteenth infantry, which was subsequently designated as the Second Connecticut Heavy Artillery and commanded Company I at

S. A. GRANGER.

the time of Lee's surrender. In 1864 he was with Sheridan in the great Shenandoah campaign. At the close of the war he accepted the position of superintendent of the New England Pin Company of Winsted and remained in that capacity for twenty-two years. In 1888 he was one of the organizers of the Morgan Silver Plate Company of Winsted, and became the secretary and treasurer. Mr. Granger was born in New Marlborough, Mass., August 12, 1839, and was educated in the common school. He acquired the trade of a carpenter, but failed to pursue it after the war. He was married December 19, 1860, his wife being Miss Carrie A. Potter, daughter of Newton C. Potter of Torrington. He has two sons, one sixteen and the second twelve years of age. In politics his position is that of an independent. He is a member of the school committee and a trustee of the Methodist church of which he has been a member since 1859. He is a past master of St. Andrew's lodge of Winsted, F. and A. M., past H. P. of Meridian Chapter R. A. M., and has attained the 32° in Masonry. He also belongs to the order of Odd Fellows, and is past grand regent of the Connecticut Royal Arcanum, and grand treasurer of the N. E. O. P. of Connecticut. He has also held the office of junior vice-commander of the Grand Army in this state.

RICHARD BULLWINKLE, Mianus (Greenwich): Stock Farmer.

Richard Bullwinkle was born in New York city, May 12, 1860, and was educated in Grammar School No. 18 and the College of the City of New York.

RICHARD BULLWINKLE.

He began the study of medicine, but was compelled to relinquish it on account of ill health. He has spent a great deal of time in traveling in this country, and is a gentleman of extensive observation and culture. He has held the office of town treasurer in Greenwich, and is a republican in politics. He is connected with the Universalist church and the Independent Order of Odd Fellows. Formerly he was of the firm of R. Bullwinkle & Co. in Greenwich, and is now president of the Volunteer Rock Drill Company at South Beach, Conn. Practically he was compelled to give up business in October, 1890, and is now spending most of his time on the stock farm which he owns at Mianus. His wife was Miss Estella A. Bowen before marriage. There are three children, all of whom are living.

———

FRANK ELDRIDGE HYDE, Hartford: Attorney-at-Law.

Frank E. Hyde, at present a member of the prominent law firm of Hyde, Gross & Hyde at Hartford, was born at Tolland January 21, 1858.

F. E. HYDE.

He was educated in the public schools of Hartford, and at Yale College, graduating in the class of 1879. After completing his college course he pursued his legal studies at the Columbia and Yale Law Schools, graduating from the latter in 1871. He was immediately admitted to the bar, and has since been in active practice in Hartford. Mr. Hyde represented Hartford in the legislature in 1887, and was re-elected for the succeeding session of 1889, being the fourth generation in his family to be represented in the general assembly of the state. His father, Hon. A. P. Hyde, served several terms in the house, representing the town of Tolland; his grandfather, Alvin Hyde, and his great-grandfather, Nathaniel Hyde, representing the town of Stafford, each in his day serving with honor and distinction. All have been democrats. The late Judge Waldo, for many years among the foremost lawyers of the state, was the grandfather of Mr. Hyde on his mother's side, and he also achieved a most honorable legislative career. Mr. Hyde has successfully followed in the footsteps of his ancestors, ably and honorably serving the interests of his constituents and clients, whether in the execution of public trusts or of his professional duties.

JOSEPH HALL BARNUM, Hartford: Editor and Proprietor "The Hartford Sunday Journal."

Captain Barnum was born in East Hartford, May 27, 1838, and received a common school and academic education. His father was Eli Barnum, who was a hatter by trade, and a cousin of the late P. T. Barnum, the family originating in Danbury. On his mother's side Captain Barnum is a descendant of Colonel Peter Harwood of Massachusetts, who served with credit in the Revolutionary army. At the age of fifteen years the subject of this sketch removed to Hartford and entered the employ of the Sawyer Silver Spoon

Works. At sixteen he went to *The Hartford Times*, where he acquired an insight into the printer's trade. From the composing rooms of *The Times* he entered the employ of *The Morning Post*, under James M. Scofield, and was in that office when the war commenced. Meanwhile he had served in the Volunteer Fire Department of the city, advancing from old No. 5 on Church Street to the assistant foremanship of the Ætna Hose Company. Captain Barnum was among the first in this city to respond to the call for troops, and enlisted April 20, 1861, in the Light Guard Infantry, Company A, First Connecticut. During the previous February he had enlisted in the Light Guard as one of the city military companies, and proceeded with it to the field, when the first call for volunteers was issued. He was in the first battle of Bull Run with his regiment. At the conclusion of the three months' service he returned home and again found employment on *The Morning Post*. In July 1862, his ardor made it impossible for him to remain longer at the case, and he became a worker in enlisting the Bee Hive Company of the Sixteenth Regiment, the old firm of Starr, Burkett & Company being especially interested in the organization. Captain

Barnum was mustered as first lieutenant of the company, August 24, the command being assigned to the left of the regiment, the second place of honor in the organization. First Lieutenant Barnum was placed in charge of regimental supplies at Arlington, when the Sixteenth started for the memorable Maryland campaign of 1862, which culminated in the battle of Antietam. After that engagement Lieutenant Barnum was promoted to the captaincy of Company H, his commission dating September 20, 1862. He was selected for this position by Colonel Frank Beach, who was one of the most impartial judges of military attainments. Captain Barnum was at Fredericksburg, serving at the head of his company. Owing to the illness of his wife he was compelled to resign, February 23, 1862, and return to Hartford. The vacancy in the company was not filled, however, and in May Captain Barnum was called to an interview with Governor Buckingham, and earnestly requested to accept the return of his old commission. Governor Buckingham supported his own wishes in the matter by referring to the personal desire of Colonel Beach that Captain Barnum should be induced to return. He was again mustered, May 12, 1863, and joined the command at Suffolk, Va., in time to participate in the Peninsula campaign of that year. During one of the protracted marches of that campaign, Captain Barnum was prostrated by the heat, and compelled for the first time in his life to fall out of line. The effects of that day's service have been felt from that time until now. When the Sixteenth was ordered from Virginia into North Carolina, January, 1864, Captain Barnum, as officer-of-the-day at the time of the regiment's departure, was called upon at a critical juncture to perform an important service. The incident referred to was in connection with the destruction of the regimental camp at Getty's station near Portsmouth, Va. The attack at Plymouth, N. C., which resulted in the capture of nine companies of the Sixteenth was commenced April 17, 1864. Three days prior to that event, Captain Barnum was selected with Company H to relieve the Union forces on Roanoke Island. Sunday morning, April 17, he started on that mission. Ten hours later the bombardment of the outpost by the rebels had commenced. During the summer of 1864, Captain Barnum remained at Roanoke, where the nucleus of the regiment was preserved, and the field and staff reports and muster rolls of the absent companies kept intact. An important expedition was made under Colonel D. W. Wardrop, the destruction of mills and property in the neighborhood of Plymouth being the objective point. Captain Barnum commanded the Sixteenth, and is deserving of the greatest credit for the work which he accomplished in its behalf. In March, 1865, he was ordered with his command to Newberne, N. C.,

and relieved the troops in that city, which were
then performing provost duty. He commanded the
escort that accompanied General Grant from Newberne to Raleigh, the object of General Grant's
visit being a conference with General Sherman.
Captain Barnum remained in command of the Sixteenth until April 19, 1865, when he was relieved by
the late Captain Thomas F. Burke of this city, the
senior line officer. June 24, 1865, the subject of this
sketch was mustered out of service, and returned
home at the head of his company. His military
career was one of strict devotion to duty. He was
one of the best disciplinarians in the regiment, and
instinctively a soldier from head to foot. After returning home he started *The Soldiers' Record* in
company with Lieutenant Wm. E. Simonds, who
has since represented the First district in congress.
Afterwards he assumed the management of *The
Gas Light*, a bright theatrical paper of the time,
and *The Travelers Journal*. In 1874 *The Gas
Light* was dropped, and in April of that year *The
Journal* was established as a Sunday paper, the
Captain becoming one of the pioneers in Sunday
journalism in Connecticut. *The Sunday Journal*
has been his life work in the field of business.
From the outset it has been a successful enterprise.
Its owner and manager is an able newspaper man,
and the success which it has attained is due to his
intelligence and administration. Captain Barnum
was unanimously elected commander of the Buckingham Rifles after the war, and served in the
National Guard for a while. His military instincts,
however, found full opportunity for development in
Washington Commandery No. 1, K. T., of which
he has long been a member. He held the position
of Captain-General in the Commandery for three
terms, and was in military command of the organization during the Chicago pilgrimage. Captain
Barnum is a 32° Mason, and is also a member of
Pyramid Temple, Nobles of the Mystic Shrine,
Bridgeport. He is a Past Chancellor of Crescent
Lodge, Knights of Pythias. Captain Barnum was
one of the vice-presidents of the great assemblage
that was held here, in recognition of General
Grant's death. He has never sought political office
of any kind, having devoted himself to his newspaper enterprises. Captain Barnum has been
married twice. His present wife, Mary A. Root,
was the daughter of Lyman Root of Westfield,
Mass. On her mother's side Mrs. Barnum is connected with the poet, William Cullen Bryant, and
with General Nathaniel Lyon. The surviving son by
the first marriage, Charles H. Barnum, is connected
with *The Sunday Journal*, occupying a responsible position in the management. Captain Barnum
has been a resident of Hartford since 1853. He is
an independent in politics, and his paper has been
guided essentially on that principle.

JAMES G. GREGORY, M.D., Norwalk.

Dr. Gregory was born in Norwalk in 1843. After
a thorough course of preparatory training in the
public schools of his native town, he entered Yale

J. G. GREGORY.

College, from which institution he graduated with
the class of 1865, and from
the New York College of
Physicians and Surgeons
in 1868. He was for two
years connected with the
medical staff of the Brooklyn City Hospital. In 1870
he returned to Norwalk,
where he has since resid-
ed and been in almost
constant practice. Dr.
Gregory represented Nor-
walk in the legislature in
1879, serving as chairman of the committee on federal relations, and a member of the committee on
claims. He was also on the staff of Governor Bigelow, as surgeon-general, in 1881–82. He has filled
various local offices in Norwalk, including that of
burgess and warden of the borough; and is a trustee on the part of Fairfield county of the Middletown Asylum for the Insane. He has taken an active part in educational interests, and has been instrumental in securing many important advantages
in this direction to the rising generation of his native town.

OZIAS HOLMES KIRTLAND, Old Saybrook: Town Clerk.

Ozias H. Kirtland has had three years of service
in the general assembly of this state. He was first
elected a member of the house in 1852, representing

O. H. KIRTLAND.

the town of Saybrook.
That year the town of
Old Saybrook was incor-
porated by the legisla-
ture. During the years
of 1882 and 1883 he rep-
resented Old Saybrook in
the house, serving on the
republican side. He was
a member of decided in-
fluence. He was born in
Saybrook, Sept. 24, 1819,
and received an academic
education. His early life
was spent in farming and
in teaching. Subsequently, he became interested
in fishing enterprises in the Connecticut river; also
on Lake Ontario in Jefferson county, N. Y., and at
Savannah, Ga. In 1860 he organized with David
W. Clark the firm of Kirtland & Clark and engaged
in shipping fish in large quantities to New York.

In 1869 the lumber business was added, being retained until the present. In 1864 Mr. Kirtland was elected town clerk of Old Saybrook and has held the position continuously since that time. He is a member of the Congregational church and held the office of deacon from 1850 to 1890. He was in the state militia for ten years. Mr. Kirtland has been married twice, his first wife, who died Feb. 3, 1879, being Miss Elizabeth R. Clark. The second wife was Miss Elizabeth R. Whittlesey prior to her marriage. The family also includes two sons and one daughter.

BENNET JERALDS, Yalesville: Contractor with the Charles Parker Company.

Bennet Jeralds was born in Watertown, October 10, 1818, and received a common school education. His life has been spent chiefly in the towns of Prospect and Wallingford.
He has held various public offices in the town where he resides, and is at present a member of the board of relief. He is also a notary public and is a republican in politics. Years ago he was connected with the state militia. At the age of 18 years Mr. Jeralds entered the employ of William Mix of Prospect, the first spoon manufacturer in

BENNET JERALDS.

the United States, and remained with him three years. When he attained his majority, he began the manufacture of britannia spoons on his own account, and continued in the business in Prospect until 1845, when he formed a copartnership with Eli Ives of Meriden and prosecuted the business until 1853. During that year Mr. Jeralds bought out the interest of Mr. Ives and subsequently disposed of the plant to Mr. Charles Parker of Meriden. He immediately became the superintendent of Mr. Parker's spoon factory in Yalesville and removed to that place in 1854. He retained the position of superintendent until 1876, when the contract system was inaugurated, and Mr. Jeralds became a contractor in the establishment. In politics Mr. Jeralds identified himself with the free-soil party and was defeated as a candidate for the legislature on the free-soil ticket in 1851 by one vote. Since the organization of the republican party he has uniformly voted for its candidates and interests. He was for years a justice of the peace in Wallingford and has been actively associated with school affairs in his community. The subject of this sketch has been married five times. The surviving wife was at the time of her marriage with Mr. Jeralds the

widow of Charles T. Sherman of West Haven. He has six children, five daughters and one son, twenty-five grandchildren, and two great-grandchildren. Mr. Jeralds is a member of the Episcopal church in Yalesville.

COL. JULIUS W. KNOWLTON, Bridgeport: Postmaster.

Julius W. Knowlton was born in Southbridge, Mass., November 28, 1838. He is the son of William S. Knowlton, and traces his American ancestry to Thomas Knowlton, who emigrated from England in 1632 and settled in Ipswich, Mass. When Julius W. was seven years of age his parents removed to Norwich, Conn., and three years later to Bridgeport, where he was educated in the public and private schools. In 1860 he engaged in business in Bridgeport, continuing until the breaking

J. W. KNOWLTON.

out of the rebellion, when he enlisted as a private in Company A, Fourteenth Connecticut Volunteer Infantry, and upon the organization of the regiment was made commissary-sergeant. He was promoted to the second lieutenancy of Company C, and was in command of that company at the battle of Gettysburg. On the third day of that battle he was wounded, and remained in a hospital on the field eleven days, when he was removed to Baltimore, and soon after to his home in Bridgeport. The following January he returned to the front, but on account of his wounds was unable to perform arduous military duty, and in 1864 was discharged for physical disability.

In October, 1866, Colonel Knowlton was one of three who purchased *The Bridgeport Standard*, organizing under the joint stock laws of Connecticut, with Mr. Knowlton as secretary and treasurer and business manager. He resigned this position in 1873, to take the superintendency of the Moore Car Wheel Company of Jersey City, N. J. In 1874 he accepted a position in the post-office department at Washington, D. C., and was later made chief clerk of the department by P. M.-General Marshall Jewell. In 1875 he received the appointment of postmaster at Bridgeport, which position he now occupies.

Colonel Knowlton is a republican, and is active and prominent in the councils of his party. He has served two terms in the legislature, has been a member of the republican state committee, and was on Governor Jewell's staff, with the rank of colonel.

He is a prominent member of the Masonic fraternity, having taken all degrees to and including the thirty-second — Scottish Rite. He is a member of the military order of the Loyal Legion of the United States, the Army and Navy Club, Grand Army, and the Seaside Club. He has been assistant adjutant-general G. A. R., a member of the National Council, and in 1880 was a delegate to the National Encampment. He is a member of the First Universalist society of Bridgeport. He married, December 17, 1866, Miss Jennie E. Fairchild, of Newtown, Conn., and they have had two children, neither of whom is at present living.

LEANDER Y. KETCHUM, Woodbury: Postmaster.

Leander Y. Ketchum was born at Clyde, Wayne county, N. Y., December 15, 1850, and was educated at Phillips Academy, Andover, Mass., and at

L. Y. KETCHUM.

Dickinson College, Carlisle, Pa. His professional studies were pursued in the medical department of the University of New York. He also took a full course in the New York College of Pharmacy, graduating from the latter in 1876. His father was Judge Leander S. Ketchum of Clyde, a lawyer of prominence in western New York, judge of the county court through successive terms, and member of the New York constitutional convention in 1869. Dr. Ketchum was educated for West Point originally, but owing to the death of his father that project was given up. Prior to 1876 he spent several years in California. After receiving the degree of M.D., he practiced in New York city, at Arcade, Wyoming Co., N. Y., and in Ansonia, finally settling at Woodbury. He is, in addition to his medical practice, the proprietor of the leading drug store in the town, postmaster, having received his appointment from President Harrison, medical examiner, and post surgeon. He is a member of the Litchfield county and state medical societies. He also belongs to King Solomon's Lodge, No. 7, of Woodbury, which possesses one of the most interesting historical structures in the state. Dr. Ketchum has been married twice. His first wife was Miss M. Belle Cothren (daughter of the Hon. Wm. Cothren of Woodbury), whose death occurred within a few years. The present wife was Miss Sophia Horton, niece of Prof. James L. Ensign of New Haven. The doctor has a large practice in the town. In politics he is a republican.

HON. JAMES L. HOWARD, Hartford: Manufacturer. President James L. Howard & Company and Hartford City Gas Light Company.

Hon. James L. Howard, Lieutenant-Governor of the State of Connecticut in 1887 and 1888, is the eldest son of the late Rev. Leland Howard, and

J. L. HOWARD.

was born in Windsor, Vermont, January 18, 1818. He received an academic education, and began his business career as a clerk in the city of New York. In 1838 he came to reside in Hartford, and in 1841 engaged in the manufacturing business on his own account, and has been a manufacturer ever since. His firm was incorporated in 1876 as James L. Howard & Company, of which he became and is now president. He is widely known to the railroad interests of the country as a manufacturer of railroad supplies.

Since his residence in Hartford, he has frequently been called to serve the city in various public capacities, having been a councilman, alderman, police commissioner, chairman of the board of park commissioners, member for many years of the high school committee, and one of the building committee in the erection of the fine high school building. In all these capacities he has won the esteem of citizens irrespective of party. His exceptional business abilities have also met recognition from the institutions of the city. Additionally to his official connection with his own house, he is president of the Hartford City Gas Light Company, a director in the Phoenix National Bank, a director in the Traveler's Insurance Company ever since its formation, and sustains the same relation to the Hartford County Fire Insurance Company, the Retreat for the Insane, the Farmington River Power Company, and several important manufacturing companies. He is also on the board of directors of the New York & New England Railroad Company. His election to the position of lieutenant-governor in 1887 was a recognition not only of his sterling qualities as a loyal and patriotic citizen, but of his practical business ability, his administrative tact, and his familiarity with parliamentary rules and usages.

Mr. Howard is a representative layman of the Baptist church of the country, his local connection being with the First Baptist church of Hartford, of which he is and has long been a deacon. He is held in high esteem and has been greatly honored by the denomination, which he represents in a wider than state limit. He was president of the Connecticut Baptist Convention from 1871 to 1876, and is now a trustee and member of its executive committee; he was one of the originators and first president (and re-elected additional terms) of the Baptist Social Union, and is now president of the board of trustees of the Connecticut Literary Institution, the leading educational corporation of the church in Connecticut; he was also president of the American Baptist Publication Society from 1873 to 1877, and of the American Baptist Home Mission Society from 1881 to 1884. He is now one of the trustees of Brown University.

Mr. Howard was originally a whig, and naturally became a republican when the party of "free men, free soil, and free speech" was organized in 1856, and has always given earnest and active support to republican principles. He is distinctively a leader in everything that goes to make up good citizenship, and in the tokens of confidence which his fellow-citizens have showered upon him.

Mr. Howard was married, June 1, 1842, to Miss Anna Gilbert, daughter of the late Joseph B. Gilbert of Hartford. There have been five children, of whom three are living; the eldest, Alice, is now the wife of Judge E. B. Bennett of this city.

FRANCIS HAYDEN TODD, NORTH HAVEN: Farmer.

F. Hayden Todd was born in the town where he still resides, August 8, 1827. He was educated at public and private schools, and has followed agricultural pursuits all his life. He was one year in the New Haven Foot Guards, but boasts no other military record. He has held many public offices, including that of selectman for four years, grand juror for nearly thirty years, treasurer of the town for the last fourteen years, and various other town offices since 1864. In 1883 he represented North Haven in

F. H. TODD.

the legislature, serving on the committee on agriculture, having been elected by the republicans. He is a Congregationalist by profession, also a member of the North Haven grange. He united in marriage with Miss Elizabeth M. Gill, who is still living, and they have three sons. Mr. Todd has had most of the grand juror business of the town since 1864, and is, with one exception, the longest in this office of any person in his part of New Haven county. His record is that of an honorable and useful citizen.

WILLIAM H. BULKELEY, HARTFORD: Dry-Goods Merchant.

General William H. Bulkeley has been a prominent citizen of Hartford for many years, conspicuous beyond the limits of the city and county, in political and business circles, first, as having occupied the second highest office within the gift of the state, and next as the proprietor of one of the most noted dry-goods houses in this section of New England. He is descended from one of the oldest New England families, the representatives of which have invariably impressed t h e m s e l v e s upon the moral, social,

W. H. BULKELEY.

and business life of the communities in which they have lived.

General Bulkeley was born in East Haddam, March 2, 1840. Seven years later, his father, the late Hon. Eliphalet A. Bulkeley, established his residence in Hartford, and remained here until his death a few years ago. The young man was educated in the district and high schools of Hartford, principal T. W. T. Curtis being one of his instructors. He left the high school before graduation, with an admirable record for scholarship and application, and entered an old and leading dry-goods establishment here as a clerk. In March, 1857, he went to Brooklyn, N. Y., and engaged in the same business with H. P. Morgan & Co. Afterwards he entered the dry-goods trade for himself, and conducted a successful business for six years on Fulton Street, Brooklyn. In 1868 he returned to Hartford and organized the Kellogg & Bulkeley Company, lithographers, of which he has since been the president. He was for several years vice-president of the Ætna Life Insurance Company, and is at present a member of its board of directors. He is also a director or otherwise officially connected with a number of the banking, insurance, and other corporations of Hartford. In 1878 he purchased the "Bee Hive," a famous dry-goods establishment, which he has since managed with great success, it being the chief secular object of his attention.

General Bulkeley has had large experience in municipal and state politics, and has been both burdened and honored with official positions. He was five years in the common council board of Hartford, serving one year as vice-president, and one as president of that body. At the expiration of his membership in the council, he was appointed a member of the board of street commissioners, retaining the position by successive appointments between seven and eight years, and proving one of the most efficient members the board has ever had. General Bulkeley was elected to the office of Lieutenant-Governor of Connecticut on the ticket with Governor Bigelow, and served through 1881 and 1882 with credit. As presiding officer of the senate, he won and received the approval of that body, irrespective of party.

General Bulkeley has a creditable war record, having been one of the first to respond to the call for troops after the attack on Fort Sumter. He was a member of the Brooklyn City Guard, G company, Thirteenth regiment, N. Y. N. G., and advanced to the front with his command, April 19, 1861. The organization was in service for four months. In 1862 he organized Company G, of the Fifty-sixth regiment, N. Y. N. G., and was elected captain. He was with his command through the Pennsylvania crisis of 1863, being in General "Baldy" Smith's division. The regiment was ordered home during the New York draft riots, after which it was disbanded, its term of service having expired.

General Bulkeley is an active member of Robert O. Tyler Post, G. A. R., of Hartford, and also of the Army and Navy Club of Connecticut. In private life he is a gentleman of superior traits of character; a member of the Pearl Street Congregational church, and a generous contributor to its charities.

S. C. BEERS, Cornwall: Merchant.

Silas Curtis Beers was the judge of probate in the Cornwall district for four years from 1880, and occupied the position of town clerk and treasurer for fourteen consecutive years, discharging the duties of the place with great efficiency and success. In 1867 he was a member of the house from the town of Cornwall, his colleagues from Litchfield county including Henry B. Graves of Litchfield, Seth Thomas of Plymouth, Nathaniel Smith of Woodbury, and the Rev. John Churchill, also of Woodbury. In

S. C. BEERS.

politics Mr. Beers is a republican. He is a member of the First Congregational church in Cornwall, in which he has held the office of deacon for a number of years. He is a member of the firm of M. Beers & Sons, and is engaged in mercantile pursuits. Mr. Beers is unmarried. He was born at Cornwall, March 13, 1827, and received a common school education. He is one of the most respected and honored citizens of the town in which he lives.

ELISHA B. GILLETTE, Canaan: Farmer.

Elisha B. Gillette was born in that town, Nov. 27, 1829, and received a common school education. His father, Joseph P. Gillette, was from Milford,

E. B. GILLETTE.

and his grandfather, Benjamin Gillette, was a soldier of the revolutionary war. The subject of this sketch was a member of the house of representatives in 1884 from Canaan, serving on the democratic side. He has been a member of the school board and school committee, occupying the position of clerk and treasurer. He has also been a justice of the peace. Mr. Gillette is a member of the Methodist church. For the past thirty years he has been engaged in the lumber and charcoal business, and in farming. The wife of Mr. Gillette was Miss Sarah L. Abells before her marriage, and is still living. The family includes five children.

CHARLES BELKNAP, Bridgeport: President of the Belknap Manufacturing Company.

Charles Belknap was born in East Randolph, Vermont, March 29, 1825. Brought up on a farm until 1841, he went to Chicopee Falls to work in a

CHARLES BELKNAP.

cotton mill. In 1844 he went to Cabotville (now Chicopee) to learn the machinist trade with the Ames Manufacturing Company. He was married in May, 1845, to Marcia C. Goddard. In 1849 he removed to Springfield and was employed in the United States Armory shops. In August, 1860, went to Bridgeport with Dwight Chapin & Co., manufacturers of brass and iron goods. In 1861 was engaged in the manufacture of army appendages. Did not go to the war and was not drafted, but wishing to be represented sent a substitute. In 1863, in company with Mr. E. G. Burnham, he organized the Belknap & Burnham Manufacturing Company for the manufacture of engineers' supplies, gas, steam, and water goods. From small beginnings this business grew to large proportions and was afterward changed to the Eaton, Cole & Burnham Co., one of the largest of its kind in the country.

In 1875, having retired from the above corporation, and having associated with him several gentlemen who had held prominent positions in the old firm's employ, the Belknap Manufacturing Company was organized to manufacture the same line of goods, in which he has held the position of president since its organization, owning the majority of the capital stock.

DAVID HENNEY, HARTFORD: President and Treasurer Hartford Light and Power Company.

Alderman David Henney was born in Onslow, Ia., Oct. 7, 1855, his parents at the time being residents of that state. One year later the family returned to Connecticut and settled in Willimantic. After a residence of seven years in that place, Mr. Henney, the father of the alderman, decided to remove to this city, where he could give his children the best of educational opportunities. It was the question of education, in fact, that determined his return east from Iowa. All of his children have been thoroughly educated,

DAVID HENNEY.

and each of the five sons occupies a responsible and influential position in the community where he resides. The subject of this sketch was educated in the public schools of this city, graduating from the Hartford High School in the class of 1874. He was a clerk in the Mechanics Savings Bank here for four years, after which he engaged in the brokerage business. In 1887 he organized the Hartford Light and Power Company and has been its president and treasurer from the start. At the session of the legislature in 1887 the company was incorporated under a special charter and was the first to introduce the incandescent system in this city. It was also the first to establish electric motors, furnishing power for industries of various kinds. President Henney was mainly instrumental in getting the electric street railroad line established. He is also the originator of the project for running electric railroad lines from West Hartford Center by way of Farmington to Unionville and from the Windsor town line on North Main street to Poquonock and Rainbow. These plans will be carried into effect as soon as acts of incorporation are granted by the legislature. Mr. Henney is the president and treasurer of the Hartford Steam Company. He also owns a valuable farm in Unionville, which is carried on under his immediate supervision. He is one of the shrewdest business men in the city. Alderman Henney has been a member of the court of common council seven

years, six of the number being spent in the board of alderman. He was chairman of the ways and means committee for four years, the position being the most important one in city government and requiring special knowledge of municipal finances and management. Mr. Henney discharged the duties of the place with complete success. He is the chairman of the eighth ward republican committee and is the only republican who has been able to win an election in that stronghold of democracy for three consecutive terms. The alderman is a member of the First Presbyterian church, and was for a number of years the president of the young people's association in that church. He has a wife and two children. The former was Miss Elizabeth Simonds of this city prior to her marriage. The brothers of the alderman are James B. Henney of Boston, formerly superintendent of motive power on the New York & New England, John Henney, Jr., superintendent of motive power on the New York, New Haven & Hartford, Charles M. and Judge Wm. F. Henney, both of whom have held influential offices in the city. The only sister resides at the family home here. Alderman Henney is a member of the Hartford Order of Elks. His career as a business man and citizen has entitled him to the honor and esteem of the entire community.

E. H. BARTRAM, SHARON: Town Clerk and Treasurer.

Ezra Harris Bartram was born in the town of Sherman, Fairfield County, Conn., July 26, 1820. He depended upon the district schools of his native town for his education, and at the age of fifteen quitted both the town and school and took up his residence in Sharon, where he has since remained. He has followed mercantile pursuits for a considerable part of his life, and has otherwise been engaged in farming. At twenty-two years of age he was married to Miss Laura Williams, who died March 9, 1884. Six

E. H. BARTRAM.

children survive her. Mr. Bartram is a member of the Methodist Episcopal church of Sharon. He is also a democrat, and has, as the candidate of that party, been frequently chosen to fill public offices in his town. He has been constable, assessor, and was a justice of the peace until excluded from further holding that office by his age. He is still a notary public, and continues to fill the important position of town clerk and treasurer. Mr. Bartram has not been conspicuously prominent in public affairs, on account of his quiet disposition and habits; but his life has been one of great usefulness, and he has the confidence and respect of all who know him.

ADDISON KINGSBURY, COVENTRY: Box Manufacturer.

Addison Kingsbury of South Coventry, senior member of the firm of A. Kingsbury & Son, is one of the most noted and successful paper box manu-

ADDISON KINGSBURY.

facturers in New England. The business includes the product from five factories which are located in South Coventry, Rockville, New London, and Willimantic in this state, and at Northampton, Mass. Mr. Kingsbury is the inventor of the machine for cutting the blanks for the boxes. The industry was started at South Coventry in 1868 and rapidly developed, becoming in the course of a dozen years one of extensive proportions and standing. Millions of boxes are now turned out annually by aid of the machinery devised by Mr. Kingsbury. In 1880, after having established an extensive plant at Rockville, the far-sighted manager of the industry located a factory at Northampton. In 1883 Arthur L. Kingsbury was admitted to the firm and has since been an active participant in its interests and business. In 1885 the subject of this sketch invented a glueing machine, which is still in use, and also the machine for cutting box blanks. These inventions have contributed materially to the firm's success. The combined production of the firm's factories amounts to upwards of ten million boxes a year, giving employment to over 150 hands and doing over $100,000 business annually. One of the specialties by which Messrs. Kingsbury achieved their success is the furnishing of printed labels with the boxes. The founder of the business is also interested in the Kingsbury & Davis Machine Company of Contoocook, N. H., which turns out the machine he invented for cutting blanks, as well as other paper-box machinery. He has spent much of his time in New York and is a gentleman of wide business acquaintance. His career has been one of superb success and may be adduced as an illustration of the prosperity that awaits ability and energy in the industrial pursuits of this country. The manufacturers of America, of whom Mr. Kingsbury is a worthy representative, are entitled to the highest credit for the part which they have performed in the

development of the American people. Mr. Kingsbury was born at South Coventry, November 15, 1835, and received a common and select school education. He began life as an accountant, but the most of his business career has been in connection with his paper box industry and inventions. In politics he is a republican. He is connected with the Congregational church. He has been twice married. The second wife, who is still living, was Miss Sara M. Scott prior to marriage. There are two children living, one of whom, Arthur L. Kingsbury, is associated with his father in the firm and business, as before intimated.

HORACE JOHNSON, PLAINVILLE: Carriage Manufacturer.

Horace Johnson was born in Decatur, Otsego county, N. Y., December 25, 1822, and received a district school education. He was only five years

HORACE JOHNSON.

old when his father died. Since that time he has made his own way in the world, working on a farm during his early years for his board and schooling. At the age of sixteen, after completing the season on a farm at three dollars a month, he made his way back to Connecticut, where his parents were born, with only seventeen dollars in his possession. The subsequent three years were spent in the town of Litchfield, where he learned the carriage-maker's trade. He then removed to New Britain and worked four years for Normand Warner, who is still remembered by many people in that locality. Mr. Johnson afterwards effected a partnership with L. S. Gladding and carried on a successful carriage business until the commencement of the war. The firm controlled an extensive business in the south and lost heavily. Mr. Johnson's partner died soon after the war was ended and the whole management of the business devolved upon him. His plant was destroyed by fire seven years ago, causing the loss of nearly one-third of his property. The works were rebuilt immediately and the business continued. Mr. Johnson manufactures only first-class goods, which are sent throughout the country, principally in the south. His "Jefferson spindle" buggy has taken several prize medals at state fairs, and is to be found in every city on the Atlantic coast. He has been a member of the board of selectmen at Plainville and treasurer of the grand lodge of Good Templars in this state. He is a prohibitionist in politics and a member of the Congregational church. Mr. Johnson also belongs to the Order of Odd Fellows. His family consists of a wife and three children. The former was Miss Susan L. Adams prior to marriage. In the management of his business since the war, Mr. Johnson has frequently visited the south and has extensive transactions in that section. His life has been characterized by the strictest business integrity, and he has thoroughly deserved the success which he has attained.

JARED W. LINCOLN, Chaplin: Postmaster.

Jared W. Lincoln was born in Windham, Sept. 8, 1823. He attended the public school at North Windham, and private schools in Chaplin and Willimantic, and, at the age of seventeen commenced teaching school. He taught fourteen winter terms. He was married to Joanna Spafford in April, 1844. They have had two children, Edgar and Clinton: the latter died in 1862; Edgar is living in Chaplin. Mr. Lincoln moved to Chaplin in 1856, and entered the store of his brother Allen Lincoln, as a clerk. Soon

J. W. LINCOLN.

afterwards he bought the store and has conducted a business in general merchandise, until within a few years, having been succeeded in the business by his son, Edgar S. Lincoln. Mr. J. W. Lincoln has retired from trade and is farming on a small scale, preferring outdoor life for health, principally, but also for comfort and independence. Mr. Lincoln has served his town in various public capacities since his residence there. He was a representative in the state legislature in 1862; was elected town clerk and treasurer in 1863, both which offices he now holds, and has held for twenty-seven years. Although a republican in politics, and the candidate of that party whenever nominated for office, he has generally received the votes of both political parties. He was appointed postmaster of Chaplin in 1863, under President Lincoln, and held the office until Mr. Cleveland's accession to the presidency. He was again appointed in 1889, under President Harrison, and is still in office. He received a notary public's commission from Governor English in 1868, and has held that office continuously since.

Mr. Lincoln is a member of the Chaplin Congregational church, of which he was elected clerk and treasurer in 1870, and has remained such to the present time, being still in office.

CHARLES H. LADD, Sprague: Farmer.

Charles H. Ladd was born in the town of Franklin, July 31, 1848, and received a common school education. Most of his life has been devoted to agricultural pursuits, and he has taken an active part in advancing the interests of the town. He is a member of the board of trade, which was organized for the purpose of reviving the industrial enterprises in Sprague, which in years past have made that town the center of so much interest. He has held the offices of selectman and justice of the peace, and was a

C. H. LADD.

member of the general assembly from the town of Sprague in 1878. The legislature of that year was the first to occupy the new capitol, spending a few days there at the last of the session. In politics Mr. Ladd is a democrat. He is a member of the Methodist church. His family consists of a wife and three children. The former was Miss Rebecca A. Steere prior to her marriage.

GEORGE AUGUSTUS HARRIS, Preston: Division Freight Agent, New York & New England Railroad.

George A. Harris was born in the town where he now resides, August 12, 1840. After graduating from the public schools, at the age of sixteen he entered the employ of Nash, Brewster & Co., lumber dealers of Norwich, as bookkeeper and accountant, remaining with the firm four and a half years. In 1861, at the close of his connection with the above firm, he began his career in the railway service with the old Norwich & Worcester Railroad Company — now a division on the New York & New England system.

G. A. HARRIS.

His service on this line has been continuous since that date, covering a period of thirty years, and embracing by successive promotions the grades of receiving freight clerk, freight conductor, passenger conductor, clerk in the ticket department, superintendent's office, president's office, freight department, agent at Norwich, and division freight agent, — which latter position he now holds.

Mr. Harris is married and has five children; his

wife was Miss Catherine Amelia Dewey previous to marriage. He is a republican in politics, and as such has held the treasuryship of the town of Preston. He is a member of the masonic fraternity, and has taken all degrees up to and including the thirty-second.

THEODORE I. PEASE, Thompsonville: Wholesale Lumber Dealer.

Theodore Isaac Pease was born in the town of Enfield, September 18, 1844, and received a thorough common school and academic education, completing the course at the  Connecticut Literary Institute. His business education was acquired at Eastman's College. In 1860–1 he was assistant bookkeeper with the Nayasset Paper Company. Subsequently, 1864–5, he served as bookkeeper with C. Blodgett & Son, wholesale lumber dealers at Burlington, Vt. In November, 1865, he returned home and assumed the

T. I. PEASE.

lumber business of Judge Seth Terry, who had been in partnership with his father, Theodore Pease, the new firm becoming T. Pease & Son. In 1869 Henry S. Pease, a brother, was admitted to the concern, which was rapidly increasing its transactions. The subject of this sketch obtained a complete knowledge of the lumber business in Michigan, Vermont, and Canada. He was president of the Pease, Robinson & Jackson Company of Stanton, Mich., for several years, till he sold out his interest in January, 1889. He is treasurer and manager now of The Quebec Lumber Company, with dressing mills at West Burke, Vt., where the company dresses and ships annually nearly six million feet of pine, spruce, and hard woods, mostly imported from Canada. To this and the management of the wholesale business of The T. Pease & Sons Company he devotes his whole time. The company keeps two salesmen on the road selling to the lumber dealers through New England, and it is known as among the largest shippers of lumber in this section of the country.

Although a very busy man, and for years carrying the burdens of a large and increasing business, he has been more or less identified with the development of the town. He is always public-spirited and interested in public matters. For years he has been an active member of the Enfield Congregational church, and early identified himself with the Christian Endeavor movement. He became the

first president of the Christian Endeavor Society formed in his church, and one of the first to move for the organization of the Enfield Christian Endeavor Union, and was elected its first president. He is now serving his third term as superintendent of the Sunday-school of his church, and is earnestly engaged in religious and benevolent work.

He has held important offices in Enfield and represented that town on the republican side of the state legislature during the session of 1874. He has held the offices of town clerk, treasurer, and registrar, and has been the clerk of the probate court. He is a member of Doric Lodge, No. 94, F. and A. M., of Thompsonville, and also belongs to the Knights of Honor. He is also a member of the Putnam Phalanx of Hartford, occupying the position of sergeant-major on the non-commissioned staff of Major O. H. Blanchard. He was married January 1, 1868, to Miss Jennie E. Ellis, and has one daughter, Miss J. Estella Pease, who was born January 15, 1874. His family hold a prominent place in the social life of Thompsonville, and have hosts of friends throughout the state.

LEWIS BISSELL, East Hartford: Farmer and Dealer in Real Estate.

Mr. Bissell was born in South Windsor, July 6, 1829, and grew up as does the average farmer's boy, dividing his time between the farm and the  district school. His early life was spent in his native town, after which he removed to Vernon, then to Manchester, and finally to East Hartford, which has since 1886 been his permanent place of abode. Early in life he married Miss Cornelia A. Palmer of Vernon, a lady of many excellent traits of character, to whom he is indebted for much of the domestic happiness

LEWIS BISSELL.

with which his home has been filled, and to whose counsel and coöperation he attributes a good share of the success he has attained in business affairs. They have one child, a son, Robert P. Bissell, who is a prosperous merchant in North Manchester, in which town he has resided since infancy, having been a native of South Windsor, as was his father.

Mr. Bissell is a member of the Congregational church at North Manchester, with which he united when a resident of that town. His life in Manchester was one of great activity, having been extensively engaged in building operations. He built the largest block in the village, containing the hall that bears his name. While there he was called to fill the office of first or second selectman of the town for six consecutive years, and was prominent in various ways in improving the town and advancing its interests. More recently he has devoted himself exclusively to his business affairs, and has declined public offices of every kind. He is a republican in politics, having been connected with that party ever since its organization. He is a good judge of values in real estate, and has made several successful ventures in this line. Since 1880 he has foreseen the advance which was likely to take place in East Hartford real estate, and has invested there quite advantageously. His sound judgment, honesty, and strict integrity are unquestioned, and his superior ability as a business man is sufficiently attested by the fact that he began life without means or influential friends, and has by his own unaided exertions accomplished the degree of success and prosperity by which he is now attended.

JOHN M. HOLCOMBE. HARTFORD: Vice-President Phœnix Mutual Life Insurance Company.

Mr. Holcombe is a native and has always been a resident of Hartford, still living in the house where he was born June 8, 1848. He prepared for college at the Hartford High School, and graduated from Yale University in the class of 1870. In 1875 he became secretary of the Phœnix Mutual Life Insurance Company, and retained that position until elected to the vice-presidency in 1889. He has been a member and president of both branches of the Hartford city government for several terms, being elected to these

J. M. HOLCOMBE.

positions by the republicans of the second ward; and is at present a member of the board of health commissioners. His business connections, aside from the official relation he sustains to the Phœnix Life, are as director in the American National Bank, the Mechanics Savings Bank, and the Connecticut Fire Insurance Company, and as vice-president of the Fidelity Company, all of Hartford. He is a member of the Center church congregation (Dr. Walker's), the oldest church organization in Connecticut.

Mr. Holcombe was married, in 1873, to Miss Emily S. Goodwin, daughter of E. O. Goodwin of Brooklyn, New York, and they have three children, two sons and a daughter.

BENJAMIN A. BAILEY, DANIELSONVILLE. Agent Quinebaug Company.

Mr. Bailey was born at Marblehead, Mass., June 19, 1828, and was educated in the public schools of Massachusetts. He is connected with the Quinebaug Company at Danielsonville and is a director in the Windham County National Bank of Brooklyn. Mr. Bailey has been engaged in the manufacture of cotton products and in mechanical interests during a large portion of his life. Since 1874 he has been the agent of the Quinebaug Company. He has resided at Great Falls, N. H., and at Biddeford and Lewiston,

B. A. BAILEY.

Me. In the latter city he was a member of both branches of the court of common council, serving as a republican. His wife, who is still living, was Miss Emily W. Burbank of Conway, N. H. They have had six children, five of whom, four sons and one daughter, are living. Mr. Bailey is a member of the Congregational church at Danielsonville.

MARCUS A. PINNEY. ELLINGTON: Dairy Farmer.

Marcus A. Pinney was born in Ellington, October 14, 1850, the son of Albert and Lavinia Pinney, grandson of the once noted Benjamin Pinney, better known as Judge Pinney, who was justice of the peace for many years, judge of probate and of the county courts of Tolland county several years; representative in the general assembly a number of times; and senator from the old twentieth district in 1833. The Pinney family is the most ancient and one of the most numerous families that ever lived in Ellington.

M. A. PINNEY.

Marcus A. Pinney, the subject of this sketch, since completing his education at the Ellington high school, has followed the same occupation as his father — dairy farming. He has always shown a natural taste and inclination in that direction, and has managed his affairs in a way which entitles him to be considered a thrifty and successful farmer. In politics he is a democrat, and was elected by that party a representative in the general assembly of 1889–90. He was one of the state delegates to the

Washington centennial at New York in April, 1889. He was one of the charter members of the Ellington grange, and is prominent in the organization, having been unanimously elected to the office of worthy master for the present year.

Mr. Pinney married Julia E. Peck of Ellington, and has one child, a son.

GEORGE E. HOWE, Meriden: Superintendent of Reformatories.

He was born in Livonia, N. Y., May 31, 1825. It was while Mr. Howe was superintendent of the public or union schools of Painesville and of Hamil-

G. E. HOWE.

ton, Ohio, from 1853 to 1859, that the attention of Governor Salmon P. Chase was drawn to him as an accomplished disciplinarian and school supervisor. The Ohio Reform School for boys, located near Lancaster, which was now in its rude incipiency, was in need of a superintendent; and Governor Chase sent forward to the Ohio state senate the name of George E. Howe for the position. The senate at once confirmed the nomination, and Mr. Howe entered in 1859 upon his life work in reformatories. He found the Ohio institution in a very crude condition. Two of the buildings were built of logs. To the great work of improvement and development, he at once gave his best energies, and so signally did his enterprise and his methods commend themselves to the state officers of the time, that they became not only the official acquaintances of the superintendent, but many of them, like Governor Salmon P. Chase and the Hon. John A. Foot, state senator from Ohio, and commissioner of reform schools, his personal friends. As soon as Mr. Howe revolved in his own mind what was the proper system for a reformatory of youth, he came to the same plans so successfully installed by the famous Dr. Immanuel Wichern of Germany. It seemed to him that the nearer a reformatory for youth could be constructed and carried on like an excellent Christian family, the more easily and successfully could it attain to its object. Accordingly he sought to apply the "family system" of Dr. Wichern to the Ohio reformatory. That system had not been known in this country, and Mr. Howe was the first to apply it. So natural a system did it prove to be, and so fraught with the best results, that Mr. Howe has had the satisfaction of seeing it transplanted into many other states. It has be-

come the popular system of the whole country, and the counsel of Mr. Howe, as the founder of the system in this country, has been sought for in establishing it in the many new institutions of the land. As soon as the achievements of the Ohio reformatory became known abroad, Mr. Howe was sought for at reformatory and prison congresses, — as in 1870, at Cincinnati, by the National Prison Reform Congress; and in 1872, in London, England, by the International Prison Congress; in 1874, in St. Louis, Mo., by the National Prison Congress; and in 1880, in Cleveland, Ohio, by the national meeting of the same distinguished body. In all of these deliberative assemblies he expounded the "family system" and its working; and at the London congress was called before the body three times, in sessions of twenty minutes each, to explain as fully as he might the system as operating in the Ohio reformatory, as well as in other reformatory institutions of the United States.

While in Europe he visited the principal reformatories of Great Britain and the continent, and at Hamburg met Dr. Immanuel Wichern, founder of the celebrated "Rauhe Haus," from whom had been derived the germinal idea which had given its present form to the Ohio institution. He also was welcomed to an interview with the celebrated De Metz, in Paris, the founder of the colony at Mettray.

At Lancaster the old and rough buildings disappeared; new, commodious, and architecturally beautiful buildings took their places; and the Ohio reformatory became a model for the erection of similar reformatories in other places, and an example of what may be done in public institutions for the building up of good character in vicious or wayward youth.

Mr. Howe has the gift of government, is able to rule by his presence, and does not need to employ the coarser means of discipline, except to a very limited extent. He teaches that all prison suggestions should be banished nearly or entirely from such reformatories, "believing that the strongest wall is no wall"; and that every family in the system should be well regulated by a kind, loving, family-like, confiding, but yet steady and firm discipline; and well supported by excellent school instruction, while yet our ambitious *esprit de corp* for good living, and reverence for things high and sacred, should pervade the whole life of the institution.

In April of 1878, Mr. Howe was called to the superintendency of the State Reform School of Connecticut, located at Meriden, and assumed the duties of the position on the 23d of that month. Here he applied the same system, and has seen similar results, similar growth, and similar pride in the institution spring up over the state. The courts no longer hesitate to send bad boys to his care and training, but rather seem to covet the opportunity.

From the Connecticut, as from the Ohio reformatory, many boys once bad have gone out to become good citizens of the body politic, and worthy members of society, some of them attaining to professional distinction. Five new large cottages, built of brick, have been erected, each one now tenanted by about fifty boys, while the large congregate department is also full, the superintendent presiding with such ease over the large farm and its appurtenances, the institution homes, and the inmates, as that not a ripple of disturbance is seen, and kind, joyous feeling prevails everywhere.

Mr. Howe has had tempting offers placed before him to draw him from his Connecticut position. In 1888 the board of managers of the State Industrial School of New York, located at Rochester, invited him to take the charge of that institution, to install there the "family system"; but he remains in charge of the Connecticut reformatory to the great satisfaction of the governing body of trustees, and of the citizens of Meriden with whom he holds relations of high esteem.

CLINTON PHELPS, East Granby; Farmer.

Mr. Phelps has been the town treasurer of East Granby for eleven years. He has been a deacon of the Congregational church in that town for eighteen years. It is needless to add that he is a highly esteemed citizen, who possesses the complete confidence and esteem of all his fellow-townsmen. Mr. Phelps is a native of East Granby, where he was born July 1, 1842. His elementary education was acquired in the common school, and supplemented with a full course of studies at Schofield's Commercial College in

CLINTON PHELPS.

Providence, R. I. He married Miss Mary J. Rising, a daughter of David Rising of Suffield, by whom he has had four children, three of whom are now living. He is more extensively engaged in farming than any other person in his town, and combines with his agricultural pursuits the milk business, milling, and dealing in grain, feed, and fertilizers. He is an owner in and patron of the East Granby creamery, of which he was for a long time the president and manager. He has also had considerable experience in the settlement of estates. Politically he is a democrat, and as such represented East Granby in the legislature in 1887. His church relations are with the Congregational society of his town, and, as already stated, he has maintained

official connection therewith for a great number of years. He now holds the office of justice of the peace, and is otherwise more or less active in the public affairs of his town.

SYLVESTER BARBOUR, Hartford; Lawyer.

Mr. Barbour was born in Canton, this state, Jan. 20, 1831, the son of a farmer of moderate means, one of a family of nine children, all of whom lived until the youngest was forty years old; the mother being a sister of Rev. Dr. Heman Humphrey, for many years president of Amherst College, and first cousin of John Brown. He spent his childhood and youth partly at hard work on the rugged farm of his father, and partly in the district school. He spent the subsequent portion of his minority in like work in summer, at school in

SYLVESTER BARBOUR.

autumn — first in the Connecticut Literary Institute in Suffield, and afterwards in Williston Seminary, East Hampton, Mass., taking a classical course, and teaching district schools in winter, to obtain means for pursuing his education. The next four years of his life were spent partly on the farm, partly at the seminary, partly in teaching select schools and academies, and partly in the study of law in the office of his brother, the late Judge Heman H. Barbour of Hartford, and in the Poughkeepsie Law School; and he was admitted to the bar in Hartford in July, 1856, having the honor of being examined and recommended for admission by the late Governor Richard D. Hubbard. In November of that year, the day after casting his first presidential vote (for John C. Fremont), he removed to Iowa, practicing in Osage, Mitchell county, until 1860, when he returned to Connecticut, practicing for a year in New Hartford, fourteen years in Ansonia, and since that time in Hartford.

While practicing in Ansonia he held many offices, such as secretary and treasurer of the Water Company, Opera House Company, Savings Bank (all of which corporations he assisted in forming), town clerk, registrar of births, deaths, and marriages, chairman of school and Congregational society committees, school visitor, and judge of probate for the district of Derby.

Politically he acted with the republicans until 1872, when he joined the liberal party, and supported Horace Greeley for president, and has since that time acted with the democratic party.

While in New Hartford he was president of the

Wide Awake Club, and in Ansonia, during the dark days of the civil war, was a member and officer of the Union Loyal League.

In 1860 he married the daughter of Hon. J. F. Collin, ex-member of Congress, of Hillsdale, New York, and she is still living, with a son and daughter, the latter being a member of the senior class in the classical department of Smith College, Northampton, Mass., with which she graduates in June, 1891.

HENRY P. HITCHCOCK, Hartford: Merchant Tailor.

Mr. Hitchcock was born in Hartford, June 1, 1837, the event of his birth occurring in the historical mansion (now demolished), corner of High

and Walnut streets, for several years occupied by Mrs. Lydia H. Sigourney. During his infancy his father's family moved to Hitchcockville in the town of Barkhamsted, and six or seven years later to Farmington, where his boyhood was chiefly spent, and where he attended the public schools and Deacon Hart's celebrated institute at Farmington, which graduated

H. P. HITCHCOCK.

in its day a great many pupils who have since become distinguished in the various walks of life. After the death of his father in 1852, the young man returned to Hartford, and, being obliged to abandon all thought of further educational advantages, turned his attention toward the means of obtaining a livelihood. Noticing in the Hartford *Courant* one morning, in startling type, the headline, "Boy wanted," he applied as directed to N. J. Brocket & Co's gents furnishing store, No. 10 State street. The vacant position was a subordinate one, but he took it and gave to the firm his best efforts, with such satisfaction and success that he was advanced step by step and continued with the house for ten years, finally resigning to accept a position with Kelsey & Carpenter, to become one year later a partner under the firm name of Kelsey, Carpenter & Hitchcock. In 1863 Mr. Carpenter retired and under the style of Kelsey & Hitchcock the remaining partners continued the business on the corner of Main and Pearl streets for nineteen years. Subsequently, after a brief period of entire freedom from business, he established himself on the identical spot where he learned the trade in 1852, and is now conducting a flourishing business there.

Mr. Hitchcock has been active in social and political, as well as business life, during the many years of his residence in Hartford. As a young republican he was one of the original "Wide Awakes" of Hartford, the parent company of that important organization which doubtless accomplished the election of Abraham Lincoln to the presidency. He has repeatedly occupied positions of honor as the candidate of the republican party, having been in the city council once from the fourth ward and four times from the first ward, and on the board of aldermen two years from the first. He is a member of the Veteran Association Hartford City Guards, and has been for thirteen years its secretary; quartermaster of the Veteran City Guard, a member of the Sons of the Revolution, second vice-president of the Young Men's Republican Club, a member of the Hartford Board of Trade, the Hartford Historical Society, and the Connecticut Congregational Club. He is a member of the Pearl Street Congregational church, and has sustained that relation since 1858.

Mr. Hitchcock was married, May 23, 1865, to Miss Charlotte F. Hunt of North Coventry. Their pleasant home is at 119 Trumbull street.

SIDNEY DRAKE, Hartford: Book Publisher and Binder.

The subject of this sketch, whose active life began in Hartford sixty-five years ago, is a native of Windsor in this state, where he was born May 8,

1811. According to the old English genealogists, the Drake family is one of great antiquity and of Saxon origin. In the land and naval service of Great Britain, in the professions and in commerce, it has furnished numerous representatives of great eminence. Among its many distinguished branches, the family which early held its seat at Ashe was ever prominent; and from

SIDNEY DRAKE.

this branch most of the Drakes of Massachusetts and Connecticut are descended. John Drake of Ashe, in Devon county, married Christian Billet in 1360. From him in the ninth generation sprang John Drake of Wiscomb, the emigrant who came to Boston in 1630, and to Connecticut before 1639, settling at Windsor. Sidney Drake is of the seventh generation from John, the emigrant. His father, David Drake, was an extensive farmer and brick maker of Windsor, ranking high for ability and judgment.

The early life of Sidney Drake was chiefly spent in the public schools of Windsor and on his father's farm. At the age of sixteen he came to Hartford to learn the trade of book-binding with D. F. Robinson & Co. In 1841 he became a partner with J. Seymour Brown, and with several changes of partners has carried on the trade on his own account for over fifty years. The establishment has always borne a high reputation for the excellence of its work, as may be inferred from the fact that among its early patrons were such noted publishers as Phillips & Sampson of Boston, G. & C. Merriam of Springfield, and Pratt, Oakley & Co. of New York; while its more recent customers have been such as are very particular in regard to the quality of their bindings. During the palmy days of book publishing in Hartford, Drake & Parsons bound millions of books from the home press, and millions more for publishers in other parts of New England and New York — their list of such customers numbering seventy different houses.

Mr. Drake's connection with the book-publishing business has been, however, a very important feature of his active business life. In 1861, being urged thereto by Mr. Drake, a purchase was made by Walter S. Williams in connection with the firm of Drake & Parsons, of the interest of Joseph Kellogg in the then existing publishing house of Hurlbut & Kellogg; and thereupon was formed the partnership of Hurlbut, Williams & Co., for continuing the publishing business. This proved to be the " tide in their affairs which led on to fortune." The war of the rebellion breaking out soon after, in 1862 the first volume of Headley's " History of the Rebellion " was published by this firm, and the sales in a short time ran up to 150,000 copies. The impulse given by this first successful issue of war literature led to the rise in this city of several different publishing concerns, the aggregate publications of which, in addition to their own, flooded with work for several years the printing office of Williams & Wiley and the bookbindery of Drake & Parsons. The firm of Hurlbut, Williams & Co., with some changes of partners, continued, doing a very successful business, till 1865, when it was organized as a joint stock company under the name of the American Publishing Company, in which Mr. Drake has always been a director; and he was largely influential in the early history of the business in procuring such books for publication as have had the largest sale. This company has been one of the most successful and widely-known subscription publishing houses in the country, and distinguished for making large sales of many of its publications. Among these may be mentioned " Headley's History of the Great Rebellion," Richardson's " Field, Dungeon, and Escape" and " Beyond the Mississippi," and Mark Twain's " Innocents Abroad."

Mr. Drake was one of the original organizers of the republican party in Hartford, and has retained

his connection therewith until the present time. In religious faith he is a Congregationalist, worshiping at the Asylum Avenue Congregational church. In August, 1842, he married Miss Catherine Brown of Bloomfield; she died May 4, 1889, in her eightieth year; there are no children.

Mr. Drake through a long career has borne an honorable and spotless name, not more for the fidelity of his work than the integrity of his dealings.

REV. FRANKLIN COUNTRYMAN, North Branford: Pastor of the Congregational Church.

Rev. Franklin Countryman is a graduate of Yale College and the theological seminary connected with that institution, completing his collegiate course in 1870. He was born in New Haven, Sept. 23, 1849, his parents being Nicholas and Louisa Countryman of that city. He is a brother of Chief Clerk Wm. A. Countryman of the Bureau of Labor Statistics in this state, and is a man of felicitous culture and training. His first pastorate was at Prospect, where he was settled in 1874, remaining for three years. In 1880

REV. F. COUNTRYMAN.

he was settled at Georgetown and remained there for two years. The call to the North Branford church was accepted in 1882 and the last eight years have been spent in that pastorate. Mr. Countryman has been the chairman and is at present the secretary of the North Branford school board and is president of the Guilford Christian Union. He is the representative of the New Haven East Consociation in the state committee on fellowship and work, and is an earnest and influential co-laborer with the clergy of his locality in advancing the interests of the church. Two of his sermons have been printed: one on " Christian Service proportioned to Ability," and a sermon preached *in memoriam* Colonel George Rose of North Branford. He has also prepared an article for a History of New Haven County to be published in the autumn. As a collegian at Yale his life was one of the sincerest fidelity to truth, the group of men in his class with whom he maintained the happiest of relationships including the Rev. E. G. Selden of Springfield, Mass., the Rev. James G. K. McClure and the Rev. Roderick Terry of New York, the Rev. John S. Chandler of missionary distinction, the Rev. Edward Sackett Hume, also of the foreign mission field, the Rev. Lewis W. Hicks, who has occupied prominent pulpits in Vermont and this state, and the Rev. Henry L. Hutchins of Kensington. A finer group of men cannot be produced by any of Yale's noted classes. The Yale associates and friends of Mr. Countryman hold him in the highest esteem. He belongs to the grange in his town and is a member of the Connecticut Society of the Sons of the Revolution. The first wife of Mr. Countryman, who was Miss Mary J. Pickett, daughter of Judge Picket of New Haven, died in 1877. The second wife was Miss Elia S. Butricks of New Haven, who is still living. Mr. and Mrs. Countryman have one child living, now eight years of age. He has of late acted with the prohibition party.

FERDINAND GILDERSLEEVE, PORTLAND: Merchant, Postmaster, President Freestone Savings Bank.

Ferdinand Gildersleeve, the fourth child of Sylvester and Emily Shepard Gildersleeve, was born on the twentieth day of August, 1840, in that part of the town of Portland now called Gildersleeve.

F. GILDERSLEEVE.

He attended the district school in his native village till nearly twelve, and was for the three following years at boarding school. He then, in 1855, at the age of fifteen, entered his father's store, and, soon after becoming twenty-one, was admitted to membership in the firm of S. Gildersleeve & Sons, ship-builders and merchants. He is now, and has been, continuously connected and identified with all the branches of the business since first entering it.

The establishment of the post-office at Gildersleeve in May, 1872, was largely the result of his efforts. He was the first postmaster, and continues to hold the office.

In 1879 he succeeded his father as president of The First National Bank of Portland, and held the office for two years; is now a director in the same bank and in The Middlesex Quarry Company; president of The Freestone Savings Bank, a vestryman in Trinity Episcopal Parish, a member of the town board of education, and for many years has been a notary public. In January, 1890, he succeeded his brother Henry as president of The Middletown Ferry Company, and is still occupying that position; he is also a director of The Portland Water Company. He has been on various committees on enterprises and improvements in the town and vicinity, and trustee for school and other funds. He was an active member and supporter of the well-known Portland Lyceum, and takes a deep interest in it now that it has again begun to hold meetings. He highly values and appreciates the advantages of a debating society, and finds his experience in the lyceum has been of incalculable benefit in many ways. He spent six months in 1864 traveling in Europe, visiting many of the places of interest in Great Britain and on the Continent, and has made various trips to many of the important cities and places in the United States and Canada.

Mr. Gildersleeve married, on the 29th of October, 1879, Adelaide Edna, born March 12, 1845, daughter of William R. and Mary A. Smith of Portland, by whom he had one child, William, born September 23, 1880. She died Sept. 28, 1880. On the 12th of September, 1883, he married Harriet Elizabeth, born Jan. 8, 1860, of Hartford, eldest daughter of Ralph and Sarah A. Northam, formerly of Portland. They have two children, Sarah, born Sept. 28, 1885, and Richard, born Oct. 27, 1889.

GEORGE S. ANDREWS, SOUTH GLASTONBURY: Farmer and Miller.

Mr. Andrews was born in South Glastonbury, March 30, 1819, and was educated in the common schools of the town and the Glastonbury academy.

G. S. ANDREWS.

In 1852 Mr. Andrews visited London under contract with the late Samuel Colt of Hartford for four years to stock firearms for the allied armies in the Crimean war. After his return home he engaged in farming in South Glastonbury. He also opened a feldspar and flint quarry in the place and built a mill for grinding the product to be used for porcelain and china ware. The enterprise is one of extensive possibilities and will increase in value hereafter. Mr. Andrews is a democrat in politics and has twice represented his town in the general assembly, being a member for the consecutive years of 1876 and 1877. He has served a number of terms on the board of selectmen and has held other local offices. He is connected with the Episcopal church. Formerly he resided in Hartford. His life has been spent chiefly in farming and mechanical pursuits. The wife of Mr. Andrews was Miss Louisa H. Killam prior to marriage, and is still living. There are three children in the family.

[Mr. Andrews died at his home in South Glastonbury, April 8, 1891, after the above sketch had been prepared. — Ed.]

EBENEZER D. BASSETT, New Haven: Ex-Minister to Hayti.

Ebenezer D. Bassett was born at Litchfield, Conn., on Oct. 16, 1833. His father was a mulatto, and his mother a pure Indian of the Pequot tribe.

E. D. BASSETT.

He attended the Birmingham Academy, and early distinguished himself as a mathematician by solving problems in the differential and integral calculus with as much ease as an ordinary scholar would perform examples in arithmetic. After finishing the course of study at this academy, he attended the State Normal School at New Britain, from which he was graduated in 1853. During the two years following his graduation he taught successfully the Whiting Street Grammar School in New Haven. At this time he availed himself of the privilege of continuing the study of the classics and higher mathematics under professors at Yale College.

In 1855 he married Miss Eliza Park of New Haven, and moved to Philadelphia, Pa., where he accepted the principalship of the Institute for Colored Youth, a school founded by the Orthodox Society of Friends for the purpose of giving a liberal education to colored youth, and preparing them to become efficient teachers. At this institution he taught the advanced classes in Latin, Greek, and the higher mathematics, and devoted himself to the education of his race. Here he exhibited marked ability as an instructor and disciplinarian. He possessed the rare quality of inspiring his pupils with an earnest desire to excel in whatever they undertook, and he therefore cultivated to a high degree the power of patient investigation and application. Mr. Bassett's scholarly ability awakened in his pupils a desire to emulate him. About this time the institute used to be visited by interested persons from all parts of the United States and even from the old world, and, as they listened to the translations of Homer, of Virgil, and of Horace, and as they saw the facility with which difficult problems in mathematics were demonstrated and solved, they would exclaim, " This is wonderful!" And this expression was not exaggerated when we consider that these results were achieved during the dark and apparently hopeless days of slavery. Through the untiring efforts of Mr. Bassett this school was made to rank with the best institutions in the country. The proficiency of his classes became a standing argument against the injustice which could keep in the darkness of ignorance

minds capable of such attainments. So much was the cause of freedom advanced and its possibilities worked out in the quiet of the school-room.

At the beginning of President Grant's administration, it was decided by the republican leaders at Washington that colored men of acknowledged ability should receive positions in both home and foreign service. Mr. Bassett was the first candidate selected unanimously by the prominent men of his own race, and supported by distinguished persons in all parts of the Union for a diplomatic appointment. In President Grant's first list of nominations Mr. Bassett's name was sent for the mission to Hayti, and the nomination was promptly confirmed by the senate. This appointment made Mr. Bassett the first colored man to represent our country abroad. Mr. Frederick Douglass spoke of it as " a significant event, the triumph of a cause — the first small wire stretched over a chasm separating two races."

After receiving from his countrymen many ovations and considerate attentions, Mr. Bassett sailed for Hayti in June, 1869. When he reached Port-au-Prince he was received with every evidence of regard and satisfaction by the Haytian government and people. Hayti was unfortunately at this time in the midst of a bitter civil strife. Mr. Bassett found himself surrounded at once by factions and intrigues, and yet, in the discharge of his duties, he won and maintained the confidence and respect of our government at Washington, by whom he was highly commended for his heroic conduct during the Salnave revolution.

Mr. Bassett's experience at this time in a country where the right of asylum had a particular force and significance, brought to him afterwards an invitation from the Kent Club of the Yale Law School, to lecture before its members on the subject. *The New Haven Palladium*, at this time, in speaking of this lecture said: " Mr. Bassett, having been our ambassador at Port-au-Prince, was peculiarly qualified for the masterly handling of ' The Right of Asylum.' The lecture was listened to by a highly intelligent and appreciative audience, among whom were many who are prominent in law circles. Those who attended had the pleasure of hearing an able and scholarly disquisition on the subject."

Mr. Bassett so won the confidence of the Haytian people by his nine years residence among them, that he was appointed by President Salomon in 1880 to be Haytian consul at New York. He faithfully discharged the duties of this office until the end of President Salomon's administration in December, 1888.

Mr. Bassett's ripe scholarship and high attainments make him distinguished among scholars. His thorough study of the classics and of the

French language shows itself in the style of his writing, which is finished and accurate. He is unassuming and cordial in his manners, thus making his social intercourse pleasant and agreeable. He could hardly fail to have an honorable position in the community at his present home, New Haven, where he is known as one of its scholarly, public-spirited and influential citizens. On many occasions he enjoys extended courtesies from New Haven's city fathers. In all the relations of life he is emphatically a good man — not passively good, but actively worthy and earnest.

HON. ROBERT GORDON PIKE, MIDDLETOWN; Lawyer.

Robert G. Pike comes of an honored and worthy ancestry, being a lineal descendant of John Pike, Esq., a Puritan, who came over in 1632, and settled

R. G. PIKE.

in Salisbury, N. H., with his two sons; of whom one was Major Robert Pike, commander of all the Massachusetts forces east of the Merrimac during the Indian wars of his time, and for a period of fifty years and more was a prominent and influential officer of the colony. The poet Whittier says " he was one of the wisest and worthiest of the early settlers of that region. He was by all odds the most remarkable personage of the place and time." He protested eloquently against all laws punishing witches and Quakers, and especially contended against clerical usurpation. Of the seventh generation from this honored ancestor, in a direct line, which is marked by clergymen and magistrates, came the subject of this sketch.

Robert G. Pike was born in Newburyport, Mass., April 14, 1822; was graduated at Harvard University in 1843; was then private secretary to Hon. Caleb Cushing in Washington, D. C.; subsequently studied law with Hon. Seth P. Staples; and was admitted to the bar in 1848. He practiced law in New York city until 1859, when important business duties in Connecticut led him to give up a lucrative practice and move to Middletown, Conn., where he still resides. August 3, 1852, he married Ellen M., daughter of Silas and Mary Miles Brainerd of Portland, Conn. By her he had six children, now living, three sons and three daughters.

Mr. Pike is a man of strong intellect, scholarly tastes, and a wide range of information. He is a fine writer and speaker, and is always instructive and entertaining. He is an accomplished lawyer

and wise counsellor. He counts among his clients many of the most prominent and wealthy families of Middletown and vicinity. Although a modest and retiring man, he has long been a prominent and highly-respected citizen, discharging with signal success the many official duties which have been imposed upon him. He has been judge of the city court, alderman, president of the board of education, eighteen or more years, president of the Russell Library from its organization, and senior warden of the Holy Trinity parish about twenty years. In all that pertains to the public schools he has ever manifested an active interest. It was largely through his influence that the new Central School building and the new Johnson school building were erected, and he was chairman of the building committee. He was also chairman of the building committee when the beautiful church building of Holy Trinity was erected. Mr. Pike also has held important state offices. He was state fish commissioner for twenty years, and chairman of the shell-fish commission from its organization. He has done much toward increasing fish-food in the state. As chairman of the shell-fish board, he did much to bring the oyster industry under proper laws and regulations, — to the lasting benefit not only of the oyster cultivators, but also of the state. His popularity with the oystermen was such that when, in 1889, he resigned his office on the board, over three hundred leading oystermen petitioned him not to resign. All the shell-fish reports were prepared by him, and they present a fund of valuable information on the subject of oyster cultivation. In establishing the boundary line between Rhode Island and Connecticut in 1887 he was unanimously elected by the commissioners of the two states chairman of the joint commission, and he discharged the duties of the office to the great acceptance of all. His ripe experience and full legal knowledge made him a valuable member of the commission. The commissioners' report to the legislature, prepared by him in 1889, is full of valuable historical information upon the disputed boundary line, and shows wide research and learning. He took an active part in reviving the Air Line Railroad enterprise and securing its bridge charter; and when the work on the road stopped for want of means, he rendered efficient aid as counsel of the company in soliciting and procuring town help for its completion, and preparing the final construction contracts. Mr. Pike has taken no very active part in politics. He has been nominated twice for mayor; but, being a strong temperance advocate, he was defeated by the pro-liquor votes. In politics he is a republican, with intermittent mugwump tendencies. He is a member of the Episcopal church, and is distinguished for his uniform courtesy, kindness, and benevolence.

HON. HOBART B. BIGELOW, New Haven: President of The Bigelow Company.

Hobart B. Bigelow, one of New Haven's citizens who has been entrusted with the administration of the highest public office within the gift of the state, was born in North Haven, New Haven county, on the 16th of May, 1834. Upon his father's side he came from the Massachusetts Bigelow stock, a family that has made its record since colonial days for producing substantial, energetic, and useful citizens. His mother was a Pierpont, a descendant of the Rev. James Pierpont, the second minister of New Haven, and one of

H. B. BIGELOW.

the founders of Yale College. Mr. Bigelow's education was that common to the sons of farmers at that time. He attended the district school of North Haven, and when, at about the age of ten, his father moved to South Egremont, Mass., his education was continued there, in the same class of school, until he was old enough to enter the South Egremont Academy, where he remained until he was seventeen.

At this age he entered upon the work of life. He began to learn the trade of machinist with the Guilford Manufacturing Company, remaining with this company until its failure, after which he went into the employ of the New Haven Manufacturing Company, then under the management of his uncle, Asahel Pierpont of New Haven, where his apprenticeship was finished. After this, and until 1861, he had charge of the machine department of Messrs. Ives & Smith as foreman, under both Ives & Smith and their successors, Wilcox & Gay. In 1861, upon the death of Mr. Gay, he bought Mr. Cyprian Wilcox's interest in the machine-shop and continued in his own name. Later he acquired of Mr. Wilcox the foundry connected with the establishment, and the business was carried on under the name of The Bigelow Manufacturing Company. At this place, under close, careful, and intelligent management, Mr. Bigelow's business grew until there was no longer space for his buildings. They had extended along Whitney avenue and through the block to Temple street, and in 1870 he was compelled to remove to a wider location. He bought a tract of land on Grapevine Point, including a disused building originally built for a machine-shop, and in this place the business has since been conducted.

Two years prior to his removal Mr. Bigelow had added a department for the manufacture of boilers,

a department for which his establishment has since become famous throughout the country. In 1875 the firm style was made H. B. Bigelow & Co., Henry Elson being received as partner, and in 1877 the partnership was extended by the entrance of Mr. George S. Barnum. Its present form is that of a corporation, The Bigelow Company, organized in 1883 under a special charter granted by the legislature of that year.

Mr. Bigelow's continuous success in his business had not passed unnoticed by his fellow-citizens, and in the period between 1863 and 1881 he was called upon to fill a variety of public stations. He was a member of the common council, as councilman in the year 1863–64, and as alderman 1864–65, under the mayoralty of the late Morris Tyler. He was supervisor 1871–74, and filled most acceptably the office of fire commissioner for the years 1874–76. He also served one term as representative from New Haven in the general assembly of 1875. So long an experience had especially fitted him to fill the place of mayor, and though belonging to the party normally in the minority in New Haven, he was, in 1879, elected for a two-years term by a very handsome majority. Mr. Bigelow's administration of this office was marked by two events of peculiar and permanent interest to the citizens of New Haven. It was under his administration, and very largely due to his support and encouragement, that the East Rock Park Commission was created and the park opened, and this great addition to the beauty and comfort of the city made possible. The other was the well planned and successful effort of the city government under his encouragement and direction for the building of the breakwaters which have been projected and are being carried on by the United States Government for the improvement of our harbor. Upon the close of his term as mayor, he was called by the majority of the citizens of the state to occupy the office of governor, a place which he filled with quiet dignity, thorough impartiality, and great good sense.

Mr. Bigelow was married in 1857 to Miss Eleanor Lewis, daughter of the late Philo Lewis, a branch of a family that has left its mark in the administration of New Haven city affairs. His family consists of two sons, both of whom are associated with him in business.

In 1882, upon the death of Nathan Peck, he was elected president of the Merchants' National Bank of New Haven, and retained that position until the fall of 1889, when he resigned — but still retains the position of director.

Since Governor Bigelow's retirement from official life, his attention has been devoted to his company, with lesser interests in a large variety of business enterprises. His career has been pre-eminently that of a business man, familiar with and skillful in modern methods of conducting large enterprises, and basing his success upon thoroughness, energy, careful and thoughtful attention to details, avoidance of speculation, and the severest integrity. His administration of public affairs has always been marked by the same characteristics. These qualities have won him the hearty esteem of his fellow-citizens, which has been deepened by a quiet, open-handed, and broad-minded practical benevolence, of which very few realize the full extent.

CHARLES ETHAN BILLINGS, HARTFORD: President of the Billings & Spencer Company.

Mr. Billings was born in Weathersfield, Vt., Dec. 6, 1835, and was educated in the common schools at Windsor in that State. He acquired the profession of a mechanical engineer, and is at present a member of the American Society of Mechanical Engineers. President Billings formerly resided in Utica, N. Y. His business life, however, has been spent for the most part in Hartford, where he has been instrumental in establishing an extensive and prosperous industry.

C. E. BILLINGS.

The company manufactures machinists' tools and drop forgings, and is at the head of that line of business in the state. President Billings is regarded as one of the foremost business men in the city, and has been for years a successful manager of industrial interests. He is the author and patentee of many useful inventions manufactured by his company, which are largely sold in this country and Europe. He is a prominent representative of the masonic order, having received all of the York and Scottish degrees. He is a past grand commander of the Grand Commandery of Knight Templars of Connecticut. His local membership is with Washington Commandery. He has also been associated with the Connecticut National Guard, formerly being a private in the First Regiment. He has been a member of both branches of the court of common council, spending four years in the board of aldermen. During the last two years was chairman of the ordinance committee on the part of the upper board, and has exerted an important influence in that capacity. He is a republican in politics, and has represented the third ward in the municipal government. Alderman Billings is connected with the Second Ecclesiastical society, the Rev. Dr. E. P. Parker's, and with the Hartford Club. He has traveled abroad, visiting Europe during the summer of 1895, and is a gentleman of the most enjoyable personal character. He has been married twice, the second wife being Miss Eva C. Holt of this city, daughter of councilman Lucius H. Holt. There are four children by the two marriages.

AMBROSE PRATT, M.D., CHESTER: Physician and Surgeon.

Dr. Ambrose Pratt of Chester, Conn., according to the genealogical record of the Pratt family, is a descendant in the eighth generation from Lieutenant William Pratt, who

AMBROSE PRATT.

came from England with the Rev. Thos. Hooker in 1632. Thos. Hooker and his companions first came to Newtown, now called Cambridge, Mass. Mr. Hooker and Lieutenant Wm. Pratt, with others, came through the forest from Cambridge to Hartford in 1636, and they were among the early settlers of the town of Hartford.

Lieutenant Wm. Pratt married Elizabeth Clark of Saybrook, and finally settled in Essex. His oldest daughter, Elizabeth, married Wm. Backus of Norwich, from which union one hundred and fifty-one descendants are recorded in the genealogy of the Pratt family.

Dr. Ambrose Pratt, son of Ambrose and Dolly (Southworth) Pratt, was born in Deep River, in the town of Saybrook, July 11, 1814. His father died the April previous to his birth, and his mother having married again, he lived with his step-father till about sixteen years old. He attended the district schools till about fourteen years old, when, being ambitious to improve every opportunity for higher instruction, he walked daily four miles and back, in the winter of 1829-30, to attend a select school. In the spring of 1830, without the advice of friends and without money, he determined to try to get a college education. He prepared for college in two years and entered Yale in the fall of 1833. By the aid of an excellent and energetic mother and other kind friends, and by teaching some in junior and senior years, he kept up with his class in their studies, and graduated with them in 1837. After graduation he was principal of Hills academy at Essex for one year, where he proved to be a very successful teacher. In the winter of 1839-40 he attended a partial course of medical lectures at New Haven. In the fall of 1840 he entered the Columbian Medical College at Washington D.C., from which he graduated in 1843. While studying medicine in Washington, he taught a classical school and devoted much time and study to the medical flora of Washington and vicinity. In 1843 he commenced the practice of medicine and surgery in Chester, Conn. In November, 1844, he married Julia M. Spencer, daughter of Dea. George Spencer, a lady of good education, good constitution, and who had a strong and steady nervous system, by whom he has now living four daughters. He remained in Chester five years, had an extensive practice, and was regarded as a skillful physician and surgeon, performing most of the minor operations in surgery called for in his vicinity. In 1848 he moved to the city of Milwaukee, Wis., and there commenced the practice of medicine. While in Milwaukee, in the spring of 1850, he opened an infirmary for the treatment of chronic diseases, introducing therein the inhalation of medicinal vapors, dieting, exercise, electro-magnetism, and the massage, and the appliances of hydropathy. In May, 1853, he was called to Chester to assist and advise in the treatment and care of a case of chronic spinal affection. At this visit to his former place of practice he was induced by friends to return to Chester and open an institution for the treatment of chronic diseases. The house he formerly occupied was very large and available, and very pleasantly situated for that use. In July, 1853, he opened a sanitarium under the name of the "Chester Water-Cure and Medical and Surgical Institute," introducing into his treatment all the improvements of the times. This institution was at once extensively patronized, requiring an enlargement of the ell part of the house. The institution continued in successful operation till 1861, when, owing to the breaking out of the war, it was closed, and Dr. Pratt, from purely patriotic motives (being too old to be subject to draft), offered his services to Governor Buckingham as surgeon of a regiment. He was accepted and commissioned as surgeon of the 22d regiment, C. V., his commission bearing date from November, 1862, and was on duty in the field every day till July 7, 1863, when the term of service of the regiment expired. Dr. Pratt also received a commission (after a competitive examination before an army medical board convened in New York) from the secretary of war as surgeon of the 83d colored regiment, dated Feb. 6, 1865, then in the service of the United States, stationed at Fort Smith, Arkansas. This commission he did not accept, owing to the prospective early termination of the war. After the close of his army service in 1865, Dr. Pratt resumed the practice of medicine in Chester, and is still one of the three physicians of the town. In addition to his professional duties he has a small farm of thirty-five acres, in one square tract, the best land in the town which

he keeps in a high state of cultivation, and has it well stocked with a choice herd of Jersey cows. Dr. Pratt inherited a strong and energetic constitution from his ancestors, and has always been a healthy, hard-working, and busy man. He has not only attended faithfully to his professional duties, but has devoted much time to study and reading. He never took a vacation, spent no time in fishing, hunting, or card-playing. He has treated the rich and poor with the same faithful attention, and as a counselor among his patients was always regarded as their confidential friend. Dr. Pratt was always a man of nerve. In the presence of the sick and wounded he is calm, cheerful, and never loses his presence of mind. He has always maintained exceptionally good habits, never using tobacco or stimulants in any form, and sustains an unblemished moral character.

Dr. Pratt has been active as one of the board of school visitors of the town for many years. He has delivered several addresses on temperance; is a member of the Grand Army, and has often addressed gatherings on decoration days, under their auspices. In politics he is a republican, but not an aggressive partisan. He is a Congregationalist by profession, and member of both church and society. He is a reader of religious works and is a man of very positive religious sentiments, though very liberal. He is anti-sectarian, opposed to all church creeds or dogmas, yet tolerant of all who differ from him in religious opinions, feeling and holding that truth, justice, and amity are higher than religious beliefs.

MORRIS B. BEARDSLEY, Bridgeport: Attorney and Judge of Probate.

Morris B. Beardsley was born at Trumbull, Conn., August 13, 1849; prepared for college at the academy in Stratford, Conn.; graduated from Yale in the class of 1870. After leaving college he attended lectures at Columbia College Law School for a year; then went to Bridgeport, and studied law in the office of William K. Seeley until June 25, 1872, when he was admitted to practice at the Fairfield county bar, and was taken into partnership by Mr. Seeley, the firm name being Seeley & Beardsley. This partnership was dis-

M. B. BEARDSLEY.

solved in January, 1874, and in the following April he was elected city clerk, and held that office for three successive terms. In 1877 he became judge of the Bridgeport probate district, and has held that office ever since. He has been a member of the board of education for three years, and was its secretary. June 5, 1873, he married Lucy J. Fayerweather, a niece of, and largely remembered under the will of, the late millionaire leather merchant, Daniel B. Fayerweather, and has three children. Politically he is a democrat. Is a member of the First Congregational church. Is a thirty-second degree Mason, an Odd Fellow, a member of the Seaside Club of Bridgeport, and of the Aldine Club of New York, and last, but not least, a "Shriner."

GEORGE LANGDON, PLYMOUTH; Merchant, Manufacturer, and Farmer.

George Langdon was born in Plymouth, Aug. 4, 1826, and graduated from Yale College in 1848, his classmates including Judge Nathaniel Shipman of

GEORGE LANGDON.

the United States district court, and Judge David S. Calhoun of the Hartford County court of common pleas. He resided in Colchester from 1849 until 1853. During the latter year he represented that town in the general assembly, his colleagues from New London County including the Hon. Jeremiah Halsey of Norwich, Judge James Phelps of Essex, ex-United States Senator W. W. Eaton, The Hon. Alfred E. Burr of *The Hartford Times*, and Major F. M. Brown were also members of the house at that time, ex-Senator Eaton occupying the position of speaker. After leaving Colchester, Mr. Langdon resided at New Brunswick, N. J., from 1855 until 1857. The balance of the time has been spent in Plymouth. In politics he is a republican. He is a justice of the peace. For ten years he was a member of the board of selectmen, and was acting school visitor for eight. He has also held the offices of town treasurer and grand juror. For thirty years he has been connected with the Connecticut State Sunday-school association, and has been actively identified with its work. He has held the chairmanship of the executive committee of the association. Mr. Langdon was one of the founders of the Novelty Rubber Company, a successful manufacturing corporation, and became one of its directors and its secretary. He was one of the incorporators of the Plymouth Wooden Company, one of its directors, and its secretary and treasurer. He was also one of the founders and a director of the Thomaston Knife Company. His family

consists of a wife and five children. The former, prior to her marriage, was Miss Elizabeth A. Chapman. Mr. Langdon is a member of the Congregational church, and an earnest religious worker.

JARVIS KING MASON, A.M., M.D., SUFFIELD.

Dr. Mason is a member of the Hartford County and State Medical Societies, and of the American Medical Association, also a Fellow of the American

J. K. MASON.

Academy of Medicine. He is the medical examiner and health officer of the town where he resides and vice-president of the Library Association. He is also the medical examiner for a number of insurance companies, including the Ætna, the Phœnix, the Mutual, the Connecticut General, and the Hartford Life and Annuity, of Hartford; the Union Mutual of Boston, the New York Mutual, the New York Life, the Mutual Benefit of New Jersey, and the Penn Mutual of Philadelphia. He is a republican in politics and a member of the Congregational church. Dr. Mason was born in the town of Enfield, November 8, 1831, and prepared for college at Wilbraham, Monson, and Easthampton. He graduated at Yale in 1855, his classmates including Hon. Lyman D. Brewster of Danbury, the Rev. Charles Ray Palmer, the Rev. Dr. John E. Todd, Theodore Lyman, P. H. Woodward, and Lewis E. Stanton of Hartford. After completing his college course he engaged in teaching in Ohio, Texas, and Mississippi. He began the study of medicine in 1858 under the tuition of Dr. J. L. Plunkett of Carthage, Miss. In 1859 he returned north and continued his studies under Dr. Clarke of Whitinsville, Mass., and Dr. Wm. Warren Greene of Portland, Me., the latter having been professor of surgery in the Berkshire Medical College, the Michigan University, and in the medical department at Bowdoin. Dr. Mason completed his medical course at Harvard, and received the degree of M.D. in 1861. He immediately settled at Suffield, where he has since continued in practice. Dr. Mason has been married three times. His first wife was Mrs. Mary R. Reynolds of Monson, Mass. She died in 1864, after a year's marriage. In 1873 he married Miss Clara K. Halladay of Suffield, who died in 1876, leaving two daughters, one of whom died at the age of seven years. In 1877 Dr. Mason was married for the third time, the bride being Miss Mary Louisa Eastman, daughter of the Rev. L. R. Eastman of Amherst. The fruit of this marriage is one son and two daughters, all of whom are living. Dr. Mason is thoroughly interested in historical and biographical literature, and has spent most of his leisure during the past thirty years in these pursuits. He is a gentleman of wide culture, and a leading resident of the town where all of his professional life has been passed.

HON. ELISHA CARPENTER, Hartford: Judge of the Supreme and Superior Courts.

Judge Elisha Carpenter was born in that part of the old town of Ashford which is now known by the name of Eastford, Jan. 14, 1824, and received a common school and academic education. He was appointed judge of the superior court July 4, 1861, and was made a judge of the supreme court in 1865. For thirty years he has been a prominent representative of the legal profession of this state, and a jurist of undoubted attainments. Prior to the appointment to the bench he had held the offices of judge of probate and

HON. E. CARPENTER.

state's attorney, and had served for two sessions in the state senate. He first became a member of that body in 1857, his colleagues including the Hon. Dwight Loomis of Rockville, who is now a judge of the supreme court, the late Governor James E. English of New Haven, and Ralph S. Taintor of Colchester. In 1858 Judge Carpenter was returned from the old 14th district. It is one of the most interesting facts in connection with the history of the Connecticut senate, that the roll of 1858 has furnished four members of the superior and supreme courts. Three of the members, ex-Judge Dwight W. Pardee of this city, the late Judge Sidney B. Beardsley of Bridgeport, and the subject of this sketch, have attained eminence and honor in the highest court in this state, while the fourth has served for years as one of the ablest jurists on the superior court bench in Connecticut. Judge James Phelps of Essex, who was the colleague of Judge Carpenter in the senate in 1858, has also served in the national congress. The incident that these four interpreters of the law were associate law-makers in the senate in 1858 is one of great value in estimating the genius and spirit of the Connecticut judicial system. Tenure of office in the higher court judgeships is practically identical with the constitutional limit. Judge Carpenter was the president *pro tempore* of the senate in 1858. In 1861 he

represented the town of Killingly in the house of representatives, serving as chairman of the military committee. During the first week of this session the legislature passed a bill confirming the act of Governor Buckingham in sending troops into the United States service without authority of law, and providing for further furnishing of state troops for such service. After his appointment to the superior court bench, Judge Carpenter removed to Wethersfield. He remained in that town several years, but eventually settled in Hartford, where he now resides. His career on the supreme court bench has been identified in an exceptional manner with public interests. Of recent years he has been called upon to prepare the most important opinions of the court relative to labor issues. The noted boycott opinion, which defined the rights of workingmen so clearly that there has been no contest in that direction since, was from his pen. The opinion relative to the forfeiture of wages in case of a violation of contract, which the supreme court enunciated two years ago, was also prepared by Judge Carpenter. This opinion presented with the utmost clearness the fundamental principles of law relative to the rights of labor. It was also Judge Carpenter's perception of the spirit and object of the secret ballot law that led the supreme court last year to a strict construction of the text, the idea of secrecy in the statute being regarded as the fundamental one. Anything outside of the strictest conformity to one course immediately destroyed the secrecy of the vote. It is in cases and issues of this nature that Judge Carpenter has rendered the public inestimable service. He is a man of absolute personal integrity, and his career has been a priceless inspiration for bench and bar during the thirty years in which he has discharged the duties of a judge in the highest courts of the state. In politics Judge Carpenter is a republican. He is a member of the Asylum Hill Congregational church, and is a typical representative of the great denomination with which his entire religious life has been identified. During the war Judge Carpenter was the firmest of supporters of the Union. Unable to share personally in the military activities of the struggle, he provided and sent a substitute into the field, though himself never the subject of any military conscription. His heart and hand were governed by an exalted patriotism, the very thought of which was an inspiration to many a man in the field. The oration which he pronounced at the funeral of Gen. Lyon in Eastford during the initial year of the war was a matchless tribute, showing that the Judge's heart was in loyal kinship with that of the fallen hero, by the side of whose grave the state was bowed in the most affectionate sorrow and reverence. Judge Carpenter has been married twice. His first wife was Miss Harriet G.

Brown of Brooklyn, Conn. She died July 3, 1874, leaving three daughters and one son. The latter died Sept. 11, 1879. The present wife was Miss Sophia Tyler Cowen, niece of the late Gen. Robert O. Tyler and daughter of the late Mrs. Cowen, whose memory will long be regarded with affection and enthusiasm in this city. There are two children by the latter marriage. One of the daughters of Judge Carpenter by the first wife is Mrs. Myron H. Bridgeman of this city.

A. C. BIGELOW, New Fairfield: Farmer.

Allen Clarington Bigelow was born January 25, 1860, in the town where he now resides, and where his life has principally been spent on the farm. He

A. C. BIGELOW.

married Miss Sarah Bell Benedict, and they have two children. He is a republican in politics, and is considered one of the best workers in that party in the town of New Fairfield. He was employed as a census enumerator in 1890, and is at the present time one of the messengers of the Connecticut house of representatives. Mr. Bigelow is a young man of many pleasing accomplishments, and an earnest and enthusiastic citizen, whose interests are all identified with the town of his nativity. He was educated at the West Center school of New Fairfield.

DAVIS A. BAKER, Ashford: Merchant.

Davis A. Baker has twice been a member of the general assembly, the first term occurring in 1867, when his colleagues from Windham county included

D. A. BAKER.

Henry M. Cleveland from Brooklyn, George Danielson from Killingly, Thomas Tallman and Lucius Briggs of Thompson, and Frank S. Burgess of Plainfield. Mr. Baker was also a member of the house in 1887. The local offices which he has held include that of acting school visitor for seventeen years, constable and collector two years, selectman five years, judge of probate eight years, town clerk and treasurer eighteen, and was postmaster under President Cleveland's administration. He is one of the leading and most successful members of the democratic party in his town. He was educated at the Ashford Academy and the State Normal school at New Britain, and began life as a public school teacher, proving himself especially adapted to that avocation. He was a contractor and builder for a number of years, but for the past decade or more he has devoted himself exclusively to mercantile interests, managing a prosperous business in that line. His two sons are associated with him. The wife of Mr. Baker, Miss Eliza H. Walbridge, is still living. Mr. Baker was born in Ashford, October 28, 1834, and has spent his life in that town, where he is thoroughly honored and esteemed.

JOHN DENNISON PAGE, Harwinton: Paper Manufacturer.

Mr. Page was born Jan. 10, 1816, in that part of the town of Manchester which was afterwards set apart and incorporated as East Hartford. After

J. D. PAGE.

acquiring his education at the public schools, he learned the trade of millwright, which business he followed in his native town for the next twenty-five years. In 1860 he gave up the business in East Hartford and engaged in the manufacture of paper at Lisbon, this state, the firm being J. D. Page & Co. This business he continued for three years, selling out at the end of that time and returning to East Hartford, where, in 1863, he became a partner in the well-known firm of Hanmer & Forbes, paper manufacturers, under the style of Hanmer, Forbes & Page. Here he remained two years. Selling his interest he removed to East Litchfield, town of Harwinton, where he has since resided, engaged in the manufacture of paper, and where he has established and built up one of the important industries of the state in his line. He has associated with him in the business his son-in-law, the Hon. George W. Dains, present senator from the Eighteenth district, the firm name being Page & Dains. His wife's name before her marriage was Mary Alvord. There have been four children, only one of whom, a daughter, is now living. She is the wife of his business partner, the Hon. George W. Dains, above mentioned. Mr. Page has never sought public office, and has never accepted it, save in 1872, when he represented his town in the state legislature of that year. He is a republican in politics and a prominent citizen, being held in high esteem by his fellow townsmen.

G. WELLS ROOT, Hartford: Wholesale Commission Merchant.

Mr. Root is senior partner in the firm of Root & Childs, a mercantile house which was established in Hartford in 1826, by A. & C. Day. Afterwards the firm became A. & C. Day & Co.; then Day, Owen & Co.; Owen, Day & Root; Owen, Root & Childs; and finally Root & Childs. Up to 1864 their business was a jobbing business, and their sales were to the principal retailers throughout New England, the northwest, west, southwest, and south. It may be said, there was not a state in the Union that merchants

G. W. ROOT.

from them did not visit Hartford for the purchase of domestic dry-goods. From that time the business gradually changed to a package commission business, sales being made exclusively to the jobbing trade. This led to their opening a store in New York city. They now occupy one of the finest stores in New York, corner Church and Leonard streets. They have a sample office in Chicago, and are represented by agents in Boston, Philadelphia, and Baltimore. Their business is very large, they selling the entire production of a large number of New England and southern mills. Mr. Root commenced with Day, Owen & Co., nearly forty-eight years ago, and Mr. Childs over thirty years ago. The Days and Mr. Owen have passed " over the river." Probably no house has been more extensively known throughout the country for the past sixty years than this house under its different organizations. It has gone through all financial panics for the past sixty years without a blemish, and its record is a very proud one.

Mr. Root was born in Augusta, Oneida county, N. Y., April 26, 1826, a descendant of Thomas Root, one of the first settlers, and a great-grandson of Jesse Root, a distinguished jurist of the revolutionary period, who was born in Coventry, Conn., and spent most of his days in that ancient town. Mr. Root spent the first eight years of his life at his birthplace, from which he went to Mount Morris, Livingston county, N. Y., and remained nine years, obtaining during these years a theoretical education at the public schools, and a three years practical education in a country store. In 1843 he came to Hartford and entered the employ of Day, Owen & Co., into which firm he was admitted as a partner in 1851. Calvin Day retired from the partnership in 1861, and the firm name was then changed to Owen, Day & Root. In 1864 Horatio

Day went out and the firm was again changed to Owen, Root & Childs. Mr. Owen soon afterwards retired from active business, but remained as a silent partner until his death. The firm then became Root & Childs, as it has since remained. Soon after entering the firm he married Miss Paulina S. Brooks, daughter of the late David S. Brooks of Hartford, who with their five children is still living.

Mr. Root was a member of the Hartford board of police commissioners for nine years, and a member of the common council one year. He is a director in the Hartford National Bank and in the Phœnix Insurance Company; president of the Sigourney Tool Company, the Taft Company, and the Mankato Pipe Company; he also holds membership in the Hartford Club and the Hartford Board of Trade. He is an active and influential member of Park church, and an enthusiastic and stalwart republican. He is a man of positive convictions and absolute frankness in their expression. His long residence in Hartford has been attended by much earnest and conscientious effort in behalf of the city and its institutions, his home-public-spirit being one of Mr. Root's strongest traits. There can be no doubt of his essential usefulness as a citizen, or of the well-earned and well-deserved confidence which is reposed in him by his townsmen and all who have the pleasure of his acquaintance.

J. H. BLAKEMAN, Stratford: Farmer and Stock Breeder.

James Henry Blakeman enlisted in the Seventeenth Conn. Vols. July 29, 1862, and served three years in the field, being a member of Company D. He was severely wounded on Barlow's Knoll during the first day at Gettysburg, and was taken prisoner by the confederate forces. Subsequently he was recaptured and removed to a place of security within the Union lines. He is the master of Housatonic Grange, No. 79, of the Patrons of Husbandry, and is one of the best known stock breeders in his section of

J. H. BLAKEMAN.

the state, paying especial attention to Holsteins. He is also engaged in general farming and the raising of small fruits. He was formerly associated with his brother, M. A. Blakeman, in dock and bridge building, but withdrew from the business after a couple of years. He has held numerous local offices, including constable, deputy sheriff in Fairfield county, tax collector, town auditor, notary public, justice of the peace, and member of the school district committee. He is connected with the Congregationalist society in Stratford. His wife, who was Miss Amelia Janette Burr, is a daughter of the late Deacon Isaac Burr of Monroe. The marriage occurred in 1866. There are two children in the family. Mr. Blakeman is a republican in politics. He was born at Stratford, November 20, 1841, and received a common school education.

GEORGE DUNHAM, UNIONVILLE: Inventor and Manufacturer.

George Dunham was born at Southington, April 7, 1830. His early life, up to the age of twenty-one, was spent in hard work upon his father's farm,

GEORGE DUNHAM.

with the exception of a few months' schooling each year until he was eighteen, when he finished with one term at Lewis Academy in Southington. As soon as he became of age he went to work at Miller's Bolt Works in Southington, heading bolts by hand for about a year and a half (this was before any machines for heading were invented). He then worked for about two years at East Berlin and Southington on Tin-man's machines. After that he was employed by the Miller Bolt Works to make tools for threading bolts and nuts. He worked at this business, having charge of the finishing department in addition a part of the time, until 1859, except in dull times, when, the factory being closed, he turned to farming and such outdoor work as could be had. In February, 1859, he went to Unionville as superintendent of Langdon's Bolt Works. In something more than a year from that time Mr. Langdon died, when, in connection with Mr. A. S. Upson, he purchased the business. He made improvements upon nearly all the machinery then used, many of these improvements being still in use. In 1865 he invented what is now called the Dunham forged nut machine, which was highly successful, and up to this time has not been superseded for this class of work, either here or in England. Having at this time no knowledge of drafting, this machine was built without drawings, the inventor carrying all the details in his head. Since then he has invented a number of machines, mostly automatic, for cheapening the product by doing several different things in one operation. Included among them is a machine for making brass tips for pocket rules; also for making brass rolls for rule joints, a bolt-header,

a paper-bag machine, a hot-working quadruple nut machine, a cold-press nut machine which makes a nut complete from the bar cold, and one for finishing nuts cold, a mechanical motion, and several others of simpler construction. He has been interested in nearly all the new business enterprises of the village, a director in most of them, president of some, and secretary and treasurer of others. He is now manager of the Dunham Nut Machine Company. He has held a number of offices within the gift of the town, including that of selectman for several years and justice of the peace since 1878. He held the office of clerk and treasurer of the Unionville Ecclesiastical Society for more than twenty years, and is a member and deacon of the Congregational church. In politics he is a strong republican. Mr. Dunham is a man of decided energy and determination, great perseverance and thoroughness in his work, and of strict integrity, quiet and self-possessed in manner. He takes great interest in the growing of fruit, of which he has a large variety; and his chief recreation in summer is in pruning and caring for it.

Mr. Dunham married Miss Isabella Bradley of Meriden in 1853, who died in 1856, leaving one daughter. In 1861 he married Miss Mary J. Johnson of Unionville, his present wife. Three sons are the result of this marriage.

OLCOTT B. COLTON, HARTFORD: Junior Partner Smith, Bourn & Company.

Councilman Colton of the second ward in this city was born at Longmeadow, Mass., January 16, 1850, and was educated in the Massachusetts public

O. B. COLTON.

schools. His first business experience was with the Medlicott Company of Windsor Locks, where he remained for three years. At the close of that period he became a clerk in the office of the Hartford Steam Boiler Inspection and Insurance Company. In 1871 he accepted the position of bookkeeper with Smith, Bourn & Company of this city, one of the largest concerns in the country engaged in the manufacture of harnesses, riding saddles, and saddlery goods. Subsequently he became a salesman for the firm, and on January 1, 1885, he was admitted to the junior partnership. The factory is located at the corner of Capitol avenue and Sigourney street in this city. It employs 200 hands. The principal depot for the distribution of its goods is in New York city. The New England market is supplied from the firm's store, No. 334 Asylum street in this city. Mr. Colton is a republican in politics and represents the second ward in the court of common council. He is a member of the Asylum Hill Congregational church, and is the superintendent of the Glenwood Union Sunday-school. His wife, who is living, was Miss Helen C. Coomes. The family includes three children. Mr. Colton is regarded as one of the most successful young business men in the city.

HON. LYMAN S. CATLIN, BRIDGEPORT: Treasurer and Secretary Mechanics and Farmers Savings Bank.

Lyman Sheldon Catlin was born at Harwinton, Litchfield county, Conn., Jan. 21, 1840, and educated in the common schools and academy of that town. He remained in Harwinton through his minority, and in 1862 enlisted as a private in the Nineteenth Connecticut Infantry Company. He remained for two years in this regiment, and, at the end of that time was commissioned as first lieutenant in the Thirteenth United States Artillery (colored) Regiment. While with the colored troops Lieutenant Catlin

L. S. CATLIN.

was in an engagement on the Cumberland River in Southwestern Kentucky, in which the entire command was captured by Forrest's Cavalry. The officers connected with the colored troops were ordered hung, but they escaped by means of a gunboat. In 1865 this command was mustered out and its first lieutenant was commissioned by Secretary Stanton as lieutenant in the Fifth United States Cavalry. He served with this command in Arkansas until 1866, when the Union army was mustered out. Since the war Mr. Catlin has passed most of the time in Bridgeport, his only absence being between 1870 and 1873. Early in 1870 he settled in Alabama as the agent of a Chicago insurance company, but was driven out by the Klu Klux in a few months. The same company then sent him to Kansas, where he remained until 1873, when he returned to Bridgeport and organized the Mechanics and Farmers Savings Bank of that city, and has since been its chief executive officer. He has filled various offices for the town of Stratford, and was elected to represent the town in the general assemblies of 1881 and 1883. The first year he served on the house committee on school funds and

in 1883 he was house chairman of the committee on banks. In 1888 he was elected senator from the Thirteenth District, and in the session of '89 was chairman of the joint committee on banks, and the committee on further accommodation for the insane. His career was one of prominence and usefulness in both branches of the legislature. Mr. Catlin was married in 1871 to Miss Helen J. Lewis of Stratford, and they have four children — two sons and two daughters. He is an earnest republican, and an influential factor, locally and statewise, in the councils of his party. He is a member of the military order of the Loyal Legion, of the Grand Army, and the Independent Order of Odd Fellows. Mr. Catlin is a thorough and successful business man and a valued citizen.

JOHN E. ANDREWS, MT. CARMEL CENTER (HAMDEN): Real Estate and Insurance.

John Edward Andrews was born in Cheshire, November 17, 1831, and received a common school education. His father was a farmer in that place, and the son at the age of twenty bought his time and spent the succeeding seven years in an axle factory. At the expiration of that period he engaged in mercantile pursuits, real estate, insurance, and building. He was one of the influential men in the community in building up Mount Carmel Center and in securing the post-office for the place. He was connected

J. E. ANDREWS.

for two years with C. A. Burleigh in the flour, feed, and coal business, and afterwards with the firm of J. E. Andrews & Son for seven years at Mount Carmel. For a period of four years he held the office of first selectman and town agent, being elected in a strong democratic town, although being himself a republican in politics. During his administration a public hall was erected at a cost of $15,000. He was one of the charter members and first master of Hamden grange, and is an influential member of the Congregational church, being connected with the finance committee of the ecclesiastical society. Mr. Andrews has been married twice. His first wife was Miss Celia Kinney of Litchfield. The son by this marriage, George L. Andrews, is the postmaster at Mount Carmel Center and has been the chairman of the republican town committee. The second wife was Miss Hannah E. Norton of Bristol. She is still living. Mr. Andrews is at present a justice of the peace and assistant postmaster.

JUDGE WILLIAM B. GLOVER, Fairfield: Attorney-at-Law.

William B. Glover, the son of Samuel and Emily H. (Brown) Glover, was born at Philadelphia, Pa., April 7, 1857. He received his early educa- 
tion at the Fairfield Academy, and prepared for college at General Russell's Military Institute at New Haven. At the age of seventeen he entered Yale University, and graduated in the class of 1878, receiving the degree of B.A. He then entered the law department of Columbia College, New York, and pursuing the course there, graduated in 1880 with the degree

W. B. GLOVER.

of LL.B., and was at once admitted to full practice as a lawyer in the courts of the state of New York. For a short time he continued in business in New York city, and then applied, and was in 1881 admitted, to practice in the courts of the state of Connecticut, since when his advancement and success in his profession have been rapid and flattering. He has been engaged in much important litigation in the courts of Fairfield county, notable among which has been the bitterly-fought contest between the town of Fairfield and the New York, New Haven & Hartford Railroad Company, involving the question of payment of the cost of separating the grades of railroad and highway at crossings. The success of the town of Fairfield, which he represented in that litigation, has more than anything else had the practical effect of settling a question which had been the subject of widespread dispute and ill-feeling for a long time.

In November, 1882, he was elected judge of the probate court for the district of Fairfield, and has received successive re-elections to that office to the present time. Judge Glover has introduced many reforms and improvements in the administration of that court, and the Fairfield probate office is to-day known as one of the model offices of the state. His opinion in matters of probate law and practice is often sought by probate judges throughout the state, and is at all times cheerfully and carefully given. In 1884 he was appointed one of the state commission formed to revise and codify the probate laws of the state. Among his associates on that commission were Judge Luzon B. Morris of New Haven and Judge A. H. Fenn of Winsted. The report of the commission was adopted by the legislature in 1885, and forms the basis of the present probate law of the state. He has three times represented the town of Fairfield in the legislature —

in the sessions of 1883, 1884, and 1889. In the legislature he has always taken a leading and honorable position, and has become one of the well-known public men of the state. In the long and difficult session of 1889 he occupied the responsible position of chairman of the judiciary committee, and was the acknowledged leader of the house. During the session he was unanimously elected speaker *pro tempore*, and when in the chair presided over the house with marked ability and success. In politics he has always been a republican.

In 1884 he married Miss Helen Wardwell of New York city, a great-granddaughter of Judge Jonathan Sturges of Fairfield, who was a member of the first congress of the United States, and for many years a judge of the superior court of this state. He has two sons.

Judge Glover is a member and junior warden of St. Paul's Episcopal church in Fairfield, and possesses in a very high degree the confidence and esteem of all classes in the community in which he lives. His judgment and counsel are greatly respected, and many private trusts are given into his care and control. Among the young men of the state there are few who give so much promise of a useful and brilliant career.

LEVERETTE W. WESSELLS, Litchfield: Merchant.

Mr. Wessells was born in the ancient town of Litchfield, in this state, July 28, 1819. He spent a few years with his colleagues in the important 
work of mastering the rudiments of the English language in the district school, and finished his educational accomplishments at the academy. Mr. Wessells began his political life at an early age, being elected to his first office, that of deputy sheriff of Litchfield county, in 1845, in which capacity he served until 1854, when he was elected

L. W. WESSELLS.

sheriff, a position he held until 1866. He was postmaster of Litchfield from 1850 to 1854. In the war he served with distinction as colonel of the Nineteenth Regiment, Connecticut Volunteers, from July 28, 1862, to September 15, 1863, having command of Second Brigade defences of Washington, south of the Potomac, from March, 1863, until the latter date, also the date of his resignation. He was made provost-marshal of the fourth district January 9, 1864, and held that position until the close of the war. In 1866 he entered mercantile life, and has pursued his avocation in this direction since. In 1870 he was elected to the house, serving on the railroad committee, and the same year was appointed quartermaster-general. In 1877 he was again chosen to represent Litchfield in the general assembly, when he was house chairman of the committee on military affairs. At present he is a member of the state board of charities, and its auditor.

EDMUND B. DILLINGHAM, Hartford: Advertising and Real Estate Agent.

E. B. Dillingham was born in West Bridgewater, Mass., Sept. 30, 1836. His residence there was of exceedingly brief duration, and from infancy until 1867 he lived continuously in Fall River, Mass. His education was acquired in the grammar school of the last-named city and in the academy at Myrickville, Mass. After leaving school he engaged in mercantile business as a clerk until 1861, and from that time untill 1866 was employed in clerical duties connected with the city of Fall River, and in the office of provost-mar-

E. B. DILLINGHAM.

shal of the 1st Congressional District of Massachusetts, being assistant marshal and enrolling officer during a considerable portion of that period, and having charge of the enlisting of men in the military service under the several calls made upon his city. From 1862 to 1865 he was United States special agent, with headquarters at Fall River. After leaving the government employ he went to Rockville, in this state, and became superintendent of the Rose Silk Company, remaining there until 1870, when he removed to Hartford, and established "Dillingham's Newspaper Advertising Agency," being the pioneer in that business in Connecticut. His agency in Hartford is among the oldest representatives of that business in the country, and sustains a reputation among the best, having the complete confidence of advertisers and publishers everywhere. In 1877 he was elected a member of the state executive committee of the Young Men's Christian Association of Connecticut, which position he still retains. In this capacity he has attended every international convention of the Y. M. C. A. since 1879. He was D. L. Moody's chief usher during that distinguished evangelist's labors in Hartford in the winter of 1878-79. As a member of the Hartford Y. M. C. A., he is on the board of trustees for the proposed new building of the asso-

ciation soon to be erected on their lot, corner of Pearl and Ford streets, which was given for that purpose by the late General Hillyer at the solicitation of Mr. Dillingham. He is a member of the Connecticut Congregational Club, chaplain of the Hartford county jail since 1879, and member of the City Mission board for several years. He has acted as temporary supply for the pulpit of nearly every country church within a radius of twenty miles from Hartford, never accepting remuneration for services thus rendered. He was chosen councilman for the Seventh ward in Hartford in 1887, and re-elected for three successive terms, representing the republicans, of which party he has been an active member since its organization. His religious connections are with the Windsor Avenue Congregational church, in the prosperity of which organization he has been an important factor.

Mr. Dillingham was married in 1860 to Miss Josephine A. Potter, daughter of the late Henry Potter of Fall River, and they have two children, Charles B. and Mabel B., the former of whom has been on the reportorial staff of one of the Hartford city dailies, was later city editor of a paper in Spokane Falls, Washington, and has recently been made private secretary to the Hon. Watson C. Squire, United States senator from that new northwestern state.

JOHN AVERY, Lebanon: Farmer.

John Avery was born in Preston, Nov. 9, 1806, and received a common school education. He is a farmer by avocation and has resided in the town where he now lives since 1823. He was a member of the general assembly from Lebanon in 1864 and has held other important offices. He has been the treasurer of the Baptist church in Lebanon since 1846 and is a member of the board of deacons. For 65 years he has been a total abstainer from the use of intoxicating liquors, and has been at the head of a temperance so-

JOHN AVERY.

ciety for a considerable period. He has been a prominent Sunday-school worker, superintendent, and has been on the committee of the church for most of the time during the past fifty years. He has also held the office of justice of the peace. His father was Colonel David Avery of Preston, who was in the revolutionary war. His mother was Hannah Avery, daughter of John Avery of Preston. Mr. Avery is the only one now living of a family of ten children. The first wife of Mr. Avery, whose maiden name was Clarissa M. Stiles, died in 1860. The second wife was Miss Almira A. Corey, who is still living. He has two children living. One daughter died in 1854. In politics Mr. Avery is a republican.

FRANK CHESTER FOWLER, Moodus: Proprietor Oak Grove Stock Farm.

Mr. Fowler was born in Moodus, December 26, 1859, and has spent most of his life there, except during his extensive travels over the South and

F. C. FOWLER.

West. He was educated at the common schools of his native town, and since his youth has been engaged in the manufacture or sale of proprietary medicines, and in the breeding of blooded horses. He is proprietor of a large stock farm, and has a business which in all departments amounts to $300,000 a year. Mr. Fowler married Miss E. H. Thompson, and they have two children. In politics he is an earnest republican, is a member of the organizations of Free Masons and Odd Fellows, and actively interested in local public affairs. He is an energetic, stirring business man, and as such has achieved remarkable success in life for one of his years.

HENRY N. CLEMONS, Danielsonville: Cashier First National Bank of Killingly.

Henry N. Clemons was born in Granby in 1824, third son (of nine sons and three daughters) of Allen and Catherine (Stillman) Clemons, on the

H. N. CLEMONS.

manor farm of his grandfather, Ferdinand Clemons (originally of one thousand acres), purchased and settled by his great-grandfather when the town was a part of Simsbury. He was educated at home, in the district school, the Granby Academy, the Suffield Literary Institute, and the Williston Seminary, Mass. He commenced teaching at the age of sixteen, and taught in Connecticut, Massachusetts, and Rhode Island, and was for a while a clerk in the office of the school fund commissioner. In 1849 he began railroading with a surveying corps on the Canal railroad in Farmington; became station agent there; and, on the extension of the road to Collinsville, first agent at the last-named place, it being then the terminus of the main line. He was also assistant postmaster there. In 1852 he became ticket agent of the Providence & Worcester Railroad at the Providence office. In 1855 he entered the Arcade Bank of Providence, and in 1856 was elected teller of the Merchants Bank of the same city, which was the exchange bank for the state of Rhode Island under the Suffolk system of state banks. While residing in Providence Mr. Clemons was a member of the Richmond Street Congregational church, was a while their clerk and treasurer, and chairman of the music committee; was secretary of the Mendelssohn Choral Union; was on city's committees, and a state secretary of a political party for two years. In 1853 he originated and co-organized the Providence Young Men's Christian Association, and was their corresponding secretary. During the war of the rebellion, though exempt by the examining surgeon, was a member of the home guard. He was elected justice of the peace in the city of Providence, and held for years a commission as notary public for Rhode Island. In June, 1864, Mr. Clemons was elected cashier of the First National Bank of Killingly, at Danielsonville; arranged its organization and commenced its banking business, and has held the office continuously to the present time. In January of this year the bank paid its fiftieth dividend, having paid to its stockholders in dividends $236,500 on a capital of $110,000. In July, 1864, he organized the Windham County Savings Bank of Danielsonville; was its treasurer and a trustee, holding the office some eleven years, in which time the deposits reached more than $1,250,000. In 1867 he arranged and superintended the erection of its present bank building and vaults. In 1876 he organized the Music Hall Company, was elected its treasurer and a director, which offices he now holds; and, as a member of its building committee, arranged the rooms and vault for the First National Bank in its block, which the bank now occupies. In 1866 he was elected clerk and treasurer of School District No. 1, and continued on its union with District No. 2, when the High school building was erected, holding the treasurer's office eighteen years. He held the treasurer's office of the Congregational church thirteen years.

Mr. Clemons has been twice married: in 1848 to Miss Mary E. Spalding of Killingly, who died in 1860, leaving two children, a daughter, now a widow, Mrs. Emily A. Merriam, and a son, Ferdinand S., now in the Merchants National Bank, St. Paul, Minn.; in 1871 married his present wife, Miss Mary L. Collyer, only child of Samuel C. and Mary (Tabor) Collyer of Pawtucket, R. I. Mr.

Clemons was a whig when made a voter, was a delegate to the whig convention at New Haven in 1852, became a republican on the organization of the party, has held his allegiance thoroughly as a temperance republican and a firm protectionist; is now all of these and a nationalist republican. Mr. Clemons has been borough treasurer and held other minor offices, and has held a notary public's commission more than twenty-five years.

EDWARD B. BENNETT, HARTFORD: Lawyer.

Edward Brown Bennett, son of William Bennett, a well-to-do farmer of Hampton, Windham County, Conn., was born in that town, April 12, 1842. He remained at home until about eighteen years of age, working on the farm summers and attending school or teaching during the winter months. In 1860 he entered Williston Seminary at Easthampton, Mass., graduating therefrom in 1862. In the fall of the same year he entered Yale College, and was graduated from that institution in 1866. At college he was active

E. B. BENNETT.

in athletic sports, and was on the Yale University crew in the years 1864, '65, '66. In 1866 and '67, after leaving college, he taught school; and at the same time studied law with the Hon. C. F. Cleveland of Hampton. He completed his law studies with Hon. Franklin Chamberlin of Hartford, being more than a year in his office; was admitted to the bar of Windham County in January, 1868, and began practice at Hampton. In April of the same year he was elected a representative from the town of Hampton to the general assembly. In the fall of 1868 he opened a law office in the city of Hartford, and soon after formed a partnership with Henry E. Burton which continued for three or four years. Since the dissolution of this partnership he has maintained his legal practice uninterruptedly until the present, unassociated. He was chosen assistant clerk of the Connecticut House of Representatives in 1869, clerk of the house in 1870, and clerk of the senate in 1871. In July, 1871, he was appointed by Judge H. B. Freeman clerk of the police court of Hartford, which office he retained for three years. In 1873 he was elected a member of the common council of that city, serving one term. In April, 1878, he was elected judge of the Hartford City Court, and continued to hold the office by successive re-elections until April, 1891. Judge Bennett was married in 1877, to Miss Alice Howard,

daughter of Hon. James L. Howard of Hartford. There are no children in the family. Judge Bennett's religious connections are with the Asylum Hill Congregational church. In politics he has always been a republican; has served on the state central committee, and was its secretary for several years. He is respected as an upright citizen, who has conscientiously and ably performed the public duties which have devolved upon him in whatever position of trust or responsibility he has been placed.

In the latter part of May of the present year, after the preparation of the foregoing sketch, Judge Bennett was appointed postmaster of Hartford, to succeed Major J. C. Kinney, deceased.

WILLIAM FRANCIS ANDROSS, EAST HARTFORD: Secretary Connecticut State Agricultural Society.

William F. Andross, born at East Hartford, Conn., June 21, 1850, has passed his entire life in that and the adjoining town of South Windsor. He received his education in various public and private schools, and was married September 21, 1874, to Irene E. Bidwell of Manchester, by whom he has three children, two sons and one daughter, few men being more fortunate in their domestic relations. As a business man, Mr. Andross has been engaged in market gardening, tobacco growing, and at present as a

W. F. ANDROSS.

commercial traveler in the fertilizer and chemical line, representing the well-known house of H. J. Baker & Brother of New York. For the past ten years he has been actively connected with the commercial fertilizer trade, acting at different times for the Bowker Fertilizer Company, the Bradley Fertilizer Company, the Soluble Pacific Guano Company, and is also at present agent for the Brockway Carriage Company of Homer, N. Y., and the Hartford Life and Annuity Insurance Company. While not specially active in politics, he is a decided republican, and has held various town offices.

Mr. Andross is perhaps best known throughout the state as secretary of the Connecticut State Agricultural Society, to which position he has just been unanimously elected for a fifth term, and has filled its difficult and onerous duties with remarkable ability and success. He is also a vice-president of the Tolland County Agricultural Society, a director in the New England Tobacco Growers' Association, the Patrons Mutual Fire Insurance Company, the Hartford County Agricultural, and the Hartford County Horticultural societies. He took an active interest in the Order of Patrons of Husbandry, and was a charter member and first secretary of South Windsor Grange, No. 28, and was for two years a member of the State Grange executive committee, having the trading arrangements of the order in hand; was also a charter member of Crescent Lodge, I. O. O. F., of East Hartford.

Mr. Andross has also been an extensive contributor to the agricultural and local press, his thorough familiarity with tobacco growing in the Connecticut valley giving his articles a more than ordinary value.

C. M. HOLBROOK, HARTFORD: Boot and Shoe Manufacturer.

Caleb Metcalf Holbrook was born in Milford, Mass., in 1822, and was educated at Shelburne Falls in that state. At the age of twenty-two he removed to Hartford and from here to Cincinnati, Ohio. The gold excitement of 1849 led him to the Pacific slope and he wears to this day a heavy gold ring which was made from the first gold found by him in the mines of California. The voyage to California was made by way of Cape Horn. In passing the latter a gale was encountered that lasted thirteen days,

C. M. HOLBROOK.

sweeping the vessel 400 miles out of its course. The trip from New York to San Francisco lasted 207 days. From the Golden Gate to Sacramento the trip was made in an open boat. Mr. Holbrook was fourteen months in the mines. The ship on which the voyage to California was made was the *Henry Lee*. Mr. Holbrook was absent about three years. Since 1852 he has been engaged in the leather business, mainly in the manufacture of boots and shoes. The original firm was Hunt & Holbrook. Subsequently it became Hunt, Holbrook & Barber, remaining under that name until the death of Mr. Barber in 1879. Since that time it has been known under the original name. Mr. Holbrook has been a director in the Travelers Insurance Company for twenty-five years and is one of the best-known business men in the city. He is a republican in politics and has served three years in the common council board. He is a member of the First Baptist church. His family consists of a

wife and two daughters. The former was Miss Anna E. Nelson prior to her marriage. Mr. Holbrook resides at No. 340 Farmington avenue, owning and occupying one of the pleasantest residences in that part of the city.

JOSEPH L. BARBOUR, HARTFORD: Attorney-at-Law.

Joseph L. Barbour was born in Barkhamsted, Litchfield county, December 18, 1846, and was educated in the Hartford High school and Williston

Seminary at East Hampton, Mass. He is a son of the late Judge Barbour of Hartford, a gentleman of eminent philanthropy, and has spent the most of his life in the city of Hartford. In 1864 Mr. Barbour was obliged to give up his plans for a college course, and engaged in teaching. This avocation was pursued for two years. In 1867 Mr. Barbour commenced a

J. L. BARBOUR.

successful career of journalism in this city, and was associated for seven years with the *Hartford Evening Post*. He retired from that paper in 1874, and has since devoted his attention to the law. Mr. Barbour is one of the ablest jury lawyers in the county, and has a large and steadily increasing practice. He is a republican in politics, and has held a number of important and responsible positions within the gift of his party. He was clerk of the common council board in this city for four years, and has held the house and senate clerkships, proving himself a man of unusual competence in these offices. Mr. Barbour's work in connection with the house and senate journals was of the highest order. For eight years he was elected prosecuting attorney by the court of common council here, and discharged the duties of that office with marked success. Mr. Barbour has been assigned to no place of public service in which he has not shown exceptional tact and ability. His best political service has been rendered on the stump through successive presidential campaigns. There is not a republican speaker in the state who can surpass Mr. Barbour as a campaigner. His reputation is not limited to Connecticut. In New York and New Jersey he has been one of the most popular favorites. In other fields his oratorical efforts have been equally brilliant. Mr. Barbour's Memorial Day orations have been models of eloquent and fascinating eulogy. He was a member of the Connecticut National Guard for six years, and is a member of the Veteran Association of the Hartford City Guard. He is also a member of St. John's Lodge, F. and A. M., of this city, and of Charter Oak Lodge, I. O. O. F. His church relationships are with Rev. Dr. Parker's, where he is a regular attendant. Mr. Barbour's family consists of a wife and three children, the former being a daughter of Assistant Postmaster Oliver Woodhouse of the Hartford post-office. A daughter of Mr. Barbour is now a student at Vassar College.

LEMUEL T. FRISBIE, HARTFORD: Merchant and Manufacturer.

Mr. Frisbie is a native of "Wintonbury," a parish of Old Windsor, the name of which is now obsolete, the parish limits being included in the present town of Bloomfield. Wintonbury was so called because its territory comprised sections of the three towns of *Wind*sor, Farmington, and Simsbury, the orthography of the word being intended to express the composition of the parish. Mr. Frisbie's first American ancestor, his grandfather on his mother's side, was Thomas Taylor, who came to America

L. T. FRISBIE.

from England about 1770, settled in Connecticut, and became a very successful farmer. He was of royal lineage, in direct descent from a reigning English sovereign through a member of his family who forfeited titles and estate by contracting a marriage outside the royal line. The subject of this sketch was born February 7, 1824. He was the son of a farmer, and was trained in all the habits of economy, industry, and thrift which characterized the New England farmer of that period. He attended the district school, and graduated from the Connecticut Literary Institution at Suffield in 1842. He thus remained at the old homestead in Bloomfield until eighteen years of age, going thence to Windsor for two years, to Hartford for four years, to West Hartford for two years, then back to Windsor, where for the fourteen years from 1850 to 1864 he was engaged in agricultural pursuits and in the meat business. Since 1864 he has been engaged in merchandizing and manufacturing in Hartford, taking up his residence here in 1874.

Mr. Frisbie was married in 1848 to Miss Caroline E. Gillett, daughter of Oliver S. Gillett of Windsor. Her ancestors were among the first settlers of Hartford, coming from Roxbury, Mass., with one of the three colonies which settled respectively in

Windsor, Wethersfield, and Hartford. Mr. and Mrs. Frisbie have had four children — two daughters died in childhood. A son and daughter remain. The former, Charles G. Frisbie, who is associated with his father in business, married Miss Belle S. Welles of Hartford, and has three children: the daughter, Ella T., married George H. Woolley of Hartford, and has four children.

Mr. L. T. Frisbie was a member of the common council of Hartford for four years, from 1878 to 1882 inclusive. He is a member of the Asylum Avenue Congregational church, and chairman of the society's committee. In politics he is, and has been since the organization of the party, a stalwart republican. He is active and influential in church affairs, a prominent and useful citizen, and has a foremost place among the prosperous business men of Hartford.

HON. ORRIN CHAPMAN, NORTH STONINGTON: Farmer.

Orrin Chapman of North Stonington, son of Elias and Eunice (Miner) Chapman, was born in the town of his past and present residence, July 6, 1834. His education was obtained in the common school. The son of a farmer, Mr. Chapman was bred to the calling of agriculture, which he has successfully followed. In 1855 he married Miss Jane D. Smith. Their family numbers two sons and two daughters. The elder son, Elias O. Chapman, is now of the enterprising young business men of Meriden. In pol-

ORRIN CHAPMAN.

itics Mr. Chapman is a republican. His superior ability has been recognized by his fellow-townsmen in the bestowal of many of the offices within their gift. He has been a member of the board of selectmen five years, three years as first selectman, in which capacity he served his constituency faithfully and well, and by his kindly efforts in behalf of the wards of the town won not only the gratitude of these unfortunates, but the commendation of all humane persons familiar with his policy. He was a member of the house of representatives in 1878, and again in 1882. Mr. Chapman's church connection is with the Third Baptist church of North Stonington, which, since 1857, re-elected annually, he has served as clerk and treasurer. With fidelity, fearlessness, honor, and justice as his watchwords, he belongs to that class of citizens which, collectively, are the strength and the security of the commonwealth.

DANIEL KIEFER, Waterbury: Die Sinker.

DANIEL KIEFER.

Daniel Kiefer was born in Germany, December 15, 1841, and received a thorough public school training. At the age of twelve years he came to New York and afterwards established himself in business in the city of Waterbury. The war of 1861 awakened in him an enthusiastic patriotism and his services were freely given for the protection of his adopted country. Daniel Kiefer is one of the best-known Grand Army men in the state, and has held important positions in the Connecticut department. He is a member of Continental Lodge, F. and A. M., of Waterbury, an organization that can boast the membership of such men as ex-Congressman Stephen W. Kellogg, Judge George H. Cowell, Colonel John B. Doherty, and Major Lucien F. Burpee of the Second regiment. He is also connected with the Odd Fellows and Concordia Singing Society of Waterbury. He has held the presidency of the board of councilmen in Waterbury, and the office of police commissioner. His wife, who is still living, was Miss Elizabeth C. Moser before marriage. There are no children. Mr. Kiefer is a republican in politics. His business is that of a die sinker.

JOSEPH B. BANNING, Deep River (Saybrook): Judge of Probate.

J. B. BANNING.

Judge Banning is a native of the town and village where he now resides; he was born December 16, 1849, the only son of Arba H. and Hannah M. Banning. He was educated in the public schools of his native town, learned the trade of shoe making, and was connected as junior partner with the firm of A. H. Banning & Son, until the death of his father in 1880, since which time he has conducted the business alone. At the age of twenty-two he married Miss Ansolette A. Smith, daughter of Charles D. Smith, Esq., of Deep River. Mr. Banning's father was judge of probate for the district of Saybrook for a period of sixteen years, up to the time of his decease. Mr. J. B. Banning was chosen as his successor, and has thus held the judgeship since 1880. He is a member of the Connecticut Probate Assembly, and has been its secretary and treasurer since the death of Judge West of Rockville. He is also a justice of the peace for the town of Saybrook.

Mr. Banning has been in the boot and shoe trade all his life. In 1886 he erected the building on Main Street, Deep River, which he now occupies both as store and residence. He is a member of the Congregational church, an undoubted republican, and a member of Webb Lodge, I. O. O. F., of Deep River.

ISRAEL HOLMES, Waterbury: Banker.

ISRAEL HOLMES.

Israel Holmes, eldest son of Samuel J. Holmes, was born in Waterbury, August 10, 1823. He received a common school and academic education, and at the age of nineteen entered the employ of the Benedict & Burnham Manufacturing Company as clerk in their general store in that place, remaining in their employ about twelve years, during the time becoming a stockholder in the concern. He was twice elected town clerk of Waterbury. In the spring of 1859 he went to Liverpool, England, to represent various manufacturing companies, remaining there twelve years, returning to his native town in 1871. His residence there included the period covered by the late war of the rebellion in this country. From the time that Mason and Slidell were taken from an English ship to the time of the assassination of Abraham Lincoln the life of a Northern man in England was anything but agreeable. In every public place, on the street, in railway cars, in fact everywhere, one heard the North denounced in unmeasured terms. Mr. Holmes narrowly escaped a personal encounter on more than one occasion, and is glad to believe that, though he did not bear arms, he was able to be of some service to his country.

In 1874 Mr. Holmes entered into partnership with Guernsey S. Parsons, to succeed Brown & Parsons; and, under the firm name of Holmes & Parsons, the connection still continues. Mr. Holmes has been a successful business man, and is a director in several of the leading manufacturing firms in Waterbury and vicinity. In politics he is a republican, and as such represented his native town in the legislature of 1870.

T. D. CROTHERS, M.D., Hartford: Superintendent Walnut Lodge Hospital.

Thomas Davison Crothers was born in West Charlton, Saratoga county, New York, in 1842. His father was a direct descendant of a noted family of surgeons who have been prominent in Edinburgh for over a century as teachers in the university of that city. His mother came from the Holmes family of Stonington, Conn., very prominent in the revolutionary war; and later they settled in Saratoga county, New York. The subject of this sketch was brought up on the farm, and prepared for college

T. D. CROTHERS.

at Fort Edward Seminary, New York. The excitement of the war caused him to give up a college course and enter direct upon the study of medicine. After a course of lectures at the medical college at Albany, N. Y., he entered the Ira Harris U. S. Military Hospital as medical cadet. In 1865 he graduated from the Albany Medical College, and continued his studies at the Long Island College until the next year, when he entered upon the practice of medicine at West Galway, Fulton county, N. Y. In 1870 he removed to Albany, and later became connected with the college as assistant to the chair of the practice of medicine and lecturer on hygiene, and instructor in physical diagnosis. In 1875 he was appointed assistant physician to the New York State Inebriate Asylum at Binghamton. In 1878 he resigned to become the superintendent of Walnut Hill Asylum at Hartford, Conn. Two years later the Asylum Association was suspended on account of the failure of the legislature to assist them in building.

A year later Dr. Crothers organized the Walnut Lodge Hospital, a private corporation for the medical treatment of alcohol and opium inebriates, over which he has had active charge up to the present time. In 1875 Dr. Crothers married Mrs. Risedorf of Albany, N. Y. In 1876 the American Association for the Study and Cure of Inebriety issued a quarterly journal devoted to the medical study of inebriety, and Dr. Crothers was unanimously elected editor, a position which he has held up to the present time. He was also elected secretary of this association, and has been ever since continued in that position.

In 1887 Dr. Crothers was one of the American delegates to the London international congress for the study of inebriety. This congress was attended by delegates from all parts of the world, and was the first great gathering of scientific men for the purpose of discussing the drink evil. The English Society for the Study of Inebriety gave Dr. Crothers a reception and dinner before the congress opened, which attracted much attention at the time. For many years Dr. Crothers has been a voluminous writer and lecturer on different phases of inebriety, and his views have been the subject of much interest and controversy. In 1888 he gave a course of lectures on inebriety before the students of the Albany Medical College, and in 1889 repeated it before the medical students of the University of Vermont at Burlington. Dr. Crothers is a member of many scientific societies both at home and abroad, and is frequently invited to present his views in both papers and lectures before them. These views, which he carries out practically in his hospital, are that "inebriety is a disease, and curable as other diseases are." Like all other pioneers, Dr. Crothers has a large circle of ardent admirers among scientific men, as well as bitter detractors. His conduct of *The Journal of Inebriety*, published by The Case, Lockwood & Brainard Company of this city, has given it a national reputation among the scientific periodicals of the day, and his private hospital has attracted widespread attention and patients from all over the country. Dr. Crothers is still a young man, and has the promise of great prominence in the future in scientific circles, if his energy and health continue.

GEORGE H. JENNINGS, M.D., Jewett City: Physician and Surgeon.

Dr. George Herman Jennings was born in Preston in this state, March 20, 1850. He fitted for college at the Norwich Academy, in 1872 pursued a a course of study in the College of Physicians and Surgeons in New York city, and in 1875 graduated from the Long Island College Hospital, Brooklyn, New York. Soon after graduation he removed to Jewett City and commenced the practice of medicine, in which he has been engaged to the present time. He was married to Miss Annie Greenwood of Bos-

G. H. JENNINGS.

ton, Mass., and they have five children. Dr. Jennings is deeply interested in educational affairs, and since 1884 has been committee of the Jewett City schools. He is connected with the Methodist church, and in politics is a republican. He is a member of the masonic fraternity, and president of the Agassiz Association of Jewett City.

CHARLES H. S. DAVIS, MERIDEN: Physician.
Dr. Charles Henry Stanley Davis of Meriden,
who held the office of mayor in that city during the
years of 1887 and 1888, was born in Goshen, Litchfield County, March 2,

1840, being the seventh in
descent from Dolor Davis,
one of the original settlers
of Barnstable, Mass.,
1634. The father of ex-
Mayor Davis, Dr. T. F.
Davis, removed to Meri-
den in 1849, when the
subject of this sketch was
a lad of nine years. Dr.
Davis had been a success-
ful practitioner at Litchfield and Plymouth. He
died at Meriden in 1870.

C. H. S. DAVIS.

Prior to the war ex-Mayor Davis, being twenty
years of age at the time, removed to New York,
and, with Charles H. Thomas, a well-known trans-
lator from the German and French, and an oriental
scholar, opened a bookstore, dealing principally in
philological works and New Church publications.
In a back room in this bookstore the American
Philological Society was started by the Rev. Dr.
Nathan Brown, who translated the Bible into
Assamese, and is now a missionary in Japan.
Rev. William C. Scott, now a missionary in Bur-
mah, Rev. F. James, and others, were members of
this society, and Dr. Davis was corresponding
secretary for several years. He soon, however,
sold out his interest in the bookstore, began the
study of medicine under Dr. William T. Baker, and
entered the Bellevue Hospital Medical School.
After a course at Bellevue, Dr. Davis entered the
medical department of the New York University,
and when he graduated received not only his
diploma but a certificate of honor signed by Dr.
Valentine Mott, Dr. John W. Draper, and the rest
of the faculty, in testimony of his having passed
one of the best examinations, and having pursued
a fuller course of study than is usually followed by
medical students. After graduating, Dr. Davis
attended a course of lectures at the University of
Maryland, and another at the Harvard Medical
School. Thus qualified by study and hospital
practice he returned to Meriden as a physician in
1862, succeeded his father in the business and soon
built up a large and lucrative practice. In 1872 he
went abroad for travel and study, remained eight
months, visiting England, Ireland, Scotland, Wales,
France, Germany, Italy, and Switzerland. Dr.
Davis is one of the honorary secretaries for the
United States of the Egypt Exploration Fund, and
is the editor of *Biblia*, an archaeological journal,
devoted to Egyptology, Assyriology, and archaeo-

logical research in oriental lands. He is also a
member of the New Haven Medical Society, Connecticut State Medical Society, the *Société
d' Anthropologie* of Paris, and the society of Biblical Archaeology of London; honorary member of
the Connecticut, Pennsylvania, Wisconsin, Buffalo,
Chicago, and Minnesota Historical Societies, New
England Historico-Genealogical, American Ethno-
logical, and American Philological societies. He
was one of the founders of the Meriden Scientific
Association, has always been director of its section
of archaeology and ethnology, from the first its
recording and corresponding secretary, and editor
of its four volumes of *Transactions*. In 1870 he
published a history of Wallingford and Meriden, a
work of a thousand pages, requiring much labor,
especially in its genealogies of old Wallingford and
Meriden families. For four years he edited, for
the American News Company, the "Index to Literature," a work which required the careful examination every month of some one hundred and
thirty periodicals. He found time also to write a
work on "The Voice as a Musical Instrument,"
published by Oliver Ditson, the distinguished musical publisher of Boston, which has had a very large
sale; also a work "On Classification, Training,
and Education of the Feeble-minded, Imbecile, and
Idiotic," which has become authority on the subject. He also edited the first volume of the Boston
Medical Register, and has contributed largely to
the literary, medical, and scientific journals. Several of his articles on the education of feeble-
minded children were translated into the Spanish
language, and published in *El Repertorio Medico*.
The catalogue of the library of the surgeon-general
at Washington enumerates over twenty articles
contributed by him to the medical press. He has
a reading knowledge of the modern languages, and
has studied Arabic, Hebrew, Syriac, Assyrian, and
the Ancient Egyptian languages.

He has been a member of the school board in
Meriden for eighteen years, occupying the chairmanship for six. He has been one of the High
School committee since its organization, and was
for five years acting school visitor. In 1873 he was
elected a member of the legislature from Meriden,
being the first democrat whom that town had sent
to the general assembly in twenty years. The
doctor served as chairman of the committee on legislation. He was returned to the house in 1885
and was again on the education committee. In
1886 he was a member of the committees on insurance and constitutional amendment. In 1888 he
was nominated as judge of probate for the Meriden
district, but declined. In 1886 he received the
nomination for state senator for the Sixth senatorial district, but, although supported by the democratic and labor parties, lost his election by thirty-

two votes, although in Meriden he ran two hundred ahead of the republican candidate. He was elected mayor by the united labor and democratic parties and was the first democratic mayor that the city of Meriden ever had. His administration was successful, and he was re-elected in 1888. Dr. Davis is one of the trustees of the State Reform School. He is a member of St. Elmo Commandery, Knights Templar, of Meriden; has attained the thirty-second degree in masonry, and is a member of Pyramid Temple, Ancient Order of Nobles of the Mystic Shrine. He is also a prominent Odd Fellow and Knight of Pythias. As a citizen, member of society, and publicist, Dr. Davis is held in the highest esteem in the city of Meriden.

CHARLES S. DAVIDSON, Hartford: Superintendent Hartford Division, New York, New Haven & Hartford Railroad.

C. S. Davidson was born in East Haven, November 9, 1829, and educated at the Lancasterian school in New Haven, under the management of John E. Lovell, a distinguished educator of that period. When he left the school in 1845, he ranked as second in scholarship, receiving in certification of that fact a silver medal, which is still retained by him as one of the pleasantest souvenirs of his boyhood. After leaving school he remained with his father two years, and then went to work in a silver and brass plating

C. S. DAVIDSON.

establishment in New Haven. In 1849 he removed to Springfield, Mass., and learned the machinist trade, on the completion of which he came to Hartford, and entered the employ of the railroad company with which he has been connected ever since, ascending through the various grades of mechanic, engineer, conductor, supervisor of construction, assistant superintendent, and finally, superintendent of the important Hartford Division of that great line. There is not a railroad manager in New England who possesses more fully than Superintendent Davidson the confidence of the public, and for the best of reasons. He has had abundant and varied experience in all departments of practical railroading, managing with consummate judgment and skill the most difficult situations; he is a man of absolute fidelity, and of courage which amounts to heroism. Those who know most of his experiences for the past thirty-odd years understand the secret of the regard which the public and the railroad company have for him, and the confidence they repose in him for every emergency.

During the administration of Mayor Sumner, Mr. Davidson was appointed a member of the Hartford board of fire commissioners, and rendered invaluable service to the city in this capacity. He was recently appointed by Mayor Dwight as a member of the board of street commissioners, the wisdom of which appointment is universally conceded. He is a director in the Dime Savings Bank, and holds other minor positions of trust. He has never been an active politician, but no man in the city has done more to promote the interests of good government. In every position in life he has been the representative of the highest type of citizenship.

Mr. Davidson is a prominent representative of the Masonic fraternity, being advanced to the thirty-second degree. He is eminent commander of Washington Commandery, No. 1, K. T.; member of Pyramid Temple; Knights of Honor; Order Red Men; Veteran Association Governor's Foot Guards; honorary member City Guards, Franklin Gun Club, etc. He is in politics an independent democrat; in religious matters his connections are with the Park Ecclesiastical society of Hartford.

Mr. Davidson was married quite early in life to Miss Catherine A. Bartholomew. They have had three children, but one of whom is living — a son — William B. Davidson, a book-keeper in the United States Bank of Hartford.

WATSON H. BLISS, Hartford: Contractor and Builder.

Watson H. Bliss was born at Chelsea, Vt., February 28, 1842, and was educated in the public schools and at the academy in East Hartford, where most of his early life was spent. He learned the trade of a house carpenter, and in 1869 established himself in business in Hartford, where he has for years been actively engaged in the building line, being the architect and builder of many of the best residences in this city. During the war he was connected with the Hartford Light Guard, and enlisted

W. H. BLISS.

in the Twenty-Fifth regiment from that organization. He has been elected to and served several years with distinction in both branches of the Hartford city government, being in 1885 a member of the ways and means committee and rendering excellent service in that capacity. He is an active and influential member of Washington Commandery, Knights Templars, having served as commander in 1881 and 1884, and is also a member of Robert O. Tyler Post of the Grand Army. He is married and has a family, one of his sons being at present engaged in business with him.

ELIJAH H. HUBBARD, MIDDLETOWN:

Elijah Hedding Hubbard is a prominent and successful business manager in Middletown, being a director of the Middletown National Bank, the

E. H. HUBBARD.

Middletown Savings Bank, the Shaler & Hall Quarry Co., the Ferry Co., and the Gas Co. in that city. He has spent most of his life in Middletown, where he has been extensively engaged in marketing business. He is a democrat in politics and has held various town offices, including that of selectman. Mr. Hubbard was born in Agawam, Mass., Nov. 13, 1810, and received a common school education. His wife, whose maiden name was Mary J. Badger, died Nov. 13, 1847, leaving three children, all of whom are living. Mr. Hubbard's life has been devoted to business in which he has met with deserved success.

FREDERICK F. BARROWS, HARTFORD. Public School Teacher.

Frederick Freeman Barrows, principal of the Brown school, Hartford, and one of the best known educators in New England, was born in Mansfield,

F. F. BARROWS.

September 4, 1821. He received a common school, select school, and academical education, and has followed the profession of teaching since the winter of 1839, although he did not enter upon it as a determined life-work until 1843. His early life was that of a farmer in his native town. He taught school winters from the time he was eighteen years of age, teaching two terms in Springfield. He taught in Willimantic for six years, and his record in equipping young men especially for a life work was so marked that attention was attracted to him in Hartford and in Norwich, both of which cities were in competition for his services in 1850. He was finally engaged as principal of the First school district in Hartford, a position which he has held for forty-one years; being the longest continual term of service of any school teacher in the state. His work in Hartford has been of the greatest value to the public of his district, which is in that part of the city known as the Fifth and Sixth wards, and has a large element of foreign population. He was the inspiring agency in the construction of the fine Brown school building named after Flavius A. Brown, who was chairman of the school committee for many years, and in close sympathy with the efforts of Mr. Barrows for the establishment of a first-class school for the masses. Mr. Barrows outlined to him what he desired, and, the district approving of his plans, the building was erected; which at the time of its construction was without doubt the finest school edifice in the state. Within a few years past the main building has been enlarged by the addition of a kindergarten department, which is carried on under the most approved modern system after Froebel, the founder of that style of teaching the young. Mr. Barrows's school numbers between 1,500 and 1,700 pupils, and requires a trained corps of thirty-five teachers and special instructors in German, penmanship, drawing, and singing to carry on the work. At a celebration of the fortieth anniversary of Mr. Barrows's connection with the school a portrait of him was presented to the school by his many friends, and some souvenirs of the occasion were given to him. Hon. M. J. Dooley, then United States bank commissioner, a graduate of the school, made the address of presentation, and most fittingly characterized the school when he said: "Mr. Barrows's genius has here reared an institution which is for the Protestant and Catholic, the Jew and Gentile, absolutely without a rival." Mr. Barrows has frequently been called upon to address teachers' conventions and educational gatherings upon his methods of teaching, and especially upon his mode of instruction in numbers, in which he has a wonderful talent amounting to genius. Graduates of the Brown school may be found in all parts of the country, and they uniformly testify to the healthful influence and wholesome results of his training. He has been a rigid disciplinarian, but tempers his school government with the rarest judgment and tact. It has been an every-day spectacle at the Brown school to see Mr. Barrows near the gateway, and hundreds of little children grasping him by the hand to say, "Good day, Mr. Barrows," as school closes. He knows children intuitively, and has had wonderful success in bringing forth from what seemed unpromising minds excellent citizens and intelligent men in all the walks of life. In 1882 his friends sent him to Europe on a tour for recreation, a kindness which he greatly appreciated. Mr. Barrows has been prominently identified with the Park Congregational church in Hartford. He has never taken any active part in political life, but has been in sympathy with the republican party from its foundation. His wife was Harriet Harris of Willimantic, and he has five children living. Volumes might be written, full of instances connected with his teaching, in which his acute knowledge of human nature and his power of "reading" persons have been most remarkable. He is as much an institution of Hartford and Connecticut as is the school system itself, and his life work has been more than ordinarily successful in that it has tended to the uplifting and betterment especially of the children of the poor of his city.

CHARLES WILLIAM BEARDSLEY, Milford; Seedsman and Stock Breeder.

Charles W. Beardsley, son of Charles Beardsley, was born in Stratford, Conn., May 27, 1829, and in the year 1844 he removed with his father's family to Milford. He is descended from William Beardsley, one of the first settlers of the town of Stratford, from whom he takes the name William; and from the Beach family through his great-grandmother Sarah, daughter of Israel Beach, 2d, of Stratford. His mother was Sarah, daughter of Hezekiah Baldwin of Milford, a descendant of one of the first settlers

C. W. BEARDSLEY.

of that town; and he regards his success in life as very largely the result of the early training and Christian advice of this mother. The first American ancestor above alluded to, William Beardsley, came from England in 1635, in the ship *Planter*, commanded by Captain Travice. He was then only thirty years of age, but had a wife and three children, all of whom accompanied him hither. He came from Stratford-on-Avon (the birthplace of William Shakespeare), and was made a freeman in Massachusetts, but afterwards, in 1639, settled in the Connecticut township, to which the family gave the name of Stratford, in honor of the English town from which they had emigrated. The town of Avon, N. Y., was also named by descendants of William Beardsley who settled there, in honor of the old river in England. William Beardsley was a deputy for Stratford in 1645, and for seven years thereafter, and was a man of much prominence in

early colonial times. He died in 1660, at the age of fifty-six, leaving three children. The succession in the line of the subject of this sketch was through Joseph Beardsley, the youngest son. The generations from Joseph were John, Andrew, Henry, William Henry, and Charles,—the latter being the father of Charles W. Beardsley, the present subject. Charles W. is the oldest of a family of eight children, the brothers and sisters being the following, all of whom are now living, and residents of Milford, except as otherwise stated: Abigail, now the wife of Charles R. Baldwin of Milford; Alvira; Hezekiah, an extensive contractor and builder in Milford; George, now residing in New Haven; Theodore, a prominent builder, of Springfield, Mass.; Sarah J., wife of Edward Clark of Milford; and Frederick, the youngest.

Mr. Charles W. Beardsley was educated in the common and select schools of his native town, and commenced learning the shoe business at the age of fifteen, which he followed for eighteen years, when, his health partially failing by close confinement in his work, he engaged in the produce business, importing the same from Montreal, Canada; and continued this business twelve years. He then bought one of the best farms in the town of Milford, and is engaged in the seed business for Peter Henderson & Company of New York city. Mr. Beardsley has bred some of the finest Jersey cattle that have appeared in America, and for which he has obtained large prices. He has held the offices of town agent and first selectman for twelve successive years, and was one of the directors of the Milford Savings Bank. He is a member of the Odd Fellows lodge in Milford, has been a member of the fire department for twenty-two years, and a member of the second company Governor's Foot Guards (organized 1775) under Governor Buckingham. He was elected a member of the house of representatives of Connecticut in 1889, for two years, and served on the railroad committee; and was commissioner on the Washington bridge. He gave a full history of the old bridge, and when the bill came before the house to have the structure made a free bridge, supported by New Haven and Fairfield counties, he made a strong argument in favor of the free bridge system,—and the bill was passed. He was re-elected a member of the house of representatives for the years 1891-92, and is again a member of the railroad committee.

Mr. Beardsley joined the First Church of Christ at Milford in the year 1850, and is esteemed in his native town and in the town where he resides, and wherever known, as an honorable and upright citizen. He married Sarah, daughter of Elnathan Baldwin of Milford, in 1850, and has the following children: Dewitt Clinton Beardsley, who married Miss Martha P. Avery of Stratford, and has three children, Medorah H., Maud C., and Stanley A. Beardsley; Sarah Etta Beardsley, who married Charles Clark of Milford, and had two children, George W. and Elwood R. Clark; and Charles Frederick Beardsley, the youngest, who resides at home, and is in company with his father in the seed business. The Beardsley family is a quite numerous one in Connecticut, and in all its branches has maintained the honorable reputation transmitted through succeeding generations from William Beardsley the venerated ancestor.

JULIUS ATTWOOD, East Haddam: Attorney-at-Law; President National Bank of New England.

Julius Attwood was born at East Haddam, February 23, 1824, and has resided in that town continuously since his birth, except from the years

1847 to 1854. He was the fifth of the seven living children left by his father, who died in 1829, five of whom are still living. He was educated in the common schools of his native town until he was twelve years of age, after which time he was employed for five years in the coasting trade and in ferrying on the Connecticut river. Not being robust, he served a four-years apprenticeship at shoemaking, but did not continue that occupation after attaining his majority. During his leisure, while an apprentice, he studied by himself and fitted himself as a teacher, and for seven years he taught in the public and higher schools on Long Island and in Maryland. Returning to East Haddam in 1854, he commenced business in a "country store" and continued in trade until 1870, when after a course in reading law, he was duly admitted to the Middlesex county bar, and has followed the profession of law since that time. In 1856 he was elected justice of the peace, which office he has continuously held ever since; and for fourteen years of that time was trial justice of the town; also from 1866 was for nineteen years town clerk and registrar of East Haddam. Elected judge of probate for the district of East Haddam in 1856, he has held that position ever since — for thirty-two years — it being probably a longer continuous period than that held by any other judge in this state now living. In 1873 and 1874 he represented his town in the general assembly, but was defeated afterwards when nominated for the office of senator for the nineteenth senatorial district, by a small plurality, there being a local panic, that

JULIUS ATTWOOD.

year among the "pound fishermen" along the sound shore. Being again nominated to that office, he declined. In 1866 he served one year as Grand Master of the Grand Lodge, I. O. O. F., of Connecticut, and represented that body in the sovereign grand lodge during 1867 and 1868. For many years he has been connected with the National Bank of New England as a director, and has been its president since 1883. Visiting Europe in 1880, he traveled extensively in France, Italy, Switzerland, Germany, Holland, Belgium, England, and Scotland. Politically, he has always been connected with the whig and republican parties. Though favoring Methodism in his youth, in his riper years he thought he could more honor the memory of its great founder by being received into the older church that John Wesley and his brother Charles never dared to forsake; and for forty-eight years he has been a communicant in the Episcopal church.

Mr. Attwood has twice married; first in 1852 to Sarah A. Gould of Stony Brook, Long Island, who died in 1860, leaving one son, Frederick J. Attwood, now a resident of Brooklyn, N. Y., who is also married and has four children. Second, in 1862, he married Catharine Palmer of East Haddam, who is still living and whose only child, Bertha Palmer Attwood, is now a student in the Yale Art School, New Haven.

A. S. BEARDSLEY, Plymouth: Mechanic.

Mr. Beardsley was born in New Fairfield, July 22, 1815, and received a common school and academic education. In 1840 he removed to Texas

and engaged in mercantile pursuits, becoming the active partner in the firm of Case, Beardsley & Co. He remained there until the death of his father necessitated his return north. For the last twenty-five years he has been in the employ of the Plume & Attwood Manufacturing Company at Thomaston, being engaged in the mechanical department. In 1874 he

A. S. BEARDSLEY.

was elected president of the Plymouth Library Association, which has trebled the number of its volumes under his management. Mr. Beardsley held a commission in the old state militia. He is a prohibitionist in politics and a member of the Congregational church. His wife, who is still living, was Miss Jane Alcott of Waterbury at the time of her marriage. The family includes four sons and three daughters.

IRA E. FORBES, HARTFORD: Journalist.

Ira Emory Forbes was born in Coventry, January 18, 1843, and received a common school and collegiate education, graduating from Yale in 1870. He enlisted in the Sixteenth Connecticut, July 21, 1862, from the town of Wethersfield, where he was working on a farm at the time for the purpose of earning funds for his college course. He remained in the service until the close of the war. At the capture of Plymouth, N. C., April 20, 1864, he assisted in the execution of plans by which the colors of the

I. E. FORBES.

regiment were kept from falling into the hands of the rebels, and at the time the battle flags of the state were removed to the corridor in the capitol, September 17, 1879, he was the only one then living who was entitled to carry the restored regimental color from the arsenal to the final resting-place of these priceless memorials. Mr. Forbes was confined in the rebel prisons at Andersonville, Ga., and Florence, S. C., during the summer and fall of 1864. He was paroled at Savannah the last of November, and spent the winter of 1864-5 in the naval academy hospital at Annapolis, Md. In June, 1865, he was discharged at Newberne, N. C., remaining there to engage in the work of the United States sanitary commission. After returning home from the war, he spent one year in completing the preparation for Yale, studying at Lyme under William A. Magill, who had been his instructor in Wethersfield. From the outset the necessary funds for the course were earned by the hardest kind of manual work. During the winter term of senior year, however, Mr. Forbes acted as principal of the Collegiate Institute at Newton, N. J. In 1871-2 he was one of the teachers at Gen. Russell's Military School in New Haven, the year after graduation having been spent in the Yale Theological Seminary. In July, 1872, he entered the employ of the *Springfield Union*, and remained with that paper until October, 1874, when he became the telegraph editor of the *Hartford Evening Post*. His connection with the *Post* was discontinued October 1, 1890. Mr. Forbes was the originator of the legislative supplement which the *Post* has issued since 1875, introducing that feature after coming here from Springfield. He succeeded the late A. S. Hotchkiss as the Hartford correspondent of the *New York Times*, and still retains that appointment. For ten years he was connected with *The Ætna*, the quarterly issued under the

auspices of the Ætna Life, his best literary work appearing in that publication. Mr. Forbes is a member of the Yale College church, Hampden Lodge of Odd Fellows, Springfield, Mass.; the Society of the Army of the Potomac, New York city; the Army and Navy Club of Connecticut; the Union Prisoners' Association; the Veteran Corps of the Governor's Foot Guard, and the Yale Alumni Association of this city. He was a member of the staff of National Commander Warner of the Grand Army, being appointed to the position from Connecticut. He has also been a member of the executive committee of the Sixteenth Connecticut. He is a republican in politics, but has not failed since he became a voter to deposit his ballot for the candidates whom he has considered best fitted for public office. July 18, 1872, he was married to Miss Sarah R. Short of New Haven, who is still living. There are no children in the family. All of his early years were spent in the towns of East Hartford and Manchester, and the first school he ever attended was in the old South district in Scotland, now Burnside.

RALPH S. GOODWIN, M.D., THOMASTON.

Dr. R. S. Goodwin was born in Litchfield, July 24, 1839. The early part of his life was largely spent in New York state, he having lived four years in Albany, ten years in Binghamton, and four years in Brooklyn. For the last twenty-two years he has resided in Thomaston, this state, engaged in the practice of his profession. In addition to the usual training at the local preparatory schools he pursued the course and graduated at the College of Physicians and Surgeons in New York, thoroughly fitting himself for

R. S. GOODWIN.

the medical profession. From 1861 to 1863 he was engaged as teacher of elocution and English language in the New York State Normal School at Albany, and from 1863 to 1865 was a tutor in the Brooklyn Collegiate and Polytechnic Institute, Brooklyn N. Y. During his residence in Thomaston Dr. Goodwin has held various local and state offices, having been acting school visitor and health officer of his town, and being at present a member of the state board of health. He married Miss Jennie Edith Irvine, and they have two children, a son and a daughter. In politics he is a republican and in religious matters a Congregationalist. He is also a member of the Order of Odd Fellows, being a Past Grand of the local lodge.

W. C. RUSSELL, Orange.

William C. Russell was born in Orange, March 13, 1835, and received a public school education. In 1871 he was a member of the general assembly,

W. C. RUSSELL.

representing the town of Orange in the house. He has held most of the offices within the gift of the town and is at present a member of the board of selectmen and a justice of the peace. Mr. Russell is a republican in politics. He is engaged in the wholesale meat business and is connected with the Peerless Attachment Co. of Tyler City, and with C. C. Andrew & Co. of New Haven. He is a member of the Congregational church and of Annawan Lodge, No. 115, F. and A. M., of West Haven, also of the Sons of Temperance order. He has been connected with the state militia. Mr. Russell's family consists of a wife and two daughters. The former was Miss Mary J. Lyon prior to her marriage. The home of Mr. Russell is at Tyler City.

LUCIUS BRIGGS, Glasgo (Griswold): Agent Glasgo Yarn Mills.

Ex-State Senator Lucius Briggs was born in the town of Coventry, R. I., Dec. 21, 1825, and was educated at Smithville Academy in that state. He

LUCIUS BRIGGS.

has been engaged through life in the manufacture of cotton goods, and is the agent and a large owner in the Glasgo Yarn Mills. He is a director in several large corporations and banks, and is one of the most prominent business men in eastern Connecticut. Mr. Briggs has been a member of both branches of the general assembly. In 1867 he represented the town of Thompson in the house, his colleague being Mr. Thomas Tallman. In 1873 he represented the old fourteenth district in the senate, his colleagues in that body including Hons. Caleb B. Bowers of New Haven, Fred W. Bruggerhoff of Darien, Thomas S. Marlor of Brooklyn, Washington F. Willcox, now member of congress from the second district, and Chauncey Howard of Coventry, subsequently state comptroller. Mr. Briggs was a presidential elector on the republican ticket in this state when General Grant was elected for the second term. He is a member of the Baptist church. The family to which Mr. Briggs belongs has been a patriotic one, his ancestors on both sides having served in the Revolutionary war. The wife of Mr. Briggs, who was Miss Harriet T. Atwood prior to her marriage, died Sept. 9, 1887. There are two children, the son, C. W. Briggs, residing in New York, and the daughter, Mrs. Floyd Cranska, in Moosup. Ex-Senator Briggs is a citizen of prominence in the state.

G. D. BATES, Putnam: President and Treasurer Putnam Cutlery Company.

Colonel Gustavus D. Bates was a member of the general assembly from Putnam in 1887, serving on the republican side of the house. He was elected

G. D. BATES.

a delegate to the national republican convention in Chicago which nominated President Harrison, and has been an active and influential participant in political interests in eastern Connecticut. He is the president of the Putnam creamery, and of the "Windham County League." He is also the founder of the Putnam Cutlery Company, which manufactures the "Old Put" knives, holding the position of president and treasurer. Colonel Bates is also a director in various corporations at Putnam. He was born in Thompson, October, 1840, and received a common school education. He has had an interesting and remarkable history from boyhood until now. His father was a farmer, and went to Grosvenordale when the subject of this sketch was but seven years of age, as "outside" superintendent for the Grosvenordale Company. The boy, rather than acknowledge a school teacher's authority, became a mill operative. When his father returned to Thompson he returned also, and worked on the farm until sixteen years of age, when he became a school teacher in Burrillville, R. I., continuing for two terms, the following year teaching for two terms at North Grosvenordale, Conn.; afterward entering a factory store at Grosvenordale. He enlisted in 1862 in the Seventh Rhode Island regiment, in which he received seven promotions; and after serving two and a half years returned disabled by exposure and wounds. Young Bates's military ardor and patriotism were so intense that he ran away from home to enlist, much to the disgust of his father, who, when he bade his son good-by, as with his regiment he started for the front, said to him quite pointedly: "Runaway boys do not generally come out very well." Grasping the paternal hand warmly, the young soldier replied: "Father, I'll make a noble exception to your rule!"—which promise he abundantly verified. From 1865 to 1875 he traveled for a Boston house, and when his health gave way returned to Putnam, where he had married Miss Ellen A. Hutchins, daughter of Benjamin F. Hutchins of Thompson. In 1877 he became a commercial traveler from Troy, N. Y., and within a year thereafter went to New York city as manager of a branch house. Thence he went to Putnam in 1884, forming a connection with the "Connecticut Clothing Company." He is at present the outside business manager of Cluett, Coon & Co., linen collars and cuffs. Colonel Bates is a member of the Baptist church, and is regarded with thorough esteem and respect in the community where he resides.

HON. JOHN HURLBURT WHITE, HARTFORD: Attorney-at-Law.

John Hurlburt White was born in the town of Glastonbury, in November, 1833. He received an academical education, and removed to Hartford in 1851, where he read law in the office of the late H. H. Barbour, and was admitted to the bar in March, 1858. He was elected auditor of the city in 1860 on the democratic ticket; continued in that office until 1863, when he was elected judge of probate for the district of Hartford, which position he retained for twenty-three years. Leaving that office in January, 1887, he

J. H. WHITE.

resumed the practice of law. He was a commissioner of the state of Connecticut to receive the votes of the Connecticut soldiers in the field in the presidential election of 1864. Since 1860 he has been connected with the First company Governor's Foot Guard, as an active and veteran member. For many years he has been a director in the Farmers and Mechanics National Bank of Hartford. He is now the president of the Connecticut probate assembly. His religious connections are with the Park church and society of Hartford, of which he has been a member since 1858. He married, in 1860, Miss Jennie M., daughter of George Cooke, Esq., of Litchfield, in this state. They have one son, Henry C. White, an artist of distinction, with whose canvases lovers of art in eastern Connecti-

cut are thoroughly familiar. Judge White is a gentleman of many accomplishments, of rare judicial ability, and possesses social qualities which are appreciated and enjoyed by a large circle of warm personal friends.

MARO S. CHAPMAN, MANCHESTER: Manufacturer of Paper and Envelopes.

Mr. Chapman was born at East Haddam, February 13, 1839, and received a thorough common school education. For three years before the war he was engaged in mercantile pursuits at Manchester, but when the demand for troops was made he enlisted, joining Company C of the Twelfth Connecticut. In 1864 he engaged in the envelope business with the Plimpton Manufacturing Company of Hartford, and has since continued in that avocation. Since the Plimpton Company received the government

M. S. CHAPMAN.

contract, Mr. Chapman has been the superintendent of the United States stamped envelope works in Hartford, and in that position has shown great executive ability and decision of character. He is treasurer of the Plimpton Manufacturing Company; president of the Hartford Manilla Company, which has a large and flourishing mill at Burnside, and an extensive business; vice-president and a director in the Mather Electric Company, and president of the Perkins Lamp Company, both of which companies are located at Manchester, and doing a prosperous business. He is connected with the City Bank of Hartford as a director, and a member of the Hartford board of trade. He has been commander of Drake Post of the Grand Army at South Manchester for eight years, and still holds that position. For upwards of twenty years he has been connected with the republican town committee at Manchester, and is now its chairman. Mr. Chapman has long been an active and greatly valued member of the republican party, and as such has often been called to serve the party and the state in places of public trust. He represented Manchester in the house of representatives in 1881, serving as chairman on the part of that body of the committee on cities and boroughs, one of the hardest-worked committees of that year. His services throughout the session were of genuine value to the state, and his influence was universally acknowledged by his associates. In the fall of 1884 he received the unanimous nomination of the republicans of his district for the senatorship, and was elected by a very handsome majority. He was a member of the republican state convention which nominated Hon. Henry B. Harrison for governor, and during the campaign was an able and influential supporter of the republican cause. He is a clear and forcible speaker, presenting his views with great earnestness and conviction, and is an admirable debater.

Mr. Chapman married Miss Lucy W. Woodbridge, who died in 1860, leaving one daughter who is now the wife of E. S. Ela, editor and publisher of the *Manchester Herald*. His present wife was Miss Helen C. Robbins of Manchester, by whom he has two daughters. The religious connections of the family are with the Center Congregational church of that town.

HENRY S. BARBOUR, Hartford: Attorney-at-Law.

Henry S. Barbour was born at Canton, Conn., August 2, 1822. After the usual preparatory course, he was admitted to the bar at Litchfield in 1849,

and began the practice of his profession in Torrington, where he resided and practiced law for twenty-one years. There he held the offices of judge of probate, town clerk, and town treasurer over fifteen years, and represented that town in the house of representatives in the years 1850 and 1863; and was senator from the then Fifteenth district in 1870, acting as chairman of the judiciary committee. He removed to Hartford in 1870 to enter into a law partnership with his brother, Heman H. Barbour, who died in 1875; since which date he has continued to practice law in Hartford. He married Miss Bartholomew of Sheffield, Mass., in 1841. They have two children, a son and a daughter; his son is the Rev. John Humphrey Barbour, a professor in the Berkeley Divinity School in Middletown. Judge Barbour is of Revolutionary stock; his father was a son of a soldier of the Revolution. His grandfather, Solomon Humphrey, was a Revolutionary soldier; his great-grandfather, John Brown of Simsbury, was also a Revolutionary soldier, and was a grandson of Peter Brown, who came over in the *Mayflower*. John Brown, the martyr, was a grandson of the above-mentioned John Brown of Simsbury, making him the second cousin of Mr. Barbour. Sylvester Barbour of Hartford and Edward P. Barbour of Ansonia are brothers of the subject of this biography.

H. S. BARBOUR.

CHARLES H. BABCOCK, Stonington: Principal of Public School No. 16.

Mr. Babcock was born in Groton in 1838, and has been engaged in teaching since he was sixteen years of age. He was educated in the seminary at

East Greenwich, R. I., preparing him for the profession which has occupied him through life. He was an instructor in the New Jersey schools for a number of years. Mr. Babcock has held numerous offices in the town of Stonington, being at present a member of the boards of education and health, and a justice of the peace. He has also been a member of the board of assessors. He is an attendant of the Baptist church, and is connected with the Masonic order, being a member of the lodge in Stonington. In politics he is a republican. Principal Babcock has a wife and three children. The present Mrs. Babcock, who is his second wife, was Miss M. Emma Gardner, of South Kingston, R. I., previous to marriage. The first wife was Miss Abbie Hinckley, of Stonington.

C. H. BABCOCK.

JOHN O'NEILL, Waterbury: Lawyer.

Mr. O'Neill was born in Canada Village, in the town of Goshen, November 5, 1841. His parents removed to Waterbury in 1848, in which city he was educated in the public schools. At the breaking out of the war of the rebellion he enlisted in the First Regiment, Connecticut Volunteers, participated in the first battle of Bull Run, and was honorably discharged at the end of his term of service. The year following he began the study of law in the office of Judge John W. Webster of Waterbury, and at the end of a three years course was admitted to the bar and soon after to a partnership with his former instructor. The law firm of Webster & O'Neill has continued ever since. Mr. O'Neill represented Waterbury in the general assembly of 1889, where he was author or chief promoter of much of the tax legislation of that session; notably the investment tax law, the collateral inheritance tax law, and the law relative to the taxation of telegraph and ex-

JOHN O'NEILL.

press companies. Mr. O'Neill has held office in Waterbury almost continuously since attaining his majority, having been a justice of the peace for thirty years, assistant city attorney ten years, and prosecuting agent of the county seven years. He is now president of the board of trustees of Bronson Library, president of the Choral Union, and a member of the secret society of the Knights of Columbus. He is a democrat in politics, and in religious faith a Roman Catholic. He is married and has five children.

DWIGHT NOYES CLARK, WOODBRIDGE: Cattle Broker.

The subject of this sketch was born in the town of Bethany in 1829. His father, Mr. Noyes Clark, and his mother, whose maiden name was Mary Abigail Clark, were both descended from the two different family lines of that name, who came early from Milford and settled in the town of Woodbridge, which then included Bethany. On his father's side he traces his ancestry back to Deacon George Clark, one of the deputies under the old Colonial government, and to Governor Robert Treat, who was governor

D. N. CLARK.

of the colonies for fifteen years, from 1686 to 1701; also to Rev. Roger Newton, the second pastor of Milford; and Rev. Thomas Hooker, the first pastor of Hartford. With such an honored ancestry, if there is anything in the old adage that "The blood tells," it might be expected that Mr. Clark would become an honored and useful citizen, and the expectation in his case is not a disappointment. He has been interested in church and society, and living near the Woodbridge line, he has been identified with the Congregational society of Woodbridge, of which the Rev. S. P. Marvin, the contributor of this article, has been settled as pastor for twenty-six years. Mr. Clark has been one of its most liberal supporters, and was one of the committee; gave valuable advice and was liberal with his means for remodeling the church, making it for the time one of the most elegant country churches in all the region.

He has been representative to the general assembly, and honored with the gift of every office in his town which he would accept. Politically he is a conservative democrat. He was in full sympathy with the government and prominent in its aid in the late war. He has always taken a deep interest in

the schools and been ready to contribute liberally for their support and improvement; also to whatever would promote the culture and refinement of society. He inherited from his grandfather a large and profitable business as a cattle broker. His affable manner, square and liberal dealing have won for him the respect and esteem of his townsmen, and of a large circle of customers who rely upon him for the purchase and sale of cattle; and is known for his extensive business transactions in all the western part of the state, as well as at Albany and Chicago. In addition to his regular business he has frequently been employed in the settlement of entangled estates, working from philanthropic rather than mercenary motives, and very often without pay, in order to retain a home for the worthy, and is justly entitled to the epithet "The burden bearer," which has often been applied to him.

Mr. Clark married Miss Althea, daughter of Hon. J. W. Bradley, a staunch republican, senator and judge of probate; also holding the first offices of the town for years in the strongly democratic town of Bethany. They have one child, a son, Mr. N. D. Clark, who has distinguished himself as a scholar in the scientific department of Yale University.

JAMES D. McGAUGHEY, M.D., WALLINGFORD:

Dr. McGaughey was born in Greeneville, East Tennessee, August 6, 1848, and is now in his forty-third year. His paternal ancestors were of Scotch Irish descent, Presbyterians, and emigrated early to America. His great-grandfather was born in Pennsylvania, and was a member of General Marion's independent brigade, being with him during the Revolutionary War, in his campaigns in the Carolinas. He was also territorial sheriff under John Sevier before the territory became a state, and served under

J. D. McGAUGHEY.

Sevier after he became the first governor of Tennessee. Dr. McGaughey's grandfather and father were born in Tennessee. The former served several times in the Tennessee state legislature, being a member at the time of the bitter fight over the removal of the capital from Murfreesboro to Nashville. His father was a merchant, doing a large business, but lost almost everything during the war, being an uncompromising unionist. The doctor's maternal grandfather, George Burkhardt, was of German descent, and emigrated to Sullivan county, East Tennessee, from Frederick City, Maryland. He built the first paper mill, and made the first sheet of paper manufactured in the state of Tennessee, the little antiquated village where the mill stood, four miles east of Bristol, being called Paperville to this day. His wife was of English descent, making the subject of this sketch a compound of Scotch, Irish, English, and German ancestry. Dr. McGaughey was educated at Greeneville College, until it was destroyed by the invading armies, after which his education was completed under private tutors. He commenced the study of medicine in 1866, and graduated from the Jefferson Medical College, Philadelphia, in March, 1870. He practiced two years in East Tennessee, when, having married a granddaughter of Deacon Lyman Cannon of Wallingford, this state, by whom he has since had five children, three now living, he removed from Tennessee, coming to Wallingford, where he has since resided, and where he has built up a large and lucrative practice. The Doctor served in the lower house of the state legislature in 1880, taking part in the debate on a final settlement of the boundary line between Connecticut and New York, which had been in dispute for over a hundred years. He is a member of the New Haven County Medical Society, and of the Connecticut State Medical Society. He holds the appointment of "medical examiner" for Wallingford under the new coroners' law, is the post surgeon for the examination of subjects for military exemption from taxes, and was registrar of vital statistics of the town for eight successive years.

JERE D. EGGLESTON, MERIDEN: Physician and Surgeon.

Dr. Eggleston was born in Long Meadow, Mass., October 28, 1853, and was educated at Williams College and the College of Physicians and Surgeons of New York city. His

professional life has been spent principally at Windsor Locks and Meriden, eleven years in all having been spent in the city. He has been a member of the board of aldermen and city physician, and is a republican in politics. Dr. Eggleston is a man of great personal energy, and attained his education by his own exertions, first earning money for the purpose of a course, and afterwards by teaching school. His father was Jere D. Eggleston, who died when the subject of this sketch was in infancy.

The death of Dr. Eggleston's mother followed while he was still a youth, leaving him dependent upon himself. He is a son-in-law of the Hon. Thomas Duncan of Windsor. He married the oldest daughter of that gentleman, Miss Libbie Duncan, in 1881. There have been four children as the result of the union, three of whom are now living. Dr. Eggleston is a member of Meridian Lodge, No. 77, F. and A. M. of Meriden, and of the order of Odd Fellows.

WALTER J. LEAVENWORTH, WALLINGFORD: Treasurer R. Wallace & Sons Manufacturing Company.

Colonel Leavenworth is a native of the town of Roxbury, Conn. He was born February 20, 1843. Since finishing his education at the public schools

of Wallingford, to which place the family removed in 1853, he has followed manufacturing, having started out as entry clerk with Hall, Elton & Co., of that place, in 1862. He afterwards became secretary of the corporation, retaining the position until 1877, when he was elected treasurer and general manager of the R. Wallace & Sons Manufacturing Company.

W. J. LEAVENWORTH.

From his first connection in this official capacity with the company, its business has trebled and is still increasing rapidly. He has been called by his fellow-citizens to occupy various public positions, including that of burgess of the borough of Wallingford for four years, chairman of the board of water commissioners for the same period, and he is now president of the Wallingford board of trade. Additionally to his business relations above specified, he is the president and a director of the Wallingford Gas Light Company, director in the First National Bank, and has membership with the Arcanum Club of Wallingford, and the Quinnipiac Club, and Republican League of New Haven. His religious connections are with the First Congregational church, and his political faith is that of the republican party. Colonel Leavenworth has a military record covering nearly twenty years. He enlisted as a private in Company K, Second Regiment, Connecticut National Guard, September 15, 1871; was appointed first sergeant on the 19th of the same month, and promoted successively to second lieutenant, December 14, 1871; to first lieutenant, August 25, 1873; and to captain, January 20, 1874; resigning January 17, 1877. He was again appointed to the captaincy of the same company, November 11, 1880, and again resigned June 16, 1882. July 26, 1882, he was elected lieutenant-colonel of the Second Regiment; and on the 16th of February, 1885, was promoted to be its colonel. This position he retained for several years, resigning from the command on the 22d of June, 1889. He was esteemed as an efficient officer and a strict disciplinarian.

Colonel Leavenworth was married to Miss Nettie A. Wallace of Wallingford, daughter of Robert Wallace, Esq., and they have had four children, three of whom are now living. It may be said that he has, during his business career, identified himself prominently with every proper interest of his town, in the line of public improvements; and has earned the reputation which attaches to him, of being an honorable and useful citizen.

CHARLES C. COMMERFORD, Waterbury: Ex-Postmaster.

Charles C. Commerford has been a well-known figure in democratic politics in the state for a number of years. He was born in New York city, June 2, 1833, and received an English and classical education in the schools of the metropolis. He was engaged in mercantile pursuits in New York until 1864, when he removed to Waterbury and entered the employ of the Great Brook Woolen Mill Company. There he became an active participant in politics, and was elected to offices of trust and responsibility, includ-

C. C. COMMERFORD.

ing that of assessor and member of the Center School district committee. His administration of the school district interests won for him great credit in the city. He was also deputy chief of the original state labor bureau in 1873. He was appointed postmaster by President Cleveland, assuming the duties of the office March 14, 1886, and retained the position until the appointment of Colonel John B. Doherty by President Harrison. Mr. Commerford has been connected with journalism and is familiar with newspaper men throughout the state. He is a gentleman of interesting personality. His father, John Commerford of New York city, was prominently identified with political interests in the metropolis, and was a candidate for congress on the republican ticket in 1860. Many of the older leaders in social and business life are the personal friends of the subject of this sketch. His wife, who was a New York lady, was Miss Eliza-

beth Hamilton, daughter of Alexander Hamilton, and a descendant of the great New York leader of that name, whose statesmanship was of so much value in the first decade of the republic. The family includes two sons and one daughter. Mr. Commerford is connected with the Episcopal church, and has been a member of the Masonic order for thirty-two years. He is a Cleveland democrat and is thoroughly in sympathy with the interests and principles of his party.

CROSSLEY FITTON, Rockville: Agent Rock Manufacturing Company.

Mr. Fitton was born in Oldham, Lancashire, England, December 19, 1839, and was brought to the United States by his parents when he was but three years of age. His father settled at Woonsocket, R. I., where he was engaged in the woolen manufactory of Edward Harris. The subject of this sketch was educated at Lenox Academy, in Berkshire, Mass., and became a woolen manufacturer, as was his father before him. Twenty-six years ago he came to Rockville, and for twenty-four years he has been

CROSSLEY FITTON.

the agent of the Rock Manufacturing Company, being the oldest in continuous service of all who have held official connection with the manufacturing establishments of Rockville. As a woolen manufacturer he ranks among the most able in New England, and during his connection with the Rock Company it has enjoyed continued success and prosperity under his management. The mills have been enlarged, the most improved machinery obtained, the force increased, and woolen goods manufactured equal to any produced in the country. Mr. Fitton was always a hard worker, and often the first man at the mill in the morning and the last to leave at night.

In public opinion Mr. Fitton occupies an influential place. In 1885 he represented the town of Vernon in the general assembly, serving on the republican side. He was an active associate on the building committee which recently erected the beautiful Union Church on the corner of Union street, in the heart of the city. He is identified with Fayette Lodge, F. and A. M., of Rockville, and with the Court Hearts of Oak of Foresters. He has been president and director of the Rockville Water Power Company, a director in the Rockville Railroad Company, the Rockville Aqueduct Company, and the Rockville Gas Light Company. He has always taken a lively interest in the Rockville fire department, and was largely instrumental in securing the first steam fire engine, which was named in his honor. Mr. Fitton married Miss Carrie R. Tarbell of Chester, Vt., and they have three children, one daughter, Mrs. P. B. Leonard, and two sons, George and James Fitton. He ranks among the eminently successful manufacturers and business men of the city and state. Being but fifty-two years of age, he is still in the prime of life; and, as a man of great public spirit, Rockville looks to his future career as certain to be one of much usefulness and honor.

[Mr. Fitton died at his home in Rockville April 29, 1891, after the above sketch had been prepared. —ED.]

HON. STEPHEN NICHOLS, BRIDGEPORT: Farmer.

Hon. Stephen Nichols, son of William and Huldah Nichols, was born September 16, 1804, in Trumbull, Fairfield county, Connecticut. He is of the eighth generation from Sergeant Francis Nichols, of London, England, who with his family removed to America and settled in Stratford, Conn., in 1639. His great-grandfather, Theophilus Nichols, who was one of the early settlers of Fairfield county, died in 1774. His grandfather, Philip Nichols, was a man of much influence in public affairs, and a magistrate for many years. He was a large landholder;

STEPHEN NICHOLS.

owned several slaves; dealt extensively in live stock, many of which he imported to the West Indies, together with produce of various kinds. He owned several vessels which were engaged in the West India trade. William Nichols, the father of Stephen, was a farmer by occupation. He was a member of the Episcopal church, and two of his sisters married Episcopal clergymen. He was twice married; eight children were born of the first marriage, and seven by the second. Stephen Nichols was one of the latter. When he was thirteen years old, having attended the public schools and acquired a respectable education, he was obliged on account of the death of his mother to seek a home for himself, which he did by going to Bridgeport where he had a married sister, with whom he made his home. He worked by the month for farmers for several years, and then learned the boot and shoe trade, which business he

followed for about twenty years. His old love of the farm returning, he gradually turned his attention again to agricultural pursuits, for which he forsook trade and in which he has since been engaged. Mr. Nichols was a whig before the organization of the republican party, but since that time has been an ardent and active republican. As such he was elected to represent the town of Bridgeport in the general assembly of 1878, being the colleague of Hon. P. T. Barnum, and serving on the cities and boroughs committee. Mr. Nichols voted in 1824 for John Quincy Adams, and has voted at every presidential election since. He voted for William Henry Harrison in 1840, was present at the succeeding inauguration ceremonies, and within thirty days thereafter attended his funeral. He has filled various public offices in the town and city of Bridgeport, having been justice of the peace, selectman, assessor, member of the common council of the city and of the town board of relief. Mr. Nichols is a member of the North Congregational church of Bridgeport, and a liberal supporter of its ordinances. Not long ago he made a cash donation of $5,000 to the Olivet church, and more recently has still further shown his generosity by a gift to the same church of valuable real estate on which a new church edifice will be erected and provision made for a parsonage. The Bridgeport *Standard*, which alluded to the first donation in very complimentary terms, afterward made the following reference to Mr. Nichols' later gift :

" Two very important warrantee deeds were executed yesterday by Attorney J. J. Rose, by which Stephen Nichols, Esq., makes another splendid gift to the Olivet Congregational church. By these deeds Mr. Nichols conveys the Hall property entire, which he recently purchased for $10,000, to the church, to be theirs forever, to be used in carrying forward their work. The first deed comprises a strip of land twenty feet wide adjoining the church property, thereby making ample provision for the location of the new church. The second deed comprises the remaining part of the Hall property, including the house, the income of which is to be applied to the general expenses of the church, provision being made, however, by which the pastor will receive his rent free, thus virtually increasing his salary. The property is conveyed free from all incumbrance, making the total gift of Mr. Nichols $15,000. Olivet church is now in possession of one of the finest properties in the city."

The liberality of Mr. Nichols in all matters promotive of moral and religious advancement, is proverbial, and his gifts seem to afford him real satisfaction. He insists that this last bestowment was one of the proudest acts of his life. He is not now in public office, and the only membership he claims, aside from church membership, is with the republican party and the Sons of the American Revolution.

Mr. Nichols was married, March 4, 1829, to Emeline Beardsley, daughter of Aaron Beardsley of

Bridgeport. She died of pneumonia, December 13, 1890, after a very brief illness. She is spoken of as a loving and devoted wife, a kind neighbor, and a most estimable lady. Of their two children, one died in childhood; the other, Stephen Marcus Nichols, served in the war of the rebellion as first lieutenant of Company B, Twenty-third Connecticut regiment, under General Banks, and died July 29, 1870.

Mr. Nichols resides in the same house to which he took his young bride in May, 1829, and where he has lived for sixty-two years. During all this time he has not been absent from the old home more than a dozen nights altogether. It has been the scene of the joys and sorrows of his wedded life, and it is not strange that his attachments to it are now very strong. It is in the vicinity of the home of his ancestors for centuries. Ten generations in a continuous line have been born, lived, died, and been buried within two or three miles, at most, of the spot where his homestead stands; and there, as the last of his family, he expects to remain until called to join the majority. Mr. Nichols has had a very sad and singular experience of bereavement. The death of his only son in 1870 was a severe blow, and left his hopes for a continuous posterity centered in Wilbur E. Nichols, an only grandson. Last December, as above stated, Mr. Nichols' wife was prostrated by a fatal illness. On the first day of last March Wilbur E. Nichols, aged twenty-six, was stricken with apoplexy while attending the service in St. John's church, and was conveyed to his home where he died a few hours later. The circumstances were particularly distressing. He had been in poor health for some time, and was intending to go to Florida the day following that on which he died. He was a young man greatly esteemed and beloved, and his loss was mourned by a wide circle of acquaintances. On the 13th day of the same month, an infant son of Mr. and Mrs. Swan B. Brewster, and a great-grandson of Hon. Stephen Nichols, died suddenly, a victim of diphtheria. And on the 22d, nine days later, Mrs. Brewster, the child's mother, and the grandchild and only remaining representative of Mr. Nichols' family, followed her infant to the grave, having been attacked with the same terrible and fatal disease. Mrs. Brewster was a young woman of amiable disposition and with many estimable qualities. She was prostrated with grief by the loss of her infant son, and was thus doubtless an easier prey to her disease. She was devotedly attached to the child, as were the entire family. He was a bright and interesting boy, the pet and pride and hope of his great-grandfather, who looked upon him as the instrumentality through whom Providence intended to transmit to posterity his blood, if not his name. [The illustration at the head of this sketch is engraved from a photograph which shows the child in the arms of his great-grandfather, the Hon. Mr. Nichols, the subject of this biography.]

Although now eighty-seven years of age, Mr. Nichols is still in the enjoyment of perfect health, with erect form, ruddy complexion, and faculties unimpaired. He looks like a vigorous man of seventy, and gives good promise of becoming a centenarian. His life has been an eventful one, and within his memory he has a fund of personal reminiscences which constitute him a most agreeable and entertaining companion. He is justly esteemed and venerated by his townsmen, and is to all his acquaintances not only a lively and interesting relic of a former generation, but a good representative of the best element of the present day.

ALBERT P. MARSH, New Britain: House Decorator.

A. P. Marsh, the prosperous and youthful proprietor of a well-known paint and house decorating establishment in New Britain, was born in Birmingham, England, July

1, 1867. When he was eighteen months old his parents emigrated to this country, and afterwards resided in Boston, Providence, New York, Brooklyn, finally settling in New Britain in 1873. From early life, or since he became eight years of age, Mr. Marsh has been compelled to rely upon his own exertions and resources. He managed

to attend school a portion of several years, though compelled to work between school hours to maintain himself. At the age of thirteen he forsook school, and commenced life in the shop, later learning the painters' trade in all its several branches, becoming practically proficient in each. When but nineteen years old he began business for himself, without capital or influential friends, and in the face of quite formidable obstacles. His obliging manners and evident knowledge of his business soon brought him patrons, however, and assured the prosperity which has almost from the first attended his efforts, and which has given his establishment a prominent place among the best in his line. In 1890 he erected a fine residence on Greenwood street, which was a significant undertaking for a young unmarried man to engage in. Mr. Marsh deals quite considerably in real estate, and in the prosecution of his business employs a large force of skilled workmen. He possesses traits of character which make him popular among those over whom he exercises authority, and which attract patrons to his place of business. Being thus "wise in his day and generation," he is likely to become a man of wealth and influence in the city of his adoption.

A. F. NASON, HARTFORD: Superintendent of Agencies, Ætna Life Insurance Company.

Almond Francis Nason, son of Rufus Nason, was born in Waterville, Me., December 14, 1841. He fitted for Waterville College (now Colby University), but, preferring mer-

A. F. NASON.

cantile pursuits, went to Boston in 1859, and engaged as bookkeeper. During the war he was a regular correspondent for the *Waterville Mail* and *Portland Daily Press*. In 1862 he made a trip as sutler on the United States steamer Rhode Island, Admiral Trenchard commander, from Boston to all the blockaded ports of the southern confederacy as far as the Rio Grande and return, arriving at New Orleans in October, while General Butler was in possession of the city. On his return to Boston he married, and re-engaged as bookkeeper. On August 1, 1864, he began his first engagement in life insurance as assistant general agent of the New York Life Insurance Company at its Boston branch office. At the conclusion of that engagement in 1867, he formed a co-partnership with L. A. Lyon, under the firm name of Lyon & Nason, as state agents for Massachusetts of the Mutual Benefit Life Insurance Company of Newark, N. J. Their agency became the largest in Boston, and the leading one of the company. In 1870 Great Britain was added to their management, and his partner visited that country to establish agencies. (This was the only foreign business ever done by that company.) In 1872 Mr. Lyon disposed of his interest to S. M. Loveridge, the firm thereafter being Nason & Loveridge. In January, 1875, Mr. Nason retired from the agency with a competency. That year he organized, in connection with his former partner, Mr. Lyon, the Shawmut Insurance Company, with the largest cash capital of any fire insurance company in Boston ($800,000), and was its first vice-president. The financial panic, beginning in 1875, so reduced real estate values that he lost heavily. In 1877 he organized the Locke Regulator Company, and was

its president. In 1879 he disposed of his interest to Mr. Nelson Curtis, — whose name the company now bears, — and came to Hartford to accept the position of adjuster for the Ætna Life Insurance Company. In 1882 he was appointed superintendent of agencies of that company, the position now held by him.

Mr. Nason has always been an ardent republican, having served as delegate to gubernatorial and senatorial conventions in Massachusetts. He is vice-president of the First Unitarian Congregational Society of Hartford. He was for ten years on the standing committee of the famous old Hollis Street church in Boston, and was a delegate to the national convention of the Unitarians in Saratoga (1873) and Philadelphia (1890). He was appointed a justice of the peace by Governor Rice, and re-appointed by Governor Washburn, for two terms of seven years each. During the past twelve years he has traveled very extensively and almost constantly over the United States and the Dominion of Canada, in connection with the responsible duties of his position with the old and well-known company with which he has so long been associated.

Mr. Nason was united (1862) in marriage to Miss Grace E. Blanchard of Boston, who died in 1886, leaving two children, a son and daughter. He is a member of the Masonic fraternity. His experience in life insurance has been wide and successful, and he is esteemed an adept in the department of which he is an active manager.

E. W. DEWEY, NORTH GRANBY: Judge of Probate.

Edward Watson Dewey was born in North Granby, October 29, 1857, and was educated at Williston Seminary, East Hampton, Mass. In 1889

E. W. DEWEY.

he represented the town of Granby in the general assembly, serving on the republican side of the house. He is the judge of probate in the Granby district, and has held other responsible offices, including that of justice of the peace. Judge Dewey has also been engaged in mercantile pursuits; has held the chairmanship of the republican town committee, and is the Worshipful Master of St. Mark's Lodge, No. 91, F. and A. M., of Granby. He is connected with the Universalist church, and is one of the most thoroughly esteemed residents of the town of Granby. Judge Dewey is without a family.

DANIEL J. DONAHOE, MIDDLETOWN: Attorney-at-Law.

Daniel J. Donahoe is a native of Brimfield, Mass., born February 27, 1853. He finished his education at Wesleyan University, Middletown, in 1872, studied law for three years, and was admitted to the bar in June, 1875. He engaged in the practice of his profession at Meriden three years, then located in Middletown, where he has since been in continuous practice. He married Margaret Burns, who died in April, 1888, leaving two young children, daughters. Mr. Donahoe is a member of the Catholic

D. J. DONAHOE.

church, and of the democratic party. He holds the associate judgeship of the Middletown city court, is a member of the city board of education, and president of the town board of health. He stands well as a lawyer before the bar of Middlesex County, is an earnest and conscientious advocate, and a gentleman of fine literary accomplishments. He is author of " Idyls of Israel, and other poems," published in 1888, and "A Tent by the Lake, and other poems," 1889. Both volumes have had a fair sale, and have been well received by the public.

HENRY M. WHITE, TORRINGTON: Editor " Torrington Register."

Henry M. White, member of the general assembly from Torrington for the current term, is the editor of the *Torrington Register*, which has

H. M. WHITE.

for years been a leading county paper in Western Connecticut. Mr. White has been at the head of the paper for nine years. In 1889 he founded the *Daily Register*, which has a handsome clientage in the flourishing borough of Torrington and the adjacent localities. Mr. White was born at Elba, N. Y., and was educated at the Shelburne Falls Academy, Mass. He was formerly engaged in the manufacture of hardware, occupying the positions of foreman and salesman. He has resided in Shelburne Falls and Northampton, Mass., and in New York. Mr. White is connected with the Congregational church

at Torrington, and is the secretary of the Y. M. C. A. in that place. He was the superintendent of the Sunday-school at Northampton. He is the president of the Mercantile Co-operative Bank, and is a member of the Knights of Honor. His wife, who is living, was Miss Minnie A. Cole prior to her marriage. There are no children.

BULKLEY EDWARDS, CROMWELL: President Cromwell Savings Bank

Mr. Edwards is a descendant of Churchill Edwards, who came from England many generations ago and settled in Wethersfield in this state, since which his descendants have mostly made their homes in the Connecticut valley. Bulkley Edwards was born in Cromwell, May 29, 1811, and during the fourscore years of his life has maintained a continuous residence in the identical house where he was born. His educational training was at the district and high school of Cromwell. He was reared in the hotel and farm life

BULKLEY EDWARDS.

which his father led until his death in 1836, and which he then took up and has since followed. He has three times married; his first wife dying in 1854 and the second in 1863; he married last Mrs. Cornelia Wilcox of Wethersfield, December 28, 1887. Of the four children who have been born to him, neither is now living. Additionally to his hotel business, Mr. Edwards is something of a farmer, owning and improving a considerable tract bordering on the Connecticut River. His farm has been cut in two twice by the locating across it of the Valley and the Cromwell railroads, and though estimated to have been thus damaged to the extent of $1,500, he regards the railroads as of more practical benefit than damage to his property. Mr. Edwards is president of the Cromwell Savings Bank, which position he has occupied for twelve years. He has been first selectman a number of terms, county commissioner four years, member of the board of assessors and board of relief, and has held various minor local offices; until at his present age he feels that he has performed his part of the public service, and has declined further public honors or burdens. Mr. Edwards was reared a Jackson democrat. When he became of age and was made an elector, he recalls that his father told him to vote as he thought best, but always to put his ballot down right side up. As a democrat he has for five different terms represented Cromwell in the legislature, and he has never given his associates or constituents reason to think that he was ashamed of his politics. He is an attendant at the Baptist church of his native town, in the support of which he is a liberal contributor.

JOHN A. CRILLY, HARTFORD: Ex-Alderman Fourth Ward.

John A. Crilly was born at Pike River, in the province of Quebec, April 22, 1847, and received a common school education, preparing him for an

J. A. CRILLY.

active and successful business career. He removed to Hartford in 1862, and has since been a resident of the city. He has been connected with the Hartford & Wethersfield Horse Railroad Company most of the time since his removal to Hartford, and has been in charge of important and responsible interests on the line for a number of years. Mr. Crilly is one of the most trusted men in the management of the company, and much of its success is due to his administration and influence. He has been a member of the court of common council in this city since 1877, when he was first elected a member of the council board from the Fourth ward, receiving a total of 627 votes. He served in that board for six consecutive years, acquiring special familiarity with municipal interests. In 1883 he was advanced to the board of aldermen, receiving a larger vote for that office than the one polled when he was first elected councilman. Mr. Crilly has served eight years consecutively in the upper board, making a period of fourteen years of active identification with the municipal government. No one in local public life has been longer associated with the city's interests, and it can be said with the utmost candor and honesty that he has been a faithful and unfaltering advocate of local progress. The different municipal departments owe a great deal to his watchfulness and supervision. From the beginning of his career he has been an intelligent observer of the effect of city legislation, and where improvements have been needed he has promptly and efficiently co-operated in their inauguration. For a number of years he has held the chairmanship of the committee on amusements, a place of decided importance, considering the fact that the chairman must be constantly on the alert against the admission of undesirable plays and companies for entertainments in the city. The matter of regulating playbills and placards

placed in public resorts is left mainly to the decision of the chairman of the committee. Ex-Alderman Crilly is a prominent Mason, being a member of St. John's Lodge, Pythagoras Chapter, Wolcott Council, and Washington Commandery, Knights Templar. He is one of the oldest members and past grand of Hartford Lodge, I. O. O. F.; member of Crescent Lodge, Knights of Pythias, and of the Hartford order of Elks. One year ago he was elected a member of the board of selectmen of Hartford, having previously served one term by appointment. He has been a member of the Fourth ward republican committee for ten years, and is also an active and influential member of the town committee. In addition to the work that has demanded his attention in connection with the horse railroad company, he has dealt extensively in real estate, and is a member of the board of directors of the Glastonbury Horse Railroad Company. Mr. Crilly is an attendant at the South Park Methodist church in this city. He has a wife and one son, John A. Crilly, Jr. Two daughters have died. Mrs. Crilly was Miss Louisa A. Smith of Wethersfield prior to her marriage. As a citizen and business man Mr. Crilly has manifested the deepest interest in Hartford, and his success in various fields of activity has been thoroughly merited.

FRANK W. MIX, NEW BRITAIN: Superintendent Corbin Cabinet Lock Company.

Major Frank W. Mix was born in Terryville, February 17, 1834. He attended the village school until he was sixteen, when he went into the factory

F. W. MIX.

with his father. What is now the Eagle Lock Company in Terryville was then Lewis & Gaylord. Here he learned the art of die-making and pressing, and obtained a general idea of machine work. At the age of twenty he left home, going to Waterbury to perfect himself as a machinist and toolmaker. At the end of six months he accepted a call from New Haven to take charge of the die and press work of the New Haven Clock Company, where he remained a year. Still having a desire to become a perfect tool-maker, he secured a position with what is now the Winchester Arms Company, then run by Smith & Wesson, as a tool-maker, remaining there until the concern failed in 1857. While in New Haven Major Mix became actively interested in musical matters, having charge of the choir and playing the organ in one of the churches. Here he was also married in 1856. After the failure of the pistol company, Major Mix went into the sewing-machine business with his father-in-law, R. B. Fuller, locating in Mansfield, afterwards in Norwich, continuing until 1860, when they sold out, the Major going to the Sharps' Rifle factory in Hartford. In the spring of 1861, his health being impaired, he removed to Michigan, where, September 1, 1861, he enlisted in the Third Michigan cavalry, with which he served for eleven months, when he was appointed a captain of the famous Fourth Michigan cavalry. While with the Third he took part in the capture of New Madrid and Island No. 10, and the battles of Corinth, Iuka, and Boonville, Miss. He joined the Fourth cavalry at Mumfordsville, Ky., and was promoted to be major for gallantry at the battle of Stone River. While he was in command of the regiment it took part in eighty-four general engagements, not to mention scores of lesser events. These included Chattanooga, Chickamauga, Mission Ridge, and most of the important actions of the western army up to the siege of Atlanta. He was severely wounded at Lovejoy's Station in August, 1864, on account of which he received an honorable discharge in the following November. He lost two horses in action, and was repeatedly named by corps and brigade commanders for gallantry, promptness, and the skillful manner in which he handled his regiment in tight places. On two different occasions the brigade commander attributed the success of his brigade " to the brilliancy and tenacity of the fighting of the Fourth Michigan, under the command of Major Frank W. Mix." It was this regiment that at the close of the war captured Jefferson Davis.

During the last twenty-five years Major Mix has resided in this state, engaged in the manufacture, as well as the invention, of locks. During that time he has probably taken out more patents on cabinet and trunk locks than any man in the country. In 1870 he brought out a padlock, known as the Mix lock, which the government adopted for mail bags, and which was manufactured by the Eagle Lock Company, where Major Mix was employed as superintendent for ten years. Since that time he has resided in New Britain as superintendent of the Corbin Cabinet Lock Company, in which position he has made a notable success, as is attested by the flourishing condition of the business at the present time. He is also half owner in the Park drug store in New Britain, which ranks among the first in the city and state. He has a wife, who before her marriage was Miss Mary J. Fuller, and three children, a son and two daughters, his only son being a superintendent of the government lock repair shop in Washington. The Major is always a republican in politics, is connected with the First

Congregational church, is a member of the Masonic fraternity, of the O. U. A. M., the Grand Army, the New Britain Club, the Army and Navy Club, and the Putnam Phalanx. He is a useful and respected citizen, and occupies, with his family, an honorable position in the community.

GEORGE FLINT, THOMPSON: Judge of Probate.

George Flint was born at Oxford, Mass., Oct. 17, 1832, and received a common school education in the town in which he now resides, all but six months of his life having been spent in that community. He has been the judge of probate in the Thompson district for nineteen years, member of the board of relief for twenty-four, and registrar of voters for four years. He has also held the office of selectman, and in every position which he has occupied he has faithfully represented the public interest. His general avocation has

GEORGE FLINT.

been that of a farmer. He has been a republican in politics since 1856. Judge Flint is a lineal descendant, on the paternal side, of Thomas Flint, who came from Wales to Salem, Mass., about 1642; on the maternal side, of John Cary, who came to Plymouth in 1635. His wife, who died Nov. 6, 1889, was Miss Gertrude I. Dowling. One son survives.

ROBERT WALLACE, WALLINGFORD: President R. Wallace & Sons Manufacturing Company.

Robert Wallace, the creator and founder of the great silver and plated-ware manufactory which bears his name, was born in Prospect, Conn., November 13, 1815. In his youth he had the advantages which the common schools of his day afforded, and with a fair education went out into the world to seek his fortune. He was under brief engagements at Watertown, Cheshire, and North Haven, but many years ago gravitated to Wallingford, where he established, at first in a small way, the industry which, under his

ROBERT WALLACE.

fostering care and management, has since become one of the most prosperous of its kind in the state. He has literally spent his life in it, devoting his time, his thought, and his energies to it, to the exclusion of all public service, and largely of active participation in the ordinary enjoyments of social life. His history is practically the history of his company and its business, with which he has always been intimately identified. Mr. Wallace was married many years ago to Miss Louisa Moulthrop, now deceased. They have had nine children, eight of whom are still living. His political affiliations are with the republican party.

REV. HORACE WINSLOW, A.M., WEATOGUE, (SIMSBURY): Congregational Clergyman.

Rev. Horace Winslow is a lineal descendant of Kenelm Winslow(brother of Governor Edward), who first settled at Marshfield, Mass., the homestead remaining in the family for four generations. Horace was born in Enfield, Mass., May 18, 1814. When he was about two years of age, his father removed to Pittsford, Western New York. Later, he was employed as clerk in a bookstore in Rochester, which city was his home until he was settled in the ministry. He was married May 8, 1850, to Miss Charlotte H. Pettibone of Simsbury, Conn. Three daughters have been born to them, two of whom are now living. He was educated at Hamilton College, from which he received the degree of A.M., and at Auburn Theological Seminary, and the Union Theological Seminary in New York city. He was ordained and installed pastor of the Presbyterian church of New Windsor, N. Y., in the spring of 1842. In 1843 he became pastor of the Second Presbyterian church in Lansingburg. In 1845 he was settled as pastor of the Congregational church of Rockville, Conn. In 1852 he resigned and accepted a call from the First Congregational church of New Britain. In January, 1858, he was installed pastor of the Congregational church of Great Barrington, Mass. Having been appointed Chaplain of the 5th regiment of Connecticut Volunteers, in February, 1862, he at once resigned his charge and joined the army. Late in the year, in consequence of ill health, being unable to follow the regiment, he resigned and returned to his home. In 1863 he became pastor of the Congregational church of Binghamton, N. Y. After five years of service there, he resigned and returned to Connecticut. For a few months he was in the service of the American Missionary Association, and also of the South church of Woodbury,

REV. H. WINSLOW.

from which he had received a call, but finally declined it and accepted one from the Congregational church of Willimantic, where he was settled in 1869. In 1876, while driving in a severe thunder storm, he was struck by lightning, thrown from the carriage, and taken up insensible. After recovering consciousness, he was for a time in a very critical condition. His people gave him a vacation for six months, after which he resumed work. Finally, after a service of a little more than twelve years, his health not being firm, he resigned his charge, and located at Weatogue, Simsbury, where he now resides. With this change his health improved, and in a short time he resumed his work in the pulpit, and has continued to the present time, supplying in Providence, R. I., for two years, in Litchfield, Hartford, and for nine months in his former church in Great Barrington, Mass.; also about three years in Simsbury.

Mr. Winslow has ever been an earnest worker in the interests and prosperity of the communities in which he has lived, in the elevation of the schools, and in village improvements. The two parks at Rockville are the outcome of his labors. The one in front of his church (as it then stood), was graded, enclosed, and, with the help of young men, set out with trees by him. Talcott park was a conception of his. He secured from the owners of the land a refusal of it for one month, for two thousand dollars. Before the time expired, the money was raised by subscription, the amount secured by a very large and generous gift (nearly one-half the amount) from Judge Phineas Talcott. While the spiritual interests of the people have been Mr. Winslow's first consideration, he has been conspicuous in renewing old church edifices and building new ones, securing in this work architectural excellence, convenience, and ventilation. His first settlement witnessed a change in the church edifice. The year following his advent in Rockville, twenty-five feet were added to the church building, with other improvements. Later on, a colony went out and formed a second church. Then a chapel with parlors was erected for the old church. When he removed to New Britain he led the people to erect a new house of worship, with the conveniences of chapel, parlors, and an audience-room seating twelve hundred people. A like work he accomplished at Great Barrington, Mass., and at Willimantic. In these new churches acoustic properties and means of ventilation were complete. He had especial care that the house should be adapted to its use; that the church edifice should have architectural excellence, the audience-room be adapted to speaking and hearing, and in all these particulars he had perfect success. In this work, also, in most cases, he had the chief business of raising money. In Willimantic, where the church building cost forty-seven thousand dollars, more than half of the amount was raised through his personal efforts. In this business of remodeling and building anew he created no burden of debt upon the society, and when a small amount was left, it was from the choice of the society. In Willimantic, when the final debt was twelve thousand dollars, and recognized as an embarrassment to the society, he took the matter up and raised the whole amount. In this building of new churches, the society was lifted into greater independence, and the church into a new spiritual life. Mr. Winslow has been an active worker in the temperance cause, and his Cold Water Army of three hundred children at Rockville became quite famous. Being an earnest advocate of human rights, he was an anti-slavery man, and at the outbreak of the rebellion an ardent defender of the Union. In the conflict of thought at the approach of the war, and since, he has given, on occasions of special interest, many discourses and addresses, which have been published. Mr. Winslow's life has been one of great usefulness to church and state, and he is united by the strongest ties of friendship with large numbers of the best men of the present and past generation.

HOMER L. WANZER, New Fairfield: Farmer.

Homer L. Wanzer was born in New Fairfield, March 3, 1850, being the son of Willis H. and Sarah A. Wanzer, and a descendant of Abraham Wanzer, who emigrated to America from Hesse Castle, Germany, and became a lieutenant in the French war in America. At the age of sixteen the subject of this sketch attended a boarding-school in Oswego village. His studies were completed in 1870 at the Chappaqua Mountain Institute in Westchester county, New York. In 1878 he married Miss Mary Alice Giddings, daughter of James A. Giddings, Jr. Mrs. Wanzer died within a few years, leaving one daughter, Miss Grace Wanzer. The subject of this sketch is a farmer by avocation. He has held the presidency of the Housatonic Agricultural Society two years, and has been a member of the board of directors and president of the New Milford Agricultural Association. He is a democrat in politics, and has been a member of the board of selectmen in New Fairfield since 1884. He is also the president of the town board of health, and is actively associated with local interests and affairs.

H. L. WANZER.

E. A. MERRIMAN, Meriden: Attorney-at-Law.

Judge Emerson A. Merriman has represented Meriden in the legislature during two sessions, serving in 1880 and 1881. He was prominently identified with the legislation of both years, being connected with important committees each year. He is a republican in politics. For thirteen years he was judge of the probate court in Meriden, serving the people of that city with marked acceptance and success. Both as judge and member of the legislature he was governed by the strictest personal honor, and his

E. A. MERRIMAN.

public career has deserved and received the most gratifying approval. He is a member of Meriden Lodge, No. 77, F. and A. M., of Meriden. Judge Merriman was born at Westfield, Mass., August 3, 1842, and was educated at Suffield, in this state, being a graduate of the Literary Institute in that place, and in the law department of the University of Michigan. His wife was Miss Frances E. Johnson before marriage. There are no children in the family. Judge Merriman is a member of the New Haven county bar, and one of the leading attorneys in Meriden.

JOHN P. WOOD, Brooklyn: Cashier Windham County National Bank.

John Palmer Wood was born in Scotland, May 30, 1833, and received a thorough common school education, preparing him for a successful business career. He was a republican in politics until 1884. Since that time he has been connected with the democratic party. He remained on the farm in Scotland until he was eighteen years of age, when he became interested in a mercantile life. From 1864 until 1870 he was in the United States treasury office in Washington. He then removed to Lynn, Mass., where he remained until 1876. Since the latter year he has been connected with the position which he now holds in the bank. He was elected judge of the Brooklyn probate district in 1890, and is now the judge of the court. Judge Wood is connected with

J. P. WOOD.

the Unitarian church. His wife, who is yet living, was Miss Sarah J. Kimball, daughter of Jacob Kimball, prior to her marriage. Mr. and Mrs. Wood have had six children, three of whom are living. The family occupy a prominent place in the community where they reside, and Judge Wood is a leading citizen of eastern Connecticut. He is a member of Moriah Lodge, No. 15, F. and A. M., of Danielsonville, one of the oldest Masonic lodges in the state.

NORRIS G. OSBORN, NEW HAVEN: Editor
"The New Haven Register."

Norris G. Osborn was born in New Haven, Conn., April 17, 1858, and his native place has always been his home. He was educated in the private schools of that city, and in Yale College, from which institution he graduated with the class of 1880. In 1886 his *alma mater* conferred upon him an honorary degree of master of arts. In 1884 he became chief editor of *The New Haven Register*, and has had the entire management of the paper since that time. Mr. Osborn served as senior aid, with the rank

N. G. OSBORN.

of colonel, to Governor Waller, during his administration, from 1882 to 1884. He is a member of many social organizations, chief of which are the Free Masons and the Sons of the American Revolution. He married, in 1881, Miss Kate Gardiner of New York city, and they have three children.

Colonel Osborn's conduct of *The Register* since he has been its editor has been as notable in its way as was that of his father, Minot A. Osborn, who practically founded the paper, and won for it a wide circulation throughout Connecticut. He has developed and broadened the scope of the paper, so as to keep in touch with the most enlightened and progressive journalistic spirit of the age. While he has always defended the sound principles of Jeffersonian democracy, he has shown that the true journalist seeks to mould, and not follow slavishly, public opinion. He has not hesitated to use his influence against prevailing tendencies in his party which he deemed unwise, and has always had the courage of his convictions. *The Register* was an earnest advocate of tariff reform some time before the action of President Cleveland made it the leading issue of his party. It has also been an admirable newspaper — enterprising and thorough in its gathering and exposition of news both in the local and national field. As

dramatic critic of the paper Mr. Osborn has shown himself a thorough and scholarly student of the drama, and displayed the insight of a keen and fearless critic.

In the councils also of the democratic party Mr. Osborn has maintained the family name and proved the worthy son of a worthy sire. Always a patriot more than a partisan, he has opposed tactics that, while they might secure a temporary or questionable advantage, sacrificed equity and justice. Mr. Osborn's winsome nature has won for him a large circle of friends, many of whom are found among his political opponents. A capital story-teller, with a cheery, responsive nature, and sterling spirit of good-fellowship, he is always a welcome comrade in any social circle.

WILLIAM BURR WOOSTER, ANSONIA: Attorney-at-Law.

Colonel William B. Wooster represented the state with honor and distinction in the field during the war, and is deserving of the highest recognition on account of his services. He was the lieutenant-colonel of the Twentieth Regiment, under Colonel Ross of the regular army, and won a brevet colonelcy for meritorious conduct. When the first colored regiment in Connecticut, the Twenty-ninth, was organized in 1864, Lieutenant-Colonel Wooster was selected by Governor Buckingham as its commander. The regiment was mustered into the service at New Haven, March 8, 1864, Colonel Wooster four days afterwards assuming the control. A few days before the organization left for the front it was presented with a set of colors by the colored women of New Haven, Fred Douglass making the presentation address. March 20th it left New Haven, under Colonel Wooster, for the front, and won the proudest of records in the field. Its behavior at the capture of Fort Harrison was especially commended. It was also particularly mentioned for gallantry on the Darby-town road, and at Chapin Farm, before Richmond. When the confederate capital succumbed, the Twenty-ninth was the first infantry to gain access to the city. Colonel Wooster's associate officers in the regiment included Lieutenant-Colonel David Torrance, now of the supreme court of errors; the late Rev. Edward W. Bacon, son of Dr. Bacon of New Haven; and Captain George H. Goodwin of the Travelers Insurance Company. After remaining at Richmond for a few days after the capture of the city the Twenty-ninth was transferred to Texas, reaching Brazos de Santiago in July, 1865. Thence the command marched to Brownsville, where it remained until ordered home in November. The organization was paid off and mustered out in Hartford, Nov. 25, 1865. Colonel Wooster returned to his home in Derby and resumed the practice of law. He is a prominent member of the Grand Army, the Army and Navy Club of Connecticut, the Society of the Army of the Potomac, and of the Connecticut Union Prisoners' Association. He was honored with the position of assistant marshal on the staff of General Joseph R. Hawley Battle Flag Day, Sept. 17, 1879, an occasion of unsurpassed military interest in the history of Connecticut. But it is not for the service alone which Colonel Wooster rendered during the war that he is to be held in honor by his fellow-citizens of the state. Prior to the war he had won place and distinction in the public service. In 1858 he was a member of the house of representatives from the town of Derby, his associates in that body including the late Governor R. D. Hubbard of Hartford, Governor Charles R. Ingersoll and the Hon. Hiram Camp of New Haven, ex-Congressman Augustus Brandegee of New London, Robbins Battell of Norfolk, A. H. Byington of *The Norwalk Gazette*, who subsequently proved himself one of the most brilliant of war correspondents; A. A. Burnham of Windham, who occupied the position of speaker; the Hon. A. P. Hyde of Hartford, and the Hon. Hezekiah S. Sheldon of Suffield. In 1859 he represented the old Fifth Senatorial District in the senate, his colleagues in that body including Judge Dwight W. Pardee of Hartford, Judge James Phelps, and the Hon. Hiram Willey of East Haddam. In 1861, the initial year of the war, Colonel Wooster was again a member of the house. Ex-Congressman Brandegee was elected to the speakership, while on the floor were such men as the late Colonel Henry C. Deming of Hartford, Thomas H. Seymour, who had been governor of the state and minister at St. Petersburg; Abijah Catlin, the late Green Kendrick of Waterbury, and Carnot O. Spencer of the school-fund office. The legislative career of Colonel Wooster reflected honor on the state. In politics he has been a republican from the outset, and the honesty and uprightness of his political views have been exemplified in every step of his career. He believed in abolition, and led his troops with the idea uppermost in mind that the war would result in the extinction of slavery. But it required great moral courage not less than loyalty to one's convictions, to assume the leadership of a regiment of colored men even in 1864. All honor is due to Colonel Wooster for the frankness and manliness of his course. He was born in Oxford, Aug. 22, 1821, and received a common school and academic education, pursuing the latter course at the South Britain Academy. He graduated from the Yale Law School in 1846, being a classmate of Tilton E. Doolittle of New Haven. He is at present a member of the law firm of Wooster, Williams & Gager. He has traveled extensively, spending upwards of three years in Europe. His wife, who is still living, was Miss Jay A. Wallace. There are no children in the family. Colonel Wooster was formerly paymaster-general of the state, and is one of the worthiest citizens of Connecticut.

HON. SAMUEL A. YORK, NEW HAVEN: Attorney-at-Law.

Samuel A. York was born in North Stonington, May 25, 1839, and was educated in the Connecticut Literary Institute at Suffield, and at Yale College, graduating from the university in the class of 1863. The members of his class included Professor William G. Sumner, William C. Whitney, secretary of the navy under President Cleveland; General Erastus Blakeslee of the first Connecticut Cavalry, now a prominent divine in Massachusetts; and the Rev. Dr. Leander T. Chamberlain. The class was a

S. A. YORK.

brilliant one and its representatives have been distinguished throughout the country. Judge York graduated from the Albany Law School in 1864 and practiced in Michigan for three years. He then returned to Connecticut and was elected clerk of the house of representatives in 1873, which was controlled by the democrats, ex-United States Senator Eaton of Hartford being speaker. In 1874 he was elected clerk of the senate. From 1867 to 1874 he occupied an editorial position on the *New Haven Register*, the manager and proprietor of the paper, the late Minot A. Osborn, being his father-in-law. He became judge of probate in the New Haven district July 4, 1876, and retained the position until Jan. 1, 1887, when he became the mayor of the city, occupying that office for two years. Judge York is a leading democrat in New Haven county, and is a gentleman of high social prominence. His career as judge of one of the most important probate courts in the state was characterized by the highest sense of honor. He is universally honored in the city where he resides.

BURTON HAMILTON MATTOON, Watertown: Merchant.

B. H. Mattoon is a native of Watertown, Litchfield county, Conn., and has lived there from infancy until the present time. He was born October 15, 1850. When he  became of age, with a thorough education obtained at the Watertown Academy and Stamford Seminary, he embarked in mercantile business in his native town, opening the store there in 1871, which he still owns and manages. In 1875 he married Miss Estella Minerva Scott; their family includes six children, three sons and three daughters. He is a member and vestryman of the Episcopal church, and a Mason of high degree. As a republican he has held the offices of town clerk and treasurer for a number of years, also clerk of the Center School district, of Watertown. He is now town clerk and treasurer, as well as registrar of births, marriages, and deaths.

C. H. MATTOON.

GEORGE B. EDMONDS, Bridgeport: Optician.

George B. Edmonds, collector of customs at Bridgeport, was born in Torrington, June 30, 1838, and was educated in the public schools of Southbridge, Mass., his people removing from Connecticut when he was but a child. He established himself in business in Bridgeport in 1875, as a manufacturer and dealer in optical goods. Prior to that period he had resided in Lowell, Mass., Pawtucket, R. I., and at Philadelphia. Collector Edmonds is an enthusiastic republican, and was instrumental in organizing the Bridgeport republican club. He has been on its executive committee for five years, and is a recognized leader. In 1886 he was elected a member of the council board from the first ward, and a member of the board of aldermen in 1887. He was appointed collector by President Harrison, April 15, 1890, the term being for four years. His first year in the office has been eminently satisfactory, the duties of the place being discharged with the utmost fidelity. He is a member of the order of

G. B. EDMONDS.

Odd Fellows in Bridgeport, and is a man of exceptional popularity in that city. His family consists of a wife and two daughters. The former was Miss Mary Hopper of Winsted, prior to her marriage. The first vote of Collector Edmonds was cast for President Lincoln.

S. P. WILLIAMS, Plainville: Principal of the Graded and High School.

Schuyler P. Williams is one of the most successful public school instructors in this state. He is the president of the Connecticut State Teachers'  Association, and an influential member of the State Council of Education. Seventeen years ago he was appointed principal of the Plainville Graded and High School, and has succeeded in making it one of the model schools of the country. When he assumed the duties of the principalship the school had no regular course of study, or high school grade, and only five

S. P. WILLIAMS.

teachers. Now the corps of instructors has been advanced to eight, and a high school grade, with a complete course of study, established. A class is graduated each year. Formerly the pupils preferred to go elsewhere and complete their studies. Under the management of Mr. Williams the town now possesses a high school whose graduates have very creditably entered Wellesley and other colleges. In 1888 the subject of this sketch was offered the principalship of the Meriden High School, but declined the position, preferring to remain at the head of the institution in which the best work of his life has been performed. Mr. Williams prepared for college at the Hudson River Institute, a military school at Claverack, and became a colonel of battalion in the military department. He entered Yale in 1869, graduating in 1873. His classmates included Judge Samuel O. Prentice of the superior court, Alderman Atwood Collins of this city, Principal A. B. Morrill of the State Normal School at Willimantic, Frank B. Tarbell, Gardiner Greene, Jr., and S. T. Dutton, formerly superintendent of the New Haven schools. His family removed to Southington when he was nine years of age, and his home was in that town during his collegiate career. After graduation he taught for one year in the select school conducted at Granby by Rev. T. D. Murphy, and in 1875 was called to the position which he has since occupied. He is an influential member of the Plainville Congregational church, and has held the chairmanship for several years of the society's committee. He was also superintendent of the Sunday-school for five years. During the current year he declined a unanimous re-election to the superintendency of the school, being compelled to adopt this course on account of increasing duties in other directions. Mr. Williams is a member of Friendship Lodge, No. 33, F. and A. M., of Southington. His family consists of a wife and daughter, the former being Miss Josephine E. Woodruff of Southington prior to her marriage. The daughter is Miss Martha J. Williams. In politics Principal Williams is a republican. He is secretary and treasurer of the Plainville Cemetery Water Company, and as a citizen of the town is held in the highest esteem.

NELSON MORSE, North Woodstock: Farmer.

Nelson Morse was born in East Woodstock, May 3, 1818, being now in the seventy-third year of his age. He is a descendant in the eighth generation from Anthony Morse, who emigrated to this country from England and settled in Newbury, Mass., in 1635. To this same line belonged also Jedediah Morse, author of the well-known Morse Geography, and Samuel F. B. Morse, inventor of the telegraph. Nelson Morse lived at home on his father's farm until he was seventeen years of age, when he left the farm and learned

NELSON MORSE.

the trade of blacksmithing and general carriage ironwork. He followed the business of country smithing several years, manufactured carriages and wagons in company with L. M. Dean, in 1840 and 1841, and for a short time afterwards alone. He changed his business later to that of carriage spring making, which he carried on until 1866 when he returned to farming, in which occupation he has since been engaged. His early education was such as the common schools of his native town afforded, and his entire life has for the most part been spent in North Woodstock. Mr. Morse is at present living with his third wife, who before her marriage was Miss Lucia A. Bass; his first wife, Pamelia Lyon, and his second, Jane Carey, both being deceased. There are three children living, Sidney Nelson, who graduated at Yale University in the class of 1890, Anna Clift, and Henry Waldo. He is a republican in politics, and has held the offices of justice of the peace, selectman, county commissioner, and representative in the state legislature.

In religious matters Mr. Morse is a Congregationalist, and a member of the Third Ecclesiastical society of North Woodstock.

L. J. NICKERSON, Cornwall: Attorney-at-Law.

Leonard J. Nickerson was born at Cornwall, October 23, 1857. After leaving the Alger Institute, in Cornwall, where he acquired his education, he taught school for several years and studied law with Hon. A. D. Warner, then of Cornwall. He was admitted to the bar April 22, 1879, a few months after becoming twenty-one years of age. He entered at once into the practice of his profession in Cornwall, and was admitted to practice in the United States courts in April, 1882. From that time on he has devoted his time almost exclusively to his legal business.

L. J. NICKERSON.

Mr. Nickerson is a republican, and as such has been called to fill various public offices. He represented Cornwall in the state legislature in 1883, and drafted the temperance law which was passed by the general assembly of that year. He was secretary of the Cornwall board of education for nine years, and has held other positions of public trust.

COMFORT S. BURLINGAME, Canterbury: Agent Brooklyn Creamery.

Comfort Starr Burlingame has been a member of the general assembly through three sessions, his first term occurring in 1879. He was returned for the consecutive sessions of 1887 and 1889. His colleagues from Windham county in 1879 were ex-Speaker E. H. Bugbee of Killingly, Clark E. Barrows of Eastford, at present deputy United States marshal for eastern Connecticut, Randolph H. Chandler of Thompson, Charles P. Grosvenor of Pomfret, William C. Jillson and John L. Hunter of Windham, and Colonel

C. S. BURLINGAME.

Wm. E. Hyde of Killingly, who served as aid-de-camp on the staff of Gov. Henry B. Harrison. Windham county has not often been represented by a finer group of men. Mr. Burlingame was appointed on the committee on manufactures, at the head of which was Congressman Frederick Miles, then a state senator from Litchfield county. His services have been of a valuable character in the legislature. In politics he is a democrat. He has for fourteen years been school visitor in his town, and is connected with the Unitarian church. He is the agent of the Brooklyn Creamery and a director of the Windham County National Bank and Insurance Company. He is also associated with the Grange. He was born at Canterbury, Jan. 5, 1853, and received a common school education. Formerly he was engaged in teaching. Most of his life has been spent in Canterbury. He is unmarried.

REV. GEORGE RUSSELL WARNER, HARTFORD : Rector St. Thomas Episcopal Church.

The subject of this sketch was born at Ellington, Conn., March 22, 1838, and is a son of Dan Warner and Mary E. (Chaffee) Warner. He was

reared on his father's farm, a portion of which had been in the Warner family for two generations.

His great-grandfather on his mother's side was a soldier in the war of the American Revolution; he enlisted in Colonel Meigs' regiment, and took part in the capture of Stony Point, where he was wounded. His grandfather was in the United States service in the Florida war. Like all farmer boys of his time, Mr. Warner received his primary education in the district school, and at the age of seventeen entered the Ellington High School, which for many years was celebrated as a college preparatory. Later on he began teaching in his native town, continuing his studies with the view of entering college. In 1858, he married Miss Sarah M. Hyde, and, as the fruit of that union, there are living three sons and three daughters. In 1862, he enlisted in the Twenty-fifth Regiment, Connecticut Volunteers, serving the full time of the regiment, and was regularly mustered out in August, 1863. Returning to his native town, he resumed teaching, and finally took charge of the Ellington High School, where he remained until 1871, when he was called to the charge of the Collinsville High School at Collinsville, Conn., and, after nearly three years service, severed his connection to accept an appointment from the American Missionary Association, as an instructor in Tougaloo University, in the state

of Mississippi. In 1875, he was ordained a Congregational minister, occasionally supplying the pulpit in his native town and elsewhere. The same year he was elected principal of the graded and high school at West Stratford (now East Bridgeport), and continued in charge six years. While located at West Stratford, he entered the Protestant Episcopal church, and, in addition to his duties as teacher, became assistant to Rev. N. S. Richardson, D.D., rector of St. Paul's Church at Bridgeport. In 1880 he was ordained deacon, and in October, 1881, was called to St. Peter's parish in the town of Monroe, Conn., and there ordained priest in 1882. After nearly three years service he was called to the charge of St. Albans' church at Danielsonville, Conn. After five years of remarkably successful work, by which St. Albans' was greatly strengthened and built up, he was elected rector of St. Thomas' parish, Hartford, Conn., where he now resides. His ministrations have been abundantly successful here. During the first two years of his rectorship, one hundred and twelve members were added to the church, of whom eighty were confirmed, and thirty-two were received by letters of transfer.

During his ministerial life he has been actively identified with the cause of education. Before leaving his native town he served three years as chairman of the school board, and school visitor, and while rector in Danielsonville he was elected chairman of the board of education, and served as special visitor of the high school.

Being of a social and generous nature, he naturally has sought and found companionship within the lines of the Masonic brotherhood, where he has won the friendship and confidence of the craft wherever he is known. He was made a Mason in Fayette Lodge, No. 69, at Rockville soon after his return from the war, and while located at Danielsonville transferred his membership to Moriah Lodge, No. 15, and since has affiliated with St. John's Lodge, No. 4, at Hartford. He also became a member of Warren Chapter, No. 12, and Montgomery Council, No. 2, at Danielsonville, and in these bodies held some of the most important offices. He has also served several terms as grand chaplain of the Grand Lodge of Connecticut. March 27, 1891, he was knighted in Washington Commandery, No. 1, Knights Templar at Hartford. These fraternities he holds in high esteem, for here he has found much to assist in strengthening the better elements of his nature and stimulating the mind to more active service in the cause of humanity and in the service of the Divine Master. There are richly blended in Mr. Warner's composition the elements of a character that fit him for successful labor in his profession, possessing, as he does, abundant zeal and tact, a kind, genial, and compassionate spirit, with earnestness in causes that he may espouse, that inspires confidence and reaches the great heart of humanity. In fact he *lives* among men, striving by his teaching and example to lift humanity to a higher and better sphere, depending.

> "Not by the helplessness of men —
> But by the strength that God supplies,
> And sends in mercy from the skies."

Mr. Warner is also a member of Charter Oak Lodge, No. 2, I. O. O. F., Robert O. Tyler Post, No. 50, G. A. R., the Army and Navy Club of Connecticut, and the Connecticut Society of the Sons of the American Revolution.

J. R. W.

GEORGE M. LANDERS, NEW BRITAIN; Vice-President "Landers, Frary & Clark."

George M. Landers, son of Capt. Marcellus Landers, and grandson of Capt. Asahel Landers (the latter having served for two years in the Revolutionary war, and having been with Gen. Wayne at the capture of Stony Point), was born at Lenox, Mass., February 22, 1813.

In Camp's *History of New Britain* we find the following sketch: "In 1820 he came to Hartford with his father, who for several years was a teacher in that city. He remained in Hartford until his father's death in 1824, when he returned to Lenox to live with his grandfather. He came to New Britain at sixteen years of age and learned the carpenter's trade, but speedily engaged in manufacturing, and in due time incorporated his business, which corporation now exists under the style of Landers, Frary & Clark, of which he was president until he retired from active business in 1870. He is still a director and the vice-president of this company, and a director and the president of the New Britain Gas Company. He was for many years a director of the New Britain National Bank, resigning to accept his appointment as bank commissioner. He was one of the incorporators of the New Britain Bank, of the gas company, the New Britain and Middletown Railroad, and the New Britain Institute, all of which received special charters from the general assembly. He has for many years been a director in the New York & New England Railroad Company. He has been identified with most of the important measures of progress in the town and city of New Britain since their incor-

G. M. LANDERS.

poration. He was one of the water commissioners when water was introduced into the borough, and was one of the original members of the board of sewer commissioners, remaining in office until the principal trunk sewers were constructed. He served for several years on the school committee. He has several times been elected to the general assembly as a democrat, being a member of the house of representatives in 1851, 1867, and 1874, and of the senate in 1853, 1869, and 1873. At this time Hartford, West Hartford, Wethersfield, Rocky Hill, Berlin, New Britain, and Southington were included in the first senatorial district. Mr. Landers was chairman of the committee that changed the original plans for the state capitol to those of the present building. He was elected to congress in 1874, and again in 1876, being a member of the forty-fourth and forty-fifth congresses. He has twice been appointed state bank commissioner, was chairman of the committee having charge of the erection of the normal school building, and has been called to other offices, in all of which he has done much to advance the interests of New Britain and of the state."

ALBERT H. BOND, HARTFORD; Life Insurance.

A. H. Bond, who for more than a score of years has represented the Massachusetts Mutual Life Insurance Company of Springfield, as its Connecticut general agent, was born in Wilmington, Mass., Oct. 14, 1834. At the age of nine his father's family moved to Colchester in this state, and three years later to Springfield, at which two last-named places, and at Andover, Mass., his education was acquired. Returning to Wilmington he was engaged for a number of years with his father in the wholesale cracker busi-

A. H. BOND.

ness; and in 1865 he entered life insurance, which has since engrossed his attention. He spent three years in Springfield in life insurance, representing a New York company, and in 1868 settled in Hartford, where he established an office and has maintained the general agency since to the present time. In 1864 he was married to Miss Mary A. Walker of Wakefield, Mass. They have one daughter, Miss Marion Walker Bond, a graduate of the Hartford public high school in the class of '93.

Mr. Bond is an ardent republican, having been a member of that party since its formation. Though positive in his convictions and earnest in his support of the principles and candidates of his party, he has declined to accept political office of any kind, giving his entire attention to business and the ordinary duties of private life. He is an attendant at the Park church.

COL. WILLIAM C. SKINNER, Hartford: Aid-de-Camp on staff of Gov. Morgan G. Bulkeley, 1889-90.

William C. Skinner was born in Malone, N. Y., January 26, 1855. He has resided in Hartford since 1872, in which year he entered Trinity College,

W. C. SKINNER.

graduating in 1876. The two winters following he attended lectures at the Albany Law School. In 1879 he became a member of the extensive wool firm of Dwight, Skinner & Co., Hartford, which connection he still retains. He is a very popular and able business man. Colonel Skinner is a director in several of the life and fire insurance companies, financial institutions, and minor corporations of Hartford. His wife, a lady of many accomplishments, is the daughter of Mr. Ebenezer Roberts, one of Hartford's most esteemed citizens.

Among the young business men of the capital city there is none who gives promise of a more useful or brilliant career than the subject of this sketch.

BYRON LOOMIS, Suffield:

Mr. Loomis was born in Suffield, May 2, 1831, in which town his entire life has been spent. His early mental training was received in the public

BYRON LOOMIS.

schools, from which he passed to the Connecticut Literary Institute of Suffield, where his education was completed. At the age of twenty-three he married Miss Elizabeth B. Cowles, daughter of the late Stephen Cowles, Esq., of Suffield, who has borne him four children, of whom three still survive — one son and two daughters. Mr. Loomis has been president of the First National Bank of Suffield, sustaining that relation for several years; he was also president of the Suffield Savings Bank for a similar period. He

was chosen a director of the Hartford & Connecticut Western Railroad Company at the first meeting of the stockholders of the corporation, continuing such until the re-organization of the company in 1875. He is a member of the Suffield Congregational church, of which he was treasurer and society's committee for some years. Among the local offices which he has held the most important are those of selectman and town treasurer. He has led a life of great activity and usefulness, and has been connected with various enterprises which have called for the exercise of mature judgment and executive sagacity. As member of various building committees he has aided in the planning and erection of many of the public edifices of Suffield, and has thus aided by word and work in beautifying and practically benefiting his native town. Mr. Loomis is held in high esteem by his fellow-townsmen as an upright and honorable gentleman and a useful citizen.

HON. MORRIS WOODRUFF SEYMOUR, Bridgeport: Attorney-at-Law.

Morris W. Seymour, son of the late Hon. Origen S. Seymour of Litchfield, was born in that town, October 6, 1842. Graduating from Yale College in the

M. W. SEYMOUR.

class of 1866, he acquired a thorough legal education at the Columbia Law School of New York, and began the practice of the legal profession at Bridgeport in the fall of 1868, in which city he has since resided. In 1870 he was elected assistant judge of the Bridgeport city court, and was also appointed that year on the staff of Governor James E. English, with the rank of colonel. The following year he was chosen city clerk of Bridgeport, and in 1872 and 1873 held the offices of city attorney and corporation counsel. He was appointed a United States commissioner in 1871, and held the position until his resignation in 1880, to accept the office of state senator, to which he was chosen in the fall election of that year. He served with distinguished credit in the upper house through the sessions of 1881 and 1882, being chairman of two important joint committees, and a member of the senate committee on contested elections. In every public position to which Mr. Seymour has been called to serve his city or the state he has discharged its duties with marked ability and a conscientious regard for the interests of his constituents and the commonwealth.

In his legal practice Mr. Seymour is in partnership with Howard H. Knapp, under the firm name of Seymour & Knapp, taking rank among the leading law firms of Bridgeport. Personally he has a great love for his profession, in which he has always been an earnest and persistent worker. He is the author of the present method of pardoning and commuting the sentence of prisoners in this state,—a system that has been commended as the best in the country by people who have investigated the subject, and which has in substance been copied by other states. His practice is such that he is quite actively engaged in the United States courts, in patent and admiralty causes; and such time as he can command from the business activities of his profession is fully occupied in those diversions which attend his position as a law lecturer at Yale University, a director in the Connecticut Industrial School for Girls, and in the exacting duties of domestic and social life.

Mr. Seymour is a gentleman of many pleasing accomplishments, an able and honorable lawyer, and a patriotic citizen. As such he possesses the esteem of a large circle of associates and personal friends.

DeWITT C. BRADLEY, WESTON: Manufacturer of Edge Tools.

Representative DeWitt C. Bradley, who was elected to the general assembly for the third consecutive term by the republicans of Weston, in November, 1890, is engaged in the manufacturing business, being connected with the firm of G. W. Bradley's Sons. This company has an established reputation for edge tools, and carries on a prosperous and extensive business. The subject of this sketch was born in Weston, Dec. 26, 1846, and received a common school and academic education. He spent two years in the regular army.

Representative Bradley is a member of Temple Lodge, No. 65, F. and A. M., of Westport, Clinton Commandery, No. 3, Knights Templar, and Washington Chapter, No. 24, R. A. M., of Norwalk. His wife was Miss Emma J. Sherwood prior to marriage. There are no children in the family. Mr. Bradley has added extensively to his circle of friends and acquaintances during the three sessions in which he has been in the legislature. He was first elected in 1886, making his first appearance as a member in the capitol in 1887. His three terms have been marked with able and conscientious service as a legislator.

14

CHARLES O. WARREN, EASTFORD: Town Clerk and Treasurer.

Charles Orville Warren was born in Vernon, July 7, 1851, and was educated in the common schools, and the Franklin academy at Somerville, Mass. In 1885 he was a member of the house of representatives from Eastford, serving on the republican side during the session. For the past three years he has been the secretary and treasurer of the Eastford creamery corporation, and chairman for eight years of the republican town committee. As a business and public man he is highly esteemed in the community where he re-

sides. He is a member of Putnam Lodge, No. 46 of South Woodstock, and has been advanced in the order to the Royal Arch degrees. Mr. Warren is an attendant of the Congregational church. His wife, who is still living, was Miss Mary Lyon Sumner, daughter of Increase I. Sumner of Illinois. There are two children — William Sumner and S. Florence Warren.

JAMES HENRY BEARD, SHELTON.

J. H. Beard was born in that portion of the town of Huntington known as the Long Hill District, January 16, 1839. He received a common school and academic education, being chiefly engaged during his minority upon his father's farm. Since becoming of age most of his time has been spent in manufacturing and mercantile pursuits in his native town, where he has always resided. He has dealt quite largely in real estate, has been engaged in the manufacture of fancy wood brackets, and during 1868 he erected

and occupied as a grocery the first store in the village of Shelton. He has been honored by his native town with most of the positions of public trust within their power to bestow, having served them as constable, selectman, member of the board of relief, registrar of electors, town agent, justice of the peace, and town auditor, covering a period of about a quarter of a century. He represented the town in the general assembly in

1883, and is now a burgess of the Borough of Shelton. His religious connections are with the Congregational church of Birmingham, and his political affiliations are with the democratic party. He was married, October 6, 1868, to Miss Emily Elizabeth Hurd of Monroe, who died January 28, 1888, leaving one child, a daughter, Helen Willard Beard. He was married to his present wife, Miss Margaret Elizabeth Blue, of the city of Defiance, Ohio, September 9, 1889.

JOHN E. SCANLAN, Hartford: Editor "The Connecticut Catholic," and Lawyer.

Probably no young man in the state, during the past few years, has been more active and influential in the democratic party than John E. Scanlan

J. E. SCANLAN.

of Hartford. He is familiar with the best methods of honest political work, is acquainted with the leading men of both of the great political parties, and enjoys the respect and confidence of them all.

Mr. Scanlan was representative from Hartford in the legislatures of 1886 and 1887 — the last of the annual sessions and the first of the biennial terms. Both years he was on the important committee of incorporations, and also chairman respectively of forfeited rights and woman suffrage. He was prominent in forwarding reformatory legislation, and in advocating the rights of the workingman. The high esteem in which he was held by his colleagues was manifested on many occasions. Every report made by him each year was adopted by the republican majority. The young legislator was elected county auditor by the Hartford county senators and representatives, and the legislature also elected him state auditor each year. He thus served the county four terms and the state three years, owing to the recent change in the constitution of the state. He was appointed clerk during the organization of the house of '86. He has been grand juror and justice of the peace several years, and a member of the board of school visitors since November, 1886.

The subject of this sketch was born of Irish parents, in Simsbury, Hartford county, this state, May 22, 1858, during a mixture of weather of hail, rain, and snow. He was educated in the district school there; in St. Peter's parochial school, Hartford; St. Charles College, Ellicott City, Md.; and Niagara University, Suspension Bridge, N. Y., from which last-named institution he graduated in 1877. He

has lived in Hartford since 1869, when his parents moved there. Immediately after graduation he began to study law in the office of Hyde & Joslyn, and was admitted to the Hartford county bar three years later. After practicing his profession for a time, he became connected with his brother, M. F., in the publication of *The Connecticut Catholic*, and has been editor of that able and influential paper since November, 1882.

In society affairs Mr. Scanlan has been prominent. He was grand knight of Green Cross Council, Knights of Columbus, two years, and has been a member of the board of government of the order, and attended all the conventions for the past six years. He was president of the 2d division, Ancient Order of Hibernians, two terms, and has been county delegate since May, 1888. He was a delegate to the national convention of this order, held in Hartford in May, 1890, and was chairman of the local general committees of arrangement and entertainment. He was a delegate from the Connecticut Weekly Press Association to the National Editorial Association conventions in Boston, June 24-27, 1890, and in St. Paul, July 14-17, 1891. He is a member of the Catholic Press Association of the United States. He was one of the three delegates, appointed by Bishop McMahon, who represented this state in the first Catholic congress of America, held in Baltimore, November 11 and 12, 1889. Mr. Scanlan is intensely American, and believes the government of the United States is the best in existence. He is glad to feel that our system of popular government is a beacon-light of freedom and liberty to all the nations of the world.

HON. EDWARD BUTLER DUNBAR, Bristol: State Senator; Manufacturer.

Edward B. Dunbar was born in Bristol, November 1, 1842. He received a common school education at home, and finished his studies at Williston

E. B. DUNBAR.

Seminary, East Hampton, Mass., on the completion of which, in the spring of 1860, he went to New York city, and engaged in the manufacture of hoop skirts. After remaining there five years he returned to his native place, where he has since been engaged in the manufacture of clock springs and small springs, under the firm name of Dunbar Brothers. Mr. Dunbar early took great interest in politics, and has been an active worker in the democratic party since he became a voter. He has been grand juror, and is now, as he has been continuously, for the last eighteen years, registrar of voters; has been on democratic town committee for the past twenty years, and chairman for the last six years. He is chairman of the board of fire commissioners, a position he has held for the last eight years, always taking great interest in the fire department and its efficiency. He is chairman of the High School committee, and has been since the institution was first established; and is a member of the third school district committee. He has always been a strong friend of educational interests, as his course in town meetings and his speeches in public meetings will testify. He has been a director in the Bristol National Bank since it was established in 1875; is at present a director in the Bristol Savings Bank; is vice-president of the Bristol board of trade; and was president of the Young Men's Christian Association four years, ending in October, 1890. Mr. Dunbar's legislative experience consists of two terms as member of the house, and two terms in the senate; having been first elected to the house in 1869, and again in 1881; and to the senate in 1884, and re-elected in 1886; on both of these occasions running more than one hundred ahead of the state ticket, in his own town. In fact, he has never yet been defeated when placed before the people for their suffrages. His legislative record gave great satisfaction to his constituents. Possessed of warm sympathy for working men, he looked well to their interests. He was one of the most earnest advocates of the weekly payment law, and inaugurated the system in his own factory before the law was passed. In 1890 his name was mentioned with others as a possible candidate for congressional honors, but he peremptorily refused its use by his friends, as his private business requires all his time. Mr. Dunbar is a member of the Congregational church of Bristol, and has been chairman of the society's committee at different times; is also a member of the Bristol Club, a social organization.

Mr. Dunbar was married in 1875 to Alice, daughter of Mr. Watson Giddings, carriage maker, of Bristol. They have one daughter, Marguerite, eleven years old; and one son, Edward Giddings, two years old. His father, the late Edward L. Dunbar, was in former years a prominent manufacturer of Bristol, and was elected representative in 1862. He established the business now carried on by the subject of this sketch and an older brother, Winthrop W. Dunbar. A younger brother, William A. Dunbar, represented the town in the legislature in 1879; he retired from the firm of Dunbar Brothers, April 1, 1890. Mr. Dunbar and his family are living in the house built half a century ago, and occupied for a time by the late Chauncey Jerome, the famous clock-maker. Three

years ago he had it remodeled, inside and out; and one of the pleasant spots in it is the library, in which are some eight hundred volumes of books which he has been collecting since his school days, and where he welcomes his friends.

WILLIAM B. RUDD, LAKEVILLE (SALISBURY): Secretary and Treasurer Holley Manufacturing Company.

General Rudd is one of the best-known business men in Litchfield county. He was born in Fredonia, N. Y., August 17, 1838. His paternal grandfather was Major Nathaniel Rudd of Vergennes, Vt.; his grandmother a sister of Judge Hopkins of Hopkinton, N. Y., for many years prominent in the politics of the states of New York and Vermont. His father, Rev. George R. Rudd, was educated at Hamilton College, was graduated in the class of 1823, prepared for the ministry at the Auburn Theological Sem-

inary, was ordained and installed by the presbytery of Cayuga over the Presbyterian church of Scipio, in January, 1827; in October of the same year married Miss Frances Beardslee of Auburn, a lady of far more than ordinary literary and social attractions. Rev. Mr. Rudd was a close student, a man of fine intellect, cultivation, and refinement. His son, William B., removed to Lyons, N. Y., with his parents, sister and brothers, in 1850. He received a common school education until sixteen, when he began his business life, first with his brother, Edward P. Rudd, of the firm of Rudd & Carleton, book publishers, New York city, later continuing in the same business in Lyons, N. Y., acting also for several years as agent for the American Express Company. He entered the army in the fall of 1861, in the Ninety-eighth N. Y. regiment, serving in the Peninsula campaign; in the spring of 1865 was appointed adjutant of the 107th regiment, National Guard, state of New York; was married in June, 1865, to Maria C. Holley, daughter of ex-Gov. A. H. Holley of Lakeville, Conn., and became connected with the "Holley Manufacturing Co." of Lakeville, on removing to that place in the spring of 1866; from the first has been its secretary, still holding that position, as well as treasurer and general manager, and is one of the directors and largest stockholders. He has been a republican since the formation of the party (his first Presidential vote being cast for Abraham Lincoln), and more or less connected with and interested in politics for many years; was a member of the state central committee for ten years; a district delegate to the Cincinnati convention in 1876, and a member of the Chicago convention in 1888. He was on Governor Bigelow's staff in 1881-82, as aid-de-camp, with the rank of colonel; and was appointed by Governor Bulkeley, in 1889, to the office of quartermaster-general of the state, holding the position more than the full term of two years, by reason of a disagreement in the matter of a successor to Governor Bulkeley at the end of his official term. He is treasurer of Hematite Chapter, Royal Arch Masons, at Lakeville, and has been a member of the Masonic fraternity since 1864. He is also a member and past commander of Orren H. Knight Post, G. A. R., of Lakeville.

General Rudd has four children. His only daughter, Fanny, is now Mrs. Martin Cantine, her husband being a paper manufacturer of Saugerties, N. Y. Alexander Holley Rudd, the oldest son, married Miss Oliver of Brooklyn, N. Y., and is connected with the Pennsylvania Railroad, with headquarters in Philadelphia, his residence being Media, Pa.; they have a son, nearly two years old, at present the only grandchild of General Rudd. The second son, Malcolm Day Rudd, fourteen years of age, is now engaged on a genealogical history of the Rudd family. He has a great love for such researches, as well as for antiques and relics. His room shows a goodly number and variety of curiosities of his own collecting. The General's youngest son, Charles Edward Rudd, is a boy of ten.

CAPT. RUSSELL FROST, South Norwalk: Lawyer.

Russell Frost is a New Yorker by birth, his native place being Delhi, the county seat of Delaware county. He is of English descent and Connecticut stock on both sides. His

mother's maiden name was Mary Griswold, and she was connected with the Connecticut Griswolds, of whom Matthew and Roger were among the earlier governors of this state. He is a great-great-grandson of General John Mead of Horseneck, now Greenwich, who was colonel of the Ninth Connecticut Infantry and general in command of the Third Connecticut Brigade in the Revolutionary war, serving under General Washington in the Connecticut and New York campaigns, and

being a personal friend and military comrade of General Israel Putnam. His paternal ancestors came to Connecticut about 1650, his great grandfather, John Frost, moving to Vermont after the war of the Revolution, and his grandfather, Russell Frost, settling in New York in 1800.

At the age of fifteen, Captain Frost was a student at the Delaware Academy in Delhi, fitting to enter college. He was induced by the president of the Delaware National Bank of that place to enter the employ of the bank, where he remained three years, being bookkeeper, teller, and acting-cashier. He then spent a year in his father's employ in the hardware business, but during this year his college hopes and ambitions, which had been slumbering, again asserted themselves, and so strongly that he gave up business and resumed his preparatory studies. At the academy again, and also under the instructions of private tutors, he fitted for college. He entered Yale in 1873, and graduated among the honor men of his class in 1877. Choosing the law for his profession, he was assistant to the district attorney for Delaware county at Delhi for two years, and conducted a prosperous private practice at that place for three years. He was then offered a position under the United States government to investigate and aid United States district attorneys in the prosecution of criminal offenses against the pension laws, forgery, perjury, false personation, and other frauds. His headquarters were for most of the time at Cincinnati, Ohio, although his work took him, at times, through Kentucky, Tennessee, Indiana, Illinois, and Missouri, where he investigated the conduct of many prominent physicians, lawyers, ex-army officers, some of very high rank, as well as public officers, whose connection with pension cases had been suspicious or criminal. He was instrumental in putting behind prison bars a number of men who had been distinguished in their respective states, besides several notorious criminals, and many others of less prominence.

After serving in this capacity for three years, Captain Frost resigned his position to resume the private practice of his profession. He chose South Norwalk as a promising field, opening an office there in 1885. He made no mistake in his choice, for his business has been active and prosperous, entirely absorbing his time and attention. Soon after going to South Norwalk, he was elected captain of Company D of the Fourth Regiment, Connecticut National Guard. He had seen no previous military service, but he took up the study of tactics and regulations with energy, and became an efficient commandant and good disciplinarian. He raised the military standard of his command to such a degree that for three successive years it has stood at the head of the Fourth Regiment in figure of merit for drills and service. He is a republican in politics, strong in his convictions, but public office never had for him as strong allurements as his profession offered, and, while often urged, he has always refused to be a candidate for office, although active in the interest of others. Captain Frost is a Free Mason, and a member of the Delta Kappa Epsilon Fraternity, which he joined at Yale. He is also a member of the University Club of the city of New York, and of the Connecticut Society of the Sons of the American Revolution. He is vice-president of the First National Bank of South Norwalk, and is connected with the Congregational church of that place. As a speaker on special literary and patriotic occasions he has been in much demand.

THOMAS A. LAKE, ROCKVILLE: Secretary and Treasurer Hartford Lumber Company.

Thomas A. Lake is a native of Woodstock in this state, where he was born June 3, 1848. His early years were spent in acquiring the rudiments of an education in the district schools of his native town. When the war of the rebellion broke out his patriotic ardor overcame his educational inclinations, and at the age of fourteen he ran away from home and joined the Eighteenth Connecticut regiment in Baltimore, on its way to the front, in the capacity of waiter for the company officers of company G. He remained

T. A. LAKE.

with the regiment through its trying experiences up to the time of the battle of Winchester, Va., in June, 1863, when he was captured with others by the Confederate forces June 15. During the excitement after the surrender he made his escape into the swamp just beyond the lines, and six days later, after a wearisome and hazardous tramp, came out at a point over the Pennsylvania border. He received from Major Matthewson a certificate stating that he was not an enlisted man, and commenced his homeward journey without means for obtaining transportation. He was put off the trains, which he boarded as a deadhead, at nearly every station between Harrisburg, Pa., and Putnam, Conn., the latter place being his objective point by railroad and but a few miles from his home. After the regiment was "exchanged," the same autumn, he returned to it and formally enlisted, and served until the close of the war. As soon as possible thereafter he engaged in business and continued with varying fortunes in Woonsocket, R. I., Worces-

ter, Mass., and for a time in Stromsburg, Neb. He married in Woodstock, Miss Martha A. Cocking, by whom he has three children. During his residence in Woodstock he represented that town for a single term in the legislature in 1885. He removed to Rockville in 1887, and at various times has held the positions of state auditor, member of the state board of agriculture, and secretary of the Tolland County Agricultural Society, the last two of which positions he still holds. His business is that of a lumber merchant, being secretary and treasurer of the Hartford Lumber Company of Hartford, and proprietor of the Lumber Yard at Rockville. His neglect to avail himself in his youth of the facilities offered for acquiring a liberal education has led him to provide carefully for the thorough education of his children. His son is in Harvard College, the elder daughter is at Wellesley College and the younger is about to enter Mount Holyoke seminary. Mr. Lake is in the prime of life, a thoroughly energetic man, and devoting earnest attention to his business, in which he has accomplished most satisfactory results. It is his intention to associate his son with him in it as soon as the young man shall graduate from college.

P. H. WOODWARD, HARTFORD.

P. Henry Woodward, eldest son of Ashbel Woodward, M.D., and Emeline (Bicknell) Woodward, was born in Franklin, Conn., March 19, 1833. His father, a distinguished physician, was perhaps even better known as an antiquarian and genealogist in matters pertaining to New England. The son inherited thoughtful and studious habits from a long line of clerical ancestors; a sturdy integrity from Puritan stock on both sides; and a natural cheerfulness of disposition, which has been of unusual service to him in

P. H. WOODWARD.

his years of dealing with his fellow-men. Beginning as do most youths of New England whose parents have the pecuniary ability, he graduated from Yale College in 1855, and afterward studied law at Harvard. Although he never engaged in active practice, his legal training sharpened and polished a mind naturally subtle and acute, and probably did much to fit him for those peculiar duties which in later life devolved upon him. Mr. Woodward's tastes are literary and scholarly, and the field of journalism was one especially congenial. From 1862 to 1865 he was the editor of the *Hartford Courant*, remaining in that position till the end of the war. At that time nothing in the disorganized south stood more in need of reconstruction than the post-office service; and, during Johnson's administration, Mr. Woodward, as special agent of the post-office department, bent all his faculties to the reorganization of that most important branch. He established, on suitable lines, railway post-offices for the distribution of through mails; and, at the end of four years, the South had a far more complete and perfect mail service than ever before. He was then employed for several years largely in important cases where it was the object of the government to discover, not to suppress or ignore, facts. In 1873 he was called from the south to New York city to conduct the investigations which led in the post-office to the overthrow of the old regime, and the incoming of Thomas L. James, afterward postmaster-general. In 1874 he was made chief of the corps of post-office inspectors, which he at once reorganized on a plan that has never since been materially modified, and which he raised by siftings and promotions for merit, to such a state of efficiency that other departments of the government repeatedly called upon him for aid in important cases. Relieved from service in the closing days of Grant's second administration, at the time Bristow and Jewell left the cabinet, one of the early acts of the Garfield administration was by telegraph to invite him to return to conduct the investigation of the Star Route robberies. The public have not forgotten the gigantic scale on which those frauds were planned and executed, or the overwhelming evidence of the guilt of certain officials and contractors. It was due to Mr. Woodward's trained mind, and his capacity for managing his subordinates, that these villainies were unearthed. He had charge of collecting and arranging the evidence, and, in his testimony before the congressional investigating committee, Attorney-General Brewster, the prosecuting attorney for the government, declared in the most emphatic way, that it would have been impossible to properly prepare the cases without the invaluable aid of Mr. Woodward. The words of Mr. Brewster, as given on page 885 of the printed report, will bear quoting: "When I first went into the case," says General Brewster, "I did not know Mr. Woodward. He was a stranger to me. After the case went on he was necessarily detailed and handed over to the department of justice. He was at the elbow of Mr. Bliss all the while, and at Mr. Merrick's elbow whenever he was needed. I do not think there was a fact in the case they did not acquire from him. When I prepared the short argument I made in the first case — the investigation and preparation indicated by this file of notes I have shown you — when I prepared that argument, I consulted a

great deal with Mr. Woodward. I had learned his value. I think without Mr. Woodward these cases never could have been instituted. I think he was, to use one word, invaluable. He is a man of remarkable intelligence; he is a man of great purity of character; he is an educated gentleman. In all my life, in an experience of over forty-six years of legal practice, I never have met with a man who could assist a lawyer better than Mr. Woodward. He understood his subject thoroughly. He understood all the bearings and relations of each point he submitted, and he would instruct himself in the law bearing upon it, by conference with counsel. He was the most valuable assistant I ever had, and I believe to him mainly is owing the fine preparation that was made in these cases, the complete and thorough preparation. The government, I think, is in debt to Mr. Woodward for his intelligence, industry, and integrity. I have learned to admire and respect him very much." Conviction in the District of Columbia was impossible, but morally the case was an overwhelming success.

With the close of the Star Route cases ended Mr. Woodward's connection with the government. Since that time he has resided with his family in Hartford. His keen intellect is never weary in exploring some fresh domain, whether of finance, science, or literature. His antiquarian bent has caused him to take delight in genealogical pursuits, and he has prepared various monographs on historical and other subjects. Some of the experiences in the secret service of himself and others he embodied in a book called "Guarding the Mails," which contains many spirited and stirring sketches of western and southern life. Much of his literary work has been journalistic, and necessarily fugitive; but it is all distinguished by that peculiar clarity and luminosity of style which betokens definiteness of thought. In 1888 Mr. Woodward was elected secretary of the Hartford board of trade, and the following year prepared a handbook of the city, which is a model of its kind. The duties of his position do not deter him, as they have not deterred him for many years, from assisting with his legal, business, and financial knowledge the many friends who are continually applying to him for advice. Such is the reflex action on character of a life of altruism and true beneficence, that once more is exemplified the truth of Shakespeare's words, "It blesseth him that gives and him that takes."

Mr. Woodward married, September 11, 1867, Mary, daughter of Charles Smith of South Windham, Conn., one of the successful leaders in the great industrial movement which began about 1820, and to which Connecticut is largely indebted for her prosperity and wealth. He has two children, a daughter and a son.

ISRAEL B. WOODWARD, Thomaston: President Thomaston Savings Bank.

The subject of this sketch was born at Watertown, March 12, 1814, and received a common school and academic education. With the exception of two years in the west his life has been spent in his native town and at Thomaston. He has been married twice. There is one child living. Mr. Woodward has held the offices of justice of the peace, grand juror, selectman, assessor, and member of the board of relief, represented Thomaston in the legislature in the session of 1879, and now holds the office of town agent. He is a member of the Congregational church, and is a republican in politics. Mr. Woodward is living in retirement, having withdrawn from active business pursuits. He was formerly a leather manufacturer. Years ago he was connected with the state militia. He has been honored with public trust in many ways, and is highly esteemed as a citizen of the town where the most of his life has been spent.

I. B. WOODWARD.

RICHARD JORDAN GATLING, Hartford: President Gatling Gun Company.

R. J. Gatling, whose name is perhaps more widely known than that of any other living American in connection with modern war enginery, as the inventor of the celebrated revolving battery gun which bears his name, was born in Hertford county, North Carolina, September 12, 1818. His father was a substantial, industrious farmer, who taught his children the necessity of labor and economy as the surest road to fortune. He received his primary education at such schools as were near his home, and when nineteen years of age taught school for a short time. At twenty he engaged in merchandising for several years, and during this time he invented the propelling wheel now used in ocean steamers, but was preceded by Ericsson a few weeks in application for a patent. In 1844 he

R. J. GATLING.

moved to St. Louis, Mo., and having invented a seed-sowing machine for sowing wheat and other small grains, engaged extensively for some time in their manufacture and sale. He was the first man to introduce this class of farm implements into the northwestern states. While engaged in this business, and during a trip by water from Cincinnati to Pittsburg, he was taken with small-pox and came very near dying — the vessel on which he was making the trip being frozen up in the ice for thirteen days, and having no physician on board. This experience induced him to take up the study of medicine, which he did for several years, attending courses of lectures at various colleges, acquiring a thorough knowledge of the medical science, and the title of "doctor," although he had no intention of undertaking medical practice. In 1849 he invented a method of transmitting power from one locality to another, through the medium of compressed air in pipes; other inventions following, previous to 1861, about which latter date, early in the war of the rebellion, he conceived the idea of making a machine gun which would, to a great extent, supersede the necessity of large armies. He made his first revolving battery gun in the city of Indianapolis, Ind., and in the spring of 1862 he fired it, in its then imperfect state, at the rate of over three hundred shots per minute, in the presence of many army officers and citizens. In the fall of the same year he had a battery of six of his guns made in Cincinnati, Ohio, and later twelve more — which were afterwards used by General Butler in repelling rebel attacks near Richmond, Va. In 1865 he made additional improvements in the weapon. Thorough tests of it were made at the Frankfort Arsenal in Philadelphia, and subsequently at Washington and Fortress Monroe, which proved so satisfactory as to induce Secretary Stanton and General Dyer, chief of ordnance, to adopt the arm into the service; and in 1866 an order was given for one hundred of the guns of various calibres. They were made at Colt's Armory in Hartford, and delivered in 1867. Since their adoption by the United States Government, Russia, Turkey, Hungary, Egypt, and England have adopted the Gatling gun, which are still made by the Gatling Gun Company at the Armory Building of the Colt's Patent Fire Arms Manufacturing Company in Hartford, which city Dr. Gatling has for many years made his home. The inventor of this pioneer in the line of revolving battery guns has devoted twenty-five years of his life to the continual improvement and final perfection of his invention, and has spent considerable time abroad testing his gun before nearly all the crowned heads of Europe. His name and fame as the inventor of something absolutely unique and revolutionary in modern warfare will be preserved and perpetuated in the world's history.

Dr. Gatling was married in 1854 to Miss Sanders, the youngest daughter of Dr. John H. Sanders, a prominent practitioner of medicine in Indianapolis, Indiana. He has one daughter and two sons. He is a member of the Hartford Club, and a republican in politics — being president of the "Harrison Veterans of 1840," an organization existing in Hartford, whose membership is indicated by its name. He is also president of the American Association of Inventors and Manufacturers of the United States.

MICHAEL F. SKELLY, Woodbury.

Mr. Skelly is a native of Ireland; was born September 6, 1837, in the village of Carrobeg Skelly, parish of Cashel, Longford county. Came to this

M. F. SKELLY.

country in 1853, and to Woodbury in 1854, where he found a home in the family of the late Joseph F. Walker, and from him learned the blacksmith trade. After six years in the service of Mr. Walker he established a business of his own, which he personally conducted in the same locality for thirty-one consecutive years. He received some education in the national school in Ireland, and in the common school in Woodbury. Since his residence in Woodbury he has for ten years occupied the office of registrar of voters; was for three years a grand juror; is now and has been for twelve years a justice of the peace; for the last eight years has acted as a trial justice; for eighteen years a member of the democratic town committee; is a member of the twentieth district senatorial committee, and for several years its chairman. He was one of the corporators of the Woodbury Savings Bank, has been one of the directors since its organization, and is now a loan agent for the bank. He is a member of the Catholic Total Abstinence Union of Connecticut, and was for three years treasurer of that organization. Is a member of the National Catholic Total Abstinence Union of America, and was a delegate to the national convention held at New Haven, August, 1883. He hates all prevalent vices of the day, but especially the vice of intemperance. He is a member of the board of school visitors, and takes great interest in the education of the youth of his adopted town. He takes a lively, active part in all that concerns the welfare of his town. Although Mr. Skelly has always been a fearless and out-spoken democrat, and was elected

to the legislature as the candidate of that party in 1886, he has the satisfaction of knowing that his election was aided by his fellow-citizens and neighbors, regardless of party lines; and during his legislative experience he did not forget that he was in the house the representative of the citizens of Woodbury, and not of any party in the exclusive and offensive sense. During the session he proved himself to be an energetic, faithful, and influential member, never absent from his duties, and giving satisfaction to his constituency of all parties. He was a candidate for state senator in the fall of 1888, and now occupies the position of assistant superintendent of the state capitol and grounds at Hartford, to which he was appointed the present year. Mr. Skelly furnishes an excellent example of what a boy, born abroad and coming to this country without money or acquaintances, can do, by the exercise of the virtues of industry, temperance, and a laudable ambition, under the benign influence of our free institutions. He has furnished an example worthy of emulation by the youth of this country, and especially by those of his own nationality.

EDWARD S. WHITE, Hartford; Attorney-at-Law.

Judge Edward S. White, of the firm of Chamberlin, White & Mills, was born in Granby, Hampshire county, Mass., March 12, 1848, and was edu-

E. S. WHITE.

cated at Wilbraham academy and Yale College, graduating from the university in the class of 1870. During the first year after graduation he taught in General Russell's Military School in New Haven, being in charge of the classical department. He studied law with the firm of Chamberlin & Hall in this city, and was admitted to the bar in 1873.

One year afterwards he was made a member of the firm, the name being changed to Chamberlin, Hall & White. This designation was retained until the death of Mr. Hall, who was a leading lawyer, in 1877, when the name of Chamberlin & White was adopted. In 1883 a new change was effected by the admission of Hiram R. Mills, who has since remained in the firm. It is one of the ablest legal concerns in this locality, and has an extensive practice. Judge White has been an indefatigable worker through life, and has won an enviable position in this community. He has manifested genuine interest in the city's educational progress, and has served on the Hartford High School committee, and the district committee of the Washington district. He was also a member of the High School building committee, serving in that capacity with Messrs. James G. Batterson and James L. Howard, and the Rev. Drs. George L. Walker and E. P. Parker. In 1883 he was elected associate judge of the Hartford police court, and retained the position until July, 1889. He is the secretary and treasurer of the Overman Wheel Company, and its legal adviser. Judge White is a member of the South Congregational church, and a gentleman of the most exemplary character. He has been married twice. His first wife was Miss Alice E. Smith of Granby, Mass., the marriage occurring Aug. 13, 1874. February 11, 1883, Mrs. White's death took place in this city. The second marriage was celebrated Oct. 28, 1885, the bride being Miss S. Adelaide Moody of Belchertown, Mass. Her death also occurred in this city, the date being Feb. 13, 1890. There are three children by the first and one by the second wife. The oldest daughter, Miss Ruth Dickinson White, is a student at the Hartford High School. Both of the Judge's wives were ladies of collegiate education, being graduates of Mount Holyoke Seminary. The first graduated in 1869 and the second in 1871. Both were regarded with the sincerest affection and esteem in this city. As a lawyer and citizen Judge White is an honored representative of the city.

ANDREW B. MYGATT, New Milford: Banker.

A. B. Mygatt, son of the late Eli Mygatt, was born in New Milford, October 31, 1820, and has always resided there. He has one son, Henry S. Mygatt, cashier of the First National Bank of New Milford, and two daughters who reside in Bridgeport. He received an academical education and prepared for college, but was unable to enter on account of trouble with his eyes. He engaged in mercantile business in 1840, at the age of twenty, and pursued it with success until 1855, when he retired owing to ill health.

A. B. MYGATT.

In 1878 he was chosen president of the First National Bank of New Milford, which position he still holds. He has always been a public-spirited and progressive citizen, and identified with most of the improvements and enterprises that have been undertaken for the benefit of the town. He laid out several new streets and built numerous houses, and is still a large owner of real estate in New Milford.

In politics Mr. Mygatt was originally a whig, casting his first presidential vote for Henry Clay in 1844. Since the formation of the republican party, he has always been one of its ardent supporters. He has been much in public life. He was a member of the state senate in 1860 and 1861, the latter year being president pro tem. of that body. In 1865 he represented New Milford in the house of representatives. From 1861 to 1864 he was state bank commissioner, and in 1865 he was appointed national bank examiner for Connecticut and Rhode Island, and served in that office with distinguished ability for twenty-two years, resigning in 1887, in the second year of President Cleveland's administration, and retiring with the cordial commendations of his superior officers, though of a different political party.

Mr. Mygatt was married June 7, 1843, to Miss Caroline Canfield, daughter of Colonel Samuel Canfield.

WILLIAM N. CLEVELAND, Andover: Farmer.

William Nelson Cleveland was born in the town of Bozrah, April 16, 1819, and received a district school education. He is a descendant of John Cleveland of Brooklyn, Conn., the early home of many of the family. The first wife of the subject of this sketch, Pamelia S. Standish, was of the seventh generation from Captain Miles Standish. Mr. Cleveland was first married when he reached the age of 22. The result of this union was five children, William Chauncey, Henry Franklin, Eliza M., Fannie F., and

W. N. CLEVELAND.

Hattie S. Cleveland. The two sons enlisted in the war, William uniting with the Tenth and Henry with the Eighteenth Connecticut. The latter returned from the field, broken in health, and died within a brief period. The remaining son is in the employ of the government at Washington, D. C. The wife of Mr. Cleveland died May 17, 1886. His second marriage occurred March 9, 1887, the bride being Miss Esther D. Phillips of Andover, sister of the Rev. James M. Phillips. The maiden name of Mr. Cleveland's mother was Mary Congdon, daughter of Daniel Congdon of Warwick, R. I. She died at Preston City, March 14, 1837. Mr. Cleveland's father died at Bozrahville, April 10, 1878. Mr. Cleveland has resided in the towns of Griswold, Norwich, Colchester, and Windham, and is

well known in those localities. He came to
Andover, his present residence, October 6, 1841.
He has spent most of his life in blacksmithing,
farming, and mercantile business. He was one of
the first republicans in Andover, and has held a
number of town offices. He is a member of the
Methodist church.

AUGUSTUS STORRS, (Brooklyn, N. Y., and Mansfield) A Retired New York Merchant.

Augustus Storrs, second son and second child of
Royal and Eunice Freeman Storrs, was born in
Mansfield, June 4, 1817. He is a lineal descendant

of the sixth generation of
Samuel Storrs, the first
resident bearing the name
of Storrs in Mansfield,
and the first in the Eng-
lish colonies. He came
from Sutton-cum-lound,
Nottinghamshire, Eng-
land, to Barnstable, Mass.,
in 1663, and removed from
there to Mansfield in 1698,
and became one of its
most active, respected,
and influential citizens.
The Herald's College of

AUGUSTUS STORRS.

London makes this family descendants of Philip du
Storrs, companion of William the Conqueror when
he entered England in 1066. Edmund Freeman,
Mr. Storrs' maternal great-grandfather, was graduated at Harvard College in 1733, and, after teaching a few years in Massachusetts, moved in 1742 to
Mansfield, where he became a practical farmer, and
was highly esteemed as an intellectual and cultured
Christian gentleman. His wife, Martha Otis, was
a daughter of Hon. Nathaniel Otis of Sandwich,
Mass., and first cousin of James Otis, the patriot
and orator, and great-granddaughter of Rev. John
Russell of Hadley, Mass., who secreted in his own
house for a long time the regicides Whalley and Goffe.

Mr. Storrs was educated in the common schools
of his native town. His father was a farmer and
a manufacturer of horn combs; but his means were
rather limited, and so both he and his wife saw to
it carefully that their six children made the most of
their time when in school; when out they were required to perform what labor they could for the
general welfare of the family, and with the two
vocations there was never lack of work; but, as
their home was always made pleasant for them,
their tasks were seldom irksome. Augustus remained at home with his father until after he reached
his majority, taking entire charge of the comb-shop
the last two years of his stay, and assisting on the
farm as occasion demanded, there acquiring

habits of industry and order, and a love of agricultural pursuits, that have never left him.

In the spring of 1839, while he was considering
in what business he would start in life for himself
(his father having decided to give up comb-making),
an unexpected opportunity presented itself. Two
men of the town, who had come into possession of
a dry-goods and grocery store in Gurleyville (Mansfield), proposed to young Storrs to " run " the store
under the firm name of A. Storrs & Co., offsetting
his work against their capital, and sharing equally
with them in the profits. In spite of the fact that
he had never had a day's experience in mercantile
life, he courageously accepted the proposition.
When he commenced business in the store he was
solicited to take the agency of the Mansfield Silk
Manufacturing Company, and he accepted that
trust also. The silk factory was in the same village, and was the first factory for the manufacture
of silk in the United States. In September of that
year he married Antoinette Abbe of Windham, by
whom he had two daughters. The Abbes were
among the early and prominent settlers of that
town. He continued in business in Gurleyville a
little over six years, giving entire satisfaction to his
partners and to the silk company. At the end of
that time the senior partner of the store died, and
the business was closed.

In April, 1846, he moved to Willimantic, and, in
company with another young man, opened a store
there. In the fall of the same year he had an advantageous offer to go as traveling agent for a
manufacturing and commission house in Hartford.
He at once closed a bargain with that firm, and
disposed of his business in Willimantic and moved
to that city. In 1851 he was employed by the same
company in New York city, and he removed with
his family to Brooklyn, N. Y. In 1854 he united
with his two brothers, Charles and Royal Otis,
under the firm name of Storrs Brothers, to carry
on a commission business in staple American goods
in New York city. On account of other business,
Royal O. found it impracticable for him to join
them in New York, and after a little he withdrew
from the firm. Augustus and Charles continued
the business under the same firm name twenty-five
years, and were sagacious, honorable, and successful merchants.

Soon after going to Brooklyn Mr. Storrs united
with Plymouth church — Rev. Henry Ward
Beecher's. He is a constant attendant there (when
in the city), and a liberal supporter. He has been
a trustee of Plymouth church twenty-six years,
treasurer eighteen years, and president of the board
of trustees six years. It is hardly necessary to say,
as he still holds these offices, that he has given
satisfaction in them — that he is a careful and
efficient business manager.

As he increased in years and means he had a longing for a rural home, where he could spend at least his summers, and his thoughts and affections reached after the home of his boyhood; and the result was that in 1875 he bought the old homestead (his parents having passed away) of his brother, R. O. Storrs. He has added to that purchase, and now owns between four and five hundred acres in the place. On commencing work on his land he determined to ascertain what and how much it could be made to produce. In a few years his large crops of grass, grain, and vegetables clearly demonstrated that, under thorough and scientific tillage, it was possible to greatly increase the productiveness of our Connecticut farms. He had been contemplating doing something for his native town and state that would be of permanent benefit to them, and had thought of various things, but could not settle upon any one thing until he had had this experience in farming. Then it seemed to him that it was as necessary for farmers to be thoroughly educated in their vocation — taught what kind of fertilizers different soils require, and the kind of crops best adapted to different places — as it was for professional men and mechanics to acquire a thorough knowledge of their business; and he decided that he could do nothing more conducive to their welfare than to give land to the state to found an agricultural school. Consequently, in April, 1881, he deeded to the state of Connecticut, for this purpose, two farms in Mansfield, near his home, containing in all 170 acres, on which were buildings sufficient for the commencement. His brother Charles, with whom he had been in company so long, was in full sympathy with the movement, and gave several thousand dollars to furnish all necessary equipments for starting such a school. It is now ten years since the " Storrs Agricultural School " was organized. The young farmers who have graduated from it think that their time was very profitably spent there, and the present indications are that the institution will prove as beneficial as Mr. Storrs and his brother believed that it would.

Until his wife's death in the spring of 1888, Mr. Storrs took his household with him each year to his Mansfield home to spend the summer. His daughter, wife of B. E. Valentine, a Brooklyn, N. Y., lawyer, with her five young daughters, joined them there every summer, filling the house with life and cheerfulness, to the great delight of their grandfather, who is exceedingly fond of his grandchildren. Harriet, Mr. Storrs' eldest daughter, a most estimable young lady, died at the age of twenty-one. Since Mrs. Storrs' death he has divided his time about equally between Brooklyn and Mansfield, going to each place as business requires, making himself useful in both places.

HENRY ROBINSON TOWNE, Stamford: Engineer and Manufacturer: President The Yale & Towne Mfg. Co.

Henry R. Towne was born at Philadelphia, Pa., August 28, 1844, where he was educated at private schools and at the University of Pennsylvania, class of 1865. He left college before graduation to enter business, but in 1887 was given an honorary degree of M. A. Entering the Port Richmond Iron Works, Philadelphia, in 1862, as a mechanical draughtsman, he was engaged for over four years on general engineering work, especially heavy marine engines for the monitors and other war vessels, the erection of

which he superintended at the Boston, Portsmouth, and Philadelphia navy yards. In 1866 he made an extensive tour of the engineering establishments of England, Belgium, and France, spending nearly six months in Paris, where he studied at the Sorbonne. In October, 1868, a partnership was arranged between him and the late Linus Yale, Jr., best known as the inventor of the " Yale Lock," whose business was then located at Shelburne Falls, Mass., and employed about thirty hands. The new enterprise was incorporated under the name of " The Yale Lock Manufacturing Co.," and Stamford, Conn., thirty-four miles from the city of New York, selected for its location. Having purchased land here, Mr. Towne began the erection of a factory building, when, December 25, 1868, Mr. Yale died suddenly, leaving the young enterprise on the hands of Mr. Towne and a son of Mr. Yale. The former became president of the corporation, and, a year later, bought out the interest of the Yale estate. Since 1869 Mr. Towne has controlled the business and has personally directed its affairs, during which time the number of employes has grown from 30 to 1,000. For several years he was entirely alone in the ownership and management of the business, but its rapid growth led him first to associate others with him in the management, and, later, to augment the capital by permitting others to subscribe for new issues of the stock. Although the Yale patents have all expired, the policy of constant experimental work has developed a series of inventions and improvements which have retained for the company a position of recognized leadership in the manufacture of fine locks of all kinds, and this department is still the most important one in the business, including not only key locks in vast variety but also time and combination bank locks, line hardware, and metal-working. Other departments are devoted to cranes and heavy hoisting machinery, to chain tackle-blocks, and to post-office equipments. In 1883 the corporate title was changed to " The Yale & Towne Mfg. Co.," and a special charter obtained from the state. Additions to the plant continue to be made almost every year to provide for the constant growth of the business.

Mr. Towne has been an active member of the American Society of Mechanical Engineers almost from its formation, a member of its council, and its president in 1888-89. In 1889 he was chosen chairman of a joint party of some 300 American engineers, civil, mechanical, and mining, which visited England and France. He is a member of the Union League and Engineers' Clubs, in the city of New York, a director in several large industrial corporations, member of the American Society of Civil Engineers, the Institution of Mechanical Engineers, London, England, and other scientific organizations.

Mr. Towne married, early in life, Miss Cora E. White of Philadelphia, and they have two sons. In politics he is a republican.

ELISHA J. STEELE, Torrington: Mechanic.

Elisha Jones Steele was born in Torrington, June 29, 1843, and received a public school education. During the war he was a member of the First Connecticut Heavy Artillery, serving from 1861 until 1865. He is a member and past commander of Steele Post, No. 34, G. A. R., of Torrington, and was one of the Connecticut aid-de-camps on the staff of National Commander Alger. He is also a prominent representative of the Knights of Honor, being a past dictator. At present he is a member of the state ex-

E. J. STEELE.

ecutive committee of the Young Men's Christian Association of Connecticut. Mr. Steele has been an active republican in Litchfield county for years. In 1887 he was a member of the house of representatives, and was appointed to the chairmanship of the committee on appropriations, one of the most important of the legislative committees. He is the president of the Young Republican Club of Torrington. Mr. Steele is a member of the Third Congregational church, and is thoroughly identified with the religious and educational work of the community of which he is so active and influential a member. For three years he was chairman of the

Torrington board of education. His business associations are with the Coe Brass Manufacturing Company, being the superintendent of the wire and tube departments. His family consists of a wife and three children. The former was Miss Sophia H. Skiff before marriage. As a soldier and citizen Mr. Steele is held in high esteem and honor in his native town.

ROBERT W. NELSON, Hartford: President Thorne Type-Setting Machine Company.

R. W. Nelson was born in Granville, Washington county, New York, September 20, 1851. He was educated at the Union School of Schenectady,

R. W. NELSON.

learned the printer's trade, became an associate publisher of the Joliet (Ill.) News, spent some years in Chicago, was for two years a merchant, and in 1882, in connection with Major O. J. Smith and G. W. Cummings, organized the American Press Association of New York city, with which he was connected for five years. He was doubtless largely instrumental in accomplishing the phenomenal success which has attended that association's progress almost from the outset. He personally introduced the patent stereotype plate matter of the association to hundreds of established newspapers throughout the country; and through his agency, and by the aid of such " matter," additional hundreds of new periodicals were started, many of which have since come into prominence and success. Five years ago, while still connected with the American Press Association, Mr. Nelson became interested in the ingenious Thorne Type-Setting Machine, then manufactured in a small way in Hartford by its inventor and patentee, Joseph Thorne. He acquired first a one-half interest in the enterprise, and a year or two later bought out Mr. Thorne altogether, and proceeded, with the aid of expert assistants to improve and at length to perfect the machine. Having accomplished this, he organized the Thorne Type-Setting Machine Company, with a capital of one million dollars, established a factory in the west wing of Colt's Armory, in Hartford, filled it with special machinery, and is now employing about seventy-five skilled mechanics in the manufacture of type-setting and distributing machines, the product of the plant being about twenty of these machines per month. The Thorne is the only type-setting machine now in use to any considerable extent. It revolutionizes the art of composition, as the introduction of power presses revolutionized the art of printing. Mr. Nelson is president of the company, and its general manager; as such, he has introduced the "Thorne" into all parts of the United States, Canada, England, Ireland, Scotland, and Australia.

Mr. Nelson is married and has one child. He is a member of the Asylum Avenue Congregational church, the Hartford Club, and the Aldine Club of New York city.

CHARLES H. LAWRENCE, HARTFORD: Secretary Phoenix Mutual Life Insurance Company.

Charles Hammond Lawrence was born in New York city, August 23, 1845. He was educated in the public schools and at the New York Free Academy; and at the conclusion of this preparatory course entered as clerk the New York branch of the Hartford firm of Smith & Bourn. In 1866, still in the employ of this firm, he came to Hartford, and for the next four years was connected with the home establishment. On the first of January, 1871, he entered into an engagement with the Phoenix Mutual Life Insur-

C. H. LAWRENCE.

ance Company, which has since continued uninterruptedly for more than twenty years. Beginning as clerk, he was advanced through succeeding grades, and in 1889 was chosen to the secretaryship of the company, his present position. In 1872 he was married to Miss Juliette H. Fisher, daughter of the late Thomas T. Fisher, Esq., of Hartford, a well-remembered and successful merchant and stock-broker, and a prominent citizen of his day. Two children, a son and daughter, have been added to the family.

Mr. Lawrence has been quite active in municipal and state politics for several years. He is a republican of pronounced type, and as such has been elected for three successive terms to the common council; also for four years on the board of aldermen; and president of the board, representing the second ward of the city. He is a conscientious political worker, and has done much to elevate the standard of local political influence in all branches of the public service. He is at present a member of the Republican State Central Committee. Additionally to his official connection with the Phoenix Mutual Life, he is a director in the State Bank, and

sustains similar relations with other Hartford corporations. He is a member, with his family, of Trinity (Episcopal) parish, and a liberal contributor to its institutions and charities.

GEORGE CURTIS WALDO, BRIDGEPORT: Journalist; Editor "Daily Evening Standard."

George Curtis Waldo was born in Lynn, Mass., March 20, 1837. He is eldest son of the late Rev. J. C. Waldo of New London, and his mother was a daughter of the late Rev. Hosea Ballou, of Boston, and a cousin of Eliza Ballou, the mother of President Garfield. Mr. Waldo was graduated at Tufts College, Mass., in 1860, studied law in company with T. M. Waller in the office of the late A. C. Lippitt at New London, and, together with Governor Waller, enlisted in the first company raised in that town for

G. C. WALDO.

the civil war, serving through the campaign of '61.

After receiving his discharge from the army he engaged, on account of impaired health, in active business in New London and Bridgeport, and in 1867 became city editor of the *Daily Evening Standard* in the latter place. In 1869 he purchased an interest in the company, and was associate editor for many years under the late Hon. John D. Candee, becoming editor-in-chief upon the death of Mr. Candee, which position he now holds.

In 1874 he married Annie, daughter of Major Frederick Frye, formerly of Bridgeport, then of New Orleans, and they have four children.

Mr. Waldo is a member of Christ (Episcopal) church, Bridgeport, and was for four years its junior warden. He was one of the founders, and for five years secretary of the Bridgeport Scientific Society; is vice-president and historian of the Fairfield County Historical Society; was first president of the Eclectic Club of Bridgeport; and is at present president of the Sea Side Club of that city, an organization of over three hundred of its most prominent citizens. He was for five years a member of the Bridgeport board of education, and for two years chairman of the committee on schools. He is a member of the board of directors of the Bridgeport Public Library, a member of the Grand Army of the Republic, and the Army and Navy Club of Connecticut. In 1889 he was appointed by Governor Bulkeley a member of the shell-fishery commission of Connecticut. He is a republican in politics.

WILLIAM J. McCONVILLE, Hartford: Judge of City Police Court.

Judge William J. McConville was born in Baltimore, Md., March 13, 1851, and was educated in the common schools of this state and the Connecti-

W. J. McCONVILLE.

cut Literary Institute at Suffield. The first years of his career in this state, which were spent in the towns of Manchester, Vernon, South Windsor, and Suffield, were attended with difficulties and obstacles, the aspirations of the lad in the direction of education far exceeding his opportunities and means. But the way was not abandoned on that account. Prior to his admission to the Hartford county bar Judge McConville learned the trade of a harness-maker, and personally earned the money which was used in carrying him through his studies. He was in the office of Judge H. S. Barbour, one of the oldest and most respected lawyers in this city, and was a careful and painstaking student. The success which Judge McConville has attained is due to the energy and perseverance which have characterized his course from the outset. These traits of character were as prominent during his early years as they have since been in manhood. Judge McConville was the clerk of the council board in Hartford for a number of years, where the reforms introduced by him in connection with the journals of the board have since been retained, and the effect of his influence is still felt in the council administration. In 1886 he was elected assistant clerk of the house of representatives, and clerk in 1887. In the latter position he was able to inaugurate improvements that will long be continued in the house relative to the journals. His analysis of the house proceedings from day to day presented in compact and intelligent form the business of the session. In 1889 Judge McConville was advanced to the senate clerkship, where his ideas and methods were again exemplified in a most satisfactory manner. The excellent work which he has performed in the house and senate clerkships entitles him to great credit from the public. He received the republican nomination for the police court judgeship from the Hartford county caucus in 1890, and was elected by the general assembly while he was the incumbent of the senate clerkship. This recognition of his ability and worth by the men who knew him best was exceedingly gratifying. The confidence reposed in his capability and judgment was not misplaced by the legislature,

the judge having proved himself an able and judicious public official. His career on the police bench has been eminently successful. The laws have been enforced without fear or favor. Judge McConville has been a member of the Center church in Hartford for twenty-two years. He is also a member of Hartford Lodge, No. 88, F. and A. M., and of Charter Oak Lodge of Odd Fellows. He is connected with the order of Red Men in the city, being a member of Wangunk Tribe; the Young Men's Christian Association, and the Young Men's Republican Club. He has been identified for years with the interests of the First ward, and was a delegate in the republican state conventions from this city during the state and national campaigns of 1888. He has traveled extensively through the United States, and is a gentleman of wide information. He was for three years an active member of the First Company Governor's Foot Guard, in this city, and belongs to the Veteran Corps of that organization. Judge McConville is without a family, never having been married. As a lawyer, Judge McConville occupies a position commanding the confidence and respect of the public. He has met with more than an ordinary share of success in life, and his practice has brought him before the supreme court on important issues and principles of law.

WILLIAM J. DICK, Newtown.

William J. Dick was born in Newtown, Sept. 12, 1822, and received a common school and academic education, completing the course at Chilton Hill

W. J. DICK.

Seminary, Elizabeth, N. J. Mr. Dick has traveled extensively through the United States, visiting nearly every state and territory in the Union. He has been engaged in mechanical and manufacturing pursuits, and was for twenty-six years the proprietor and manager of the hotel at Newtown. He retired from business, however, some time ago. In politics Mr. Dick is a republican, and is connected with the Episcopal church. He has held various local offices, being at present a member of the burgess board of Newtown, a justice of the peace, and president of the Cemetery Association. The wife of Mr. Dick, Mary E. Beardsley, was a cousin of Governor Isaac Toucey of this state, who was subsequently United States Senator from Connecticut, and the secretary of war in President Buchanan's cabinet. There were four children, all of whom have died.

M. W. TERRILL, MIDDLEFIELD.

Moses Weld Terrill was born in Morristown, Vt., October 2, 1826, and is son of the late Moses Terrill and Matilda (Weld) Terrill. His paternal great-grandfather was born in East Canaan, Conn., and is believed to have descended from Roger Terrill, who was one of the first settlers of Milford, Conn., in 1639, and who later joined the colony from that town which settled New Milford. His mother was a descendant of Joseph Weld, who came from Wales and settled in Roxbury, Mass., in 1638. Mr. Terrill's ed-

M. W. TERRILL.

ucation was obtained for the most part in the common schools of his native town. This was supplemented by one term in the academy in Johnson, Vt., and two terms in a private school taught in his own town. He finished his studies just at the completion of his eighteenth year, and taught school the following winter. In the spring of 1845 he entered a country general store as clerk, in which occupation he spent three years. In March, 1848, in company with another, he embarked in mercantile business in Wolcott, Vt. At the end of one year the business was sold, and Mr. Terrill removed to his native town and engaged in the same line. This business was continued until 1861, when he removed to Middlefield, and with the late David Lyman, Esq., joined in establishing under the joint stock law of Connecticut, the Metropolitan Washing Machine Company (now the Metropolitan Manufacturing Company), for the manufacture and sale of washing and wringing machines, and other laundry utensils. Mr. Terrill was president of the company until Mr. Lyman's death, in 1871, when, upon the re-organization of the company, he was elected treasurer, which office he still holds.

Raised on a farm, Mr. Terrill's inclinations toward agricultural pursuits were so strong that he bought land in Middlefield, and erected a full set of buildings thereon. Since 1864 he has continued to conduct this farm on the lines of general agriculture and the breeding of thoroughbred cattle (Short-horn and Jersey breeds). At present he has a large and valuable herd of Jersey cattle. He has also given attention to fruit culture, especially to the culture of the peach, and at this time he has a young orchard of one thousand trees. In his native town he held the office of constable and collector of taxes, and assessor, and twice represented the town in the state legislature. In the home of his adoption he has served several years as selectman, as-

sessor, member of the board of relief, since 1865 as school visitor, and for many years as justice of the peace and notary public. He also occupied a seat in the Connecticut legislature in the years 1866 and 1867, also in 1883. In his legislative experience he has served on committees of claims, state prison, and agriculture, three times as chairman.

In July, 1848, Mr. Terrill was married to Miss Almira O. Ferrin, also of Morristown, Vt., sister of Hon. W. G. Ferrin of Montpelier, Vt. Their children are three sons and two daughters, all of whom are living at the present time. By temperament, mental structure, and inheritance, Mr. Terrill is a republican. His father supported James G. Birney and successive candidates of the liberty party until it grew into the republican party in 1856. Mr. Terrill's first national vote was cast for Van Buren and Adams in 1848; also for J. P. Hale in 1852. In religious conviction and association he is a Methodist. He has occupied various responsible positions in this church, and at present is a trustee. He is also a supporter of the principle of prohibition of the liquor traffic.

ALEXANDER SEMPLE, BROAD BROOK (EAST WINDSOR): Agent Broad Brook Company.

The subject of this sketch is a remarkable illustration of the strength of purpose which is so often found in "self-made men." He was born at Johnstone, Renfrewshire, Scotland, on the 8th day of May, 1835, and is descended from the family of Lord Semple (1560), of the ancient family Semple, Barons of Elliestoun (1214), on the father's side, and from the Buchanans of the family of the distinguished reformer and Latin poet, George Buchanan (1506), on the mother's. His parents were in humble circumstances, and be-

ALEXANDER SEMPLE.

yond the plain rudiments of an English education Semple had no advantage over the other boys of his native town. Like them he had to contribute to the income of the household, and at an early age went to work learning the business of a weaver. At the age of thirteen years he emigrated to New York state, finding employment in a cotton mill. Seeing an opportunity to better himself, he secured work as a weaver in the woolen mill at Warehouse Point; then was engaged as loom fixer in the mills at Broad Brook. In this place and position he determined to seize every opportunity in which to become a manufacturer, little thinking that years hence he would be called upon to take the management of the same concern. After a few years sojourn at Broad Brook he removed to Dracut, Mass., thence to Amesbury, thence to Windsor, Conn., and thence to Lee, Mass. During these changes he was mastering one after the other the details of the business, and in 1862 was engaged by the Globe Woolen Mills, Utica, N. Y., as their superintendent and designer, which position he creditably filled for seven years. At the end of this time he was engaged by the Broad Brook company as their mill manager, in which position he is widely known as one of the most successful manufacturers in the United States, his goods more than holding their own in the most fastidious mart. He entered a woolen mill at the age of thirteen years, and has worked continuously ever since, a period of forty-three years. He is proud of his perseverance, and to this inestimable quality he attributes his success in life. His mind is quick and penetrating in its perceptions, and his directness of action, combined with his insight and force of character, would make a man of real worth among any people.

GEORGE H. HOYT, Stamford: Banker.

George H. Hoyt is a prominent citizen of Stamford and has served three terms in the general assembly of the state. He was first elected to the house by the democrats in 1876. In 1881 he was chosen for the second time and was returned again in 1883. He made many friends in the state during his legislative career. He occupied the office of burgess for six years in Stamford and has served on the board of education for five. He is a vestryman and treasurer in St. John's Episcopal church at Stamford and holds a prominent place socially in the community. Mr. Hoyt is the president of the Stamford Savings Bank, vice-president of the Stamford National Bank, director and treasurer in the Stamford Water Company, member of the board of managers of the New York Transfer Company, and a director in the Stamford Safe Deposit Company. He was connected with the New York & New Haven road from 1857 until 1873, when he resigned to devote his entire attention to the banking business. The wife of Mr. Hoyt, who was Miss Josephine E. Bailey prior to marriage, is living. There are also two children. Mr. Hoyt was born in Stamford, December 11, 1838, and was educated in the public and private schools of that town and of Darien.

G. H. HOYT.

JOHN MILTON NEWTON LATHROP, Franklin: Farmer.

Mr. Lathrop was born in Franklin, May 20, 1830, and is a direct descendant of the Rev. John Lathrop, who came to this country from England in

J. M. N. LATHROP.

the *Mayflower* in 1634, settling first in Scituate, and afterwards in Barnstable, Mass. The spelling of the name has undergone various changes, the early records showing it to have been Lowthroppe, again Louthroppe, and later, Lathrop, as at present, John Louthroppe of England being the great-grandfather of the Rev. John Lathrop, above mentioned. Israel Lathrop, the third in the line of descent from the Rev. John Lathrop, was born in 1687, in what was then called Norwich East Farms; afterwards, in 1786, being incorporated as the town of Franklin. He married in June, 1710, and about this time settled on the eastern declivity of Blue Hill, in the southwestern part of the town of Franklin. Just how much land Israel possessed is not known, but there are about one hundred acres originally owned by him which is now held by his lineal descendants, having never been deeded, but inherited from generation to generation to the present time, and a part of which is now owned by the subject of this sketch. Ezekiel, the son of Israel, and the grandfather of Mr. Lathrop, born Sept. 5, 1724, fought throughout the Revolutionary war, his death occurring at his home in 1796, from the effects of the exposure and hardship endured therein, leaving his family without support, no aid from the government in the way of pensions in those days being possible. James, the son of Ezekiel, and father of our subject, completes the lineage, he being born February 27, 1789, in Franklin, on a part of the old ancestral estate. John M. N. Lathrop received his education in the district schools of his native town, and at the Phillips academy, Andover, Mass. He has generally been engaged in the business of farming, and has been twice married. First to Lydia Eliza, daughter of Samuel A. Gager of Bozrah, now deceased, and by whom he had one son, Charles Edwin, born in 1855, now living in East Orange, N. J.; and second to Lucretia, daughter of Col. J. S. Hough of Bozrah, now living, and by whom he has had two children, one born in 1882 and the other in 1887. Mr. Lathrop has no military record, the family being represented in the war of the rebellion by his only brother, who gave up his life in the service, leaving the surviving son no alternative but to remain at home to care for the aged parents and the homestead. Mr. Lathrop has held about all the offices in the gift of the town, including those of first selectman, grand juror, assessor, and collector, retaining them all at the present time, with the exception of that of selectman. He also represents his town in the legislature at the present session, being a republican in politics. His life has been spent almost entirely at home, where by his energy, and integrity, and other sterling qualities, he has won the confidence and esteem of all his fellow-townsmen. He is a member of the Bozrah Congregational church, New Concord Society, and of the Farmers' League.

HENDRICK HUDSON WILDMAN, New Fairfield: Farmer and Road Contractor.

H. H. Wildman was born at New Fairfield, March 25, 1830, and has always resided on the old homestead and farm where he was born. He attended the district school until twelve years of age, and afterwards until sixteen was a pupil at Peck's academy and a boarding-school in his native town, working Saturdays and on all spare moments daily while at the academy, but always keeping up with his classes. From sixteen until he became of age he was employed on his father's farm. The two years following he

H. H. WILDMAN.

worked at farming and jobbing, and in 1853 commenced farming for himself, alternating it with teaching district school winters in his own and adjoining towns. He taught on the old " boarding 'round " plan for upwards of twenty winters, which proved a great aid to him in studying human nature. For six years, from 1870 to 1876, he was contractor and superintendent of all the town's poor of New Fairfield. In addition to his farm and other labors since 1877, he has been contractor for the repair of the town highways, and he is generally considered " a good road-maker." For the last twenty-five years he has had considerable practice as counsel in the justice courts of his own and adjoining towns, although not a lawyer by profession. There is rarely a legal trial in his vicinity in which, if not sitting as judge, he is not employed on one side or the other; and he often acts as assistant counsel at the higher courts. He is acknowledged to be " a good associate " by all the professional lawyers of Fairfield County. Mr. Wildman has been a member of the board of school visitors since 1857, most of the time acting visitor and examiner,

and now chairman of the board. He has been justice of the peace since 1861, registrar of voters ever since the office was created, auditor of town accounts for sixteen years; has held the offices of constable and collector of taxes, has been a member of the board of relief, has served as a grand juror in the United States court, and quite frequently in the superior court and court of common pleas in his own county. He represented New Fairfield in the general assembly in 1863, 1879, and 1885, taking an active part in the debates of these sessions, in which he was characterized as " a perfect sledge-hammer " by Hon. Henry B. Graves. In his legislative experience he has rendered effective service in debate, as well as in committee work on the educational and state prison committees.

Mr. Wildman is a member and trustee of the Methodist Episcopal church; a member of Samaritan Lodge, No. 7, I. O. O. F., of Danbury, having passed or holding the offices of conductor, treasurer, secretary, V.G., N.G., and P.G., and is a member of the Grand Lodge of the state. In politics he is a democrat, generally taking an active part; has been a member of the town committee thirty years, most of the time its chairman; also has been on county and senatorial committees several times. He was married Oct. 17, 1852, to Miss Eveline Pearce, daughter of Matthew L. Pearce of New Fairfield, who died in 1885. He has not again married. He has two sons and two daughters living — one daughter and both sons married. The elder son, Hendrick H. Wildman, Jr., is now constable of the town, having been elected the first time the day after he became twenty-one years of age, and continuously re-elected ever since.

STREET WILLIAMS, Wallingford: Farmer.

Mr. Williams was born in Wallingford, July 9, 1833, and was educated there in the public and private schools, and at the State Normal School at New Britain. He has spent his life in agricultural pursuits since attaining his majority, and has made farming a success in the best sense of the word. He was married in 1864 to Miss Julia A. Blackman of Huntington in this state, an estimable companion and helpmate, who is still living, and to whose advice and coöperation he attributes much of his happiness and suc-

STREET WILLIAMS.

cess in life. He has filled various town and school-district offices for many years, and is now, and has been for five years, assessor of the town. He has

15

been from his youth a member of the Episcopal church of Wallingford; has served for a long term of years as treasurer and vestryman of the parish, and superintendent of its Sunday-school. Politically, he is an ardent republican.

NELSON ADAMS, NEW HAVEN: Merchant and Manufacturer.

Mr. Adams is a direct descendant of the colonial Adamses of Massachusetts, and was born in Hubbardston, Worcester county, July 6, 1831. As a

NELSON ADAMS.

scholar in the public school of the place, he had few equals. At seventeen years of age the chair factories of Gardner, Mass., were the first attraction, but more purely mercantile pursuits were his desire; and, with no introduction or assistance, he found employment first in the Bacon works, near Boston, and next held a responsible place in the stock yards of Brighton, which led to the business of dressing and curing Provisions for the markets of Fitchburg and vicinity. Then going to New Haven in 1856, and adding Bone and Fertilizer business, followed that line of trade and manufacture to the present time, having been thirty-eight consecutive years in business, depending only upon his own resources. During that time he has been honorably connected in his line of the manufacturing business in several cities, including New York, Hartford, Bridgeport, and Springfield.

An active, busy life must of necessity attend these various interests, requiring a fair degree of judgment to keep the several mercantile trusts entirely solvent during so long a period. Mr. Adams might be classed as an expert in his lines of trade and manufacture, no one in the state — probably few in New England — having been for longer time or in a more familiar way connected with that industry. That he has been a busy man may be inferred from the fact that never since he was twenty-two years old has he been a day without business of some kind. When he was twenty-four he built and owned a house free and clear, without financial assistance from anybody. He has always relied upon himself financially, and has never had a just debt that he was not ready to pay when asked to, or before.

In character Mr. Adams is of a pronounced type, as were his ancestors, and in habits, more natural than acquired, has an inherent disfavor for narcotics and their like. He has owned and driven horses from youth, and has a good word for them, and for their more considerate treatment; also a kind act and word for the helpless among all creatures. He takes an interest in the work of the Humane Society, having been a member of the Connecticut society since it was chartered.

In 1868 he married Jennie E., daughter of Thomas P. Dickerman of New Haven. They have had three children, one son and two daughters, but one of whom, a daughter, is living. Mr. Adams is one of the directors of the New Haven Cooperative Savings Bank and Loan Association, and one of its incorporators, it being the pioneer association of its kind in the state. He has always held republican principles, and voted that ticket, but has never favored receiving political or local office, yet taking a lively interest in the affairs of the country and in local enterprises. He has had considerable coast-wise traffic by water, and his library contains quite a large volume of canceled bills of lading. In all Mr. Adams' transactions it has never been said the dollar was the all-absorbing thought of life, and it may be added that he is more than willing to refer all inquiry as to his past or present dealings to his partners in business in each of the above-named cities who may be living at the present time.

JOHN ADDISON PORTER, POMFRET: Journalist, Editor "The Hartford Post."

John Addison Porter, eldest son of Professor John Addison Porter, first Dean of the Sheffield Scientific School of New Haven, and of Josephine Earl

J. A. PORTER.

Sheffield, a daughter of the founder of the school, was born in New Haven, April 17, 1856; was educated at the Hopkins Grammar School of that city, and at Yale University, from which he was graduated in the class of 1878. After leaving college, Mr. Porter studied law in Cleveland, Ohio, but afterwards entered journalism. He has been connected in various capacities with the *New Haven Palladium, Hartford Courant, New York Observer, New York Tribune*, and other newspapers, and has written many articles for the principal magazines, including the *New Englander* and *Century*. He has also been a contributor to "Appleton's new Cyclopedia of American History," and is the author of several monographs and books.

In 1884 Mr. Porter removed his residence from

New York city to Washington, D. C., and for two years there conducted a book-publishing business. During a session of congress he served, by appointment of Senator Platt, as clerk of one of the senate's special committees. During the past five years Mr. Porter has resided with his family at Pomfret, Conn., excepting when occupied with business in Hartford. In 1888 he purchased an interest in *The Hartford Evening Post*, and became its managing editor, and in 1889, having bought a majority of the stock of the Evening Post Association, he became the editor-in-chief. *The Hartford Post* continues to be a vigorous and progressive exponent of sterling Connecticut and national republicanism. Mr. Porter was elected first representative from the town of Pomfret in the autumn of 1890, and during the following session of 1891 was one of the leaders of the party, serving as a member of the house committee on canvass of votes for state officers, and as house chairman of the committee on education.

Mr. Porter was married, December 20, 1883, to Miss Amy Ellen Betts, daughter of George F. Betts, a prominent lawyer of New York city. They have had two children: the first, Constance Elaine, a very promising child of four years, died in June, 1889; the second, also a daughter, was born March 7th of the present year.

CHARLES H. SMITH, Union City (Naugatuck): Postmaster.

Mr. Smith was born in Milford, December 16, 1844, and received a public school education, preparing him for a successful business career. He remained on the farm until he reached the age of eighteen, when he became a clerk in a Waterbury dry-goods establishment, remaining in that place for three years. He then accepted a position with the dry-goods firm of Wilcox, Hall & Co. of New Haven, where he continued in business until 1871. During that year he established, in company with F. L. Andrew of

C. H. SMITH.

Naugatuck, a general store at Union City, the firm being Andrew & Smith. In 1877 Mr. Smith purchased the interest of Mr. Andrew, and has since managed the business himself, meeting with success and accumulating considerable property. He has been the postmaster at Union City since 1879. He has also been actively associated with the Naugatuck board of selectmen. He is a member of Shepherd's Lodge, No. 78, F. and A. M., of Nauga-

tuck, and also belongs to the Ancient Order of United Workmen. Mr. Smith has a wife and one son. The former was Miss Ella A. Andrew prior to to her marriage. In politics Mr. Smith is a republican.

CHARLES W. LOUNSBURY, Darien: Merchant.

Mr. Lounsbury was born at Eddyville, Ulster county, in the state of New York, in 1842, and the same year moved to Norwalk, Conn., with his parents. The first twenty years of his life were spent in Norwalk, Wilton, and New Canaan. At the latter place he learned the tin and stove business. He was educated at the public schools in the two places first named, and in the twenty-first year of his age enlisted in Company A, Seventeenth regiment, Connecticut Volunteers, as a private, for three years, or during

C. W. LOUNSBURY.

the war, at Norwalk, August 11, 1862. In June, 1864, on account of disability for active service, he was by general order of the war department detailed to serve in the medical purveyor's department at Baltimore, Md., where he remained two months after he was mustered out, which was at Baltimore, August 28, 1865. In the following year he took up his residence at Darien, where he opened a tin and stove store, later on adding other goods, in which business he is still engaged. In 1868 he was married to Miss Torrington of the city of Baltimore, Md., and they have three children, two sons and one daughter. Mr. Lounsbury has been a resident of Darien for twenty-five years, and for more than twenty years has held various public offices in that town. He was first elected constable, then school committee and treasurer of his district, and has served on the town school board. He has acted as administrator and executor of various estates; has twice been appointed commissioner by the probate court, and once as a superior court committee, covering a period of six months' service. He has been for twenty years the principal trial justice of his town; has twice been the republican nominee for the legislature, and is now a notary public. He is a member of the South Norwalk Baptist church, also of the Odd Fellows and the Masonic fraternity. He enjoys a reputation among his townsmen for strict honor and integrity in all his dealings, and in his official capacity his duties are always performed with absolute conscientiousness and a determination to treat every man and every cause with impartial justice.

PLINY JEWELL, HARTFORD: President Jewell Belting Company.

The name of Jewell is a distinguished one among the honorable names of the sons of Connecticut, both living and dead; and its mention revives

PLINY JEWELL.

always the recollection of our late lamented Governor Marshall Jewell, than whom no citizen of the state was in life more honored and beloved, or in death more sincerely lamented. Pliny Jewell, the subject of the present sketch, and an elder brother of the late Governor Jewell, is a descendant in the eighth generation from Thomas Jewell, his first American ancestor, who was a native of England, and emigrated to America about 1639, settling in Boston. Pliny Jewell, the second son of Pliny and Emily (Alexander) Jewell, was born at Winchester, N. H., September 1, 1823, which ancient town appears to have been the birthplace and residence of the Jewell family for several generations. Pliny Jewell, senior, carried on business as a tanner in New Hampshire for many years. He was an active member of the Congregational church, and was politically identified with the old whig party, by which he was elected several times to the state legislature. In 1845 he removed to Hartford, Conn., continuing the tanner's trade, to which he added the manufacture of leather belting. He was associated in this business with two of his sons, including the subject of this biography, from 1848 onward until his death in 1869, under the style of P. Jewell & Sons. The present Pliny Jewell is now the sole survivor of the original firm. He was at different dates joined by his two brothers, Lyman B. and Charles A., the firm continuing under the old style until its organization as a joint stock corporation, April 16, 1883. The old factory on Trumbull street is still occupied, but it has been greatly enlarged and new structures added, until the plant is now one of the largest of its kind in the country, leading nearly every other similar establishment in the extent and volume of its business. There have been developed from this industry the Jewell Belt Hook Company, the Jewell Pad Company, and the Jewell Pin Company, Pliny Jewell being a stockholder in and president of all these corporations. He is also a director of the Hartford National Bank, and the Travelers Insurance Company, and a trustee in the Hartford Trust Company. His whole active life has been spent in the leather business, with all the details of which he is intelligently familiar, and in which he has been very successful. Mr. Jewell is a republican of the stalwart kind, having been one of the original organizers of that party in this state, and since prominently identified therewith. His religious connections are with the Pearl Street Congregational church and society. He is one of the vice-presidents of the Hartford board of trade, and a member of the Hartford Club.

Mr. Jewell was married, September 5, 1843, to Miss Caroline Bradbury, and they have two children: Edward Jewell, born January 26, 1847, now residing in Boston; and Emily Maria Jewell, now Mrs. Walter Sanford of this city.

LYMAN B. JEWELL, HARTFORD: Vice-President Jewell Belting Company.

The subject of this sketch was born in Winchester, N. H., August 29, 1827. Following the universal New England custom, his parents kept him in

L. B. JEWELL.

the district school summer and winter until fifteen years of age, where he acquired a solid preparation for the active duties of life. After leaving school he was variously employed during the remaining years of his minority, and ultimately engaged in the dry-goods commission business, which he followed in New York and Boston for sixteen years, from 1856 to 1872. During this period, in January, 1858, he married Miss Charlotte Williams of Boston. In 1873 he removed to Hartford, and became associated with his brothers in the firm of P. Jewell & Sons, now the Jewell Belting Company, of which he is at present a director and the vice-president. Since his residence in Hartford he has become connected, officially and otherwise, with various industrial and financial corporations. He holds the vice-presidency of the four incorporated industries which have developed from the parent house of P. Jewell & Sons, namely, the Leather Belting Company, the Pin Company, the Belt Hook Company, and the Pad Company; and is treasurer of the Detroit Leather Company, which is practically an offshoot of the Hartford establishment. He is also a director in the Phœnix Insurance Company, the American National Bank, and the Southern New England Telephone Company, and a member of the Hartford Club. His political connections are with the republican party, and in church affairs he favors the Episcopalians.

Mr. Jewell inherits in a marked degree some of

the notable characteristics of his ancestors. He is thoroughly independent and outspoken, sometimes to the verge of abruptness, and in his intercourse with others expects that a spade will always be called a spade, and by no other name. He "stands four-square to all the winds that blow."

CHARLES A. JEWELL, HARTFORD: Treasurer Jewell Belting Company.

Charles A. Jewell is the youngest son of Pliny and Emily Jewell, one of a family of ten children, of whom the late Governor Marshall Jewell was the third,—the family being of English descent, and strictly a New England family since 1639, when Thomas Jewell, the first American ancestor, settled in Boston. Charles A. Jewell was born in Winchester, N. H., March 29, 1841, and four years later removed with his parents to Hartford, which city has since been his continuous abode to the present time. He was

C. A. JEWELL.

educated at the district and Hartford Public High schools, graduating from the latter to enter the leather belting manufactory of P. Jewell & Sons, first as a clerk and apprentice, and subsequently as a partner. He entered military service during the first year of the war as adjutant of the Twenty-second Connecticut regiment, serving until honorably discharged at the close of his term of enlistment. When the Jewell Belting Company was organized under its charter as a joint stock corporation, in April, 1883, he became its treasurer, and has since held that office. He is also treasurer of the Jewell Pin Company, and sustains official relations with the other corporations to which are attached the family name, and whose operations are conducted in one or another of the cluster of factories which constitute the plant of the Jewell Belting Company, the parent establishment. He is a director in the City Bank, and in the Hartford Chemical Company, vice-president of the Hosmer Hall Choral Union, and a member of the prudential committee of the Hartford Theological Seminary. Mr. Jewell is a member of the First (Center Congregational) church of Hartford, one of its society's committee, and superintendent of its Sunday-school. He is active in all religious work, and a useful and valued member of this ancient Christian institution. As vice-president of the Hartford Young Men's Christian Association, and for ten years its president, he has been one of the chief promoters of its religious activities, as well as one of its most liberal benefactors. The association is largely indebted to his prudent councils and wise direction, as well as his personal influence, for its high standing before the public, and the comparatively prosperous condition of its finances. Mr. Jewell was married in 1866 to Miss Julia W. Brown, daughter of Roswell Brown, Esq., of Hartford. There are no children in the family. It is hardly necessary to add that the subject of this sketch is a republican; no member of the family in the present generation, at least, has been suspected of other political affiliations. He is also a member of the Loyal Legion.

NOAH PORTER, D.D., LL.D., NEW HAVEN.

The venerable ex-president of Yale University was born in the ancient town of Farmington, December 14, 1811. His father, whose name is borne by the subject of this sketch, was for sixty years pastor of the only church in Farmington, of which one of his ancestors was among the first settlers in 1640. It was in his study that the American Board of Commissioners for Foreign Missions was organized, and held its first meeting September 5, 1810. The boy early manifested so great an interest in books,

NOAH PORTER

and his progress in the English branches of education was so rapid, that at eight years of age he was permitted to begin the study of Latin. In his sixteenth year he left home to enter college as a freshman, immediately took a high rank as a scholar, and graduated in 1831. He became the rector of the old Hopkins Grammar School shortly after his graduation, was elected tutor in Yale College in 1833, serving in that capacity for two years. In 1836 he became pastor of the Congregational church in New Milford, and about the same time was married to the daughter of Dr. Taylor, his instructor in theology in the Yale Divinity School. Mr. Porter's pastorate in New Milford lasted seven years, and at its close he entered into the same relation with the South Congregational church in Springfield, Mass., where he remained for four years, when he was chosen, in 1846, Clark professor of mental and moral philosophy in Yale College. After occupying this chair for twenty-five years, on the resignation of President Woolsey, in 1871, he was elected president. During his administration the college was very prosperous. Several costly buildings were erected, the corps of instructors was much enlarged, and the different departments of the institution came to be officially recognized by the corporation as having "attained to the form of a university." His incumbency of the presidential office continued until 1886, when physical infirmity compelled his resignation.

Dr. Porter has, during all his life, been a voluminous writer. His published works are too numerous to even be mentioned here by their titles. He has been a constant contributor to the press, and the editor of all the later editions of Webster's Unabridged Dictionary. He will rank in history as among the foremost of American authors and scholars.

JOHN N. STICKNEY, ROCKVILLE: A Retired Manufacturer and Journalist.

John Newton Stickney was born in Vassalboro', Me., January 17, 1818, and was educated at the Hallowell Academy. In 1837, after having

J. N. STICKNEY.

spent a few years in the store of Dole & Stickney in Hallowell, he removed to New York city, and in May, 1839, was married to Miss Mary S. Hale, daughter of the founder of *The New York Journal of Commerce*. The young couple removed to Union City, Branch county, Mich., where they resided between three and four years. Two children were born to them, while living in Union City, one son and a daughter. The first born died there, but the daughter, Miss Caroline Alathea Stickney, attained womanhood, and is now Mrs. J. K. Creevey of Brooklyn, N. Y. From Union City Mr. and Mrs. Stickney removed to Marshall, Calhoun county, Mich., where the second daughter, Laura Hale, now Mrs. H. L. Hall, was born. In 1846 the family removed to Rockville, in Tolland county, and have since been residents of this state. Frank Hale Stickney, now residing in Longmont, Colorado, and Mrs. Jeannie Rose Carson of Pelham Manor, Westchester county, N. Y., are the children of Mr. and Mrs. Stickney who were born in Rockville. Mrs. Stickney, who was a lady of the most attractive and loveable character, died April 23, 1885. For over forty years Mr. Stickney has been a prominent and influential citizen of Rockville, and has been actively identified with its progress and prosperity. He has been treasurer of the Rockville Gas Light Company since 1863. He is one of the foremost laymen in the Congregational Church of this state, occupying at present a

responsible position in the general conference of Congregational Churches, and being a leading member of the Congregational Club of Connecticut. He has been a director in the Missionary Society of Connecticut, and a trustee of the Fund for Ministers, since 1865; to which offices he has been annually re-elected by the General Conference of Connecticut. He has also been a trustee of the Hale Donation Fund since 1877. He was the senior deacon in the First Congregational church in Rockville at the time the Union church was organized, and retains the office in the new church. The subject of this sketch, while not having been a public office-holder in the general sense of that term, has been one of the most reliable and trusted representatives of town affairs in Rockville in the town of Vernon. He has possessed abundant means through life, and has used his wealth for the advancement and benefit of the community in which he has been for so long a time an honored resident and business manager.

PATRICK McGOVERN, HARTFORD: Alderman Third Ward.

Alderman McGovern was born October 23, 1849, and received a university education. The whole of his public life has been spent in this city. He has

PATRICK McGOVERN.

been a member of the court of common council for fourteen years, all but two of the number having been passed in the upper board. For the past three years he has been the acting president of the aldermanic organization, making him the chief executive of the city during the mayor's absence. He has had the unanimous vote of his republican associates in the board for the place, occupying the position through three consecutive terms. He was chairman of the fire department committee for a number of years, and has held the most important special committeeships during the whole period in which he has been connected with the municipal government. His work has been invaluable on these committees. The details belong to the history of the city's administration during the past dozen years, but the mention of the work belongs properly to a personal history of the alderman. He has held positions of great responsibility in the town and city apart from his connection with the court of common council. He has been a member of the republican town committee for years, occupying the chairmanship since 1887. He has been a member of staff under every republican marshal in this city since 1876. He is the republican town auditor, and his work in that capacity has been performed with the utmost accuracy and fidelity. During the last presidential campaign he was one of the founders of the Henry C. Robinson troop, and is actively interested in the later history and work of the organization. On various important occasions he has represented the republicans in conventions and public assemblages. Mr. McGovern is a member of the Ancient Order of Hibernians, and of the order of Elks in this city. He belongs to St. Peter's church, and is one of the staunchest friends of the working classes in the city. He occupies a position of great trust and responsibility in the Ætna Life Insurance Company, and is a gentleman of the strictest business habits and training. Mr. McGovern is married, his wife being Miss Vitaline Dumont prior to marriage.

THOMAS J. THURBER, Putnam Heights: Artist.

Thomas Jones Thurber was a member of the general assembly in 1882, representing the town of Putnam. His legislative career was one of credit and success. The felicitous qualities of heart and head of which he is the possessor won for him a cordial place among his associates, and he is remembered as one of the pleasantest gentlemen in eastern Connecticut. He is a republican in politics. He is at present a justice of the peace and an agent of the Connecticut Humane Society. He is also the collector and treasur-

T. J. THURBER.

er of the First Congregational church society at Putnam. Mr. Thurber is interested in scientific research, and has devoted considerable time and attention to independent investigation. He has also executed meritorious work as an artist, his oil paintings meeting with decided favor and acceptance. His time and money have been cheerfully expended in behalf of temperance interests, and his life in various ways has been a benefaction to the world. Mr. Thurber was born in Providence, R. I., May 20, 1831, and was educated in the Providence high school. In 1852 he accepted a position with the New England agency of the Delaware & Hudson Canal Company, retaining it for four years. Subsequently he represented Edward Harris, the Woonsocket woolen manufacturer, in New York city for thirteen years, being allowed an interest in the business

during the last three years of his term. He then established a connection for four years with Gardner, Brewer & Co.'s New York house, and afterwards with A. T. Stewart & Co., having charge of the domestic woolen mills owned by the firm. He retired from business in 1873, and has since resided at Putnam Heights. The wife of Mr. Thurber, who is still living, was Miss Esther A. Carey of Providence. There is one son, Charles H. Thurber, who is engaged in business at Newark, N. J.

COL. JOHN B. DOHERTY, Waterbury: Postmaster.

Colonel Doherty was born in Westmoreland county, New Brunswick, Sept. 10, 1853, and was educated in a private academy at St. John, New Brunswick, and in the public schools of Waterbury. He is an accountant by profession. He is a member of the Quinnipiac and Republican League of New Haven, Continental Lodge, F. and A. M., and Clark Commandry, Knights Templar, of Waterbury. He also belongs to the Odd Fellows, the Knights of Pythias, the Red Men, and the Waterbury Club.

J. B. DOHERTY.

He has taken an active part in politics and occupied the position of first selectman in Waterbury for two years, the term of service beginning October, 1886. He was appointed postmaster under President Harrison. Colonel Doherty has also been considered as a candidate for position on the state ticket. But as colonel of the Second Regiment he has been brought into deserved prominence during the past eighteen months. In the first place his way was made from the ranks to the highest position in the command. In addition to this his management of the Second during two encampments at Niantic proved his promotion to be a meritorious one. He enlisted as a private in Company A of the Second, January 22, 1872, and became second lieutenant May 20, 1880. He was commissioned first lieutenant, June 2, 1882, captain, August 1, 1883, and major, February 16, 1885. January 24, 1887, he received his commission as lieutenant-colonel, and was promoted to the command of the regiment, July 1, 1889. Colonel Doherty is one of the best officers in the National Guard. Under his leadership the Second has lost none of its prestige. The wife of Colonel Doherty died Nov. 29, 1882. There are no children. He is connected with the Second Congregational society in Waterbury.

EDWARD W. THOMPSON, New Britain: Druggist.

Edward Willet Thompson is engaged in the drug business in New Britain, where he has a large and lucrative patronage. He is a member of the New

E. W. THOMPSON.

Britain club, and is connected with the First Congregational church. In politics Mr. Thompson is a republican. He was born at Broadalbin, N.Y., November 1, 1850, and received a common school education. He removed to New Britain a number of years ago, and succeeded to one of the best drug establishments in the city, reorganizing the business under the firm name of E. W. Thompson & Co. Mr. Thompson has a wife and two sons, the former being Miss Ella M. Andrews of New Britain. Mr. Thompson resided in New York city prior to his removal to Connecticut.

C. E. JACKSON, Middletown: Banker, Vice-President Middlesex Banking Company.

Charles Eben Jackson was born in Middletown, January 25, 1849. He was educated at St. Paul's School, Concord, N. H., receiving a thorough

C. E. JACKSON.

preparation for the business activities of life. After leaving school he engaged as a clerk in a mercantile establishment, and later in a banking office in New York city. In 1872 he made the acquaintance of Miss Evelyn Quintard, daughter of E. A. Quintard of New York city, whom he married in 1873, and by whom he has had eight children, seven of them now living. Mr. Jackson has for a number of years been at the head of the Middletown banking house of C. E. Jackson & Co., well known among the reputable financial institutions of the state. He is also vice-president of the Middlesex Banking Company, treasurer of the Berkeley Divinity School, and of the Russell Library Company, and has minor official connection with other institutions of Middletown. He is by religious faith and profession an Episcopalian, being a member and senior warden of Holy Trinity parish.

He has been connected with the republican party, but latterly his political inclinations are decidedly " mugwumpian."

It may be said without impropriety that Mr. Jackson has a well-founded reputation in business circles as an able and honorable financier, whose business methods and management entitle his firm to the utmost confidence of the community.

GENERAL SAMUEL E. CHAMBERLAIN, Wethersfield: Warden Connecticut State Prison.

S. E. Chamberlain was born Nov. 28, 1829, at Center Harbor, N. H., and was educated in the public schools of Boston. He served as an enlisted

S. E. CHAMBERLAIN.

man in the First United States Dragoons, during the war with Mexico, and took part in the storming of Monterey, Sept. 21, 22, and 23, 1846, and the battle of Buena Vista, Feb. 22 and 23, 1847. He afterwards served with Rangers in Sonora and Arizona, in suppressing Apaches' outrages, employed by the governor of Durango. In the fall of 1853 he was a member of Walker's expedition to " extend the area of freedom " in Lower California, and participated in the affairs at La Paz, San Thomas, and La Encinada. On the breaking out of the civil war he was, on April 17, 1861, commissioned first lieutenant Company C, Third Regiment, Massachusetts Volunteer Militia, at Cambridge, Mass. On his return from the three-months campaign he enlisted as a private in the First Massachusetts Cavalry, was commissioned captain Nov. 28, 1861; major, Oct. 30, 1862; lieutenant-colonel, March 5, 1864; colonel, Sept. 30, 1864; and breveted brigadier-general for gallant and meritorious service in covering the retreat of Gregg's Division of Cavalry, at the disastrous battle of St. Mary's Church, Va., June 25, 1864. He was wounded seven times, was engaged in thirty-five battles, besides numerous cavalry affairs. After the close of the war he was stationed in Texas, and was finally mustered out October, 1865. He served on the staffs of Governors Bullock and Claflin of Massachusetts, as assistant quarter-master-general, with the rank of colonel. He was appointed warden of the Massachusetts State Prison in 1871, resigned in 1881, and was appointed warden of the Connecticut State Prison March 17, 1885, which office he still holds.

General Chamberlain married Miss Mary Keith, and they have three children. Among the military and other associations with which he is connected may be mentioned the military order of the Loyal Legion of the United States, the Grand Army of the Republic, and the Masonic fraternity. In politics he is identified with the republican party. His military life and habits, his wide familiarity with all phases of humanity, and his quick perceptive instincts, admirably qualify him for the proper discharge of the important and peculiar duties of his present position at the head of the chief penal and reformatory institution of the commonwealth.

ADOLPH KORPER, WILLINGTON: Paymaster with Gardiner Hall, Jr., & Co.

The subject of this sketch is a native of Bohemia, Austria, where he was born in February, 1846. He was educated in the public schools, and at the age of twenty-one emigrated to America, taking up his residence in Willington, in which town he has ever since resided, engaged as bookkeeper and paymaster for the firm of Gardiner Hall, Jr., & Co. of South Willington since 1869. He married Miss Mary I. Brigham of Tolland, and four children have been born to them — a daughter and three sons.

ADOLPH KORPER.

When the project of a post-office at South Willington was carried out and an office established, Mr. Korper was appointed postmaster, but subsequently resigned, owing to the pressure of other duties, and his wife was appointed as his successor. He is in ardent sympathy with New England ideas, though not a native, and interests himself actively in all schemes for public improvement. He has held various elective offices in his town, being chosen thereto by the republicans, of which party he has been a member since becoming an elector. He was grand juror, constable, registrar of electors, and auditor several years, and represented Willington in the state legislature in 1879; was appointed notary public that year and re-appointed each year since; is now first selectman, town agent, and agent of the town deposit fund, having held these offices continuously since 1886. It is but just to say that in whatever position Mr. Korper has been called to serve the public, he has rendered conscientious service, and has given complete satisfaction to his constituents. He is a director of the Stafford Springs Agricultural Society, a member of the Stafford Springs Business Men's Association, and a member also of Uriel Lodge, No. 24, Free and Accepted Masons.

DWIGHT W. TUTTLE, EAST HAVEN: Attorney-at-Law.

Representative Dwight W. Tuttle was born in Hamden, and is forty-four years of age. He was educated in the common schools and in the law school connected with Yale University. He has held the offices of town clerk, justice of the peace for twenty-two years, prosecuting agent for nine years, grand juror, and member of the board of relief. He was originally elected to the legislature in 1881, and in 1889 was returned by the republicans of East Haven. Last fall he was elected for the third term and was placed

D. W. TUTTLE.

on the judiciary committee, his standing as a republican lawyer entitling him to that position. He is at present school visitor in East Haven, chairman of the republican town committee, and justice of the peace. He is the senior warden of Christ Church in East Haven, a member of the Masonic order, the Grange, and of the Sons of Temperance. The wife of Representative Tuttle, who is still living, was Miss Bertha Lancey prior to her marriage. There are no children. In addition to his law practice Mr. Tuttle is interested in farming in East Haven and in Florida.

M. A. HART, RIVERTON: Merchant.

Myron A. Hart, at present representative in the general assembly from Barkhamsted, was born in that town, January 17, 1849, and was educated at Wilbraham Academy, graduating from that institution in 1869. He engaged in mercantile business at Riverton and was for years at the head of the firm of M. A. & L. C. Hart. He was assistant postmaster from 1867 until 1883, and postmaster from the latter year until 1890. He has also held the position of first selectman and town agent, justice of the peace, town

M. A. HART.

auditor, member of the school board, and board of relief, discharging the duties of each office with promptness and efficiency. Mr. Hart is a democrat in politics. He is associated with the Congregational society at Riverton. In May, 1890, he disposed of his mercantile business, and resigned as secretary and treasurer of the Tunxis Creamery Association. He is at present connected with a manufacturing company at Chicago, Ill., engaged in the manufacture of machinery for mining. The wife of Representative Hart, who was Miss Carrie A. Ransom prior to marriage, died January 12, 1890, leaving to him the care of four daughters.

JAMES NEWTON LOOMIS, Granby: Merchant.

Mr. Loomis is senior member of the prosperous firm of Loomis Brothers, who are proprietors of the principal store in the town of Granby. He is a native of Southwick, Mass., where he was born September 16, 1832. His attendance at the district school and at the academy in Southwick was nearly continuous up to the time when he reached the age of fourteen, when he was put out to live with an uncle on a farm for six months,—which experience he yet retains a lively recollection of on account of the severe and

laborious tasks which were imposed upon him. At the end of this term of farm service he went to Granby and engaged as a clerk for G. H. Dibble, and has retained his residence in that town up to the present time. He formed a business connection, later, with J. J. Phelps, which continued until 1856, when he joined his brother, C. P. Loomis, and, under the style of Loomis Brothers, the business has since been successfully conducted for thirty-five years. During the war of the rebellion both himself and his brother were drafted, but both furnished substitutes. Since 1856 the office of postmaster of Granby has been held continuously by one or the other of the brothers — J. N. holding the commission until 1868, and resigning in favor of C. P. in order to accept the office of representative in the state legislature to which he was elected by the republicans the fall previous; and the latter similarly resigning when he was elected to the same office in 1879. Mr. J. N. Loomis was selectman of Granby for several years, and has filled other minor town offices. He is a member of the South Congregational church; also of the Masonic fraternity, including St. Mark's Lodge, No. 91, and La Fayette Chapter. He has twice married: first Catherine Pratt of Middleboro, Mass., who died in 1885; and subsequently Estelle M. Deming of Granby. He has three children — two by first and one by his last marriage. Dr. Frank N. Loomis of Birmingham is his eldest son.

The firm of Loomis Brothers has met with some hard luck in business, having suffered by a disastrous conflagration in 1877, but by perseverance and plenty of hard work they have conquered obstacles and achieved a splendid success. They have recently completed a new edifice for their business, which will give them one of the finest country stores in the state.

CHESTER P. LOOMIS, Granby: Merchant.

The subject of this sketch was born at Southwick, Mass., November 20, 1834, the younger of two brothers, whose relations, both business and social, have been most intimate from childhood until the present time. He received a good rudimentary education at the district school, finishing at Dickinson Academy, an excellent institution of that town. Here he laid a foundation for the success which he achieved in later life, in mercantile pursuits, to which he seemed to be adapted and which was clearly in the line of

his taste and ambition. He left home at eighteen years of age to become a clerk in Lee, Mass., in which position he worked faithfully until he became of age, when he removed to Granby, Conn., and shortly afterward entered into partnership with J. N. Loomis, his elder brother, in the establishment of a general country store in the village of Granby, the firm being Loomis Brothers. This connection has continued uninterruptedly from that time until the present, and the establishment has become one of the best known and most prosperous and extensive in that part of the state. During the war Mr. Loomis was engaged in business in Newberne, North Carolina, for upwards of four years, maintaining the while his connection with the Granby firm. In addition to his personal and partnership affairs, he has found time to serve his fellow-citizens in various capacities. He has been town clerk since 1872, and still holds that office. He represented Granby in the general assembly in 1880, and previous to that date was postmaster for nearly or quite ten years. He has been republican town committee, and otherwise active in promoting the interests of that party, by whom he was elected to his seat in the legislature. He is a member of the South Congregational church, also of St. Mark's Lodge, No. 91, F. and A. M. Mr. Loomis is married and has two children. His wife was Miss Eliza L. Harger, daughter of the late Deacon John W. Harger of Canton. A younger brother, George L., lives in Northampton, Mass.

ASA SINCLAIR COOK. Hartford: Manufacturing Machinist.

Asa S. Cook, eldest son of John and Sarah (Sinclair) Cook, was born at Sandwich, N. H., Jan. 10, 1823. His father, a sturdy and respected farmer, recognized the importance of mental as well as physical culture for his children, and thus the slender advantages of the district school were supplemented in his case by several terms at the high school then taught by Daniel G. Beede, an instructor of ability and considerable local distinction. At the age of eighteen he started out to seek his fortune, his chief and almost sole

A. S. COOK.

equipment being a fair education, robust health, and a resolute will. Having determined to learn the trade of a machinist, he served a regular apprenticeship, and spent his first five years as a journeyman at Gloucester Point, N. J., during which time he was sent by his employers to Tuscaloosa, Ala., to assist in setting up the machinery of one of the pioneer cotton mills of the south. In 1850 he moved to Hartford, Conn., and entered the employ of the Colt's Patent Fire Arms Company, where as workman, foreman, or contractor, he remained during the next fifteen years, with the exception of a few months given to the cause of freedom in Kansas, during the border-ruffian imbroglio of 1858. In 1865 the petroleum excitement drew him to the Canadian oil regions, where he spent three years somewhat fruitlessly. Returning to Hartford he at once entered into an engagement with the National Screw Company to make, from their patterns and drawings, machinery for the production of wood screws. When a few years later this company was absorbed by its powerful rival in Providence, R. I., he began to manufacture wood-screw machinery for the trade, from designs of his own, introducing several important improvements for which he secured letters patent. Since then he has equipped many screw factories in America and Europe. In 1872 Mr. Cook began to manufacture Stephens' patent parallel vise, of which he has since turned out over thirty thousand. He has also made special machinery to order, employing from fifty to a hundred men at his establishment in Colt's armory building, and disbursing from $50,000 to $75,000 a year in wages. He has had a business career of remarkable prosperity, and has accumulated a handsome property, the result of patient industry, wisely directed efforts, and honorable dealing.

In politics Mr. Cook is a republican, and has been a recognized leader in the councils of his party in all affairs of municipal government. He served two years in the common council of Hartford, and four years as alderman, representing the Fourth Ward. When the Hartford board of trade was organized in 1888, he was selected for one of the directors. He is also a member of the American Society of Mechanical Engineers; and has been for some years a director of the Pratt & Whitney Company. He has traveled extensively south and west, and has made at least one trip abroad, combining in these journeys the interests of his business and his personal gratification.

Mr. Cook married, Oct. 31, 1850, Mary J., daughter of John and Harriet (Coburn) Cole, of Lowell, Mass., to whose wise counsels and hearty coöperation Mr. Cook attributes very much of the happiness and prosperity that have fallen to his lot. They have had five children, all but one of whom are now living. Two of the children are married, namely, John F., to Josephine E. Garrison, and Harriet E., to Philemon W. Robbins, both families residing in Hartford. The sons, Albert S., and Millard F., are both unmarried. The latter, with his brother, John F., both practical mechanics, assist their father in carrying on the business; thus giving assurance that the establishment and its success will be perpetuated through succeeding generations.

Mr. Cook's pleasant home in Hartford is on Charter Oak Place, overlooking the valley of the Connecticut, with its delightful landscapes; and, for a summer residence, he has recently erected a cottage on an island in Squam Lake, in Moultonborough, N. H., near the home of his boyhood.

JOSEPH F. GILPIN. Ansonia: Master-mechanic.

Joseph Frederick Gilpin, superintendent of the copper mill, wire mill, and wire covering department of the Ansonia Brass and Copper Company, began life as a millwright and machinist. By ability and industry he has attained the position of master-mechanic with the company, and is held in high esteem in the community where he resides. He is a member of the board of burgesses of Ansonia, and was elected fire marshal in 1890. He was born in England, July 18, 1837, and received a thorough school educa-

J. F. GILPIN.

tion. He learned the trade of an engineer and wheelwright. He arrived in New York in April, 1864, and in January, 1866, removed to Ansonia.

where he has since resided. He first engaged in work with the Farrell Foundry & Machine Company. October 15, 1866, he became connected with the Brass and Copper Company, and has remained in its employ since then. He belongs to the Masonic and Odd Fellow fraternities, and is a member of the Ansonia Club. He is a republican in politics, and is a member of the Episcopal church. His wife, who is still living, was Miss Sarah Simpson before marriage. The family consists of three children, two daughters, and one son. Mr. Gilpin is a popular citizen of Ansonia.

SAMUEL J. P. LADD, Canterbury: Postmaster.
    The subject of this biography is of New London county origin, having been born in the town of Franklin. The date of his birth is recorded as

S. J. P. LADD.

September 9, 1822. He was brought up on a farm, and educated at the district and select schools of Franklin. His father died when he was a lad of thirteen, and after that the responsibilities of the farm were largely on him. Naturally robust, his habits of life tended to his best physical development, and he reached his maturity with a constitution and power of endurance worth more to him than any pecuniary outfit could be as a preparation for the stern duties of life then before him. At the age of twenty-two he went to Ashtabula county, Ohio, bought a drove of three hundred and fifty-five head of cattle, and drove them to his farm in Franklin, being forty-eight days on the road. He has from that time onward dealt more or less in cattle and horses, and very largely in real estate. In 1846 he contracted to draw from Norwich to Coventry all the granite of which the Hale monument was constructed, which he did with an ox-team, personally driving the team on the several trips necessary, back and forth, twenty-two miles each way.

In 1845 he married Miss Philena B. Hazen, daughter of Colonel Henry Hazen of Franklin, and a graduate of Wilbraham academy. She died in 1860. He married, second, in September, 1861, Catherine G. Kenyon of Plainfield, a cousin of the late Hon. David Gallup. By his first marriage Mr. Ladd had three children: Philena Josephine Ladd, now Mrs. Lowell K. Smith of Willimantic; Samuel Pierrepont Ladd, now the leading physician and surgeon of Moosup; and Arthur C. Ladd, now postmaster at Jewett City.

In 1856, and for some years afterward, Mr. Ladd was temporarily a resident of Hartford. During this time he became a member of the old Fourth church. He was actively instrumental in assisting to organize the republican party in that year, and became prominent among the politicians of Connecticut in the first Lincoln campaign. In 1861 he represented the town of Franklin in the state legislature. It was during this year that the new town of Sprague was created from adjoining portions of the old towns of Franklin and Lisbon. Mr. Ladd went to the legislature a citizen of Franklin; he returned to his home at the close of the session a citizen of Sprague. Previous to this time, when Governor Sprague (senior) of Providence first contemplated the purchase of water powers and erection of a manufacturing plant on the Shetucket River, where the village of Baltic now stands, he employed Mr. Ladd to accomplish the difficult feat of buying all the real estate contemplated in the proposed purchase, at a given price, from the twenty-seven owners who then held it. This Mr. Ladd succeeded in doing, obtained the twenty-seven deeds, and was directly instrumental in the creation of the village of Baltic. Some years after the Baltic privilege was taken up, he was employed by the younger Spragues to secure all the water rights between Baltic and Willimantic, being fifty-five feet fall,— equal to two such privileges as Baltic,— which would have been occupied if the Spragues had not met with financial reverses.

In 1868 he sold the old homestead and removed to Windsor Locks, purchasing a farm there, on which he resided five years. During this period, as before, he was employed as purchasing agent and as adjuster of claims against the Hartford, Providence & Fishkill Railroad (now the New York & New England), serving in this and similar capacities for some twelve or fifteen years. He was also engaged in various outside work and speculations for firms and corporations, involving good judgment and experimental knowledge of men and things. Lawyers in the employ of companies and corporations which employed him valued his services in carrying on suits at law, in preparing the cases brought to trial, for which he received many compliments from them. Some years ago he removed to the town of Canterbury, having bought the house on "Canterbury Green" which occupies the site of the old Judge Judson residence, long ago demolished. On his premises is "Cobble Hill," the eminence from which the cannon was fired nearly a century ago, when the valiant citizens of Canterbury succeeded in driving Prudence Crandall out of the town for the offense of teaching colored children in her school. Mr. Ladd has held various town offices here and elsewhere, and is now the postmaster of Canterbury. His religious connections are now with the Congregational church of Plainfield.

Mr. Ladd is of choice Puritan stock, being the ninth in direct descent from Elder Brewster, the famous leader of the pilgrim band who landed on Plymouth Rock from the *Mayflower* in 1620. The record of his lifework abounds with practical achievements for the public welfare in the various localities in which his lot has been cast, and he has the satisfaction of seeing results which abundantly demonstrate that he has worthily served his day and generation.

SIDNEY W. CROFUT, DANIELSONVILLE: Fire Insurance Agent.

Mr. Crofut was born Oct. 17, 1847, in the town of Ossining, Westchester county, N. Y. He was educated at a military academy, and afterwards made his home in Brooklyn, N. Y. He began his business career as a clerk in the office of an insurance company in New York, and later on occupied official positions for several years. He served in the National Guard of that state for the full term of seven years. He removed to Danielsonville in 1884, and bought an interest in a fire insurance and real

S. W. CROFUT.

estate agency. In 1886 he acquired the entire insurance interest. He has continued the business with success, conducting a large agency, and representing several of the best and leading companies. He has been president of the People's Library Association, has served the borough in the capacity of a burgess, and in 1888 was elected warden of the borough. Re-elected in 1889, and again in 1890, he is now holding the office his third term. During his administration the most notable things accomplished have been the entering into of contracts for a system of fire hydrants throughout the borough, and lighting its streets by electricity, both of which are now in operation. It has been written of him: "The intelligence and executive ability exhibited by him in that office (warden) have proven him thoroughly competent to fill offices of greater importance." Mr. Crofut is also vice-president of the Windham County Savings Bank, chairman of the school district committee, and treasurer of the Baptist society. In politics he is a republican, and was the acting chairman of the executive committee of the local campaign club in 1888. He is a member of the Baptist church; is married, and has one child, a daughter.

CHARLES ARNOLD, THOMPSON: Cashier of the Thompson National Bank.

Mr. Arnold was born in Coventry, R. I., September 12, 1843, and was educated at the common schools, and at the Westerly, R. I., high school. He followed the business of a carpenter in early life, but for the most part has been a bookkeeper, and latterly a banker. He was bookkeeper for the Grosvenordale Company at North Grosvenordale, for twelve years, and has been connected with the Thompson Bank for five years. At present he is cashier of the Thompson National Bank, and treasurer of

CHARLES ARNOLD.

the Dime Savings Bank of that place. He is a republican, but has never held public office. He is a deacon of the Baptist church in Thompson, and is connected with the Putnam Council, Royal Arcanum. His wife was Annie A. Sweet, and they have one son and two daughters. Mr. Arnold is as well known as any man in the northeastern section of the state, is recognized as a financier of more than average ability, and has the respect of business men everywhere.

A. W. SPAULDING, HARTFORD: Merchant.

Alva W. Spaulding, who has held the office of sheriff in Hartford county for ten years, was born in Morristown, Vt., March 1, 1825, and received a common school education. In 1865 he removed to New Britain, and in 1870 represented that city in the legislature, his colleague being T. W. Stanley. Sheriff Spaulding held the office of deputy sheriff for nine years, receiving the appointment originally from Westell Russell of Hartford. He was chief of police at New Britain for ten years prior to his election as county

A. W. SPAULDING.

sheriff. He had also held the offices of constable and bailiff. He was first elected sheriff in 1880, and served consecutively through three terms, the latter being for four years. His official career has been thoroughly satisfactory to the public. In retiring from the position which he occupied with so much of honor and success he carried with him the sincerest respect and esteem of the community. Mr. Spaulding is widely known throughout the county and state. He is now connected with the furniture business, owning a half interest in the firm of C. C. Fuller & Co. Sheriff Spaulding has a wife and adopted son, Clinton E. Spaulding. His wife was Miss Josephine A. Beckley of New Britain, but formerly of Berlin. Sheriff Spaulding and wife were members of the Center church in New Britain before removing to Hartford. After settling in this city they transferred their membership to the Windsor Avenue Congregational church. The sheriff was formerly an Odd Fellow in New Britain, but has not been affiliated with any society organization for a number of years.

—

HENRY A. WHITMAN, HARTFORD: President Hartford Life and Annuity Insurance Company.

The subject of this sketch was born in the town of Farmington, being a son of the late Judge Lemuel Whitman, a prominent lawyer of ability and reputation throughout the county, occupying important civil and judicial positions in the state, and representing the commonwealth four years in the national congress.

H. A. WHITMAN.

Mr. Whitman was graduated at the then famous "Hart Preparatory School" in his native town, and early in life entered upon what has proved to be a successful business career. In 1851 he removed to Hartford, and entered the employ of one of the largest wholesale commission houses of the state. Five years later he was admitted a partner in the dry-goods commission house of Day, Griswold & Co.; and in 1863, when this firm was dissolved, he, together with Messrs. Wareham Griswold and Daniel F. Seymour, continued the business in Hartford and New York. This firm was succeeded by Griswold, Whitman & Welch, afterwards Whitman & Welch, and still later Whitman & Co.— all successful and well-known houses.

Mr. Whitman is now president of the Hartford Life and Annuity Insurance Company, one of the prosperous institutions of the state, with which he has been connected for over a quarter of a century as director, holding the office of vice-president for more than a decade previous to his election to the presidency. He is also a director in other well-known financial institutions, such as the National Fire Insurance Company and the First National

Bank, both of Hartford. In 1863 Mr. Whitman married Miss Emma C. Griswold, daughter of his then senior partner, an amiable and accomplished lady, well known in Hartford society, her name being prominently connected with many worthy charitable and benevolent undertakings.

Mr. Whitman has never sought political preferment, often declining such honors, preferring to confine himself closely to those walks of business life which were his early choice, and in which he has reaped the harvest of a generous competency.

WILLIE ARTHUR COUNTRYMAN, HARTFORD: Journalist.

Willie Arthur Countryman was born in New Haven, July 4, 1852. His christian name was Willie, after Willie P. Mangum, a North Carolina statesman, but wrongfully believing it to be invariably a diminutive, at manhood he changed it to William, having for a while called himself Willis, out of his mother's regard for Nathaniel Parker Willis, poet and journalist. The Arthur was conferred out of a similar esteem for Timothy Shay Arthur, the author. He is the second of the children in this list,

W. A. COUNTRYMAN.

all born at New Haven: Franklin, Willie Arthur, Charles Lewis, Edwin, Louisa, Robert Eugene, and Stella Elsie (who died in infancy). His parents are Nicholas Countryman, born in the town of Stark, near the village of Starkville, Herkimer county, New York, October, 1825, and Louisa (Talmage) Hine, born in Prospect, New Haven county, Connecticut, 1825. On his father's side he descends from John, Fred Conterman — afterward corrupted to Countryman — who settled near Catskill, N. Y., in 1709, coming with many others from the German Palatinate, which had been devastated by Louis XIV. The family afterward removed to the Mohawk Valley, where they remained through the French-Indian war and the butcheries of Butler and Brant during the revolution. The maternal grandfather of Nicholas — Jacob Eckler — was taken captive by the Indians to Canada during one of the border raids, and held seven years. His paternal great-grandfather, Jacob Countryman, was in the militia of Tryon county in the revolution, under Herkimer, and was probably with his company at Oriskany. On his mother's side William Arthur is of English ancestry — the Talmages and Hines coming to this country from England in 1640 or thereabouts, and living for the most part in New Haven county, Connecticut.

After schooling at John E. Lovell's later school, corner State and Court streets, opened about 1860, at Sydney A. Thomas's on St. John street, and at the Business College, managed by Thomas A. Stevens, under Music Hall, Crown street, New Haven, Mr. Countryman became bookkeeper at his father's sash, door, and blind factory on Water street, and was taught the trade of a sash and blind maker. He had also a short apprenticeship at carpentering. In the spring of 1871, as his aims had been literary and newspaperial, Major Minott A. Osborn, editor and proprietor of the New Haven *Evening Register* employed him as city editor. When the New Haven *Daily Union* was established by Alexander Troup some two years and a half later Mr. Countryman transferred his duties to that journal. A few months afterward he was invited to become the assistant of Frank D. Root, in the city department of the New Haven *Palladium*, whose editor was Edward Butler. After five years' service there he was re-called to the *Register*, where he remained until July, 1883. During this time he was also editor of the *Educator*, a small monthly publication devoted to literary and educational themes. Then he removed to Hartford to become a general writer, with special attention to literary and legislative matters, on the Hartford Evening *Post*. His newspaper experience was characterized by severe application, astonishingly rapid work, and a persistent and generally successful inquiry after facts. Upon the *Post* he became the gatherer of its " Old Days in Hartford " papers, and was generally its authority on economic subjects. During the secret ballot agitation he advocated the Australian system with pen and voice, in the newspaper and before the legislature. He was otherwise identified with the interests of the working people. In August, 1889, by appointment of Commissioner Hotchkiss, he became chief clerk of the State Bureau of Labor Statistics. In 1890 he was chosen first president of the Hartford Press Club, and has been secretary of the Connecticut Press Association. He is a member of the Connecticut Sons of the Society of the American Revolution and of the Grand Council of the Royal Arcanum, which is a coöperative insurance society, and has Masonic (Adelphi lodge No. 63, Fair Haven,) and Odd Fellowship (Harmony lodge No. 5, New Haven) affiliations.

December 23, 1874, he married Mary Adella Perry, born January 16, 1850, fourth child of Samuel Perry (born Montville, Connecticut, October 19, 1811; died in Fair Haven, September 26, 1880; and Emeline Chapin, born in Chicopee Falls, Mass., February, 1819). Her ancestry thus goes back to the early days of Massachusetts, Rhode Island, and

Connecticut; to the ancestry of the Perry of naval fame and the Chapins of Springfield, Mass. Her brothers and sisters are: Harriet Elizabeth, born Springfield, 1844, married John P. Augur, wholesale spice dealer, New Haven; George Elbert, born Fair Haven, 1846, now of Providence, R. I.; Genevieve Isabella, born Fair Haven, 1848, married Elbridge F. Barnes, proprietor Barnes Tool Co.; Emma Sarah, born Fair Haven, 1852, died July 2, 1872; B. Frank, born Fair Haven, 1854, died 1859; Frederic Chapin, born Fair Haven, 1860.

He has two children, Emeline Perry, born New Haven, August 28, 1882, and Willis Arthur, born Hartford, November 16, 1884.

MARVIN H. SANGER, CANTERBURY Judge of Probate.

Marvin Hutchins Sanger was born in Brooklyn, in Windham county, April 12, 1827. In his infancy his parents removed to Canterbury, where he was educated in the public schools, and at Bacon Academy in Colchester, and was kept at home assisting his father upon the farm until he reached the age of eighteen. Then followed two years of experience in a country store as clerk, which served as a preparation for the business of general merchandizing which he followed in Canterbury for twenty years, from 1849 to 1869,

M. H. SANGER.

since which latter date he has not been actively engaged in any business. November 14, 1855, he was married to Miss Mary J. Bacon, daughter of the late Benjamin Bacon of Plainfield. They have had two children, both daughters. Mr. Sanger has been a lifelong democrat, and for many years an active and influential member of his party, performing much service in its behalf and receiving many honors through its agency. He has long been a justice of the peace and has thus been much occupied in the trial of criminal cases. He was elected town clerk and treasurer in 1852, and has been re-elected ever since with the exception of two years. He has been judge of probate for about a quarter of a century, and was postmaster at Canterbury for fifteen years under various presidential administrations. He has been on the board of directors of the Brooklyn Savings Bank, and now for several years has been its president. He represented Canterbury in the state legislature in 1857, 1860, 1872, 1877, and 1889; was secretary of state for four successive years, from 1873 to 1877; and was democratic candidate for state treasurer in the autumn of 1890, receiving an apparent majority of all the votes cast, but failing to receive official recognition from the house of representatives at its session the following January, owing to a disagreement between the two branches of the legislature as to the accuracy or validity of the returns,—as was the case with all the candidates on the democratic state ticket, with the exception of the comptroller.

Mr. Sanger is a member of the Congregational ecclesiastical society of Canterbury, and of the Masonic fraternity, his local connection being with Mount Moriah lodge of Danielsonville. He is one of the most prominent members of his party in Windham county, and among the foremost citizens of his town.

THEODORE H. SUCHER, New Haven: Merchant.

Captain Theodore H. Sucher was born in New Haven February 26, 1850, and was educated in the public schools. He has pursued the avocation of a

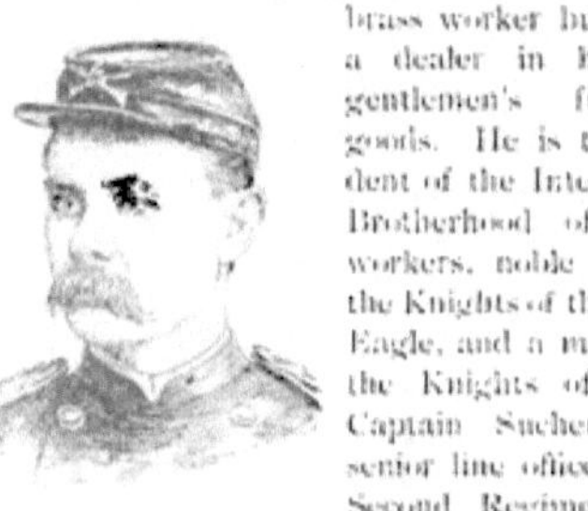

T. H. SUCHER.

brass worker but is now a dealer in hats and gentlemen's furnishing goods. He is the president of the International Brotherhood of Brassworkers, noble chief of the Knights of the Golden Eagle, and a member of the Knights of Labor. Captain Sucher is the senior line officer in the Second Regiment, Connecticut National Guard. His commission as the commanding officer of Company E, of the Second, dates from December 13, 1884. He has been in the National Guard service fourteen years. Captain Sucher has risen from the ranks. He enlisted as a private in Company E, May 7, 1877, and was made corporal May 1, 1879. He was discharged May 6, 1882, and re-enlisted the next day, retaining his rank as corporal. He was commissioned second lieutenant March 5, 1883, and first lieutenant March 4, 1884, retaining that position until December, when he received his captain's commission. His company ranks among the first in the National Guard of the state. Captain Sucher is a member of the Lutheran church in New Haven and is a republican in politics. He has been a member of the court of common council in his native city and is a popular leader. He has a wife and two children. The former was Miss Hertha Hax before her marriage.

DR. ALFRED R. GOODRICH, Vernon: President Mutual Benefit Life Company of Hartford.

Dr. Goodrich is a direct descendant of Ensign William Goodrich, who, with his brother, John Goodrich, settled in Wethersfield about the year

A. R. GOODRICH.

1636. His grandfather, George Goodrich, served in the revolutionary war, and after its close removed to the town of Gill, Mass., where he died at the advanced age of 92 years. A large family of children survived him, but his wife, Lucinda Wells, died in 1814. Alfred Goodrich, the father of Alfred R. Goodrich, was born in Gill in 1787, and occupied the old homestead, where he also reared a large family of children. He died in 1866, at the age of seventy-nine. His wife was Abigail Howland, daughter of Solomon Howland, of Greenfield, Mass. She died in 1821, leaving three sons, of whom the subject of the present sketch was the youngest. He was born at Gill in 1818, and was educated at the Deerfield Academy. Subsequently he became an associate teacher and principal in the institution. In 1843 he commenced the study of medicine under the instruction of the late Alden Skinner, M.D., and graduated in 1846 with distinction from the Berkshire Medical College. He practiced for some time in New York city, and remained there during the terrible epidemic of ship fever. Dr. Goodrich was himself prostrated by the disorder, but finally recovered from the attack. After his restoration to health he went to Vernon, and has since been engaged in his profession there, entering also into mercantile and manufacturing interests. In 1870 Dr. Goodrich was elected as the first democratic representative from his town, receiving, as he has invariably done when a candidate for public office, a very flattering vote from his political opponents. In 1871 he was the democratic nominee for congress in the First District, and came very near securing his election. Dr. Goodrich was elected state comptroller in 1873, and was re-elected for the three succeeding terms, discharging the duties of the office with fidelity and honor. He was successful in largely reducing the expenses of the state. Since 1874 he has been president of the Mutual Benefit Life Company of Hartford, which was chartered by the legislature in 1866. Previous to 1874 he was vice-president of the company. In 1870 he was elected president of the Connecticut State Medical Society, but declined a re-election. He is also a member of the State board of agriculture, a director in the Rockville Savings Bank, a member of the Tolland County and State Medical societies, chairman of the town board of education, a justice of the peace, and on the building committee which has charge of the proposed new high school building in Rockville, in the town of Vernon. Dr. Goodrich was treasurer of the state of Connecticut in 1883-84, having been elected to that office by the democratic party on the state ticket headed by Governor Waller. He has been almost constantly in office in the town of Vernon, rendering important service wherever placed. He was on the building committee which erected the fine memorial hall in Rockville, and served in a similar capacity on the committee which had in charge the recent expensive enlargement of the town almshouse.

Dr. Goodrich married Charlotte Dobson, daughter of the late Hon. Peter Dobson, the founder of cotton manufacturing interests in Vernon. He has one son, George Dobson Goodrich, who is treasurer of the life company in Hartford of which his father is president.

WILLIAM WALLACE LEE, Meriden: Machinist.

William Wallace Lee was born in Barkhamsted, July 20, 1828, and received a common school education. He learned the machinist trade with Taylor & Whiting of Winsted, and has worked at his trade in the city of Meriden, where he has resided since 1862. Prior to that period he worked in Guilford, Colt's Manufactory in Hartford, Ansonia, Bridgeport, Westville, and Birmingham. He represented Meriden in the general assembly in 1885 and 1886, and was assigned to important committees each year. Mr.

Lee has served four years on the board of aldermen of Meriden, and is prominently identified with political interests in that city. He was a delegate to the first republican convention held in Connecticut in 1856, and was a free soiler in 1848. He voted for President Lincoln in 1860, and in 1872 cast a vote for Horace Greeley, considering these votes as the proudest acts in his political life. Mr. Lee has never knowingly missed an opportunity for recording his vote in favor of equal rights, temperance, and good morals. It has been his aim to give, so far as his vote can effect that result, an equal chance for every man to make the most of himself. He is one of the most widely known secret society representatives in the state. He has been a member of the Sons of Temperance since he was eighteen years of age, and has held all the offices of importance in the order in this state, and was for thirty-five years connected with the national organization. He was grand master of the Connecticut Grand Lodge of Odd Fellows in 1877 and 1878. His masonic career was begun in 1852. In 1875 he was knighted in St. Elmo Commandery of Meriden, and was grand master of the grand lodge in 1874 and 1875. Prior to that he had held the office of grand high priest in the grand chapter of this state, occupying the position in 1872 and 1873. For the past twelve years he has been the president of the Masonic Veteran Association of the state of Connecticut. He is a member of the order of Red Men. In the various orders with which he is connected he possesses the fullest confidence of his associates, and is a man of decided personal popularity. Four brothers of the subject of this sketch served in the army during the war, two of them dying on the field. The grand army post at New Hartford is named in honor of one of Mr. Lee's brothers, and the principal address on the occasion of its flag presentation was delivered by the ex-representative. Mr. Lee also delivered an interesting address at the Barkhamsted Centennial a few years ago. The only surviving brother, Major B. D. Lee of the Second Heavy Artillery, is a member of the bar at St. Louis, Mo. Mr. Lee is the secretary and treasurer of the Lee Association, which was organized in this city in 1884 by the descendants of John Lee, who came to Hartford in 1635 from England, and in 1641 removed to Farmington, becoming one of the original proprietors of the town. The gentleman whose life is the subject of this sketch is a grandson of David Lee of Farmington and of Joseph Somers of Milford, and a great-grandson of Andrew Hays of Simsbury and of Elihu Crane of Killingworth, all four of whom were private soldiers in the army of the revolution. In view of this fact it is but natural that he should feel a genuine interest in the Sons of the American Revolution. He is a charter member of the Connecticut society and was a delegate to the national body, which met in Hartford April 30. Although holding so many positions, he has never sought office or even asked anybody to support or vote for him. The two brothers of Representative Lee who were killed in action during the war for the Union were Captain Edwin R. Lee of the Eleventh Connecticut, and Lieutenant Henry B. Lee of the Seventh. Representative Lee enlisted himself in the service, but was rejected on account of physical disability. He was formerly a lieutenant in the state militia. The wife of Mr. Lee was Miss Mary Jane Carrington of New Haven. She is still living. There is one daughter in the family.

LOVELL HALL, A.M., LL.B., MIDDLETOWN: Attorney-at-Law.

Lovell Hall is a practicing lawyer at Middletown. He was born May 12, 1844, at East Hampton (town of Chatham), Conn., which is within the ancient limits of Middletown; and in these two places the family have lived for nine generations. His first American ancestor, John Hall, helped settle Cambridge, Mass., in 1633; Hartford in 1635, and Middletown in 1650. His great-grandson, Giles Hall, Esq., married a sister of Supreme Court Judge Jabez Hamlin, and their son, John Hamlin Hall, settled in the east

LOVELL HALL.

part of his native Middletown, now East Hampton. Other branches of the family removed to Vermont, from whom sprang Hiland Hall, congressman, governor, and supreme court judge of Vermont, and U. S. commissioner to settle land titles in the (then) territory of California; and to New York state, whence General Amos Hall of that state. The whole family have always lived on the land, and been interested and informed on public questions, and often public men, when the surrounding population happened to hold views according with their own; which are public-spirited and thoroughly independent, based on experience, reflection, and reading, and not on appetite and clamor, and always heading the same way, no matter how the tide runs. It would be hard, perhaps, to find a family more uniform in many states and through nine generations, — books on the shelves and something on the table from the family orchard and garden. Mr. Hall's grandfather was a Baptist, that is, for religious toleration, — his father an abolitionist, Hiland Hall a free-soiler, long before the world wheeled into line, and would have continued had it not wheeled into line at all; and, had fruits not improved, it is probable that apples would be growing on the family property to-day, the descendants of cions brought by John Hall from England in 1633.

Mr. Hall's mother is from a Massachusetts family equally old; latterly, to a considerable extent, clergymen; they were, earlier, sea captains on Cape Cod, descended from Robert Lovell, who settled in Weymouth, Mass., in 1635; and this bent, to some extent, re-appears in L. N. Lovell, New York manager of the "Fall River Line" (steamers).

Lovell Hall was fitted for college in the Fall River high school, ranking first in his class, having spent his youth in East Hampton in the district school and at his father's farm and factory, where,

and later, his hands have become familiar with every farm operation, and many of those of manufacturing, from using a pair of pliers to an engine or 52-inch Hoe saw. He has carried his dinner-pail to the brass shop and lumber woods, as well as eaten New England society dinners at Delmonico's. In 1862 he stood first for one term in the class of 1866 at Wesleyan University, Middletown, and then entered the same class at Yale, with which he graduated. Here, as later in New York city, he cultivated his tastes in every direction, and is at least passable company for a great many different kinds of men. He was organist at the First Baptist church, New Haven, president of Linonia, a high oration man in scholarship, Townsend literary prize man, and divided the Yale literary prize medal; and contributed to the intellectual life of his class with such men as Geo. C. Holt of Pomfret, Prof. Hincks of Andover, Chas. H. Adams of the *Hartford Courant*, Judge John M. Hall, and others of his class. He also wrote the class song, and was active in founding the *Yale Courant*. After graduation he was tendered and declined a nomination to the assistant-professorship of ethics at the Annapolis naval school. His love and tastes drawing him rather to the old homestead and an open, country life, in 1866 he was acting postmaster and town clerk at East Hampton; in 1867 taught the principal's studies in a ladies' school at Canandaigua, N. Y.; in 1868 entered Columbia College law school, New York city, graduating in 1870, meanwhile being admitted to the bar there on examination in 1869, and singing in St. Bartholomew's church. The years from 1870 to 1875 he spent at East Hampton, developing the family real estate under the new conditions of the Boston & New York Air Line Railroad, now the Air Line Division of the New York, New Haven & Hartford Railroad, losing heavily and financially crippled by delays in its building, etc., but being the main instrument in locating its station to the convenience of the public and the family property, and confirming his health by air, labor, and horseback riding. Since 1875 he has been engaged in law practice at Middletown, keeping up oversight of the family farms at East Hampton — sometimes spending every night there. Here he is quietly developing a country home, such as old-time Connecticut professional and public men enjoyed. Choice poultry, registered Jersey stock that well know their master's hand, smooth gardens and fruit trees for which he has cut the cions with his own hands from the tallest trees, and long distances away; wild berries with their flavor, forest flowers, nuts, brooks, and forest trees trimmed and culled to avoid crowding and monotony, are here. And the old brick oven, crane, and five-foot fireplace, are safe at least in his day. Here, one-half mile from the station on a main

New York and Boston traffic artery, behind ancestral shade trees, with scores of neighbors in a stone's throw, a hundred men might stand a siege of a hundred years against famine, pestilence, and a thousand human follies, and want not shelter, food, fuel, clothing, nor the outward ministrations to thought, nor the inner ones to beauty, while the waves of the world, its follies, fashions, prejudices, controversies, broke outside and sent within hardly a ripple. A visit is like what the Catholic clergy call a "retreat," and gives what Emerson sought when he wrote :

"Good-bye, proud world, I'm going home."

And frequenting it for years, and may be generations, breeds those staying powers by which Mr. Hall has been able to work forty-two hours on a stretch, or walk twenty-five miles in a day.

Mr. Hall won his first case for the most unpopular man in Middlesex county against its two foremost lawyers, and has always taken a just case, no matter what the standing of either party.

In 1879 he was appointed prosecuting agent of Middlesex county, and so continued most of the time, and latterly sole officer until July, 1887, when he was succeeded by a more active party man. He carried out of office the hearty written endorsement of nearly every prominent and conservative man interested in that matter in every town of his county, save one, where there had been no call for his functions. At the close of his course he gained seventeen successive cases, — and lawyers know if that be easy, — and many sections of the statutes are in the very language prepared by him.

In 1883 Mr. Hall was appointed county coroner under the new law, and held that office two terms till 1889, the state's attorney meanwhile going out of office, and judge dying who had caused his nomination and confirmation. In this office, under a new law which first gave that power and duty to a single man, he held Arthur Jackson for the suspected murder of Seymour A. Tibbals. In this case, Mr. Hall was petitioned against, caricatured, and the jailer finally served with a writ of *habeas corpus* to be heard by Chief Judge Park. The labor of defending this Mr. Hall escaped by working forty-two hours on a stretch, finishing his investigation, finding probable cause against Jackson (and others), and thus devolving the responsibility on other officers who released Jackson before the hour of hearing the *habeas corpus*. But Jackson, later, cut his wife's throat, and it was generally conceded that he killed Tibbals.

Finding, at the end of his term, that others, more active politicians, were seeking the place, Mr. Hall made no contest for a further appointment, believing that the record of his painstaking cases and the fact that the medical examiners whom he had selected and for six years trained into the new law,

were to a man re-appointed, was a sufficient endorsement, partisanship aside, of his career. He was succeeded as coroner by Stephen B. Davis, of Davis Bros., coal dealers, Middletown.

As a public officer, Mr. Hall considered each man as an individual to whom justice, restraint, or mercy, was due, and not the class, clique, or society to which he belonged. If he thought it his duty to strike, he struck, no matter how large a hornet's nest might be behind the offender. Though knowing well that the "popular" officer appears busy and dutiful by whacking the poor and isolated only, when a sense of duty had made him take hold, a sense of fear never made him let go.

His scholarship made him a member of the Phi Beta Kappa Society, and he is a warm-hearted Psi Upsilon, but never carried his feelings towards those inside to the extent of injury to those outside. He was raised in the Baptist church, but attends in Middletown the old mother church (Congregational) founded by his ancestors. He has friends in all classes and churches, giving full appreciation, though by no means adhesion, to the Catholic church, the old mother of all, and values the table which she spreads for her sons, though himself choosing more modern housekeeping. Mr. Hall never looks down upon any class of men, though keeping out of the way of the filthy, drunken, and profane; and admires any man who has mastered his calling (if useful), no matter what it is. He has never aimed solely to attain "success," or to follow the various openings which might lead to it; but first to live the solid life of his fathers (having no brother with whom to divide it), and to do whatever else duty and opportunity may present beside.

JAMES M. THOMSON, HARTFORD: Dry Goods.

James M. Thomson was born in Perthshire, Scotland, November 28, 1838, and spent several years in the common schools. At the age of fifteen he left school, going to Glasgow in 1853, to learn the dry-goods business. He served an apprenticeship of four years with Arthur & Frazier, remaining with them until 1860. In August of that year he landed in Boston, having accepted a situation from Hogg, Brown & Taylor. He continued with them until 1866, when, in company with Frank S. Brown and Wm. McWhirter, the dry-

J. M. THOMSON.

goods firm of Brown, Thomson & Co. was organized in Hartford, and has continued unchanged in name ever since, although its personality has been changed by the retiracy of Mr. McWhirter in 1878 and of Mr. Frank S. Brown in 1891. On the first of January, 1891, a new partnership was formed by Mr. Thomson admitting to the company George A. Gay, Wm. Campbell, Harry B. Strong, and George M. Brown, still under the same firm name of Brown, Thomson & Co. This firm is known all over the state for its straightforward business principles. It is a well-known fact that they have the largest store and carry the largest stock of dry and fancy goods in the state. Mr. Thomson is still in the prime of life, is active in business, and has every reason to anticipate a long and prosperous future. For the last seventeen years he has made West Hartford his home, having one of the most attractive suburban residences in the neighborhood of Hartford. Politically he is a republican, and in church matters a Congregationalist. He married Miss Cornelia Catharine Hotchkiss, and their family includes three children.

WILLIAM L. BIDWELL, Windsor: Paper Manufacturer.

The subject of this biography was born in the village of North Manchester, in June, 1838, being now in the fifty-third year of his age. He received

a common school, academical, and business training in his youth, and has since maturity been actively engaged in the manufacture of paper. Since 1864 he has held the important position of treasurer and manager of the Springfield Paper Company of Rainbow, Conn. For the last thirty-four or five years he has resided in Windsor, and in politics has always acted with the republican party. His personal popularity was attested in the fall of 1876, when he was elected to the state legislature on the republican ticket, the town being at that time nominally democratic by a hundred majority. Mr. Bidwell has, during his residence in Windsor, been interested in all matters relating to the public schools and church. He has three times made extensive trips through the south and west for rest and recreation, the first being in the winter and spring of 1876, at which time he visited the Bahama Islands; next in the winter and spring of 1885 he traveled south to Florida, and west to California and the Pacific coast; and again during the recent winter and spring of 1891 he made quite a protracted and agreeable sojourn in the extreme southern states.

CHARLES B. WHITING, Hartford: President Orient Insurance Company.

Charles B. Whiting, a son of Jonas Whiting of New Hampshire, was born in Greenbush, Rensselaer County, New York, Sept. 3, 1828. He is a

descendant from Rev. Samuel Whiting, first minister of Lynn, Mass., who came to America from England in 1636. The wife of Rev. Samuel Whiting was Miss Elizabeth St. John prior to her marriage, a sister of Sir Oliver St. John, lord chief justice of England under Cromwell. She was an own cousin of Oliver Cromwell. The father of the subject of this sketch was a merchant, and the youthful career of the lad was partly in the store and partly at school, his educational experience being first at the public schools, and finally at a boarding school in Williamstown, Mass. At the age of twenty-one he left home and entered the employ of the Boston & Albany Railroad Company at East Albany, remaining three years, after which he had two years' experience in steamboating with the " People's Line " of Hudson River steamers. In 1855 he went west and settled in the town of DeSoto, Wisconsin, on the Mississippi River, where for nine years he was variously engaged as railroad and steamboat agent, postmaster, and local agent for the Ætna Insurance Company of Hartford, Conn. In 1866 he went to New York and formed a connection with the Accidental Insurance Company of that city. In October of the same year he was engaged by the executive committee of the national board of fire underwriters, and became its secretary, remaining such until May, 1870. At that time the Home Insurance Company offered Mr. Whiting the position of state agent of that company for New York, and he thought best to accept it. He served the company faithfully for ten years, when he was forced to resign on account of the condition of his health. A few months of rest followed, when he again went into active service, for the Springfield (Mass.) Fire and Marine Insurance Company; but in October following, having been unanimously elected secretary of the Hartford Fire Insurance Company, he removed his residence to this city. He remained with the Hartford until called to the presidency of the Orient in May, 1886, in the duties of which latter position he is at present engaged. His successful management of the Orient, in connection with his associates, is well known.

Since his advent into the business in 1866, Mr.

Whiting has been quite a prolific writer on insurance matters; he has also delivered several addresses upon this theme, one before the New York State Association of Supervising and Adjusting Agents at Niagara Falls, and others before the Connecticut State Firemen's Association in 1888; also one of special note before the Northwestern Association. At the annual meeting of the national board of fire underwriters in 1890 he contributed a paper which attracted much attention.

Mr. Whiting has held various positions of public trust. He was supervisor of the town of Wheatland, Wisconsin, in 1863; in 1865 was a member of the Wisconsin state convention which nominated Hon. Jeremiah M. Rusk to the first state office he ever held. Here in Hartford he is vice-president and a director in the City Bank, director in the National Life Insurance Company and the Perkins Electric Lamp Company, chairman of the finance committee of the Hartford Board of Trade, a member of the Historical Society and of the Sons of the Revolution. He is a member of the Asylum Hill Congregational society, and in politics an independent republican. He married in 1856 Miss Sarah E. Fairchild, daughter of Frederick Fairchild of Greenbush, N. Y. They have had two children; both died in infancy.

HON. HOMER TWITCHELL, NAUGATUCK: Manufacturer.

Senator Homer Twitchell is an active and influential democratic leader in his section of the state. In 1884 he was a member of the house of representatives, and was in the senate during the session of 1889, representing the Fifth senatorial district. He was returned to the senate of 1891. In 1884 he was a delegate to the national democratic convention in Chicago which nominated President Cleveland. The senator has held numerous local offices, including that of first selectman, justice of the peace, member

HOMER TWITCHELL.

of the boards of assessors and relief in his town. He has also been prominently connected with business interests, having been president of the Naugatuck Savings Bank, president of the Naugatuck Water Company, and being now director in the Naugatuck National Bank, trustee of the Naugatuck Savings Bank, and manager of the extensive manufacturing firm of H. Twitchell & Son. Since 1870 he has been engaged in the manufacture

of umbrella trimmings and shield pins. He is a member of the Congregational church, and a past master of Shepherd Lodge, No. 78, F. and A. M., of Naugatuck. The wife of Senator Twitchell, who is still living, was Miss Lavinia Mason of Coventry. He has one son, who is engaged with him in business. The senator was born in Oxford, August 19, 1826, and received a common school education. He lived on a farm until he was eighteen years of age, when he began work in a pocket cutlery establishment. His success in life has been due to his personal exertion and management.

HON. HENRY E. SHOVE, WARREN: Farmer and Salesman.

Mr. Shove is a descendant in the fourth generation of the Rev. Seth Shove, who came to this country from England about 1700, and was the first settled minister in Danbury, Conn. He was born January 22, 1831, at Warren, Conn., where he has spent the greater part of his life as farmer and salesman. He was for a number of years previous to 1885 associated with the firm of Richards & Shove, at Brewsters, N.Y., where his son, L. A. Shove, still carries on business. Mr. Shove has held the office of selectman for a number

H. E. SHOVE.

of years, assessor for six years, collector, grand juror, and justice of the peace for thirteen years, which office he still holds; also a member of the school board — all of which he has filled with credit to himself and to the entire satisfaction of his constituents and fellow-townsmen. In the numerous suits that have come before him as justice he has always been guided by the strict principles of equity in rendering his decisions, which have been to the general satisfaction of all parties concerned. He is always ready to help those who are willing to help themselves, liberal in his donations and in his views. He has been associated with the Methodist church forty years, and has always been very active in all temperance movements. In 1851 he was married to Miss Fannie Lain of Kent, Conn. The fruit of their union is five sons and one daughter, all of whom are living and filling honorable positions in four different states. In 1879 Mr. Shove received a nomination as representative for the town of Warren to the general assembly by the democratic party, and was elected by the largest majority ever given to any candidate in that town. He filled the office with credit, and to the great satisfaction of his constituents. He has been frequently called upon to officiate at special religious gatherings, for which service he seems specially qualified. He is a man of great kindness of heart, urbanity of deportment, and of the strictest integrity. As such he commands the respect and confidence of all with whom he becomes associated in the active duties of life.

JOHN HENRY HURLBURT, BRIDGEPORT, Insurance and Real Estate.

J. H. Hurlburt was born in Wilton, Fairfield County, Jan. 21, 1840. He was educated at Wilton academy, and spent two years in Trinity College,

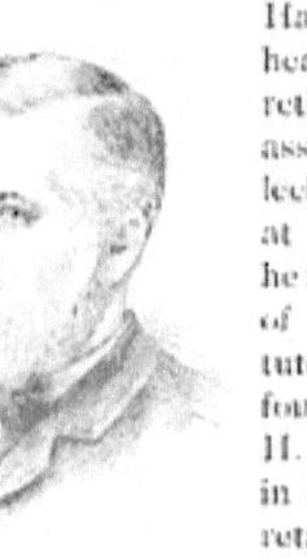

J. H. HURLBURT.

Hartford, from which illhealth compelled him to retire. In 1860 he became assistant to Mr. C. M. Selleck in his famous school at Norwalk, from which he resigned to take charge of "Rocky Dell Institute," a private school founded by Hon. William H. Barnum at Lime Rock, in 1864, which position he retained until January, 1887, at which latter date he was appointed internal revenue agent under President Cleveland. He resigned the agency July 1, 1889, at the request of the Harrison administration, under the frank avowal that the place, being one paying a good salary, was much sought after and desired for some friend of the new administration. For fifteen years he served as secretary of the school board of Salisbury, bringing the public schools of that town to a high degree of efficiency. During his long connection with educational institutions and affairs he accomplished great results in the enlightenment and discipline of youth, and acquired a wide and honorable reputation, not only as an instructor, but also for his able management of the public schools. In the fall of 1881 he was chosen a member of the legislature from Salisbury, and served on the committee on education. After resigning from the government service he was obliged on account of the loss of an eye to relinquish the charge of the school he had held through assistants up to that time. At present he is residing at Bridgeport, and acting as special agent of the Mutual Life Insurance Company of New York.

Mr. Hurlburt has been twice married; first to Miss Rebecca Maria, daughter of B. O. Banks, of Norwalk, by whom he had two children; and second to Roxana Sophia, daughter of C. H. Glens of Salisbury, by whom he has five children.

REV. J. H. CHAPIN, Ph.D., MERIDEN: Universalist Clergyman, and Professor of Geology and Mineralogy in St. Lawrence University, New York.

Dr. J. H. Chapin is a descendant of the eighth generation of Samuel Chapin, who came from Wales to Dorchester, Mass., in 1636, and finally

J. H. CHAPIN.

settled at Springfield in 1642, where some of his descendants still reside. He was born Dec. 31, 1832, at Leavenworth, Ind., but spent his youth in Illinois, whither his father removed in 1839. He graduated at Lombard University, Galesburg, Ill., in 1857, and was for several years an instructor in mathematics and natural science in that institution. In 1859 he was ordained to the ministry in the Universalist church, and was settled at Pekin, and afterwards at Springfield in that state. During the war of the rebellion he was in the service of the United States Sanitary Commission, and crossing the Rocky Mountains in the spring of 1864, canvassed the greater part of the Pacific coast from Mexico to British Columbia for funds for the commission, supplementing the work that had been so well begun by Rev. T. Starr King just before his death. In the autumn of 1865 he went to Boston as secretary of the New England Freedmen's Aid Society, of which Governor John A. Andrew was president, and while holding that position made several tours of inspection of the schools in the Southern States. In 1868 he became financial secretary of the Universalist convention, with headquarters in Boston, and during the centennial period of that church was instrumental in raising the larger part of the "Murray centenary fund," now held for missionary purposes. In 1871 he became professor of geology and mineralogy in St. Lawrence University in New York, which position he still holds. In 1875 he was elected president of his alma mater at Galesburg, Ill., but after due consideration declined to go. In 1873 he resumed regular pulpit ministrations, and became pastor of the Universalist church at Meriden, Conn., and continued in that relation till 1875, when, finding himself overloaded with professional duties, he resigned. He is a member of the school board in Meriden, and from 1880 to 1887 was acting school visitor; and it was during this period that the high school was established, and the present capacious building erected. He is an active Fellow of the American association for the advancement of science, and one of the founders of the association of American geologists. He has been president of the Connecticut convention of Universalists for a dozen years, and was for a long period, preceding his recent absence from the country, chairman of the committee on missions in the national convention of that church. He belongs to the free masons and odd fellows, and among the former holds the rank of knight templar. He has been twice married — first in 1857 to Helen M. Weaver of Alstead, N. H., and again in 1878 to Kate A. Lewis of Meriden, Conn., and has one daughter, Mary A., born in 1863. Dr. Chapin has made several tours in foreign lands, and not long since returned from a tour around the world. He is the author of several volumes, among them " The Creation, and the Early Development of Society," which had a large sale for a scientific work ; and one recently from the press entitled " From Japan to Granada," is well received both by the press and public. He has been identified with the republicans since the organization of the party, but never held a political office till elected to the house of representatives in 1888.

HON. HEZEKIAH SIDNEY HAYDEN, Windsor: Judge of Probate.

H. Sidney Hayden — a descendant in the seventh generation from William Hayden, the American ancestor — was born at Haydens, in the town of Windsor, January 29, 1816. In boyhood he developed no very marked traits to distinguish him from his brothers, except possibly that into the dull routine of farm and school life he infused more enthusiasm, and managed to find a quicker market and drive a little sharper bargain than his associates when trying to dispose of the wild game which they captured each

H. S. HAYDEN.

autumn, and on which they were largely dependent for pocket money. At the age of about sixteen he left the farm and entered a country store, from which he graduated two or three years later, and joined his brother in Charleston, S. C. Here, with untiring energy, he applied himself, under the leadership of his elder brother, and on the retirement of that brother in 1843 took the lead of the business himself. After successfully conducting the business in Charleston about fifteen years, he returned to Windsor in 1858, where he has since resided. He has served in both branches of the Connecticut

legislature — in the senate in 1866, where he served as chairman of the joint special committee for the care and education of the orphans of soldiers; and in the house in 1868 and 1872, where he was on the joint standing committee on the school fund. He was judge of probate for the district of Windsor for twenty-seven years, or until disqualified by the seventy-years limit set by law for all judicial officers. He was appointed one of the trustees to select a site and erect buildings for a hospital for the insane; has been chairman of the trustees and of their building committee, and has had supervision over the erection of nearly all the buildings now composing the Connecticut Hospital for the Insane at Middletown, which have cost the state a million dollars. His services have been gratuitous (as have been the services of the other trustees), and he has devoted much time to the interests of the institution. In July, 1889, Mr. Hayden voluntarily retired from the board of hospital trustees, which action called forth the following expression from his associates a few months later:

RESOLUTION IN REGARD TO H. SIDNEY HAYDEN.

THE CONN. HOSPITAL FOR THE INSANE.,
MIDDLETOWN, CONN.

We, the trustees, desire to have entered upon our records an expression of our regard at the voluntary retirement of Mr. Hayden from our board, and our appreciation of his long and valuable services. To no citizen of our state is a greater debt of gratitude due for the amelioration of the condition of its insane than to Mr. Hayden. From the very inception of the plan for the founding of our insane hospital before 1865 to last July, when he retired, he has been untiring in his devotion to, and work for, the afflicted in mind of the state. The present condition of this hospital, of which we are justly proud, is in a great measure due to his unflagging zeal. No weather was so inclement, or call so inconvenient, that he could not attend to his charitable duties here; in the early days, when the income was not always sufficient to meet the expenses, loaning his personal credit, and aiding all by his advice and mature judgment. His absence will long be felt at our meetings, and his memory ever be held in affection and esteem.

Resolved, That the above resolution be entered upon our records, and that the secretary transmit an engrossed copy of the same to Mr. Hayden.

Attest: J. W. ALSOP,
                        Secretary Board of Trustees.
Middletown, Conn., Nov. 5, 1889.

Soon after Mr. Hayden's return from Charleston to Windsor he prepared and furnished suitable buildings for a young ladies' seminary, an institution which has been well sustained, and is still in the full tide of success, with Miss Julia S. Williams as principal. He is one of the trustees and the treasurer of the Loomis Institute, an educational institution ultimately to be established with its large fund at the old Loomis homestead in Windsor. His enterprise and investments have added much to the growth and attractiveness of the historic old town of Windsor, in which he takes a commendable pride as the home of his ancestors from its early beginnings. He has been a large contributor to Grace (Episcopal) church in Windsor, of which he is a devoted member and senior warden.

Mr. Hayden married, October 9, 1848, Miss Abby S. Loomis, daughter of Colonel James Loomis of Windsor, and a descendant of one of the first settlers of the town. They have one (adopted) daughter, Sarah Elizabeth Hayden, who married H. T. Haskell of Chicago, Ill.

F. F. STREET, East Hartford: Insurance Agent.

Frederick Ferdinand Street was born in Cheshire, Conn., January 26, 1830. The family ancestry on both sides is traced back to English origin — on his

mother's side to the Hon. Henry Wolcott, who came from Tolland, England, and settled in Windsor, Conn., and whose grandson was Governor Roger Wolcott of the Connecticut colony; also to the Rev. John Davenport, one of the original settlers of New Haven. In the paternal line Mr. Street is of the sixth generation from the Rev. Nicholas Street, who came from Taunton, England, in 1630, or thereabouts, settling in what is now the city of Taunton, Mass., naming the place after his native town. The Rev. Samuel Street, son of the emigrant, came to this country with his father, was educated at Cambridge, Mass., and settled in Wallingford, this state, being the first minister in the town, and one of the original settlers there. In his early life the subject of this sketch was for eight years engaged in extensive farming, and the West India trade in New Haven, especially during the winters; alternating this occupation with the manufacture of brick during the summers. For the following seven years he was in the india rubber business in Naugatuck, being one of the superintendents of what is now the Goodyear Metallic Rubber Shoe Company, where he still retains an interest. He afterwards went on to the road as commercial traveler for a Philadelphia house, journeying through the northern and southern states for several years. After this Mr. Street settled in Harrisburg, Pa., in the building and brick business, under the firm name of F. F. Street & Co., where he continued until 1868, when he came to Hartford and established himself in the fire insurance business, where he has since remained.

During his business life in Hartford Mr. Street has been often engaged in promoting or establishing business enterprises and manufacturing concerns, among them being the Hartford Machine Screw Company, previous to its present organization, and others on the west side. He is one of the auditors of the Pratt & Whitney Company, a director of the Pratt & Cady Company, and secretary and treasurer of the Tucker Stop Motion Company. Mr. Street's early education was acquired at the common schools and the Cheshire academy. His wife previous to her marriage was Miss Mary Abbott Chapman, daughter of the late Reuben Chapman of East Hartford, and they have one adopted daughter. Mr. Street resides with his family in East Hartford, where he is a member of the First Congregational church, and a director in the Raymond Library. In politics he is a republican, but has always refused to accept public office. He is also a member of Hartford Lodge of Masons.

N. A. MOORE, Kensington: Landscape Artist.

Nelson Augustus Moore was born in Kensington in 1824, in the paternal homestead owned by his grandfather, probably one hundred and fifty years

ago, and still standing, though in a dilapidated condition. He is a lineal descendant of John Moore, his first American ancestor, who emigrated from England to America in 1630, and settled in Dorchester, Mass., removing thence to Windsor, Conn., in company with Dr. Wareham, in 1636. Nearly thirty years ago the subject of this sketch erected his present residence in the vicinity of the ancestral mansion above referred to, and to its natural beauty of situation he has since, by the aid of nature and art, added such adornments as to entitle it now to considerable distinction among the picturesque residences of New England. Mr. Moore's father was a manufacturer, of the firm of R. Moore & Sons, who were the first to make and successfully introduce hydraulic cement as an article of commerce into the markets of this country. He was a man of some means, and anxious that his son should take a collegiate course at Yale; but, though the latter received what was then considered a liberal education, he neglected to avail himself of the higher advantages contemplated by his father, which neglect he has in his later life often regretted. From the age of eighteen to twenty-five his occupations were thoroughly varied. Much of his time was spent at the mills, and he thus acquired a facility for turning his hand to almost any mechanical work. One of these years was spent in railway service, in 1846, when railroading in this country was in its infancy. His position was that of local agent at the Berlin station on the New Haven & Hartford Railroad, which then had its termini at these two cities. During all these years he found more or less time to gratify his taste for drawing and painting; and when at the Berlin station, he maintained a studio in the attic of the little depot building, where he painted gratuitously a few portraits for his friends. Of these it might be said there was a resemblance to their subjects! Although he always had a love for pictures, his first strong impulse to paint was when a portrait painter (the father of the present state labor commissioner, S. M. Hotchkiss,) invited him to assist in painting by candle-light a portrait (or a study for one) of a little girl who had met with a fatal accident. His "assistance" was that of holding the light and watching the progress of the study. This was when he was eighteen years of age. After that he embraced every opportunity to practice in a crude way the art of painting. After leaving the service of the railroad company he decided to study in New York, and went into the studio of Thomas S. Cummings, now the only survivor of those who first organized the National Academy, of which Mr. Cummings was treasurer, and afterwards vice-president. Later, Mr. Moore entered the studio of D. Huntington, now and for many years the president of the Academy. After leaving New York he continued to practice his art at his home in Kensington; and soon his love for natural scenery drew him from the practice of portrait and figure painting to that of landscapes, which he has followed all his life with great assiduity. Few artists have spent as much time in out-of-door study, in painstaking fidelity to nature, as Mr. Moore. His sketches comprise a great variety of subjects, including all seasons of the year. Much of his summer life has been at Lake George. Since he built his house in Kensington his home has always been there, although before that time he lived several years in Hartford, and has since spent four years in that city in order that his children might enjoy the advantages of its excellent schools. Much of his adult life has also been spent in New York, his studio at one time being in the Y. M. C. A. building in that city. His canvases have been exhibited in the academy more or less for the past twenty-five years. He has painted to order for many leading and wealthy men, and his works are scattered from his own state even to Japan, where several are now owned by gentlemen who consider themselves critics as well as *connoisseurs* of art. As a landscape artist he has an established reputation, and has among his patrons some of the most noted picture buyers of the country.

Mr. Moore was married in 1853 to Miss Ann Maria Pickett, of Litchfield, Conn., who with their four children, is now living. There are three sons and one daughter; the oldest son, a figure and animal painter, has reached a high degree of success in the department of art to which his attention has been chiefly devoted.

RUSSELL L. HALL, New Canaan : President First National Bank.

Mr. Hall was born in Warren, Litchfield county, Conn., August 18, 1832, being now in his fifty-ninth year. He is a descendant in the seventh generation from Francis Hall, who came from Milford, county of Surrey, England, in 1639, settling first in New Haven, afterwards in Fairfield, and finally in Stratford, where he was engaged in the practice of law until the time of his death, which occurred in March, 1689 or 1690. The subject of this sketch, after completing his education, which was acquired partly at the 

public and partly at private schools, learned the trade of cabinet-maker in Goshen, Conn., removing from there soon afterwards to New Canaan, where he has since resided. He has always been active in public affairs, is president of the First National Bank of New Canaan, which position he has held since 1879, is also treasurer of the New Canaan Savings Bank, and a member of the firm of R. L. Hall & Brothers, dealers in furniture.

The family of Mr. Hall consists of his wife, who, before her marriage, was Miss Betsey A. Jones of New Canaan, and two children, son and daughter, the former of whom, Lewis C. Hall, is a member of the present senior class at Yale University. In politics Mr. Hall is a republican, and he has held many local offices, being at present republican registrar of voters, as well as chairman of the republican town committee, which latter position he has held for nearly twenty years. He has been repeatedly chosen town assessor, has been deputy sheriff, and held other offices of minor importance. He is a member of the Methodist Episcopal church of New Canaan, of the order of Odd Fellows, and the Sons of Temperance, a man of wealth, sterling qualities, and of the highest standing, socially and intellectually.

ARTHUR H. DAYTON, Naugatuck: Banker.

Mr. Dayton was born at Waterbury, November 24, 1854. He finished his education at Wilbraham (Mass.) academy, and at the age of sixteen entered

the bank at East Haddam, Conn., as clerk. After a few years of clerical service he was chosen cashier of the institution, retaining that connection until 1883, when he was appointed cashier of the Naugatuck National Bank, which position he still occupies. In 1885 he was elected treasurer of the Naugatuck Savings Bank, and holds the office at the

A. H. DAYTON.

present time. He is also president of the Naugatuck Electric Light Company, and assistant treasurer of Goodyear's Metallic Rubber Shoe Company of Naugatuck. He is a member of the Protestant Episcopal church, is a republican in politics, and has membership in the Odd Fellows and Masonic fraternities. Mr. Dayton is married, and has one son. His wife was Miss Millie C. Bliss of Longmeadow, Mass.

WILLARD A. COWLES, Torrington: Dairy Farmer.

Willard Albro Cowles of Torrington was born in that town Sept. 17, 1858, and was educated in the Torrington high school and at the Claverack col-

lege and Hudson River Institute. With the exception of a brief period at Waterbury his business life has been spent in Torrington, where he is engaged in the milk trade as a member of the firm of Patterson & Cowles, wholesale and retail dealers in milk and cream. Mr. Cowles is a republican, and has been an assistant in the town clerk's office at Torrington and

W. A. COWLES.

census enumerator. He has also held the position of tax-collector, member of the board of assessors, and secretary of the school board, of which he has been a member for nine years. He represented Torrington in the legislature in '89–90, and served as clerk of the joint select committee on constitutional amendments. He is at present a commissioner of the superior court. His religious associations are with the Congregational church,

and he is a member of the Patrons of Husbandry and of the Knights of Pythias. His wife was Miss Mary E. McKinstry of Chicopee, Mass., prior to her marriage. There are no children in the family, their only child having died in infancy.

E. J. SMITH, Hartford, Merchant.

Edwin J. Smith was born in Washington, Litchfield county, Jan. 19, 1844, and was educated in the Brown School of Hartford, and in the Harris Mili-

tary Institute. The parents of Mr. Smith moved from Washington when he was a mere lad, residing at first at Cabotville, Mass., and afterwards in East Hartford. They also lived for a number of years in this city. At the outbreak of the war the subject of this sketch was employed in the clothing trade with William F. Whittelsey. Being under age at the time, he met

E. J. SMITH.

with considerable difficulty in his attempts to enlist. After rejection in the Sixteenth on account of his minority, he waited until the organization of the Twentieth, when he succeeded in his desire, becoming a member of Company K of that command. The Twentieth, which was commanded by Colonel Ross of the regular army, was a participant in the great battles of Chancellorsville and Gettysburg, and subsequently took part in Sherman's march to the sea. Mr. Smith was made a sergeant in his company, and served with credit through the war. After returning home he accepted of a business situation with Messrs. Dunning, Tooker & Co., New York city, and remained one year with that firm. He then returned to Hartford, and was associated with H. W. Conklin as clerk or business partner until the organization of the firm of Covey & Smith, of which firm he was the senior member. After a few years Mr. Smith purchased the interest of Mr. Covey in the business and has since been at the head of the company. He has visited Europe twice in the interest of the house. Mr. Smith has been prominently identified with republican politics in this city, and has held the office of councilman from the seventh ward, member of the board of fire commissioners for twelve years, occupying the position of president during the last five; member of the republican town committee and fire marshal three years. In the fall of 1890 he was elected a member of the board of selectmen, and assumed the duties of the office in January. He was originally appointed fire commissioner by Mayor Sumner. He was reappointed twice by Governor Bulkeley, and once by Mayor Root. As president of the fire board he proved himself an invaluable official. The present development of the department has been largely due to his energy and intelligence. He has been the president for two years of the Interstate Polo League, and is the president of the Hartford Amusement Association. He is a member of the Veteran City Guard, Robert O. Tyler Post, G. A. R., and of the Army and Navy Club of Connecticut. He is connected with the highest Masonic bodies in the state, having taken all the degrees of York and Scottish Rite masonry. He is also a member of the Mystic Shrine, and belongs to the Hartford Club. One year ago he was elected a member of the North School District building committee, and has taken an active and influential part in securing the new school structure in that district. Commissioner Smith has a family of five children. His wife, who was Miss Sarah H. Moses, daughter of Luther M. Moses, died May 9, 1890. The oldest son, Harry C. Smith, is connected with the Hartford *Courant*, and the daughter, Miss Gertrude C. Smith, is a student at the Hartford high school. The family are attendants at the Park Congregational church.

E. O. GOODWIN, East Hartford: Leaf Tobacco Dealer.

Edward O. Goodwin of East Hartford was born in that town May 22, 1839, and received a public school and academic education. He was a member of the Connecticut house of representatives from East Hartford during the session of 1886, serving as clerk of the railroad committee, and has held most of the offices within the gift of the town. He has been a trial justice for nearly twenty years, member of the board of relief, treasurer of the center school district eight years, clerk of the board of health, and treasurer

E. O. GOODWIN.

of the Street Light Association since its organization in October, 1881. He has served two terms on the democratic state central committee, and is one the most prominent democrats in his town. He is engaged in the tobacco business, being the agent since 1868 of the successful New York firm of E. Rosenwald & Bro., leaf tobacco dealers. He was acting first assistant foreman of Charter Oak, No. 1, when the volunteer fire department in this city was disbanded. He is a member of the Veteran

Firemen's Association, the East Hartford Bicycle Club, and is the president and treasurer of the East Hartford Gun Club. He is one of the past masters of Evergreen Lodge, F. and A. M., past grand of Crescent Lodge, I. O. O. F., and is an ex-member of the Putnam Phalanx. The wife of ex-Representative Goodwin was Frances L. Sanford of Hartford, prior to her marriage. There are no children in the family.

REV. DANIEL M. MOORE, Colebrook: Pastor of the Congregational Church.

Daniel M. Moore was born in Athol, Mass., July 31, 1848. His father died when he was but nine weeks old. His mother, a thrifty, energetic, and capable woman, took the entire care and responsibility of his early years. Most of the time up to his eleventh year was spent in his native village. About this time his mother married again and he was taken to live with his step-father in Winchendon, Mass. Here and at Orange, Mass., whither his parents soon removed, he had a somewhat severe drill in farm-

D. M. MOORE.

ing. At about the age of sixteen, not succeeding in getting apprenticed to a trade, he took a clerkship in a country store. He continued at this until the proprietor closed out his business. Soon after this, receiving the offer of a somewhat tempting job in a furniture manufactory, he engaged in this with considerable success for about two years. In the fall of 1868, at the earnest solicitation of a cousin, he entered with him Kimball Union Academy, Meriden, N. H. He expected to spend only a term or two at school and then engage in business, but it had been his mother's earnest desire for several years that he should get a thorough, and, if possible, a collegiate education. The favorable opportunity seemed to have come. He continued his studies, graduating at Kimball Union Academy in the class of 1871, at Amherst College in the class of 1875, and at Yale Divinity School in the class of 1878. May 12, 1878, Mr. Moore was invited to preach at the Congregational churches in Canaan and Falls Village, Conn. This led to an engagement with these churches which continued until Nov. 1, 1887. In the winter of 1886-7 Canaan was visited by a great revival. There were very few families that did not feel the blessed influences of the Spirit. In several cases whole families were led to publicly confess their new found faith. As the fruit of this work large additions were made to the membership of the Methodist and both the Congregational churches.

May 17, 1881, Mr. Moore married Mary I. Hurlbutt, youngest daughter of Joseph W. Hurlbutt of Stamford, Conn. Two children, a son and a daughter, have been added to the family.

Mr. Moore held the office of school visitor for several years in Canaan and is at present school visitor for the town of Colebrook.

JOHN HENRY HALL, HARTFORD: Vice-President and Treasurer Colt's Patent Fire Arms Manufacturing Company.

J. H. Hall was born at Portland, in this state, March 24, 1849. He is a son of Alfred Hall, and is of the ninth generation of the family in the

J. H. HALL.

United States. He attended the public school at Portland, and afterward Chase's school at Middletown, finishing at the Episcopal a c a d e m y at Cheshire. When others of his class entered college, he turned his attention to business, entering into an engagement with Sturgis, Bennet & Co., 125 and 127 Front street, New York, at that time the largest importers of tea and coffee in the United States, which connection he maintained for five years. After a brief and not very satisfactory experience in business alone, he purchased a large interest in the "Pickering Governor," at Portland, and made a success of what had previously been a small enterprise. Afterwards, on leaving Portland, the same business, formerly carried on as a partnership under the name of T. R. Pickering & Co., was organized as a corporation, Mr. Hall retaining his proprietary interest and holding the position of treasurer. In 1884 he was elected president of the Shaler & Hall Quarry Company of Portland, of which he was a large stockholder, and has held that office ever since. He went to Hartford in April, 1888, to assume the position of general manager of Colt's Patent Fire Arms Manufacturing Company. He has since been elected vice-president and treasurer, and holds these offices at the present time. He is a director in the Phœnix Insurance Company and Phœnix Mutual Life Insurance Company of Hartford, and of the First National Bank of Portland, besides sustaining other similar official relations with various institutions of Hartford and vicinity. He was appointed on the Hartford City board of water commissioners in April, 1890, for the term of

three years. He is a member of the Hartford Club of that city, and of the Manhattan Club, the New York Athletic Club, and Engineers' Club of New York city.

Mr. Hall married, Feb. 8, 1871, Miss Sarah G. Loines of New York; they have two children living, Clarence Loines Hall, 18 years of age, now at Trinity College, and Grace Loines Hall, aged 12 years. He has always been a member of the Episcopal church, and is now connected with the parish of the Good Shepherd in Hartford. Politically he is with the democratic party, in the interests of which he has been often unsuccessfully urged to accept nominations for both branches of the state legislature. He has taken no active part in politics, being too deeply absorbed in business.

REV. FLORIMOND DeBRUYCKER, WILLIMANTIC: Rector of St. Joseph's Roman Catholic Church.

The Rev. Fd. DeBruycker was born in the city of Ghent, Belgium, October 6, 1832. He was ordained to the priesthood at Ghent, December 20,

REV. F. DeBRUYCKER.

1856. In October, 1860, he began a course of studies in the American College, Louraine, preparing himself and others for the American missions. On August 1, 1862, he left Antwerp for London and Liverpool. In Liverpool he was delayed by missionary work during three months. On November 5th he sailed for New York and Providence. After attending, during six months, to the spiritual wants of the French and German Catholic population of Connecticut and Rhode Island, which two states then formed the diocese of Hartford, on May 11, 1863, he was assigned by the late Right Rev. Bishop McFarland to the Willimantic parish and mission, where he has ever since remained as rector. The Willimantic mission contains at present upwards of 3,500 Catholics; of which number one-third at least are French Canadians; the remainder, with the exception of a few English and German, are of Irish nationality or descent. In the diocese of Hartford Reverend Father DeBruckyer occupies positions of great responsibility, being a member of the board of consultors to Bishop McMahon, and a member of the board of examiners of clergy. The two positions indicate the high esteem in which he is held by the dignitaries of the church. The members of his parish at Willimantic regard him with the utmost appreciation and affection.

OLIVER S. FRANCIS, South Canterbury: Postmaster.

Oliver S. Francis is a native of the town of Griswold, New London county, Conn., where he was born in 1829. He was educated in the public schools, and has been variously engaged in agricultural and mercantile pursuits since leaving the home of his childhood. His life has chiefly been spent in Plainfield and Canterbury, in which latter town he now resides, and holds the office of postmaster. He has been selectman and constable, and has filled other town offices with ability and credit. Mr. Francis is a

O. S. FRANCIS.

widower; his wife, who died some time ago, was Miss Sallie Ann Brown before marriage; and he has two children living. He is a democrat in politics, of which party he has always been a member, and by whose votes he has been elected to the town offices above mentioned.

GEORGE ULRICH, Hartford: Banker.

Mr. Ulrich came to this country at an early age from Germany, where he was born August 13, 1831. He has lived the greater part of his life in Hartford, where he was educated in the public schools. For upwards of 20 years he has been engaged in the banking business, most of the time with the State Savings Bank of Hartford. In politics Mr. Ulrich is a democrat, but not of the ultra kind. He is a member of the town committee, also an alderman from the fourth ward, and chairman of the committee on ways and means.

GEORGE ULRICH.

That he is popular with those who know him is evident from the fact that he was elected in the last city election from a strongly republican ward by a handsome majority, being the first democrat ever elected from that ward. As a member of the city government he is conservative, always found to favor just measures of economy and reform, and insists upon a strict and rigid enforcement of the laws, and proper attention to business by all city officials. He has a strong antipathy to what is known as "ring rule." In private life he rides various hob-

bies: Is a capable art critic; writes with fluency and keenness; is skilled in the graphic and plastic arts, and has held the title of state chess champion. He is an active member of the South Congregational church (Dr. Parker's), is a charter member of the Wangunk Tribe of Red Men, and is interested in numerous political and social organizations.

EDWIN IRVING BELL, Portland: Proprietor of the Connecticut Steam Brown Stone Works.

E. I. Bell was born in Portland, Middlesex county, Conn., September 17, 1848. He is a graduate of the district school of that town and of Eastman's Business College, Poughkeepsie, N. Y., in the year 1866. His first occupation was in the capacity of timekeeper in the Middlesex quarry. At the age of nineteen he entered into partnership with his brother, five years younger than himself, in the retail grocery trade, using the firm of E. Bell & Sons, being too young to responsibly conduct business under their own

E. I. BELL.

names. After continuing this relation successfully for eight years, he sold his interest in the store to his brother in 1876, and started the wholesale flour and feed business under the name of "The Valley Mills." This mill was burned in 1884, and the same year he established the "Connecticut Steam Brown Stone Works," and built mill number one near the ferry. Business increasing, in the winter of 1886–87 he built mill number two in the Middlesex quarry. This is one of the best stone-cutting plants in the United States, having cost about $75,000. Among the many fine buildings which Mr. Bell has erected, or for which he has furnished the dressed stone, is the United States custom house and post-office in Bridgeport, the United States custom house and post-office at New Bedford, Mass., and the Dunmore school at Dunmore, Pa.

Mr. Bell, in addition to his business, above stated, is president and two-thirds owner of the Washington Steam Stone Company of Washington, D. C.; president and two-thirds owner of the James Mann Steam Stone Company of Philadelphia, Penn.; trustee of the Freestone Savings Bank of Portland; director in the Middlesex county National Bank of Middletown; vice-president of the Shaler & Hall Quarry Company of Portland; secretary and treasurer of the Portland Wharf Company; and president of the Portland Building Association. He represented the town of Portland in the legislature in 1880, having been elected by the largest majority ever given in that town; is on the board of relief; is a member and president of the Portland club; is and has been for thirteen years treasurer of Warren Lodge, F. and A. M., of Portland; and is a member of the Putnam Phalanx of Hartford.

Mr. Bell has twice married. His first wife was Miss Hettie M. Cooper, by whom he has one son living; his second marriage was to Miss Elizabeth Ronald of Middletown, and they have one daughter.

THURLOW B. MERRILL, Hartford: Superintendent of Agencies, Ætna Life Insurance Company.

Mr. Merrill is a native of Cassville, Oneida county, N. Y., born April 11, 1841. He received a common school education, and a two-years course at the Saquoit academy. He lived with his parents on the farm until he reached his majority, when he engaged for a time in the commission business, afterwards with the publishing house of Henry Bill & Co. of Norwich, Conn. Having developed a fitness for soliciting, and being fond of arithmetic, he entered the service of the Charter Oak Life Insurance Com-

I. B. MERRILL.

pany of Hartford, May 1, 1865, as special agent for A. M. Ward, the company's general agent for New York state. After one year's service in that state he accepted the general agency of the Charter Oak for the state of Iowa, removing, with his family, to Davenport. After establishing a most successful agency in Iowa, he disposed of his interest in the business, and in July, 1870, accepted the position of home office agent for that company, continuing for one year, when he was appointed superintendent of agencies of the Charter Oak, to succeed E. O. Goodwin. After another year's service he removed with his family to Chicago, and purchased an interest in the Illinois agency, that being the largest agency of the company. During the first year the business increased from less than $500,000 to $2,500,000 insurance written and delivered; but, owing to the depression following the 1873 panic, the business of life insurance became demoralized, and at the urgent request of the company he sold out his interest in that agency, and was re-appointed superintendent of agencies, which position he held continuously until 1884. After the re-organization of the Charter Oak in 1880 he removed with his family to Hartford, and, in addition to his other

duties, looked after the large real estate interests of the Charter Oak in the western states. When the company ceased writing new business the agency department was in a most flourishing condition, a large majority of the general agents having been selected by Mr. Merrill, who received a compliment from Governor Jewell, after he was elected president of the company, as having the best and most successful corps of agents he ever met connected with any corporation.

Mr. Merrill resigned his position in January, 1884, to accept an engagement with the Ætna Life Insurance Company as manager for New York state. After reorganizing the company's business in that state, and making it one of their most successful agencies, and selecting a manager to succeed him, he was appointed in January, 1888, superintendent of agencies, which position he now holds. Mr. Merrill is thoroughly familiar with all departments of practical life insurance, and is regarded as one of the most efficient organizers connected with the profession.

HON. NICHOLAS STAUB, New Milford: State Comptroller.

Hon. Nicholas Staub has had an extensive legislative experience, having been a member of the general assembly during five sessions, serving two terms in the senate. During the five terms he was was not absent an hour consecutively during business. A record of this kind cannot be surpassed. He was a member of the house in 1876, serving on the committee on banks, and assisted in reporting an important savings bank bill. In 1884 he also sat for New Milford, and was placed on the committee on insurance. He was

NICHOLAS STAUB.

returned again in 1885, when he was given the house chairmanship of the committee on new counties and county seats, serving also on the committee on railroads. He was elected to the senate in 1886 for the first time, representing the Nineteenth district. In 1887 he was returned for the first biennial term of the legislature. Comptroller Staub was nominated by the democrats at their state convention in this city, September 16, 1890, and was elected by one of the largest majorities ever given a candidate for the comptrollership. It may be truthfully said that he is the only state officer in this commonwealth at present universally recognized as holding his office legally. He has held important offices and positions outside of politics, and is the president of the State Firemen's Association. He is one of the past masters of St. Peter's Lodge, No. 21, F. and A. M., of New Milford, a Knight Templar, member of the order of Odd Fellows, Knights of Honor, and Hartford Lodge of Elks. He has been a prominent tobacco dealer in the Housatonic valley, and is a member of the hardware firm of Soule & Staub in New Milford. Comptroller Staub was born in Alsace-Lorraine, now Germany, February 1, 1841, and removed to the United States when sixteen years of age. He enjoyed the advantages of a common school education, fitting him for the successful business and political career which he has had. For thirty years he has been a resident of New Milford, and possesses the fullest confidence and esteem of that community. He is connected with the Congregational church. His wife was Miss Nancy J. Peck previous to her marriage, and is still living. There are three sons in the family. The official career of Mr. Staub has been one of which any citizen might be proud.

REV. JOHN C. WILSON, Stonington: Pastor First Congregational Church.

Rev. John C. Wilson was born in the city of Philadelphia, May 9, 1862, and was educated at Rugby Academy in that city, and at Amherst College, graduating from the latter in 1885. His theological studies were pursued at the Yale Seminary in New Haven, from which he received the degree of B.D. in 1888, and of M.A. from Amherst College in June of the same year. He was immediately installed as pastor of the Stonington church, and is regarded as one of the ablest of the younger

REV. J. C. WILSON.

preachers in the Congregational pulpit in Connecticut. He is a gentleman of admirable scholarship, and has edited a commentary on Sunday-school lessons. Some of his sermons have been published in the *Christian Union*. He also edited *The Young Christian* in Philadelphia, in 1876-80. He spent one year in the south, in 1880-81, had charge of the Home Mission work in Virginia during the summer of 1886, and has traveled through the west. He is married, his wife being Miss Lilian A. Barton of Washington, D. C., prior to her marriage. Mr. Wilson is an independent in politics.

J. GILBERT CALHOUN, Hartford: Attorney-at-Law.

Joseph Gilbert Calhoun was born in Manchester, July 20, 1856, and was educated in the Hartford High school, class of 1874, and at Yale, graduating from the university in 1877, his classmates including James P. Andrews, one of the leading members of the bar in this city; Thomas Dwight Goodell and Arthur H. Gulliver, both of whom have been able instructors in the Hartford high school; and William Milo Barnum of Salisbury. The subject of this sketch occupies one of the first places among the younger mem-

J. G. CALHOUN.

bers of the Hartford county bar, and is an able lawyer. He was clerk of the city police court here from 1883 until 1889, and is at present a member of the council board from the first ward. His services have been of great value to the city. Councilman Calhoun is a republican in politics, and an intelligent observer of public affairs and interests. He is an attendant at the Center Congregational church. He is a son of Judge David S. Calhoun, and has received from him traits of character deserving of the highest recognition. Councilman Calhoun married Miss Sarah C. Beach of Brooklyn, N. Y. They have no children.

MOSES F. GRANT, Norfolk: Farmer.

Moses F. Grant was a member of the Connecticut house of representatives in 1878, his colleagues from Litchfield county including the Hon. Charles B. Andrews, now chief justice of the state, and Judge A. P. Bradstreet of Thomaston. The Hon. Charles H. Briscoe of Enfield was speaker of the house, and the roll of members included the names of the Hon. Lyman D. Brewster of Danbury, the Hon. W. W. Wilcox of Middletown, the late Dwight Marcy of Vernon, ex-Speaker John H. Perry of Fair-

M. F. GRANT.

field, Increase W. Carpenter of Norwich, ex-Mayor Henry I. Boughton of Waterbury, and County Commissioner Thaddeus H. Spencer of Suffield. Mr. Grant served on the republican side, discharging his duties ably and successfully. He is at present the first selectman of Norfolk, and has served as selectman for fourteen years. He was postmaster at Grantville for seventeen years, and has been a member of the board of assessors. He has also been associated with the settlement of various estates. Mr. Grant is a member of Western Star Lodge, No. 37, F. and A. M., of Norfolk, and is thoroughly devoted to the interests of Masonry. His wife, whose maiden name was Mary Ann Gilbert, is still living. There is one daughter, Miss Lillie E. Grant. Mr. Grant is a native of Norfolk, where he was born, June 26, 1835; obtained his education in the common schools, and has been chiefly engaged in lumbering and farming.

GEORGE MAHL, HARTFORD: Contractor and Builder.

Alderman George Mahl was born in New York city, February 26, 1848, and was educated in the public schools of Norwich in this state, the family

GEORGE MAHL.

removing from New York to Connecticut when the subject of this sketch was but a lad. Mr. Mahl remained in Norwich until he was twenty-four years of age, acquiring there the avocation of a practical plumber and steam-fitter. He became a resident of Hartford not far from twenty years ago and has since resided here. In company with his brother, Frederick Mahl, he established himself in the plumbing business on Main street, and met with success from the outset. At the end of four years he purchased his brother's interest and has since conducted the business alone. Ten years ago he engaged in building enterprises, buying land and constructing dwellings thereon both for private residences and tenements. In this way he has erected upwards of forty structures in the city, realizing a handsome income from the course which he has pursued. He has been, in fact, one of the most successful builders in the city. He was the first to build on Florence street, developing one of the most attractive sections of the city. Six years ago he engaged in politics, and was elected to the council board from the seventh ward. He held the office of councilman for two years, and was then elected to the board of aldermen, where he has served for four consecutive years. During the whole of this period he has been the chairman of the city hall committee. He is also the chairman of the seventh ward republican

committee and is an influential member of that party in the city. Alderman Mahl belongs to St. John's Lodge, No. 4, F. and A. M. of this city, and is a member of Washington Commandery, Knights Templar. He is also connected with the National Provident Union. January 1, 1873, he married Miss Ellen L. Hills of this city, who is still living. The family of Mr. and Mrs. Mahl consists of six children, two sons and four daughters. They are members of the Windsor Avenue Congregational church. As a business man and citizen Mr. Mahl is regarded with high esteem in this city.

STEPHEN GOODRICH, HARTFORD: Druggist.

Bank Commissioner Stephen Goodrich of this city was born in Simsbury, April 13, 1836, and received a common school education. In 1852 he re-

STEPHEN GOODRICH.

moved to Hartford, where he acquired the profession of a druggist, beginning his career in the place of business which has been under his management and proprietorship for a number of years. He is one of the best-known druggists in the state and has occupied the highest positions attainable in that avocation. Mr. Goodrich was one of the founders of the Connecticut Pharmaceutical Association, and one of the first presidents of the organization. He was also influential in the movement resulting in the organization of the State Board of Pharmacy, and held the place of commissioner for three years, the appointment being an executive one. As a commissioner his work was invaluable to the druggists of the state. He insisted on a higher standard of examinations, and was instrumental in elevating the scholarship and attainments of the profession throughout the state. Commissioner Goodrich has served in both branches of the court of common council in this city and has served eight years as a member of the board of police commissioners. His career as a member of the city government was one of great credit and success, his influence in both boards being recognized as that of a man of unfaltering personal integrity and judgment. In the police board his work has been equally important and valuable to the city. He has been resolute in his demands for the best service, the efficiency and *morale* of the department receiving his special attention. In 1889 he was appointed bank commissioner by Governor Bulkeley for the term of four years, and the appointment was confirmed by the senate with a unanimity that reflected the utmost credit upon the standing of Mr. Goodrich as a public citizen. He has discharged the duties of the office with complete acceptance, and has been a faithful custodian of the interests that have been committed to his care and watchfulness. The office of bank commissioner is one of the most important in the state, requiring exceptional adaptation and judgment in the incumbent. Mr. Goodrich has fully exemplified his fitness for the position. In politics he is a pronounced republican and is a staunch supporter of the principles and achievements of that party. He is a member of St. John's lodge, F. and A. M., of this city, and has attained the Scottish Rite degree. The wife of Commissioner Goodrich, who is still living, was Miss Alice G. Kellogg prior to marriage. The only child of Mr. and Mrs. Goodrich is the wife of Capt. Wm. B. Dwight of the First regiment. The family are connected with the Park church in this city and occupy a high social position in the community. Commissioner Goodrich is at the head of the drug firm of S. Goodrich & Co.

W. L. SQUIRE, New Haven: Treasurer New York, New Haven & Hartford Railroad Company.

William Lyman Squire was born in West Granville, Mass., October 1, 1831. His education was acquired principally in the old Hartford Grammar School and the Hartford Public High School. At eighteen years of age he engaged as clerk in the grocery store of Messrs. Collins & Co., Meriden, remaining there until December, 1851; from that date until July, 1853, he was employed in a cotton commission house in New Orleans, La.; from September, 1853, until July, 1865, was paymaster for the Hartford & New Ha-

W. L. SQUIRE.

ven Railroad Company; from that time until February 1, 1879, was with the Charter Oak Life Insurance Company in Hartford; and from 1879 until the present time has been treasurer of the New York, New Haven & Hartford Railroad Company. He was united in marriage to Miss Lucy Cowles Butler of Meriden, and they have three sons,— Wilbur H., in insurance business at Meriden; Allan B. and Frederick N., both in the service of the N. Y., N. H. & H. R. R. Company. Mr. Squire is a member of the United (Congregational) Church of New Haven. In politics he is a republican.

LUCIUS M. GUERNSEY, Mystic: Editor of "The Mystic Press."

Lucius M. Guernsey was born in East Hartford, February 17, 1824, removing with his parents in early childhood to Northampton, Mass., where he secured the foundation of an education in the common schools, adding thereto by study while learning and working at his trade there, and afterwards with book open upon the hand-press while printing, in the office established by G. & C. Merriam in Springfield, Mass. He commenced business for himself in that city as a book and job printer, removing thence to New

L. M. GUERNSEY.

Britain, in this state, in 1854, where he established the first permanent newspaper of the place, *The North and South*, Elihu Burritt, the "Learned Blacksmith," being its editor, and advocating through its columns his scheme of "compensated emancipation"— the United States government to pay the owners for their slaves when given their freedom by the several states — a plan afterwards publicly endorsed by President Lincoln and others. The name of the paper was subsequently changed to *The True Citizen*, Mr. Guernsey becoming sole editor and publisher, the present *Record* being its successor. He removed from New Britain in 1868, and after some three years spent in Cromwell and Middletown went to Mystic River (now Mystic), where in 1873 he established *The Mystic Press*, an independent republican newspaper, of which he is still editor, cylinder pressman, and sometimes compositor, notwithstanding he has been more than fifty years in a printing office.

Mr. Guernsey was married at Springfield, Mass., in 1850, to Mary A., youngest daughter of Captain John Beaumont, a native of Lebanon, this state, who is still living, with two sons, George M. and John B., who are his assistants in his business. In religious faith he is a Baptist, having been actively identified with a church of that denomination and its Sunday-school work in every place where he has lived since the age of sixteen years. In politics he was in early days an anti-slavery whig and free-soiler, and subsequently a republican from the birth of that party. Always an advocate of liberty and temperance, he believes and maintains that the party of which he is a member is called in the name of God and humanity to give the negro whom it has freed his rights under the laws of the land, and, as far as practicable by law, to free that land from the curse of intemperance. He has filled various offices in churches and societies, and also in the towns where he has resided; has for several years been a justice of the peace and an officer of the board of health for Mystic, in the town of Groton; is corresponding secretary of the Mystic Valley Board of Trade, and is proud to be identified with all the interests of that delightful locality by the sea.

JOHN LATHROP HUNTER, WILLIMANTIC: Attorney-at-Law.

John L. Hunter was born in Gardiner, Me., March 13, 1834. His father and mother were both lineal descendants of the pioneer stock of Maine.

J. L. HUNTER.

He attended school at Gardiner and Wiscassett (Me.) academies; entered Bowdoin College in 1851, and graduated there in 1855; studied law at Gardiner, Me., with Hon. Charles Danforth, LL. D., who was one of the judges of the supreme court of that state from 1864 to his decease in March, 1890. He was admitted to the bar in Maine in 1859; practiced law in Gardiner several years, residing in the adjoining town of Farmingdale, where he was supervisor of schools. In 1863, in connection with his law practice, he edited *The Age*, a long-established democratic weekly newspaper, published at Augusta, the capital of Maine, and of which the present chief justice of the United States had been an editor. He went to Willimantic, in this state, and entered upon the practice of law, in 1871, and has continued his legal practice at that place ever since. He is married, and has two daughters.

In politics Mr. Hunter has always been a democrat, and for twelve years was one of the democratic state committee of Connecticut. He represented the democracy of his congressional district in the national democratic conventions of 1872 and 1876. He was elected to the legislature of Connecticut in 1879, his democratic colleague on the democratic ticket, although a popular man, being defeated by a large vote. The legislature was strongly republican, but the speaker placed Mr. Hunter on the judiciary committee, where he did effective work, as well as on the floor of the house, in accomplishing the change from the old technical common law forms to the present form of practice. He has been town and borough attorney, under democratic régime; has served many years on the school board of his town, and is at present the chairman of the high school committee.

B. P. BEACH, WASHINGTON: Builder.

Benajah Peck Beach was a member of the legislature in 1867, his colleagues in the house including Seth Thomas of Plymouth, ex-Governor Waller,

B. P. BEACH.

Hon. John T. Wait of Norwich, ex-Congressman George M. Landers, and States Attorney Tilton E. Doolittle of New Haven. Mr. Beach served on the democratic side of the house. He has held the offices of grand juror, justice of the peace, and constable. He is a builder by avocation. He was born in Woodbridge, November 27, 1820, and received a public school education. Most of his early life was spent in the towns of New Haven and Woodbridge. Since 1842 he has resided in the town of Washington. His wife, who is still living, was Miss Huldah A. Titus. There are two children in the family.

JAMES BOLTER, HARTFORD: President Hartford National Bank.

The subject of this sketch, now at the head of the oldest banking institution in Connecticut, was born at Northampton, Mass., June 27, 1815. Most of

JAMES BOLTER.

his early life was spent in his native town, and there his education was acquired in the public and private schools. With the exception of two years in St. Louis, Mo., since leaving Northampton, Mr. Bolter has resided only in Hartford. His first business experience here was as a clerk in the grocery establishment of C. H. Northam. Afterwards he entered the Phœnix Bank as discount clerk, occupying that position for a few months. He then formed a partnership with Mr. Ellery Hills in the wholesale grocery business, under the firm name of Hills & Bolter. In 1843 he became a partner with his old employer, C. H. Northam, and the firm of C. H. Northam & Co. continued until 1860, when Mr. Bolter was made cashier of the old Hartford Bank, afterwards reorganized as a national bank, with a present capital of $1,200,000. This connection continued until 1874, when he was promoted to the presidency of the institution, which position he still holds. During his administration of its affairs, the history of the Hartford National Bank has been one of almost phenomenal prosperity, giving it rank among the very foremost of the banking institutions of the city and state. Mr. Bolter is by political faith a democrat, though rarely engaging actively in politics, and never seeking public office. His only acceptance of public preferment, on record, was that of membership on the board of aldermen, some years ago. His time and attention are chiefly devoted to his duties as president of the bank, though he holds a directorship in the National Fire Insurance Company, the Dime Savings Bank, the Hartford County Mutual Fire Insurance Company, and the P. & F. Corbin Company of New Britain; he is also a member of the Hartford Club. His religious connections are with Christ church (Episcopal) of this city. Mr. Bolter was married, in 1846, to Miss Mary S. Bartholomew, and they have three children, one son and two daughters, the younger daughter being the wife of John W. Gray, Esq., of Hartford.

PROF. HENRY A. PARSONS, SALEM: Teacher of Music.

Among the distinguished names of the Revolutionary era, and in later days, which have shed a lustre upon the country, that of Parsons stands prominent. The subject of this sketch was born in Franklin, Delaware County, New York, July 7, 1839. His childhood days were spent in the common school, which experience was supplemented by a thorough course in the Delaware Literary Institute at Franklin, New York, to which was added a finishing course in music in Brooklyn, N. Y. He be-

H. A. PARSONS.

gan teaching music in his native town in 1860, and to study art while teaching. He has taught painting more or less during the past twenty-five years. In Oxford he taught music two years; in Richmond, Va., two years; in Cooperstown, N. Y., one year; in East Greenwich, R. I., six years; and in New London, Conn., until failing health caused him temporarily to abandon his chosen profession and enter a new field more for recreation than profit, that of the "Tribune Fresh Air" work, traveling in New York, New Jersey, Pennsylvania, Vermont, Massachusetts, and Connecticut, making arrangement for the work to be done in each of the states named, and entertaining children. This

new field of labor has proved of great physical advantage to him. He married, May 30, 1866, Hattie R. Miner, youngest daughter of the late Rev. Nathaniel Miner, at Salem, Conn. She died March 24, 1888, in Salem, at the residence of her brother, deacon N. E. Miner. Professor Parsons is a republican, believing that the principles of that party are conducive to the best interests of the country. In local affairs he is in the habit of giving his support to the men best qualified for minor offices, irrespective of party. He has never been an office-holder, preferring honors that are the direct result of patient study in his chosen profession. He is an intelligent Christian gentleman, a useful and respected citizen, and a self-made man in the best sense of the term.

A. M. PARKER, PUTNAM: Boot and Shoe Merchant.

Alfred M. Parker was born at Boston Highlands, Mass., October 26, 1853, and was educated in the Dearborn School in Boston and at the High School in Medford. He has been engaged in the boot and shoe trade for twenty-two years, serving with one of the leading wholesale houses in Boston for a long period and also with the largest firm in St. Louis, Mo., residing in the latter city from 1869 until 1873. He is a brother of H. B. Parker of Boston, senior member of the wholesale boot and shoe firm of Parker, Holmes &

A. M. PARKER.

Co. In 1877 the subject of this sketch succeeded the firm of Houghton & Crandall in Putnam, and has since been engaged in business there, controlling one of the best trades in his business in eastern Connecticut. He was formerly an officer in Company G, of the Third Regiment, Connecticut National Guard, and was an aid-de-camp on the staff of Gen. Graham for two years, ranking as captain. His selection for staff service was a high compliment, showing the confidence that was placed in his ability as a national guardsman. He resigned when the military troubles began in the state in 1890, retiring from the service with his chief. Captain Parker is a republican in politics. He is a prominent Mason, being worshipful master of Quinebaug Lodge and past high priest of Putnam Chapter Royal Arch Masons. He is connected with the Congregational church at Putnam, and is married. There are no children in the family.

MYRON P. YEOMANS, ANDOVER: Attorney-at-Law.

M. P. Yeomans was born in Columbia, Tolland county, Conn., April 1, 1837. He spent the entire term of his minority in his native town, where he

M. P. YEOMANS.

was first a pupil at the district schools, afterwards studying at the Connecticut Literary Institute at Suffield and the Wesleyan Academy at Wilbraham, Mass. After graduation he was three years in Charleston, Mo., whence he returned to Connecticut and established himself in the practice of law at Andover, which has been his residence for thirty years. He was admitted to the bar of Tolland County in 1862, and has been a prominent practitioner in all courts most of the time since that date. He has been judge of probate for his district, represented Andover in the Connecticut legislature in 1875, is a justice of the peace, and has held many other public offices. He is a democrat in politics, and always occupies an influential position in the councils and activities of his party. He is a member of the Andover Congregational church and society, also of the Masonic fraternity, and is a Granger. He is at present secretary of the Andover Creamery Company. Mr. Yeomans is married and has two children, his wife being Miss Marion A. Cheney before their marriage.

CLIFTON PECK, FRANKLIN: Farmer.

Clifton Peck was born in Canterbury, July 11, 1844, and received a public school education. He also pursued a business course at Eastman's College

CLIFTON PECK.

in Poughkeepsie, N. Y. He has devoted his time principally to farming and teaching, pursuing the latter avocation from 1861 until 1869, when he engaged in the wood and lumber business. In 1882 he removed to Franklin, where he has a large and profitable farm under his control. He is one of the directors of the Lebanon Creamery, in which he takes a great interest. He is a member of the Lebanon Grange of the Patrons of Husbandry, the Franklin Farmer's League, and the Lebanon Lodge of the Ancient Order of United Workmen. He is a firm believer in legislation in favor of the farmers. In 1873 Mr. Peck represented the town of Canterbury in the legislature, serving on the democratic side of the house. He was a member of the board of selectmen from 1869 until 1873, assessor and member of the board of education in that town. He is at present first selectman in Franklin and has been a member of the board of relief. Prior to his removal to Franklin Mr. Peck was connected with the Reade Paper Company in Sprague for one year. October 5, 1870, Mr. Peck married one of his pupils, Miss Hulda M. Preston, and has four daughters, one of whom became the bride of E. A. Hoxie of Lebanon last February. January 12, 1891, Mr. Peck lost his left arm while running an Ensilage cutter, the injury requiring amputation below the elbow. In politics he is an independent.

TRACY B. WARREN, BRIDGEPORT: Proprietor Atlantic Hotel.

Tracy Bronson Warren, who was a member of Governor Harrison's staff, is one of the best-known National Guardsmen in the state. In 1872 he was

T. B. WARREN.

a lieutenant in the New Haven Grays, and is a member of the Veteran Association of that command. He had served as adjutant of the Fourth regiment prior to his appointment as an aid-de-camp by Governor Harrison. He is a gentleman of great personal popularity in military circles, and belongs to the Old Guard of New York, in addition to his Connecticut connections. He is a prominent republican in Bridgeport, where he has served for two terms in the board of aldermen, and held the position of city treasurer. He is a member of Corinthian Lodge, No. 104, of Bridgeport, F. and A. M., and is connected with the higher Masonic bodies of the state. For fourteen years Colonel Warren has been a vestryman of St. John's church in Bridgeport. He was born at Watertown, December 20, 1847, and was educated at the Collegiate and Commercial Institute in New Haven. He is the proprietor of the Atlantic Hotel in Bridgeport, and is the son-in-law of John F. Mills of the Parker House in Boston, his wife being Clara A. Mills. There are four children in the family. The Colonel is a member of the Seaside Club, the finest organization of the kind in Bridgeport, and also of the Scientific Society in that city.

CYRUS B. NEWTON, M.D., STAFFORD SPRINGS;
Physician and Surgeon.

The subject of this sketch is an able and widely-known physician, who stands in the front rank of his profession in eastern Connecticut. Dr. Newton was born in Ellington in 1831. He received his preparatory training in the high schools of Somers and Ellington, attended the Connecticut Literary Institute at Suffield, and graduated from the medical department of Yale College in 1856. In the latter year he came to Stafford Springs, where he has since resided. During this time he has devoted himself to a con-

C. B. NEWTON.

stantly increasing medical practice and has performed more surgical work than any other physician in this part of the state. Dr. Newton is by natural inclination a student and he has kept well abreast with the best work of scientific discovery as it pertains to his chosen profession. This is especially true of the advances made in his favorite studies, chemistry, botany, physiology, and hygiene. His interest in the latter subject has led him into the examination of sanitary questions, the conclusions from which have been from time to time published in the medical journals of New England. Dr. Newton has long been an active member of the state medical association, and has frequently presented papers before the medical conventions of Connecticut and Massachusetts, and the county medical societies, advancing new methods of treatment; among others, one upon Pneumonia, and one concerning improved methods of using plaster splints in the treatment of fractures of lower extremities, read before the State Medical Society of Connecticut. An article upon the thermometer published in the *New England Medical Monthly*, and one entitled "Our Armamentarium," published in the Philadelphia *Medical and Surgical Reporter* in 1884, were prepared by Dr. Newton. He has also written sketches of the life of Dr. Orson Wood of Somers, of Dr. Joshua Blodgett and Dr. William N. Clark of Stafford.

In 1880, Dr. Newton was appointed a director of the State Prison at Wethersfield, and has been continued by re-appointment in that office ever since. He is also actively interested in the public affairs of Stafford and has been chairman of the board of selectmen and chairman of the board of school visitors during various years.

Dr. Newton married, in 1856, Caroline, daughter of John Fuller, Esq., who was prominently identi-

fied with the early growth and development of Holyoke, Mass. Four children have been born to them, one of whom died in childhood. Dr. Newton has enjoyed remarkably good health, and during thirty-five years of exacting professional service has lost scarcely a fortnight from active personal attention to his business.

EDWARD GRISWOLD, GUILFORD; Merchant.

Mr. Griswold is a native of the town where he now resides; was born June 30, 1839. He studied in the public schools, and graduated at the Guilford Institute. When the civil war broke out he was twenty-two years old, and in September, 1861, he, with another resident of Guilford, enlisted thirty-four of the young men of that place as members of the First Light Battery, and served with them as a private soldier in that organization three years. At the end of that time his record showed that he had

EDWARD GRISWOLD.

participated in one more engagement than any other member of the battery. Returning from the war, he was solicited by the late Governor Buckingham and by Generals Russell and Kellogg to recruit a section of artillery for the Connecticut National Guard. This he did, the condition of many enlistments being that he too should become a member, and upon organization he was unanimously elected commander — a position he most satisfactorily filled six years. It was the first battery that ever appeared with the state militia fully equipped for mounted service. He has been an active member of the Grand Army from its organization. For upwards of twenty years he has kept a "country store" of general merchandise, and for several years was business manager of the Guilford Canning Company. He has held various minor offices in his town and borough, and in 1882 and 1883 represented Guilford in the Connecticut legislature. He voted for the "parallel road" in the house, and cannot resist the impression that this action cost him the bitter personal ill-will of some of the active opponents of the measure. He has always been a republican in politics, and cast his first vote for Abraham Lincoln; but he now classes himself as an independent. He is married and has three children, his wife being Miss Annie E. Parmelee prior to her marriage. His church membership is with the First Congregational society of Guilford.

HERMAN W. HUKE, Torrington: General Foreman and Assistant Superintendent Excelsior Needle Company.

Herman W. Huke was a member of the general assembly in 1889 and acquitted himself with credit on the republican side of the house. He was born

in Torrington October 2, 1854, and was educated at the Torrington High School and Yale College of Business and Finance, preparing himself for a business career. He is a member of the Board of Education in his town and is connected with a number of industrial enterprises, including the Excelsior Needle Company, the Torrington Cooperative Company, and

H. W. HUKE.

operative Company, and the Alvord & Spear Manufacturing Company. He has been in the employ of the Excelsior Needle Company for twenty years, occupying the position of general foreman and assistant superintendent for the past fifteen years. He is the president of the Torrington Cooperative Company. Mr. Huke is a member of the Third Congregational Association at Torrington, and is a republican in politics. His wife, who was Miss Nellie H. Allen prior to her marriage, is the daughter of Sheriff Allen of Litchfield county. There is one child, a boy of seven years.

ERWIN O. DIMOCK, Tolland: Attorney-at-Law.

E. O. Dimock was born in Stafford, October 6, 1842, and received a good common and select school education. He served with the Twenty-

fifth Connecticut regiment in the late war, and spent a year at General Banks' headquarters after the regiment returned home. He engaged in farming and lumbering a few years, and afterwards took up the fire insurance business and the study of law, and was admitted to the Tolland county bar in 1871, and engaged in the practice of law in Stafford till 1873, when he estab-

DIMOCK.

lished himself in Tolland, and has been in practice there to the present time. In 1875 he was appointed assistant clerk of the superior court for Tolland county, and was appointed clerk the following year, which position he now holds. He has also held several town offices. He was a liberal republican in the Greeley campaign, and a St. John prohibitionist, and is now acting with the republican party.

Mr. Dimock married Miss Mary E. Sparrow. She died June 15th of the present year. He has no children. He is a member of the Congregational church in Tolland; also of the Masonic fraternity, Patrons of Husbandry, Grand Army of the Republic, and Sons of Temperance.

HON. OSCAR LEACH, Durham.

The subject of this sketch was born in Madison in 1831. He had the advantages of the common schools and academy, and an acquaintance early in

life with all the prominent people of the community through his father, Hon. L. W. Leach, who was long a leading citizen of Middlesex county. The senator removed to Durham when young, and became a successful merchant. He was early interested in the success of the republican party, and filled many local positions of honor and trust. He was appointed postmaster

OSCAR LEACH.

at Durham at the opening of President Lincoln's first term, and was removed during the last year of Johnson's term, but was re-appointed the next year, under President Grant. He held the office until his resignation in October, 1883. In 1866 he represented Durham in the house, being the colleague of William Wadsworth, and serving upon the committee on incorporations. In 1869 he was elected to the state senate, and became a conspicuous member of a body in which were Hon. David Gallup, Hon. Heusted W. R. Hoyt, Hon. Charles B. Andrews, Hon. Carnot O. Spencer, Hon. George M. Landers of New Britain, and ex-Mayor Lucien W. Sperry of New Haven. In 1887 Senator Leach was returned to that body, and was made senate chairman of the committee on cities and boroughs, and served with distinction throughout the session.

Senator Leach has been always in politics, and has probably exerted a more controlling influence in the deliberations of his party associates, locally and statewise, than almost any of his contemporaries. He is entirely at home in legislative affairs, is a fluent speaker, and has a most happy faculty for impressing his audience with the righteousness of his cause, which he adopts conscientiously and advocates with great persistence and profound earnestness of manner and language. Senator Leach married, in December, 1853, Miss Eliza J. Hickox, daughter of L. C. Hickox of Durham, and they have two children.

HON. THOMAS CLARK, NORTH STONINGTON: President Norwich & New York Transportation Company.

Hon. Thomas Clark is the only son of Hon. Thomas A. Clark of Lisbon, Conn., and was born in that town, December 26, 1830. His early boyhood was spent at home. He received his education at the common and select schools, and from a private teacher. At sixteen years of age he taught school in his own district, and was so efficient that the same board chose him again for teacher the following winter. When eighteen years old he left home, spending a year at Norwich and a year or two in Mata-

THOMAS CLARK.

gorda, Tex., as merchant's clerk. In the autumn of 1853 he returned north and opened a store temporarily in North Stonington, where he married Miss Sarah E. Wheeler, only daughter of the late William R. Wheeler, and where he has since resided. He was educated a democrat, but his sojourn at the south and other influences decided him to work with the republican party from the day of its organization. He has ever since been its staunchest friend, and one of its most earnest workers.

For many years he pursued an energetic and successful career as a manufacturer. At the time of the war, and for several years succeeding, his health was much impaired. He sent a substitute, and with his zeal and purse gave all the aid in his power to the cause in which he so thoroughly believed. Subsequently his physicians recommended a voyage across the ocean and entire rest from business as the only means of saving his life. In 1870 he made the trip to Europe, spending several months on the continent and placing himself under the care of Sir Henry Thompson. This course resulted, after long debility, in an entire cure.

In 1861, 1862, and 1866, he was a member of the house, and in 1867 a member of the senate. In 1868 he was a delegate-at-large at the national republican convention at Chicago, acting in place of the late Hon. H. H. Starkweather, and as secre-

tary of the Connecticut delegation. In 1889 he was elected president and manager of the Norwich & New York Transportation Company, which position he now holds. In 1882 he was nominated for the office of judge of probate for his district, but declined the honor. He was comptroller of the state in 1887-88, having been elected on the state ticket which had the Hon. P. C. Lounsbury at its head. He discharged the duties of this office with signal ability, his ripe judgment and experience in business affairs serving to good purpose in enabling him to decide promptly and wisely concerning the responsibilities and obligations of this important trust. His church connections and membership are with the Congregational society. He has one son, Wilfred A. Clark, who is a lawyer in New York city.

Mr. Clark is a gentleman of pleasing social qualities, and his wide circle of personal friends hold him in the highest esteem.

HENRY W. WESSELLS, LITCHFIELD: Druggist.

Henry W. Wessells was born in New Milford, July 13, 1845, and was educated at the "Gunnery" in Washington. He is the son of General L. W. Wessells of Litchfield, who was a prominent soldier in the field during the war, and is actively connected with the Connecticut Division, Sons of Veterans. When the C. O. Belden camp, No. 31, was organized at Litchfield, Oct. 5, 1887, he was elected captain and held the position until January, 1890. In May, 1889, he was elected lieutenant-colonel of the Connecticut

H. W. WESSELLS.

division and was advanced to the command in February, 1890. February 5, 1891, he was chosen lieutenant-colonel and commander of the Arm Battalion of the division. He is also at present the captain of Belden Camp. He was the first dictator of the Litchfield lodge, Knights of Honor, and is a member of the New York Commandery, Loyal Legion. Colonel Wessells is a republican in politics and has held the office of assessor in Litchfield. He is a member of the Episcopal church in that place. He is engaged in the druggist business, being a member of the firm of Wessells, Gates & Co., and is also the secretary of the Litchfield Mutual Fire Insurance Company. He was lieutenant Company H, Fourth Regiment, C. N. G., for three years, resigning in 1875. The wife of Colonel Wessells was Miss Anne E. Dotterer prior to marriage. There are no children in the family.

WILLIAM F. J. BOARDMAN, Hartford: A Retired Merchant and Manufacturer.

W. F. J. Boardman, a representative of one of the oldest and most honorable families of Hartford, was born in Wethersfield December 12, 1828. He is a descendant in the seventh generation from Samuel Boardman (originally spelled Boreman), who was born in Banbury, Oxfordshire, England, and emigrated to America about 1637, settling in Ipswich, Mass., where he was a land owner in 1639, and whence he removed to Wethersfield, Conn., in 1640. He was a deputy from Wethersfield to the

W. F. J. BOARDMAN.

general court for thirty-four sessions, and during his lifetime there occupied many positions of honor and trust within the gift of his township and the colony. "Few of the first settlers of Connecticut (says Hinman) came with a better reputation, or sustained it more uniformly through life, than Mr. Boardman." From the original American ancestor, Samuel, down through six generations, in the line of the subject of this sketch, the Boardmans have without exception been natives of Wethersfield, and during their lives prominently identified with that ancient town, where each has, in one or another official capacity, served with distinction his day and generation, leaving an honorable and patriotic record. The father of the present subject, William Boardman, was born at Lenox, Mass., but removed to Wethersfield with his father the year of his birth. He was by trade a printer; was a book and newspaper publisher, and afterwards a merchant and manufacturer for forty-six years. He came to Hartford in 1853, and until his death in 1887 was a prominent and useful citizen, as many of the residents of Hartford of the present day will well remember.

William F. J. Boardman received his primary education at the public schools of his native town, and graduated from Wethersfield Academy in 1846, where he had studied under the preceptorship of Noah B. Clark and S. A. Galpin, distinguished educators of that day. On leaving school in the spring of 1846, he entered the coffee and spice manufactory of his father in Wethersfield, to learn the business in detail. Four years later, upon the removal of the business to Hartford, he purchased a one-third interest therein and it was continued under the firm name of William Boardman & Son. On the seventh of January, 1852, he was married to Jane M. Greenleaf, daughter of Dr. Charles

Greenleaf of Hartford. In 1853 his brother, Thomas J. Boardman, was admitted as a partner in the business, and the firm removed to larger quarters; its name was changed to William Boardman & Sons, and its operations extended to include importing, manufacturing, and jobbing in teas, coffees, and spices, with a wholesale trade throughout New England and other states. The financial part of the business being under the care of W. F. J. Boardman, his father attended to the buying, and his brother to the manufacturing and packing department. This business connection continued with uninterrupted success until 1887, when Mr. Boardman, senior, died, and one year later W. F. J. Boardman retired, having been connected with the firm continuously for thirty-eight years.

Mr. Boardman was one of the original members of the Putnam Phalanx under its permanent organization in 1859. In 1863 he was elected a member of the Hartford common council from the third ward, in which he was a member of the highways committee and chairman of the committee on the horse railroad then being constructed. As a member of the council he did his whole duty, acting for the city's good without fear or favor. In 1861 he was chosen a director of the State Bank of Hartford, serving several years and giving to the institution the same conscientious attention that he did to his own business. This was during the war of the rebellion, when the "old State" Bank was called upon by Governor Buckingham, perhaps more freely and extensively than any other institution in the state to furnish the "sinews of war," which it did to the extent of many times its capital. In 1868 Mr. Boardman's health suffered serious impairment, and he was obliged temporarily to retire from active business; but, regaining it to a considerable extent, he gave renewed attention to the affairs of the firm. The establishment was again moved to larger quarters on State street, and in 1871 the fine "Boardman Building" on Asylum street was erected at a cost — including machinery, etc., — of over $100,000, the firm occupying the new building in 1872. In 1887 he went abroad, visiting parts of England, Scotland, and France, in the hope of confirming his still imperfect health, and taking with him his medical adviser. The trip was not entirely successful, and as a matter of physical necessity he concluded on his return in 1888 to abandon all business activity, which he did by selling to his brother his entire interest in the old firm July 7, 1888, as above intimated, after an experience of forty-two years, thirty-eight of which was with the firm already specified. During his business life Mr. Boardman has been actively engaged in promoting or establishing many enterprises, including the Hartford & New York Steamboat Company, the Merrick Thread Company of

Holyoke, Mass., and the Hudson River Water Power and Paper Company of Mechanicsville, N. Y. He has also assisted many young men in establishing themselves in business. In 1863-64 he in company with others built a number of sailing vessels, for the coasting and foreign trade, among them the *William Boardman*, the *M. M. Merriman*, the *Sarah A. Reed*, and the *A. J. Bentley*, with a considerable proprietory interest in many others. He has often served on commissions, has settled estates, operated in real estate considerably, attended to the construction of some of the best buildings in Hartford, and has generally led an active life. He has made it a point never to incur an obligation which he could not meet at once or on maturity of his promise, and has thus acquired and maintained a reputation for integrity which none can call in question. He is and always has been a democrat, inheriting that political faith from ancestors whose patriotism has been inflexibly loyal and solid in all emergencies. He has held no public office for several years, nor does he seek any. He has until recently retained his connection with the Phalanx, and is still a member of the Connecticut Historical Society, and of the Sons of the American Revolution.

Mr. Boardman's family consists of his wife and an only son, William Greenleaf Boardman, who was born in Hartford June 29, 1853, and still resides in this city.

EDWARD MILLER, Meriden: Manufacturer of Brass and Iron Goods.

Edward Miller was born in Wallingford, in this state, August 10, 1827. When he was two years of age his parents moved to Canistota, New York, eight years later return-

ing to Connecticut and settling in Meriden, where his life has since been spent. His education was acquired chiefly at the public schools of Meriden, with a brief subsequent academical experience. After leaving school he engaged in mechanical pursuits, and ultimately established himself in Meriden in the manufacture of kerosene burners, lamps, bronzes,

EDWARD MILLER.

sheet brass, and various forms of utensils made from that metal; making and putting upon this market the first kerosene burner, for burning kerosene oil made from distilled coal. He is now the president and senior member of the house of Edward Miller & Company, one of the important industrial establishments of that city.

with offices and salesrooms in Boston and New York. This house was established in 1844, and incorporated under the laws of the state in 1866. Mr. Miller has never sought public office, though having occupied various positions of trust within the gift of his townsmen. He is a republican in politics, and a member of the First Baptist church. He has a wife and three children living, two sons and a daughter. Mrs. Miller was Miss Caroline M. Neal prior to her marriage, and a native of Southington.

S. Y. BEACH, Seymour: Paper Manufacturer.

Sharon Yale Beach is a descendant of the Rev. Benjamin Beach, an influential clergyman of New Haven county. His father, Giles Beach, was born in North Haven, where the subject of this sketch was also born, May 21, 1809. On his mother's

side he is a descendant of Captain Jonathan Dayton, who was a justice of the peace and an officer in the revolutionary war. An interesting fact in connection with the military service of Captain Dayton is that his four sons were members of the company which he com-

S. Y. BEACH.

manded. The wife of Captain Dayton was Mary Yale, the latter name appearing in Mr. Beach's. Mr. Beach has four sons, who with himself compose the S. Y. Beach Paper Company of Seymour. The oldest of the sons, Mr. G. W. Beach, is also the superintendent of the Naugatuck division of the New York, New Haven & Hartford railroad system. The second, A. Y. Beach, is engaged in the coal and grocery trade. The third, Sharon D. Beach, is the manager of the paper company, while the fourth, Theodore B. Beach, is the railroad station agent at Seymour. The first wife of Mr. Beach, who died February 18, 1871, was Miss Adeline Sperry of Orange, sister of the late Dr. Isaac J. Sperry of Hartford. The second wife, who is now living, was Miss Julia L. Hine of Orange. There is also one daughter in the family. Mr. Beach has made his own fortune in the world. He began life on a North Haven farm and was afterward a clerk in a grocery store. Subsequently he spent about twelve years in a cotton factory at Humphreysville, now Seymour, and there began the manufacture of paper. In the latter industry he met with decided success. When the Ansonia Baptist church was organized, Mr. Beach was chosen its first deacon, and the office is still retained by him at the earnest solicitation of the people. He was the superintendent of the Bible-school until he was seventy years of age. Deacon Beach has been a member of the Baptist church for more than sixty years. He was a democrat originally, but abandoned the party on account of the extension of slavery and united with the republicans. At present he is an active supporter of the prohibition party. He has held the offices of selectman, justice of the peace, and chairman of the board of education. During the war he was chairman of the republican town committee of Seymour and called the first meeting in the town favoring President Lincoln. He also presided at the last meeting in the town held in consequence of the struggle. His life has been one closely identified with public interests.

ELIPHALET B. HULL, Noroton Heights (Darien).

Eliphalet B. Hull, who is the sole survivor of the party that attempted to convey assistance to the passengers of the burning steamer *Lexington* January 13, 1840, was born in the town of Westport February 4, 1820, and educated in the common schools of that section of the state. At the age of sixteen he was apprenticed to the carpenter's trade. At the end of his apprenticeship he was employed for two years in Fairfield and Bridgeport. It was towards the end of his apprentice days that the event referred to

E. B. HULL.

above occurred. Young Hull was not twenty years of age at the time. With three others he manned a yawl boat at Southport and started for the rescue of the burning steamer's passengers. It was an act of great gallantry, the four men taking their lives in their hands, ready to sacrifice themselves in the effort to rescue the *Lexington's* passengers from the terrible calamity that engulfed them. The rescuers labored with a will to reach the ill-fated steamer but were unable to make much more than half of the distance before the vessel sank out of sight. In 1842 Mr. Hull entered the employ of the Stamford Manufacturing Co., being assigned to wheelwright and machinery work, and remained with the establishment for twenty-eight years. From the close of that period until within a few years he was engaged in his regular trade. Mr. Hull served in the state militia in the town of Fairfield. He is a member of the Methodist church and a republican in politics. He has been twice married. His present wife was Miss Sarah C. Hyde. There are three daughters living, by the first wife.

REV. SAMUEL M. HAMMOND, Torrington: Pastor Methodist Episcopal church.

Samuel M. Hammond was born in Brookhaven, N. Y., March 10, 1833. He supplemented an academic education by a theological course in the

S. M. HAMMOND.

Methodist Biblical Institute at Concord, N. H., graduating in 1859. When a young man he taught in the south, and, during the war, spent some time in the service of the Christian Commission. He became a minister in the Methodist Episcopal church in 1860, and has spent part of his ministerial career in Brooklyn, New Rochelle, New Haven, New Britain, and Ansonia, going to his present charge at Torrington in the spring of 1888. In 1859 he was married to Miss Fannie A. Howell of Mattituck, L. I., a lady in all respects well adapted to assist him in the prosecution of the work to which he has devoted his life. They have been blessed with ten children, three sons and seven daughters. Mr. Hammond is a most sympathetic and faithful pastor, and a logical, instructive, magnetic, and very earnest preacher. He has an excellent gift of language, is never at a loss for words to express either his thoughts or feelings, and, when fully aroused, in using either tongue or pen, not seldom reaches an eloquence that touches every emotion and awakens every sympathy. He is a man of clear, well-reasoned, strongly-grounded conviction, and therefore a man of great moral courage, who is never afraid to stand with a despised minority, in defense of any cause that he deems right. He is well known throughout Connecticut and in other states as a fearless and uncompromising enemy of the American grog-shop. During one of his pastorates on Long Island he took such an active part in pushing the temperance cause and suppressing the illegal sale of liquors, that the worshipers of Bacchus and Gambrinus, instead of canonizing him for the good work he had accomplished, cannonaded him by firing a national salute, out of joy for his departure, the day he left for a new field of labor. When a young man he became deeply interested in the anti-slavery question, was a stout advocate of freedom, and an ardent member of the republican party; but when, in 1872, his party in the sixteenth resolution of its national platform, joined hands (as he believed) with the liquor interest, he became convinced that the drink evil could only be effectually dealt with by a political party organized for that purpose. He assisted to organize the prohibition party in Connecticut in 1884, and during the four years following was one of its most able and aggressive leaders. The productions of his pen were scattered broadcast over the state, arousing the hostility of some, carrying deep and permanent conviction to others, and giving new inspiration and courage to those who had already entered the prohibition ranks. In 1888, he was sent as a delegate at large to the national prohibition convention at Indianapolis. He there became satisfied that the party as officered and managed stood as much for woman-suffrage as for the abolition of the drink evil, and, being strongly opposed to that measure, he was reluctantly compelled to leave the party; but he never lets slip a good opportunity to strike a blow at the liquor traffic and its political protectors. Physically, Mr. Hammond is not what would be called vigorous, but intellectually and spiritually he is thoroughly equipped for his important work. He is a sincere, manly man, who "abhors that which is evil, and cleaves to that which is good."

GOULD SMITH CLARK, MIDDLEBURY: Farmer.

Mr. Clark, now in his seventy-eighth year, was born in the town of Prospect, March 12, 1814. He was reared a farmer, in an agricultural neighborhood, where the educational facilities were few, and at a remote date when school-houses were of very primitive design exteriorly and interiorly, in striking contrast with the public schools of to-day and the buildings in which pupils are now taught. He was married in 1840 to Miss Maria H. Skilton of Watertown, by whom he has had three children. His married

G. S. CLARK.

life has been spent almost entirely in Middlebury, where he has owned and managed the farm upon which he now resides, and where he has held nearly all the offices within the gift of the town, being elected thereto by the republicans, of which party he has been a member since 1856. He is a member of the Congregational church of Middlebury, and has been one of its deacons since 1864. He represented that town in the legislature in the years 1857, 1871, and 1872, and was appointed by Governor Andrew as one of the appraisers of the state prison property in Wethersfield. Deacon Clark has had a long, useful, and honored life. He was of sturdy New England stock, and in his person and character exemplifies the noblest and best traits of a Puritan ancestry.

NATHANIEL LYON KNOWLTON, ASHFORD: Farmer.

N. L. Knowlton was born in Ashford, May 19, 1844. After acquiring a solid education at the public schools he engaged in mechanical and agricultural pursuits, which have since occupied his attention. He represented Ashford in the legislature in 1872, and was postmaster at West Ashford from 1881 till 1887. He was married in 1868 to Miss Sarah S. Wright of Ashford. He is a democrat in politics, and by that party has been raised to the various positions of trust and honor which he has held. Mr. Knowl-

N. L. KNOWLTON.

ton is of distinguished ancestry, being a nephew of General Lyon, the brave and lamented soldier who lost his life in the service of his country, during the war of the rebellion, at Wilson Creek, Aug. 10, 1861; and also a descendant of Colonel Thomas Knowlton of revolutionary memory, who was killed in the battle of Harlem Heights, Sept. 16, 1776.

AMOS S. BLAKE, WATERBURY: Inventor and Manufacturer.

Amos S. Blake has been a member of the general assembly during three sessions. He was originally elected to the house from Waterbury in 1869, and was returned during the two successive years of 1874 and 1875. In politics Mr. Blake is a democrat. He has also held public offices in Vermont and Michigan. For a number of years he was one of the judges of jail delivery in the former state, where the law until recent years authorized imprisonment for debt. He was a county commissioner for three years in the state of

A. S. BLAKE.

Michigan. Mr. Blake is an inventor of distinction, his inventions being covered by nineteen patents. During the winter of 1830-31 he constructed the first locomotive ever seen in New England. The model was small, being designed to illustrate the principles of railroad construction. It was able to carry two persons around a hall on a circular track. The design was very generally exhibited through the northern states,

by Asa Harrington of Middlesex, Vt. During the
war Mr. Blake was the superintendent of the American
Flask and Cap Company at Waterbury. In one
year the concern delivered one hundred tons of
percussion caps to the government. Mr. Blake
has employed not less than 3,000 persons for himself
and others in various kinds of work. He was
born at Brookfield, Vt., January 18, 1812, and was
educated at Southmade Academy and Scott's Military
School at Montpelier, Vt. He was a captain
in the artillery service for two years. The maiden
name of his wife, who is still living, was Eliza Cordelia
Woodward. Two daughters are also living.
The subject of this sketch has spent his whole life
in the profession of dentistry and in mining and
manufacturing.

JEROME B. BALDWIN, WILLIMANTIC: Merchant.

Mr. Baldwin was born in the town of Mansfield,
September 14, 1843. The common schools of the
town afforded him his education, and at the age of

J. B. BALDWIN.

eighteen he enlisted as a
private in Company D,
Twenty-First regiment
Connecticut Volunteers,
serving three years; rose
to the rank of sergeant,
was in all the principal
battles of his gallant regiment,
and was seriously
wounded in the second
day's engagement in front
of Petersburg. Returning
from the war, after
three years' active service,
he turned his attention
to mercantile pursuits, and for many years was
senior member of the firm of Baldwin & Webb in
the clothing and furnishing goods trade, doing
business in Willimantic. For the last few years,
since the retirement of Mr. Webb from the firm, he
has conducted the business alone. He married
Miss Ella M. Adams, and has three children, daughters.
Mr. Baldwin filled the position of town and
borough assessor for three years and was on the
board of water commissioners for a similar term,
which latter position he still occupies. He is a
member of the republican party, and as such was
elected to represent the town of Windham in the
state legislature in 1885, serving as chairman of the
engrossed bills committee and also on the committee
on military affairs. He is a member of the
Grand Army organization in Willimantic. Mr.
Baldwin is a highly-respected citizen, and though
never an aspirant for public office, takes an active
interest in whatever promotes the public
welfare.

HON. EDWIN HOLMES BUGBEE, PUTNAM.

Edwin H. Bugbee was born in Thompson, Conn.,
in 1820, the son of James Bugbee, born in Woodstock
in 1788, a descendant of Edward Bugby,

E. H. BUGBEE.

who settled in Roxbury,
Mass., in 1634, sailing in
the ship Francis, from
Ipswich, England. The
family home of the immigrant
was Stratford-Bow,
then a suburb of London,
but now within the corporate
limits of that city.
The subject of this sketch
was educated in the public
schools of the town,
and was early a clerk in
his father's store. In
1839 he entered the employ
of the Lyman Manufacturing Company at their
mills in North Providence, R. I., as clerk and bookkeeper.
In 1843-44 he obtained a lease of the
mills, and commenced business on his own account.
The business of those years proved successful for
manufacturers, and at the close of 1844 he returned
to Thompson, having in the meantime purchased
a farm in his native town. In 1849 he removed to
Killingly, entering the employ of the Williamsville
Manufacturing Company, at their factory in Killingly,
remaining with them till 1879. He early
took an active interest in the political affairs of the
town, and in 1855 received the nomination for representative
to the general assembly. The exciting
question in the several towns of the county at that
time was that of the proposed incorporation of a
new town to be formed from portions of Thompson,
Killingly, and Pomfret, to be called Putnam. Mr.
Bugbee having earnestly advocated the cause of
the friends of the proposed new town was defeated,
because of that advocacy, by a majority of fourteen
votes. In 1857 he was again a candidate and was
elected by a handsome majority; he was also
elected a representative from Killingly in 1859, '61,
'63, '69, '71, '73, and 1879. In 1865 and 1868 he was
senator from the Fourteenth District, and in 1868
was elected president *pro tem*, of the senate. He
served eight terms as chairman of committees, and
in 1871 was speaker of the house. In all these
years he proved an active member on the floor of
either house. Mr. Bugbee is a republican, having
acted with that party since its organization, but
disclaims being a partisan. He is represented as
being in favor of tariff and civil service reform,
and is strenuously opposed to the so-called "Lodge
Force Bill" of the Fifty-first congress. He contends
that the country's greatest need at the present
time is for more patriots and fewer partisans.

Mr. Bugbee was married in 1857, his wife surviving less than one year. Since 1882 he has been a resident of Putnam, having retired from business. He has been a director of the Putnam National Bank since the year of its organization, and is vice-president for Connecticut of the New England Historic-Genealogical Society, and is much interested in genealogical research.

JOHN D. BROWNE, Hartford: President Connecticut Fire Insurance Company.

John D. Browne is a native of Connecticut, having been born in the town of Plainfield, Windham county, in 1836. The old homestead, first occupied by his great-great-grand-father, is still in the family, and now occupied by an elder brother. Mr. Browne comes of long-lived, hardy, Puritan, and revolutionary stock; the kind which broke up the rugged soil, built the public highways, and the school-houses and churches, and fought the battles for liberty and national independence. His grandfather, John

J. D. BROWNE.

Browne, enlisted as a musician in the patriot army in 1776, serving, with two of his brothers, through the long and trying period of the war, and was promoted while in service to the position of fife-major of his regiment. His father, Gurdon Perkins Browne, was a hard-working farmer, who reared his family in habits of industry and frugality, and did not forget to inculcate by precept and example those principles of robust morality and patriotism in which he had himself been trained. He was also a school teacher of considerable celebrity, beginning to teach at the age of seventeen, and continuing in that profession through thirty-six winters. He was an ardent democrat of the old school, always performing his duties as a patriotic citizen, and voting at every election in his town until the very close of his long life, dying at the advanced age of eighty-three years. Mr. Browne's mother was a woman of rare qualities, deeply solicitous for the intellectual and spiritual culture of her children, and earnestly devoted to her family. The early environment of the subject of this sketch was, therefore, of a healthy sort, in both its material and mental aspects, favorable to the formation of correct habits and a manly character, and promotive of the best development of the natural gifts which he had inherited from a long line of sturdy and honorable ancestors.

Mr. Browne's youthful life was devoted to the farm and the district school, and at the age of nineteen he taught one of the schools of his native town. But the duties of a school teacher were not congenial as a life work; and, having in 1855 made a visit to the then far-off territory of Minnesota, he made a second journey thither in the spring of 1857, and located in Minneapolis. He was for two years connected with the Minneapolis Mill Company, and aided in the development and improvement of the magnificent water-power at that point. Afterwards he went to Little Falls, then a town of a few hundred inhabitants, located on the Mississippi River, about one hundred and twenty-five miles north of Minneapolis, where he spent a year as director and agent of the Little Falls Manufacturing Company, engaged in developing the water-power there by the construction of a dam across the Mississippi.

While in Minnesota Mr. Browne was actively prominent in local and state politics, aided in organizing the republican party in Minnesota, and held intimate relations with the dominant party at the national capital throughout the administration of President Lincoln, for whose election he had been an enthusiastic and effective worker. He was often a delegate to county and state conventions, and was elected an alternate delegate to the national republican convention which nominated Mr. Lincoln. His republicanism was known to be of the most pronounced type, and his political activity and enthusiasm constituted him an important factor in all the councils of his party throughout the greater portion of the period of eight years over which his residence in Minnesota extended.

At the close of the presidential campaign, in the autumn of 1860, he was elected messenger to take the first electoral vote of Minnesota to Washington, in which city he remained during the succeeding winter, having been appointed to a desk in the interior department at the capitol under Jo. Wilson, then commissioner of the general land office. He returned to Minnesota in the spring of 1861, and for four years, during Lincoln's administration, was chief clerk in the office of the surveyor-general of public lands at St. Paul, to which city the office had been recently removed from Detroit.

In 1865 Mr. Browne returned east, and soon afterwards entered upon insurance work, in 1867 becoming permanently connected with the Hartford Fire Insurance Company as its general agent and adjuster. In 1870 he was elected secretary of that company, in the duties of which office he was engaged for ten years, or until called to the presidency of the Connecticut Fire in 1880. His incumbency of this latter office still continues. It is but just to Mr. Browne to say that since his elevation to its chief executive office the Connecticut has abundantly maintained its high standing among the solid and prosperous institutions of its class in this insurance center, while its progressive tendency is illustrated by the fact that the volume of the company's yearly business has doubled since he assumed its management.

Mr. Browne sustains official relations with various business and social organizations in Hartford. He is a director in the Phoenix Mutual Life Insurance Company, the National Exchange Bank, the Board of United Charities, the Humane Society, and the Connecticut State Prison Association, with which latter society he is further connected as a member of its committee on visitations and discharges. He is also a member of the Connecticut Historical Society, and of the Connecticut Society of the Sons of the American Revolution. He was married, October 23, 1861, to Miss Frances Cleveland, daughter of Luther Cleveland, Esq., of Plainfield. They have two children, the elder being now the wife of Francis R. Cooley, son of Hon. F. B. Cooley of this city.

OLIVER MARKHAM, MIDDLETOWN: Gunsmith.

The subject of this sketch was born in Middletown, of which city, either as a municipality or a township, his ancestors for five generations were natives and residents. Mr. Markham is able to trace his descent in a direct line through nine generations to Sir Robert Markham of Nottinghamshire, England, who was seventeenth in descent from Claron de Markham, the Saxon chief, of West Markham, England, the first of the name, who died in the year 1006.

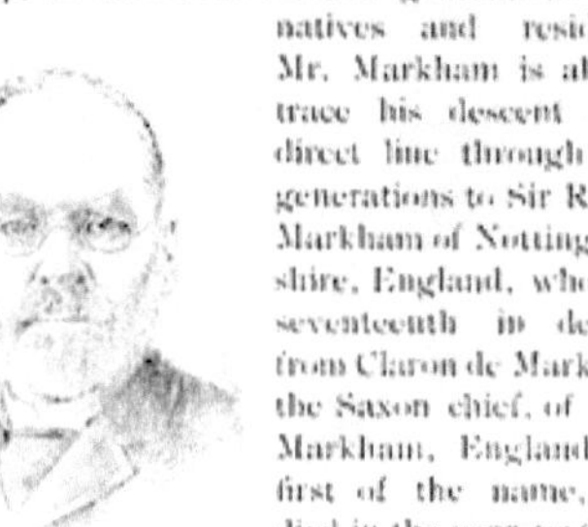

OLIVER MARKHAM.

Oliver Markham was born in Middletown, as before stated, July 17, 1825. He learned the trade of gunsmith from his father, John Markham (the last owner of Markham's mills), at Savage's factory in Middletown. He went to Windsor, Vt., in 1848, took a contract for locks for Robbins & Lawrence, and when that firm removed to Hartford under the name of "Sharps' Armory," he went with them there, and subsequently to Bridgeport, being a contractor with the corporation during its entire existence. He was an inventor of sundry parts of guns, and acted as draughtsman for the concern. While in Hartford, Mr. Markham was a member of the common council in 1862. He is now a director in the Central National Bank of Middletown, to

which city he removed in 1869, and has since maintained his residence there. He was married, July 23, 1848, to Sarah Ann Clark, daughter of Ambrose Clark of Middletown. They have two sons living, one of whom is Dr. E. A. Markham of Durham.

CALEB J. CAMP, WEST WINSTED: Retired Merchant and Financier.

C. J. Camp was born in the town of Winchester, where he has spent his whole life. His early education was that of the common school, with a winter or two at the village academy by way of finish. This, however, was the foundation only. Reading and observation, and constant contact with able men have since made him a self-reliant and versatile man of affairs, judicious and sagacious. At fifteen he began his business career as clerk in the general store of Lucius Clarke. At nineteen he was a member of the firm

C. J. CAMP.

of M. & C. J. Camp, who were Mr. Clarke's successors. Such was the enterprise and energy of this young firm that they soon not only surpassed all local competitors, but in amount of sales distanced every other mercantile establishment in Litchfield county. The management, largely, of this store soon came into this young man's hands, who not only made a grand success of it, but also a first-class training school for many a clerk, who was there drilled to do his very best, and taught habits of strictest integrity. In public enterprises he has often been a leader — always an active promoter. His strong characteristics have been an inborn business sagacity, a clear insight into the intricacies of almost any kind of enterprise, and the possession of that rare tact which enabled him to disarm prejudice, and secure for his own ideas an enthusiastic approval, or at least a respectful consideration. He has been a successful organizer and an influential man at all times. During his career as village merchant Mr. Camp was progressive, and the promoter of various schemes which long ago resulted in making Winsted one of the most attractive boroughs in the state. The firm of which he was a member were active in the establishment of several manufacturing enterprises. For thirty-five years they were the owners of the Union Chair Company of Robertsville; they built the first large brick block in Winsted containing a public hall, which was at that time regarded as in advance of the demands of the village. To Mr.

Camp's individual efforts the borough was indebted for its flagging stone walks, and he was the first mover in the introduction of gas works. He was also the founder of the Winona Savings Bank at Winona, Minn., of which the late Secretary Windom was president at the time of his death. While president of the Connecticut Western Railroad Company he evinced the same ability to master the affairs of railway enterprises that he had manifested in mercantile and manufacturing pursuits. Under his management the securities of the company advanced in value more than one hundred per cent. In politics Mr. Camp has been a life-long republican, a firm believer in high tariff and protection, and a consistent temperance man. For many years he has been a member of the Congregational church, and an earnest and active supporter, and not only of the church but of every benevolent and worthy cause. He is always recognized as a friend and helper of the minister and the missionary, and as taking cognizance of the needs and bestowing judicious benefactions upon the deserving and unfortunate poor. He is known and honored not less for his marked ability than for his courtesy and kindliness of heart and unquestioned integrity, while his home is proverbial for its genial and generous hospitality.

LUKE M. HEERY, Versailles: Woolen Manufacturer.

Mr. Heery is a native of Ireland, where he was born in 1848. His father's family removed to this country and settled in Hinsdale, Mass., in 1858. At the age of twelve years, after earlier training in the public schools, he went to work in the woolen mills at Hinsdale, and rose through the various grades of employment to the superintendency, which position he held six years, until 1876, when he formed a partnership with James Walton, who owned and operated the Methuen Mills. This partnership

L. M. HEERY.

was dissolved two years later, when Mr. Heery assumed sole management and control of the extensive business. In 1878 he was owner of the West Chelmsford mills, near Lowell, Mass., and in 1880 bought the Versailles Mill. A year later he also purchased mills in Monson, Mass., and for several years operated the several establishments in the manufacture of cassimeres and worsted goods, being probably the largest individual woolen man-

ufacturer in New England. In 1889 he suffered quite heavy losses through parties to whom he consigned his goods, and shortly afterward contracted his business and disposed of the Versailles and Chelmsford establishments. In partnership with his brother he is now confining his attention to the Monson Mills, in the same lines of manufacture, the establishment being incorporated under the laws of Massachusetts, and known as the Monson Woolen Company. Mr. Heery is an active, energetic man, who will conquer success in the face of great obstacles. He was an aid-de-camp on the staff of Governor Waller in 1883-84, with the rank of Colonel.

GEORGE M. REDWAY, Hartford: Marble Dealer.

Lieutenant-Colonel George M. Redway occupies a prominent position in the Order of Odd Fellows in Connecticut, and is widely known throughout the state. He became a member of Charter Oak Lodge in Hartford, September 23, 1874, and united with Midian Encampment in 1876. He held all of the offices in that organization, occupying that of Chief Patriarch in 1881. He has been the treasurer of the encampment for a number of years. He was a charter member of Canton Capitol City, Patri-

G. M. REDWAY.

archs Militant, and was elected captain of the organization in 1887. During that year he was also advanced to the position of major of the Second Regiment; December 22, 1889, he was elected lieutenant-colonel of the regiment, and still retains that position. September 23, 1890, the decoration of Chivalry, the highest degree in the order, was conferred on him in Hartford on the occasion of the annual field-day of the Connecticut Patriarchs Militant. October 21, 1890, he became an officer of the Grand Encampment, I. O. O. F., of the state of Connecticut. Lieut.-Col. Redway is one of the most exemplary of Odd Fellows, and is governed in all respects by the principles of the order. He has for years been an influential participant in the work of the different organizations with which he is associated, and was one of the originators of the Odd Fellow Memorial Day. He was born in Trenton, N. J., July 12, 1832, and was educated in grammar school No. 3, New York city. He removed from New York to Hartford, Nov. 16, 1848, going to Mobile, Ala., in 1853. He remained in that city not far from four years, and returned to Hartford in 1857. He engaged in the employ of the Hon. James G. Batterson as a marble engraver, and remained with him until 1879, proving himself one of the most competent men in the state in his avocation. After retiring from the employ of Mr. Batterson in 1879, he established the monument business on North Main street, where he has since remained. In 1857 he married Miss M. Elizabeth, daughter of Elijah Bibbins of Windham, and has resided in this city since his marriage. There are no children in the family. As a citizen and business man Lieut.-Col. Redway possesses the fullest confidence of the public and is deserving in every way of the positions which he has attained in life.

LUZON B. MORRIS, NEW HAVEN: Attorney-at-Law.

Hon. Luzon B. Morris was born in Newtown, April 16, 1827, and received a collegiate education at Yale, being a member of the class of 1854. His

L. B. MORRIS.

life at the outset was environed with difficulties from which men of less spirit and determination would have shrunk in despair. The means for defraying his college expenses were earned by himself, and the diploma that was awarded him by the great university of which he has been a loyal son was merited in the highest degree. Within a year of his graduation from Yale, he was elected a member of the legislature from the town of Seymour, was returned from that town in 1856, and in 1870 represented New Haven in the same body. In 1874 he was a member of the state senate from the old Fourth district, and in 1876 again represented New Haven in the house, as he has since for one or two sessions. He was the candidate of the democratic party for governor in 1888, and again in 1890, receiving at each succeeding election a large plurality of the votes cast,—and by the face of the returns a majority in 1890. But his inauguration in regular form was defeated by the republicans at the opening of the legislative session following, in January, 1891, on technicalities which are still occupying the attention of the courts at the present writing. Judge Morris is a distinguished member of the New Haven county bar and the president of the Connecticut Savings Bank of New Haven. His career has been an exemplification of the results attainable in New England by men of genius and perseverance. As a young man he

worked at the blacksmith's forge in Roxbury and in an edge tool factory at Seymour, earning the means to send him through college. In the mature years of life he has been one of the state's most trusted counselors, and the honored standard-bearer of a great political party. In every position he has been a citizen deserving the utmost honor and respect. His family consists of a wife and six children, three sons and three daughters, each of the latter being a graduate of Vassar. The maiden name of Mrs. Morris was Eugenia L. Tuttle.

GEORGE LUCIUS BEARDSLEY, BIRMINGHAM: Physician and Surgeon.

Dr. Beardsley is the son of Dr. Lucius N. Beardsley (deceased) of Milford, where he was born May 12, 1848. At the High School in that town, and

G. L. BEARDSLEY.

subsequently at the Hopkins Grammar School, New Haven, Dr. Beardsley prepared for Yale College, graduating with high honors in 1870. In 1873 he received, also, the degree of A.M., and in the same year was graduated at the Bellevue Hospital Medical College, N. Y. From 1871 until 1873, Dr. Beardsley was assistant to the distinguished surgeon, Dr. A. B. Mott, and the chief of his clinic in the " Outdoor Poor Department, Bellevue Hospital." In 1874 Dr. Beardsley commenced his practice in Birmingham, where he now resides. He was appointed assistant surgeon of the Second Regiment, C. N. G., and served five years under Colonels Smith and Graham. For the past seven years he has been post surgeon for Derby.

Dr. Beardsley is now the acting school visitor of Derby, and has been elected to the office four times. He has been a member of the town board of education thirteen years. For five years Dr. Beardsley has been the medical examiner of the town of Derby, being rated by Coroner Mix as one of his best. He is a member of the town board of health, has been twice elected a burgess of the borough of Birmingham, and is an officer of the Derby board of trade. His political preferences are republican; his religious tendencies, Methodist. As a writer he has contributed several medical essays of merit, is the medical examiner for seven life insurance companies, and president of the local medical society. His wife is a daughter of Mr. A. H. Alling, the senior member of the firm of A. H. & C. B. Alling, wooden manufacturers of Birmingham.

CHRISTIAN HAUSER, Waterbury: Clothing Merchant.

Christian Hauser was born at Wurttemberg, Germany, June 6, 1848, and was educated in the common schools of that country. He removed to the United States in 1865, and resided for a number of years in the town of Southington, where he held at one time the office of tax collector. For the last four years he has resided in Waterbury, and is at present chairman of the board of relief. In politics he is a democrat. For the last twenty years he has been engaged in the ready-made clothing business, and is the pro-

CHRISTIAN HAUSER.

prietor of the Waterbury One Price Clothing store, being one of the leading establishments in that city. Mr. Hauser has been the grand master of the German Order of Harugari of this state, and a prominent member for sixteen years. He has been the president, and is now the treasurer, of the Concordia Singing Society of Waterbury, one of the favorite German societies in Connecticut. The wife of Mr. Hauser, who was Miss Mary C. Erbe of Southington, is still living. The family includes three children.

ANDREW T. SMITH, Hartford: Superintendent of Agencies Hartford Life and Annuity Insurance Company.

Mr. Smith is a native of the city of Bridgeport, Conn., where he was born on the 15th of October, 1851. His father early removed to New Haven, and the son was educated in the schools of that city. After graduating, Mr. Smith was for a time associated with his father in manufacturing, but soon turned his attention to special work in life underwriting, in which business he has been engaged for nearly twenty years. In 1879 he became associated with the late H. P. Duclos in perfecting and intro-ducing the safety fund

A. T. SMITH.

plan of life insurance, which was shortly after adopted by the Hartford Life and Annuity Insurance Company. Upon the adoption of that plan by the company, Mr. Smith, together with Mr. Duclos, took charge of the agency department, and

18

during their administration the company's business became an exceedingly popular and progressive one. Upon the death of Mr. Duclos in 1885, Mr. Smith became sole superintendent of agencies, which position he has since held, and in which his wide experience, together with his ability, energy, and push, find full scope.

In 1872 Mr. Smith married Miss Mary E. Perkins of New Haven, and has four children, the oldest being seventeen years of age, and the youngest an infant daughter. His home is in the western part of Hartford, on Prospect avenue, a handsome suburban villa, with artistic surroundings, overlooking the capital city.

HON. JOSEPH W. ALSOP, Middletown: Physician and Farmer.

Dr. Joseph W. Alsop was born in New York city August 20, 1838, and was educated in the Yale and Columbia Scientific Schools and in the medical school of the University of New York. He is a descendant of New England stock, being the third of the name belonging in Middletown. Dr. Alsop's father was born and brought up in that city, and on his mother's side he is a Bostonian by descent. Most of his active life has been in Middletown where he has held important and responsible public trusts. He has

J. W. ALSOP.

served in both branches of the court of common council and represented the city in the general assembly, serving on the democratic side of the house in 1873. During that year he was assigned to the chairmanship of the school fund committee and discharged the duties of the position with great credit and fidelity. He was elected to the senate from the Middletown district for three consecutive terms, during two of which terms he was chairman of the committee on agriculture, the six years of continuous services beginning in 1881. As a state senator Dr. Alsop won the approval of all parties, his course from first to last reflecting honor on his district and state. He has been a member of the State Board of Agriculture since 1881, and is now a member of the state commission on the diseases of domestic animals. He is a trustee of the Connecticut Hospital for the Insane at Middletown, having held the position since 1880, and being at present the secretary of the board, and has been a director of the Connecticut Industrial School for Girls at Middletown since

1881. He is also a director of the Russell Library Company, and of the St. Luke Home in Middletown for aged and indigent women. Dr. Alsop was nominated for lieutenant-governor by the democratic state convention, which was held in this city September 16, 1890, and received a majority exceeding 500 in number at the election November 4th. The personal popularity of the Doctor, who is known and honored throughout the state, added strength to the democratic ticket. In addition to his professional life he is a special partner in the firm of C. E. Jackson & Co.; he is also one of the most successful stock breeders in the state. The truth is the Doctor is a genuine farmer and values the avocation for its own sake. At the election last fall the farmers extended to him a most gratifying support. Dr. Alsop has five children living.

[Dr. Alsop died in Fenwick, June 24, 1891, after the above sketch had been prepared.— ED.]

WILLIAM H. HAMILTON, DANIELSONVILLE: Publisher " The New England Fancier."

William Hunter Hamilton was born at Winsted January 8, 1857, and was educated in the Killingly High School. He is a printer by avocation but has

for a number of years published *The Fancier* at Danielsonville. This periodical is devoted to poultry interests and is an ably-conducted journal. Mr. Hamilton is an authority in his line of research and is prominently connected with poultry associations throughout New England, being a member of the American Poultry Association,

W. H. HAMILTON.

the Bay State, the North Middlesex, and the Quinebaug Valley Associations, and is a member of the American Langshan Club, the American Pekin Bantam Club, the American Brown Leghorn Club, and the American White Wyandotte Club, being one of the founders of the first-named of these clubs at Boston in 1887. He is known all over the country for the work which he has accomplished in behalf of the breeding and raising of poultry. Mr. Hamilton is connected with various orders, including the American Mechanics, the Ancient Order of United Workmen, and the Odd Fellows. His life has been spent at Winsted, Worcester, and Danielsonville. He is a republican in politics and is connected with the Episcopal church. His wife, who is living, was Miss Marceline P. Dumas. The family consists of three children, two sons and one daughter.

D. W. C. SKILTON, HARTFORD: President Phœnix Insurance Company.

DeWitt Clinton Skilton was born in that portion of the present town of Thomaston which was then known as Plymouth Hollow, on the 11th of January,

1839. His first American ancestor was Doctor Henry Skilton, who was born in the parish of St. Michael, Coventry, England, November 19, 1718, and sailed for America in a " gun ship," April 1, 1735, in his seventeenth year. He left the ship the same year on its arrival in Boston, boarded awhile in Roxbury, and is next heard of in Preston, Conn.,

D. W. C. SKILTON.

where he was married in 1741 to the daughter of Joseph Avery of Norwich. He removed to Southington in 1750, ten years later to Woodbury, and finally in his old age to Watertown, where he died in 1802 at the age of eighty-four. Henry Skilton was the first physician to commence the practice of medicine in Southington. He built a house in Southington which is still standing. Mr. Skilton's ancestors were among the early and most distinguished settlers of Hartford county, including such historical names as Hon. John Steel (who came to Hartford with Rev. Thomas Hooker from Massachusetts in June of the year 1636), Hon. John Wadsworth (the half brother of Captain Wadsworth who is said to have removed and concealed the Connecticut charter in the old charter oak), Sir William Southmayd, Hon. Matthew Allyn (one of the original parties to the royal charter), and Hon. John Allyn (who is called in the " History of Connecticut " " the great secretary "), William Pynchon, Esq., Governor Thomas Welles, Captain William Judd, and Timothy Judd, Esq., the last two the representatives of Waterbury in the colonial government almost continuously for forty years,— and many others of equal prominence in colonial and state history.

The subject of this sketch removed from Plymouth Hollow to Hartford in 1855, and began his business career in the dry-goods trade. In October, 1861, he first entered the insurance business as a clerk in the office of the Hartford Fire Insurance Company. In 1862 he joined Company B, of the Twenty-second Regiment, Connecticut Volunteers, and was elected second lieutenant, serving with distinction in the army until he was mustered out, having been promoted in the meantime to first lieutenant. On his return from the army he resumed his old position with the insurance company. In November, 1867, he was elected secretary of the

Phœnix Insurance Company, and remained in that capacity until August 1, 1888, when he was elected vice-president and acting president; and February 2, 1891, was elected president of the company. He ranks unquestionably among the expert underwriters of the country, and the Phœnix owes much of its success to his able management.

Mr. Skilton was married, August 8, 1865, to Miss Ann J. Andrews, daughter of Lyman Andrews of Hartford. They have had two children, a son and daughter, neither of whom is now living. In addition to his official connection with the Phœnix Insurance Company, Mr. Skilton is a director in the Hartford National Bank, a corporator and trustee of the State Savings Bank, president of the National Board of Fire Underwriters, a member of the Military Order of the Loyal Legion of the United States, a member of the Grand Army of the Republic, and of the Hartford Club. He held the office of committeeman of the West Middle school district in Hartford for several years. He is a republican in politics, and his religious connections are with the Asylum Avenue Congregational church, of which he has long been an active member.

E. K. CHRIST, New Britain: Teacher of Drawing and Penmanship.

Ernest Konrad Christ is a native of Germany, where he was born September 10, 1848. He was educated in the public schools and the gymnasium in his native country, and at the age of twenty left Germany to evade conscription for military service and came to the United States. He settled in New York, made artistic pen work a specialty, and engaged in teaching drawing and penmanship to private pupils and in the public schools. He removed to New Britain in 1871, where he has since remained, engaged in the

E. K. CHRIST.

same profession. He now holds the position of supervisor of drawing and penmanship and teacher of German in the public schools. He is often called upon to engross resolutions and testimonials, which he does in an exceedingly artistic and attractive style. Mr. Christ was a member of the New Britain court of common council in 1878, and has held other public positions. He is a member of the Odd Fellows and other benevolent societies, of the First Church of Christ in New Britain, and of the republican party. He is married, his wife being Miss Jennie B. Wilson before marriage, and they have six children.

HOXIE BROWN, Colchester: Farmer.

Hoxie Brown, who is one of the most successful and influential farmers in his locality, was born in South Kingston, R. I., Nov. 1, 1819, and resided there until he was ten years of age, when he removed to Lebanon, in this state. He was educated in the common schools of Rhode Island and Connecticut, amply preparing him for business life. Mr. Brown resided at Lebanon until 1865, when he transferred his interests to the town of Colchester, where he has since lived. In 1879 he represented that town

HOXIE BROWN.

in the general assembly, being a member of the house. His associates from New London County included such men as Senator Robert Coit and ex-Mayor George F. Tinker of New London, ex-Mayor Increase W. Carpenter and Jabez S. Lathrop of Norwich, and William T. Cook of Ledyard. Mr. Brown was associated with the democratic side of the house. He has been the recipient of many recognitions from his townsmen, and has occupied public office most of the time since he became a resident of Colchester. In early life he was connected with the state militia. His wife, Mrs. Esther Hoxie Brown, is still living at the age of sixty-nine years. Three children are also living.

EDWARD E. CULVER, Winsted: Lumber Dealer.

Edward E. Culver was born in Colebrook, April 19, 1828, and received a common school education. The first twenty years of his life were spent in Colebrook, three years were passed in Litchfield, and the remainder of his career has been identified with Winsted. He has been a member of the board of selectmen four years and of the board of water commissioners for thirteen. He is connected with the Second Congregational church and is a member of the republican party. He is also a member of the Royal Ar-

E. E. CULVER.

canum and the American Mechanics. His wife, who is still living, was Miss Mary Ann Bowker prior to marriage. There are three children, one son and two daughters, in the family.

ELI DEWHURST, Bridgeport: A Retired Contractor.

Eli Dewhurst, eldest son of James and Elizabeth Dewhurst, was born in Berry, Lancashire, England, July 24, 1824. When three years old his parents sailed from Liverpool in the *Mayflower* bound for Plymouth, Mass. After landing they immediately proceeded to Pawtucket, R. I., where the father soon found employment in the woolen mills as a superintendent of the loom department; from thence they removed to Andover and remained there until 1833, when they took the stage for Boston, and

ELI DEWHURST.

thence from Boston to the old Franklin Inn at the corner of State and Main streets, Bridgeport. Although Bridgeport had not yet become a city, the Bunnells woolen mills had made the place known throughout the trade, and here the father again obtained employment; and it was at this time that the lad Eli, then but nine years of age, formed an attachment to the place in which the greater part of his life was to be spent. From Bridgeport they moved to Zoar Bridge, and from thence to Birmingham. During these years he had learned that industry and the practice of temperance and economy were the necessary requisites to prepare for the comforts of old age. Shortly after his arrival in Birmingham he met the helpmeet of his life, Elizabeth Simpson, whom he married in 1845. In 1849 they removed to Woodbury, where Eli and Mr. Simpson purchased a farm, which they worked together; afterwards he moved to Waterbury and from there to Watertown; and notwithstanding he had become proficient in his trade as a spinner, he foresaw the future of the sewing-machine business and abandoned his trade to accept a position as screwmaker in the Wheeler & Wilson Manufacturing Company. At that time the company employed only one other person in that department. In 1856 the factory was removed to Bridgeport, and Eli, having formed an attachment for its new locality, willingly came with them. As the business increased, instead of working by the day he took the work by contract and had in his employ at times upwards of sixty employés. During his contract of twenty-five years with the company, having commenced saving from his individual hard earnings in youth, with careful investments he had accumulated sufficient in 1881 to retire from active business. Not only did his employers regret to lose his valuable and trustworthy services, but his

employés also who had worked for him many years equally regretted the change. He was a man who always demanded a fair price for his services, and also believed that the laborer was worthy of his hire, and paid his workmen liberally for their services, which the writer can personally testify to. While his early days were spent in the mill or on the farm, and no opportunity offered for educational training such as is open to the lad of to-day, yet he embraced every opportunity to acquire what self-education and training he could. He is a keen observer of human character, and has delight in assisting those who have tried to help themselves. He has served in the common council of the city, and for sixteen years served as one of the board of fire commissioners. He is a firm believer in pure and simple democracy. He is and has always been ready and willing to labor for the good and welfare of the beautiful Park City. A few years ago he built two substantial brick blocks on Harriet street, and then selected a commanding site on the corner of Barnum avenue and Noble street, facing on Washington park, where he erected a home under which roof during the summer months he enjoys the results of the labors of youth and early manhood. While not a devotee of society, yet those who enjoy his friendship can testify to the hearty and whole-souled hospitality that is dispensed to the intimates of his household. The time is approaching for them to celebrate their golden wedding; and of the many who start in life with good resolutions and promises to each other, if success attend them and they reap the golden harvest, few appreciate the same as fully as does Eli and his wife; the writer can truthfully say that they have worked together, they have lived for one another, and their greatest delight is to see each other happy.

He was made a mason in King Solomon lodge of Woodbury, but afterwards became a charter member of Corinthian lodge, No. 104, of Bridgeport. They helped the late Rev. Dr. N. S. Richardson to plant St. Paul's Protestant Episcopal parish of East Bridgeport. Eli has been an active worker in its vestry and Mrs. Dewhurst has gone along continuously doing good among the needy in a quiet unostentatious manner. They are firm believers in the pure and simple form of worship as promulgated in the book of Common Prayer, and strenuously oppose all invasions that tend toward high ritualism.

May their lives be spared for years to come so that they may enjoy many more winters in Florida, as has been their custom of late, and their pleasant and happy home in Bridgeport during the summer; and may the purity of their lives and character prove a living example of a life well spent, is the earnest desire of the writer.   W. H. C.

ALFRED T. RICHARDS, Hartford: General Agent Connecticut Mutual Life Insurance Company.

Mr. Richards was born at Pembroke, South Wales, August 28, 1843. While attending the country school of his native place, one day a strolling gypsy came into the schoolroom and sought to tell the fortunes of the teacher and pupils. She fixed her eye on young Richards, and pointing at him exclaimed: "That boy will go to America and get rich!" The prediction did not so far overcome the lad as to occasion any neglect of his studies, but it proved true so far at least as his emigrating to this country was concerned.

A. T. RICHARDS.

Mr. Richards received from his parents a careful religious training. His mother impressed upon his young mind the importance of a strict adherence to the truth, and of living a God-fearing life. The teachings and example of a Christian mother generally have a more restraining and controlling influence upon a child's life than any other agency can accomplish; and in the case of the subject of this sketch it is certain that his mother's kindly and oft-repeated precepts have been the guiding star of his early and later career.

Before coming to the States, Mr. Richards was for some time a resident of New Brunswick, where he held the office of postmaster. He came to Hartford in 1871, and was for some years engaged in mercantile pursuits, a part of the time as the business representative of the firm of Keney & Roberts. Latterly for several years he has represented the Connecticut Mutual Life Insurance Company as general agent for Connecticut, and he is also president of the Connecticut Life Underwriters' Association. As general agent of the Connecticut Life, with headquarters at the home office, he has labored most earnestly and conscientiously, and to the great satisfaction of the management. His ideas and methods are entirely in harmony with the honorable policy which distinguishes this company, and his habits of persevering industry have been rewarded with a degree of success which still further strengthens the attachments that bind him to his principals.

Mr. Richards is a republican in politics, and has acted with that party since becoming a voter. He is a member of the Asylum Avenue Congregational church, in which he holds the office of deacon. He has a wife and four children, three of whom are daughters. Mrs. Richards was Miss Laura R. Johnson prior to her marriage; a graduate of Mount Holyoke Seminary, and a most estimable lady. Mr. Richards is a man of excellent literary instincts, and an enthusiastic admirer of Carlyle, Ruskin, and Emerson. He is not unaccustomed to public speaking; his addresses on special lines of research have been particularly interesting. He is in every way a valued citizen of Hartford.

GEORGE DANIEL COLBURN, Union: Farmer and Lumberman.

George D. Colburn was born at the old homestead in Stafford, February 11, 1819, is of the fifth generation in descent from Daniel Colburn, who was one of the twelve original settlers of the town in 1718, and the seventh from Daniel Colburn who landed in Boston in 1631. He removed to New Haven with his parents in 1828; was educated in the common and private schools of that city; served three years at a trade; at nineteen was working as a journeyman; at twenty-two went into business; at

G. D. COLBURN.

twenty-five married Elizabeth, daughter of Gardner Wallace of Holland, Mass., and had four children born to them, three of whom are living, all daughters. In 1848, on account of his health, he removed to the town of Union, and engaged in farming and lumbering. He returned to New Haven in 1853, and again engaged in manufacturing. Health again failing, in 1856 he went back to the farm in Union. In 1862 (at the urgent request of his brother, the late Colonel Ledyard Colburn of the 12th Connecticut Volunteers) he went to New Orleans and took the position of superintendent of construction on the railroad running from New Orleans to Brashear City, Colonel Colburn having been detailed by General Butler as military superintendent of all the roads in the department. In 1863–64 he also assisted Colonel Colburn in building transport steamers for government use. By order of General Banks, one was finished and put on commission, and was so useful that it was kept in service longer than any other vessel of its class in the department. He experienced some exciting times and had several narrow escapes during his service on the road. He returned home just before the close of the war, and has since been, and is now, actively engaged in farming and lumbering, at the age of seventy-two. He has held numerous town offices, and has been five times honored with a seat in the general assembly — 1857, 1858, 1862, 1866, and 1870. He also had the honor of being defeated for the state senate. He is a Protestant, but no bigot: joined the Odd Fellows in 1843; is a Patron of Husbandry, and an uncompromising enemy of rum. He cast his first presidential vote for Wm. H. Harrison in 1840, and his last for his grandson, Benjamin Harrison, in 1888.

GEN. THOMAS L. WATSON, BRIDGEPORT: Banker and Broker.

Thomas L. Watson was born at Bridgeport, Dec. 13, 1847. He was educated in his native city and at the Military Institute at New Milford, with a view to West Point, but owing to a temporary physical injury this design was abandoned. The *Connecticut Guardsman* in a recent issue gives an admirable sketch of General Watson, which states that "his business career began as a clerk in the Farmers' Bank of Bridgeport; from there he went to the City National Bank, and left there to become a partner in the private

T. L. WATSON.

banking and brokerage business, with the late Daniel Hatch. The firm began Nov. 1, 1866, as Hatch & Watson, and has been continued since the death of Mr. Hatch by General Watson, as T. L. Watson & Co. General Watson extended his business to New York city in 1879, and became head of the firm of Watson & Gibson, which firm is in successful operation. General Watson has held many positions of responsibility and trust, both in Bridgeport and New York. Since the completion of the Boston & New York Air Line Railroad he has been a director and secretary of the company. The General has for several years been vice-president and a director in the Consolidated Stock and Petroleum Exchange of New York, and chairman of its finance committee. He accepted the position of paymaster on the staff of Colonel R. B. Fairchild of the Fourth Regiment, C. N. G., and was commissioned with the rank of first lieutenant, May 25, 1877. He was promoted aide-de-camp to General S. R. Smith, commanding the Connecticut National Guard, with rank of captain, July 6, 1878. He was promoted brigade-quartermaster, with rank of major, Jan. 30, 1879, and while occupying this position was elected colonel of the Fourth Regiment, C. N. G., and commissioned April 23, 1884. General Watson was tendered the position of adjutant-general of Connecticut by Gov-

ernor Lounsbury, but declined the honor, preferring his earnest work of maintaining the high standard of excellence in his regiment. In politics he is a republican, and has declined nominations to public office on several occasions. He is a member of the Union League and other leading clubs of New York and Bridgeport. He lives most of the year in a handsome residence at Black Rock, and, although part of his business connections are in New York, he is thoroughly identified with Connecticut interests. He was senior colonel of the brigade when, on March 1, 1890, he was appointed brigadier-general commanding the Connecticut National Guard, by Governor Bulkeley, and ordered to assume command, which position he has since filled, bringing to its duties that same earnest attention to all the details which has characterized his nearly fourteen years of service in the Guard. He has always at heart the interests of his command, and is constantly working to build up and promote its advancement. The press of Connecticut, during and after the last encampment at Niantic, pronounced it to be as fine a camp as the state had ever held."

General Watson was married May 4, 1874, to Miss Alice Cheever Lyon, daughter of Hanford Lyon of Bridgeport, and his family includes two children, one son and one daughter. His religious connections are as a member and vestryman in St. John's Episcopal church of Bridgeport.

CALEB HOPKINS, ELLINGTON: A Retired Builder and Public Official.

Mr. Hopkins was the youngest of eight children, born in Springfield, Mass., on the ground where the Church of the Unity now stands, July 9, 1813.

CALEB HOPKINS.

He was educated at the district school and High school of Springfield, until he was seventeen years of age, when he learned the trade of a joiner and builder, working for Colonel Ithamar Goodman of that city, a noted builder. Mr. Hopkins built the first house in Brightwood, Springfield, in 1834. In September of that year he married Miss D. H. Holton of Ellington, who

died July 31, 1877. She was a great-great-grand-daughter of Governor Roger Wolcott. He removed to Manchester in 1835, and to Ellington in 1837, since which time he has resided there. He has held various town offices, constable, school committee, justice of the peace; was postmaster for twelve years, judge of Ellington probate district, including Ellington and Vernon, for twelve consecutive years, and has been station agent on the Connecticut Central & Western road for five years. At his advanced age he does but little, occasionally writing a will or a deed, and doing light work at his trade of a joiner. He is a republican. He has had three children, but all have died.

WM. PHIPPS BLAKE, New Haven: Mining Engineer.

William P. Blake, whose residence is at Mill Rock, in the city of New Haven, was born in New York city, June 1, 1826. He is a direct descendant from William and Agnes Blake,
who sailed from Plymouth, England, and arrived in Dorchester, Mass., in 1630. He was among the first students in the department of philosophy and the arts of Yale College, and was graduated there Ph.B.— Bachelor of Philosophy — in 1852, in the same class with the present professors, Brewer and Brush, and in 1861 received the

honorary degree of M.A. from Dartmouth College. While devoting his time largely to purely scientific pursuits, and to the organization and administration of great international exhibitions, Mr. Blake has followed the occupation of mining engineer and adviser with respect to the value and the working of mining properties, in which capacity he has visited repeatedly nearly all of the great mining centers of the United States, particularly the gold and silver regions of California, Nevada, Montana, and Arizona, and has reported upon the chief gold and silver mines. In 1851 and 1852 he was mineralogist and chemist of the New Jersey Zinc Company. In 1853 he projected the mineral department of the New York International Exhibition and resigned to accept an appointment as mineralogist and geologist of the United States Pacific Railway surveys in California, and made extensive reports upon the geology of California and other portions of the West. In 1857 he made an exploration in Texas and New Mexico, and was also editor of the *Mining Magazine;* in 1860 and 1861 he visited the silver mines of the Comstock Lode and introduced the Blake crusher in the gold mills of California and silver mills of Nevada. In 1862 was appointed mining engineer to the government of Japan, and with his associate, Mr. Raphael Pumpelly, organized the first school of science in Japan and gave

lectures on geology and mining. From there he went to China and went up the Yangtse to the interior of China and returned to America by way of the Aleutian Islands and Sitka; accompanying a Russian government expedition up the Stickeen River, where he found and described several glaciers, before undescribed. Reaching San Francisco in the summer of 1863, he engaged actively in examinations of critical questions of structure upon the Comstock Lode and explored many of the principal mines then in full work. In 1865 he was appointed professor of geology and mining in the department of science of the college of California, by the organization of which the congressional grant of land to the agricultural and mechanical art college was secured to that institution, afterwards the University of California. He resigned in 1867 to go as commissioner from California to the Paris exposition of 1867, and on his return was appointed by Secretary Seward editor of the reports of the United States commissioners, which were published by the government in six octavo volumes, to which Mr. Blake was a large contributor. At the close of this work he was selected by the state department as the geologist of the Santo Domingo commission, and headed an expedition across the island of Santo Domingo. He next devoted his energies to the promotion of the great International Expedition of 1876, commencing in 1871 as commissioner alternate of Connecticut and continuing in this work as commissioner and as secretary of the Connecticut board until 1878 when he went as United States commissioner from Connecticut to the Paris Exposition of 1878, where he served on the international jury of awards, was secretary of the scientific commissioners, and made several reports, among them one upon the exhibits from the state of Connecticut, a list of awards, etc. At this exposition he received from the French government the cross of the Legion of Honor of France in recognition of his services to the mining industry and to great expositions.

Mr. Blake has been a frequent contributor to the pages of the *American Journal of Science* and to the " Proceedings of the American Institute of Mining Engineers." He was editor of, and chief contributor to, the " History of the Town of Hamden, Conn.," published after the centenary of the incorporation of the town. He is a member and correspondent of many learned societies in America and Europe. As chairman of the committee on classification of the exhibition in 1876 he became familiar with this important department of exhibitions, and was recently called by the Columbian commission to assist in the preparation of the classification for the Columbian exposition at Chicago.

Mr. Blake was married, in 1855, to Miss Charlotte

Haven Lord Hayes, daughter of Hon. Wm. A. Hayes of South Berwick, Maine, and has four sons and one daughter. He is still active as a mining engineer and mine expert after forty years of service, and has great familiarity with the mineral resources of the United States, having, before the advent of the railroad, traveled thousands of miles in the saddle and by stage coach, and since then has crossed the continent frequently, and is perhaps more generally and extensively known west than east of the Rocky Mountains.

Mill Rock, a rugged and picturesque spur of East Rock, was chosen as a place of residence by Mr. Blake in 1871, who made it accessible by well-graded roads and built the first house upon its summit before East Rock was thought of as a public park. The site affords most extensive and delightful views of New Haven harbor, Long Island sound, and the surrounding country.

D. W. PLUMB, Huntington: A Retired Manufacturer.

David W. Plumb of Shelton, in the town of Huntington, has served half a dozen sessions in the general assembly, being a member of the house fifty-three years ago. It is just half a century since he represented the old Fifth district in the state senate. He resided in Derby until 1868, and during the five sessions which he served in the house he represented that town. He was first elected in 1838, and in 1841 was honored with a seat in the senate. The subsequent years in the house were 1852, 1860, 1862, and 1864.

His colleagues during the latter year included John M. Douglas of Middletown; Seth Thomas, founder of the great clock industry at Thomaston; Ira G. Briggs of Voluntown; the lieutenant-governor, David Gallup of Plainfield; Colonel Dwight Morris of Bridgeport; O. H. Platt, the present United States senator; the late O. H. Perry of Fairfield; John F. Trumbull of Stonington, who was a leading abolitionist in his day; Roger Welles of the patent department in Washington; ex-Speaker Charles H. Briscoe of Enfield; the late President George H. Watrous of the Consolidated road; the late David B. Booth of Danbury; Senator Homer Twitchell of Naugatuck; and President Samuel E. Elmore of the Connecticut River Banking Company of Hartford, who was then the representative in the house from South Windsor.

Mr. Plumb has been one of the leading manufacturers in the Naugatuck Valley. He started in the woolen manufacturing business in Birmingham in 1836, removing to Ansonia in 1848. This plant was sold to the Slade Manufacturing Company in 1865. Mr. Plumb then removed to the new village of Shelton, establishing his home there in 1868. Of recent years he has not actively participated in manufacturing interests, though he still remains a stockholder in a number of corporations. He has been engaged from its commencement in aiding the development of the Ousatonic Water Company. He is a director in the National Bank, the Ousatonic Water Company, the Shelton Water Company, and several local manufacturing companies. He is at present interested in the development of River View Park in Shelton, and has been one of the commissioners in charge of the work since its inception. Mr. Plumb was born in Trumbull, October 13, 1808, and remained on a farm during his minority. He received a common school and academic education, preparing him for the successful business and public career which he afterwards pursued. He has been married twice. His first wife, Miss Clarissa Allen, was united with him in wedlock in 1841, and died in 1865. His second wife, who is still living, was Louise Wakelee, the marriage occurring in 1875. There are no children. Mr. Plumb has been a man of large influence in his community, and much of the manufacturing success of that locality is due to his enterprise and foresight. He is held in high esteem in Shelton, where he has resided for the past twenty-three years.

E. J. HOUGH, Wallingford: Farmer.

Elijah J. Hough was born in Wallingford, July 28, 1829, and was educated in the common schools. He is a farmer by avocation, and is at present largely interested also in peach growing. He was a member of the board of selectmen for three years, being elected for the first time in October, 1887. He has also served on the board of relief for three years. Mr. Hough is a member of the Wallingford Grange, and has been its treasurer since the date of organization in May, 1885. His wife, who was Ruth Blakeslee prior to marriage, is still living. There are also two daughters and one son. Mr. Hough is a democrat, and connected with the Baptist church.

THOMAS SEDGWICK STEELE, Hartford: Artist and Author.

Thomas Sedgwick Steele was born in Hartford, Conn., June 11, 1845. He was a descendant of John Steel (spelled in old times with only two e's), one of the founders of Hartford, who came to this country in 1635, and who was afterwards town clerk of Farmington. Mr. Steele's father, Deacon Thomas Steele, was one of the committee who called Dr. Horace Bushnell to the old North church (afterwards Park church), of which he was deacon some twenty-six years. Mr. Steele was educated at the public

T. S. STEELE.

High school while T. W. T. Curtis and Samuel M. Capron were principals; entered the jewelry business and was partner with his father in 1866, the style of the firm being T. Steele & Son, which business was continued fifty-two years.

Mr. Steele very early developed a taste for drawing and painting, and at odd hours, in and out of business, was plying the pencil or brush; in fact, at one time he almost ruined his eyes in trying to paint by gas light. His paintings have been well received by the public, and the compliment of having " hung on the line" at the National Academy of Design, New York, in 1877, was one of the results. In 1880 and 1882 Mr. Steele published two books on the woods of northern Maine, entitled " Canoe and Camera," and " Paddle and Portage," and compiled a map for their illustration, the result of his many explorations of those wilds. In 1887 he closed out the jewelry business and gave his entire time to the long-desired profession of painting. In 1890 he was honored by election to the Boston Art Club, and had his celebrated trout painting, entitled " Net Results," etched by a Boston publishing company. He has also been invited to exhibit his work before the Union League Club of New York city.

Mr. Steele has been twice married; first in 1868 to Miss Annie Eliza Smith, daughter of Captain Joseph E. Smith of Stonington; she died about six years after, leaving no children. His second marriage was October 26, 1876, to Miss Sarah Cole Goff, daughter of the late Hon. Darius Goff, a distinguished citizen and extensive manufacturer of Pawtucket, R. I. There is one child by the second marriage, Annie Lee Steele, born August 21, 1877. Mr. Steele is a member of the Park Congregational church at Hartford; was once superintendent, and for seventeen years a teacher in its Sunday-school.

JAMES HUNTINGTON, Woodbury: Attorney-at-Law.

Judge Huntington was born at South Coventry, June 4, 1833. He graduated from the State and National Law School of Poughkeepsie, in August, 1857, and was at the same time admitted to the bar of New York. Having determined to practice in Connecticut, he entered the law office of Waldo & Hyde of Tolland, read law under their direction for a year, and was admitted to the bar of Tolland county at the April term of the superior court in 1859. He immediately thereafter located in Woodbury, where he has

JAMES HUNTINGTON.

remained in active practice to the present time, being now professionally associated with Arthur D. Warner, in the firm of Huntington & Warner. He was elected judge of probate for Woodbury district in 1861, and continuously held that office for thirty years. He has held the appointment of states attorney for Litchfield county since June, 1874, and is also president of the Litchfield County Bar Association. In politics Judge Huntington is a democrat, and as such represented Woodbury in the legislature of 1874 and 1875, and was state senator from the old Sixteenth district in 1877 and 1878.

NATHANIEL C. BARKER, Lebanon: Merchant.

Mr. Barker was born in Middletown, R. I., August 31, 1838, attended the common schools, and graduated at Lebanon academy. He has been honored by his fellow-citizens by being chosen town clerk and treasurer for five years, and in 1886 was elected as a republican representative from that town to the lower house of the legislature. He is also a justice of the peace. He is prominently connected with the Baptist church, with the Masonic fraternity, and the Ancient Order of United Workmen. He is engaged in

N. C. BARKER.

mercantile pursuits, being at the head of the house of N. C. Barker & Co., in the village of Lebanon. His wife was Maria F. Sweet, and they have three children.

HON. EPHRAIM H. HYDE, Stafford: Ex-Lieutenant-Governor of Connecticut.

The name of the Hon. Ephraim H. Hyde of Stafford is familiar to the people of this state as that of a leading politician, an agricultural scientist, and

E. H. HYDE.

a thoughtful student of social economy. In every of these capacities he is no less widely than favorably known, and his many years are crowned with many honors. He was born at Stafford, on the first day of June, 1812. He married Hannah Converse Young Sept. 27, 1836. Six children were born to them, three of whom died in infancy, another at the age of four years; the other two, Ellen E., wife of Ernest Cady, of the Pratt & Cady Company, and E. H. Hyde, Jr., of the firm of Hyde & Joslyn, are now living at Hartford. His wife died Feb. 26, 1862, and, on Oct. 19, 1869, he married Miss Mary S. Williams of Hartford, who now survives.

Attendance at the district school in his native town, and about six weeks of study at the academy in Monson, Mass., comprised his entire school education. His boyhood was passed in the manner common to the boys of that time; work on the farm, accompanied by general service in an old-time hotel connected with the farm and known as the half-way stage station between Worcester and Hartford, and about four months as a stage driver between Stafford and Sturbridge, filled up the years between school and the commencement of his active business life. He took an efficient and active interest in the Universalist Society of Stafford, serving therein as sexton, organist, and leader of the choir for fifteen years. Entering a country store as a clerk in his eighteenth year, he became proprietor of the same in his twenty-first year, and from that time on he has been closely identified with the business interests of the town. He was interested in a blast furnace business for about eight years; in his twenty-ninth year he was the chief promoter of a cotton mill at Stafford Springs; he was for many years interested in the business of manufacturing satinets, as one of the firm of Converse & Hyde, and he has been actively engaged in many other industrial enterprises. His energies have been devoted principally, however, to promoting the agricultural interests of the state and to breeding blooded stock.

About the year 1842, having become the owner of two or three large farms, all of which he retained until within a few years, and most of which he still owns, he commenced the careful breeding of stock from imported and native cattle, and thus entered upon a course that was to make his name familiar as a household word to the leading agriculturists throughout the country. He began with Devons, and afterwards experimented with Ayrshires, Durhams, and Jerseys; but believing the Devons to be the best adapted to this part of the country, he applied himself to the scientific selection and breeding of that class, and as a result he greatly improved the stock and produced herds of rare beauty and excellence, the winners of many a sweepstake medal and prize. He will be known in the years to come as the pathfinder for Devons in this country. Animals from his herds have gone to all parts of the country, and it can be said with truth that the improvement of the stock in his native state is owing in a large measure to his care and wisdom as a breeder of pure-blooded Devons.

He early became concerned in the general agricultural interests of the state, and has been an active and zealous participant in all movements for their protection and advancement. Fully comprehending the needs of the farmers, and also the necessity of arousing them to a realization of the benefits to be derived by the adoption of more intelligent and scientific methods of farming, he zealously devoted the best years of his life to the interests of agriculture, giving his time, money, and talents without stint, and bringing to the service an indomitable will and energy that prosecuted its aims with a patient industry that was untiring. It was largely owing to his influence and enterprise that the Tolland County Agricultural Society was organized in 1852. He was its president from its organization to 1860, and again from 1864 to 1868; and Hyde Park at Rockville was thus named in his honor, and in recognition of his services to the society. He was president of the Connecticut State Agricultural Society from 1858 to 1881, vice-president of the New England Agricultural Society from its beginning, vice-president of the State Board of Agriculture from its organization in 1866 to 1882; and was chosen again in 1890, and is now vice-president; chairman of the commissioners on diseases of domestic animals for thirty years, which office he still holds; president of the American Breeders' Association from 1863 until it resolved itself into sections for each breed; president of the Connecticut Valley Agricultural Association, comprising Connecticut, Massachusetts, New Hampshire, and Vermont; corporator of the Connecticut Stock Breeders' Association; vice-president of the Dairyman's Association; chairman of the committee to publish the first volume of the American Herd Book; president of the Tolland County East Agricultural Society, from its organization in 1870 to 1876; and one of the trustees and vice-president of the Storrs School, a position which he still retains. He had long been in favor of a school in which the science of agriculture should be taught, and was one of the first two persons who consulted the Storrs brothers in regard to the project of establishing the school at Mansfield. The scheme met his approval; and that the plan was finally adopted, and that the school has been able to maintain itself against the numerous attacks that have been made upon it by friends and foes alike, is largely owing to his indefatigable efforts and earnest support. At a meeting of the trustees in 1889 he was chosen one of the building committee to erect the beautiful and commodious structures which have been completed at about the estimated cost of $50,000.

His labors to secure reform in the management of prisons and houses of correction have been extensive and persistent. He is one of the founders and directors of the Prisoners' Friend Association, and a director, also, of the Industrial School for Girls; and has been more or less active in the direction of the state board of education, especially in 1867, 1868, and 1869.

When the United States Agricultural Convention met in Washington some time since, he attended as delegate from the New England Agricultural Association.

He has also been called to numerous other offices by the citizens of his town and state. He was county commissioner for Tolland County in 1842-43; a member of the house of representatives from Stafford in 1851-52; a delegate to the national democratic convention at Baltimore; and in the presidential campaign of 1860 he took a prominent part, identifying himself with the state rights faction, whose head and candidate was Breckinridge, and was made an elector on their ticket. He was a state senator and president *pro tem.* of the senate in 1876 and 1887, and lieutenant-governor in 1867 and 1868. While occupying the latter position the office of commissioner of agriculture at Washington became vacant, and he was strongly pushed for the place, every member of the legislature then in session, irrespective of their party affiliation, signing the petition, and nearly all the state delegation in congress. He took an earnest and lively interest in the Connecticut Experimental Station, and was chosen vice-president of the board of control at its organization March 29, 1879, and still retains the office. He presided at the one hundred and fiftieth anniversary of the primitive organization of the Congregational church and society in Franklin, Conn., Oct. 4, 1868. He was president of the Tolland centennial celebration in 1876, delivering the opening address, and he has occupied many other offices of more or less importance.

In all his public life, covering a period of nearly half a century, his aim has been to subserve the interests of the state, and not the shadow of a suspicion rests on his honored name. His conduct, motives, and methods have been straightforward and honorable, and his record is one of which he may well be proud.

Ex-Lieutenant-Governor Hyde has filled a large place in the state, but his name will be best known as that of the eminent breeder, who by his enlightened efforts materially assisted in raising the farming industry of the state to a higher level, and in vastly increasing the value of its dairy farms and stock.

In the course of years he is now aged; but few are the men of half his age who are to be compared with him in activity and endurance. Always strictly temperate in his habits, he has saved himself from the infirmities that so often overtake public men in their declining years. With a tall and slender form, a well-bred face, a flowing white beard and the graceful courtesy of an elder day, he presents a striking figure. Affable and agreeable, fond of society and companionship, kind and considerate of others, with a pleasant smile and a cheerful greeting always, he has as large a circle of personal acquaintances and friends as any man in the state, and no one is more highly esteemed.

NELSON A. BROWN, North Stonington; Farmer.

Mr. Brown is a native of North Stonington, and was born Feb. 16, 1847. He received a common district school education and has followed the business of farming in North Stonington except for two years, when he resided in Westerly, R. I. He has always acted with the republican party, politically, and has held the office of selectman and assessor for a number of years, his re-election for ten successive years showing the esteem in which he is held by his fellow-townsmen. He is generally recognized as a man

N. A. BROWN.

of strict integrity, sound judgment, quick perception, and executive ability. He is a prominent member of the Baptist church and was chosen deacon at the age of twenty-four years. He was superintendent of the Sunday-school for three years, during which time the school was prospered greatly. His wife was Louisa K. Crary, and they have one son.

HON. SAMUEL FERDINAND WEST, Columbia: Farmer.

Mr. West was born in Columbia, Conn., December 13, 1812. He was the son of Colonel Samuel West, who was a lineal descendant of Francis West,  who came from England and settled in Duxbury, Mass., in the early settlement of New England, and died 1694, aged eighty-six. His mother was Rebecca Little, a lineal descendant of Thomas Little, a lawyer, who came from Devonshire, England, and settled in Plymouth 1630. He received his education principally in the common district school, with the exception

S. F. WEST.

of one term in a select school; labored on his father's farm during the farming season, and taught district schools during the winter, from the winter of 1830–31, to the winter of 1835–36. In November 1835, he left home and the state of Connecticut and went westward into Ohio and made a stopping point at Delaware in that state. In the spring of 1836 he joined a partnership with Nathaniel W. Little of that place, under the firm name of Little & West, in mercantile business, which business he pursued until the spring of 1841. In the fall of 1841, at the earnest solicitation of his father, he returned to Columbia, Conn., and went on to and managed the ancestral farm where he was born and where he still resides. This farm has been unincumbered in the West family since 1773. Tilling the soil and the cultivation of fruit has been his principal occupation. September 28, 1837, he married Miss Charlotte Porter of Columbia, who is yet living; have had eight children, three only of whom are now living, Samuel Brainard West, who now manages the farm, and two daughters who are married and living in Providence, R. I.

Mr. West has been selectman, justice of the peace, and has held other minor town offices. In the spring of 1847 he was chosen to represent the twenty-first senatorial district in the Connecticut legislature, and faithfully performed the duties of that position in the Connecticut general assembly during its session in May, 1847. He was county commissioner for Tolland county in 1855 and 1856; had a large share in the oversight of the building of the present county jail at Tolland. In December, 1864, he was appointed assistant assessor for the ninth division of the first district of Connecticut, which position he filled until July, 1868. This division embraced the south part of Tolland county, including the town of Willington. He has been

president of the Tolland county Agricultural Society and a member of the State Board of Agriculture. Has been a director in the Willimantic Savings Institute, and a trustee in that institution for many years, a place he still occupies. Politically, in the early part of his life, he was an unwavering whig; ever since the formation of the republican party he has been identified with that party. He and his wife, then Miss Charlotte Porter, united with the Congregational church in Columbia in 1831; in 1838 removed their relationship to the Presbyterian church in Delaware, Ohio. In 1842 returned to the membership of the Congregational church in Columbia.

Mr. West has been a live, active, stirring, energetic citizen, interested in all the advancements and improvements of the times.

REV. EDWARD PAYSON HAMMOND, Hartford: Congregational Clergyman.

Edward Payson Hammond, son of Elijah and Esther Griswold Hammond, was born in Ellington, Tolland county, Conn., in 1831. At the age of  seven his parents removed to Vernon Centre, which was his residence thenceforth until he removed to Hartford, but a few years ago. Mr. Hammond's paternal American ancestor was Thomas Hammond, who came to America in 1635, and settled in Hingham, Mass. His mother was a descendant of George Griswold, of Kenilworth, Warwickshire, England.

E. P. HAMMOND.

Connecticut received two governors from this family — Matthew Griswold, who held the office from 1784 to 1786; and Roger Griswold, who was the incumbent in 1811, and died in office, serving one year and five months. It will thus be seen that on both father's and mother's side Mr. Hammond has some of the best New England blood in his veins.

Rev. E. P. Hammond is a graduate of Williams College, Mass. After his graduation he studied theology for a while in New York city, then finished his studies in the seminary of the Free Church at Edinburgh, Scotland. While a student at Edinburgh he was invited to hold meetings in a vacant church six miles distant. Here he labored so earnestly, zealously, and wisely, that there was a great religious awakening; hundreds were converted. Ministers in Edinburgh, Glasgow, Aberdeen, and other cities heard of this wonderful revival; they recognized in this youthful evangelist a man called of God to a special work; they invited him to their pulpits; they encouraged him to hold special services, at which they assisted him, in halls that would hold immense audiences. Thousands and tens of thousands, who never entered the churches, were drawn to these meetings, and many of them became Christians. After laboring thus two years in Scotland, going only where the ministers and churches invited him to go, not setting himself up as a leader, but yielding to the urgency of the ablest and best men of the land, that he should use the gift with which God had endowed him, in the special department of ministerial work to which he was so manifestly called, he returned to his native land. Here his experience was the same. Wherever he went the people thronged to hear him, and multitudes were brought to Christ. After five years of evangelistic labor in New England and the Middle States he again went abroad. He has spent six years and a half on the other side of the Atlantic, having been there at three different times. In 1856 he, with his wife, visited the Holy Land, and at that time he wrote Sketches of Palestine. Since his return from Europe the second time he has held meetings in towns and cities from Minneapolis in Minnesota, to Galveston, Texas; and from the shores of Lake Erie to Denver, among the mountains. He has gone to none of these places without a special invitation. Wherever he has gone the various evangelical churches have been drawn together in brotherly love and cordial coöperation, and in every place conversions have followed his labors, not a few of the subjects being men and women who previously had been notoriously wicked. One of the most successful of Mr. Hammond's series of meetings was in St. Louis. The largest halls in the city were crowded day after day, and one of the pastors afterwards stated that over five thousand persons were added to the churches of St. Louis as the result of these special services. Mr. Hammond was for nine weeks in San Francisco, holding about two hundred meetings, and speaking to more than two hundred thousand people. His efforts there were blessed abundantly.

And so the good work has gone forward for more than thirty years, and eternity alone will reveal its extent and blessedness. The winter of 1890–91 Mr. Hammond spent in evangelical work in Washington, D. C.; the previous winter he was in the mining districts of Colorado — two fields in as strong a contrast as can well be imagined, but neither without a harvest. Mr. Hammond has written about a hundred tracts and books, most of which have been published both in this country and in Great Britain. Numbers of them have been translated into various languages. They are usually distributed judiciously among his audiences, and thus often become a valuable auxiliary to his oral work.

Mr. Hammond is a gentleman of marked personality. He has a nervous temperament, with quick observation, keen perceptions, and intuitive judgment. Physically, as well as mentally, he is alert and active, possesses a thoroughly vigorous constitution, an erect and portly figure, with pleasing and impressive features. He is esteemed at home and abroad no less for his high personal traits than for his distinguished services in the advancement of Christianity throughout the world.

GEORGE W. BURR, Middletown: President of the Middlesex County National Bank.

George W. Burr was born in Haddam in this state, April 12, 1816, the son of a farmer, to which calling his early years were largely devoted, while acquiring his education at the common schools of his native town. At the age of seventeen he passed a successful examination before the board of education in Middletown, where he was for a time employed in teaching. Two years later he engaged in selling books by subscription in the eastern counties of New York state, and at the age of twenty went to Charleston,

S. C., and thence to Augusta, Ga., spending one year in southern Georgia in the book trade. Returning north on the decease of his father, he arranged the settlement of the ancestral estate, and afterwards returned south, traveling and selling books in most of the southern states. He subsequently came back to Connecticut and located at Middletown, where he became a director of the Meriden Bank, trustee of the Middletown Savings Bank, and director of the Middlesex County Bank. He was elected president of the Middletown Savings Bank, and during his incumbency of the office, covering a period of twenty years, the deposits in that institution increased under his wise and careful administration from $1,700,000 to $6,000,000. He was afterwards elected president of the Middlesex County National Bank, which position he now holds, having been on its board of directors for thirty years. He is also president of the Connecticut Brown Stone Quarry Company of Cromwell, and a director of the Middlesex Mutual Assurance Company of Middletown. His religious connections are with the South Congregational church of Middletown; politically he is a republican. He married Miss Annie E. Sage of Cromwell, and they have two children, George B. and Annie M. Mr. Burr is a gentleman of mature judgment in financial affairs, and has proved a most successful manager and able counselor for the various institutions with which he has been or still is officially connected.

WILLIAM B. CLARK, HARTFORD: Vice-President Ætna Insurance Company.

Vice-President Clark is the senior insurance officer in this city in years of actual service with the Hartford companies. He was born here, June 29, 1841, and was educated in the old North school, completing his course at the New Britain high school and at N. L. Gallup's College Green school in this city. The latter institution was located on Trinity street, opposite Trinity College, and fitted students for a collegiate course of study. The father of Vice-President Clark was the late A. N.

W. B. CLARK.

Clark, one of the proprietors of the *Hartford Courant* prior to the war, the name of the firm being A. N. Clark & Co. After spending one year in the *Courant* business office, Mr. Clark, the subject of this sketch, became a member of the clerical corps of the Phœnix Insurance Company in 1857. August 27, 1863, he was elected secretary, and remained with the company until December 1, 1867, when he was elected assistant secretary of the Ætna. The latter position was retained under President Hendee through a period of nearly twenty-one years. Assistant Secretary Clark became familiar with the vast detail connected with the Ætna's business, and was regarded with the utmost confidence and trust by his chief, who was one of the most successful insurance managers Hartford has known. The demise of President Hendee, September 4, 1888, necessitated a number of changes in the administration of the company. Mr. Clark was advanced to the vice-presidency, September 26, 1888, receiving the unanimous vote of the board of directors for the position. As vice-president of the company his course has been characterized by ability and judgment of the highest order, entitling him to a foremost place among insurance managers in New England. Vice-President Clark occupies a number of important offices in business and public institutions in the city. He was elected a director of the City Bank January 14, 1879; director in the

Travelers Insurance Company July 6, 1875; trustee in the Mechanics Savings Bank July 18, 1883; and a director of the Retreat for the Insane April 10, 1890. He is also a member of the corporation of the Hartford hospital. April 5, 1880, he was elected a member of the board of aldermen from the Third ward, and served two years in that position. He was the aldermanic chairman of the ordinance committee, the mayor holding the chairmanship *ex officio*. At the conclusion of his term in the board of aldermen he was appointed a member of the board of water commissioners, and has held that office for nine years, being one of the ablest members of that commission. Vice-President Clark is a member of the First Baptist church in this city, and has been clerk of the society and member of the society's committee for twenty-five years. He is also a member of the Connecticut Historical Society. He values the fact that he was one of the original Wide Awakes as the most interesting reality connected with the first years of his citizenship. In point of accuracy, he had not attained his majority when he became an active participant in that noted organization. It is not necessary to add that his republicanism has as true a ring in it now as in the great presidential campaign of 1860. Vice-President Clark was married May 13, 1863, his wife, who is still living, being Miss Caroline H. Robbins, daughter of the late Philemon F. Robbins. The family includes three daughters. Two sons have died. As a citizen, as well as the representative of great business interests, Mr. Clark has but few equals in the community. The people of Hartford regard him with the highest esteem and honor.

HEZEKIAH SPENCER SHELDON, SUFFIELD.

Mr. Sheldon was born in Suffield June 23, 1820, and was educated in the common schools and in the Connecticut Literary Institute. He has given

H. S. SHELDON.

a large amount of time to research concerning the history of Suffield, and is one of the best-informed men concerning local history in the state. His work appears in the "History of Hartford County," and in independent volumes, showing the thoroughness and reliability of his researches. His library of old and rare books and town histories is extensive and valuable.

Mr. Sheldon has held numerous places of trust and responsibility in Suffield, of which town he is and has long been one of the best-esteemed and leading citizens. He represented that town in the general assembly in 1858, 1881, 1887, and again in 1889. In 1881 he was a member of the committee on banks, where he proved himself, as always, an able and conscientious legislator. During the session of 1887, the first biennial session, he served with marked ability on the judiciary committee and as chairman of the state library committee — in both of which positions he was continued when called to the legislative duties of the succeeding session in 1889. In whatever capacities he has served the state, or in local affairs, his duties have been performed with fidelity and success. His personal character and honorable record entitle him to the high esteem with which he is regarded by his associates in public service, and by his fellow-citizens without distinction of political party or religious sect.

EDWARD CHARLES NEWPORT, M.D., MERIDEN; Physician and Surgeon.

Dr. E. C. Newport was born in Halle, Germany, July 1, 1837. His early paternal ancestors were Englishmen, who during the Cromwellian era drifted from England into Holland, and thence into Germany. His mother's ancestry dates back to Martin Luther's family. She died when the subject of this sketch was six years of age. Dr. Newport was one of a family of four brothers, the others being Augustus, William, and Otto. Their father was a political agitator and participator in the revolutionary disturb-

ances of 1848, who, on account of this, was compelled to forsake his native country. He came to America, taking with him his sons Augustus and William, leaving Edward and Otto in the care of an uncle and aunt in Halle. Edward was kept at school quite closely from his sixth to his fifteenth year. After that he pursued the study of lithography very successfully, and combined therewith the study of music, anatomy, and physiology, taking great delight also in mastering the English language and familiarizing himself with its literature. In 1859 he emigrated to America, and the December after his arrival in this country he went to Windsor Locks, where his brother Augustus was already employed in the Medlicott Mills; and, as he had no pecuniary resources, he engaged as a cutter in the same establishment with his brother, remaining in that position for nearly two years. On the first of January, 1861, he was married to Miss Carrie Jeanette Norton of Suffield, who died in

February, 1875, after fourteen years of happy wedded life. By this marriage there were four children, namely: Mary, now Mrs. Dr. S. D. Otis, residing in Meriden; Herbert, who is a druggist in the same city; Belle, at present studying music in the conservatory of Xavier Scharwenka in Berlin, Germany; and Gussie, who is at home in Meriden. There is a fifth child, Alice, a daughter, by a second marriage.

In 1862, when the call for nine-months volunteers was issued by President Lincoln, Dr. Newport and several of his personal friends enlisted in Company C, Twenty-fifth regiment, C. V., in which company he was made a corporal, and afterwards promoted to be chief bugler of the regiment. January 13, 1863, he was ordered to general headquarters as brigade bugler, with rank of sergeant. He went through all the skirmishes and battles in which the brigade was engaged, including the sanguinary engagements at Irish Bend on the Mississippi, until the investment of Port Hudson by the Union army. On May 27, 1863, after the first general assault on the fort had been made, he was taken sick, sent to the hospital, and after more than two months of suffering was sent home, arriving contemporaneously with his regiment, whose term of service had expired. On regaining his health Dr. Newport began the study of medicine, and attended the New York Homœopathic Hospital College until 1868, when he graduated from that institution with the degree of M.D. He was more or less in practice, however, from 1865 to 1868 as assistant to Dr. Pierson of South Hadley Falls and Holyoke, Mass., whose delicate health and advanced age largely incapacitated him from the active practice of his profession. In the latter part of 1868 Dr. Newport went to California, where he remained nearly a year; but within that period came east again, and settled in Meriden, his present home. Here he established at once an extensive practice, which he has maintained to the present time. In June, 1874, he visited Germany and England, spending about three months abroad. The same year he was elected alderman of the city of Meriden, which position, and that of president of the board, he retained one year. In 1875 he was elected medical director of the state encampment of the Grand Army of the Republic, which office he held through the regular term. Since that he has never sought or accepted any office, his large and increasing practice demanding all his time and attention. Having lost his wife by death, as before stated, in February, 1875, Dr. Newport was again married on June 23, 1886, to Miss Ann Ellsworth Horton, daughter of Eli Horton of Windsor Locks, a celebrated inventor and manufacturer. Mrs. Newport is a lady of many accomplishments, of Puritan ancestry, and a lineal descendant in the eighth generation from John Alden and Priscilla (Mullens) Alden of primitive New England celebrity, whose romantic courtship and marriage have become a familiar story to every descendant of the Puritans. Mrs. Newport's father's family, the Hortons, is an ancient and representative family of New England, prominent in political and civil affairs ever since the first settlement of the colonies.

Dr. Newport is connected with the following Masonic orders: Apollo Lodge, No. 59, of Suffield; Meridian Chapter, No. 8, O. E. S., Keystone Chapter, No. 27, R. A. M., Hamilton Council, No. 22, R. and S. M., St. Elmo Commandery, Knights Templars — all of Meriden; and Pyramid Temple, A. A. O. N. M. S., of Bridgeport. He is also a member of Merriam Post, No. 8, G. A. R.; Teutonic Lodge, No. 95, I. O. O. F.; Montowese Tribe, No. 6, I. O. R. M.; Silver City Lodge, No. 3, A. O. U. W., and the Meriden Scientific Association — all of Meriden. He also holds the office of medical examiner for a number of life insurance companies and societies.

J. M. BAILEY, DANBURY. Journalist; Proprietor "Danbury News."

James Montgomery Bailey is one of the most popular writers in this state. For years his humorous productions have been the delight of circles far

J. M. BAILEY.

beyond the boundaries of Connecticut, and his name is a household word throughout the country. Mr. Bailey is not only an admirable humorist, but he is also a first-class business man. At the meeting of the state board of trade in January, 1891, he was elected first vice-president, and he holds the position of president of the Danbury board. He was born in Albany, N. Y., Sept. 25, 1841, and received a public school education. He began business life as a carpenter's apprentice. In 1860 he removed to Danbury and in 1862 enlisted in the Seventeenth Connecticut regiment, serving in that command for three years. He is a prominent Mason, belonging to all the bodies in the order, from the blue lodge to the mystic shrine. He was the first president of the Danbury Hospital Association and is a member of the executive committee of the Danbury Relief Society. Mr. Bailey is one of the most active and influential citizens of the new city of Danbury and is thoroughly interested in its progress and prosperity. He is connected with the Baptist church. His wife, who is still living, was Miss Kate D. Stewart prior to her marriage.

ORLANDO C. OSBORN, OXFORD: Farmer.

Orlando C. Osborn was a member of the legislature in 1889, representing his town on the democratic side of the house. He has been a member of

O. C. OSBORN.

the board of selectmen, justice of the peace, and school visitor, and is still the incumbent of the latter position. He is a farmer by occupation, a member of the grange, and a progressive manager, being one of the first in his locality to adopt farming improvements. He is a member of Morning Star Lodge, No. 47, F. and A. M., of Seymour. The wife of Mr. Osborn was Miss Idella J. Andrew prior to marriage and is still living. The family includes two sons and two daughters. Mr. Osborn is connected with the Episcopal church. He was born in Oxford March 23, 1847, and received a common and high school education. Most of his life has been spent on the farm that has been in the family for generations. It is crossed by the New York & New England road, the station being located on a portion of the estate that has descended to him.

THOMAS NEARY, NAUGATUCK: Wholesale and Retail Merchant.

Thomas Neary is a native of Ireland, having been born in county Kilkenny, April 1, 1833. At a very early age he left home and friends in search of fortune, with scarcely a dol-

THOMAS NEARY.

lar in his pocket, and no reliance on anybody or anything except his own clear head and strong hands. He first went to England, but afterwards sailed for America, landing in New York. Almost immediately after his arrival in this country he settled in Naugatuck, Conn., and at the age of twenty-one he was married. In 1858 he rented a small house in Naugatuck, and started a retail trade in spirituous and malt liquors. By careful management and strict attention to business he built up a prosperous trade, and was soon able to open a wholesale department. The small house which he rented became his own property, and in due time all the surrounding ones were his also, as well as the land connected therewith. His trade increased, and he may be said to have had thirty-three years of uninterrupted prosperity. He has been all the time acquiring additional real estate, until now he is the largest individual taxpayer in Naugatuck. His present place of business is perhaps the finest and most elaborate of its kind in the state, occupying a handsome block in the center of the town. By its side, and a little in the rear, stands the old building in which as a poor young man he first began business. It is preserved as a memento of his humble beginnings, and visitors often note and comment upon the contrast between the two, and the change which thirty-three years have wrought under Mr. Neary's skillful management. From a pecuniary standpoint, his life has indeed been a marvelous success.

Mr. Neary is a democrat in politics, and exerts a powerful influence in his party. He has never sought public office, preferring to remain in the ranks. He is an earnest and generally a triumphant worker for the success of the party and the candidate in whose behalf his influence and labors are enlisted.

ALBERT BARROWS, WILLIMANTIC: Farmer.

Albert Barrows was born in Mansfield, June 27, 1825, and received a common school education. With the exception of four years in Norwich and two in this city, his life has been spent in Tolland county. He has been engaged in the meat business and farming as an avocation. Mr. Barrows was one of the original members of the Putnam Phalanx, and served fourteen years in the battalion. He has been married three times. The first and second wives, Mary J. and Angeline M. Slate, were daughters of

ALBERT BARROWS.

the late Deacon N. Slate of Mansfield. The third, Fanny M. Case, was the daughter of the late Luther Case of Norwich. She died on the 4th of April of the present year. There are three children, one son and two daughters. One daughter resides in Lowell, Mass., and the other at Mansfield. Mr. Barrows is a member of the Baptist church, and is a republican in politics, having united with that political organization after the repeal of the Missouri compromise. Prior to that act he was a democrat. In 1857 he represented the town of Mansfield in the legislature. He was a member of the school board in Windham for

nine years, and truant officer for the same period; assessor of the town and borough for fourteen years; and has occupied other minor offices. His father, the late Deacon Samuel Barrows, was one of the first settlers of Willimantic.

JAMES U. TAINTOR, HARTFORD: Secretary Orient Insurance Company.

James Ulysses Taintor, fourth son of Ralph Smith and Phœbe Higgins (Lord) Taintor, is a native of the town of Pomfret, Windham county, Connecticut. He was born October 23, 1844. He traces his ancestry to Captain Josiah Burnham, who was master of the brig-of-war *Oliver Cromwell* of revolutionary memory; and to Thomas Lord, one of the first proprietors of Hartford, from whose family the section of the city familiarly known as "Lord's Hill" received its name. The American ancestors

J. U. TAINTOR.

of Mr. Taintor on both sides were Pilgrims; and one of them, Rev. Ralph Smith, is mentioned in colonial history as having preached before Governor Winthrop and Governor Bradford on the occasion of an important conference between these notable representatives of Massachusetts and Plymouth colonies.

Mr. Taintor's stay in the town of his nativity was brief, for in his fourth year the family moved to Colchester, where he spent his early years in solving the mysteries of the district school. Later he prepared for college in the reputable Bacon academy of Colchester, and entered Yale in September, 1862, graduating from the university in 1866. The summer before his graduation he was elected assistant clerk of the Connecticut House of Representatives — a unique experience for a college student — was clerk of the House the succeeding year, and in 1868 was called to the clerkship of the Senate. In January, 1869, he became interested in the principal fire insurance agency in the city of Meriden. In July of the same year he became adjuster of losses for the Phœnix Insurance Company of Hartford, and continued in that position until the autumn of 1881, when he was called to the home office of the company. He remained in the service of the company until June, 1888, when he became secretary of the Orient Insurance Company, which position he now holds.

Mr. Taintor is an earnest republican, and during periods of his life has been thoroughly active in political affairs. At the invitation of Mayor Root in 1888 he became, and still is, a member of the Board of Street Commissioners of Hartford, but holds no other public office. He is married and has two children, both sons. Mrs. Taintor was Miss Isabel Spencer, of Hartford.

JONATHAN FLYNT MORRIS, HARTFORD: President Charter Oak National Bank.

Jonathan F. Morris, fifth son of Edward Morris of Belchertown, Mass., and of the seventh generation from ancestor Edward Morris of Waltham

J. F. MORRIS.

Holy Cross Abbey, in the county of Essex, England, and Roxbury, Mass., was born at "Kentfield Place" in Belchertown, March 20, 1822. After the death of his father, in 1824, he lived with his maternal uncle, Rufus Flynt, in Monson, until 1836. In April of that year he went to New York city, where he attended school and filled clerkships until October, 1843, when he went to sea as supercargo of a vessel engaged in the Haytian trade. He spent most of the four succeeding years in commercial establishments at Port de Paix and Gonaives; but in the autumn of 1847, having become reduced in health by an attack of yellow fever, which was followed by a relapse, he was compelled to seek a change of climate, and returned to New England. He soon recovered his health, and obtained a situation in the cashier's department of the Western Railroad — now Boston & Albany — at Springfield, where he remained until March, 1850, when he was offered and accepted the position of teller in the Tolland County Bank of Tolland, in this state. He remained with this institution until chosen cashier of the Charter Oak Bank of Hartford, September 13, 1853. He entered upon the duties of his new position on the first opening of the bank, October 3, 1853, and remained in it until chosen its president, September 3, 1879, which latter position he continues to fill.

In politics Mr. Morris has been a whig and a republican. With the latter party he continues to act. He was one of the nine persons who met in Hartford, February 4, 1856, to take the first step toward the formation of the republican party in Connecticut. Of these nine gentlemen only three are now living, viz.: General Hawley, now United States senator; Judge Shipman of the United States district court, and the subject of this sketch. In

educational affairs Mr. Morris has always manifested a lively interest, and during his residence in Hartford has borne an active part. He is, and has been for years, treasurer of the Wadsworth Athenaeum, treasurer of the Hartford Theological Seminary, and treasurer of the West Middle school district. He is a member of the Connecticut Historical Society, and for many years has been its treasurer also. In business matters, additionally to his duties as president and director of the Charter Oak National Bank, he has filled the position of trustee for the Society of Savings on Pratt street for thirty-four years, and has been for thirty years an auditor of the same institution. He is also a director in the National Fire Insurance Company, and one of the original members of the Cedar Hill Cemetery Association. He has during the same time served as trustee or executor in the settlement of several important estates. He was one of the founders of the Connecticut Society Sons of the American Revolution. He is a member of the Asylum Hill Congregational church.

Mr. Morris married May 8, 1855, Harriet, youngest daughter of Samuel Hills of Springfield, Mass. She was for many years an invalid, and died March 3, 1879, leaving two daughters. The elder, Anna, married Rev. Alfred Tyler Perry of Ware, Mass.; and the younger, Alice, is the wife of Rev. Charles Smith Mills of Andover, Mass.

CHARLES B. SMITH, HARTFORD: Senior Partner Smith, Bourn & Co., Manufacturers Harness and Saddlery.

Charles B. Smith was born in Hartford July 31, 1811. His parents were Normand and Mary Boardman Smith; Normand Smith was the fifth

C. B. SMITH.

son of William, who had eight children. The father of William was John Smith, who was born in Liverpool, England, in 1680; married to Anna Allwood of Glastonbury, England, in 1722, and emigrated to America the same year, settling in Boston. In 1726 he moved to Hartford, but died in Liverpool, England, in 1729. He had three children — George, Mary, and William. The subject of this sketch was the ninth child of a family of fifteen children. One brother was Deacon Thomas Smith, who died in Hartford in 1882. Rev. James Allwood Smith, who died in Unionville in this state the same year, was also his brother; and another was Doctor

Andrew Kingsbury Smith, surgeon in the United States army for many years until he was retired with the rank of colonel in February, 1890.

Charles B. Smith was educated at Lenox, Mass., and at Hartford. As early as December 1, 1833, when, at the age of twenty-two, he embarked in business, becoming a member of the firm of Smith, Hubbard & Co., at New Orleans, which was established as a branch of the Hartford house in 1816 — the oldest, or one of the oldest business houses in the southwest, then known as Smith & Bigelow. A few years after engaging in business at New Orleans, his interest commenced in the present Hartford firm of Smith, Bourn & Co., then T. Smith & Co., where he has for many years been the senior partner. This firm is one of the oldest engaged in the saddlery business in the United States,— dating from 1794. The files of Hartford papers published during the early days of the firm, contain their advertisement, in which the location of the establishment is described as "six yards from the state house." In 1870 Mr. Smith withdrew from the New Orleans house of Smith & Brother, as the firm was then styled. He had previously opened a branch of the Hartford house in New York city, at No. 10 Old Slip, in 1842, under the name of T. Smith & Co.; afterward located at 101 Maiden Lane, also on Beekman street, and afterward on Broadway. Of late years its location has been at No. 40 Warren street, under the firm name of C. B. Smith & Co., succeeded later by Smith, Worthington & Co., which firm is still actively engaged in business.

Mr. Smith has twice married. His first wife, to whom he was married November 5, 1844, was Miss Frances M. Humphrey, daughter of Lemuel Humphrey of Hartford. After her decease he married, October 3, 1855, Miss Eliza A. Thayer of Westfield, Mass., whose father was Dea. Lucius F. Thayer. Her grandfather was Dr. Nathaniel Thayer. Mr. Smith has one daughter, Mrs. Frances Eliza (Smith) Miller, and four grandchildren.

Mr. Smith is a member of the Asylum Hill Congregational church. In politics he is a republican. His life has been one of continued activity, covering a business experience of nearly sixty years, through periods of wonderful vicissitude in civil and financial affairs. He has been a participant in, as well as an observer of, the financial crises which have come to the commercial world from one cause or another within the last half century, but has maintained an unimpaired credit for himself and his firm, which is still strong and solid financially, as it is high in honorable reputation among the commercial houses of the country. It cannot be regarded as adulatory to say that wherever Mr. Smith is known his name is a synonym for personal integrity, rectitude of motive and action, and honorable citizenship.

JAY H. HART, Waterbury: Manufacturer.

Mr. Hart was born in Berkshire county, Mass., Dec. 11, 1847, and educated in the common schools and at the South Berkshire Institute. He lays claim to the fact that the town of Hartford was named from one of his ancestors who first had a ferry or fording place on the Connecticut River, near the present site of the bridge, which was called "Hart's ford," and finally became the name of the town and city. Mr. Hart is a manufacturer and has lived in Great Barrington, Mass., New Haven, Bridgeport,

J. H. HART.

and Waterbury, Conn., and is now connected with the Platt Brothers & Company, and secretary of the Patent Button Company. He is a republican, and has been tax collector of the city of Waterbury for four years, and a member of the board of fire commissioners and common council. He is connected with the Congregational church, the Waterbury Club, and the Masonic and Odd Fellows fraternities. His wife was Bertha L. Platt, and he has six children. He is recognized as one of the pushing, go-ahead men of the "Brass City."

M. B. DUNBAR, Torrington: Treasurer Union Hardware Company.

Marcene B. Dunbar has made his way from the bench to the position which he now occupies. He learned the trade of wood turning and was advanced step by step in the company, the past eighteen years having been spent in its employ. Mr. Dunbar was born in Torrington, April 17, 1850, and received a common school education, completing a thorough training at the Eastman Business College in 1867. In 1872 he spent the year in Chicago. Mr. Dunbar is a democrat in politics and holds the position of town auditor.

M. B. DUNBAR.

He is a member of Trinity Church, Seneca Lodge, No. 45, F. and A. M., and of the Grand Lodge I. O. O. F. of Connecticut; has recently been elected one of the Grand Officers of the Royal Arcanum for Connecticut. He is also treasurer of the Torrington Club. The Union Hardware Company of which he is the treasurer, employs a force of 250 hands, being one of the leading manufacturing industries at Torrington. Mr. Dunbar has a wife and three children, one son and two daughters. Mrs. Dunbar prior to her marriage was Miss Helen D. Smith. Treasurer Dunbar is an able business man, and is regarded with genuine favor in the community where he resides.

A. N. BELDING, ROCKVILLE. Secretary Belding Bros. & Co., and Manager the Rockville Mills.

Alvah Norton Belding, one of the best known manufacturers in the state, was born in Ashfield, Mass., March 27, 1838. His education was in

A. N. BELDING.

the common schools and in the high school. At seventeen years of age he removed to Michigan, where he cleared wild land and founded the town of Belding. In company with his brother, Hiram H., he began the sale of sewing-silk from house to house, the material being supplied by another brother in the east, Milo M. The business soon became so large that it required several teams and controlled a great part of the jobbing trade of the section. Three years after they started a house in Chicago, Milo M. joining them. In 1863 the brothers formed a partnership with E. K. Rose of Rockville for the manufacture of silk, renting the first floor of what was then the Glasgow Thread Company's mill in Rockville. This partnership came to an end in a few years, and afterwards the Belding Brothers bought the mill, and have since run it, in connection with other manufacturing concerns in Belding, Mich., Montreal, Northampton, and San Francisco. Mr. Belding has not been an active politician, but was once elected representative to the lower house in the Connecticut legislature in 1882, being elected by the largest proportionate vote of electors ever given in his town. He is a republican. He was married January 6, 1870, to Lizzie S. Merrick of Shelburne Falls, Mass., and has two children, a son and a daughter. Mr. Belding's wide interest in manufacturing and business affairs can best be understood by a glance at the various official positions he holds. He is secretary of the Belding Bros. & Co. Silk Mill; a director in the Belding, Paul & Co. Silk Mill of Montreal, director in the Carlson & Courier Silk Manufacturing Company, San Francisco, Cal.; president of the Belding Manufacturing Company, refrigerators, Belding, Mich.; president

of the Belding Land and Improvement Company, Belding, Mich.; director in the Miller Casket Company, Belding, Mich.; director in the Hall Brothers Manufacturing Company, furniture, Belding, Mich.; director in the Belding Savings Bank, Belding, Mich.; director in the St. Lawrence Fiber Pulp Company, Governeur, N. Y.; director in the Rockville National Bank, and People's Savings Bank of Rockville; director in the American Mills Company, woolens, Rockville; and a stockholder in several other companies. Despite his various interests, he finds time to devote himself to the welfare of the city in which he resides, and is one of its most popular citizens. He is a typical, energetic New England business man, who has the rare ability to do a great many things, and do them all well. An instance showing the pluck of the Belding Brothers in their enterprises is that of the attempt to bore an artesian well in the vicinity of their mill in Northampton. After a depth of 3,700 feet had been reached through the sandstone, and $32,000 had been expended, the firm abandoned the attempt, for the first time in its business career having been baffled. Mr. Belding is also interested with his brothers in the development of the new south, owning 75,000 acres of land in North Carolina and Tennessee, teeming with almost inexhaustible wealth in timber and minerals. The record of the Belding Brothers is certainly a remarkable one, and one of the leading spirits of the firm is Alvah N. Belding, the subject of this sketch.

HON. JOHN G. ROOT, HARTFORD. President Farmers and Mechanics National Bank.

John G. Root is a native of Westfield, Mass., where he was born April 20, 1835. He came to Hartford in 1855, and has resided in the city continuously since that time.

J. G. ROOT.

His first financial experience was with the old Bank of Hartford County, now the American National Bank, with which he was first officially connected as cashier, being elected to that position in 1871, and retaining it until 1883, when he was chosen president of the Farmers and Mechanics National Bank, which relation still continues. He was for a time treasurer of the Hartford Trust Company. He is one of the trustees of the Mechanics Savings Bank, a director in the Orient Insurance Company and several other corporations, and prominently connected with civic and military organizations in Hartford. During the war he held the rank of captain in the Twenty-second Connecticut regiment, and is now one of the leading members of Robert O. Tyler Post of the Grand Army and a trustee of the Post fund. He is connected with the highest orders of the Masonic fraternity in the state, and has held the office of grand treasurer of the grand lodge for a number of years. He delivered the oration in Cedar Hill cemetery when the handsome monument in honor of Thomas H. Seymour was dedicated a few years ago, which effort reflected permanent credit upon him as an author and orator. For years he has held an honorable place in the First Company Governor's Foot Guard, and is an influential member of the Veteran Association. In all these positions of civil and military comradeship he has been the ideal representative of good feeling and manliness. He was elected to the mayoralty of Hartford in 1888, and proved himself an able and conscientious chief magistrate of the municipality. His administration was one of marked success, and the review of his career as mayor increases the great public respect which has been felt for him since his residence in the city. His uprightness of character and frankness of intercourse with men secure for him the confidence and esteem of his townsmen in a very eminent degree.

SAMUEL ALLEN, NEW HARTFORD: Justice of the Peace.

Mr. Allen is a native of Barkhamsted, where he was born March 15, 1823. He was the third son of Joel and Rosanna Case Allen, whose children were eight in number. He received his education in the district schools of his native town, finishing with a few terms at the North Canton academy. At the age of twenty-one he removed to Pine Meadow — which has since been his home — and worked for six years in the rule shop of H. Chapin. In 1850 he formed a partnership with his brother, Philemon Allen,

SAMUEL ALLEN.

in a brass foundry, and two years later he bought out his brother's interest. In 1867 he sold his foundry business, and associated himself with another brother, Anson J. Allen, in mercantile business in Pine Meadow. For twenty-one years Mr. Allen retained an interest in this store as senior partner. In 1887 he retired from business on a handsome competency, gained partly from his successful and

upright mercantile course, and partly from a large interest in Iowa lands, of which, in 1855, he purchased some nine hundred acres. Mr. Allen is a republican, having joined that party in 1856. He was in earlier years a democrat, but joined the American party in 1855, and was by them sent to the general assembly of that year. He was again elected to the legislature in 1889, by the republicans, and served on the appropriations committee. He has held various offices of trust in New Hartford, has been grand juror, is now and has been for twelve years a justice of the peace, and is a member of the board of relief. He was the last captain in his native town in the old state militia, holding his commission until the disbanding of the organization, about 1844. He has the esteem and respect of all parties in the town, with whose interests he has been identified for nearly fifty years. In May, 1846, Mr. Allen married Miss Eveline U. Case of North Canton. They have no children.

E. C. DENNIS, STAFFORD SPRINGS: Flour and Grain Merchant.

Ebenezer C. Dennis was born in Hardwick, Worcester County, Mass., July 26, 1834, and received a public school education. He represented the Twenty-fourth senatorial district during the sessions of 1881, 1882, 1883, and 1884, serving as chairman of the committee on claims during a portion of the time. His senatorial career was marked by the strictest devotion to the interests of the state, and was creditable in every sense of the word. Ex-Senator Dennis formerly resided in Worcester. For twenty-four years he was

E. C. DENNIS.

engaged in the wholesale hide and leather business, but a number of years he has been at the head of an extensive flour and grain trade. Mr. Dennis is a republican in politics, and has held the office of assessor at Stafford for several years, is chairman of the board of selectmen, and has been a director of the Stafford National Bank for many years. He has also been warden of the borough of Stafford, and has taken a prominent part in local affairs. He is a bank director, and a man of thorough business training. He is a member of the Business Men's Club and of the Grange. His religious associations are with the Congregational church. The ex-senator's family consists of a wife and one son. The former was Miss Sophronia M. Fuller prior to her marriage.

FREDERICK JESUP BANKS, Bridgeport: Cashier City National Bank.

Frederick J. Banks has always resided in Bridgeport, where he was born, July 20, 1854. He was educated in Strong's Military Institute, where he

F. J. BANKS.

received ample preparation for the business career which he has since developed. His first start in business life was as bookkeeper and teller for the banking firm of Hatch & Watson for three years. His faithfulness gained him promotion to a position in the City National Bank in 1874 as a bookkeeper, from which he was advanced to be the receiving teller, and later for ten years the courteous and very efficient paying teller. He now fills the honorable and very responsible position of cashier, most acceptably to the institution, and to the gratification of his many friends. Mr. Banks married, January 23, 1889, Miss Julia L. Whitehouse of Brooklyn, N. Y., and their beautiful and hospitable home is on Clinton avenue. Mr. Banks has never sought public honors or distinctions; he is, however, the trusted treasurer of the Bridgeport hospital, and is deeply interested in its welfare — as of everything that tends to promote the social, moral, and charitable interests of his native city. He is a member of St. John's Episcopal church of Bridgeport.

HENRY R. ADKINS, Winsted: Harness-maker.

Henry R. Adkins has spent most of his life in the business of harness-making. He is a well-known resident in his section of the state. He com-

H. R. ADKINS.

menced life in the old town of Plymouth, and afterwards removed to New Hartford. Thence he transferred his interests to Winsted, where he has since resided. He is a member of the First Congregational church of that place, and a man of exemplary life and character. His wife, who is still living, was Miss Ruth Ann Baker prior to marriage. Both of the children, the fruit of this union, are dead. Mr. Adkins was born in the town of Plymouth, January 30, 1813, and received a common school education.

GEORGE H. CLOWES, Waterbury: Manufacturer of Sheet Brass and Copper, Seamless Brass and Copper Tubing, Brazed Tubing, etc.

George H. Clowes was born in Clinton, Oneida county, N. Y., June 17, 1842, at which place his father, the Rev. Timothy Clowes, LL.D., was

G. H. CLOWES.

principal of the Clinton Liberal Institute. A year later his parents moved to Philadelphia and resided there about four years. From that city they went to Hempstead, L. I., where they resided until he was about eleven years of age. During this time he attended school at the Hempstead Seminary, and later on at Jamaica Academy at Jamaica, L. I. At the age of eleven he was sent to Thetford Academy, Thetford, Vt., and remained there until he became fifteen years of age. He then went to De Pere, Wisconsin, and spent one year in the banking office of his brother there. Subsequently he attended St. Lawrence University at Appleton, Wisconsin. His father died in 1847, and a few years later his mother removed to Brooklyn, which city was chiefly his home up to the year 1875.

Shortly after the commencement of the war he took a course of military instructions under Col. Tompkins, who was appointed by the U. S. Government to fit officers for positions in the army. Having passed a creditable examination before the board of the U. S. Government examining officers, he received the appointment of adjutant of the McClellan infantry, then under the command of an experienced French officer (Col. Levy). After spending several months and considerable money in helping to raise the regiment to the number of 600 men, there was an order from the war department to stop recruiting and to consolidate all incomplete regiments. His regiment was consolidated with one of about 400 men, and the whole staff of the larger contingent thrown out; owing entirely, as is believed, to political influence. The young adjutant became somewhat chagrined at the treatment he had received and determined to let army matters alone. On the second call for troops, however, he joined the 47th regiment, N. Y. N. G., and shouldered a musket. Shortly after joining the regiment he was appointed sergeant-major and held the position until mustered out of the three months service for which the regiment was mustered in. In the spring of 1863 he accepted a position as paymaster's clerk on board the U. S. gunboat *Flambeau*, doing duty off the coast of North and South Carolina, Georgia, and Florida, during a period of about one year and a half. Shortly after the evacuation of Charleston he was transferred to a similar position on the United States store ship *Home*, and had charge of the accounts and naval stores on board that vessel and several smaller ones, and held this position until all were ordered home in the summer of 1864. After settling his accounts with the government, he became engaged in the large manufacturing hat house of Gardner & Co., New York, where he remained two years, at first as a bookkeeper and subsequently as salesman. This position he gave up to accept one with the Middlefield Fire and Building Stone Co., whose works and office were situated at 1269 Broadway, New York. After remaining about two years with this company, he received an offer of the appointment of paymaster's clerk on the U. S. gunboat *Juanita*, ordered to the European station, which position he accepted, and went on board the vessel twenty-four hours after the appointment. The vessel sailed for the European station July, 1869, and did not return to the United States until July, 1872. His next position was with the New York Loan Indemnity Co. as loan and discount clerk. During the two years he was with this company he influenced to it deposits to the amount of upwards of a quarter of a million of dollars, more, it is believed, than its president, secretary, and nineteen directors combined. January 1, 1875, he became head bookkeeper of Brown & Brothers and held that position up to the time of change in management, when Franklin Farrel assumed control of the company, at which time he was reappointed office manager and assistant treasurer, and remained in such position until they made an assignment in January, 1886. After the assignment Mr. Clowes remained several months with the trustees of the company or up to the time when he purchased that portion known as their seamless tube, brazed tube, and boiler business. After building this part of the business up to what was generally considered a great success and outgrowing the occupied premises, the present partners (Randolph & Clowes) purchased the old rolling mill of Brown & Brothers, and the remainder of the property. The past two years have been devoted to getting that part of the plant in a good condition for doing a successful business, and the proprietors have good reason to feel satisfaction and pride in the results they have achieved. They started in April, 1886, with about 50 men and one clerk, with a small office about fourteen feet square; they now employ nearly 400 men and have three depots, one in New York, one in Chicago, and one in Boston. It is understood that they paid the trustees of Brown & Brothers for the property they bought of them, in all, about

$125,000, and have expended in improving the property about $275,000 more, making the cost of the plant to them about $400,000. Had the business not been made a success the original cost of the property would have been considered large; but, having made a success, the additional expenditure for putting the property in good shape has given it a value more than double the amount actually expended on and for it. From starting with about 200 customers on their books, they now have nearly 3,000, a remarkable result to have accomplished in so brief a period. Although Mr. Randolph has been more than liberal in his assistance in furnishing the large capital necessary ($800,000) to carry on the business, yet he has given no time to the management of the business; and, beyond his financial aid, Mr. Clowes has had no assistance whatever. It is owing entirely to his energy, great executive ability and perseverance, that Randolph & Clowes to-day stand second to none in their line. This success is all the more marked and creditable, from the fact that he has succeeded where others had failed who were supported by a large coterie of encouraging and admiring friends.

F. S. CROSSFIELD, HARTFORD: Physician and Surgeon.

Dr. Fred S. Crossfield was born in Keene, N. H., July 29, 1854, and received an academic education, completing his general studies at the Keene High School and Dean Academy in Franklin. He pursued a thorough medical course in New York and has been engaged in practice in Hartford for thirteen years. He is the medical director of the National Life Association and belongs to the City, Hartford County, and State Medical Societies, and is also a member of the American Medical Association. He is assistant 

F. S. CROSSFIELD.

surgeon on the Putnam Phalanx staff, and is connected with the Order of Red Men. Dr. Crossfield is one of the vestrymen of Christ church. In politics he is a republican. His wife, who is still living, was Miss L. I. Hill, daughter of Hon. E. B. Hill of Glastonbury, prior to her marriage. There are no children in the family. Dr. Crossfield occupies a prominent position professionally in this city and is regarded with the most genuine esteem by his associates. He is equally honored as a citizen.

S. W. HAUGHTON, Bozrah: Farmer.

Mr. Haughton was born in Utica, N. Y., September 30, 1831, and was educated at Christ Church Hall, Pomfret, Conn. He has followed farming for the greater part of his life, and has resided in Boston, Buffalo, and Bozrah, being assistant postmaster in the latter town during the Cleveland administration. He is of the democratic political faith, and religiously connected with the Episcopal church. His wife was Harriet W. Smith, and she is still living. They have no children. Mr. Haughton is a gentleman of excellent ability and earnest convictions. He is careful and methodical in all business affairs, and his life thus far has been one of great usefulness. He is highly esteemed by his townsmen and all who enjoy his acquaintance.

S. W. HAUGHTON.

GEORGE E. ELLIOT, Clinton: Merchant.

Mr. Elliot was born in Killingworth (now Clinton) April 17, 1819, and comes of noted ancestry. His father was Ely A. Elliot and his mother Susan M. Pratt of Old Saybrook, and he is the direct descendant in the seventh generation from John Eliot of Roxbury, Mass., well known as the "Apostle to the Indians," and the first to translate the Bible into the native tongue of the American aborigines. The subject of this sketch was educated in the public schools and at Amherst, Mass., Academy, and has been a successful merchant in Clinton for many years. He has been justice of the peace, judge of probate, and postmaster, but at present holds no public office except that of member of the board of school visitors, which he has held from 1844 to the present time. He was one of the original trustees of the famous Morgan school of Clinton, and is its secretary and treasurer. He was a member of the lower house of the Connecticut legislature in 1853. He is connected with the Union Manufacturing Company, and with the Clinton Paper Company. In politics he is a democrat. He is connected with the Congregational church in Clinton, and is influential in

G. E. ELLIOT.

its work. His wife, who was Cornelia C. Redfield, is living, and they have four children. Judge Elliot is very well known in that stretch of towns on the Sound line, and has also an extensive acquaintance in all parts of the state. He is universally esteemed for his upright character, and for his earnest interest in educational affairs.

JOSEPH HUTCHINS, Plainfield.

One of the most respected and honored citizens of the ancient town of Plainfield, in Windham county, is Joseph Hutchins, the subject of this sketch. He is a native of the town, and was born March 4, 1820. During his youth he attended the district school, and completed his education at Plainfield academy, one of the oldest and most reputable institutions of its class in the state. He became a farmer, from the active pursuits of which avocation, however, he retired some years ago. At the present time

JOSEPH HUTCHINS.

he is a director of the Uncas National Bank of Norwich, agent of the Plainfield Town Deposit fund, and trustee of the David Gallup fund of that town. He is also a trustee of the Chelsea Savings Bank of Norwich, of the Ecclesiastical Society fund of Plainfield, and of various personal estates. In 1858 and 1875 he was a member of the Connecticut house of representatives, a legislative experience repeated in 1885. He was elected to the state senate from the Seventeenth district in the fall of 1886, and in the session which followed he was appointed on the committees on banks and on constitutional amendments, being the senate chairman of both. He has held many local offices, including first selectman, and has enjoyed the confidence and esteem of his townsmen through an uninterrupted business career covering over half a century. Senator Hutchins was originally a whig, but became a republican when the latter party was organized, and has remained a consistent member of it ever since. He married Lucy R. Woodward, daughter of Lemuel Woodward of Plainfield, and she is still living. They have one daughter, born May 22, 1853; she is the wife of Mr. Joseph C. Noyes of Cincinnati, Ohio, where they now reside. Mr. and Mrs. Hutchins have spent considerable time in Cincinnati since that city became the home of their daughter.

The church membership of Mr. Hutchins is, and has long been, with the old First Congregational

Society of Plainfield. He has no membership with clubs or fraternities. His early life was full of business and social activity, but for the last few years he has been quietly enjoying the fruits of his success, and devoting his time to the intelligent direction and management of his own affairs and of various accepted trusts.

JOHN G. BAIRD, Ellington: Congregational Clergyman.

Rev. John G. Baird was born in Milford, Conn., November 27, 1826. He was educated at the Milford High school, graduated at Yale College in 1852, and at the Andover Theological Seminary. His life has been spent in ministerial and educational work. He taught in Ellington from '52 to '54; was a student at Andover from '54 to '57; was pastor of the Second Congregational church in Saybrook from '59 to '65; was in educational work in New Haven from '65 to '78; resided in Hartford, in same occupation,

J. G. BAIRD.

from '78 to '83; resigned his position in the office of the state board of education in '83, and removed to Ellington in 1884, where he has since resided. His wife was Miss Eliza Hall of Ellington. They have no children. Mr. Baird is a republican, but has never held any elective office. He is a member of the First church in Hartford.

SETH BARNES, Bristol: Clock-Maker.

Seth Barnes was born in Norfolk, March 13, 1846, and was educated in the common schools at Torrington, where his early years were passed. His father died in 1853, and at the age of fourteen he commenced work on a farm, where he remained for three years. He then engaged in the employ of the Seth Thomas Clock Company. On the 13th of March, 1866, when he was twenty years of age, he entered the employ of the E. Ingraham Clock Company at Bristol, where he has since remained. He has been an active

SETH BARNES.

and influential citizen of the place, and has been a member of the High school committee since 1887, and of the building committee, which has had the erection of the High school in charge, the structure costing $30,000. He was a member of the Bristol fire department for fifteen years, serving as assistant chief engineer during the last two years of the time. Mr. Barnes is a past master of Franklin Lodge, No. 56, F. and A. M., of Bristol, and is a prominent representative of the order. He holds the office of a trial justice of the peace. He is a republican in politics, and has been a member of the town committee for a number of years. His wife, who was Miss Margaret E. Phetzing prior to marriage, died in June, 1890, leaving two sons, Arthur S. and Fred H. Barnes. The former is a member of the junior class in Yale, while the latter is studying at Bristol. Mr. Barnes has taken an active interest in education, and has served as committee of his district for a number of terms, in addition to the place which he has held on the High school committee. He is a public-spirited citizen, and is held in high esteem in Bristol.

GEORGE AUSTIN FAY, Meriden: Attorney-at-Law.

The subject of this sketch was born at Marlboro', Mass., Aug. 29, 1838. His early life was spent at home upon the farm, and afterwards at the bench in the manufacture of shoes. He received his education in the common schools of his native town, graduating finally at the Marlboro' High school. In 1859 he left his native place and went to Meriden, Conn., where he has since resided. During his early residence in Meriden he was employed as a clerk in the office of the Adams' Express Company, and was at the same

G. A. FAY.

time the Western Union telegraph operator at that place. Two years later, in May, 1861, he entered the law department of Yale University, where, in 1862, he was graduated as LL.B. After his graduation he entered the office of Hon. O. H. Platt, now United States senator, where he remained a year. In May, 1863, he was admitted to the Connecticut bar as an attorney-at-law, since which time he has practiced in that profession. In 1865 he married Jennie M. Curtis, only daughter of Alfred P. Curtis of Meriden. In 1871 he was elected by the republicans to the state senate from the Sixth senatorial district, where he served as chairman of the committee on incorporations, and also as chairman of the committee on elections, to determine who was elected governor of the state. The canvass for state officers during the preceding campaign had been an exceedingly exciting one, and resulted, as will be remembered, in a declaration of the election of Hon. James E. English of New Haven, on the face of the returns, by a majority of thirty-nine votes. On account of alleged frauds in the vote of the Fourth Ward of New Haven, the election of Mr. English was contested and an investigation instituted, with the result of unseating him, and awarding the gubernatorial office to Hon. Marshall Jewell, who was duly inaugurated governor of Connecticut. Mr. Fay has a very proper sense of gratification still, that he was able to participate officially in the action of the committee by and before whom this important investigation was conducted. Since that legislative term he has not taken any active part in politics, beyond casting his vote for the candidates of the republican party, feeling obliged to devote his time wholly to his profession. Mr. Fay is a member of the Masonic fraternity.

REV. S. H. HOWE, D.D., NORWICH: Pastor of Park Congregational Church.

Rev. Samuel Henry Howe was born in Fleming county, Ky., December 18, 1837. He graduated from Hanover College in Illinois in 1861. He taught

S. H. HOWE.

Greek and mathematics for two years previous to his graduation in McNair's academy in Louisiana. He pursued a course of theological studies at Princeton, graduating from the Theological Seminary there in 1864. In 1865 he was ordained as a Presbyterian minister, and has occupied four pastorates in the Presbyterian church. His first field was at Vincennes, Ind., where he remained for two years. In 1867 he was settled at Independence, Mo., occupying the pastorate there until 1869. In 1870 he removed to Cortland, N. Y., and in 1872 he accepted the pastoral charge of the church in Georgetown, D. C., and continued his pulpit ministrations there until 1883. In 1877 he received the degree of D.D., his scholarship and attainments entitling him to that recognition. He became the pastor of the Park Congregational church in Norwich in November, 1883, and has since remained there. He is a member of the New London association, and has one of the largest churches in eastern Connecticut. The membership is about 800 and the cost of the church edifice was $125,000. Dr. Howe was married in 1873, and has a family of four children.

DAN A. MILLER, BRISTOL: General Manager Burner Department, Bristol Brass and Clock Company.

Dan A. Miller was born in that part of the town of Farmington which is now known as Avon, December 5, 1823, and received a common school

D. A. MILLER.

and academic education, completing his studies in the old Hartford academy. He is an accountant by profession, and in 1867, also in 1871, represented the town of Southington in the general assembly, serving on the democratic side. He has held various offices in Bristol, including member of the board of selectmen, board of relief, and assessor, and is at present a notary public. Mr. Miller is a past worshipful master of Franklin Lodge, No. 56, F. and A. M., of Bristol and is held in high esteem in the fraternity. He has been identified with the settlement of different estates in Bristol and is an honored business man in the community. He was married in 1847, November 26th, to Miss Sarah M. Bishop, who is still living. Mr. and Mrs. Miller have three sons. Their home is at Forestville.

ANDREW J. GARDINER, DANIELSONVILLE: Cotton Manufacturer.

Andrew J. Gardiner, whose name is quite familiar to a large number of cotton manufacturers and business men in Connecticut, Rhode Island, and

A. J. GARDINER.

Massachusetts, was born in Windham, Ct., January 18, 1832, and received his education in the common schools. The activity that has characterized his life from boyhood up has placed him in the front ranks in his line of business. He earned his first money in the cotton mill at the age of thirteen years. Mr. Gardiner in 1850 entered the employment of Paul Whitin & Son of Whitinsville, Mass., the well-known and extensive builders of cotton machinery; and by force of his ability and character soon rose to prominent positions in their employ, and remained with them upwards of twenty-five years. In 1879, on the organization of the Danielsonville Cotton Company, Mr. Gardiner was engaged as the resident agent, and the excellent success of that company during the eleven succeeding years is due in no small degree to his practical skill and business experience as a manufacturer. Mr. Gardiner is one of the stockholders originally forming this company, which interest he still retains. He is also president of the Suffolk Manufacturing Company, a large corporation in Boston, Mass.

Mr. Gardiner is a member of the Congregational church, and in politics a staunch republican. His activity in business has always prompted him to decline all political honors. He takes great interest in all improvements in the locality where he resides, and is a gentleman of excellent judgment and valuable opinions and views respecting financial affairs. He married Miss Annie F. Andruss, and they have three sons. He is a member of the Masonic fraternity.

SAMUEL GREGORY BEARDSLEY, Trumbull: Town Clerk and Justice of the Peace.

Samuel G. Beardsley was born at Long Hill, Trumbull, December 7, 1824, where his home has ever since been. His father, Samuel Beardsley, Esq., was confessedly one of the ablest and most prominent men his native town ever produced, having been twice representative, once state senator, sheriff, and commissioner of Fairfield county, trial justice for many years, largely employed in the settlement of estates, having acted as executor or administrator of more than one hundred, and was universally respected

S. G. BEARDSLEY.

and esteemed. The subject of this sketch was educated in the common schools of his own, and the academies of adjoining towns; was admitted a member of Yale College, but was compelled to discontinue study through failure of sight; taught school several terms, engaged in the manufacture of cotton in partnership with the late Alonzo Sherman for six years, and afterward, on the death of his only brother, assisted his father in farming, which has since been his chief occupation. He has held numerous town offices; was a member of the general assembly of 1865, and of the centennial senate of 1876, defeating for the latter position Hon. David B. Plumb, a distinguished citizen of Shelton, whose father, Noah Plumb, Esq., was also beaten for the same office by his father just forty years before; and now holds the office of justice of the peace, which he has held since 1860, and of

town clerk, to which he has been elected thirty consecutive times. He has been entrusted with the settlement of many estates, and earnestly seeks to deserve the character of an honest, upright man. He married, early in life, Mary, youngest daughter of Dea. Ephraim Wells Beach, who is now living, and from whom was born one son, Morris Beach Beardsley, now serving his fifteenth year as judge of probate for the district of Bridgeport, and two daughters, one unmarried and the other the wife of Lewis B. Curtis, of the firm of Curtis & Curtis, manufacturers at Bridgeport. He is a member of the Congregational church, and in politics is, and ever has been, an unswerving democrat.

HON. EARL MARTIN, Danielsonville: Attorney-at-Law.

Judge Earl Martin was born in Chaplin, Windham county, in 1820, and received a common school education, the ordinary training of the school being supplemented by instruction under private tutors. He studied law with the late J. D. Richmond, and was admitted to the bar in 1847. Two years afterwards he located at Danielsonville, where he has since resided. His entire business life has been devoted to the law, which he has practiced honestly and conscientiously. In 1872 he was elected to the legislature from the town

EARL MARTIN.

of Killingly by the democrats, and in 1874 he was advanced to the superior court bench, occupying the position for eight years. The Judge was for years the contemporary of Judge Carpenter of the supreme court at Danielsonville, the two men being considered the leading lawyers of that part of Windham county. Both were connected with the higher courts of the state at the same time, constituting an interesting incident in the life of each of them. Judge Martin has also held the office of judge of probate in the Danielsonville district, and is regarded with profound respect and esteem in the community where he resides. He is a member of the Episcopal church, and has been connected with the democratic party since 1841. His wife, who is still living, was Miss C. J. Champlin of Niantic prior to her marriage. There are no children in the family. The career of Judge Martin on the superior court bench was one of honor and of strict personal devotion to the duties of the office.

CHARLES F. MARTIN, ELLIOTT (POMFRET): Merchant.

Charles F. Martin was a member of the house of representatives in 1887, his colleagues from Windham county including Messrs. Milton A. Shumway, now of the senate, Marvin H. Sanger, and C. S. Burlingame of Canterbury, and J. Griffin Martin of Windham. He was a member of the National Guard from 1876 until 1881, being connected with Company F of the Third Regiment. He has held various town offices and is at present a grand juror. In politics Mr. Martin is a republican.

C. F. MARTIN.

He is a member of the Unitarian Society of Brooklyn and belongs to the Knights of Pythias, Royal Arcanum, and Masonic orders. He was married in 1882, his wife being Miss Catharine C. Elliott. There are two children. Mr. Martin was born in Brooklyn March 3, 1857, and received a common school education. Since 1876 he has been engaged in mercantile pursuits.

[Mr. Martin died at his home in Pomfret, on the 24th of March, 1891, after the above sketch had been prepared. — ED.]

DAVID HENRY MILLER, GEORGETOWN (REDDING): Vice-president and Secretary Gilbert & Bennett Manufacturing Company.

Mr. Miller was born in London, August 12, 1831, and received a private school education. At the age of fourteen he removed to New York, remaining in the metropolis for ten years. He then became a resident of Connecticut and has since retained his citizenship here. Major Miller has had considerable military experience. He served five years in the New York State Militia, being a member of the Washington Greys, Eighth Regiment. He was captain in Company E, Eighth Regiment, Connecticut Militia,

D. H. MILLER.

and was the major of the Twenty-third Connecticut during the war under Colonel Holmes of Waterbury. He is an old member of James E. Moore Post, G. A. R., of Danbury. Major Miller is a member of Ark Lodge, No. 39, F. and A. M., of Georgetown,

Crusade Commandery, Knights Templar, and Pyramid Temple. He is also connected with the Fairfield County Historical Society, and the Army and Navy Club of Connecticut. For the past twenty-two years he has been the treasurer of Ark Lodge. Mr. Miller is a justice of the peace, notary public, and treasurer of the school district at Georgetown. He is an Episcopalian and a republican. In 1881 he was a member of the general assembly, representing the town of Redding in the house, and made many friends in that body. His wife, whose maiden name was Catherine Welling, and nine children constitute the family.

WILLIAM L. CAMP, WEST WINSTED: Merchant.

William Lewis Camp was born in Michigan in 1846. His father was Seth Lewis, a Michigan pioneer settler. When the subject of this sketch had reached the age of six years his parents consented to his adoption by Moses Camp, a relative, then at the head of the best known and most successful mercantile firm in Litchfield County. After a few terms in the public school of the village the boy was given a brief course of study at the Winchester Institute, then under the direction

W. L. CAMP.

of the Rev. Ira Pettibone, and at the South Berkshire Institute, New Marlboro', Mass.; and, though he attained good standing in his classes, it soon became evident that in business, rather than books, lay his future success. At the age of sixteen he became a clerk in the store of M. & C. J. Camp & Co., a few years later being admitted to membership in the firm. From that time until Camp's block was burned out, in January, 1889, Mr. Camp was one of the principals in the mercantile business at the same "old stand," the firm name changing successively to Woodford & Camp and Camp & Clark. The new Camp's block, which rose, phoenix-like, from the ashes of its predecessor, is owned by Mr. Camp, and is said by insurance inspectors to be one of the most substantially built brick blocks in the state. Mr. Camp has recently taken on the business harness again, being now proprietor of the "Broadway Shoe Store," one of the model establishments of its kind in the state. He does not allow his business affairs to monopolize all his time, however, and interests himself only with its general features, leaving the details to his son, Lewis M. Camp. Mr.

Camp is the owner of some of the choicest building sites within the borough limits, and has also a choice tract of frontage on the west shore of Highland Lake, where his summer cottage is charmingly ensconsed among the forest trees.

Mr. Camp has four sons and one daughter, and a pleasant home on Hinsdale avenue, his wife being one of Winsted's most popular ladies — formerly Miss Nellie Brown of Des Moines, Iowa. He is a trustee of the Winsted Savings Bank, member of the board of burgesses of the borough, prominently identified with the board of trade, treasurer of the Winchester Memorial Park Association, and a member of the board of trustees of the Gilbert fund (about $1,200,000 left by the late William L. Gilbert for free High school and Home for Friendless Children). In politics Mr. Camp is a republican, though not a strenuous partisan.

EDWARD F. BIGELOW, Portland: Editor and Publisher.

Edward Fuller Bigelow, editor and proprietor of the *Middlesex County Record*, the *Observer*, and the *Colchester Advocate*, has demonstrated that new enterprises in newspaper fields in Connecticut need not of necessity prove unfruitful. In addition to the three papers which he controls and manages, he has a large printing and job office at Portland that is meeting with gratifying success. The energy shown by Mr. Bigelow in his work has entitled him to the success that has crowned his way. He

E. F. BIGELOW.

was the pioneer in newspaper enterprises in Portland. Associated with him was the late William A. Chapman, who, like the subject of this sketch, possessed the instincts of the born newspaper man. The *Observer*, which is one of Mr. Bigelow's ideas, is the only paper of the character issued, being devoted especially to natural history. It has met with remarkable success, many scientific people, naturalists, and microscopists in particular being interested in it. The *Colchester Advocate* is also a popular publication, and has a successful patronage. Mr. Bigelow is a member of the board of education, and is connected with the Episcopal church in Portland. In politics he is a republican. He belongs to the Ancient Order of United Workmen, the Odd Fellows lodge, and the Order of United American Mechanics. He was born at Colchester, January 14, 1860, and was educated at

Bacon, academy. From the age of sixteen until twenty-six he was engaged in teaching, principally in Colchester and Portland. He has a wife and three children. The former was Miss Mary A. Pelton of Portland prior to her marriage with Mr. Bigelow.

REV. ABRAM J. QUICK, South Coventry: Congregational Clergyman.

The subject of this sketch was born at South Branch, N. J., March 11, 1832. He was educated at Williams College and Union Theological Seminary, and has been engaged in the gospel ministry, with pastorates in New York, New Hampshire, and Connecticut. His wife, who was Miss Frances Merritt prior to marriage, is a native of Boston. The family includes four children, two sons and two daughters. The elder son is a mechanical engineer with the West End Electric Railway Co. of Boston;

A. J. QUICK.

the second son is civil engineer for the city of Providence; the daughters are students at Mt. Holyoke Seminary. Mr. Quick is a conscientious Christian gentleman, devoted to his work, and highly esteemed by his associates in the ministry as well as the community in which he labors. His political affiliations are with the republican party.

E. S. GREELEY, New Haven: Manufacturer and Importer of Railway and Electrical Supplies.

Gen. Edwin Seneca Greeley was in the military service of the United States Government from August, 1861, until September, 1865, receiving the rank of brigadier-general United States Volunteers. He is a distinguished member of the Army and Navy Club of Connecticut, and is regarded with universal admiration by the veterans of the war. While not a native of Connecticut, he has spent thirty-five years in New Haven, and is one of the best-known representatives of that municipality. He has been a mem-

E. S. GREELEY.

ber of the city government, serving in the board of aldermen, and is the president of the New Haven Republican League. He is a director in the Yale

National Bank, C. Cowles & Co., The Edgewood Company, and in the New Haven Palladium Company. Gen. Greeley is the president of the E. S. Greeley & Co. corporation, which controls extensive lines of railroad and electrical supplies. He is a member of the Church of the Redeemer, and is prominently identified with the best interests of the city. Gen. Greeley was born at Nashua, N. H., May 20, 1832, and received a district school education. He learned the trade of a machinist. The family of Gen. Greeley consists of his wife and one child. The former, prior to marriage, was Elizabeth Anthony Corey of Taunton, Mass.

JAMES T. MORGAN, Winsted: General Manager Morgan Silver Plate Company.

James T. Morgan was born at Haddam Neck, July 24, 1839, and received a common school education, preparing him for a successful business life.

J. T. MORGAN.

The father of Mr. Morgan was engaged in the blacksmith business, and he was made familiar with the trade. At the age of seventeen, however, he entered the employ of L. Boardman & Sons in East Haddam, manufacturers of silver-plated ware, and learned that trade. He was ultimately advanced to the position of superintendent in one of the company's establishments, remaining there until 1870. From East Haddam Mr. Morgan removed to Winsted, engaging with the Strong Manufacturing Company of that place. In 1871 he was made a member of the board of directors, and superintendent of the hardware department in 1874. In 1887 he disposed of his interest and organized the Morgan Silver Plate Company for the manufacture of undertakers' supplies, and has been the general manager from the outset. Mr. Morgan has been one of the best-known fanciers in Litchfield county, and was the originator and manufacturer of the celebrated phosphorated poultry food. At the age of twenty-six he married Miss Ellen V. Mitchell, of Moodus, Conn., and, besides his wife, the family consists of two sons. Mr. Morgan is a member of the First Congregational church at Winsted, and is held in high regard in the community where he resides. In politics he has always been a republican. Among the fraternal and benevolent orders to which he belongs are the Odd Fellows, the Royal Arcanum, the United Workmen, and the New England Order of Protection.

ERASTUS BRAINERD, Portland: President Brainerd Quarry Company.

Erastus Brainerd was born in Portland (formerly Chatham), July 27, 1819, and was educated in the schools of that town, afterward at the High School

ERASTUS BRAINERD.

in Boston, and prepared for West Point with Rev. L. H. Corson of Windham, Conn. He has resided in his native town all his life, and since 1845 has been the manager of the well-known Brainerd Quarry Co. in that town, carrying on a large business in Portland brown stone, shipping from that point to all parts of the country. He is president of the company, and has cared for its interests until it has assumed extensive proportions, and is one of the best known quarries in the country. Mr. Brainerd, although deeply interested in politics, has declined political honors, except that he was a presidential elector in 1880, casting his electoral vote for Garfield and Arthur, in accordance with his party principles, which were formerly with the whigs, but afterwards with the republicans. He is a prominent member of the Protestant Episcopal church in Portland. His wife was Emily H. Churchill, and he has one daughter. Mr. Brainerd is regarded as one of the influential and forceful business men of Middlesex county, and would have been honored frequently in political life, but has made it a rule to decline.

JASON C. FENN, Terryville: Clerk and Trustee.

Mr. Fenn has always lived in Terryville; was born there October 27, 1838, in the house he now owns, and which has been in the family over one

J. C. FENN.

hundred years. He attended the common school and academy as a boy and youth. For the past twenty-five years his time has been spent principally in clerking; and he is now, as for the past twenty years, with W. H. Scott & Co. He married Mary O. Johnson, daughter of the late Capt. Augustus S. Johnson, and granddaughter of Benoni Johnson, a revolutionary pensioner of Harwinton. He is a member and deacon of the Congregational church; has always been a republican; served as republican town committee a number of years, and represented the town of Plymouth in the House in 1886. He has had experience as constable, justice, member board of health, and notary public, and for a number of years selectman; and to him the town is indebted for the invention and erection of the best bridges for the money in the state, as they are built of old railroad iron, which combine cheapness with strength and beauty. He divides his time between service for the firm with which he has been so long, and labor in the settlement of estates,— adding sundry public duties, he now being notary public, selectman, health officer, and clerk of board of health. He also holds a number of estates either as trustee, guardian, or administrator, has been appointed to serve as commissioner on various estates, and has assisted on many soldiers' and widows' pensions.

ERNEST ARTHUR MARKHAM, Durham: Physician.

Dr. Markham is a native of Windsor, Vermont, the son of Oliver and Sarah Ann (Clark) Markham of Middletown. He was born October 16, 1853. Dr. Markham is of the eighth generation from Daniel Markham, who emigrated from England to America in 1665 and settled in Cambridge, Mass., but in 1677 removed to Middletown, Conn., where five generations of his descendants in a direct line to the subject of this sketch were born.

Dr. Markham was in his boyhood a pupil at the Wadsworth Street School in Hartford, also in the Hartford Public High School; and graduated from the Middletown High School in 1871. He studied at Wesleyan University, Middletown, which institution conferred upon him the degree of A.B. at graduation in 1875, and A.M. in 1885. He was also a student in the Eclectic Medical College of New York city, graduating therefrom in 1877; and took a non-resident course in the Illinois Western University, graduating as Ph.D. He married, April 21, 1876, Miss Annie Dering Brown, daughter of Addison Brown of Sag Harbor, L. I. They have two sons and one daughter. He is a member of the Church of the Epiphany, of which he has been a vestryman since 1884. Politically he favors the democrats. Societywise he is associated with the New York City Eclectic Medical Society, Royal Arcanum, Knights of Pythias, Sons of the American Revolution, and various local

orders. He has practiced medicine in Glastonbury and Durham, and in New York city during the time he was connected with the Eclectic Medical College, where he held the chair of Chemistry. At present he is permanently located in Durham.

HON. DWIGHT LOOMIS, Rockville: Supreme Court Judge.

Judge Dwight Loomis of the Supreme Court in this state was born in the town of Columbia July 27, 1821, and received a common school and academic education, completing his classical course at the Monson and Amherst academies. He was admitted to the bar in Tolland county and immediately won distinction in his chosen profession. In 1851 he represented the town of Vernon in the general assembly and was elected to the senate in 1857 from the old twenty-first district. His colleagues in the senate in-

cluded the Hon. Elisha Carpenter, who is now associated with him on the supreme court bench, and the late Governor James E. English, who subsequently served with him in the national congress. In 1859 Judge Loomis was elected by the republicans of the first congressional district and was re-elected April 1, 1861, thereby serving through one of the most important epochs in the history of the country. His colleagues during the first term in congress were the Hons. John Woodruff of New Haven, A. A. Burnham of Windham, and O. S. Ferry of Norwalk. Congressman Ferry took a prominent part in the war and was afterwards elected a United States senator. His place in the congressional delegation of 1861 was taken by the late George C. Woodruff of Litchfield, father of Railroad Commissioner George M. Woodruff. Ex-Governor English represented the second district and Congressman Burnham the third. The work of the thirty-seventh congress was of incalculable importance and Judge Loomis as the representative of one of the staunchest of Union states was not without a most creditable part in it. During the spring of 1864 he was appointed a judge of the superior court and has been on the bench since that time. He was advanced to the supreme court in 1875. In June, 1891, after twenty-seven years of judicial service, he retired from the Supreme Court bench, being within two months of the age at which he would be thereby disqualified for re-appointment. He returns to the general practice of law, and will also occupy a position as instructor in the Yale University Law School. Judge Loomis has been an able and conscientious expounder of the laws of the state, and his opinions have been characterized by great force and accuracy of judgment. His career altogether has been one of eminence and honor to the state. He is a prominent member of the Congregational church and deeply interested in its prosperity and success. Judge Loomis was married on the 26th of November, 1845, to Miss Mary E. Bill, who died June 1, 1864. He was again married on the 28th of May, 1866, to Jennie E. Kendall, who died March 6, 1876. One child, a daughter by the last marriage, is living.

J. H. BARLOW, SHELTON: Superintendent Packing and Shipping Department of the Shelton Company.

John Henry Barlow, who has held the highest position in the Grand Lodge of Connecticut, F. and A. M., was born in Ridgefield, November 7, 1852,

and received a common school education. In 1849 he removed to Birmingham, and remained there until 1889, when he transferred his residence to Shelton. He was the borough clerk for ten years at Birmingham, and is at present chairman of the board of relief in the town of Huntington. Mr. Barlow holds the place of superintendent of the Packing and Shipping

Department in the Shelton Company, which is engaged in the manufacture of tacks and bolts, and is a man of superior business ability. He is a member and associated with the vestry of the Episcopal church, and is held in high regard by the community where he resides. For thirty years he has been the secretary of the Odd Fellows lodge in Birmingham, but his highest honors in this direction have been attained in the Masonic fraternity. He is one of the past masters of King Hiram Lodge, No. 12, of Birmingham, and has held the exalted office of grand master of the Grand Lodge of the state, entitling him to permanent membership in this important and influential body. At the last meeting of the Grand Lodge in Hartford Mr. Barlow was present as one of the representatives of King Hiram Lodge, and served on one of the special committees during the conclave. In politics he is a republican, though originally and for many years connected with the democratic party. He has been twice married. His first wife, who

was Miss Emeline Gilbert, died in 1875, after a married life of fourteen years. Mr. Barlow's second marriage occurred in Ansonia, May 29, 1877, the bride being Miss Lina Ells. He has one daughter, twenty-six years of age, and one son, nineteen. The second wife is also living.

HON. D. S. CALHOUN, HARTFORD: Judge, Court of Common Pleas.

David Samuel Calhoun, who has occupied the judgeship of the Hartford County Court of Common Pleas since 1876, was born in Coventry, Sept. 11,

1827, and graduated from Yale College in 1848, being a classmate of Judge Shipman of the United States court. After graduating he taught school in Ravena, O., for one year. Subsequently he studied law in the office of the late Chief-Justice Seymour, in Litchfield, and settled in Manchester in 1852. In 1856 he was elected to the senate from the old Second dis-

trict, his colleagues that year including the late Governor James E. English; Orris S. Ferry, who subsequently represented Connecticut in the United States senate; Gideon H. Hollister, the historian of Connecticut; and Lucius J. Hendee, for years the president of the Ætna Insurance Company. In 1862 Judge Calhoun was again elected to the senate from the Second district; United States Senator Platt, and ex-State Comptroller John B. Wright of Clinton, associate members. The Judge was then as now a republican of the sincerest and clearest convictions. He occupied the probate judgeship in Manchester for twelve years. In 1870 he removed to Hartford, and has since been a resident of this city. He was formerly in partnership with the late Mahlon R. West, the firm being West & Calhoun. In 1876 Judge Calhoun was advanced to the bench, being elected judge of the Court of Common Pleas in this county. He is the vice-president for Connecticut of the Scotch-Irish Society of America, and is a member of Manchester Lodge, No. 73, F. and A. M., of Manchester. He is an attendant at the Pearl Street Congregational church. The father of Judge Calhoun, the late Rev. Dr. Geo. A. Calhoun of Coventry, was one of the best known Congregational divines in the state in his day. Judge Calhoun and wife, in company with his sons, J. G. and David Calhoun, spent the summer of 1888 in Europe, traveling in Great Britain and on the continent. The young gentlemen made an extensive bicycle tour. The Judge is a man of the most delightful culture and companionship, and is held in universal honor in this city. He has been married twice. His first wife, Harriet A. Gilbert of Coventry, died in 1868. In 1870 he married Miss Eliza J. Scott of Manchester, who is now living. There are besides the sons two daughters in the family. The professional life of Judge Calhoun has been one of marked distinction. As judge of the court of common pleas his opinions have but seldom been controverted. For years he has been one of the most polished and scholarly men on the bench in this state.

EDWIN E. MARVIN, HARTFORD: Clerk United States Circuit and District Courts.

Edwin E. Marvin was born in Tolland, October 8, 1833, and was educated in the schools in Tolland and at Suffield. His profession is that of a lawyer. He enlisted in the Fifth regiment, Connecticut volunteers, and was captain of Company F in that regiment, which was the first company from Tolland county in the war of the rebellion which repulsed a rebel charge and captured rebel prisoners. He served during the campaigns of 1861 and 1862, and resigned for disability and came home early in 1863. He after-

E. E. MARVIN.

wards wrote the history of the regiment, which was highly appreciated by its members. He has at various times resided in Tolland, Colchester, Rockville, and Hartford, engaged in the practice of the law. He was for many years the secretary of the Tolland County Agricultural Society, has been grand juror, justice of the peace, and United States commissioner. He is now clerk of the United States Circuit and District courts for Connecticut, United States commissioner, and Extradition commissioner for the state, occupying those positions with a great deal of ability, hearing many of the criminal cases coming before the United States courts in this state upon the preliminary hearing, and acting as Examiner and Master in Chancery in the majority of civil cases. He is a dignified gentleman, of fine personal appearance, and has a host of friends. He has always been a democrat in politics. He says he is devoted to all churches, alike, which make it their business to teach virtue and rebuke wrong; and is a regular attendant at Trinity church in Hartford. His wife was Cynthia Waldo, daughter of the late Judge Waldo. They have one son.

20

WILLIAM JESUP JENNINGS, REDDING: Pastor Congregational Church.

William J. Jennings was born at New Canaan, Conn., April 7, 1822. His father was a farmer of limited means, and soon after the birth of his son removed to his native place, Green's Farms, now a parish in the town of Westport. There the subject of this sketch spent his early life, helping his father when old enough during summer on the farm. He prepared for college at the Green's Farms academy under the tuition of that eminent instructor, Mr. Ebenezer B. Adams. He was graduated from Yale College

W. J. JENNINGS.

in 1843. The next two years were spent in teaching in the academy at Miller's Place, L. I. In 1848 he was graduated from Yale Divinity school. In August, 1849, he commenced preaching in the new Congregational church at Black Rock, Conn. The church was soon formed, and April 10, 1850, he was ordained its pastor. It being deemed expedient that he should remove from such close proximity to the sea, he was dismissed October 6, 1857, and immediately went to Seneca Falls, N. Y., and was installed pastor of the Presbyterian church in that village December 1, 1857. In May, 1862, having been released from his pastoral office he commenced ministerial labors with the Congregational church in North Coventry, Conn., of which he was installed pastor September 3, 1862. November 5, 1879, he was dismissed and at once removed to Redding, Conn., and was installed pastor of its Congregational church December 17, 1879, and still occupies that office.

March 26, 1850, he was united in marriage with Miss Miranda Dimon Greene of Miller's Place, L. I., who was graduated at Mount Holyoke Female Seminary in 1848. She is still the light and joy of his home. Of their eight children five are still living. Of these the three sons were graduated at Yale College, two of them in the academic department, and the other in the Sheffield Scientific school. The oldest, John J., is a lawyer in Bristol, Conn., one is the principal of the large Union school in Huntington, L. I., and the other is connected with the United States Geological Survey, and has his residence in Washington, D. C. One of the daughters is a graduate of Mount Holyoke Female Seminary, and one passed two years in that institution.

While he was at Seneca Falls, N. Y., he was one of the commissioners of Auburn Theological Seminary. For several years he was one of the trustees of the Hartford Theological Seminary. He was acting school visitor in the town of Coventry seventeen years, and has occupied the same position in Redding ten years. He is now one of the directors of the Missionary Society of Connecticut and one of the trustees of the Fund for Ministers.

EDWARD F. JONES, Branford: Secretary and Treasurer of the Branford Lock Works.

Edward F. Jones was born in New Jersey in 1821, and resided in New York city from 1844 to 1868, where for fifteen years he was connected with

E. F. JONES.

one of the largest jobbing or wholesale boot and shoe houses in the city,— removing thence to Branford, of which town he has since been continuously a resident. He was chosen by the republicans to represent the town in the general assembly of the state in 1878, when he was appointed and served on the committee on insurance and on special railroad committee, enjoying the distinction of being the first republican representative ever elected in Branford. In 1878 and also in 1880, he was a delegate to the republican state conventions, and he has been frequently on the republican state central committee from his district. He was on the electoral ticket at the last presidential election. In 1880 he was chosen state senator from the sixth district, occupying the seat during the sessions of 1881 and 1882, and serving as chairman of the school fund and contested elections committees. He has held from time to time the local offices of auditor and member of the board of relief of Branford. He has been one of the New Haven County auditors, and was one of the incorporators of the Guilford Savings Bank, as well as a trustee of that institution. Mr. Jones has been long and actively in politics, and a leader among the republicans of the state. He is a member of the Republican League Club of New Haven. His legislative career has been highly creditable, and has won for him the hearty esteem and approval of his associates and constituents.

Mr. Jones's business connections are with the Branford Lock Works, of which he is secretary and treasurer, having held the former position for more than twenty years. This company represents the most important industry of Branford, its works being quite extensive and giving employment to a large number of operatives.

CHARLES E. BRAYTON, Stonington: Physician and Surgeon.

Charles Erskine Brayton was born in Stonington, February 11, 1851, and was educated in the College of Physicians and Surgeons, New York city. The

C. E. BRAYTON.

most of his life has been spent at Stonington, where he has engaged in the practice of medicine and surgery since 1873. In 1881 he founded the drug firm of Dr. C. E. Brayton & Co. He is connected with a number of societies, including the Royal Arcanum, in which he holds the position of medical examiner, the Knights of Columbus, and the Royal Society of Good Fellows. He has been a member of the board of burgesses and the health committee of the borough since 1885. Dr. Brayton is a democrat in politics, and a member of the Second Congregational church. He is unmarried.

— —

JOHN B. LEWIS, M.D., Hartford: Surgeon and Adjuster Travelers Insurance Company.

John B. Lewis, M.D., whose personal record in the military service of the government throughout the late war of the rebellion is one of distinguished

J. B. LEWIS.

honor and efficiency, comes of patriotic and soldierly stock. His father (John) was a teacher at West Point, his grandfather (Benjamin) a soldier in the war of 1812–14, and his great-grandfather (Eleazur) a soldier in the war of the revolution. John B. Lewis was born in Suffolk County, N. Y., March 10, 1832. He was educated at Powellton Seminary, at Newburg, N. Y., and afterward pursued his professional studies in New York city at the University Medical College, where he was graduated March 10, 1853, on his twenty-first birthday. Shortly thereafter he located in Vernon, Conn., having formed a business partnership with Dr. Alden Skinner, and here for several years he had a full share of that laborious practice of medicine and surgery which falls to the lot of a country doctor.

At the outbreak of the war of the rebellion, and when the president's call for volunteers occasioned the organization of Connecticut troops, he was offered a surgeonry by Governor Buckingham, and later he accepted an appointment as surgeon of the Fifth Connecticut Infantry, with rank from date of commission, July 3, 1861. He at once reported for duty with his regiment, which was then in camp at Hartford, and with the regiment left for the seat of war. The next spring he was commissioned by the president, brigade surgeon U. S. V., and ordered to report to Major-General Banks, department of the Shenandoah, and was assigned to the second brigade, Shields' division. Soon afterward he was promoted to be medical director of the division, and remained in service in that capacity up to the time when the division was incorporated with General McClellan's army at Harrison's Landing, when he was assigned to temporary duty. The invasion of Maryland by General Lee occurred soon afterward, and, September 15, 1862, while in charge of a field hospital, he received orders to proceed without delay to the headquarters of General McClellan and report to Surgeon Letterman, where, during September 17th and 18th, he was on duty at the battle of Antietam.

This terminated his field service. A few days later he was assigned as surgeon in charge of United States general hospital No. 6, at Frederick, Md., and was in charge of this hospital until its discontinuance in February following. By command of Major-General Schenck, middle department, February 18, 1863, he was assigned surgeon in charge of U. S. general hospital at Cumberland, Md., upon which duty he remained until after the close of the war. While in charge of this hospital he also served a while as medical director of the department of West Virginia, and in such official position, in company with Major-General Crook commanding, visited and inspected the military posts and hospitals within the department.

In his field service Doctor Lewis was present in thirteen skirmishes and battles, and during the same period was many times in charge of field hospitals. He was subsequently commissioned brevet lieutenant-colonel United States volunteers. He was retained in service after the close of the war, in order that he might have charge of the sale of the large property belonging to the government which had been used for hospital purposes at Cumberland; and when he had completed these duties he forwarded a written request to be mustered out "at the earliest date consistent with the interests of the service." By special orders from the War Department October 7, 1865, he was "honorably discharged out of the service of the United States."

In the latter part of 1865 he returned to Rockville, Conn., and resumed the general practice of his profession, remaining there about three years, when he removed to Hartford with his family, and

soon afterward went to Europe. On his return in 1869, he entered the service of The Travelers Insurance Company of Hartford, as medical director for that company and in charge of its claims department. His time has ever since been occupied with the duties of that position to such an extent that he has wholly withdrawn from the general practice of his profession.

Doctor Lewis was married, in 1855, to Miss Mary K. Mann, daughter of Hon. J. N. E. Mann of Dedham, Mass. They have three children, a son and two daughters. The former, Dr. William J. Lewis, is also connected with the Travelers Insurance Company as its consulting surgeon.

LEWIS A. CORBIN, ROCKVILLE: Contractor and Builder.

Lewis A. Corbin was born in Dudley, Mass., September 18, 1822, where the first eighteen years of his life were spent as a poor boy, managing a part  of the time to get a few months' training each year in the district school. At eighteen years of age he struck out into the world for work, "going west" as far as New York state, and meeting no success until he encountered a job in Warrensburgh at nine dollars per month for sixteen hours' work per day. He relinquished this munificent contract after a single winter, to

L. A. CORBIN.

undertake an apprenticeship at the stone cutter's trade in Cranston, R. I. In due time he became master of this trade, and returned to his native town to practice it in connection with building operations. In the fall of 1846 he went to Rockville, in this state, where he found employment on the Rock mill. Subsequently he became a master builder, and successively erected the American, the New England, the Leeds, and the Hockanum mills in Rockville, and the Windermere in Ellington. In 1851 he went to California, but after two years returned to Rockville, and soon afterwards associated himself with Cyrus White, first in the perfection of an envelope machine, and afterwards in the manufacture of envelopes, under the firm name of White & Corbin, afterwards incorporated as "The White, Corbin & Co.," of whose stock he is a one-third owner.

Mr. Corbin has held the offices of first selectman and assessor of the town of Vernon, is a member of the Methodist church in Rockville, and in politics is classed as a "temperance republican." He married Miss Mary H. Upham, who, with their three children, is still living. He is a man of economical habits, in a lifelong practice of which he has risen from a penniless boy to a man of large and increasing fortune.

WATSON GIBBONS, HARTLAND: A Retired Farmer and Merchant.

Watson Gibbons of East Hartland was born in Granville, Mass., February 18, 1812, and received a common school education. He has held the

offices of judge of probate, selectman, town clerk and treasurer, and is a republican in politics. In 1881 he was a member of the general assembly. He is a member of the Congregational church, and of St. Mark's Lodge, F. and A. M. Mr. Gibbons has been married twice. His first wife was Miss Elizabeth C. Parsons, daughter of Oliver Parsons of Granville. The

WATSON GIBBONS.

maiden name of his present wife was Almira H. Colton, of Granby. At the time of her marriage with Mr. Gibbons she was the widow of Darius Emmons of Hartland. There are no children in the family. The subject of this sketch has devoted nearly fifty-five years of his life to mercantile pursuits.

REV. CHARLES NELSON NICHOLS, ANDOVER: Baptist Clergyman.

Rev. C. N. Nichols was born in Trumbull, this state, August 15, 1832. He received his education in the common schools, and at a select school in

Bridgeport. After engaging in mercantile and mechanical pursuits, he entered upon the work of the gospel ministry in connection with the Baptist denomination, May, 1858. He was ordained in New Hartford, September, 1862. He has held pastorates in New Hartford, Cromwell, Old Lyme, Colchester, Tariffville, and other places in this state; and on Martha's

C. N. NICHOLS.

Vineyard and at Chatham, Mass. His present field of labor is Andover, Conn. He has been successful in his calling; precious revivals have fol-

lowed his labors; and he is still preaching faithfully the same old gospel. Nearly all of his life thus far has been spent in this state, which he ardently loves. He is also well known as an earnest and zealous temperance advocate, and a frequent contributor to the temperance and religious press. In politics Mr. Nichols is a strong prohibitionist. He served as postmaster for a time during the present administration of President Harrison. In January, 1868, he was married to Miss Sarah A. Dibble of Old Lyme. She is still living. They have had no children.

Mr. Nichols has a wide circle of acquaintances and friends throughout the state, and is highly respected and esteemed, and prizes very much the love and companionship of those among whom he has so long lived and labored. Mr. Nichols is one of the oldest Baptist pastors in this state, so far as it relates to ministerial service in Connecticut.

HON. ROBERT J. VANCE, NEW BRITAIN: Journalist; Editor "New Britain Herald."

Hon. Robert Johnston Vance of New Britain, who represented the first Connecticut district in the fiftieth congress, is a leading member of the

democratic party in this state. He was a member of the Connecticut delegation in the national democratic convention at St. Louis in 1888, and was president of the state democratic convention at New Haven during the same year. At the state convention, which was held in Hartford, September 16, 1890, Mr. Vance

R. J. VANCE.

made one of the ablest speeches in that body, eliciting enthusiastic approval from the delegates. The ex-congressman began his political career as the city clerk of New Britain, occupying the position from 1878 until 1887. In 1886 he represented New Britain in the legislature with decided ability and success. For the past ten years he has been a member of the democratic state central committee and is at present chairman of its executive board. This fact alone indicates the sense of confidence and trust which is felt in his ability and leadership. Mr. Vance is the editor and associate proprietor of the *New Britain Herald*, and is one of the ablest newspaper men in the state. He was the staff correspondent of the *New York Sun* in Washington during the winter of 1889-90. Aside from his editorial work he is actively connected with business interests in New Britain, occupying the presidency of the New Britain Electric Light Company and directorship in other business concerns. He is a member of Harmony Lodge, No. 20, F. and A. M., of New Britain, and is also a member of the order of Odd Fellows in that city. The family of Mr. Vance consists of a wife and one child. The former was Miss Matilda O'Conor prior to her marriage. The ex-congressman was born in New York city March 15, 1854, and is now in the very prime of manhood. He was educated in the New Britain High school and has traveled extensively, spending considerable time in Europe. He is a gentleman of the most delightful personality and is the possessor of hosts of friends in this state.

HON. W. H. H. COMSTOCK, New London: Retired Merchant.

William H. H. Comstock was born in that portion of Lyme that is now known as East Lyme, March 20, 1819, and was educated in the public and select schools of that period. He engaged in mercantile business early in life and has spent much of his active career in New London. Prior to his removal to that city he was treasurer and postmaster in East Lyme. In 1848 he was elected a member of the house of representatives from East Lyme, and the year after he was appointed paymaster-general on the

W. H. H. COMSTOCK.

staff of Gov. Clark Bissell of Norwalk and was confirmed by the senate. In 1854 he represented the old ninth district in the state senate, his associates in that body including the late United States Senator James Dixon of this city, Hon. Henry B. Harrison of New Haven and Hon. Wm. T. Minor of Stamford, both of whom became governors of the state, John Boyd of Winsted, Chauncey Rowe of Farmington, and Clark Greenman of Stonington. In 1859 Major Comstock was returned to the house from East Lyme, Augustus Brandegee of New London, Jeremiah Halsey and ex-Judge James A. Hovey of Norwich, and the late Daniel Chadwick of Lyme being associate members from New London county that year. The Major is a member of the New London board of trade, a director in the New London City Bank, and is connected with the Sons of the Revolution in that city. While he was a member of the state senate in 1854 he was associated with the corporation of Yale College, being one of the six senators entitled to that distinction. The wife of Major Comstock, whose

maiden name was Miss Eliza A. Smith, daughter of Doct. John L. and Fanny Smith, died December 4, 1876. One daughter, Mary C., wife of C. J. Viets, is living. Gen. Comstock is a member of the First Baptist church in New London. His political affiliations are with the republican party.

LEWIS A. LIPSETTE, Meriden: Journalist.

Lewis Allen Lipsette, editor of *The Meriden Journal*, was born in New York city February 18, 1852, and was educated in the public schools of the metropolis. For the past fifteen years he has been engaged in journalism in this state and is one of the most successful newspaper representatives in the commonwealth. Mr. Lipsette, or "Lew Allen," as he is universally known in newspaper circles, was the city editor of *The New Haven Union* up to four years ago, when, with Francis Atwater, who had for years been

"LEW ALLEN."

in the newspaper and job printing business, T. L. Reilly, who had been the city editor of *The Meriden Republican*, and Frank E. Sands, who had recently graduated from the Sheffield Scientific school, he organized "The Journal Publishing Company" of Meriden and started *The Meriden Daily Journal*. It was a pronounced newspaper success from the start. The company now own their own building, a fine web-perfecting press, stereotyping equipment, job printing department, electrotype plant, and book bindery, all fully fitted to turn out the best class of work; and *The Journal* all the while is growing in popular favor as a well-conducted and profitable newspaper, second to none in any city of the size of Meriden. Of this newspaper Mr. Allen has acted as editor, Mr. Reilly has had charge of the city news, Mr. Sands has been treasurer, and Mr. Atwater general manager, especially of the several mechanical departments, for which his long experience so well fitted him. The company have not far from fifty employes at present.

Mr. Lipsette has been a member of the city council in Meriden, and is an independent in politics. He was in the Connecticut National Guard for five years, serving in Company I of the Second Regiment. He is connected with the Episcopal church in Meriden and is a member of the Royal Arcanum. During the time that he was connected with *The New Haven Union* he was one of the best known state correspondents of New York and Boston papers. He has been one of the leading members of the Connecticut Press Association, and his newspaper success has been exceedingly gratifying to his friends in the profession throughout the state.

CHARLES E. HILL, STAMFORD: Retired Merchant.

Charles Edwin Hill was born in Great Falls, Strafford County, New Hampshire, Feb. 27, 1827, and was educated in the public schools. When a child he lived in York County, Maine, and his youth and early manhood were spent there in woolen manufacturing. He begun business on his own account in the city of Philadelphia in connection with United States ex-Senator Chase of Rhode Island, as a drygoods commission merchant. Subsequently he entered the China trade in New York city, and for

C. E. HILL.

twenty years, including the war period, was at the head of a large business in teas and other China products, during which time he was a stockholder and director in various banking, transportation, and manufacturing corporations. In 1880 at the instance of the Chamber of Commerce of New York, he was appointed chief special agent of the United States census bureau to gather the statistics of the manufacturing industries of that city and continued in that great work for over two years. In 1876 he came to this state and settled in Stamford. He has been a frequent contributor to the press on topics of political and social importance. In religion Mr. Hill is a Quaker, still adhering to the fundamental doctrines of that sect, though worshiping with other Christian denominations, chiefly with Methodists. In politics, from the inception of the republican party till the present time, an unflinching devotee of its principles and an earnest worker for its success. He was elected a member of the lower house of the Connecticut legislature for 1889, and served as chairman of the insurance committee on the part of the house, and also as a member of the committee on education. His term of service was notable for the active part he took in the stirring debates of that session. He made notable speeches on the petition of the Housatonic Railroad for authority to build a parallel railroad from New York to New Haven, upon the resolution granting commutation of death sentence to John H. Swift, upon the resolutions in honor of John Bright, and took an active part in the movement to secure the

act which made it possible for the policy-holders of the Phoenix Mutual Life Insurance Company to defeat the designs of McFarland of Philadelphia, which he regards as one of the most important legislative acts of the session, carried as it was, over the veto of the executive. Mr. Hill was mentioned in connection with the republican candidacy for lieutenant-governor in 1890, but would not allow the use of his name. His career has been one of activity and honor, and he retains the good will and esteem of a large number of citizens of the state.

ORRIN E. MINER, NOANK (GROTON): Physician and Druggist.

Dr. Orrin E. Miner is one of the best-known physicians in his section of the state. He was born at North Stonington, September 29, 1834, and received a classical education at Greenwich, R. I. At the age of sixteen he began teaching, but in 1855 gave up that profession for the study of medicine. After reading medicine in the office of Dr. L. W. Kinney of North Stonington, he continued the study at Castleton Medical College in Vermont and in the medical department of the University of New York city, graduat-

O. E. MINER.

ing in 1858. He also received a diploma from Bellevue Hospital. Dr. Miner located at Groton soon after his graduation, and has remained in practice there since. He also has a large practice at Mystic Island and at Fisher's Island during the fashionable season at these places. He is the senior member of the drug firm of O. E. Miner & Son at Noank, which was originally established in 1867. The son, O. E. Miner, Jr., was admitted to the partnership in 1874. Dr. Miner was postmaster from 1869 until 1886, and has been a notary public since 1860. He has also been a commissioner of the superior court, and is the medical examiner. He has always been identified with the republican party. The Doctor is a member of Relief Lodge, No. 71, F. and A. M., of Mystic Bridge, and is an influential representative of the order in southeastern Connecticut. His family consists of a wife and two children, a son and a daughter. The latter is a member of the senior class at Mt. Holyoke College, and the son is a railway postal clerk on the Providence & New London road. Mrs. Miner was Miss Abbie J. Latham, daughter of James A. Latham, Esq., of Noank. The marriage occurred in 1859.

CHARLES B. POMEROY, Windham: Farmer.

Charles B. Pomeroy of Willimantic (town of Windham), sheriff of Windham county, was born at Somers, May 15, 1832, and was educated in the common schools of that locality. Most of his life has been spent in farming. He has occupied important public positions, serving on the board of selectmen, and representing his town in the general assembly. In 1886 he received the republican nomination for sheriff in Windham County, and was elected by a plurality of 936. This fact expresses the

C. B. POMEROY.

popularity of the man in the county of which he has been for years a resident. He is an able and efficient officer, and his public career has been thoroughly satisfactory. Sheriff Pomeroy is a member of St. Johns Commandery, Knights Templar of Willimantic, and also of the order of Odd Fellows. His family consists of a wife and six children. Mrs. Pomeroy was Miss Mary E. Palmer before marriage. Sheriff Pomeroy and family are connected with the Congregational church in Willimantic.

JOSEPH KELLOGG WHEELER, Hartford: Grand Secretary of the Masonic Grand Bodies of Connecticut.

Mr. Wheeler was born in Bloomfield, Conn., on the 27th of August, 1834, and was christened Joseph Kellogg, the last name indicating the line of descent on his mother's side. It is through the Kellogg family his genealogy is traced to Samuel Kellogg, one of three brothers who came to this country from Scotland, in 1600. Their names were Joseph Kellogg and Samuel Kellogg, who located in Hatfield, Mass., and Daniel Kellogg, who located in Norwalk, Conn. His ancestors on the Wheeler side were among

J. K. WHEELER.

the early settlers in Keene, N. H., the record going back to Abraham Wheeler, who was born about the year 1700, of English or Welsh parents, supposed to be Welsh, as Wheeler is a very common name in Wales. He was raised a farmer's son in the town of West Hartford, being early accustomed

to the labors which came naturally to one in his position. He received a common school education only, with the addition of two terms in an academy located in his native town, and at the age of nineteen was employed as teacher of a district school in the vicinity of his home. In 1854 he engaged as clerk in the grocery business in the city of Hartford, and finally entered the business for himself, which he conducted for many years, until the duties of the office of grand secretary absorbed so much of his time that he was obliged to relinquish all business.

He was made a Master Mason in St. John's Lodge, No. 4, of Hartford, May 30, 1860. He was exalted as a Royal Arch Mason in Pythagoras Chapter, No. 17, of Hartford, May 9, 1862; received the degrees of the Cryptic Rite in Wolcott Council, No. 1, Hartford, April 3, 1863, and was knighted in Washington Commandery, No. 1, of Hartford, July 28, 1863. He received the degrees of the Scottish Rite to the thirty-second in Rhode Island, September 28, 1863, and was created a grand inspector general, 33°, in Boston, Mass., May 18, 1865. He was elected master of St. John's Lodge, No. 4, Hartford, January 3, 1866, and held the office two years, those years being marked with great prosperity. He was elected high priest of Pythagoras Chapter, No. 17, January 3, 1868, and served two years; elected thrice illustrious master of Wolcott Council, No. 1, January 4, 1872, and eminent commander of Washington Commandery, No. 1, January 2, 1877, having filled the subordinate offices in those bodies. He was one of the original members of Charter Oak Lodge of Perfection, which was organized at Hartford in 1870, and for ten years or more was its presiding officer, and helped to constitute Hartford Council, Princes of Jerusalem, and Cyrus Goodell Chapter of Rose-Croix, serving as presiding officer over each. In the grand bodies of Connecticut he holds the following official positions: He is grand secretary of the Grand Lodge, having been first elected May 8, 1867; grand secretary of the Grand Chapter, to which office he was first elected May 7, 1867; grand recorder of the Grand Council, his first election being May 7, 1867, and grand recorder of the Grand Commandery, his first election being March 21, 1882.

In all these positions of labor and responsibility he proved himself to be the right man in the right place, and his services have been productive of the best results in all the departments where his thought and energy have been applied. He is an enthusiastic craftsman, and loves freemasonry for its truths, principles, and symbolisms, not less than for its social feature and practical helpfulness. His conservative opinions, his generally correct judgments, his catholicity of sentiment, and his devotion to the best principles represented by the Masonic system and organization, have given him a justly-earned and widely-extended reputation among intelligent brethren. Mr. Wheeler was a member of the city council of Hartford in 1873-4; belongs to the Windsor Avenue Congregational church; the Connecticut Society of the sons of the American Revolution, his great-grandfather, Daniel Kellogg, having served in the war, enlisting first in the fall of 1775 under Captain Bulkeley of Colchester; and acts with the republican party. He is married, and has three children.

GEORGE WASHINGTON HODGE, Windsor: Paper Manufacturer.

George W. Hodge was born at Seymour, Conn., July 5, 1845. He received his education at the Connecticut Literary Institution at Suffield, and a

G. W. HODGE.

further preparation at Eastman's Business College at Poughkeepsie, N. Y. He learned the business of tissue paper manufacturing in the mills of his father at Rainbow, to which place his father's family removed from Seymour in 1853. He was married to Miss Jennie A. Clark of Tivoli, N. Y., in August, 1865, and admitted into partnership with his father in 1866, continuing business as a firm until 1874, when he sold his interest and was out of business until 1876. He then purchased a one-third interest with House & Co., manufacturers of press paper; in 1882 he further purchased the interest of one of his partners, and in 1889 the interest of the remaining partner, and is now conducting the business personally, though under the old name of House & Co.

In 1881 Mr. Hodge represented the town of Windsor in part in the house of representatives. In 1883 he was elected selectman, and served for five consecutive years. In 1889 he was elected to the state senate from the third senatorial district. At present he holds no public office. He has always belonged to the republican party, and as their candidate was elected to both branches of the legislature as above specified. He joined the Baptist church when a lad of twelve years, and has been connected with that body ever since. He was one of the leading agencies in the organization of the church, and in building the house of worship and parsonage at Rainbow. He belongs to the Masonic fraternity, having been a member since 1866.

OLIVER GILDERSLEEVE, Portland: Ship Builder.

Oliver Gildersleeve, son of Henry and Emily F. Gildersleeve, was born on the 6th of March, 1844, in that part of the town of Portland now called Gil-

OLIVER GILDERSLEEVE.

dersleeve. He received his education at the Hartford High school, and at the age of seventeen entered his father's shipyard, where he soon acquired the art of practical shipbuilding, and to-day is the fifth generation of shipbuilders in that place. At the age of twenty-one he became a partner, since which time he has largely increased the business, having added a marine railway, capable of hauling vessels of eight hundred tons burden, and built a large ice-house, provided with steam machinery and the necessary appliances for gathering ice from Connecticut river for shipment to New York and southern ports. In 1881 he became a member of the firm of S. Gildersleeve & Co., shipping and commission merchants, 84 South street, New York, he being the active managing owner of the fleet of vessels controlled by that house, and principally then owned by the Gildersleeve family. As a young man he was very desirous of seeing the world, and at the age of twenty-seven had visited the principal cities of his own country, Europe, and Canada. Possessing an excellent memory, he acquired a fund of information, which has been utilized to good advantage in his business. In works of charity and benevolence he has fully sustained the reputation of the Gildersleeve family. He is senior warden of Trinity Episcopal church of Portland, and has variously officiated as lay-reader, Sunday-school superintendent, and teacher. He is a trustee of the Gildersleeve high school fund, also of the Freestone Savings Bank, and has served three years on the district school committee, also as one of the building committee in the erection, in 1890, of the elegant new school building in district No. 1; was also for many years a prominent debater and officer in the Portland lyceum. In 1887, in connection with the late Horace Wilcox of Meriden, he established the Gildersleeve & Cromwell Ferry, and has ever since been the president of the company. In 1889, in connection with Wheeler & Parks of Boston, he organized the Portland Water Company and built its works, which, with its twelve miles of piping, now supplies the citizens of Portland with the purest and best of water. He has been president of the Water Company ever since its organization.

On the 8th of November, 1871, he married Mary Ellen, daughter of the Hon. Alfred Hall of Portland; by her he has had eight children: Alfred, born August 23, 1872; Walter, born August 23, 1874; Louis, born September 22, 1877; Emily Hall, born June 9, 1879, died August 12, 1880; Elizabeth Jarvis, born June 6, 1882, died January 18, 1883; Charles, born December 11, 1884; Nelson, born September 14, 1887, and Oliver, Jr., born March 9, 1890.

HON. JAMES PHELPS, Essex: Judge of the Superior Court.

James Phelps was born in Colebrook, in the county of Litchfield, in 1822. He is a son of Dr. Lancelot Phelps, who was for many years a prominent citizen of the state and one of its representatives in congress in the administrations of Jackson and Van Buren. The subject of this sketch received a thorough academic education, and entered Washington, now Trinity, College, but sickness prevented the completion of his course. He acquired a legal education in the law department of Yale College, and in the

JAMES PHELPS.

offices of the Hon. Isaac Toucey and the Hon. Samuel Ingham, and was admitted to the bar at Middletown, in October, 1844, and practiced his profession at Essex where he has resided during all his professional life.

Besides holding other prominent local positions, he was a member of the state house of representatives in 1853, 1854, and 1856, and of the state senate in 1858 and 1859. He was elected by the general assembly in 1863, a judge of the Superior court for the regular term of eight years, and was re-elected in 1871; and in 1873 was elected a judge of the Supreme court of errors, which office he resigned in 1875 on his election to the forty-fourth congress of the United States from the second congressional district, composed of the counties of New Haven and Middlesex. He was re-elected to the forty-fifth, forty-sixth, and forty-seventh congresses, and declined further congressional service. While in that body he was placed on several of its most important committees, including ways and means, foreign affairs, reform in the civil service, investigation of the Louisiana election, etc.; and in the contest in the special session of the forty-sixth congress, between the executive and the legislative departments of the government respecting the appointment and service of deputy U. S. marshals,

and the stationing of U. S. soldiers at the polls while elections were being held, he was selected as one of the joint committee of democratic senators and representatives to consider and recommend suitable legislation with reference to those important questions.

Soon after his retirement from congress he was again appointed a judge of the Superior court and is still discharging the duties of that position.

September 30, 1845, he married Lydia A., daughter of Hon. Samuel Ingham, who still survives. They have had two sons, viz: Samuel Ingham Phelps and James Lancelot Phelps. The former died at Chattanooga, Tennessee, January 10, 1891.

Judge Phelps has been for many years a member of the Protestant Episcopal church in Essex, to which his liberal support and benefactions are well known.

EMIL C. MARGGRAFF, Watertown.

Emil C. Marggraff is a native of Germany, and was born May 25, 1841, in Landstuhl, in the Bavarian Palatinate, a locality celebrated in history as the birthplace of Francis of Sickingen, the valiant knight who assisted Martin Luther in the Reformation. Mr. Marggraff came to America when a boy of twelve years. He attended General Russell's military school in New Haven, and acquired a thorough elementary education with a good knowledge of English literature and the sciences. At the breaking out of

E. C. MARGGRAFF.

the war of the rebellion on the 16th of April, 1861, he enlisted in Company E, First regiment Connecticut Volunteer Infantry, for three months, under the first call of President Lincoln for 75,000 volunteers. He served the full term and was mustered out July 30, 1861. Shortly afterward he again enlisted, joining Company B, First Connecticut Volunteer Cavalry, for three years. He went through numerous engagements, and was severely wounded at the battle of Winchester, September 19, 1864. After the close of the war he became editor of a German newspaper, but resigned his position when the paper changed its politics from republicanism to democracy. In 1868 he came to Watertown, where he engaged in the harness business. Mr. Marggraff has followed literary and musical pursuits quite extensively, being the author of several musical compositions, and having written and published several war stories, under the title of "Reminis-

cences of a German Officer." In 1869 he was
married to Miss Sarah Dutton, by whom he has
three children living. He is a staunch republican
in politics, and has been chairman of the republican
town committee of Watertown for the past seven
years. He has also been a member of the school
committee for three years.

Mr. Marggraff is known to be highly educated in
music, having studied harmony and counterpoint
under some of the most eminent and successful instructors and masters. He is thoroughly literary
and musical in his tastes, and devotes all his leisure
time to the further study of his favorite topics.

HON. BENJAMIN NOYES, New Haven.

Mr. Noyes was born in New Canaan, Conn., and
is now a little past sixty-eight years of age. He was
the son of Dr. S. S. Noyes of New Canaan, who
was great-great-grandson
of the Rev. Joseph Noyes,
whose ministerial services
continued with the Center
church in New Haven for
forty-five years; and his
tablet forms one of the
seven now ornamenting
the inside walls of the
church. Mr. Noyes came
to New Haven into the
college book store of General Howe in very early
youth, and when seven-
teen years of age became

BENJAMIN NOYES.

half owner in the establishment; and a few years
after became sole owner, up to 1847, when he sold
it all out by dividing it up and putting it into the
hands of others. He then devoted himself to the
study of life insurance in New York for one year,
and prepared the charter of the American Mutual
Life Insurance Company, which was organized
with Professor Benjamin Silliman as president and
Mr. Noyes secretary, in 1849. Mr. Noyes, as a result of his reading and studies, believing that the
average longevity of man was increasing in the
United States, succeeded in inducing the directors
to reduce the then standard rates of premiums for
life insurance. The company thrived about
twenty-eight years, and accumulated a fund of
more than one million dollars, over and above all
losses and expenses, and built the insurance building. In 1857 the legislature of Connecticut, without his solicitation, appointed him a bank commissioner for three years, which office he held the full
term under Governor Buckingham. In discharging
these duties Mr. Noyes examined personally every
bank and savings bank in the state, and made a
personal balance sheet each year of each one of

them, and reported the same to the legislature.
During this period the country was carried into the
suspension of specie payments, and his recommen-
dations to the legislature and the banks were so
uniformly complied with by both, that the banks
were enabled to reduce their circulation from
twelve million of dollars down to about four millions without disaster to the banks or the public.
Mr. Noyes was appointed the first insurance commissioner of the state by Gov. Buckingham for
three years, and was re-appointed by Gov. English
for the same term. Full annual reports of the administration of nine years of official life as bank
and insurance commissioner by Mr. Noyes to the legislature were presented and printed every year,
which are now much sought after as valuable contributions to banking and insurance. During the
period of Mr. Noyes' public life he was active in
the affairs of men, and was the author of many
charters, among them the following: Four insurance charters, three railroad charters, and three
bank charters, all of which were organized and went
into business. He re-insured three life insurance
companies by combining them with his own. Among
other things, he wrote the charter and constructed
the Fair Haven Water Company, and built four
large reservoirs. He was a member of the board
of education for several years, and participated in
legislation in Washington, Albany, Massachusetts,
and Connecticut; and at the breaking out of the
war of the rebellion, after the banks in Hartford
and New Haven had declined to advance any
money to Governor Buckingham, towards sending
into the field the first two regiments, under the
requisition of President Lincoln, Mr. Noyes in less
than one hour raised the necessary amount, to wit:
$200,000; by his own insurance company, $50,000,
from Mechanics Bank, $50,000, and from Elm City
Bank, $100,000, which money was immediately sup-
plied to Governor Buckingham, and the regiments
were at once gotten up, equipped, and sent to the
war without the delay of calling the Connecticut
legislature together. The accumulations of the insurance company under the management of Mr.
Noyes, after paying losses and expenses, was
largely devoted towards the erection of stores,
factories, and houses, and assisting with cash,
enterprises, to large amounts of money, which
neither private capital nor banks would supply;
and it is a fact worthy of mention that not one dollar of principal or interest thus loaned or invested
during twenty-eight years of uninterrupted management was lost, and it contributed largely to the
growth and advancement of the city of New
Haven. Mr. Noyes is now engaged in writing and
printing a volume of 400 pages, octavo, exemplify-
ing constitution, laws, and legislation, under a republican form of government, to the end that the

people shall better understand how to protect and enforce their rights, including an exposé of the scandal of state requisitions as practiced by the governors of most of the states, as he says, without the authority of the constitution of the United States.

In early life Mr. Noyes married Miss Bates of Sharon, Conn., and they had five children. After her death he remained a widower six years, and then married Miss Maryland Virginia Gardner, daughter of Ira Gardner of Gardnerville, N. Y. Their beautiful daughter, Birdie, died at five years of age, of malignant diphtheria. Four of the first children are now living, and three of them are married.

FRANCIS RUSSELL CHILDS, HARTFORD: Professor of Latin and Greek.

Professor Childs was born in East Hartford, April 19, 1840, and is one of the best-known educators in the capital city. He prepared for college at the Hartford Public High school, entered Yale in the class of '69, graduating with honors, having an oration stand. He was also salutatorian of his class in the High school. After graduating at Yale he took a post graduate course of two years. He was principal of the Thompsonville High school for one year, and for a short time was principal of the West Middle

F. R. CHILDS.

District school of Hartford. In 1870 he became a teacher in the Hartford Public High school, his *alma mater*, and continued in that service until the fall of 1896. For a number of years he had charge of the senior class, and was instructor in Latin and Greek in the preparatory course for college. His success in instilling into the minds of his pupils a love for the classics and thorough scholarship is one of the traditions of the school, and his "boys" in college have uniformly made that progress which can only be made upon sound foundation principles of study. Professor Childs has hosts of friends in the alumni of the Hartford Public High school, who are all willing to cordially testify as to his conscientious work as a teacher. He has also been secretary of the alumni associations of the school since its formation. While a resident of East Hartford he was school visitor for some fifteen years, and for the most of the time was secretary of the board. Professor Childs married Adèle Amélie Dunham of Windsor; she died

November, 1886, leaving one child, a son. He has for the most part been connected with the democratic party, so far as politics go, but has not taken any especially active part. He is a Congregationalist.

RALPH I. CRISSEY, NORFOLK: Farmer.

Mr. Crissey is a native of Norfolk, and has spent almost his entire life there. He was born February 4, 1833, and educated in the public schools, finishing at Norfolk Academy. He has one daughter, Mrs. Winthrop Cone. His present wife was Miss Mary E. Buell of Colchester. He has held nearly all the local offices within the gift of his town, repeatedly, and now holds that of selectman and justice of the peace. He was a member of the general assembly, representing Norfolk in 1867 and again in 1883,

R. I. CRISSEY.

serving on the committee on probate districts, and on contested elections. He has always acted with the republican party and has been their town committee for several years. For more than twenty years he has been the business agent for his section of the Barnum Richardson Company of East Canaan. Mr. Crissey is a member of the Norfolk Congregational church, and of the Masonic fraternity.

STEPHEN WALKLEY, SOUTHINGTON: Manufacturer.

Stephen Walkley was born at Southington, June 27, 1832. At the age of eighteen, owing to his father's financial reverses, he left Lewis Academy, where he was nearly fitted to enter college, and entering a factory learned the machinist's trade. He also studied land surveying, and was appointed county surveyor. He enlisted as private in Co. A., 7th Conn. Vols., in September, 1862, and served three years. For most of this time he was detached as clerk in the adjutantgeneral's department at the headquarters of Maj.

STEPHEN WALKLEY.

Gen. A. H. Terry. On the organization of the Peck, Stow & Wilcox Company, in 1870, he was appointed its secretary. After holding this position three years, he resigned and bought out the *South-ington Reporter*, now the *Southington Phenix*. In 1876 he gave up newspaper work and was appointed treasurer of the Peck, Stow & Wilcox Company, which office he has held ever since. He was a member of the legislature in 1875, and again in 1887 and 1888. Has been a selectman, and for fifteen years chairman of the board of school visitors in his native town, and for twenty years a deacon of the Plantsville Congregational church. He is now treasurer of the Peck, Stow & Wilcox Company, and also of the Southington & Plantsville Electric Tramway Company.

In 1855 he married Ellen A. Hobart, daughter of John M. Hobart of Southington, who died in October, 1888; has reared three children, one son and two daughters.

WASHINGTON SMITH, Canterbury: Blacksmith and Wagon-maker.

Washington Smith was born in Canterbury, January 10, 1834, and received a common school education. At the age of eighteen he was apprenticed

WASHINGTON SMITH.

at the blacksmith's trade, and within a year after completing his time he purchased the business. In 1870 he was obliged to give up the more burdensome part of the business on account of impaired health. Ten years later his son became associated with him under the firm name of W. Smith & Son, resuming the blacksmithing department in connection with the branch of wagon-making which he had carried on in the interval from 1870. Mr. Smith has spent the whole of his business career in Canterbury and is highly esteemed in that community. He has been often solicited to take office, but has steadily resisted the appeals of his townsmen in that direction. On one occasion, however, he accepted the position of justice of the peace. He is a member of the Congregational church, occupying the position of society's treasurer for twenty years, and is also connected with the Golden Cross, Knights of Pythias, and Helping Hand societies. He was married when twenty-three years of age, his wife being Miss Mary A. Brown of Jewett City, who is still living. There have been four children. Of these, one son, Charles F. Smith, died in 1885, at the age of twenty-two; and one daughter, Mary E. Smith, died in infancy. A son, George W. Smith, and a daughter, Ruth K. Smith, still survive.

NATHAN TROWBRIDGE PULSIFER, Manchester.

N. T. Pulsifer was born in Newton, Mass., October 27, 1851, and was educated at the Newton High and Grammar schools. He has at different periods

N. T. PULSIFER.

of his life resided at Newton, New York city, and at Manchester. He has followed the business of paper-making, and is, in addition, interested in electric manufacturing. He is treasurer of the Oakland Paper Company, general manager of the Mather Electric Company, and president of the Lawson Valentine Company of New York. His energetic business methods have won for him the esteem and confidence of his fellow-townsmen, who have shown their appreciation of his ability by electing him president of the Manchester Board of Trade. He is looked upon as one of the leading business men in the paper trade in the state. He is connected with the Congregational church. In politics he is a republican, but more interested in business than in politics. He is a member of the Hartford Club, the New York Electric Club, and of the Connecticut Sons of the American Revolution. His wife was Almira Houghton Valentine, of New York city, and he has two children.

EDMUND WILKINSON, Greenwich: Manufacturer.

Mr. Wilkinson was born in that portion of Pomfret which was included in Putnam, when that town was incorporated by the legislature in 1855,

EDMUND WILKINSON.

the date being October 12, 1815, and was educated in Rhode Island and Massachusetts. His grandfather, father, and uncles from Rhode Island built at Putnam, in 1806, the first cotton mill erected in Connecticut, and Mr. Wilkinson, the subject of this sketch, continued the business until 1868. His efforts in securing the incorporation of Putnam, the plans being inaugurated in 1840, were of great importance. At first the idea was strenuously opposed, the opponents of the measure winning the victory in four different sessions. But in 1855 Mr. Wilkinson and his associates bore away the palm. The justice of the cause has been proved time and again since, the town of Putnam having become one of the most prominent centers of trade and industry in eastern Connecticut. Mr. Wilkinson was also an earnest supporter of the New York & New England line, and was instrumental in establishing the National and Savings banks in the town. He has been actively interested in the Merrick Thread Company, and has spent a portion of his life in France in connection with his business. His wife, who is not now living, was Miss Harriot Augusta Thayer before her marriage. There are four sons living. Mr. Wilkinson is a member of the Episcopal church, and in politics a republican.

TRACY PECK, NEW HAVEN: Professor of the Latin Language and Literature in Yale College.

Tracy Peck, twelfth child of Tracy and Sally (Adams) Peck, was born in Bristol, May 24, 1838. His direct male ancestors since Paul Peck, who came to Hartford with Rev. Thomas Hooker in 1636, have lived and died in Hartford county. He prepared for college at the Bristol Academy, and at Williston Seminary, East Hampton, Mass., and graduated at Yale in 1861, the valedictorian of his class. After graduation he desired to become a soldier in the civil war, but, dissuaded by the state of his health, he

TRACY PECK.

went to Europe, for nearly three years residing and studying, mainly in Germany, Italy, and France. On his return he taught mathematics and Latin, four years as tutor in Yale and one year in the Chickering Institute, Cincinnati, Ohio. He was professor of Latin in Cornell University from 1871 till 1880, since which time he has held the same position at Yale. He has been greatly interested in the movement to restore to Latin its ancient pronunciation, writing several articles in its support and introducing the reform both at Cornell and at Yale. He has contributed many papers to various critical, educational, and philological periodicals. With Professor C. L. Smith of Harvard College, he is editor-in-chief of a new series of annotated Latin books for college use, of which series four volumes have already appeared. Since 1883 he has been a trustee of Williston Seminary. He was president of the American Philological Association for 1885–86. He is a member of the Con-

gregational church, and in politics is an independent.

December 22, 1870, in Plymouth church, Brooklyn, N. Y., he married Miss Elizabeth H. Hall of Hadleigh, England, by whom he has a daughter (Teresina, born Nov. 9, 1872) and a son (Tracy, born April 1, 1874).

REV. JAMES M. PHILIPS, ANDOVER: Baptist Clergyman.

James Monroe Philips was born at Griswold, Conn., February 24, 1818, and was educated at the Plainfield Academy and Suffield Literary Institute. His younger days were spent in Plainfield. When seventeen years of age he began teaching school, and taught twelve terms with excellent success. In 1844 he was settled as pastor of a Baptist church in Russell, Mass., where he was ordained in 1845. He has held pastorates in Noank, Mystic, Greeneville, Niantic, Clinton, Easton, and Willington, covering a period of forty

J. M. PHILIPS.

years, all but three of which were spent in Connecticut. Since 1885 Mr. Philips has been living in Andover, as he says, " on the invalid list." Rev. Mr. Philips has been a tremendous worker in his field, performing what would now be regarded almost as impossibilities. He has preached 3,800 sermons, conducted as many prayer-meetings, and officiated at some 300 funerals. In the early part of his ministry it was common to preach three times on Sunday, frequently during the week at school-houses, and almost invariably at funerals. In addition to his duties in the ministry, he has been acting school visitor in Groton, East Lyme, Russell, Mass., and a member of the school board of Norwich when he was settled as pastor in Greeneville. He is an earnest prohibitionist, and even at his advanced age takes a keen interest in the movements of the prohibition party. He was married to Joanna M. Fish of Voluntown, December 9, 1845. She died in 1878, and Mr. Philips was again married September 9, 1879, to Rosetta P. Adams of Colchester, who is still living. He has never had any children. Rev. Mr. Philips is well known and sincerely beloved by his denomination in the state, and has many friends in all religious connections. His ministry has been a very able and successful one. In connection with his labors there have been precious and blessed revivals of religion. He is a man of intellectual attainments and spiritual power, and held in the highest esteem by his associates in the ministry; a man of clear judgment and fine executive ability. He has served as moderator of the Stonington Union and New London Baptist associations; also as clerk of both bodies. His record is a most worthy one.

CHARLES PAGE, North Branford: Town Clerk and Congregational Minister.

Charles Page of North Branford was born in that town May 21, 1830. He received a thorough education, pursuing his studies at the Guilford Institute, the Normal school at New Britain, and at the Yale Theological Seminary. In 1859 he commenced teaching in the public schools, devoting his attention to this avocation winters, and working on the farm during the summer. This method was continued until 1870. He was chosen a member of the board of school visitors in 1862, and held the position

CHARLES PAGE.

continuously for twenty-one years. He was chosen justice of the peace in 1870, and remained in office until 1887. In 1871 he was elected town clerk, treasurer, and registrar of births, deaths, and marriages, and has held these offices from that date until the present. In 1874 he represented the town of North Branford in the general assembly, his colleagues in the house being the Hon. Allen Tenny of Norwich, School Fund Commissioner Jeremiah Olney of Thompson, E. S. Day of Colchester, Edwin A. Buck then of Ashford, Colonel Charles M. Joslyn of Hartford, J. Dwight Chaffee of Mansfield, F. W. Bruggerhoff of Darien, ex-Congressman George M. Landers of New Britain, ex-Senator T. M. Maltbie of Granby, ex-Speaker William C. Case, Lynde Harrison of New Haven and Charles Durand of Derby, Tilton E. Doolittle of New Haven, and ex-School-Fund Commissioner Henry C. Miles of Milford. The experience in a house composed of such leaders of public thought and policy was invaluable. Mr. Page studied theology at the Yale Theological Seminary in New Haven, 1882-1885, attending lectures daily, and reciting with the class. He was licensed to preach Sept. 30, 1884, by the New Haven East Association, and has occupied pulpits in his locality as opportunity has presented itself. In politics Mr. Page is a republican. His wife, who is still living, was Miss Ellertine A. Dudley before marriage. There are three children in the family.

WILLIAM C. PIKE, Sterling: Town Clerk.

William Campbell Pike was born in Sterling, September 4, 1832, and was educated at the Plainfield academy and at the Smithville seminary in

W. C. PIKE.

Rhode Island, preparing him for an active and influential business life. He has been the town treasurer of Sterling, and represented that town in the legislature during the session of 1887, serving on the republican side of the house. He is an accountant by avocation, and is connected with the Sterling Dyeing and Finishing Company. He holds the office of town clerk of Sterling. During the time that he held the responsible position of town treasurer, and while holding the office of town clerk, his duties have been performed with intelligence and fidelity, and in a way to secure the approbation of the entire town. He is held in high public esteem in eastern Connecticut. Mr. Pike is without a family.

T. R. MARTIN, Waterbury: Superintendent Waterbury Brass Company.

Thomas Richards Martin was born in New York city, April 27, 1839, and received a common school education. He was advanced from the bench to

T. R. MARTIN.

his present position in 1881. He was a member of the council board in Waterbury from 1883 until 1886, and has since been a member of the board of aldermen. He has also been a police commissioner since 1884, and is a popular public official. In politics Alderman Martin is a republican. He served with merit during the war, advancing from the ranks to the captaincy of Company D, Fifth New York Volunteers. He enlisted as a member of Company D of this regiment in April, 1861, the command being known as Duryee's Zouaves, and was mustered out in 1863 on account of expiration of term of service. Since the age of thirteen years Superintendent Martin has been dependent upon his own energies for success. He has resided at Haverstraw, N. Y., Rahway, N. J., Brooklyn, New York city, and Philadelphia, being in the latter city from 1870 until

1874. For the past sixteen years he has lived in Waterbury. He is connected with the Episcopal church, and is a member of the order of Odd Fellows in Waterbury. His family consists of a wife and two daughters. The former was Martha M. Freeman prior to her marriage with Commissioner Martin.

DAVID PLATT, West Haven: Agriculturist.

David Platt was born in Naugatuck, Conn., December 5, 1830, his father, Nathan Platt, having moved from West Haven, his native place, to that town a short time before.
In the spring of 1831 his parents returned to West Haven, where nearly all of Mr. Platt's life has been spent, and where he now resides. He is the fourth child of a family of ten, six brothers and four sisters, all of whom are living. His ancestors were active in the revolutionary war and the war of 1812. An uncle of his on his mother's side built at his

DAVID PLATT.

own expense the war-ship *The Wasp*, used in the latter war. In early youth Mr. Platt manifested that energy and intelligence which have characterized him through life. In 1852, having been attacked by the "gold fever," which was then so prevalent, he journeyed to California to try his fortunes in mining there. After two years he left California for home, carrying with him not huge nuggets of gold, but a sum of money sufficient to give him a start in life in the east. In 1856 he married Miss Melissa Shenehon of New Haven. They have three children, all daughters. He purchased in 1857 the place in West Haven upon which he now resides. This place is beautifully located on Long Island Sound. The lawn is well shaded by fine elms and maples, and there grows among them a grand old cedar tree, dear to the family because that Mr. Platt's father in his boyhood, having been sent to clear a wood-lot, spared a sturdy little cedar that gave promise of being unusually fine, and this is the tree on his son's grounds, without doubt the largest cedar in Connecticut. Mr. Platt is a representative New Englander, a man of sterling business integrity, one whose "word is as good as his bond," of great energy and keen insight. Above all this, he is emphatically the poor man's friend. No wayfarer ever goes hungry from his door, and to many a man endeavoring to make some headway in the world has he extended a helping hand. He is himself what is termed a "self-

made man," having been thrown upon his own resources in boyhood, and having made for himself, if not a fortune, at least a competency. He has been mainly engaged in agriculture, and in that pursuit is well known as a practical and successful man. He is a very young looking and appearing man for his years, with a shrewd, intelligent face, lighted up by fine dark eyes, which seem to read one's thoughts, they are so bright and searching, although very pleasant in their expression. In politics he is a Jeffersonian democrat, and is a faithful and earnest worker for the success of the democracy in all its departments. He is a public-spirited man, and has served his town in various offices, having been for many terms upon the board of selectmen. He has not represented his town in the state legislature, his party having been in the minority; but he has had the honor of the nomination a number of times. The republicans now have a majority of over one hundred; still in last November's election Mr. Platt was a candidate for representative, and made a fine run, being defeated by the small number of six votes. But, although he has not been an active member of the legislature, he and several of his fellow-townsmen have worked zealously in different sessions of that body for their town's good in the settlement of several legal claims and disputes, and their efforts have met with success.

FRANK W. ETHERIDGE, Thomaston: Judge of Probate.

The subject of this sketch was born in Montville, Conn., March 31, 1858, and was educated in the High school at Hartford, in which city he resided for several years, prior to 1880. In 1880 he was admitted to the bar after a thorough course of study in the office of Johnson & Prentice, and soon after removed to Thomaston, where he is now connected with the law firm of Bradstreet & Etheridge. He has been prominent in public life in Thomaston, serving as clerk of the probate court from its organization in that district

F. W. ETHERIDGE.

in 1882, until he was elected judge of that court in 1890. He is a member and secretary of the board of education and of the board of health of the town, and is a justice of the peace and assistant town clerk. Judge Etheridge is a republican, taking an active part in the affairs of the party, and devoted to its principles. He is a member and one of the trustees of the Methodist church, and is connected with the fraternal organizations in Thomaston, being a member of Franklin Lodge, I. O. O. F., of Thomaston, and of Columbia Encampment of the same place. He married Ellen Mathews, and has four children. Judge Etheridge is looked upon as one of the rising young men of the western part of the state.

WASHINGTON R. GARDNER, WATERFORD: Farmer.

Mr. Gardner was born at Waterford, March 1, 1842. His elementary education was acquired at the district schools in his native town, to which in

later years was super-added an academic course in the Bartlett high school in New London. Mr. Gardner has descended from choice New England ancestry, his paternal and maternal progenitors having been men of note and identified with the early history of the state. They were all residents of New London or Newport for many generations, as is determined by tracing

W. R. GARDNER.

back through the genealogy for over two hundred years. His father, the late Henry Gardner, 2d, was the esteemed postmaster of Waterford for thirty years. The present residence of the widow of Mr. Henry Gardner, known as the " old Bulkeley tavern stand," was bought in 1832, and has remained the family homestead to this day. In 1864 Mr. Gardner married the youngest daughter of Gurdon T. Chappell, Esq., a gentleman of note in Waterford, and who at least once (in 1857) represented that town in the legislature. The maternal grandfather of Mrs. Gardner, Griswold Avery, Esq., was evidently a prominent figure in the early history of Waterford. He was a justice of the peace at the time of the incorporation of the town in 1801, and in that capacity warned its first town meeting, of which he was appointed the moderator. Afterwards, in 1806-7, he was elected representative to the general assembly. His son, Griswold Avery, 2d, succeeded him in 1808, and Charles Avery, a brother, in 1815-16-18. Others of the family have from time to time held positions of trust within the gift of their townsmen, including frequent elections to the legislature. The roll of representatives, as recorded at the state capitol, discloses the interesting fact that during the last century Mr. Gardner's family has been represented by one or another of its members, in the legislature, no less than twenty-eight times. Mr. Gard-

ner is a democrat in politics, inherited from father and grandfather, of the Jacksonian type, and a pronounced advocate of temperance. His first election to the position of a legislator was in 1882, when his majority was greater than the entire vote of his opponent. His re-election the succeeding year was a still greater triumph, inasmuch as he received the total vote, not only of his own party, but of the republicans, who at their caucus indorsed unanimously the democratic nominee. This action was chiefly attributable to the satisfactory record of Mr. Gardner on the prohibitory amendment before the legislature in 1883, which received his active support. Mr. Gardner is at present a justice of the peace for the town of Waterford, and a member of the board of relief. He carries on the farm upon which he resides, the homestead of Rev. Gurdon T. Chappell, deceased, and additionally is engaged more or less as a carpenter and builder. He has discharged the duties of all public positions to which he has been called with singular fidelity, and to the entire satisfaction of his constituents.

REV. GEORGE M. STONE, D.D., HARTFORD: Pastor of Asylum Avenue Baptist Church.

Dr. Stone is the son of Marvin E. and Hannah (West) Stone, and was born at Strongsville, Ohio, December 10, 1834. He commenced a business life

at an early age in Cleveland, but shortly after united with the Second Baptist church in that city, and changed his plans for life, deciding to take a course of study preparatory to the Christian ministry. He spent some months at Williston Seminary, Easthampton, Mass., in 1854, and then entered Madison (now Colgate) University, at Hamilton, N. Y., and

G. M. STONE.

graduated in 1858. His theological course was also taken at the Hamilton Theological Seminary.

Dr. Stone's first settlement was in Danbury, Conn., where he was ordained in September, 1860. The next year he married Miss Abbie E. Seeley, daughter of Deacon Nathan Seeley of the Danbury church. His pastorate in Danbury continued seven years and was highly prosperous, the last year an accession being made to the church of over ninety members. A failure of health at this time led him to seek a change of climate, and he removed to Minnesota in September, 1867, becoming pastor of the First Baptist church in Winona, serving this church for two years. In 1870 Dr. Stone was called to the charge of the Jefferson Street Baptist church in Milwaukee, Wis. In 1872 he received the honorary degree of Doctor of Divinity from the Chicago University. After a pastorate in Milwaukee of three and a half years, he returned to the East and was settled with the Baptist church in Tarrytown-on-Hudson, N. Y., in September, 1873. During his residence here, a beautiful new stone church edifice was erected. Dr. Stone gave special attention during this pastorate to the public reading of the Bible, occasionally devoting a whole service to the simple reading of the Scripture without comment. In June, 1879, he accepted a call to the Asylum Avenue Baptist church in Hartford, Conn., which pastorate he still holds (1891), after a period of twelve years. Dr. Stone has made three tours to Europe; the first in 1862, the second in 1882, and again in 1889, the latter including a visit to Turkey, Italy, Egypt, and Palestine. In 1884 a journey was made by Dr. Stone through the Yellowstone National Park, an account of which was given in a series of letters to the New York *Examiner*. He also went to Alaska in 1886. Dr. Stone has lectured extensively upon various subjects, notably his journeys, with stereopticon views on Alaska, Constantinople, and Palestine. He has rendered efficient service in Sunday-school institutes, the especial line in which he is particularly suggestive and fresh being in methods of Bible study. His studies in the public reading of the Bible, which had been continued for several years previously, were gathered together in 1890 in a volume entitled, "The Public Uses of the Bible; A Study in Biblical Elocution." This book, now issued by A. D. F. Randolph & Co., New York, has received the highest commendations from the press and from Christian ministers and teachers. Dr. Stone has been a prolific writer for the press, in which branch of activity he is still constantly engaged. He was elected chaplain of the house of representatives of the Connecticut general assembly in 1883, and re-elected in 1884.

A recent notice in the *New York Herald* makes mention of Dr. Stone in these words: "A few weeks since, one of the most prominent churches in that centre of the great empire of the West, Minneapolis, invited him to their pastorate, but he has decided to remain in his present position, to the great satisfaction of his church and the entire state. His counsel is eagerly sought in all local and state moral and educational and religious work, and he is ever at the front in all movements for the good of men, holding positions in all the important boards of the denomination. In the pulpit he is an attractive, forceful preacher, and his utterances are always marked by sweetness of spirit, keenness of analysis, breadth of view, and the persuasiveness of one who loves his fellow-men."

21

CALVIN M. LEETE, GUILFORD: Farmer.

Calvin M. Leete of Leete's Island, in the town of Guilford, has served three terms in the legislature from that town, representing that constituency in the house in 1856, 1862, and 1878. He is a republican in politics, and has held the office of registrar of voters for twenty-two years. He is a farmer by avocation and is one of the trustees of the Guilford Savings Bank. With the exception of two years in Meriden his life has been passed on Leete's Island, where he was born October 18, 1816. He is at present a member 

C. M. LEETE.

of the school board in Guilford and belongs to the Third Congregational church in that place. His wife, who is still living, was Miss Lucy M. Leete. There is one son in the family. The subject of this sketch is widely known throughout the state on account of his legislative associations. He is one of the oldest and most respected residents in Guilford.

HON. CYRUS G. BECKWITH, NEW LONDON: Merchant.

Cyrus Grosvenor Beckwith was born at Waterford, Conn., December 3, 1841. In early boyhood he studied in the common schools of his native town, and graduated in 1858 from the Bartlett High school at New London. He gradually became interested in mercantile pursuits, and was a commercial traveler for fourteen years, up to 1880, when he established his present business, the firm now being Beckwith & Keefe. In 1864 he was elected a member of the New London court of common council, and in 

C. G. BECKWITH.

1884 elected again for a term of three years. In 1886 he was elected to represent the Ninth senatorial district in the upper house of the state legislature, serving on the democratic side. Mr. Beckwith has membership with the Free Masons, Odd Fellows, and Red Men. He some years ago married Miss Augusta A. Dart, and they now have one child. His business and public career have been such as to entitle him to the respect and gratitude of his fellow-citizens.

PRENTICE O. SMITH, Franklin.

Prentice O. Smith, born August 3, 1817, in that part of Groton which is now Ledyard, moved in early manhood to Franklin, Conn., where he has

P. O. SMITH.

since resided. Having learned the trade of carriage-making, he carried on the business in partnership with his brother for about twenty years in Franklin. He then took the general agency for New York city for the successive editions of the atlas published by Mitchell & Bradley, holding the field to the satisfaction of all parties for a full quarter of a century.

He married, April 29, 1840, Miss Eliza J. King of Lebanon, Goshen society. They have two sons and two daughters.

Mr. Smith was a member of the Connecticut legislature in 1865. He has always been active in forwarding every measure which has given fair promise of benefiting the community, and has been especially earnest in sustaining the local church. A few such men in each of our country towns would soon arrest the decadence of which many complain.

JOHN N. LEWIS, Voluntown: Accountant.

Mr. Lewis was born in Exeter, R. I., April 23, 1847. He is a son of Deacon James Lewis, a prosperous farmer, and a grandson of Colonel

J. N. LEWIS.

Nathan B. Lewis, a veteran of the war of 1812. In his boyhood he worked on the farm summers and attended school winters, receiving his education in the public schools, select schools, and at Schofield's Commercial college. After leaving school he taught for several terms with good success. In 1870 he was United States census gatherer for Exeter, and in 1872 was elected

justice of the peace by the Rhode Island legislature. In October of that year he came to Voluntown, where he has been with the firm of Ira G. Briggs & Co. and their successors, to the present time.

He was postmaster of Voluntown under the Hayes and Garfield and Arthur administrations, but was removed by President Cleveland. He has been a member of the school board of the town for

many years, and is now town clerk and treasurer, and registrar of voters. He was elected to the lower house of the Connecticut legislature for 1889, by 99 majority out of 203 votes, and served on the committee on appropriations. He was returned to the house at the last election, and is now a member of that body, and chairman of the committee on unfinished business. Mr. Lewis is an ardent republican and a worker for the success of the party. He professes no religion, classifying himself as a materialist. He is a Mason and an Odd Fellow and stands high in those orders. His wife was Nietta Lee prior to marriage, and they have one child. Mr. Lewis is one of the active business and political forces in his part of the state.

WILLIAM HENRY FISHER, New Haven: Locomotive Engineer.

William H. Fisher, one of the best known lay preachers and workers in the state, was born in New York, Sept. 25, 1836, and when he was eleven

W. H. FISHER.

years of age his parents removed to New Haven. His education was in the public schools of New York, and the famous Lancasterian school of New Haven, under the veteran educator John E. Lovell. He has followed the profession of a locomotive engineer, and is well known to railroad men in all parts of the state. For several years he was engaged in the

work of an evangelist in the city of New Haven, and his labors were blessed by a great deal of lasting good. For the past eight years he has confined his public efforts to speaking in connection with the gospel temperance work. He is connected with the Methodist church, and the work in which he has been engaged is a guarantee that he is an honor to that body. During the civil war he was connected with the Union League of the United States of America, holding the highest office in the council to which he belonged and preserving, as a memento, its charter. He is a member of the Knights of Pythias, Sons of Temperance, O. U. A. M., Temple of Honor, and Masonic orders. He is an engineer on the New York, New Haven & Hartford Railroad, and is also a chaplain in the Brotherhood of Locomotive Engineers. His wife was Agnes Hitchen Miller, daughter of Doctor Richard Miller, and granddaughter of Captain Samuel Hitchen, founder of "Wheel of Fortune" Copper Mine, in Cornwall, England. They have one son and a daughter. He is a republican.

REV. EUGENE F. ATWOOD, Bloomfield: Pastor of Congregational Church.

Rev. E. F. Atwood is a descendant of Dr. Thomas Atwood, who came from Essex, England, in 1640, to Plymouth, Mass., and settled in Wethersfield, Conn., about 1660. On one line he is a direct descendant from Solomon Stoddard of North Hampton, Mass., and Rev. John Warham, the first pastor of Windsor. He was born in Woodbury March 14, 1847. He is married and has two children, a boy and a girl. He enlisted at fifteen years of age from the district school July 14, 1862, in Company A, Fifteenth Connecticut

E. F. ATWOOD.

Volunteers. He has served two years as state chaplain of the G. A. R., was also commander of D. S. Cowles Post, and delegate to the national encampment of the G. A. R. in California.

After the war he began a course, preparatory to entering college, in a private school in Woodbury. In 1868 he entered Madison University (now Colgate), Hamilton, N. Y. In 1870 he removed to Oberlin, Ohio. After two years in the college he entered the Theological Department, and graduated in August, 1875. In December, 1875, he was ordained and installed pastor of the Congregational church at Arcade, N. Y. In the summer of 1877 the society voted to tear down the old church and build a new one at a cost of $6,000, and granted Mr. Atwood a leave of absence for six months. He immediately entered the government employ as assistant superintendent of construction, and with a party he assisted in laying out Fort Keogh on the Yellowstone river. In the fall he returned, and, finding some dissatisfaction arising from his activity in raising the money for the new church, he at once resigned his pastorate to accept a call to Rodman, N. Y. Here a great revival followed his labors, and the church was repaired at a cost of $3,000. The Home Missionary Society extended him a call to the pastorate of the Congregational church at Deadwood, Dakota, and to supervise their new work in the Black Hills. In the fall of 1878 he accepted this call. Here he found full opportunity for the exercise of his natural organizing and financial ability. He assisted in organizing and procuring pastors for nine churches. This association of churches voted to locate a college in that region and appointed Mr. Atwood their financial agent. A college charter was secured, the first granted by the territory of Dakota. A preparatory school was sustained, forty acres of land secured at a value of

$8,000, and a building erected at a cost of $3,000 more. A bill was introduced in the territorial legislature to establish a Normal school in connection with this school at Spearfish. The bill was so amended as to include three other Normal schools, locating two in North and two in South Dakota; these are now in successful operation.

The position of county superintendent of schools was offered Mr. Atwood, but his health began to fail under his multiplied labors, and he was obliged to resign his pastorate and to return East. After a few months' rest he accepted a call to a small country church in Bridgewater in this state, where he remained three years, and then accepted a call to the church in East Canaan. A division in the society as to location of the church arose, and Mr. Atwood resigned. Soon after one party withdrew and formed the Plymouth church of North Canaan.

After supplying a few months in Harwinton, he accepted the call to his present pastorate in Bloomfield in May, 1887. Mr. Atwood has taken much interest in photographing the historic homes of old Connecticut, and is at present the accredited lecturer of the Connecticut Historical Society. He is frequently called to read papers pertaining to the history of Connecticut before learned societies in other states, and is much in demand for memorial and other addresses in locations where he is known.

EDWIN AYER, Old Saybrook: Farmer.

Edwin Ayer was born in Saybrook (now Old Saybrook), Oct. 15, 1824, and is of the seventh generation in direct descent from John Eyre (*pronounced Ayer*), who migrated from Norwich, in England, to Newbury, Mass., in 1637. He received his education in the common schools of his town, and at the academies of Saybrook and Essex. He has followed farming through life to some extent, and also lumbering; is now president of the Saybrook Bank of Essex.

In 1849 he went with

EDWIN AYER.

the crowd to California by way of Cape Horn, and was absent about three years. Was married in October, 1852, to Miss Abbie M. Youngs of Farmington, who died in 1882, leaving three sons and two daughters; two of the sons and one daughter are now residents of the state of Washington. He married for his second wife, in 1883, Miss Carrie E. Youngs, who is now living. He held the military office of major of the Sixth regiment Conn. militia when he left for California, and has subsequently held various civil offices, such as selectman, assessor, chairman of school board, and justice of the peace for some twenty-five years, and represented his town in the legislatures of 1872 and 1873. He is now living at his ancestral home, of which his family have held successive title since its first occupation by the English colonists.

HON. JOHN ALLEN, Old Saybrook : Senator.

John Allen of Old Saybrook, Middlesex county, Conn., was born in Meriden on the 6th day of February, 1815. He was the eldest of four children of

JOHN ALLEN.

Levi Allen, a farmer and prominent citizen of that place. He is a lineal descendant of Roger Allen of New Haven, who was a contemporary of Rev. John Davenport and deacon in his church. His grandfathers, Archelaus Allen and Aaron Hall of Wallingford, were patriots of the revolution, and served in the war for our national independence. After receiving a good academic education he was placed in the store of Major Elisha A. Cowles, in his native town, where, under the several changes in the style of the firm, he served a clerkship from the age of fourteen to twenty. In the spring of 1836 he removed to New York, and entered the employ of Perkins, Hopkins & White, wholesale merchants, then extensively engaged in the dry-goods jobbing business with the South. He remained with that firm in confidential relations through a period of unusual instability and difficulty in the mercantile affairs of the country, during which time, by active participation in the business, he gained valuable experience in laying the foundation of his future prosperity. Upon the re-organization of that firm in 1842, he became interested as a partner with Perkins & Hopkins; and upon a subsequent re-organization, was of the house of Hopkins, Allen & Co. It was, however, as a member of the last-named firm, whose high reputation was a fitting tribute to its enterprise, integrity, and success, that he became prominently known to the business world.

On the 10th day of November, 1847, he was married to Mary Ann Phelps, daughter of the late Hon. Elisha Phelps of Simsbury. His intercourse with the people of the South made him familiar with their views and policy in reference to the institution of slavery, and perceiving the growing antagonism between free and slave-labor, which foreshadowed serious difficulty to the country, he resolved to withdraw from mercantile business (then conducted largely upon credit), and established a residence in the town of Old Saybrook, where his family now resides. Being in active sympathy with the government of the United States in its efforts to maintain its integrity and suppress the rebellion, he received an unsought nomination to represent the nineteenth senatorial district in the state senate of Connecticut, and was elected thereto in 1863, and again in 1864, and in both years was chairman of the joint standing committee on finance, whose labors were of the highest importance in that critical period of public affairs, when the state was raising money for the war. The financial measures recommended by that committee and adopted by the legislature, not only enabled the state to creditably place its full quota of men in the field, but established a policy in the revision of the tax laws which has met the approval of the people of the state for twenty years, and reduced to a minimum amount the public debt. The present equitable method of taxing railroad property, on the basis of what it will sell for, by which the market value of its stock and bonds is made the measure of value of such property for purposes of taxation, was suggested by him.

On the 17th day of June, 1864, Mr. Allen introduced into the Connecticut legislature the first resolution in favor of the abolition of slavery by constitutional amendment. He was one of the delegates from Connecticut to meet a convention of loyal Southerners at Philadelphia, on the third day of September, 1866, called to give expression to the sentiments of the people in support of congress against the defection of Andrew Johnson. He was prominent in the movement that arrested the " peace flag " heresy at Saybrook, or the raising of any flag not representing all the states of the Union. He was one of the fellows of the corporation of Yale College while he was senator, in the years aforesaid, the odd law being that the six senior senators were members *ex officio* of that corporation. In the Hayes presidential campaign of 1876, Mr. Allen was a republican presidential elector in this state. In 1867 he was elected president of the Peoria, Pekin & Jacksonville Railroad Company, of the state of Illinois, which position he held in the active administration of the property for twelve years.

In 1883 he was again elected to the state senate from the 21st district, formerly the 19th, and served during the sessions of 1884 and 1885 as chairman of the joint standing committee on railroads. He was chairman of the legislative committee in charge of the public services at the inauguration of Warner's statue of William A. Buckingham in the battle-flag vestibule of the capitol. For many years he has been identified with the public library in Old Saybrook, and president of the organization.

In matters of church government he is a Congregationalist, in theology a Unitarian, but he attends the Episcopal church with his excellent wife. In politics he is a republican. He has two sons and four daughters. His second daughter is the wife of Hon. William Hamersley of Hartford.

WILLIAM WALES PECK, Woodbridge: Farmer.

The subject of this sketch was born in the town of Woodbridge, June 29, 1832, where his entire life has been spent. He has been a farmer from his youth, but managed to get a good education at the common schools, and at the Literary Institute in Suffield. He represented Woodbridge in the legislature in 1880 and 1881, being elected by the republicans. For seven years he was a selectman and town agent, and for ten years grand juror. He was prevented by sickness from personally joining the military service of the country during the war of the rebellion,

W. W. PECK.

but did the next best thing by providing and sending a substitute. Mr. Peck is a member of the Congregational church. His family consists of a wife and five children. Mrs. Peck, who is still living, was Miss Mary Jane Fairchild before their marriage.

HON. DAVID TORRANCE, Derby: Judge of the Supreme Court of Connecticut.

Judge David Torrance was born in Edinburgh, Scotland, March 3, 1840, and removed to this country in 1849. He received a common school education. His active life was commenced as a paper maker, that avocation being given up in the end for the law. In July, 1862, he enlisted as a private in Company A of the Eighteenth Connecticut, and served as second sergeant until December 22, 1863, when he was appointed to the captaincy of Company A of the Twenty-ninth Connecticut colored regiment. He received

DAVID TORRANCE.

the appointment of major in July, 1864, and lieutenant-colonel in November of that year. He was

mustered out of the service at Brownsville, Tex., October, 1865. While a member of the Eighteenth he was taken prisoner and was confined in Libby prison and on Belle Island for a short period. Judge Torrance is a distinguished member of the Army and Navy Club of Connecticut and is connected with the Grand Army. He represented the town of Derby in the legislature during the years of 1871 and 1872, and was secretary of state under Governor Charles B. Andrews, the present chief justice of the state. He was appointed judge of the New Haven county court of common pleas for the four-years term, beginning in 1881. In 1885 he was advanced to the superior court bench and in 1890 was appointed a judge of the supreme court of errors by Governor Bulkeley. His term will not expire until 1898. Judge Torrance is a member of the Congregational church and a republican in politics. He is also a member of King Hiram Lodge, No. 12, F. and A. M., of Birmingham, and is recognized as one of the most valued members of the fraternity in this state. His wife was Miss Annie France prior to her marriage. There are three children in the family.

WILLIAM R. HARTIGAN, Burlington: Manufacturer.

William Robert Hartigan was born in Burlington, March 10, 1852, and was educated in the Unionville High school. The education which he received was the result of his personal efforts, the funds necessary for his maintenance in the High school being earned and saved during the summers. At the age of fourteen he commenced the trade of wood-turning under John N. Bunnell of Unionville. When he was seventeen he established himself in business in the town of Burlington. After six years of

W. R. HARTIGAN.

success, he met with the loss of every dollar which he had placed in the enterprise, the establishment being destroyed by fire. Undaunted in courage, he resumed the old lines, and gradually recovered from the misfortune. He is a skilled mechanic and inventor, being especially successful in wood turning, machine work, forging and enameling in all colors on wood or metal. Mr. Hartigan is now the owner of a prosperous and successful plant. In politics he is a republican, and is town registrar. He is a member of the Episcopal church. He has a wife and one child. The former was Miss Annie S. Barnes prior to her marriage.

CHARLES H. PINNEY, M.D., DERBY: Physician and Surgeon.

Dr. Charles Hitchcock Pinney was born in South Windsor, April 25, 1831, and received a collegiate training. He prepared for Harvard at the Rogers Academy in East Hartford, and matriculated in 1850. From Harvard he went to New York, becoming a student in the College of Physicians and Surgeons in that city. He was also a private pupil of Dr. Willard Parker. He graduated and received his diploma from the New York institution in 1853, and commenced the practice of his profession immediately at Derby.

C. H. PINNEY.

His wife, who is still living, was Miss Maria Watson, daughter of Royal I. Watson of New Hartford. There is one son, Dr. Royal Watson Pinney, who is associated with the subject of this sketch as a practitioner. The doctor is a member of the New Haven County and State Medical Societies, and of the American National Medical Association. In politics he is a republican. He has invariably declined office, devoting the whole of his time to the duties of his profession. Dr. Pinney is universally honored in Derby, and is a gentleman of exceptionally agreeable personality.

R. W. PINNEY, M.D., DERBY: Physician and Surgeon.

Dr. Royal Watson Pinney was born in the town of Derby, Dec. 25, 1863, and prepared for Yale at the Birmingham High school, and under the private tutorship of John W. Peck. He graduated from the Sheffield Scientific department in the class of 1885, receiving the university diploma at the June commencement. In September of that year he entered the college of Physicians and Surgeons of New York city, and graduated in April, 1888. He sailed for Europe immediately after graduation, and spent the remainder of the year until December at Vienna,

R. W. PINNEY.

where he pursued a special course of study in the hospitals of that European metropolis. In December he returned to New York to take the place of house surgeon at Bellevue Hospital, having received the appointment prior to his departure for Vienna. From April, 1886, to October of that year, he had studied with Dr. Gustave Bögel in Lüneburg, Germany, not only to familiarize himself with the language, but also with German methods of treatment. In July, 1890, he left Bellevue Hospital, and has since been associated with his father, Dr. Charles H. Pinney, in the practice of medicine at Derby.

JULIUS CONVERSE, STAFFORD SPRINGS: Treasurer Mineral Springs Manufacturing Company.

Julius Converse, himself one of the leading manufacturers of Stafford, is the son of Solva Converse, who was one of the pioneers in the manufacture of woolens in Connecticut. He is a descendant from Asa Converse of Huguenot stock, who settled in Stafford about the middle of the last century. Julius Converse is a native of Stafford, born there March 1, 1827. After leaving the public school he attended the Ellington High school and the Quaboag Seminary at Warren, Mass. Later he entered the employ of the Mineral

JULIUS CONVERSE.

Springs Manufacturing Company, and acquired a thorough practical knowledge of manufacturing. He was then transferred to the office as clerk, subsequently became both agent and treasurer, and finally the sole owner of the property. In addition to his manufacturing interests, he is prominently connected with many other important business concerns. He was one of the incorporators of the Stafford National Bank; also of the Savings Bank of Stafford Springs; and is a director in the Hartford Life and Annuity Insurance Company.

Mr. Converse is a prominent member of the republican party, by whom he has been elevated to various public positions. He represented Stafford in the state legislature in 1865-66, was a Grant elector in 1872, elected to the state senate from the twenty-fourth district in 1877, was candidate for state treasurer in 1884, and delegate to the national republican convention at Chicago in 1888. He has a wife, who was Miss Myra C. Lord prior to her marriage, and four children living. His religious connections are with the Methodist Episcopal church of Stafford Springs, of which he is a generous supporter by his personal influence and private means. He is a man of eminent public spirit, as is evidenced in his large and frequent contributions to the improvement and advancement of his native town. His own private residence, "Woodlawn," is a charming spot, where he dwells in great comfort, and dispenses liberal hospitality to his friends.

FRANK M. MESSENGER, Thompson: Cotton Manufacturer.

The subject of this sketch is occupying the responsible position of agent of the mills of the Grosvenor Dale Company, one of the largest cotton manufacturing corporations in the state, and located at North Grosvenor Dale, in the town of Thompson. He has performed the duties of this office since 1884, and in so efficient a manner that during this term the capacity of the mills has been increased fully twenty-five per cent. Mr. Messenger is a native of Stoddard, N. H., where he was born April 3, 1852.

F. M. MESSENGER.

He remained with his father on the farm until fourteen years of age, attending school a part of each year. The following two years he continued his studies while working in a chair factory; and afterward for a period of three years divided his time between clerking and work in a cotton mill. Entering a cotton factory at Winchendon, Mass., at the age of nineteen, he was promoted from card grinder to second overseer, and finally, after a short period spent in the employ of the Amoskeag Company in Manchester, returned to Munsonville in the capacity of overseer. He afterwards filled the same position successively in several Massachusetts manufacturing concerns, his longest stay being in Manchaug, where he spent four years. At the expiration of this period he went to Shirley, Mass., as superintendent of the Phœnix and Fredonian mills, which he in turn resigned to accept, in November, 1884, the position which he now occupies in Grosvenor Dale. Mr. Messenger is one of the directors of the Thompson National Bank, a member of the Fredonia Lodge of Odd Fellows, a member of the Baptist church of Manchaug, Mass., and was for three years the superintendent of its Sunday-school. He is a republican in politics, and takes active interest in all religious, social, and educational affairs in his neighborhood. He married first, Eliza J. Smith of Winchendon, Mass., who died within a year; and second, Mary A. Young of Newton, Mass. Their children, three in number, are Frank M., Mabel W., and Don E. Messenger.

LEWIS SPERRY, East Windsor Hill (South Windsor): Attorney-at-Law.

Lewis Sperry was born in the town of South Windsor, January 23, 1848. He has always resided at East Windsor Hill. He prepared for college at Monson Academy in the class of '69, and graduated from Amherst in 1873. He studied law in the office of Waldo, Hubbard & Hyde, in Hartford, and was admitted to the bar March 30, 1875. He opened an office in this city shortly after, and has continued in legal practice here ever since. He was married, November 7, 1878, to Miss Elizabeth Ellsworth Wood,

LEWIS SPERRY.

daughter of Dr. Wm. Wood of East Windsor Hill, and they have two children. Mr. Sperry held the appointment of county coroner for Hartford county from June, 1883, to April, 1891, when he resigned. In politics he is a democrat; in religious sympathies a Congregationalist, though not a church member. He was elected November 4, 1890, to represent the first district in the national house of representatives, taking his seat at the assembling of the fifty-second congress.

HON. JAMES GRAHAM, Orange: Brass Founder.

Hon. James Graham, a resident of Orange, with business connections principally in New Haven, is one of the best-known manufacturers and public men in the state. He was born in Albany, N. Y., January 23, 1831, and educated at the public schools. He moved to Branford, Conn., in 1852, and was employed by the Squire & Parsons Lock Company for nearly ten years. In 1861 he started the business of a brass foundry in New Haven, and is now the senior member of the firm of James Graham & Co.,

JAMES GRAHAM.

carrying on an extensive business. He is also a director in the New Haven & West Haven Horse Railroad Company; president of the Bear Valley Irrigation Company, of Redlands, California; and a director in the West Haven Water Company. Mr. Graham is a thorough-going republican and has

for many years been prominent in the councils of
that party in the state. In 1878, 1885, and 1886 he
represented the town of Orange in the Connecticut
legislature, the last year serving as chairman of
the committee on railroads on the part of the
house. He was elected state senator from the seventh district for 1887-8 and again for 1889-90. His
familiarity with railroad legislation naturally
fitted him for the chairmanship of the railroad committee, in which position he served both terms,
during sessions in which the struggle between the
Consolidated road and the Housatonic system was
at its fiercest. Mr. Graham is an example of persistent, energetic endeavor in all that he undertakes, and he has the universal esteem and respect
of the people of the state.

J. B. MERROW, Merrow (Mansfield): Manu-
facturer and Merchant.

Joseph Battell Merrow was born in East Hartford, June 12, 1819, and is one of the best-known
men in the eastern part of Tolland county. He

was educated in the com-
mon schools, and has fol-
lowed manufacturing and
mercantile pursuits. He
removed from East Hart-
ford to Mansfield, where
he has since been engaged
in various branches of
stockinet manufacture,
carries on a large mer-
cantile business, has been
postmaster and station
agent at that point, as he
says, pretty much ever
since, the post-office and

J. B. MERROW.

railway station being named after him. He is the
oldest station agent on the New London Northern
road in point of service. He is at present senior
partner of the firm of J. B. Merrow & Sons, doing
business at Merrow and at Norwich, manufacturing knit goods, and now engaged in building special machinery for this manufacture in Norwich.
He has been a selectman of the town of Mansfield,
and a justice of the peace for several years. In
1867 he represented his town in the lower house of
the legislature, and was in the senate in 1873. His
first vote was cast for William Henry Harrison for
president in 1840, and he has been a republican
since the organization of the party. His wife was
Harriet L. Millard of Manchester. They have five
children, one of the daughters being the wife of
Prof. Washburn, principal of the Rhode Island
Agricultural College. He has been an active, energetic man, and has his full share of friends, both
in business and socially.

REV. STEPHEN B. CARTER, Westminster:
Pastor Congregational Church.

Stephen B. Carter, son of Adin and Polly C.
Carter, was born in Brooklyn, Conn., Sept. 2, 1839.
At the age of four years his parents removed to

Westminster in the town
of Canterbury. Here he
attended the district
school near his home both
summer and winter un-
til he reached the age of
twelve years, after which
he worked on a farm
summers, attending
school during the winter
months until he became
eighteen years of age. He
then commenced teaching
winters, continuing his
labors on the farm during

S. B. CARTER.

the summer seasons. At the age of twenty-three
he began work as a moulder in one of the iron
foundries of Westminster, and followed this occupation for about three years. He then resumed
the profession of teaching, in which, being very
successful both as an instructor and a disciplinarian,
he continued almost without interruption for
several years. He was married, Sept. 3, 1865, to
Miss Louisa Button, an estimable lady of Westminster. Two children are the fruit of this marriage, Edwin M., born February 26, 1870, and
Annie E., born July 12, 1873.

In the spring of 1872, he removed with his
family to Brooklyn, where he held the position of
principal of the East Brooklyn Grammar School for
nine successive terms. In 1874, he returned to
Westminster, where he resided till January, 1876,
when, having given some attention to the study of
theology, and been licensed by the Windham
County Association of Congregational ministers, he
received a call to become acting pastor of the
church in Ekonk, commonly known as the Congregational church of Voluntown and Sterling. He
continued his pastorate here for five years, having
been ordained in August, 1879. In January, 1881,
he resigned this position, and again returned to
Westminster. He was called to take the pastoral
charge of the Congregational church in this place in
March of the same year, in which relation he still
continues.

Mr. Carter has been eminently successful as a
teacher in an experience of more than thirty terms.
By the clearness and simplicity of his illustrations,
by his power to awaken the interest and arouse the
energies of his pupils, and by the healthfulness of
his own moral character, he has left an influence
for good upon the minds of many of the youth of
his charge which will never be lost. He possesses

a well-balanced mind, and is master of his mental powers. He is a deep thinker, with rare powers of memory. As a man he stands high among men. As a minister, he is highly esteemed; and his sermons, which are much admired, are all largely and some of them wholly unwritten. His early and frequent practice as a debater in the lyceums of his own and other towns have made him a close and logical reasoner, while as an extemporaneous speaker he ranks among the best. He also enjoys a very pleasant local reputation as a poet.

Mr. Carter has always been closely identified with the republican party; he has also for several years been a member of the school board of Canterbury, and for a part of that time acting school visitor.

F. B. NOYES, Stonington: Dealer in Western Securities.

Franklin Babcock Noyes was born in Westerly, R. I., June 22, 1831, and received a common school education, preparing him for an active and successful business life. He has held the positions of secretary, ticket agent, and paymaster on the New York, Providence & Boston railroad, and is one of the burgesses of the borough of Stonington. In politics Mr. Noyes is a republican. He has also held an agency for western loans, and is at present engaged in that business. Formerly he was engaged in business in

F. B. NOYES.

New York, and resided in that state for nine years. He is a member of Asylum Lodge, No. 57, of Stonington, and of the Royal Arcanum. He has been married twice, his first wife being Miss Harriet A. Thompson of Ithaca, N. Y. The second was Mrs. Harriet E. Palmer of Chicago, formerly Harriet E. Wilder of Lancaster, Mass. There is one child living. Mr. Noyes is a member of the Congregational church. His father was a volunteer in the war of 1812. He has the commissions of his grandfather as lieutenant, 11th Co., Second regiment, R. I., dated August 26, 1776, and signed by John Hancock; first lieutenant artillery, dated May 29, 1777; second major, senior class, May 7, 1792; first major, senior class, May 6, 1793, and lieutenant-colonel, commanding second-class regiment, May 12, 1794. His great-grandfather, Dr. Charles Phelps, was one of the first physicians in Stonington. He is also a great-grandson of Col. Henry Babcock of the revolutionary army. Mr. Noyes is an active and influential business man in the community where he resides.

CHARLES H. STILLSON, Ansonia: Real Estate.

Charles Hubbell Stillson was born at Newtown February 18, 1843, and was educated at the Newtown academy. At the age of twenty-one he removed to Ansonia, where he began business as a joiner and carpenter, and has since resided there. He is a republican in politics and a member of the board of assessors. He took an active part in securing the division of the old town of Derby two years ago. Mr. Stillson has been a member of the order of Odd Fellows for twenty-four years and is also a member of the An-

C. H. STILLSON.

sonia Club. He is engaged in the real estate business, being especially interested in that line. He is a member of the Episcopal church. His wife was Marion E. Kelley prior to her marriage. There is one son living.

HENRY B. CARTER, Wolcott: Farmer.

Mr. Carter was born in Wolcott, New Haven county, December 2, 1839. He is the eldest son of Deacon George W. Carter, who in his time represented that town in the Connecticut house of representatives, and the fifth senatorial district in the senate. Mr. Carter's whole life has been spent in his native town. His education was obtained at the district school. Early in life he married Mary R. Hotchkiss, only daughter of Stiles L. Hotchkiss of Wolcott. He has followed farming as an occupation chiefly, but has also made

H. B. CARTER.

quite a business of light and heavy teaming. He is a member of the Wolcott Congregational church, of which he was appointed deacon soon after the death of his father, who held that office before him. For many years he has been superintendent of the Sunday-school connected with his church; also has been, and now is, on the list of the society's committee. He has held the office of president of the Wolcott Agricultural Society for several years, and was re-appointed at its last annual meeting. He is chairman of the republican town committee; is first selectman of Wolcott; is chairman of the board of education; has served the town as assessor and road commissioner; and is at present master of Mad River Grange, No. 71, Patrons of Husbandry. He represented the town of Wolcott in the general assembly twice — in 1883 and 1884 — serving the first term on the committee on new towns and probate districts, and the last session on the joint select committee on temperance.

HON. HENRY B. GRAVES, Litchfield: Attorney-at-Law.

Henry B. Graves was born in Sherman, Conn., and is sixty-eight years of age. He had a common school education and spent one year in the academy

at Westfield, Mass. He was admitted to the bar in April, 1845. He has been a judge of probate in Litchfield and Plymouth. Mr. Graves comes of legislative ancestry, his grandfather, Ezra Graves, representing New Fairfield in the general assembly several sessions, and his father, Jedediah Graves, representing Sherman many times.

H. B. GRAVES.

His father was also a member of the constitutional convention of 1818, and one of the last survivors of that memorable body of men. In 1849 Mr. Graves was clerk of the state senate, in 1854 executive secretary; was clerk of the superior and county courts of Litchfield county in 1854-55, and has been a justice of the peace for forty-four years. His legislative career has been as remarkable and as useful as that of any man in the state. He was a member of the lower house for the first time in 1858, when he served on the judiciary committee and on contested elections; in 1867, again on the judiciary committee; in 1869 he declined service on the judiciary, and at his own request served on the committee of education; and was active in support of the law making the schools free. Governor English gave him the credit of being largely influential in the success of that measure. In 1876, after an interval of eight years, he again entered the legislature, and was house chairman on railroads and chairman on contested elections. In 1877 he was again a member of the judiciary committee, and also in 1879. In 1889 he was house chairman on the school fund. Many of the existing statutes were drafted by him, notably the act to prevent frauds in the sale of patents. This act Governor Hubbard pronounced one of the best specimens of legal mechanism. In 1889 he strongly advocated the bill to protect the policy-holders of the Phœnix Mutual Life Insurance Company, and when the veto of Governor Bulkeley came into the house it was on his motion passed over the veto, without debate and nearly unanimously. In 1879 he defeated a resolution that had passed the senate without dissent, concerning an order on the state treasury for $118,000, in favor of the policy-holders of certain defunct insurance companies of New Haven. Subsequently the senate unanimously rejected the resolution. It will be seen from his record that he has made an unusual impress upon the legislation of the last thirty years in this state, which argues well for his ability and his untiring devotion to a cause when once enlisted, and for his energetic individuality. He has enjoyed a large practice at the bar and has been counsel in most of the important cases in Litchfield county, both civil and criminal. He is a democrat, but has never received honors from his party except in election to the legislature. His acquaintance throughout the state is very extensive, and he is universally considered one of its ablest lawyers and a man of integrity and honor.

EDWARD MORTON BULKLEY, Southport: Sea Captain.

Edward M. Bulkley was born at Southport January 31, 1827. He received his education at the academy in Danbury, also some nautical instruc-

tion, for which he evinced an early fondness. Probably the circumstances surrounding his early life had a tendency to confirm his tastes, as his father for many years followed the sea and was largely interested in shipping, while a majority of the men of his town were or had been commanders of vessels. Edward Bulkley sailed, first, on the brig *Edward* as cabin boy, and when

E. M. BULKLEY.

nineteen years of age took command of the vessel, running from Boston to Savannah. He was successively master of the ships *Julia Howard*, *Henry P. Russell*, *Maria Morton*, and the steamers *Carolina*, *Zodiac*, *Virgo*, and *Cleopatra*. A strange fatality seemed to attend the vessels which he abandoned, as after he left them three were almost immediately destroyed. Captain Bulkley married, for his first wife, Miss Alvord of Southport, by whom he had four children, two sons and two daughters; for his second wife, Miss Hadlock of Vermont, grandniece of Colonel John Lovewell, whose name was made famous by his fight with the Indians, which battle was afterward commemorated in verse; also a descendant of Lord Mansfield. Two children were the result of this marriage. Captain Bulkley was the means, during his long service at sea, of saving the lives of many, having rescued several crews of disabled or wrecked vessels. He was particularly fortunate in his nautical experience, never meeting any serious losses or accidents, and has had many testimonials given him by passengers in recognition of his courage and great presence of mind at a time when such qualities are most needed and appreciated. It has been said of Captain Bulkley that to really know and appreciate his sterling qualities one must be with him at sea in command of his own vessel. Captain Bulkley retired from the water in the year 1879, the *Cleopatra* being the last vessel he commanded. In politics he is a democrat, but always intends to vote for the best man irrespective of party ties or prejudices. He has held one or two minor town offices, is a member and vestryman of Trinity church, and at the age of sixty-four is enjoying the best of health and often wishes to tread again the deck of some good vessel.

CHARLES F. BROOKER, TORRINGTON: Manufacturer.

Charles F. Brooker was appointed one of the alternate commissioners for the world's fair from this state in 1890 by Governor Bulkeley, and is

amply fitted by training, travel, and experience for the position. Mr. Brooker has spent a great deal of time in Europe and the West Indies in the interest of the Coe Brass Manufacturing Company, with which he has been prominently associated for the past twenty years. He has made as many as a dozen trips abroad during that period. He is a member of the Union League Club of New York and also of the Engineers' Club of that city. Mr. Brooker is a prominent republican, being a member of the state central committee from his section of the state. In 1872 he was a member of the general assembly from Torrington, his colleagues from Litchfield county including Henry Gay, the Winsted banker, and State's Attorney James Huntington of Woodbury. Mr. Brooker is director in various banks and manufacturing corporations, being one of the most active business men in western Connecticut. He was born at Torrington March 4, 1847, and was educated in the common schools of old Litchfield county. He is a member of the Congregational church and is unmarried.

GEORGE D. STANTON, STONINGTON: Physician and Surgeon.

Dr. George Dallas Stanton was born in Charlestown, R. I., April 13, 1839, and was educated in the common schools until he was thirteen years of age,

when he entered the select school of Dr. David S. Hart of Stonington, remaining there for five years. He was trained in the languages, surveying, and civil engineering, and pursued that profession until he was twenty-three years of age. He then commenced the study of medicine in the office of Dr. William Hyde of Stonington, and completed his course at Bellevue Hospital Medical College, graduating in 1865. Since 1847 Dr. Stanton has been a resident of Stonington. In 1867 he married M. Louise Pendleton; three sons, two of whom are living, being the result of this union. Mrs. Stanton died in 1871, and in 1875 he married Miss Annie Whistler Palmer, youngest daughter of the late Dr. George E. Palmer, and a niece of Major George W. Whistler, one of the pioneer railroad engineers in this country and Russia. One son is the result of the latter union. Dr. Stanton has been in official position, either as health officer, warden of the borough of Stonington, or selectman of the town, most of the time for the past twenty years. He is at present first selectman and agent of the town deposit fund. He is also medical examiner for the town of Stonington, and has held the place since the present coroner system was established. The Doctor is a Democrat of the old school. He was chairman of the executive committee of the Cleveland clubs at Stonington during both of the campaigns in which Mr. Cleveland was the candidate for the presidency. President Cleveland appointed him postmaster, the appointment being confirmed by the senate, but, owing to the fact that local affairs of first selectman and agent of the town deposit fund could not be held in conjunction with the postmastership, he declined the latter. The matter of salary entered in no way into the decision, as the offices which he retained in preference to the government appointment were without salary. Dr. Stanton is a past master of Asylum Lodge, No. 57, F. and A. M. of Stonington. He has been deputy grand lecturer, district deputy grand master, and senior grand deacon of the Grand Lodge of A. F. and A. M. of Connecticut. Dr. Stanton is connected with the Protestant Episcopal church, and is held in the highest honor and respect by the community in which the whole of his professional life has been spent.

CHARLES E. THOMPSON, Hartford: With Connecticut Mutual Life Insurance Company.

Lieutenant-Colonel Charles E. Thompson, whose career as a National Guardsman is deserving of the highest admiration and approval, was born

C. E. THOMPSON.

in Rockville February 26, 1847, and was educated in the Rockville High school. He resided in Rockville until 1863, when he removed to Hartford, remaining in the city for ten years. He was in the city of Providence for two years, but returned to Hartford in 1875 and has since resided here, being engaged with the Connecticut Mutual Life Insurance Company. In August, 1865, he enlisted as a private in Battery D, Light Artillery, which was attached to the First Regiment, C. N. G. He was appointed corporal January 20, 1868, and was discharged July 24, 1871. He was the originator of Company K of the First Regiment, enlisting in the command February 10, 1879. On that date he was elected to the first lieutenancy. January 31, 1883, he was elected captain of Company F, Hartford City Guard, of the First Regiment, and was advanced to the lieutenant-colonelcy of the regiment January 22, 1885. During the period that Captain Thompson commanded the City Guard the company stood at the head of the brigade in figures of merit. The credit and distinction which he won as a line officer were accorded to him without dissent throughout the National Guard as a field officer of the First. In personal honor, instinct and training, Lieutenant-Colonel Thompson is the ideal military leader. In March, 1890, he was elected major-commanding the Veteran City Guard. In 1889 he was captain-commanding Company K, Veteran Corps. He has also been the military instructor at the West Middle school in this city, holding the position for one year. During the presidential campaign of 1888 he was in command of the Harrison and Morton battalion of this city, ranking as major. Lieutenant-Colonel Thompson originated the present signal for calling out the city companies in case of emergency, the call being made by means of the alarm fire bell. At the time of the Park Central hotel disaster the signal was sounded for the first time, being ordered by Governor Bulkeley, and within twenty minutes one hundred men were en route from the armory in uniform and armed for the scene of the calamity. The service rendered by the Guard at that time under command of Colonel Cone and his associate field officers was invaluable.

Lieutenant-Colonel Thompson is one of the most respected citizens of Hartford. For six years he was assistant superintendent of the Center church Sunday-school, and was treasurer for one year of the Connecticut Temperance Union, of which Governor Buckingham was the first president. He declined a second term on account of increasing business duties. For the past eleven years he has been a member of the board of deacons and treasurer of the Asylum Hill Congregational church. He is also a member of the board of managers of the Young Men's Christian Association. Nine years of his business life were spent with the Cheney Silk Manufacturing Co. The past fifteen years have been passed with the Connecticut Mutual Life, where he holds a responsible position in the bond and mortgage department. The wife of Lieutenant-Colonel Thompson, who is still living, was Miss Abby Frances Allen prior to her marriage. There are three children in the family, the oldest of whom is connected with the *Hartford Courant* in this city.

AUGUSTUS HOWARD JONES, Meriden: Manufacturer of Brass and Bronze Goods.

A. H. Jones was born in New York city Dec. 21, 1850, and has resided there and in Connecticut, following the occupation of a brass moulder. He is

A. H. JONES.

indebted to the common school for his education, and to his own enterprise and grit for his business success and prominence in the affairs of his adopted city. He is a staunch republican, and has been a member of the city council and board of aldermen of Meriden, but at present holds no public office. He is connected with the Knight Templars, with the Home Club of Meriden, and also with the Congregational church. He is in business under the firm name of the Meriden Bronze Company, manufacturers of beautiful art goods, notably of the "Meriden lamp," which is made in a great variety of artistic designs. He is married, and has one child.

HON. S. W. ROBBINS, WETHERSFIELD: Stock Farmer and Breeder.

Hon. Silas Webster Robbins is one of the ablest business men in this locality and is known throughout the country as a successful breeder of thoroughbred cattle, including Short Horn, Jersey, and Guernsey stock, Cotswold, South Down, and Shropshire Down sheep. For thirty years he has been a director of the American National Bank of Hartford. He is also a director in the Phœnix Life Insurance Company, trustee of the Mechanics Savings Bank, president of Johnson, Robbins & Co.; also of

S. W. ROBBINS.

the A. D. Vorce Co., and is a director in the Merrick Thread Co. of Holyoke, Mass. He was born in the town of Wethersfield October 2, 1822. His great-grandfather, on his mother's side, was a brother of the father of Noah Webster, the lexicographer — hence his middle name — while his paternal great-grandfather, John Robbins, sat in the legislature for twenty-one years as a representative of Wethersfield, and was otherwise a noted man in the community. Step by step back to the settlement of the old town and to John Robbins can be traced the genealogy, thence it passes to the north of England. The character of the family has always been high. The subject of this sketch was educated under the tutorship of the Rev. Joseph Emerson, who was at the head of a successful private school in Wethersfield sixty years ago. Mrs. Emerson, the principal teacher, was a sister of Mrs. Hazeltine, principal of the famous Bradford (Mass.) academy. Her methods were so incomparable that among the other scholars attracted during Mr. Robbins' course of instruction there were a niece of Henry Clay and one of Francis P. Blair. After completing his education, he became a clerk in the provision store of Fox & Porter, on Central row, but before he was twenty he established a general store in Wethersfield, retaining the management of it for nearly forty years. He was instrumental in establishing the seed firm of Johnson, Robbins & Co., which gained a national reputation. He was one of the incorporators of the Hartford & Connecticut Valley Railroad, and of the Hartford & Wethersfield Horse Railroad Co. In politics he is a republican. In 1888 he was elected to the state senate from the second district and served with marked acceptance in that body. He has held the offices of postmaster and town treasurer in Wethersfield, and is held in the highest personal esteem in the community in which the whole of his life has been spent. Ex-Senator Robbins has one son and three daughters. His wife, who was Miss Sophia Jane Johnson of Wethersfield, the daughter of one of the most prominent citizens of the town, is not living. Mr. Robbins and family have been members of the Congregational church in Wethersfield from the outset, and are among the staunchest representatives of the denomination in Hartford county.

ERASMUS D. AVERY, GROTON:

Mr. Avery is now eighty-three years of age, having been born May 12, 1808. Groton is the place of his nativity. In childhood he attended the village schools there, afterward spent some time at Plainfield Academy, and finished his education in the private school of Rev. Timothy Tuttle in Ledyard. At the age of eighteen he embarked in the mercantile business in New York city, continuing there for about ten years, when, his health failing, he went to Florida and engaged in similar business at Pensacola.

E. D. AVERY.

He regained his health, established a prosperous trade, and remained until 1861, when at the breaking out of the war of the rebellion he was compelled to leave suddenly and abandon a very considerable property, entailing great pecuniary loss. Returning to Groton, he established his residence there, and has maintained it ever since, although his business connections are mostly with New London, just across the Thames. Mr. Avery was one of the incorporators of the Mariners' Savings Bank in New London, in 1867, and has been one of its directors ever since; he is, and has been for several years, a director in the New London City National Bank; also a trustee of the New London Savings Bank. He has been connected with the settlement of upwards of twenty different estates, and is now the agent and trustee of various properties. He is trustee and treasurer of the Bill memorial library, director and treasurer of the Groton Cemetery Association, and president of the Groton Monument Association. Mr. Avery has represented his town or district six times in the legislature, three times in the senate and the same number of times in the lower branch. He was a member of the Groton war committee for raising troops throughout the entire period of the civil war. As a member of the general assembly he has assisted in the election of three United States senators. — Hon. LaFayette S. Foster of Norwich, Hon. James Dixon of Hartford, and Hon. Orville H. Platt of Meriden. He has been assessor and auditor of accounts in his native town for a number of years, and for a some time clerk and treasurer, as well as committee-man, in the Groton Congregational church, of which he has been eight years a member. His life has been one of great activity and usefulness, and his public services to the town and state have been of inestimable value. Mr. Avery married Miss Sarah Hinckley, who, with three of their four children, is still living. He was formerly a Henry Clay whig, but since the organization of the republican party has been prominently identified therewith.

C. W. HALL, SOUTHINGTON: With The Peck, Stow & Wilcox Company.

Charles Williams Hall was born in Watertown, Conn., and removed to Southington in early life. He was the son of Peter Hall, formerly of Wallingford, and is a lineal de-

scendant from John Hall, the immigrant, who came to New Haven in 1650 and settled in Wallingford, of the sixth generation. He received a common school education, mostly in the town of Cheshire, where he spent some years of his early life. He has worked at tinman's machines and tools, with the exception of the time devoted to public affairs. He con-

C. W. HALL.

nected himself with the Roys & Wilcox Company of East Berlin, in 1847, and was one of the first contractors when they started business. He returned to Southington in 1873, where he has since resided, being connected with the Peck, Stow & Wilcox Company. He is a staunch republican, professing to be "dyed in the wool," and has been a selectman for ten years, three in Berlin and seven in Southington. He has been fire commissioner since the organization of the Southington department. He is connected with the Congregational church and has been Sunday-school superintendent, and successfully conducted a mission school in East Berlin and in Southington. He is a member of the Masonic fraternity, and a director in the Mutual Benefit Association of that order; is a member of the Order of United American Mechanics, the Southington Agricultural Society, Union Grange, and president of the South End Cemetery Association. He married Mary A. Newell of Southington, April 26, 1848, daughter of Asahel Newell,

and author and publisher of the Newell genealogy, who is still living. He has no children living, but has one grandchild. Mr. Hall has always been noted for his activity, push, energy, and for thoroughness in all his undertakings.

DANIEL CHAPMAN SPENCER, OLD SAYBROOK: Farmer and Merchant.

Among the descendants of Girard Spencer, who came to this country about 1610, and settled at what is now Cambridge, Massachusetts, is Daniel C.

Spencer, the subject of this sketch, who was born in Saybrook in this state on the 3d of December, 1823. He attended the public school until he was nine years of age, when he went to work on his father's farm, where he continued until he was twenty-two. During this period he enjoyed further educational privileges at the Saybrook Academy, covering only the winter

D. C. SPENCER.

months while he was "in his teens." He might have lived and died a farmer, but what appeared to be a providential misfortune changed the whole current of his life. While working in the field he suffered a sunstroke, the effects of which compelled him to abandon farming, and for three years he filled a clerkship in the stores of his native town and of Westbrook. This was the stepping-stone to his subsequent advancement. He next entered the employ of L. L. Bishop of New Haven, as traveling salesman, into which business he entered enthusiastically and soon acquired a reputation that extended beyond the limits of his own state. Upon the earnest solicitation of Messrs. Moulton, Plympton, Williams & Co., one of the leading wholesale dry-goods firms of New York, he assumed the entire charge of their fancy goods department, in which capacity he served them for two years, and then entered the establishment of Claflin, Mellen & Co., at that time located at No. 111 Broadway. His experience here was so satisfactory to the firm that at the end of his first year Mr. Claflin voluntarily presented him with a check for $1,000 in addition to his salary. During Mr. Spencer's connection with this house, covering a period of thirteen years, the establishment advanced in the volume and extent of its transactions until it became the largest dry-goods house in the United States, the sales exceeding those of its most distinguished rival by several millions of dollars. Mr. Spencer had made almost superhuman efforts to reach this result, and the strain proved too great for his powers of endurance. In the fall of 1867 his health broke down completely, and he was compelled to give up business altogether on the first of January following. Upon his retirement he was presented by his associates with a superb silver service, appropriately inscribed, as a token of their appreciation and regard.

Mr. Spencer had previously purchased a number of acres contiguous to the old homestead property in Saybrook, known as the Chalker farm. Here he retired to spend his days. The old place was enlarged and improved, and the surroundings made attractive and healthful by the expenditure of much money and the exercise of infinite taste. Amid these environments he soon recovered his health, and again became active in affairs. He engaged in projects for public improvements, and became a power for good in the advancement of numerous worthy enterprises. He is a life member and auditor of the Acton Library Association of Saybrook, and one of the auditors of the town accounts. He was one of the pioneers in the Connecticut Valley Railroad, and was instrumental in securing the present location as the terminus of the road. He is a director in the company, and has been for many years. He was largely instrumental in the erection of the beautiful stone building occupied by the Grace Episcopal church of Old Saybrook, and one of the largest contributors to the building fund. He has been an earnest and devout member, and a liberal contributor to its support since he became connected with the church, in which he holds the office of junior warden, and where he had previously been clerk and treasurer for a number of years. He was previously for several years a member of St. Timothy Episcopal church in New York city, in which he held a similar official position.

On the 12th of October, 1851, he married Emily Maria, daughter of William Stokes, Esq., of Westbrook, one of the most ardent and enthusiastic patriots and a volunteer in the war of 1812. He was one of the brave men who shouldered his musket and intercepted the retreating British troops after the burning of Essex in 1814. The issue of Mr. Spencer's marriage with Miss Stokes was eight children: William David, the eldest, born in 1852, became a practicing physician; Ella Maria, born in 1856, married Dr. B. W. Leonard, a prominent dentist of Saybrook; Daniel Stokes, born 1860; Grace Emily, born 1861, married John C. Wood of New York City, prominently connected with the H. B. Claflin Co.; George Jarvis, born 1866; Edmond Chapman, born 1869; Frederick Clarence, born 1870; and Henry Russell, born 1875, died in infancy.

Mr. Spencer's present business connections are as director in the Deep River National Bank and the Stoddard Lock and Manufacturing Company. He is an earnest republican in politics, and as such has been twice chosen to represent Old Saybrook in the state legislature, once in 1885, when he was chairman of the State Library committee, and again in 1886 when he served on the committee on railroads. His extensive knowledge of affairs and his ripe judgment constituted him a valuable factor in state legislation, and enabled him to do conspicuous service for his constituents and the state.

Mr. Spencer is a man of strong and positive convictions, but of great kindness of heart, always seeking to promote the public good and increase the sum of individual happiness. His life affords a striking example of what the young men of this country are capable of accomplishing under our benign institutions. Commencing the battle of life at nine years of age, by untiring energy he conquered all difficulties, and in his declining years is leading a quiet life of retirement in the enjoyment of a sufficient competence to place him beyond the possibility of want during the remainder of his days.

— — —

ALBERT C. GREENE, WESTMINSTER: Farmer.

Albert C. Greene of Canterbury (Westminster,) was born in Plainfield, Sept. 24, 1829, and received his education in the common schools. He has followed mechanical, mercantile, and farming pursuits in Boston, Killingly, and Canterbury. He enlisted as private in Company A, Eighteenth Regiment, Connecticut Volunteers, and served with that body from 1862 to 1865, sharing the tremendous service of that regiment in the last year of the war west of the Blue Ridge, in West Virginia. He has always

taken a great interest in matters pertaining to the veteran soldiers, and is a member of G. A. R., Post No. 77, of Central Village. He has served many years on the board of education of his town, but otherwise has not held elective office. He was an enumerator for the eleventh census. He is a republican in political faith, and active in the councils of the party. He is a deacon of the Congregational church in Westminster, and is highly esteemed for his probity and his neighborly kindness. His wife was Mary E. Bemis of Oxford, N. Y., daughter of A. N. Bemis, Esq. She is still living, and they have seven children, five sons and two daughters.

HENRY W. PECK, Bethlehem: Clothing Merchant.

Henry W. Peck has been a member of both branches of the general assembly, representing the town in which he resided in 1853 and 1862, and be-

H. W. PECK.

ing a member of the state senate from the old sixteenth district in 1865. His colleagues in the latter body included Judge Edward I. Sanford of New Haven, the Hon. Lynde Harrison, ex-Congressman John T. Wait, and the Hon. Robbins Battell. Mr. Peck was postmaster at Bethlehem from 1845 until 1867, and has been town clerk for thirteen years. He has also held various minor offices, including that of town treasurer, member of the board of selectmen, registrar of vital statistics, and justice of the peace. In politics he is a republican. He is a member of the Congregational society. He is engaged in the clothing business, and is connected with the Star Pin Company of Birmingham. Mr. Peck has been married twice. His first wife was Miss Mary Brown and the second was Miss J. E. Crossman prior to marriage. The latter is still living. There are also two children. Mr. Peck was born in Woodbury Jan. 10, 1819, and received a common school education. He has been a resident of Bethlehem since he was twenty-one.

WILLIAM F. PALMER, Scotland: Merchant.

William F. Palmer was born June 29, 1824, in Scotland, Windham county, Conn.; and, with the exception of seven years in Springfield, Mass., has

W. F. PALMER.

passed the whole of his life in his native town. After an elementary education received at the schools near his home, he engaged until the age of twenty-two in labor on the farm. He was then for a brief time employed in teaming, and subsequently entered the service of the Hartford, New Haven & Springfield Railroad Company. In 1854 he returned to Scotland, and for a time engaged in farming. Mr. Palmer, at a later date, in connection with a partner, embarked in mercantile ventures, and in 1882

purchased the entire business interest, which he now controls. In 1866 he was elected by the republicans to represent his town in the state legislature, and in 1872 was appointed postmaster, which he held until January 1, 1891, when he resigned the office to accept the state senatorship for the seventeenth district. He also for many years held the office of justice of the peace, and has been since 1874 town treasurer and town clerk. He is a trustee of the Willimantic Savings Institute, and is frequently called upon to act as executor, trustee, and administrator. He is a member of the First Congregational society of Scotland, and treasurer and clerk of the society. Mr. Palmer was married October 14, 1850, to Susan B., daughter of Thomas Webb of the same town. They have one daughter, Ella Brewer, the wife of James H. Johnson.

HENRY P. STAGG, Stratford: Town Clerk.

Henry P. Stagg was born in Stratford August 23, 1836, and received an academic education. At the outbreak of the war in 1861 he was connected

H. P. STAGG.

with the Seventh New York Regiment and was mustered into the United States service with that command at the first call of President Lincoln for troops. The presence of the Sixth Massachusetts and the Seventh New York in Washington prevented the capture of the city by the confederates at the opening of hostilities. Mr. Stagg is a member of Elias Howe, Jr., Post of the Grand Army at Bridgeport, and is president of the Veteran Association of Stratford. He served as a member of Company K of the Fourth Regiment, C. N. G., for five years, and is a member of the Connecticut Society of the Sons of the Revolution. He is also a member of St. John's Lodge, No. 6, F. and A. M., of Stratford, which contains the name of Representative Stiles Judson, Jr., on its roll. Mr. Stagg has held the office of town clerk since 1879, and has been a member of the school committee. He is a republican in politics, and is the secretary and manager of the Stratford Oyster Company. He was with the firm of Booth & Edgar, sugar refiners of New York, for twenty-five years. The wife of Mr. Stagg was Miss Mary E. King of New York. The family consists of four children. Mr. Stagg is connected with the Congregational church and an active participant in every interest that pertains to the welfare of the community.

SAMUEL J. BRYANT, West Haven: Real Estate and Fire Insurance.

Mr. Bryant was born in West Stockbridge, Berkshire county, Mass., June 26, 1851. His father was a Congregational clergyman, the seventh of eight children, and a native of Sheffield, Mass. His mother was the first of ten children and was a native of Canaan, N. Y. He therefore claims to be of good eastern blood. He graduated from Oberlin College in 1873 and from Yale Theological Seminary in 1876. His struggles for an education are typical of the American youth who is determined to make a place for himself in the world. While at Oberlin he sawed wood

S. J. BRYANT.

and worked gardens to earn money to put himself through the college course. In 1869-70 he began teaching school winters and taught successively in York, Medina county, Ohio, Briar Hill, Trumbull county, Brownhelm, Lorain county, and in Oberlin during the long vacations in 1872-3. While in the Theological Seminary at New Haven in 1873-4 he taught school in Weston, Windsor county, Vermont, keeping up his studies in the seminary meanwhile. During the last year of the seminary course he preached every Sunday. In July, 1876, he was settled as pastor of the Congregational church of South Britain, where he remained until July of 1883. He then removed to West Haven. He is identified with the Maltby, Stevens & Curtiss Co. of Wallingford as a director, and was until recently secretary and assistant treasurer. He is now a member of the firm of Bryant & Main, transacting business in real estate, loans and fire insurance. Mr. Bryant is a republican and represented the town of Orange in the lower house in 1889, and was clerk of the committee on humane institutions, and house chairman of the committee on contested elections. He is one of the burgesses of the borough of West Haven, and for several terms has been a member of the school board. As may be gathered from the above he is a Congregationalist, and is deacon of the church in West Haven, superintendent of the Sunday-school, and member of both the church and ecclesiastical society standing committee. May 23, 1876, Mr. Bryant married Ellen E. Tyler, daughter of Dr. David A. Tyler, for forty years a leading practitioner of New Haven. They have had four children, two sons and two daughters, three of them still living, one daughter having been taken. Mr. Bryant is one of the live citizens of West Haven,

and is enthusiastic in the promotion of all things which are for the best good of the town. He is a Master Mason and Knight of Honor, is one of twenty-five members of the Bisby Club in the Adirondacks owning land for hunting and fishing purposes, the Bisby being one of the most complete organizations of the kind in the wilderness.

WILLIS R. AUSTIN, Norwich: Retired Cotton Dealer and Banker.

Willis Rogers Austin was born in Norwich, January 31, 1819, and was educated for the bar, being a graduate of the Yale Law School. He spent a number of years in Texas after his graduation from the university, being engaged chiefly in cotton speculation. Subsequently, he engaged in the banking business in Philadelphia. Success was met with in each of these enterprises, enabling him to retire from active pursuits a number of years ago. Mr. Austin traveled extensively in this country and Europe before

W. R. AUSTIN.

finally returning to his old home in Norwich for a permanent residence. In 1874 he was elected a member of the general assembly from the town of Norwich, his colleague being the Hon. Allen Tenney. His associates in the house that year from New London county included Railroad Commissioner Wm. H. Hayward, Erastus S. Day of Colchester, chairman for four years of the republican state central committee, and the Hon. Benjamin Stark of New London. In 1875 Mr. Austin was re-elected by the largest majority that had been given up to that time to a representative in the legislature from Norwich. The centennial period was also a most fortunate one, politically, for Mr. Austin. After having carried the city of Norwich by the largest majority ever received there by a republican representative, the natural step was advancement to the senatorship in the old eighth district. In 1876 Mr. Austin was elected senator from that district, his colleagues in the senate including Gen. S. E. Merwin of New Haven, Edward W. Seymour of Litchfield, now of the supreme court, Washington F. Willcox, now member of congress from the second district, Charles C. Hubbard of Middletown, subsequently state comptroller, and ex-Lieutenant-Governor E. H. Hyde of Stafford. Mr. Austin has also served as a member of the republican state central committee. He has been the president of the agricultural society, member of the state board of charities, and is at present a director of the Second National Bank of Norwich, and vice-president of the Dime Savings Bank in that city. He was on the staff of General Bacon, having the rank of lieutenant-colonel. He is a member of the Episcopal church. His wife was Miss Mary McComb prior to marriage. She is still living; also one son. In 1883 Mr. Austin, with his family, spent the year in Spain; 1884 was passed in Northern Africa, and 1885 in traveling generally through Europe. It goes without saying that Mr. Austin is one of the most cultivated men in the state. He is a clear and forcible speaker, when the occasion requires, and his judgment is entitled to the fullest deference.

CHARLES F. BROWNING, Middletown; Manufacturer.

Mr. Browning was born at Griswold, in this state, April 22, 1822, being a son of Hon. Welcome A. Browning, farmer. He was educated at the public

C. F. BROWNING.

and private schools of the town, taught school about two years, and at the age of twenty-three went to Middletown, and began a mechanical education with the Sanseer Manufacturing Company. He filled every position there, including the presidency of the company, and finally sold out the factory and business in 1871. He has manufactured iron castings, machinery, and numerous other articles in that line. In 1849 he was married to Sarah P. Lewis, only child of Elias Lewis of Middletown. She is still living. They have no children. He is connected with the society of the South Congregational church, Middletown; has no connection with orders or clubs. He was reared in the old democratic party and continued to act with that party until they abandoned the principle of free soil. In 1850 and '51 he became disgusted with both the old parties, and in '52 voted for John P. Hale for the presidency. Early in 1856 he was one of the few who organized the republican party in Middletown, and has continued to act with that organization ever since. He has held various local offices in the town; was selectman for seven years, city councilman and alderman nine years, and a member of the board of education nine years. He is at present, and has been for the last fourteen years, treasurer of the city school district of Middletown. Early in the history of "the Industrial School for Girls" Mr. Browning was invited to accept the position of a

director in that institution; soon after was appointed treasurer, which position he now holds. For some years he had especial charge of the new buildings, during and after their erection. Three of the large buildings and the reservoir were constructed under his supervision. By taking advantage of the market, and close personal attention, he succeeded in reducing the cost of a home from $22,000 to $10,500. He was formerly a director of the old Hartford & New York Steamboat Company, also of the Middlesex Quarry Company, and the Middletown Ferry Company, a director and president of the Middlesex Manufacturing Company, and is connected with several others in various capacities. He retired from active life as a manufacturer in 1877, and has been since that time occupied with settling estates and the other matters above referred to.

Mr. Browning was major of the old Eighteenth Regiment, Connecticut state militia, at twenty-one years of age. In the late war of the rebellion he was an ardent supporter of the government, contributing liberally to the cause, though unable to take an active personal part in military service. He placed a man in the navy at his own expense, while he remained at the factory and made battery trimmings for the army.

HON. JAMES D. SMITH, Stamford; Banker.

Mr. Smith is a native of New Hampshire, having been born at Exeter, in that state, November 24, 1829. He was educated at Wilton academy with a view to entering Yale College, but finally decided on a business life, and has achieved exceptional success in the branch to which he turned his attention. He commenced his business career at Ridgefield, but removed soon afterwards to New York, where he became cashier and first bookkeeper with the firm of Hoyt, Sprague & Co. Subsequently, he became a member of the Wall street firm of Jameson, Smith & Cotting, with which he was associated for upwards of twenty years. The style of his present firm is James D. Smith & Co. He is one of the ablest business men and financiers in Connecticut, with large and successful experience, covering a wide range of operations and many years of earnest personal application to his business. He is a member of the New York Stock Exchange, and was for two years its president. He has also held membership in the Produce Exchange, the New York Mining Exchange, directorship in the New York Elevated

Railroad, and in a number of large corporations, including the Pacific Mail Steamship Company, the Union Pacific, and the Kansas Pacific Railroad companies, the Panama Railroad Company, the Quicksilver Mining, and the Atlantic and Pacific Telegraph companies. He was one of the founders of the Woodlawn cemetery, and was largely instrumental in its success. He has visited Europe a number of times, and among the first-class securities which he has successfully placed abroad, may be mentioned $2,000,000 of St. Louis City Park and Sewerage bonds, $4,000,000 of Mississippi and Illinois River Bridge bonds, and $6,000,000 of North Missouri first mortgage bonds. In 1882 he was appointed treasurer of the state of Connecticut, and discharged the duties of that important office with singular ability and fidelity — the previous year having served the state in the capacity of representative in the general assembly from the town of Stamford. His eminent fitness for both these positions was heartily recognized throughout the state, and the appointment met with the unanimous approval of republicans and democrats.

Mr. Smith's personal popularity and influence in New York were exemplified in the most gratifying manner during the presidential campaign of 1880. He organized and was the president of the Bankers and Brokers New York Stock Exchange Garfield and Arthur Club, one of the most powerful and influential organizations in the campaign, and labored most efficiently at its head. This club furnished the impetus for the organization of the Produce Exchange and Dry Goods Exchange Garfield and Arthur clubs, and developed largely the sentiment among business men throughout the country that national prosperity and success depended upon the retention of the republican party in power. Mr. Smith has always been an ardent republican, and is a representative of the party's best impulses and purposes.

Mr. Smith is a gentleman of the most agreeable social traits, as exemplified in his numerous affiliations with the most celebrated and reputable social organizations of New York and other cities. He has been for five years president of the New York Club; a member of the Union League Club, of the New York Club, the Players' Club, the Athletic Club, the Manhattan Athletic Club, commodore for two years of the New York Yacht Club, all of New York; and of the Stamford Club of Stamford, Conn. He was owner of the celebrated yacht *Estelle*,—the envy of New York yachtmen—with one of the fastest records of the New York fleet.

Mr. Smith's religious connections are with the Presbyterian church, of which he is an honored and influential member and a generous supporter. He married Miss Elizabeth Henderson, now deceased, and has two children, a son and a daughter.

H. G. COLT, WINSTED: Agent Strong Manufacturing Company.

Henry G. Colt was born in Torrington, November 2, 1832, and received a common school and academic education, completing his course at Williams Academy in Stockbridge, Mass. During the war he served in the Second Connecticut three months volunteers. In 1863 he was a member of the house of representatives from Torrington. Mr. Colt is independent in politics. He is the agent of the Strong Manufacturing Company at Winsted and a director in several manufacturing enterprises in that place.

He is associated with the Second Congregational church in West Winsted. His wife, whose name was Annette Griswold prior to marriage, is not living. There are three children in the family. Mr. Colt has resided through life at Torrington and Winsted.

JOHN PIERCE, SOUTHBURY: Farmer.

John Pierce of South Britain (town of Southbury) was born in that place, May 31, 1839, and received his education in the Western Reserve College of Ohio. He is one of the most noted farmers and breeders in the state, owning a tract of 1,000 acres, a large part of which he keeps under cultivation. He is perhaps better known by his efforts to improve the breed of coach and draft horses in this country, having followed the business of importing and breeding French coach and Percheron horses, in

which he is assisted by his son, the firm being John Pierce & Son. He has been town treasurer of the town of Southbury for eight years, and in 1878 and 1880 represented that town in the legislature. He has always been an earnest republican, and active in the affairs of his party in that section of the state. In religious faith and membership he is a Congregationalist. His wife was Caroline E. Garlick, and they have five children living. At present he holds no public office, but he is esteemed by the citizens of his immediate neighborhood for his business qualifications and honorable dealing, and as a man of public spirit.

REV. S. K. SMITH, NAUGATUCK: Methodist Episcopal Clergyman.

Rev. Sidney Ketcham Smith was born in Huntington, L. I., March 14, 1838, and graduated from the Wesleyan University in 1863. He entered the

S. K. SMITH.

Methodist ministry immediately after his graduation, uniting with the New York East Conference. He has been assigned to pastorates in Middlefield, Clinton, Simsbury, Torrington, Watertown, Westville, Middlebury, and Naugatuck. In all of these fields he has met with marked success. Mr. Smith has a wife and five children. The former was Miss Mary Frances Barnard of Marlboro, Mass., prior to marriage. In politics Mr. Smith is a prohibitionist. He has served on the school boards in Clinton, Torrington, and Watertown. His pulpit appointments have been of a high order, indicating the standing which he holds in the conference.

DAVID STRONG, WINSTED: Manufacturer.

David Strong is one of the leading manufacturers in Winsted, being associated with the Strong Manufacturing Co., the Winsted Hosiery Co., the New

DAVID STRONG.

England Knitting Co., the Winsted Silk Co., and the Winsted Shoe Manufacturing Co. He is also connected with the Winsted First National bank, and with M. H. Tanner & Co. He is a member of the First Congregational church, and is a republican in politics. He has held the offices of selectman, warden of the borough, and has served two sessions in the general assembly. In 1872 he represented the town of Winchester in the house, his colleagues from Litchfield county including Railroad Commissioner George M. Woodruff of Litchfield, ex-Senator I. N. Bartram of Sharon, and the late N. Taylor Baldwin of Plymouth. The distinguished members from other localities in the state included the late Governor English of New Haven, ex-Governor Waller, Judge John M. Hall, and Colonel John A. Tibbits. The subject of this sketch was born in Chatham, August 17, 1825, and was educated in the district school at East Hampton. During the war he held

a commission in the Twenty-fourth Connecticut, being the first lieutenant of Company C of that command. His life has been spent mainly in farming and manufacturing. His wife, who is living, with three children, was Miss Emerette L. Colt prior to her marriage.

LESTER L. POTTER, HARTFORD.

Lester L. Potter was born in Colebrook, Litchfield county, March 30, 1858. His father, the Rev. C. W. Potter, was for fifty years an honored Bap-

L. L. POTTER.

tist clergyman in country parishes of Connecticut. Mr. Potter left home at the age of fourteen years, and became literally the architect of his own fortune. His education was secured at Burnfield Academy, the Connecticut Literary Institute, and at Rochester Theological Seminary.

After leaving the seminary at Rochester he taught Greek and Latin at the Everett Seminary, near Boston, and supplied the churches of Everett and West Newton, Mass. He was called from there to succeed the Rev. Dr. George B. Ide at the First Baptist church in Springfield, Mass., where he ministered till the spring of 1885. As early as his second year at Springfield the church building became too small to accommodate the congregation at many services. The organ was taken from the rear and placed in front, in order to secure a larger seating capacity. Newspaper comments show the popularity of his ministry, and his strong hold upon the people of Springfield. In April, 1885, he accepted a call to the First Baptist church in Hartford, but resigned in December, 1887, on account of a change of views as to the tenets of the Baptist denomination. He was immediately called to the North church in Springfield, the Park church of Hartford, and received the unanimous vote of the committee of the Union church in Boston. In February, 1887, he began his ministry with the Park church in Hartford, as the successor of the Rev. N. J. Burton, D.D., continuing this charge until his resignation about four years later. Under the name of "Forrest Linwood," Mr. Potter has written upon art and nature for many papers, religious and secular. He has also lectured with success in New England and other northern states. His printed addresses and sermons in *The Watchman* of Boston, *The Examiner* of New York, *The Springfield Republican*, and papers of Hartford, have appeared frequently through the past eight years.

CHARLES GRISWOLD, Guilford: Banker.

Mr. Griswold is a native of the town where he now resides, and was born July 20, 1841. He was educated at Guilford Institute, and has followed the mercantile and banking professions. He served in the Union army three years and a half, or during the greater part of the civil war, and was mustered out of the service as captain. He has lived for the greater part of his life in Guilford, and has been honored by the citizens of that town by an election to nearly every office in their gift. He was postmaster for seventeen years, and represented the town in the lower

CHARLES GRISWOLD.

house of the legislature in 1887, serving on the committee on banks. He was treasurer of the Guilford Savings Bank ten years. He was appointed bank commissioner in 1890 and still holds that office, winning the respect and esteem of the banking men of the state by his thorough knowledge of banking and his sense of honor in conducting the examinations connected with his office. He is a republican, a member of the Grand Army of the Republic, and is connected with the First Congregational church of Guilford. He is married and has two children.

JOSEPH PEABODY, Jr., Waterford: Farmer.

Mr. Peabody was the second lieutenant of Company A of the Twenty-sixth Connecticut Regiment during the war, and commanded the company at Port Hudson, both of his superiors being wounded during the siege. He was born in Salem, Nov. 16, 1833, and received a district school education. He is a democrat in politics, and represented his town in the legislature in 1889. He has been a member of the board of selectmen, occupying the office for seven years, and is now a member of the board of relief and of the school

JOSEPH PEABODY, JR.

committee. He is a member of Union Lodge, No. 31, F. and A. M., of New London, and also belongs to the Grand Army of the Republic. Mr. Peabody, with the exception of one year in Wisconsin, has been a resident of Connecticut. His family consists of a wife and four children. The former was Miss Marietta Austin prior to her marriage.

ISRAEL PRIOR, Stamford: Physician.

Dr. Israel Prior of Stamford was born at Perth Amboy, N. J., Dec. 7, 1842, and was educated in the Stamford High school. Subsequently he pursued a course of medical studies, and commenced the practice of his profession in Danville, Ill., where he remained for five years. Returning east he established himself in North Stamford, continuing there for eighteen years. Three years ago he removed to the borough of Stamford and has since resided there. He was originally a student under Dr. Trow-

ISRAEL PRIOR.

bridge of Stamford, and also under Professor Wood of New York. Dr. Prior is connected with the order of United American Mechanics, and is medical examiner in the order of the Iron Hall. His family consists of his wife and three children, the former being Miss Mary F. Brown prior to her marriage with the Doctor. They are associated with the Congregational church and society in Stamford. He is a republican.

E. STEVENS HENRY, Rockville: Banker.

The subject of this sketch is a descendant of the first settlers of the town of Coleraine, Massachusetts, and was born in Gill in the same state in 1836, removing at an early age to Rockville, and receiving his education in the excellent public schools of that city. He has resided continuously in Rockville, and been intimately connected with the business interests of that enterprising city, especially with its financial institutions. He also has large investments in local real estate, is a successful farmer and

E. S. HENRY.

breeder of thoroughbred stock, and has been uniformly successful in all his business undertakings. Mr. Henry has also found time to occupy many positions of public trust. He was an active trial justice for fifteen years prior to the adoption of a city charter in Rockville. He represented the town of Vernon in the house of representatives in 1883, and the twenty-third senatorial district in the senate of 1887-1888, serving as chairman of the committee upon appropriations, also as chairman of the temperance committee, obtaining in the first-named position an intimate knowledge of the financial necessities of the state. He was a delegate-at-large to the republican national convention at Chicago in 1888, was elected state treasurer in 1888, and received the somewhat unusual honor of a re-nomination for the same position upon the republican state ticket in 1890, being the only one of the state officers elected in 1888 to receive a re-nomination. This unexpected and unsolicited honor was doubtless due to Mr. Henry's successful administration of the treasury office, in which he claimed and demonstrated that direct state taxes in Connecticut were not only impolitic, but unnecessary; that, properly administered and collected, the state possessed ample revenues from other sources, especially from taxation of corporate franchises granted by the state. Mr. Henry is an earnest student of economic questions, and has been greatly interested in the reform of the crude, and often unjust, system of taxation at present prevailing in Connecticut. As a member of the general assembly he gave his influence to needed reforms; and the passage of the somewhat novel "investment tax law" by the general assembly in 1889, was largely due to his influence. Although a lifelong republican, Mr. Henry has always been honored by receiving the votes of many of his fellow-citizens of the opposite political faith, whenever a candidate for local or state office.

HON. D. WARD NORTHROP, Middletown: Attorney-at-Law.

David Ward Northrop was born in Sherman, Conn., February 10, 1844, and is of Scotch descent. His early life was spent on a farm, and he attended the district school in his native town. Afterwards he prepared for college at Amenia Seminary, New York, and entered Wesleyan University in the class of '68, graduating with honors. For a year afterwards he taught languages in Fort Edward Institute, New York, at the same time reading law. He graduated at the Albany Law School

in 1870, and was that year admitted to the bar in Middlesex county. In 1873 Mr. Northrop was elected judge of probate for the district of Middletown, and served in that capacity until 1881, when he declined to be again a candidate. In 1871 he was elected to the legisla-

ture, and again in 1881 and 1882, and was recognized as a leader of the democratic side of the house. He was secretary of state during the administration of Governor Waller in 1883–84; was elected mayor of Middletown in 1884–85; and was appointed postmaster of Middletown by President Cleveland, serving from 1886 to 1890. Aside from his various public positions, he has enjoyed a large law practice, and is president of the Middletown Electric Light Company, and of the Great Barrington, Mass., Electric Light Company. He is a prominent member of the Reform Club of New York, and takes an active interest in all forward movements in politics and in the Methodist church, to which he belongs. He is an earnest democrat, but enjoys an unusual degree of popularity with all classes. He was married in 1870 to Mary A. Stewart, and has four children.

REV. SUMNER ABRAHAM IVES, Thompson: Pastor Baptist Church.

The subject of this sketch was born in Suffield, Conn., Oct. 21, 1839. When he was five years of age his father, Dr. Sumner Ives, (a brother of Rev.

Dwight Ives, D.D., pastor of the Suffield Baptist Church,)died, leaving him the only son in a family of five children. Soon after this, his mother, Sarah Humeston Ives, removed to Holyoke, Mass., and this place continued to be his home until manhood. After attending the district schools and academy of Holyoke, he became a student successively of Williston Seminary, East Hampton, Mass., Bridgewater Normal School and Newton Theological Seminary, from which latter he was graduated in 1873. Eleven years previous to this date, on July 30, 1864, he had received an unsolicited license to preach from the First Baptist Church of Holyoke, of which he had been a member for some years. This same church also ordained him after graduation. His first pastorate was at Alfred, Maine, where he remained from Sept., 1875, to June, 1884. On Sept. 19, 1881, he was united in marriage to Alice Dunbar, daughter and youngest child of Rev. A. Dunbar of Alfred. Two sons, now living, were born there. From Alfred he removed to Barnston, P. Q., Canada, where he remained nearly four years, and was instrumental in much good. His third and present pastorate is at Thompson, Windham County, Conn.

REV. FRANCIS WILLIAMS, Chaplin; Pastor Congregational Church.

The Williams genealogy in this country, almost without exception, is traced through Robert Williams, who came from Wales to Roxbury, Mass.

FRANCIS WILLIAMS.

The family held a high position in the mother country, and it is said no name in this country shows as many graduates from Oxford and Cambridge, England, and the colleges in this country, as the name of Williams. The ancestry of Oliver Cromwell was Williams, one of his not distant forefathers taking a change of name that a large estate might come to him, his name being enrolled upon the public document, "Cromwell, *alias* Williams." The grandfather of the subject of this sketch, Ephraim Williams, Esq., was one of the original settlers in Ashfield, Mass. Both himself and his wife were from families of wealth and position. On their marriage trip from eastern Massachusetts, two ox carts were connected by long timbers (ox wagons not then being in use), the furniture needful for housekeeping was placed upon it, the bed, table, and chairs arranged for use, two large yokes of oxen were attached to the extemporized home, food taken, and the happy bride and groom set out on their long journey. When mealtime and bedtime came, the oxen were turned out to browse, while they enjoyed the honeymoon in their cosy home. With sparkling eye he said to a wealthy granddaughter, as she set out after her wedding, "You cannot have such a delightful wedding trip as we had." When ninety years of age, he had on the list of his descendants ten children, sixty-seven grandchildren, and forty-seven great-grandchildren, and all within six miles of him, whether living or in their graves. He gave all his sons and sons-in-law a good farm, and enjoyed the late evening of a Christian life with the somewhat pleasant title by which he was known, "Rich Ephraim." Capt. Israel Williams, his son, was the father of the subject of this sketch. His mother, Lavinia Joy, was the daughter of Capt. Nehemiah Joy of Cummington, Mass. He was a successful teacher, and his daughter and William Cullen Bryant were pupils under his instruction. Rev. Francis Williams was born in Ashfield, Mass., January 2, 1814. He was one of a family of nine sons and two daughters. Neither the father nor one of his sons ever used tobacco, or strong drinks after the temperance question began to be agitated. Before this, it was thought necessary in having sea-

son and washing sheep, of which he had a flock of three or four hundred. At this time only were intoxicating drinks thought necessary or desirable. He prepared for college at Sanderson Academy in Ashfield, at Amherst Academy, and the academy at Shelburne Falls. He entered Williams College in 1834, graduating in the class of 1838, delivering an oration at commencement. He was one of the prize speakers in his junior year, and had also a junior oration. He was president of the three principal college societies of which he was a member. He immediately after graduation entered the theological seminary at East Windsor Hill, Conn., where he graduated in August, 1841. During his educational course he taught in Coxsackie, N. Y., and two terms in Hawley, Mass. During the winter of his senior year he was principal of Sanderson Academy in his native town of Ashfield, and while a member of the theological seminary was principal of the Windsor Academy at Windsor, Conn. He was licensed to preach by the Franklin Association, was ordained and installed over the Congregational church in Eastford, September 20, 1841, Dr. Bennett Tyler of the seminary preaching the sermon; Dr. Nettleton, also, was to take part, but was prevented by sickness. Gen. Lyon of Eastford graduated from West Point at about the same time, came to his old home, he and his mother's new pastor became warm personal friends; he offered the prayer at the general's funeral. In 1851 Mr. Williams received a call to settle in Bloomfield, Conn., Rev. Milton Badger, D.D., uncle of Mrs. Williams, preaching the sermon. In 1858 he accepted a call to settle in Chaplin, where he still labors. Prof. E. A. Lawrence of the seminary preached the installation sermon. For many years he has been a director of the Connecticut Home Missionary Society, and trustee of the ministers' fund, and for more than thirty years a trustee of the Hartford Theological Seminary. Since the death of Newton Case, Esq., he is the senior trustee. For more than forty years he has been a member of the school board and acting school visitor in the towns where he has resided. In 1876 he was a member of the legislature, and a member of the committee on temperance.

On the 22d of October, 1841, he married Miss Mahala R. Badger, daughter of Enoch and Betsey Nash Badger of Springfield, Mass. She was sister of Rev. Norman Badger, a classmate of Stanton, the great war secretary, a professor in Gambia College, Ohio, president of Shelby College, Kentucky, and died while chaplain in the army. They have had five children, four sons and one daughter. Two sons died in infancy. Edward F. graduated at Williams College in the class of 1868, taught for a short time, when failing health compelled him to return to his home in Chaplin, where he died October 6, 1869, aged twenty-four. Charles H. graduated at Eastman's Business College at Poughkeepsie, N. Y., became a member of Haight's Engineer Corps, took a severe cold while at Rondout surveying the Hudson River railroad, had severe hemorrhage of the throat, and died at his home in Chaplin, December 19, 1874, at the age of twenty-six. Mary Elizabeth, their only daughter, graduated at Mt. Holyoke Seminary in the class of 1871, taught select school after graduation, married Rev. William H. Phipps, October 10, 1872. He has been pastor of the Congregational churches at East Woodstock, Poquonock, and Prospect, Conn., where he has been pastor for about twelve years, and where he still continues his labors.

Seven sermons of Mr. Williams have been printed in pamphlet form, and several in part or in full in the newspapers. No ecclesiastical council has ever been called to adjust any difficulty with the church or minister where he has labored, and no vote in church or society was cast against his settlement in either of the three fields of his labors. In a few months, if life is spared and ministerial labor is continued, will occur the fiftieth anniversary of his graduation at the seminary, his ordination, and his marriage. His present pastorate of thirty-three years is exceeded by that of only four of the Congregational ministers in the state, and there has been no day during his ministry when he was not under his regular salary.

RAYMOND N. PARISH, Montville: Lumber Dealer.

Mr. Parish was born in Montville, March 31, 1834. After completing a substantial education in the common schools he followed the business of farming until 1872, when for ten years he was engaged as a hardware merchant, and since that time has been a manufacturer and dealer in domestic lumber. With the exception of ten years as merchant in Norwich, his life has been spent in Montville, where he has held the offices of assessor, selectman, and treasurer. He represented Montville in the lower

R. N. PARISH.

house of the legislature in 1866 and in 1882, and was elected senator from the eleventh district in 1889, serving on the state prison committee and as chairman of the temperance committee. He has also been honored with various minor offices connected with the community in which he has lived;

has been clerk of the probate court, president of the Raymond Library since its organization twelve years ago, treasurer and collector of the Congregational Society, school district clerk, and the executor and administrator of a great many wills and estates. The esteem in which Mr. Parish is held is shown by the fact that all these offices have been gratuitously bestowed, as he has never solicited a nomination or an election to any office in any case. In the varied walks of life he has won the confidence of the community in which he lives to a more marked degree than happens to the lot of the average man. He has always been a republican, but holds to independent action in political matters when necessary. His wife was Susan C. Huntington, and they have one child.

BYRON TUTTLE, Plymouth: Judge of Probate.

Byron Tuttle is of Welsh descent and the eighth generation from William Tuttle, who came from Devonshire, England, in the ship *Planter*, and

BYRON TUTTLE.

landed in Boston in 1635. He removed to New Haven in 1639, and lived on and owned the land where the Yale College buildings now stand. Mr. Tuttle was born in Plymouth, Conn., August 23, 1825, the son of a farmer, and his early years were spent at home with the best of life training, that of a New England farmer boy; having the advantages of the common district school of those days. On the 26th of August, 1847, he entered the carriage establishment of Augustus C. Shelton of Plymouth, afterward entering into partnership with him under the firm name of Shelton & Tuttle. In 1854 Mr. Tuttle went to Chicago and established a carriage repository for the sale of their carriages in that city. Later, repositories were opened at New Orleans, La., and Burlington, Iowa, where he spent a portion of his time for a number of years. The venture proved successful, and the firm made money. In 1864 they built a repository on Madison street, Chicago, which was burned in the great fire of 1872, without much loss to the company, when the property was sold and Mr. Tuttle retired from the business.

Mr. Tuttle was married to Candace D., daughter of Oliver Smith, Esq., of Plymouth, April 10, 1853; they have two children, Hattie A. and William B. Aside from private business Mr. Tuttle has occupied a prominent place in the affairs of the town, having been elected justice of the peace in 1864 and selectman in 1878, which offices he has filled continuously to the present time. Also for a number of years he has been the agent of the town, having filled this position with ability before the legislature and the courts in cases where the interests of the town were involved. He has been judge of probate for ten years in the district where he resides and is a prominent member of the community and among the leading men of the town. In politics he is a republican. He is a member of the Congregational society and has served with credit as society's committee.

Mr. Tuttle's characteristics as a business man are energy, promptness, thoroughness, and integrity. It is perhaps the secret of his general success in life, that in whatever he engages he observes the same rules of conduct that govern him in the management of his business affairs.

JULIUS B. SMITH, WHIGVILLE (BURLINGTON): Manufacturer.

Mr. Smith was born in Whigville, October 14, 1843, and was educated at the common schools. He has always resided in his native town. In 1866 he established the wood-turning business, the firm name being Bunnell & Smith. In 1879 Mr. Bunnell sold his interest, and since that time the firm name has been Smith Brothers. Mr. Smith enlisted in Company G, Sixth regiment, Connecticut volunteers, September 4, 1861, and served three years, being wounded in the charge on Fort Wagner, July 18, 1863.

J. B. SMITH.

At the formation of the Connecticut National Guard he was commissioned first lieutenant of Company K, First regiment, serving five years. Mr. Smith has been a member of the republican party ever since he became a citizen, and prominent in the organization in his own town, and a member of the town committee. He is a constable. He is also connected with the Masonic lodge in his town, with the Grand Army, and is a member of the Grange. He was married November 21, 1865, to Miss Alvina E. Curtiss of Bristol, Conn., who died in 1877, leaving one son. He was again married to Miss Alice E. Beach, daughter of B. S. Beach of Terryville, in 1879, and has one son by his latest marriage. Mr. Smith is an example of that New England persistence which induces a man to remain in a place and make for himself an honored name and a fine business record.

JOHN HYDE PECK, NEW BRITAIN: Principal of High School.

John H. Peck was born at Norwich, Conn., Sept. 7, 1838. After teaching two winters in Franklin, he entered the Normal school, where he was graduated in 1856. Two years of teaching in Portland followed, and, after a brief course at Wilbraham academy, he entered Yale College, from which he was graduated in 1863. He then had the charge of a very prosperous select school in Milford, which position he resigned in 1865, to become principal of the High school in New Britain. This position he still retains. Distin-

J. H. PECK.

guished educational critics speak of Mr. Peck as one of the most able and successful instructors in the state. At various times he has served as secretary and president of the Hartford County Teachers' Association; treasurer, secretary, and president of the State Teachers' Association; and president of the State Council of Education. He held the office of alderman in New Britain in 1877, but declined a renomination. He is a member and deacon of the South Congregational church of New Britain.

He married his present wife, Mrs. Sarah F. Waterman of Toledo, Ohio, in 1874, and they have two sons.

ROBERT HEALEY, SEYMOUR: Farmer.

Mr. Healey was born in London, England, February 24, 1842. He came with his parents to the city of New York in 1847, and to Seymour in this state in 1851. The latter place has since been his home. He was living in the state of Louisiana at the outbreak of the war of the rebellion, but passed through the southern lines and joined the Twenty-second Regiment, Indiana Volunteers at Jefferson City, Mo., on the 15th of September, 1861. He served under Fremont until Curtiss took command, and

ROBERT HEALEY.

was in the three-days battle of Pea Ridge, Ark., in March, 1862. From this place his regiment was sent to Corinth, Miss., and took an active part in the siege. After the retreat of Beauregard he was attached to Buell's command, and was in the battle of Perryville, Ky., October 8, 1862, where he received four wounds and was taken prisoner, but was left on the field, the rebels retreating the next morning. He has carried a rifle ball in his body since this battle, which at times is somewhat troublesome. After an absence of nine months he rejoined his regiment and served until the close of the war, re-enlisting at Knoxville, Tenn., December 23, 1863. He was color guard, but acted as bearer from the time he rejoined his regiment until the final muster out. His regiment was actively engaged in the battle of Chickamauga, Mission Ridge, the Atlanta Campaign, taking an active part in the bloody charge of Kennesaw Mountain, June 27, 1864; was on Sherman's march to the sea; also in the battle of Averysborough and Bentonville, N. C., and remained in Sherman's command until the final muster out, serving four years in all. Returning to his home in Seymour, August 6, 1865, he entered the employ of the Douglass Manufacturing Company. September 13, 1866, he married Alice J. Bassett, eldest daughter of Amos Bassett, Esq.; their family consists of six sons. Mr. Healey has served his town as selectman many years, also as assessor and a member of the town board of education. He is representing his town in the house of representatives this year for a second time, having been a member of that body in 1889. He is a past post commander in the G. A. R. organization of Seymour.

THEODORE HALL McKENZIE, Southington: Civil Engineer.

T. H. McKenzie was born in Wallingford, Conn., in 1845, a son of Wm. McKenzie of Scotch origin, as the name indicates, who was a well-known con-

tractor for railroad and other public works. His mother, Temperance Hall, was of Puritan stock and a native of Wallingford. Mr. McKenzie was educated in the common schools and in the Meriden High school, the Connecticut Literary Institute at Suffield, and a special course of one year at the Sheffield Scientific School. For two years, 1867–68, he assisted his father,

who had charge of the construction of the Farmington River bridge on the New York, New Haven & Hartford railroad at Windsor, the construction of the masonry for the factories and water power of R. Wallace & Sons, and the brownstone Episcopal church at Wallingford. At the age of twenty-

one he engaged with the New Haven & Northampton Railroad Company as rodman on the extension of the road to New Hartford. At the end of six months he was promoted to assistant engineer on construction of the same road. At the age of twenty-three he was appointed division engineer on the third division of the Connecticut Valley railroad from Middletown to Higganum, and remained with the company in that capacity for two years. He was first assistant engineer on the location of the Massachusetts Central railroad from Clinton to Boston, fifty miles ; was first assistant engineer on the location and construction of the Providence & Springfield railroad, twenty-six miles ; also located branches of the same road to Woonsocket and Chepachet, R. I. ; was one of a commission to apportion the water powers of the Woonasquetucket river in Rhode Island ; was for one year street commissioner and three years city engineer of the city of Meriden, during which time he made the surveys and plans for a sewerage system for the city, and was engineer of the increased water supply for the city in 1876–7. He was also engaged on a very important water power damage lawsuit between G. I. Mix and the Wallingford community. He removed to Southington in 1878, and was for nine years secretary of the Peck, Stow & Wilcox Manufacturing Company, and devoted about two-thirds of his time to the business of that company, and the remainder to engineering work. He was chief engineer of the Southington water works, constructed in 1883–4, and also secretary and treasurer of the same company. Made the surveys and plans for the Plainville water works, and numerous plans for smaller public works ; and was engaged as an expert in several water power lawsuits and other court cases. He was chief engineer of the Naugatuck and Litchfield water works, and made surveys and plans for water works at Terryville, Norfolk, and New Hartford. Made surveys and plans for sewerage systems for Litchfield, Bristol, and Southington ; also in 1890 made surveys and reports on the various proposed plans for a new water supply for the city of Meriden ; and was employed as consulting engineer on the South Manchester water works. He was for several years school committee, fire commissioner, secretary of agricultural society, and secretary and treasurer of Electric Light & Tramway Company. He was the leader in organizing the Southington board of trade, and has since its organization been the secretary of the board. He is a member of the American Society of Civil Engineers, of the New England Water Works Association, first vice-president and member of executive committee of the Connecticut Society of Civil Engineers. For the last four years has been a member of the State Board of Civil Engineers. He is a member of The Home

Club of Meriden, is a Freemason, and a member of the Wallingford Baptist church. Was married at the age of twenty-four to Miss Mary E. Neal, daughter of the Hon. R. A. Neal of Southington; four children, two boys and two girls, are the fruit of the union. He is a republican in politics, and his present business connection is as secretary, treasurer, and superintendent of the Southington Water Company. He is also chief engineer Naugatuck Storage Reservoir, South Manchester Sewerage, Westport and Saugatuck Water Works, and for designing sewerage disposal works for the city of Meriden; and consulting engineer Wallingford Water Works, and Union City Bridge over the Naugatuck River.

HON. C. EDWIN GRIGGS, CHAPLIN: Preacher and Teacher.

C. Edwin Griggs was born in Pomfret, Abington Society, Conn., July 21, 1827, and removed to Chaplin in 1831, where he still resides. He received an academical education at Monson, Mass., and entered Amherst College, from which he graduated in 1856. He then took a course in theology at the Union Theological Seminary in New York, from which he graduated in 1859, and was licensed to preach by the Third Presbytery of New York. On account of impaired health he never entered

fully into the work of the ministry, though he has supplied pulpits in his vicinity for terms varying from a few Sabbaths to more than a year. He has taught school twenty terms, and fitted several young ladies and gentlemen for college. Mr. Griggs was state senator from the thirteenth district in 1868; assistant to the United States Marshal in taking the census in 1870; school visitor from 1862 until the present time; a member of the house of representatives in 1885; has served on the board of relief, and many times as juror of the superior court for Windham County; has been a grand juror of the United States Circuit Court; a registrar of voters; a judge of the probate court for the district of Chaplin, one term; first selectman two years; is now trustee of the Dime Savings Bank, Norwich; auditor of the town of Chaplin, and clerk of the court of probate. He has always acted with the republican party since its formation. Mr. Griggs has been a member of the Congregational church in Chaplin more than fifty years, having

united with the church in 1840. In 1859 he married Mary Jane Hall of Chaplin; and they have three daughters, all of whom are graduates of Mt. Holyoke College. Mr. Griggs is a lineal descendant of Thomas Griggs, who came from England with two sons and settled in Roxbury, Mass., about 1635, and whose grandsons were among the first settlers of what is now Woodstock, Conn.

E. G. SUMNER, M.D., MANSFIELD CENTRE: Physician.

Edwin G. Sumner was born in Tolland, in this state, May 15, 1839. He was educated in the common school until he was sixteen, at which time he went to the Ellington Academy and afterwards to the academy at Wilbraham, Massachusetts. After having served as clerk in the city of Hartford for a little more than one year, he commenced the study of medicine in the same place, and continued his studies at the New York University, and at the end of three years graduated in the medical department at

Yale College, and commenced practice in Mansfield. He afterwards practiced three years in the old town of Farmington. In 1860 he went to St. Louis, Mo., and was there at the breaking out of the war, after which he returned to Mansfield, in time to be drafted. He received a commission from Governor Buckingham as assistant surgeon in the 21st Connecticut regiment, but owing to sickness was not able to go into the field at that time. He afterwards moved to Ohio, where he was engaged in business at Dayton for some ten years, returning in 1871 to Mansfield, which place has since been his permanent residence. In 1875 he was elected by the republicans to represent Mansfield in the state legislature, to which he was returned in 1883, at the latter date receiving the appointment of county commissioner in Tolland county for the term of three years.

Dr. Sumner is a member and deacon of the Baptist church at Willimantic. He is also president of the Mansfield school board, and a member of the Masonic fraternity. He married Miss Ellen M. Hinckley of Mansfield, and they have two daughters — one married and living in Dayton, Ohio, and the other in Oberlin College in the same state. His business connections are with a wholesale notion house in Dayton, as special partner, with the Dime Savings Bank and Natchaug Silk Company of Willimantic, the National Thread Company of Mansfield, and the Underwood Belting Company of Tolland; in all which corporations he is a director. He is still engaged to some extent in the practice of his profession. He has always manifested a lively interest in church affairs and the Sunday-school work, and has sustained active official connection with both church and Sunday-school for a great number of years.

JOHN P. KINGSLEY, Plainfield: Merchant.

John P. Kingsley was born in 1823, in Canterbury, Conn., the son of Captain John Kingsley, and grandson of Captain Hezekiah Kingsley,

J. P. KINGSLEY.

who did service in the war of the revolution. His mother, Mary, was daughter of Joseph Raymond. His educational opportunities were such as were offered at the common schools, supplemented by a course of instruction at the Manual Labor High school in Worcester, Mass. At the age of twenty-one he bought a farm in Norwich Town, two miles from the city, and was engaged in farming about twelve years. For the next twelve years was in the real estate business in Norwich. In 1869 he returned to his native town, Canterbury, and entered the mercantile business, and in 1871 opened a branch store at Plainfield Junction. In 1874 the firm of J. P. Kingsley & Sons was established, and their store has become one of the largest in Windham county. In 1844 he was married to Clarissa Mathewson of Woodstock, who died in 1849, leaving one son, Milton Kingsley. He was married again, to Elizabeth Scholfield, daughter of John Scholfield, whose grandfather, John Scholfield, manufactured the first yard of woolen cloth that was made by machinery in this country, and also manufactured and presented to President Madison the broadcloth from which his inaugural suit was made. He not only manufactured the cloth, but also the machinery with which the cloth was made. Mr. Kingsley by his last wife had one son and four daughters: Walter, Mary, Emma, Carrie, and Lizzie. Mary died at the age of eight years. His son Milton was married to Hattie Ames, daughter of Deacon William Ames of Plainfield. His son Walter married Belle Clark, daughter of Deacon Thomas Clark of Canterbury. His daughter Emma married William E. Tunison of New York, son of the Rev. William Tunison of Orange, N. J.

His daughter Carrie married Alex. M. Purdy, M.D., son of the Rev. Alvah Purdy of Canterbury. In Canterbury Mr. Kingsley was judge of probate and town treasurer for several years; also a member of the legislature two years, and postmaster for sixteen years. At fifteen years of age he united with the Baptist church in Worcester, Mass., and afterwards at Packersville (Plainfield), where he is now a member.

The immediate descendants of Captain Hezekiah Kingsley, who remained in Canterbury, in the vicinity of the ancestral estate, for many years, were among the best esteemed people of the town, distinguished for their inflexible integrity, and their consistent moral and religious life. The subject of this sketch is now the sole male survivor of his generation in Windham county, and he worthily perpetuates the good name which he received as an inheritance and will transmit to future generations.

EDWARD F. PARSONS, Thompsonville: Physician and Surgeon.

Dr. Edward Field Parsons was a member of the house of representatives from the town of Enfield, in 1887, and was appointed on the committee

E. F. PARSONS.

on insurance. He was born in Enfield, Nov. 21, 1833, and received a classical school education, completing his studies at Williams College. Subsequently he graduated from the College of Physicians and Surgeons, New York city. His life has been devoted to his profession, and he is one of the best known practitioners in his section of the state. He is post surgeon at Enfield, medical examiner, member of the board of school visitors and of the district committee, and is connected with the First Presbyterian church in that town. In politics Dr. Parsons is a republican. He is associated with the Good Templar, Knights of Honor, and Temple of Honor organizations, and is an active public leader. He has resided in Farmington, Williamstown, Mass., and New York city. The most of his professional life, however, has been spent at Enfield. Dr. Parsons has been married three times. His first wife, Mary H. Bowman, of Brooklyn, N. Y., died Feb. 15, 1875, and the second, Ellen M. Bates of Worcester, Mass., died Aug. 13, 1879. The third, Margaret J. Harrison of New York city, is living. There are no children in the family.

ISAAC NEWTON BARTRAM, Sharon: Architect and Builder.

Isaac N. Bartram is of Scotch descent. His father, Isaac Bartram, was a son of Isaac Hamilton Bartram, who, with three brothers, served through the revolutionary war from the town of Redding. His mother was Lydia Platt, daughter of Isaac Platt, who was an artificer from that town during the same trying period in the country's history. Isaac N. Bartram, the subject of this biography, was born in Redding, March 25, 1838, where, and in the town of Sharon, his whole life has been spent, and of which

I. N. BARTRAM.

latter town he has been since 1864 a prominent and influential citizen. He received a common school and academic education, the latter having been acquired at Redding Ridge Academy. His marriage was with Miss Helen D. Winans, which union has been blessed by two daughters. Mr. Bartram's business connections have been as an iron founder, architect, builder, and contractor. He is now superintendent of the Sharon Water Company. His religious affiliations are with the Methodist Episcopal church, and in politics he is an ardent democrat. He is a member of the Masonic fraternity, the "Old Put Club" association, and the Connecticut Sons of the Revolution, and was elected last May one of its directors. He has held numerous public offices, having served his town as selectman, treasurer, and in several minor capacities. His legislative record is one of long, important, and almost continuous service for more than a score of years. He represented Sharon in the general assembly in 1868, 1872, 1876, 1886, 1887, and 1890, and is again serving as a member of the house the present year. He represented the nineteenth district in the state senate in 1889, when he was chairman of the committee on roads and bridges, and took an active part in making the old Hartford bridge a free avenue of public travel. He presented the bill for making all bridges dependent upon the counties in which located for their support and maintenance. The towns on the Housatonic River are indebted to him for the bill making their bridges free, under support by their respective counties. He is a strong believer in and advocate of the farmers' rights, and was the only democratic senator in the session of 1889 that voted to pass the farmers' bill over the governor's veto. In the house he served on various committees, including the state prison committee of 1876, origi-

nating the plan of extensive improvements on the state prison buildings, which was subsequently carried into effect. He also originated and introduced the resolution respecting the Putnam encampment that secured to the state the gift of land and erection of the monument near his old home in the town of Redding. Mr. Bartram was appointed by Governor Lounsbury one of the commissioners to take charge of the encampment and erect the monument. He carried out the plans with great satisfaction, and was again appointed by Governor Bulkeley as chairman of the commission; was subsequently elected superintendent of the encampment, taking an active charge of the same, and devoting much time and careful attention to improving and beautifying the grounds and approaches.

Mr. Bartram's distinguished service at the state capitol has given his name prominence at all caucuses and nominating conventions of his party; and at the senatorial convention in Falls Village last October, he was unanimously nominated for senator from the nineteenth district, which honor, however, he thought best to firmly but respectfully decline, although realizing that his election would follow his acceptance beyond the shadow of a doubt. But his townsmen felt that his services were needed in the legislature the present year, and insisted on his representing them in the house, which he consented to do. Mr. Bartram is a man of positive opinions, frank and outspoken sometimes almost to the point of abruptness; but he intends always to be right, and very properly holds that firmness is an important factor in the effective advocacy of a righteous cause.

CHARLES McNEIL, Torrington: Druggist.

Mr. McNeil was born in Litchfield, Feb. 25, 1829, and received a common school education. In 1850 he removed from Watertown, where he had spent a number of years, to Torrington, and established the drug business, which he has since managed. Mr. McNeil is the oldest druggist in the Naugatuck Valley, and is at the head of one of the largest drug houses in Litchfield county. He is a lifelong democrat and has taken some part in politics. In 1873 he was elected to the legislature from Torring-

CHARLES McNEIL.

ton, and was returned in 1874. He was also a member of the house centennial year, his colleagues from Litchfield county in 1876 including Henry B.

Graves of Litchfield, Nicholas Staub of New Milford, John Cotton Smith and Isaac N. Bartram of Sharon, and Henry Gay of Winchester. He was appointed postmaster under President Cleveland, being the first of the democratic appointments in this state. Prior to President Cleveland's administration, he had been in charge of the office for twenty-five years. He was also in charge of the Western Union telegraph office from the time of its establishment in Torrington until he became postmaster. He was one of the incorporators of the Torrington Savings Bank, and secured the passage of the act incorporating the Torrington Water Company. He was also one of the original promoters of the Torrington Electric Light Company, and has been actively associated with the business interests of the town. Mr. McNeil has visited Europe twice, the last trip occurring two years ago. He is an Episcopalian, and belongs to Seneca Lodge, No. 55, F. and A. M., of that place. His wife was Emeline Loveland prior to her marriage. The two sons are associated with him in business.

MAJ. NATHAN R. GARDNER, Baltic: Cotton Mill Agent.

Nathan R. Gardner was born in South Kingston, R. I., April 15, 1839. He was educated at the Kingston Classical Seminary. For six years he was paymaster of the extensive woolen mills owned by the late General Isaac P. Rodman, a leading manufacturer of that town. He enlisted early in the war of the rebellion. President Lincoln appointed him captain and commissary of subsistence. At the close of the war President Johnson brevetted him major "for faithful and efficient services in the subsistence department of the U. S. army." Directly upon his return from the army, in August, 1865, he took the position of paymaster of the Baltic cotton mill, one of the largest plants belonging to the Spragues of Rhode Island. In 1880 he was appointed by the trustee, agent of the Baltic mill estate, which position he now holds. For twelve years he held the office of treasurer of the town of Sprague, and has been elected to other minor offices. Has been secretary and treasurer of the Sprague Butter and Cheese Company since its formation. In politics he is a republican, and has held the office of chairman of the republican town committee for twenty-five years. He became a

N. R. GARDNER.

Freemason twenty years ago. His wife, a lady of many accomplishments, is the daughter of Geoffrey Watson, one of Sprague's most esteemed citizens. His only child, a daughter, who is highly cultured, completed her education at the New England Conservatory of Music. Major Gardner has held responsible and important positions of trust, etc., all his life, and besides the integrity of his character, he is a man of most kindly disposition, of generous impulses, a true and manly friend, broad in his sympathies, and fair in his judgment.

RUFUS WARREN BLAKE, Derby: Piano and Organ Manufacturer.

Mr. Blake was born in Norfolk, Mass., May 3, 1841, the son of a farmer of moderate means. The activity and energy that have characterized his life were potent in him as a boy, and the dull routine of farm work didn't suit him. He earned his first money as bobbin boy in a cotton factory, in which position he remained until he was 15 years old, attending school during the winters. He then learned the painter's trade, afterwards (in 1861) taking up the cabinet-maker's trade. And here really began his connection

R. W. BLAKE.

with the music business. In 1863 Taylor & Farley of Worcester were manufacturing melodeons, in a small way, and Mr. Blake engaged with them. Here he had excellent opportunity to learn the reed business in a thorough manner, for as the firm employed only three men, each one became familiar with all points. He continued here until about 1867, when he formed a partnership with Mr. J. W. Loring, under the firm name of Loring & Blake (afterwards Loring & Blake Organ Company), and commenced the manufacture of organs. The business was prosperous, but in 1873 Mr. Blake took advantage of the opportunity he saw of purchasing an interest in the Sterling Company, of Derby, Conn., with which he has been actively identified ever since, and of which he is now president.

Mr. Blake possesses great mechanical ingenuity, and much of the success of the Sterling Company is due to the fact that he is able to do his own designing. In this line he has few equals. His styles always seem to meet the popular taste, but he is ready to receive suggestions from the trade and make the required changes. As a financier he has had many opportunities to test his abilities, and always successfully. A few months after he entered the business came the demoralizing Black Friday; then, in 1875, the fire that swept away the entire plant. In 1887 came the McEwen failure that involved the Sterling Company to the extent of $75,000; but through Mr. Blake's skillful financiering the company pulled through without any great loss. So it will be seen that in the past seventeen years there have been many stormy times in the financial life of the Sterling Company, but Mr. Blake has been at the helm, and the ship is now sailing in calm water. At the last annual election, August, 1890, the capital stock was increased to $210,000.

Mr. Blake is an active business man, whose only recreation seems to be a spin behind his spirited horses, a handsome pair of Hambletonians which don't take anybody's dust. He has held several public positions of trust and honor, and discharged the duties to the satisfaction of all. He is one of the burgesses of the borough of Birmingham, is a member of the Baptist church, and in politics is a republican. He is still in the very prime of life, and full of the enthusiasm that is part of every successful man's make-up.

GEORGE E. TAFT, Unionville: Attorney-at-Law.

George E. Taft was born in Sheffield, Mass., November 4, 1855, and was educated at the Connecticut Literary Institute. His parents died before he was seven years of age, necessitating his removal to the town of Harwinton, where he received the care of an uncle, the late L. U. Olmsted of that place. He studied at the Torrington High school, and after completing his course at the institute, he entered the law office of Judge G. H. Welch in Torrington. From 1878 until 1883 Mr. Taft was

G. E. TAFT.

engaged in teaching in the towns of Litchfield, New Hartford, Simsbury, and Canaan. He completed his legal studies in the office of Judge A. T. Roraback in Canaan and was admitted to the Litchfield county bar. He immediately removed to Unionville, where he has since resided. In 1878 he married Miss Julia M. Barber of Harwinton, who died April 27, 1891, and three children survive her. He has been a member of the board of selectmen in Farmington and is now a justice of the peace and one of the prosecuting agents for Hartford county. In 1887 and 1888 he was a member of the republi-

can state central committee from the fourth district. He is connected with the Congregational church at Unionville, and is a member of the insurance firm of Hitchcock & Taft.

J. W. WINCH, Mashapaug (Union): Merchant.

John Wesley Winch represented the town of Union in the general assembly of 1886, serving as a republican. He was a member of Company F, Fourth Massachusetts Cavalry, during the war, and was forage master of the Cavalry Brigade, Army of the James. For the past six years he has been the commander of D. P. Corbin Post, G. A. R., at Union, and belongs to Wolcott Lodge, No. 65, F. and A. M., of Stafford. He founded the Union Post and is greatly interested in Grand Army affairs. Mr. Winch is con-

J. W. WINCH.

nected with the Methodist church. He was born at Fall River, Mass., March 31, 1838, and received a common and high school education. Since 1875, he has resided in Connecticut, and is engaged in the business of a merchant and farmer. The wife of ex-representative Winch, who is living, was Helen M. Moore. There are two children in the family. Mr. Winch has held every office within the gift of his townsmen and is at present constable, notary public, and commissioner of the superior court.

E. C. STEVENS, Norfolk: Hotel Proprietor.

Edward C. Stevens, who is one of the best known hotel managers in Litchfield county, was born in East Sheffield, Mass., August 29, 1837, and received a common school education. He remained at home on the farm until he was twenty years of age, when he removed to Winsted and engaged in the hotel business with his brother, remaining there for nine years. In connection with the hotel and livery establishment, he managed the stage line between Canaan and Hartford. After spending a couple of years in

E. C. STEVENS.

Michigan he returned East and spent two years in a hotel at Fulton, N. Y. Afterwards he engaged in the hotel business at Waterbury and at Morris

Cove. He then returned to Winsted, remaining there until nine years ago, when he assumed the management of a summer hotel at Norfolk. During the summer of 1890, in company with his son, Harry Stevens, he visited the Pacific Coast, spending a portion of the time in Washington. Thence he proceeded to San Diego, where he remained until the time for returning East. The wife of Mr. Stevens, who is still living, was Miss Sarah L. Deming of Winsted. There are two children, a son and a daughter, in the family. In politics Mr. Stevens is a democrat. He belongs to the Masonic order and the Knights of Pythias, and is a gentleman of most enjoyable personality.

WILLIAM SHERIDAN TODD, M.A., M.D., Ridgefield: Physician and Surgeon.

Doctor Wm. S. Todd, one of the best known and most successful physicians in the town of Ridgefield, was born in Coleraine, Mass., January 1,

W. S. TODD, M.D.

1840. He was the son of a Methodist minister, and his education was picked up in the various towns where the itinerant system placed his parents. He finished his preparatory course at Deerfield academy, entered Wesleyan University at Middletown in 1860, graduating therefrom in 1864, his course having been disturbed by the excitements of the war. In 1864-65 he was principal of Hills academy in Essex, and commenced the study of medicine with Dr. Chas. H. Hubbard of that place. In 1866, 1867, and 1868, he was a teacher in W. O. Seymour's school in Ridgefield, still pursuing his medical studies. In 1869 he graduated from the College of Physicians and Surgeons in New York city, since which time he has been practicing his profession in Ridgefield. May 6, 1873, he was married to Miss Mary Jane Conklin, daughter of Deacon Gamaliel Conklin of Essex, who is the mother of his two boys. Doctor Todd has held no political office, except that of representative in the state legislature, to which he was elected in 1888, when he served as chairman of the committee on humane institutions. He has, however, officiated for several successive years as school committee, has been president and treasurer of the "Ridgefield Press Printing Company," and a frequent contributor to the editorial columns of the local paper. He is now a member of the school board, and deeply interested in all efforts for the improvement of the public school system and

management. He is a member of the Twilight Club of New York, Pilgrim Lodge, I. O. O. F., Jerusalem Lodge, F. and A. M., and its secretary for several years; member of the Fairfield County Medical Society, Danbury Medical Society, and the American Academy of Medicine. In religious belief and church membership he is a Congregationalist, and in politics a republican.

GEORGE F. TILLINGHAST, Canterbury: Farmer.

Geo. F. Tillinghast comes of Revolutionary stock. He was born in Griswold, this state, December 31, 1838, the son of a farmer of moderate means. He

G. F. TILLINGHAST.

was the fourth child in a family of seven. His father died when he was but five years of age, and for several years thereafter he was "a boy of most all work." He received a common school education, remaining on his mother's farm until he was seventeen years of age, when he became an operative in a woolen mill. He took a deep interest in the stirring events of 1861; and, neglecting bright business prospects, was one of the first men to enlist from his native town at the earliest call of his country for volunteers. He was a member of Company B, under Captain Chester, Second Regiment, Connecticut Volunteers, under command of Colonel A. H. Terry. He participated with his regiment in the first battle of Bull Run, the Connecticut brigade being one of the last to leave the field of battle, partially covering the retreat and saving millions of dollars' worth of public property for the government. After being discharged from the three months' service he re-enlisted for three years in the Eleventh Connecticut Regiment, familiarly known as the "fighting Eleventh." He served as a non-commissioned officer in Company D, following the fortunes of this regiment up to the siege of Petersburgh. He was honorably discharged on the 26th day of November, 1864, by reason of expiration of term of service. In the fall of 1865 he started on a journey southward, as a traveling agent, and traveled through many of the southern and western states. In 1867 he spent his time in Nebraska and took an active part in the capital contest which resulted in wresting the seat of government from Omaha and making Lincoln the capital of the state. It is generally conceded that he contributed his full share in various ways to accomplish that result.

He has held real estate in Lincoln ever since the city was founded, which is now very valuable. In the summer of 1868 he returned East in quite poor health. Was for several years engaged with his brother, Gideon G. Tillinghast, Esq., in the book trade. Since the year 1876 he has followed the occupation of a farmer; has lived in Canterbury the last ten years. Mr. Tillinghast married Miss Rosa Wilcox of Griswold, by whom he has two sons and one daughter. He has held public positions of trust and discharged the duties to the satisfaction of all. He believes in and tries to follow the golden rule. He is an attendant and supporter of the Baptist church at Packersville, of which his wife is a member. He acted with the republican party until 1888, when he became an ardent prohibitionist. He regards the open saloon as the greatest curse to the laboring man, and the sum of all villainies. He is a member of Sedgwick Post, G. A. R., and also of Canterbury Grange, No. 70. He enjoys a reputation for sound practical sense and good judgment.

F. P. BISSELL, TURNERVILLE (HEBRON): Farmer.

Frederick Phelps Bissell was born in Hebron, April 23, 1822, and received a common school education. He has pursued the business of farming, insurance, and teaching, devoting his attention to the latter during his early years. He was formerly connected with the state militia, holding a lieutenant's commission in an independent company. He was one of the original members of the Know Nothing party, and was actively connected with it as an organization. In 1862 he represented the town of Hebron in the

F. P. BISSELL.

house, serving on the republican side. In 1871 he was elected to the senate from the old twenty-first district. He was also judge of probate in the Hebron district for a number of years. Judge Bissell is a prominent member of St. Peter's Episcopal church in Hebron, and has been connected with it in an official capacity since 1844. He was a vestryman until 1854, and has been one of the wardens since the latter year. He has also been the treasurer of the church for twenty-nine years. His wife, who is still living, was Miss Almira J. Carver, daughter of Joseph Carver, Esq., of Hebron. There is one son living. Mr. Bissell has been a public-spirited citizen through the whole of his life, and has been honored practically with

every office within the gift of his town. In all of the public positions which he has held his career has been characterized by the strictest loyalty to his constituents and the state.

SAMUEL FITCH, ROCKVILLE: Manufacturer of Stockinets and Plushes.

The progenitors of Mr. Fitch were of French descent. His father, Samuel Fitch, was born in Bolton, Tolland county, and removed to Albion, N. Y., where his death occurred. He married Nancy Atwell of Montville, Conn., and had one child, Samuel, the subject of this biography, was born December 2, 1821, in Enfield, Hartford county, where the greater portion of his youth was spent. After several terms at the common school, he pursued his studies at North Wilbraham, Mass., and until his twenty-second year

SAMUEL FITCH.

continued the healthful employment of a farmer. He then engaged in the sale of merchandise in New England, frequently extending his trips to the Canadas, where he received furs in exchange for other commodities. Mr. Fitch finally, becoming weary of the nomadic life which his business necessitated, settled in West Stafford, and, renting a factory, embarked in the manufacture of knit goods, continuing for thirteen years in this location. During the years 1858 and 1859 he was selectman of that town. He then removed to Rockville, and, renting a factory, engaged in manufacturing at that point. In 1874 he purchased his present site, which has since that date been greatly enlarged and improved. Here he continues the production of a great variety of knit goods, certain specialties of which have given the mill a deservedly high reputation.

Mr. Fitch was, on the 9th of January, 1845, married to Mariette, daughter of Daniel Spencer of Enfield. Their children are Spencer S., Sarah E. (wife of C. H. Strickland), and Fred. H. (deceased). The son is identified with the business which is now a corporation under the firm name of "The Samuel Fitch & Sons Co." Mr. Fitch was formerly a whig, and later became an exponent of the principles of the republican party. He has held various local offices, and during the years 1860, 1861, and 1877, represented his town in the state legislature. He was from 1863 to 1869 state railroad commissioner. He was also one of the incorporators and is a director in the People's Savings Bank of Rockville. In 1889 he was chosen vice-president of the " United States Central Railroad Company," and in the same year, on the 2d of December, his sixty-eighth birthday, he was elected the first mayor of the city of Rockville for the term of two years. Mr. Fitch was a supporter of the Second Congregational church of Rockville during its existence, and Mrs. Fitch was a member.

GILES POTTER, New Haven: Agent of the State Board of Education.

Giles Potter, son of Elisha Payne and Abigail (Lathrop) Potter, of good Puritan stock, was born in Lisbon, Conn., February 22, 1829. Attending  the common school, working on the farm or at carriage-making in his father's shop, and teaching school, he at length found his way through Leicester academy, and graduated at Yale College in the class of '55, winning honors in mathematics and the sciences; and engaged in teaching — 1855–56 at East Hartford, 1856–59 as instructor in natural science at the

GILES POTTER.

Connecticut Literary Institution (Suffield), 1859–64 as principal of Hill's academy, Essex. He then went into manufacturing for a short time, resumed teaching at the Essex seminary, and in 1870 took up the insurance business.

Mr. Potter is in politics a firm but quiet republican, doing his duty in the caucus and at the polls, but never troubled by political ambition. However, the people of Essex found it their pleasure and profit to bestow upon him many local offices — selectman, justice of the peace, school visitor, etc. — keeping him always in the two latter offices, well knowing that Mr. Potter has almost a weakness for serving his fellows and not himself. For the years 1870, '71, and '72 they elected him representative to the state legislature. Quite naturally, he was assigned to the committee on education. This committee, in 1872, being instructed to revise the school laws, formulated the present compulsory system, Mr. Potter, as chairman, presenting the report. In the fall of 1872 he became agent of the state board of education, and for the last eighteen years it has been his office to look after the enforcement of those same beneficent laws which he had so large a share in compiling. He has brought into this work rare tact, energy, and love. For instance, if he happens to buy a paper of a small-sized newsboy he is apt, in a kindly way, to ask the boy's name and age, and where he goes to school. Quiet and conciliating in manner, preferring mild means where possible, never withholding stronger ones where necessary, the delinquent employer and selfish or brutal parent have learned that Mr. Potter brooks no trifling. For Agent Potter to be in town means business. He has, therefore, won the esteem and respect of the many prominent men in all parts of the state with whom his duties bring him in contact; has largely by the diligence and enthusiasm with which he fulfills his office contributed to the present creditable showing of Connecticut in regard to popular education — this despite the increasing foreign character of the population, and the vast growth of the factory interest — and seems well to bear out the truth of these words, uttered in reference to him on the floor of the United States senate : "One of the most efficient men in the state is appointed to enforce the law."

Mr. Potter is an active supporter of public worship; long time deacon of the Essex Baptist church; twenty-three years superintendent of the Sunday-school. He is now a deacon of Calvary church, New Haven, whither he removed in 1884. He was married in 1857 to Martha Hubbard Wright, daughter of Rev. David Wright, and has four children living.

GEORGE MILTON MORSE, Putnam: Cotton Manufacturer.

George M. Morse was born at Central Falls, R. I., August 25, 1830. He was educated principally at the public schools of his native town and of the  city of Providence. He has been engaged in manufacturing, merchandizing, and in real estate operations in Woonsocket Falls, Valley Falls, and Providence, R. I., and in Putnam, Conn. He is now president of the Powhattan and the Morse mills manufacturing corporations, which are among the leading cotton manufacturing concerns in

G. M. MORSE.

the Quinebaug Valley. He has held and worthily filled various offices within the gift of his townsmen, including that of representative to the general court, to which he was chosen at the last state election. He is a member and deacon of the First Baptist church of Putnam, and in politics is an ardent republican. Mr. Morse married Miss Melora Whitney, of the adjoining town of Killingly, and has reared a family of nine children.

J. E. PINE, Winsted. Marble Cutter.

John Edgar Pine was born in Riverton, in the town of Barkhamsted, in 1841. After spending a few years at the schools of his neighborhood, he served an apprenticeship as stone cutter with his father, who was then in the marble business. From 1872 till 1884 he was junior partner with his father, conducting the monumental and marble business under the firm name of S. W. Pine & Son at Winsted. In 1884 the senior partner retired, and John E. Pine has since that date conducted the business alone, the

J. E. PINE.

establishment being designated and known as the Winsted Monumental Works. The many fine monuments in the vicinity of Winsted which have been furnished by this house indicate that the proprietor is master of his business. Mr. Pine is a member of St. James' Episcopal church. He is also a Mason, and in politics a republican. He has held various town offices, such as water commissioner, school committee, etc.; and in whatever capacity called to serve the public he has proved a trusty and useful public officer. He has a wife, but no children living.

CHARLES P. STURTEVANT, Norwich. Woolen Manufacturer.

The subject of this sketch was born in New York city in 1844 and received an academic education. His father was Hon. A. P. Sturtevant of Norwich, one of the great manufacturers of eastern Connecticut. Mr. Sturtevant has held nearly all the offices in the gift of his townsmen; was elected to the house of representatives in 1878 and was state senator from the eleventh district in 1881-82. He is a Congregationalist, and has been prominently identified with the republican party of his section of the state.

C. P. STURTEVANT.

He is engaged in manufacturing and is agent and secretary of the Niantic Mills Co. and connected with the Clinton Mills Co., the Norwich Woolen Co., and the Glen Woolen Co. He has for some years been prominent in the fraternal societies,

being a 32d degree Mason, an Odd Fellow, and a member of the Knights of Pythias and of the Improved Order of Red Men. He is married and has five children. Mr. Sturtevant is deservedly popular among a host of friends and in his various business interests has a most extensive acquaintance.

JAMES ANDREW PICKETT, New Britain: Ex-Mayor and ex-President of Several Manufacturing Corporations.

J. A. Pickett, one of the most honored and respected of New Britain's citizens, a son of Albert Pickett, was born in New Milford, Litchfield county, March 9, 1829. He was educated at the public schools in New Milford and private schools in Bridgeport, and in 1851 went to New Britain to enter the employ as bookkeeper of the A. North & Son Saddlery Hardware Manufacturing Company. In 1855 he, with L. F. Judd, bought a one-half interest in the establishment. He has been twice married: first, September 9, 1857,

J. A. PICKETT.

to Miss Caroline E. Stanley; and a few years after her death, second, to Miss Emma C. Lawrence. He has one child, a daughter, who is now Mrs. Anna M. Rockwell of Birmingham.

In 1876 Mr. Pickett was elected president of the manufacturing company of Landers, Frary & Clark, and held the office by repeated re-elections until his resignation in 1889. He was also president of the Union Manufacturing Company from 1878 to 1891. He was vice-president and director of the Shelby Iron Works, Alabama, and was for many years director and vice-president of the New Britain National Bank. He is a director in the Mechanics National Bank, Russell & Erwin Manufacturing Company, American Hosiery Company, Stanley Rule and Level Company, Union Manufacturing Company, and the New Britain Savings Bank. He has been repeatedly called to offices of trust and responsibility by his fellow-citizens. He was elected town assessor for several years; was city auditor in 1871 and 1872. On the adoption of the system of sewerage by the city he was appointed one of the sewer commissioners, and held the office from 1874 to 1882, inclusive. He was elected mayor of the city in 1883, 1884, and 1885, and represented the town in the legislature in 1884, when he was chairman on the part of the house of the committee on insurance. He is a member of the Center church of New Britain, and a liberal promoter of its interests and supporter of its charities. His rank as a public officer, business man, and citizen is very high, and has met practical recognition from his townsmen on every opportunity. By his knowledge of business and insight into the needs of the town and city, he has been able in all the various positions he has occupied to contribute much to the welfare and prosperity of the place.

CHRISTOPHER M. SPENCER, Windsor: Treasurer Spencer Arms Company.

Christopher Miner Spencer was born in Manchester, Conn., June 20, 1833. In 1845 he went to live with his grandfather, and there developed a

C. M. SPENCER.

great fondness for mechanical work. From early childhood he had a passion for firearms, and the first gun he owned was his grandfather's old musket, a revolutionary relic, which he improved by sawing off the barrel with an old case-knife converted into a saw by hacking it on the edge of an axe. In 1847 he left his grandfather's farm and went to work in Cheneys' silk mill, and in 1848 entered a machine shop at Manchester Center as an apprentice. The year following he again entered the Cheneys' employ as a machinist, and remained about three years. In 1853 he went to Rochester, N. Y., where he worked in making machinists' tools. Returning to Hartford he was a year with Colt's Firearms Company, where he first conceived the idea of radical improvements in repeating firearms. Later, while with the Cheneys, he invented an ingenious automatic machine for winding silk, which was adopted by the Willimantic Thread Company. About this time he invented and patented the " Spencer Seven-shooter," which was adopted by the U. S. government, and a company, known as the Spencer Repeating Rifle Company, was organized for its manufacture. The success of this new arm is now a matter of history. At the close of the war the company sold its entire plant to the Winchester Repeating Arms Co. of New Haven. In 1869 Mr. Spencer moved to Hartford, and in company with Mr. Charles E. Billings began the manufacture of drop-forgings. While here he invented a very successful machine for turning sewing-machine spools, which later suggested to him the idea of a machine for turning metal screws automatically. He kept this invention a se-

cret until he had obtained his patents, and then applied the device to a machine in the Billings & Spencer shop. The result was a complete success, and so great was his enthusiasm that he determined to commence the manufacture of screws automatically as a new enterprise; and, severing his connection with Mr. Billings in 1874, he hired a room and set his first screw machine to work. In 1876 the Hartford Machine Screw Company was formed from this nucleus, with Mr. Spencer as superintendent, the ultimate result of which is one of the largest and most profitable enterprises in the city of Hartford, with a plant valued at half a million dollars.

During all these years Mr. Spencer's mind was exercised with the idea of still further improving modern firearms, and he determined to produce a repeating-gun that should excel all others in rapidity of firing. The result of his thought on the subject has been what is now known as the " Spencer Repeating Shot-Gun." Models were shown, capitalists interested, and a company was formed for their manufacture, known as the " Spencer Arms Co.," with its works located at Windsor in this state, of which Mr. Spencer is the treasurer. This gun has an established reputation among sportsmen, and many thousands are in use in the United States and other parts of the world. His latest achievement is the invention of an automatic screw machine, which produces finished screws direct from a coil of wire.

ELIJAH MANROSS, Bristol: Clock Manufacturer and Constable.

Mr. Manross is a native of Bristol, having been born there June 20, 1827. He received a common school and academic education, completing his

ELIJAH MANROSS.

course of study at Williston Seminary, East Hampton, Mass. Upon entering active life Mr. Manross learned the clock business, and was a manufacturer until 1867, when, owing to ill health, he was obliged to retire and give himself over to absolute rest. After rugged treatment, including a year and a half passed in the wilds of the Adirondacks, he regained his strength, and now enjoys good health. The father of Mr. Manross was a pioneer in the manufacture of brass clocks in America, with which industry he was prominently identified. Three of his brothers served in Connecticut regiments during the war of the rebellion, one of whom (Captain Newton S. Manross) was killed while leading his company into the sanguinary field of Antietam. Sergeant Eli Manross of the Fifth Connecticut was wounded at Chancellorsville, and John Manross, also a brother, was disabled at Cold Harbor. The subject of this sketch has twice represented Bristol in the legislature, in 1880 and 1882. He has held the office of justice of the peace, has served repeatedly on the republican town committee, and for fifteen years has been constable, in the duties of which office his time is now chiefly occupied. He has been a republican ever since the formation of that party. His wife, who before her marriage was Miss Ellen S. Woodruff, is living, and they have three children.

CHARLES F. LINCOLN, ANDOVER: Postmaster and Merchant.

Charles F. Lincoln was born in Columbia, Oct. 4, 1854, and was educated at the public schools. He came to Andover in 1873 as clerk for Henry F. Cleveland, and in May, 1880, bought the business and carried it on until 1888, and between those dates he held the offices of town clerk, treasurer, registrar, and treasurer of the Andover Creamery Company. He represented Andover in the legislature in 1886. In 1888 he entered the employ of Durkee, Stiles & Co., of Willimantic, as commercial traveler, con-

C. F. LINCOLN.

tinuing with that firm for about six months until he again went into business for himself, buying out the establishment of Palmer Brothers in Fitchville, town of Bozrah. He continued that business until 1889, and since that time has been a commercial traveler for New York grocery and specialty houses. In this line he has been very successful, and is ranked as a first-class salesman. His instincts and abilities are of a high mercantile order. He was assistant postmaster and postmaster at Andover for three years, and assistant postmaster at Fitchville one year. Mr. Lincoln has always been a republican, and has received honors from the hands of his townsmen as a member of that party. He married, in June, 1883, Miss Nellie A. Daggett, youngest daughter of W. H. H. Daggett of Hartford. She died Sept. 21, 1887. Mr. Lincoln is a wide awake sort of a man, who succeeds in whatever he undertakes.

R. W. CHADWICK, OLD LYME: Farmer.

Richard William Chadwick was born a farmer, and has followed that occupation through his life. He was solidly educated at the public schools, and had the additional advan-

R. W. CHADWICK.

tage of a course of training at Lyme Academy. He has held various town offices, to which he has been elected by the republicans, of which party he has been a member since old enough to vote. For about a quarter of a century he has been a deputy sheriff, and by virtue of his office was instrumental in capturing the notorious Bridgeport gang of boy burglars in 1885; and at that time narrowly escaped death by a bullet from the pistol of one of the burglars while effecting his arrest. Mr. Chadwick was a member of the Connecticut house of representatives from Old Lyme in 1873, and again in 1889, during the latter session serving on the fisheries committee. He also holds the office of selectman of his town at the present time. He is a member of the Odd Fellows and Masonic fraternity; is married, and has two children living. His wife was Miss A. M. Rowland before her marriage.

WILLIAM C. SHARPE, SEYMOUR: Editor and Publisher "Seymour Record."

Mr. Sharpe is a native of Southbury, where he was born October 3, 1839. He was educated at the Seymour High School and Wesleyan Academy at Wilbraham, Mass. After his graduation he engaged in teaching, and was thus employed for ten years, in Massachusetts, Connecticut, New Jersey, and Pennsylvania, his last work of this kind being as principal of a graded school at Derby in this state. He became the editor and publisher of *The Seymour Record* in 1871, and has sustained that relation for

W. C. SHARPE.

twenty years. He was united in marriage some years ago to Miss Vinie A. Lewis, daughter of Harry Lewis of Monroe, by whom he has had two children, a son and a daughter. Mr. Sharpe has held a number of public offices in Seymour, having been a member of the school board for nine years, secretary and acting visitor six years, a trustee of the Methodist Episcopal church fifteen years, and superintendent of the Sunday-school. He is now a member of the Congregational church at Seymour. He is a republican, and connected with various social organizations, including several Masonic bodies, New Haven Commandery, Knights Templar, Red Men, Knights of Pythias, New England Order of Protection, and others. Additionally to his literary work on the *Record*, Mr. Sharpe has found time for much other similar labor. He is author of the "History of Seymour" in two volumes; "Annals of Seymour M. E. Church," "History of Oxford," "Genealogy of the Sharpe Family," "Dart Genealogy," etc. He is also a member of the Connecticut Historical Society of Hartford. Mr. Sharpe is a thoroughly industrious man, a careful editor, and a conscientious author.

CYRUS WHITE, Rockville: President, Treasurer and Manager of the White Manufacturing Company, President of The White, Corbin & Company.

Mr. White was born at Richford, Vt., Nov. 18, 1814, the eldest of eight children of a farmer of moderate means. He was early inured to the toils

and privations of life in a newly-settled region, and thereby gained a hardy physical development and laid the foundation of industry, frugality, and self reliance, which has served him so well in his subsequent career. With the limited educational privileges of a few weeks each year in the district schools, he gained a fair knowledge of the rudimentary sciences (reading, writing, and arithmetic), and at the age of nineteen started out to learn the blacksmith's trade, serving an apprenticeship of three years in the little hamlet of East Enosburgh, about ten miles distant from the parental home. Here he learned, literally and figuratively, to strike while the iron is hot, a practical lesson to ever keep in mind. At the close of this term, in November, 1836, the chances for obtaining employment in Northern Vermont being less favorable than in other localities, he made an engagement with a man in Ware, Mass., and went there to find that his intended employer had died suddenly a few hours before his arrival. This left him without business, among strangers with only three dollars in his pocket; but providentially he heard of an opening for employment at Vernon

Center in this state, with a chance to work his passage thither by helping a drove of cattle to that place. There he remained until April 1, 1838, receiving about eighty cents per day and his board for his services, from which during the seventeen months he managed to save $25, in cash; and with this capital he hired a shop at Rockville and employed two assistants, thus commencing business for himself. On the 1st day of January, 1839, meeting with some success, he engaged in a matrimonial partnership with Miss Sarah A. Grant of Ware, Mass., formerly a school companion in Vermont. This union proved a very fortunate and happy one, and still continues. Of five children born to them, three are now living. During the next few years he acquired considerable real estate and built his present residence, also White's opera house and other buildings. In 1848 he bought a half interest in the iron foundry business, and about two years later the firm of C. White & Co., which had at this date bought tools and started a machine shop business in connection with the foundry and smithing business, with Milton G. Puffer employed as a patternmaker and ingenious mechanic, inaugurated a series of experiments which resulted in the production of an improved machine capable of folding and pasting 10,000 letter envelopes per day. Mr. White, discovering in this a chance for a permanent and profitable enterprise, began to lay the foundations for the eminently successful business of C. White & Co. In this his partner had less faith, and in 1855 sold his interest to L. A. Corbin, when the firm was changed to White & Corbin, and the foundry and blacksmith shop were sold, a waterpower purchased, and early in the spring of 1856 a four-story building, 83 x 39, was erected for an envelope factory.

On the fourth of the following July three or four of these improved envelope machines were started in the new factory, and the business was placed on a more permanent basis, Mr. White devoting his time exclusively to the general management of the business, and to the building up of a trade in envelopes and paper. Sales were small and means also; hence the firm had to proceed slowly. A business of about $8,000 the first year more than doubled the next, and so continued to increase until a condition was reached where sales amounted to $325,000 in a single year. Machines were added as fast as they could be made by the company with their limited facilities. In 1866 William H. Prescott, who had been their bookkeeper for several years and who by his ability and strict attention to business had made his services indispensable to the firm, was, at the instance of Mr. White, admitted as a partner, with an equal interest with the two former partners, when the firm became White, Corbin & Co. In May, 1870, Mr. White having other business requiring his attention, retired from the management of the envelope and paper business, since which time the managerial duties have devolved upon Mr. Prescott. The business continued to develop to such an extent that in 1881 it gave occasion for the purchase of the "Florence mills," one of the largest and finest mill buildings in Rockville, and which it became necessary to enlarge by extensive additions some years later, in order to accommodate the still increasing business, which is now among the most extensive of its line in the world. As ability, integrity, and success had given value to the name of Cyrus White, it was frequently sought as a means of obtaining credit by others less fortunate. By his kindness of heart which too often led him to disregard warnings to avoid suretyship, he became involved, by the failure of parties he had assisted during the autumn of 1869, in liabilities amounting to nearly $200,000. This necessitated taking certain mill properties, assuming prior incumbrances thereon, and likewise a further outlay to make the property available as a source of income for reimbursement for obligations he had assumed. This led to the commencement of the business of the White Manufacturing Company, which was started with sixty looms, and has been extended, until now it operates four hundred and eighty-eight looms and other machinery requisite to run them, with capacity to make 14,000 to 15,000 yards daily of ginghams and ladies' dress goods of various designs and superior quality. In addition to the business of the White Manufacturing Company, of which Mr. White is principal owner and manager, he also holds a one-third interest in The White, Corbin & Company. Mr. White also owns the Highland farm, located within the city limits, which is carried on and managed by him. He takes great pleasure in improving its well-tilled fields, and in its fine herd of cows and young stock. He also owns a large farm in Enosburgh, Vermont, well stocked, together with two fine sugar orchards of over two thousand trees.

In Rockville he does a large grain and milling business, the extensive "city mills" being run by the White Manufacturing Company. The various enterprises with which Mr. White is and has been identified have kept him a very busy man. Notwithstanding he is almost an octogenarian, he still attends to the direction and general management of his business with the energy and vigor of a man in the prime of life. A recital of the struggles and triumphs through which he has passed affords a fine picture of a life which illustrates the possibilities of undaunted confidence and earnest effort in making a success of enterprises undertaken under adverse circumstances, and in some cases almost without any previous practical knowledge of their

details. His success is not measured by his own personal profit only, but in the advancement of the interests of others with whom he has been associated, and in contributing largely to the material wealth, prosperity, population, and industries of his adopted city, notwithstanding the many obstacles that would discourage or dismay the average man, but which the subject of this sketch has resolutely met and overcome. He still looks on the bright side of life with undimmed vision, and spirit apparently as buoyant as in earlier days; and while he carries a full share of the burdens and responsibilities of life, he extends the hearty greeting of a friend, and richly deserves the reputation he has won and the magnificent success he has achieved.

[Mr. White died at his home in Rockville, May 10, 1891, after the above sketch had been prepared. —ED.]

WINTHROP M. WADSWORTH, FARMINGTON: Farmer.

Mr. Wadsworth is one of the most favorably known of public officials in Hartford county. He has been a member of the general assembly through four terms, and introduced there the constitutional amendment changing the sessions of the legislature from May to January. The amendment when submitted to the people was carried by a large majority. Mr. Wadsworth also introduced the resolutions some years ago, discountenancing the back pay scheme which had been carried through the na-

tional congress. These resolutions were copied and passed by the legislatures of several of the states, and produced a marked impression on the public. For twenty-eight consecutive years Mr. Wadsworth was the first selectman of his town. He has been the president of the Dairymen's Association, and president of the Farmington Creamery Company, the first established in New England. He was a justice of the peace for a number of years, and has been prominent in town interests for fifty years. He was a Hartford county director in the State Agricultural Society, and is the president of the Farmington Savings Bank. Mr. Wadsworth is a republican and a member of the First Congregational society. He has twice married. His first wife was Lucy A. Ward, who died in 1853. The second wife, Elizabeth F. Wadsworth, is still living. There are four sons in the family. The eldest,

Adrian R. Wadsworth, remains on the farm which has been in the family for five generations. The remaining sons, Harry H. and Frank H., lawyers, and Frederick A., real estate manager, reside in Minneapolis. Mr. Wadsworth owns a farm of three hundred acres, which he has managed personally until within a short period, in addition to his extensive public duties. It has been a marked advantage to the town of Farmington, and the state at large, in fact, that so capable and honest a man has been willing to bestow so much of his time and experience to the public service.

Mr. Wadsworth was born in Farmington, November 27, 1812, and received his education in the public schools and at Farmington Academy. His long life has been one of great honor and usefulness, and for a great many years there has been no one in his community whose advice and counsel was more sought after or depended upon.

WILLIAM M. STANLEY, EAST HARTFORD: Farmer.

Mr. Stanley was born in East Hartford November 18, 1817, and received a common school and academical education, and in early life followed the

W. M. STANLEY.

business of bookbinding, but since 1840 has been farming in East Hartford, one of the finest farming towns in the state. Mr. Stanley is a republican, casting his vote for William Henry Harrison in 1840, and by virtue of that act is an influential member of the Harrison Veterans of Hartford. He has often been honored by the votes of his townsmen, and for fourteen years was the first selectman of the town, from 1856 to 1870. He was justice of the peace from 1853 until 1887 when he was disqualified from age, serving one of the longest terms in that capacity of any man in the state. He has the confidence of the financial men of central Connecticut, and is a trustee of that honored institution, the Pratt Street Institution for Savings in Hartford, the strongest savings bank in the state. Mr. Stanley's wife was Mary E. Newton, and they have three children living. He is prominently connected with the Congregational church in East Hartford. Mr. Stanley is one of the Sons of the American Revolution, and takes pride in the fact that his grandfather, Theodore Stanley, was among the patriots who hurried to Boston in response to the Lexington alarm in 1775.

WARREN W. WOODWARD, DANIELSONVILLE: Druggist.

Mr. Woodward was born in Brooklyn, Conn., in 1834, and is a graduate of the Brooklyn academy. He is a druggist, and has resided in Brooklyn, Lisbon, and Danielsonville.

W. W. WOODWARD.

His business career was begun in Brooklyn as a news dealer, afterwards in a general store, and for two years in Eagleville (Lisbon) he kept a general store and was postmaster. Since 1868 he has been in the drug business in Danielsonville in his own name. He has been a republican from the date of the organization of the party. He has been a grand juror of the town of Brooklyn, and has served as juror in the United States District Court at Hartford. He has been prominently connected with the Baptist denomination in the eastern part of the state, being one of the organizers of the Baptist church in Danielsonville, and for several years was a member of both the church and society committees, and clerk and treasurer of both organizations. He was a member of the building committee when the church was erected. His wife was Anna E. Ross, and they have three children.

ASHER S. BAILEY, EAST HARTFORD: Flour and Grain Merchant.

Mr. Bailey, who is one of the best-known business men of East Hartford, was born in Haddam, Conn., January 6, 1851. He was educated in the

A. S. BAILEY.

common schools of Haddam, and spent his life there until he was twenty-six years of age, working at his trade of a carpenter and joiner, when he removed to East Hartford. Since residing in the last-named town, he has been justice of the peace and school committee for ten years, and is well known for his active interest in public affairs. He is an earnest republican. His religious connections are with the First Baptist church of Hartford. He has been in mercantile business for the past twelve years. He is without any family, having lost by death his wife and only child.

JAMES H. BEACH, New Britain: Ex-Probate and City Court Judge.

Judge Beach was born in Litchfield, Feb. 10, 1819, and was educated at the common schools of that town. For thirty years he followed the trade of a carpenter and joiner, and has lived sixteen years in Litchfield, nine years in Waterbury, twenty-five in Plymouth, and twenty-two in New Britain. He has been constable and deputy sheriff for eighteen years, selectman for two years, justice of the peace for seventeen years, judge of probate six years, and judge of the New Britain city and probate court for four

J. H. BEACH.

years. In all these public capacities he has won the esteem of the citizens whom he served, and is one of the honored residents of New Britain to-day. He has been an attendant of the Episcopal church for many years, always taking an interest in its affairs. He is a democrat in politics. His wife, who is still living, was Ann M. Coy, and he has had five children, of whom four are now living. Mr. Beach is thoroughly known and respected by a large circle of friends in the central and western part of the state.

H. D. PATTERSON, Naugatuck: Merchant.

Henry De Witt Patterson was born in Seymour, November 2, 1834, and is a graduate of the Connecticut Literary Institute at Suffield. He enlisted as a private in the First Connecticut Artillery May 23, 1861, and served with that famous regiment until October 5, 1865, holding the rank of lieutenant and brevet captain when he was mustered out. Naturally he takes a great deal of interest in all matters connected with the veteran soldiers, and is an enthusiastic member of the Grand Army of the Republic. He has

H. D. PATTERSON.

followed the business of a merchant in Seymour, New Haven, and Naugatuck, dealing in general dry-goods on his own account. Although an earnest republican, he has found no time for public office. He is an Odd Fellow and Mason, a member of Shepherds Lodge, Allerton Chapter, Clark Commandery, and Lafayette Consistory,

reaching the thirty-second degree. He is a Congregationalist in religious faith and membership. His wife was Ellen R. Potter, and they have two children. Mr. Patterson is an active man, and has a host of acquaintances in the Naugatuck Valley.

SIMEON ABEL, Fitchville (Bozrah): Farmer.

Simeon Abel, a native of Bozrah, was born in 1822 and educated in the common schools. He is a farmer, and is prominent in the community in which he has been so long a resident. In the days of the old state militia Mr. Abel held the commission of a lieutenant. He is a republican in politics and has been assessor, member of the board of relief, selectman, constable, and collector, the latter for twenty years. In 1869 he represented Bozrah in the legislature, serving on the committee on banks. He was the

SIMEON ABEL.

census enumerator in his town for 1880 and 1890, and is now a justice of the peace. These offices he has filled with great acceptance to his constituents and the town, whose interests he has always earnestly striven to promote to the best of his ability. He is a member of the Congregational church, and its clerk. His wife, who is living, was Fanny E. Stark, and he has three sons.

HON. RALPH S. TAINTOR, Colchester: Farmer.

The Hon. Ralph Smith Taintor was one of the prominent organizers of the republican party in this state. In 1857 he represented the old ninth district in the senate, his colleagues including Judges Carpenter and Loomis of the supreme court. Mr. Taintor was born in Colchester, Nov. 13, 1811, and was educated at Bacon Academy. With the exception of nine years from April, 1839, which were spent in the town of Pomfret, he has resided in Colchester. He is a direct lineal descendant from Michael Taintor,

R. S. TAINTOR.

one of the original nine incorporators of that town in 1698, and for twenty-six years a delegate to the general court of Connecticut. Ex-Senator Taintor was married June 2, 1834, at Lyme, to Miss Phœbe Higgins Lord, who was born in that town June 11, 1814, and died December 16, 1890. There were eight children in the family, seven of whom are still living. The sons include Judge Taintor of New York city and Secretary James U. Taintor of the Orient Insurance Company, both of whom are graduates of Yale College. Mr. Taintor was a lieutenant in the old state militia. He has held various local offices, including that of selectman. He is a member of Wooster Lodge No. 10, F. and A. M. of Colchester, and also of Grange No. 78. He has pursued the avocation of a farmer most of his life, and has been an earnest representative of the farming interests in the state. He has also been an extensive purchaser of wool on commission, and has been widely known in business circles. He was originally a Whig, but has been identified with the republican party since its formation; and during his active political life was frequently delegate to the state, congressional, and senatorial conventions of his party. He is a member of the Congregational church at Colchester, and is held in the utmost respect and esteem in the community where he resides.

WILLIAM F. DANIEL, Stamford: Stock Broker.

William F. Daniel is one of the active citizens of the Borough of Stamford, and the captain of Company C, Fourth regiment, C. N. G. On

W. F. DANIEL.

October 8, 1880, he enlisted as a private in the Seventh regiment, N. G. S. N. Y., and was made corporal, January 13, 1882. October 20, 1885, he was discharged from the command. He was one of the organizers of Company C of the Fourth in this state, and became captain of the company, December 26, 1884. With the exception of Captain Sheridan of Bridgeport, he is the ranking line officer in the regiment. Captain Daniel was born in Stamford, December 30, 1855, and received a high school education. He is engaged in the brokerage business, being the senior member of the firm of Wm. F. Daniel & Bro., with office at No. 62 Broadway, New York city. Captain Daniel spent one year at sea as purser between New York and the West Indies. He is a member of the Manhattan Athletic Club, one of the crack clubs of the metropolis, the Republican Club, and the New York Wheel Club. He was at one time president of the Young Men's Re-

publican Club of Stamford. He is a director of the New York Consolidated Stock and Petroleum Exchange and a director of the clearing house connected therewith. He is associated with St. John's Episcopal church in Stamford, and is unmarried.

WILLIAM CONRAD WILE, A.M., M.D., Danbury: Physician.

This well known physician and surgeon was born in Pleasant Valley, Dutchess county, N. Y., January 23, 1847. He was the son of the Rev. Benja-

W. C. WILE.

min F. Wile, a noted Presbyterian m i n i s t e r, and Betty Buckley, a lady from one of the prominent families of the state.

His early education was acquired under the direction of the Rev. Edgar Poe Roe, who occupied at the time a prominent place among the teachers of that state, and among whose pupils were numbered many who have since gained prominence and reputation. Under this efficient tutorship he remained several years, acquiring an extensive knowledge and proficiency in various branches of learning. In 1871 he was married to Miss Eliza Scott Garrison of New York, who, after several years of devoted companionship, succumbed to disease of the lungs, perpetuating, however, in an only daughter her many prominent and endearing qualities. At the beginning of the rebellion he responded to the urgent demands of the occasion, and became a member of Company G, 150th New York volunteers, serving as private for two years and eight months, during this time marching with Sherman to the sea. In accordance with a long-cherished desire to practice medicine, he began in 1865 the study of that profession, and in 1870 received his degree of M.D. from the medical department of the University of the city of New York. After graduation he engaged in medical practice in New Brunswick, N. J., and Highland, N. Y., but afterwards removed to Newtown, Conn., where for years he was engaged in professional work, which was distributed over a large territory, and of which surgery formed a prominent feature. During this period he conceived the idea of founding a medical journal, and the outcome was the *New England Medical Monthly* — a publication which, by reason of its many distinctive features, soon acquired popularity and took a foremost position among the medical journals of the day, its circulation in this (the tenth) year of its existence being equaled by few medical publications of this country.

His professional and literary attainments were destined ere long to receive further recognition, for in 1887 he was tendered the professorship of Mental and Nervous diseases in the Medico-Chirurgical College of Philadelphia, where his success as a practitioner and his skill in imparting information rendered him a highly popular and valued teacher. Yet, as might be inferred, this specialty and the conditions attending city life were not wholly congenial; so that, having received urgent inducements to go elsewhere, he removed to Danbury, Conn., where he has ever since been engaged in the duties of his profession. Soon after his return to Connecticut he was united in marriage to Miss Hattie Adele Loomis of New Haven, an accomplished lady, who, with his daughter, Miss Alice, supply all the pleasant features of domestic life, and dispense their hospitality with a lavish hand.

The specialty of surgery has always received from him more or less attention, and by reason of his knowledge of anatomy and his marked mechanical ingenuity he has made, from time to time, valuable contributions to this department of medicine. His success in nearly all the major operations, as well as in the specialty of abdominal surgery, have likewise added to his reputation, and given him an extended consultation practice throughout the southern portion of the state. He holds the positions of Medical Examiner of the town of Danbury and surgeon of both the Housatonic and New England railroads. His deep interest in medical organizations of various kinds is well known, and has gained for him an extended acquaintance among the members of the profession, both in this country and Europe. Among the offices which he has held may be mentioned those of vice-president of the American Medical Association, president of the American Medical Editors' Association, president of the Fairfield County Medical Society, president of the Danbury Medical Society, secretary of the Section of Anatomy of the Ninth International Medical Congress, as well as member of the British Medical Association (to which he has been a delegate), member of the Medico-Legal Society, Connecticut State Medical Society, and various other organizations.

Dr. Wile is a prolific writer, and has contributed to these societies, and to the medical publications of this and other countries, many important papers upon surgical, medico-legal, and other subjects. In addition to such work, he is occupied with the editorship of the *Monthly*, and another more recent publication entitled, *The Prescription*, which has already acquired a large circulation. His literary acquirements, which are of a high order, and his interest in educational matters, have won

for him a deserved recognition from the Central College of Kentucky, which a few years ago awarded him the honorary degree of A.M. Dr. Wile is likewise well known in social circles. He is a prominent Knight Templar, and Thirty-Second Degree Mason, and a member of many fraternal and business organizations. In politics he has always been identified with the republican party.

His wide professional knowledge and executive ability have won for him a foremost place in the medical profession, while his many attractive qualities of mind and heart have placed him high in the esteem of all who know him.

J. J. B.

JOSEPH HOWARD NORTH, M.D., Goshen: Town Clerk and Registrar.

Dr. North has resided in Goshen since the fall of 1873. He graduated from the Long Island College Hospital, June 26, 1873, and immediately established himself in practice in the town where he now resides. He was born at Cornwall, January 15, 1846, and received a thorough English education at Alger Institute in Cornwall, then managed by Colonel Pettibone, and in the public grammar schools of New York city. While in the metropolis he was especially influenced by Dr. Jackson Bolton, father of

H. Carrington Bolton, Ph.D., (who was until recently identified with Trinity College of Hartford, as Professor of Chemistry,) and by Col. B. S. Alexander of the United States Engineer Corps. The former was a relative by marriage of the Doctor's father, Mr. Joseph North. Colonel Alexander desired the lad's matriculation at West Point, but the outbreak of the war interfered with the plan. In 1868 Dr. North commenced the regular study of medicine under the direction of his uncle, Dr. B. B. North of Cornwall, remaining under his instruction until 1871. He then removed to Potter county, Pa., with a brother-in-law, L. N. Whiting, and engaged in business. There he married Miss Mary C. Hurd, daughter of Harry Hurd, Esq., of Genesee, Pa., and returned to Connecticut. He has taken an active part in public affairs, and has held numerous local offices, including that of constable and school visitor in Cornwall, town clerk in Goshen, and member of the legislature from that place in 1884, serving with credit on the democratic side. He belongs to the Patrons of Husbandry, and is a member of the Litchfield County Medical

Society and the Connecticut Medical Association. There are three children in the family, two sons and a daughter.

RODNEY DENNIS, Hartford: Secretary Travelers Insurance Company.

The subject of this sketch was born at Topfield, Mass., January 14, 1826; the son of a Congregational clergyman of considerable distinction in his

RODNEY DENNIS.

profession, whose ministry covered a period of fifty years. Within a few years after the birth of this son, the family removed from Topfield to Somers, in Tolland county, Conn., where the young man spent several years in acquiring an education at the public schools. At the age of sixteen he came to Hartford, and for ten years was engaged in mercantile pursuits, first as a clerk, and later in business on his own account. He afterwards spent two years in business in Augusta, Ga., and was for a short time a resident of Albany, N. Y. Returning to Hartford in 1855, he engaged with the Phoenix Bank of this city as an accountant, continuing this connection for nine years. In 1864 the Travelers Insurance Company of Hartford was chartered; and at the request of its president, Mr. J. G. Batterson, and the newly-elected board of directors, Mr. Dennis became secretary of the company, and has ever since held that position, — a period of twenty-seven years. He was by education and training admirably qualified for the duties of his office, and brought to this comparatively untried field of insurance effort a vigilant and active mind which quickly and easily grasped every situation; a tenacity of purpose which pursued every possible advantage to a successful issue; a painstaking and methodical habit which enabled him to present always a lucid and orderly solution of all the intricacies of his department; a disposition disciplined by experience, which made him an agreeable official with his associates and patrons; and an inflexible sense of honor and rectitude, which secured for him the implicit confidence of the company and the public. He has been a conscientious and earnest worker, and any intelligent analysis of the phenomenal success which has attended The Travelers Insurance Company during the last quarter of a century must include his efforts among those which have contributed thereto most effectively.

Mr. Dennis is prominently identified with various charitable and humane enterprises and institutions in Hartford. He is, and has been since its foundation, president of the Connecticut Humane Society; auditor and member of the executive committee of the Connecticut Bible Society, and chairman of its finance committee; vice-president of the Young Men's Christian Association; a director in the Connecticut Fire Insurance Company, and one of the three American trustees of the Lion Fire Insurance Company of London; a trustee in the Society for Savings and the Hartford Trust Company; a director in the Hartford City Gas Light Company and the Farmington Power Company; and is officially and otherwise connected with various other financial institutions in which The Travelers is interested. In politics Mr. Dennis is a republican of the truest type. His religious connections are with the Center church (Dr. Walker's) of Hartford.

CHAUNCEY B. WEBSTER, Waterbury.

Chauncey B. Webster was born in Burlington, June 19, 1826, and received a common school and academic education, completing the course in the

C. B. WEBSTER.

academy at Harwinton. He has served two years in the general assembly, and has held numerous public offices in the city of Waterbury. For ten years he was a member of the board of aldermen, two in the council and eleven on the board of assessors. He is at present chairman of the Center school district finance committee. In politics Mr. Webster is a democrat. He was a charter member of the City Guard in 1854, and has been prominently associated with the Masonic order for years, being a member of Harmony Lodge in Waterbury and of Clark Commandery, Knights Templar. He is also a member of the order of Odd Fellows, Knights of Pythias, and Red Men. He is connected with the Congregational church in Waterbury, and has retired from business. His various occupations have included that of house painter, carman, and coal dealer. He removed to Waterbury in 1843 and has since resided in that city. From the time he was nine years of age until his removal to Waterbury he worked on a farm. His success in life has been due to his personal energy and management. His wife, who is now living, with three children, was Miss Louisa Thayer prior to her marriage.

GEORGE W. ROUSE, Voluntown : Postmaster.

George W. Rouse was born at Griswold, February 20, 1847, and received a public school education. His boyhood was spent in a cotton-mill at Voluntown, but at the age of sixteen he obtained employment in a Norwich hotel. One year later he enlisted in the Twelfth Connecticut and served with that command at New Orleans and in the Shenandoah under Sheridan, being in the hottest of the fight at Cedar Creek. He is a member of the Grand Army and is actively interested in the welfare of

G. W. ROUSE.

the soldiers. Mr. Rouse is a member of Mount Vernon Lodge, No. 75, F. and A. M., of Jewett City, and is connected with the order of Odd Fellows and the Ancient Order of United Workmen. The family of Postmaster Rouse consists of his wife and four children, three sons and one daughter. The former was Hattie Maynard before her marriage. He has held the offices of grand juror, notary public, and registrar of births, deaths, and marriages. He is a republican in politics. He is engaged in the grocery and confectionery business.

HON. MICHAEL J. HOULIHAN, Newtown: Hotel Proprietor.

Michael J. Houlihan is a native of Newtown, where he was born January 7, 1858, and educated at the common schools and academy. He has always been a resident of Newtown, and has followed the business of hotel keeping, his hostelry being one of the best known in southwestern Connecticut. He has held the esteem of his fellow-townsman to a great degree, having been town clerk since 1887, registrar of voters, clerk of the probate court, representative in the lower house of the legislature in 1885, and

M. J. HOULIHAN.

senator from the district in 1891. During this latter term he was chairman of the labor committee and of the committee on military affairs. Mr. Houlihan has always been a democrat, and for the last three campaigns has been upon the state central committee of that party, and during the campaign of 1890 was on the executive committe, representing Fairfield county. His wife was Annie M. Slavin, and he has two children. He is prominently connected with the Knights of Columbus, the Foresters, and the Brotherhood of Elks. He is in religious belief and membership a Catholic. Mr. Houlihan is one of the most popular men in the democratic wing of the senate. He is proverbial for his hospitality, which was very gracefully extended to his colleagues of the senate at a reception held by him at his hotel in Newtown last February, and greatly enjoyed by his distinguished guests.

WILLIAM B. SPRAGUE, Andover: Farmer.

William B. Sprague of Andover represented the twenty-third senatorial district in the state senate during the session of 1889, being chairman of the important committees on agriculture and labor. In both of these positions his services were of great value to the working classes. He is a republican in politics, and has held important local offices, including that of first selectman and town agent. He is one of the trustees of the Storrs Agricultural School, and a member of the building committee, and superin-

W. B. SPRAGUE.

tended the building of the new school buildings which were built in 1890. He is also superintendent and treasurer of the Andover Creamery Company. Ex-Senator Sprague is a member of the First Ecclesiastical society in Andover. He is the owner of Maple Grove Farm, and is the master of the Andover Grange. His business pursuits have required him to travel extensively through the south and west. He was formerly connected with the newspaper advertising department of the firm of Dr. J. C. Ayer & Co. of Lowell, Mass. The senator was born in Andover, May 6, 1849, and was educated in the public schools and at the Natchaug High school in Willimantic. His father was Benjamin Sprague, who represented the town of Andover in the legislature in 1857; and the Rev. Dr. William B. Sprague, for forty-one years the pastor of the Second Presbyterian church in Albany, N. Y., was his uncle. He was formerly a resident of Manchester, living in that town for four years and a half. He was married Nov. 19, 1872, to Miss Lizzie S. Lathrop, who is still living.

T. W. HANNUM, Hartford. Principal of Hannum's Hartford Business College.

T. W. Hannum was born in central New York, town of Preble, Cortland county. His parents were born in New England, his father in Massachusetts, his mother in Connecticut.

His father, though not a college graduate, taught school while a young man, and also evening classes in singing. He was one of the earliest abolitionists, and at one time was the only one in the town where he lived. When the subject of this sketch was ten years old, the family moved to the adjoining town of Homer,

'T. W. HANNUM.

where he grew to early manhood, attending the common school summer and winter, until he was sixteen, and winters only, afterwards, for two or three years. In the public schools he was specially commended for his improvement in penmanship when the committeemen came around on their annual tour of examination. Being skillful in making and mending the quill pens that were formerly in use, he had considerable of this part of the teacher's work to do. The last two years before he was of age he was engaged in mechanical work with his father, who was a fine mechanic, and was paid wages during his twenty-first year. While thus engaged, every newly-planed board offered an invitation to indulge his taste for penmanship, which he accepted, and with chalk or pencil covered its surface with off-hand letters.

In those days he attended evening singing schools, and readily learned to read music. While at his daily work he used to indulge his fancy by seeing himself, in imagination, as a teacher of singing schools and leader of choirs, which was afterwards realized to some extent. At this time he also undertook the construction of a violin, but gave it up for want of proper facilities. These things are mentioned as showing how the dreams of youth are often prophetic of what is realized in later years. About this time he became a Christian, and joined a Congregational church. Having a desire to extend his education as a means of usefulness, he started, with money that he had earned, in company with the son of a neighboring abolitionist, for New York Central College, an institution that had been recently founded, at McGrawville, upon anti-slavery principles, and on the same plan as Oberlin College. This classmate was M. E. Cravath, who afterwards became a minister, and later president of Fisk University. The

principles and spirit which brought the college into existence were naturally shared by the students who were drawn to it, who were of an unusually thoughtful class. Among them was a talented sister of Gen. J. R. Hawley. While in attendance at the college he found time to take lessons in instrumental music and in penmanship, two branches in which he felt an especial interest. At vacation he extended his lessons in penmanship by taking what was called a teacher's course. He made such proficiency in the art that at the end of his course he went home to instruct neighborhood classes in penmanship. In his morning class were sisters of F. C. Carpenter, who has since become famous as the painter of " Lincoln and his Cabinet." To the evening class came loads of young men and women riding in lumber wagons, with their hay racks on, as they had been used in the fields during the day.

On his return to college he was employed by the faculty to instruct students in the preparatory department; at the same time he instructed others on his own account, by which he more than paid his college expenses. After a year and a half at the college, finding that the change from physical exercise to the confinement of study was impairing his health, he decided to give up attendance at the college and do what good he could in the world as a teacher.

While at the college, and in vacations, he had given lessons in vocal music, which he thought to make his life work, in preparing for which he afterwards spent a good deal of time and money. But finding himself adapted to teaching penmanship, and successful in it, he continued in that work. Early in his experience as a teacher he found a way to relieve students of rigidness in the arm, wrist, hand and fingers, which has proved invaluable to hundreds of business men. After teaching a few years in some of the large villages and small cities of southern and western New York, finding that in each place where he taught he had to contend with the influence of incompetent and unprincipled teachers who had preceded him, he decided to locate in some city large enough to sustain a teacher continuously, and chose Hartford as the city. Here he opened a school for instruction in penmanship alone, at first, afterwards was associated with teachers of other commercial branches, and was engaged as a special teacher in several of the public schools.

About the time of the commencement of the civil war, Bryant & Stratton opened a business college in Hartford, which was a link in the chain of fifty or more business colleges known as " The Bryant & Stratton Chain." Mr. Hannum was engaged to conduct the department of business penmanship and correspondence, and to take charge of the college paper which was published in the interest of the institution. After a few years Mr. Stratton, who was the traveling member of the firm, died; and just before his death most of the colleges were sold to the resident principals. About this time Mr. Hannum left the college and established what was known as Hannum's Commercial School. The Bryant & Stratton college was discontinued after a few months, leaving Mr. Hannum in sole possession of the field. He was assisted at first in the bookkeeping department of his school by a brother of Judge Carpenter, and was afterwards associated with the late Prof. H. F. Klinger, who was a thorough scholar and capable teacher. In 1876 the school was removed to the new Batterson building, corner of Asylum and High streets, enlarged and changed to a regular business college, which took the name of Hannum's Hartford Business College. Mr. F. A. Stedman, who after five years' experience in business had taken a course at the former school, and developed an unusual talent for bookkeeping and mathematics, was employed, first as an assistant, and afterwards became a partner and associate principal. The college had a steady growth from the first, which has been largely increased during the last few years. Mr. Hannum is an educator in the best sense of the word. About the time of his coming to Hartford he became acquainted with the principles of Pestilozzian teaching, which he has applied, as far as practicable, to his teaching of commercial branches. He draws out the minds of his students and helps them to a true and harmonious development of their powers, and thus assists them to make the most of themselves. He has always taken a great interest in young people who show that they have a purpose in what they do, and a desire to make the most of their opportunities for improvement. Hundreds who are now holding prominent positions got their start by the help of his training. Last year (1890) he delivered the address on "Business Correspondence" at the twelfth annual meeting of the Business Educators' Association of America, held at Chautauqua, N. Y.; this year he is to speak on "First Lessons in Penmanship," at the same place.

Mr. Hannum is a member of the Fourth Congregational church, of which he has been a deacon about twenty years.

When a boy he learned to play the violin, and has always taken much interest in the instrument. In 1874 he saw the late Dr. S. G. Moses making a violin, and said to the doctor, "I wish I could make a violin." The doctor told him he could, and that he would assist him if he needed assistance. With the doctor's help he made one, and while away on a vacation made another. After he had made three or four, the doctor said to him one day, "I have been looking over your last violin, and

have made up my mind that if you continue making violins you will some day make as good ones as have ever been made." At first the difference in tone of violins which looked alike was a perfect mystery; but he had the patience to work out the problem, point by point, until the making of a first-class instrument was mastered. In spare moments, on Saturdays, and during vacations he has made fifty-three violins. His instruments have attracted much attention and are highly prized by those who own them. One of them was owned by the late G. Edward Bishop, violinist and teacher, who was well known in Hartford; he became so attached to this violin that in his last sickness he kept it within reach on his bed, and at his funeral it was placed upon his coffin. Having made violins as a recreation, and not as a business, his aim has been to make as perfect an instrument as possible, in all respects. In addition to beauty of form, he has succeeded in putting into them that emotional quality of tone which moves the feelings of both player and listener. He carried the same desire for perfection into his violin work that he has always shown in his teaching, and some who have seen his later instruments think the prediction of Dr. Moses is likely to be verified. It has been said, by one who has looked into the matter thoroughly, that only one or two men in a century combine all the qualifications necessary for the making of a violin that is first-class in all respects. Mr. Hannum had the advantage of a mechanical talent, the use of tools, patience to investigate and caution in working out the results of investigation, sufficient knowledge of the instrument to be a judge of tone, and an eye trained to curves and beauty of form by the work of his profession. He has also had the advantage of examining, from time to time, some of the most perfect instruments of the celebrated Cremona makers, in the collection of Mr. R. D. Hawley of Hartford.

He made the selection of violin wood a careful study, and did not varnish any of his instruments until he had learned the secret of making the finest amber oil varnish, with dragon's blood color incorporated. The increase of his business college work now leaves him but little time for work on violins, but he hopes to be able to make one or two a year in vacations.

Mr. Hannum was married in 1859 to Miss Elizabeth T. Wright, of Elmira, N. Y. There has been but one child, a son, T. W. Hannum, Jr., who is at present in the office of the Connecticut Mutual Life Insurance Company in this city. He inherits musical tastes from both father and mother, is a cultured vocalist, and has for some time taken charge of the music at one of our Congregational churches.

By a strictly temperate life, and attention to matters of health, Mr. Hannum has kept himself young in feeling and appearance. He was never more active, mentally or physically, than at the time this sketch is written.

O. A. HISCOX, WOODSTOCK: Grain and Lumber Dealer.

O. A. Hiscox was born in Woodstock Valley, August 21, 1854, and received a public school and academic education. He is the master of Crystal

Lake Grange, and is the chairman of the republican town committee in Woodstock. He is regarded as one of the most active young republicans in his section of the state. He has held the offices of justice of the peace, constable, and grand juror. In 1883 he was one of the messengers in the House, and in 1886 occupied a similar position in the Senate. He is the owner

O. A. HISCOX.

of saw and grist mills at Woodstock Valley, and is also engaged in farming. Mr. Hiscox is a descendant of the earliest settlers in that locality. His grandfather, Lieutenant David Hiscock, was in the revolutionary army under General Samuel McClellan. Mr. Hiscox was married in 1884, his wife being Miss Lillian E. Briggs of Pomfret. He is a gentleman of great energy and perseverance, and unquestionably has a successful future before him.

CHARLES PHELPS, ROCKVILLE: Lawyer.

Charles Phelps, who holds the Tolland county coronership, and is the city attorney of Rockville under the municipal government, was a mem-

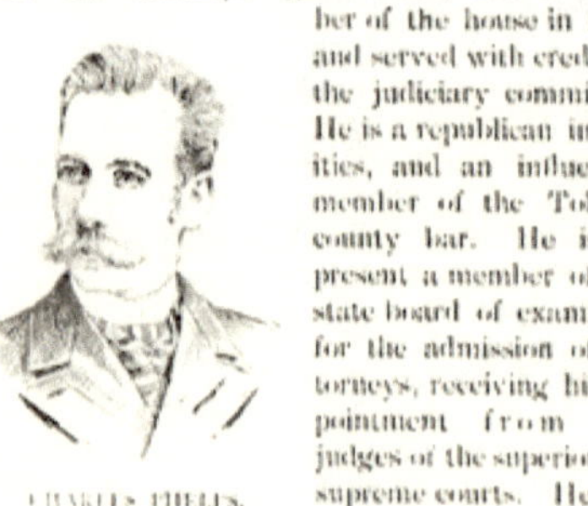

ber of the house in 1885, and served with credit on the judiciary committee. He is a republican in politics, and an influential member of the Tolland county bar. He is at present a member of the state board of examiners for the admission of attorneys, receiving his appointment from the judges of the superior and supreme courts. He is a member of the Methodist

CHARLES PHELPS.

church, and a graduate of Wesleyan University. While in college he was a member of the Psi Upsilon fraternity, and is now connected with the order of Odd Fellows. The wife of Mr. Phelps, who died

Sept. 30, 1888, was Miss Leila L. Bill, daughter of States Attorney Benezet H. Bill, and niece of Judge Loomis of the supreme court. The father of Coroner Phelps was the Rev. B. C. Phelps, a Methodist clergyman, who is still living at the age of eighty years. The subject of this sketch was born in East Hartford, Aug. 10, 1852, and has resided at Wethersfield, East Greenwich, R. I., Middletown, and Rockville. He is a gentleman of superior training, and is held in marked esteem by the members of his profession.

HENRY R. PALMER, STONINGTON: Journalist; on editorial staff of "Providence Journal."

Henry Robinson Palmer is a native of Stonington, and was born Oct. 15, 1867. He is a son of Ira Hart and Harriet Trumbull Palmer, and a direct

descendant of Roger Sherman of Connecticut, who signed the Bill of Rights, the Declaration of Independence, the Articles of Federation, and the Constitution. He is a grandson of the Hon. John F. Trumbull, who was well known throughout the state as an antislavery and early republican leader. Mr. Palmer is also a nephew of Hon. Henry C. Robinson of

H. R. PALMER.

Hartford. He is a prohibitionist in politics, and was nominated for secretary of state by that party in 1890. He received the highest vote of any candidate on the ticket. He has been the president of the Clinton B. Fisk club at Stonington since its organization in 1888, and was the prohibition candidate for the legislature in Stonington the same year. He is a member of the Second Congregational church in that town, member of the Connecticut Society of the Sons of the American Revolution, and of the college Delta Kappa Epsilon fraternity. Mr. Palmer is a graduate of Brown University, receiving his diploma in 1890 a few weeks prior to his nomination for secretary of state. He was chairman, while in college, of the board of editors of *The Brunonian*, and editor-in-chief of *The Brown Magazine*, the literary monthly of the university. He was the class poet of 1890, and a speaker at commencement, and his literary qualities are of a superior order. At graduation he was offered and accepted a position on the editorial staff of *The Providence Journal*, the leading newspaper in Rhode Island, and will probably make journalism his life profession. But few young men in the state possess a brighter future.

B. C. PATTERSON, TORRINGTON: Wholesale and Retail Grain Merchant.

Burton C. Patterson was born in Cornwall, September 10, 1839, and received a common school education. He is engaged in the retail and wholesale lumber trade, in addition to his business as a builder and farmer. He was a member of the legislature in 1884, representing the town of Torrington in the house, and is a republican in politics. He has also been a member of the board of selectmen, and is at present the town auditor. Mr. Patterson is prominently associated with the Patrons of Husbandry, being treasurer

B. C. PATTERSON.

of the Mutual Fire Insurance Company belonging to the order, and is chairman of the State Grange executive committee, and State Grange purchasing agent. He is also a member of the United Order of American Mechanics, and is thoroughly interested in the elevation of the working classes. Mr. Patterson has been married twice. His first wife was Miss Hattie M. Beach, daughter of Amzi Beach of Goshen, Conn. The second wife, who is still living, was Miss Annie M. Merwin, daughter of Samuel T. Merwin of New Milford. There is one son by the first wife and two by the second. Mr. Patterson is connected with the Congregational church in Torrington, where most of his life has been spent.

S. H. SEWARD, PUTNAM: Attorney-at-Law.

Major Samuel H. Seward was in the Fourteenth Connecticut regiment during the war and won a most creditable record in the field. He was wounded four times in action, losing his left arm; and after leaving active service in the field, and in recognition of his gallantry, he received the rank of major and was assigned to the paymaster's department. He is at present one of the leading members of the Grand Army in eastern Connecticut, and during 1886, and again in 1890, was judge advocate of

S. H. SEWARD.

the Department of Connecticut. He was born in Guilford, Conn., April 16, 1835, and was admitted to the bar in New Haven county in 1869. The most of his professional life has been spent at Stafford and Putnam. Since 1885 he has been the clerk of courts for Windham county. In 1881 he represented Putnam in the legislature, winning more than commonly falls to the lot of members during the first session. He was an able debater on the floor and his influence was felt from the beginning to the end of the legislative proceedings. Major Seward is a descendant of William Seward, who emigrated from England to Lowell, Mass., prior to 1643 and removed to New Haven in 1651. Soon afterwards he settled in Guilford, where the family has been represented from that time till now. The grandfather of Major Seward, Timothy Seward, was a soldier of the revolution. The wife of the major, who is still living, was Miss Sarah M. Watson of Beloit, Wis. There is one son, who is now engaged in business in California, being located at San Francisco. Major Seward is a republican in politics and a member of the Congregational church.

WILFRED HOPKINS NETTLETON, BRISTOL: Manufacturer of Clock Parts and Sewing Machines.

W. H. Nettleton was born in Waterbury, June 2, 1825. After attendance at the public schools of Waterbury and Bristol, to which latter place his parents removed when he was twelve years old, he went to work in a clock factory at the age of seventeen, engaging to remain for one year at eight dollars per month and board. After the expiration of his apprenticeship he entered into a contract to make certain parts of clock movements. In the execution of this contract he conceived the idea of automatic machinery for

W. H. NETTLETON.

making the "pillars," "shafts," and "arbors," and by patience and perseverance succeeded in perfecting machines, and obtaining patents thereon, which saved about one-half the labor and performed the work much better than by the old hand method. For many years he supplied nearly all the clock manufacturers in the country with those parts; also with the finer wire-work which regulates the striking part of the clock movement, called "lock-work," using on an average about half a ton of clock wire per day — which will give some idea of the number of clocks made in this country. About the year 1859 he engaged in manufacturing sewing machines in Brattleborough, Vt., with Charles

Raymond, who had been his machinist and inventor for several years. After building up a very profitable business, he sold out, rather than to leave Bristol and his clock business. Soon after, the sewing-machine business was removed to Guelph, Ontario, where Mr. Raymond has been very successful, employing two hundred workmen or more. After prosecuting the clock business in Bristol about twenty-five years, Mr. Nettleton sold out, on account of poor health, to George A. Jones, of New York, who removed to Bristol and conducted the business.

Mr. Nettleton is married. His wife was Miss Harriet Newell Tuttle. They have no children. He is a member of the Bristol Congregational church, and of the republican party. He is a director in the Bristol National Bank, and has been since its incorporation. He has social connections with the Republican League Club of New Haven and with the Masonic fraternity.

SAMUEL L. BLOSS, BETHLEHEM: Farmer.

Mr. Bloss is a native of Bethlehem, and was born July 1, 1826. His education was in the common and high schools of Bethlehem and Woodbury,

S. L. BLOSS.

and he has followed agricultural pursuits. He held a military commission as lieutenant in the cavalry in the old "training days" of 1842–43. He is a democrat, and was appointed a justice of the peace when quite a young man, trying a large proportion of the cases in the town. He has been often honored by the votes of his townsmen, and has held nearly every office in their gift. In 1860 he was a member of the lower house of the Connecticut legislature, and in 1875 was elected to the state senate. After holding the office of justice of the peace for twenty years, Governor Jewell forwarded to him a commission as notary public, unsought. He has been a member of the Crocodile Club of Hartford county and its vice-president since its organization in 1876. This is a social club of some 300 members, who meet annually in the early part of September at Compounce Lake, in the town of Southington, for a sheep bake or barbecue. He is also a member of the Legislative Club of 1875. Mr. Bloss has been twice married, his second wife, who is still living, being Mary Tyler of Middlebury. He has five children, one son and four daughters, all living. He is connected with the Congregational church. In politics a democrat.

HENRY E. H. GILBERT, COVENTRY: Merchant and Farmer.

Mr. Gilbert was born December 17, 1822, in Mansfield, and received his education at the neighboring school and academies. He then entered his

H. E. H. GILBERT.

father's store, and at the age of eighteen engaged in teaching when his presence was not required upon the farm, which he superintended. In 1859 he removed to Coventry. As a republican he has served in most of the offices in the gift of his townsmen. He was elected to the house of representatives for the sessions of 1868, 1872, and 1883, and in the latter was house chairman of the committee on temperance. He has been a member of the Congregational church for forty years, and for an equal length of time either treasurer or committee of the ecclesiastical societies of North Mansfield and Coventry.

P. B. SIBLEY, BROOKLYN. Deputy Sheriff and Jailer Windham County Jail.

Preston P. Sibley was born in Eastford, June 25, 1840, and received a common school education, following the occupation of farmer and mechanic

P. B. SIBLEY.

for the most part. He resided in Eastford till March, 1881, when he removed to Brooklyn, Ct., and took charge of the jail. While in Eastford he was honored many times by his fellow-citizens, holding various offices within the town and county, and representing the town in the legislature in 1873–74; and is one of the best-known men in eastern Connecticut. He was first appointed deputy sheriff under Prescott May, and reappointed by C. H. Osgood, which position he held until called to take charge of the jail. His services at that institution have been highly appreciated. Although having had no previous experience in prison management, he has proved a valuable officer. His business interests are extensive. He is a director in the Brooklyn Savings Bank, director in the Windham County Fire Insurance Company, and its agent; and secretary, treasurer, and director of the Brooklyn

Creamery Company. He is connected with the Congregational church and society, and is clerk and treasurer for both organizations. He has been connected with the republican party from its organization, has been a member of the State Central Committee, and has always worked for the advancement of its principles. He is a member of the Ancient Order United Workmen. He has a wife and three children. Sheriff Sibley has a host of friends, won by long continued efforts both in public and private business affairs, and is regarded as one of the most genial and companionable of men, and a force in all matters of public progress.

MARTIN H. SMITH, Suffield.

The subject of this sketch, who has been connected with the Travelers Insurance Company of Hartford since 1889, has spent most of his life in educational work. He graduated from Williams College, Williamstown, Mass., in 1857, and spent the following two years as instructor in mathematics at the Connecticut Literary Institute, at Suffield, Conn., where his preparatory course had been pursued. In 1859 he became the principal of the Maysville Literary Institute at Maysville, Ky., an institution chartered with col-

M. H. SMITH.

legiate privileges, and remained there until 1880, when he returned to Suffield, having been elected principal of the institute by the board of trustees. Mr. Smith remained at the head of the school for nine years. Prior to his withdrawal from the position he declined the chief clerkship of the Bureau of Labor Statistics, which was offered to him by Commissioner Hotchkiss. In 1871–2 he was the grand commander of Knights Templar in Kentucky and stands high in Masonry. The wife of Mr. Smith, who is still living, was Miss Nancie G. Thompson, daughter of Hon. E. P. Thompson of East Granby. There are two daughters, one being the wife of Charles L. Spencer of Suffield, and the second is the wife of Elmer E. Bailey and resides at San Mateo, Fla. Mr. Smith has written extensively in connection with his life work. He is a member of the Baptist church and is connected with the republican party. He was born at Suffield, August 5, 1833. His parents were Henry and Lydia Smith. His father was a farmer of moderate means, and the family were held in the most thorough esteem in the community where they resided.

CHARLES H. MAIN, North Stonington. Farmer.

Charles Henry Main, first selectman of the town of North Stonington, has been a member of the legislature through two sessions, the first being in 1883, and the second in 1887. His colleagues from New London county included Colonel Wm. H. Bently and Bryan F. Mahan of New London, N. Douglass Sevin of Norwich, now of the state pharmacy commission, Eben P. Couch of Stonington, the Hon. Stephen A. Gardner of New London, and E. Burrows Brown of Stonington. He has been a member of the

C. H. MAIN.

board of selectmen for nine years, and belongs to the democratic party. He is connected with the Baptist church, and occupies a leading position in the denomination. Mr. Main has been married twice. The first wife was Miss Louisa Miner, who died September 12, 1875. The second wife was the twin sister of the first, Lovisa Miner, and is still living. There are four children in the family. Mr. Main was born January 3, 1837, and received a common school education. His business is that of a farmer.

NORMAN A. WILSON, Harwinton: Farmer.

Norman Addison Wilson is a descendant of Rev. John Wilson, who emigrated from Windsor, England, and was the first one of the name in New England, arriving in Boston in 1630. The subject of this sketch was born in Harwinton, December 16, 1819, and received an academic education, completing his studies in Western Reserve College in Ohio. Mr. Wilson has been engaged in farming and the lumber trade, and is a prominent business man in his locality. With the exception of one year,

N. A. WILSON.

which was spent as a book agent in the South, Mr. Wilson has resided at Harwinton. He was married June 30, 1841, his wife being Miss Harriett Latham Griswold, only daughter of Oliver Griswold of Windsor. She was born May 7, 1819. The golden wedding of Mr. and Mrs. Wilson occurred in June of this year. There are six children in the family, four sons and two daughters. One daughter died in September, 1890. Mr. Wilson has held numerous town offices, including that of grand juror for nine years, first selectman for eight, justice of the peace for twenty, and registrar of births, deaths, and marriages for ten. He has been a trial justice for a great many years, and his aim has always been to do to others as he would like to be done by. He is at present a commissioner of the superior court, and has been a member of the board of relief. In 1869 he was a member of the general assembly from Harwinton, serving as a republican in that body. He was an original member of the know nothing party in this state. His religious connections are with the Congregational church. Mr. Wilson is a valued correspondent of several Litchfield county papers, and is held in high esteem in the community where he resides.

REV. R. P. STANTON, Norwich: Congregational Clergyman.

Rev. Robert Palmer Stanton was born in Belchertown, Mass., January 20, 1818, and was educated at Monson Academy and Yale College, graduating from the latter institution in 1843. His classmates included the Hon. Benj. T. Eames of Providence, R. L. W. L. Kingsley of New Hampshire, W. W. Atterbury of New York, E. W. Gilman of New York, the Hon. Gardner Greene of Norwich, Rev. Sylvester Hine of Hartford, and Rev. Geo. A. Bryan of Scotland. After completing his college course Mr. Stanton grad-

uated from the Theological Seminary and was settled as pastor of the Presbyterian church at Cohoes, N. Y., remaining there for five years. He then accepted a pastorate in Derby and was called from that town to the pastoral charge of the Fourth Congregational church in Norwich which he occupied for twenty-four years. He still resides in Norwich and preaches frequently, but is without pastoral charge. In 1852 he was a delegate to the general assembly of the Presbyterian church of the United States from the Presbytery of Albany, and was a delegate to the National Congregational Council from the New London Association in 1886. He is a member of the Eastern Connecticut Congregational Club. Mr. Stanton is a republican in politics. His wife, who is still living, was Miss Harriet Jones, daughter of Dr. Timothy Jones of Southington. There are two daughters. Mr.

Stanton has been a school visitor in Norwich for thirty-three years, and is thoroughly interested in educational work.

AARON THOMAS, Thomaston: President Seth Thomas Clock Company.

Aaron Thomas was born in the town of Plymouth, in Litchfield county, March 13, 1830, and received a common school education. He is associated and

closely identified with the extensive clock industries in that locality, and is known throughout the country as the head of the great manufacturing interests which the family have established in Thomaston, the place itself being named in their honor when it was incorporated by the legislature in 1875. Mr. Thomas was born in that part of Plymouth that was included in the new town. He has been prominently identified with local interests during the entire period of his adult life. He is one of the principal managers of the noted Seth Thomas Clock Company and has been its president for the last thirty-two years. In politics Mr. Thomas is a republican; his religious connection is with the Congregational church. His family consists of a wife and three children. The former was Miss Phœbe A. Hine prior to her marriage. Mr. Thomas is one of the most honored and respected citizens of Litchfield county.

WALTER P. WHITE, Putnam: Farmer.

Walter Peregrine White is of the tenth generation in descent from Peregrine White, the first child of European parentage born in New England. He

is a member of Quinnebaug Lodge, No. 106, F. and A. M. of Putnam, also of the American Order of United Workmen, a director of the Putnam Dairy Company, and of the Connecticut Dairymen's Association. He is prominently associated with the Farmers League, being the president of the local and one of the treasurers of the national organization. He has been the first selectman of the town, occupying that office in 1888; and has also held the position of secretary and president of the board of health. He is a member of the Congregational church, and is a republican in politics. June 5, 1890, he was married to Julia Demarest, the only daughter of Abraham Demarest, of the engraving firm of A. Demarest & Son, No. 249 Broadway, New York city. He has served for seven years in Co. G, of the Third regiment, C. N. G., and is a well-known National Guardsman. Mr. White was born in Putnam, May 17, 1859, and received an academic education, completing his course in the Putnam High school. He is engaged in dairying and market gardening.

DEACON THOMAS WATSON, Winsted. (Deceased.)

During the last twenty years of his life, from 1856 to 1876, no resident of Winsted was so conspicuous in some respects as Deacon Thomas Watson. A few of his local cotemporaries were better known to the outside world — Elliot Beardsley, John Boyd, and George Dudley — but in the realm of intellectual activity Deacon Watson possessed characteristics r a r e l y found in the man of business. He was born a farmer's son, and lived at the family homestead in the adjoining town of New Hartford until past

THOMAS WATSON.

fifty years of age, when he removed to Winsted, making the change that he might be relieved from the care of his large farm, and to derive the social advantages a village like Winsted offered; and here, at the age of fifty-five, he engaged in the lumber business. And though he was diligent in it, and gave to it the careful attention which brought him pecuniary success, Deacon Watson was always regarded by those who knew him intimately to have mistaken his calling, either in remaining upon the farm or in engaging in active business. Had a phrenologist indicated the channel in which he would come to his highest usefulness, he would most likely have said it would be through the divinity school. It is said to have been one of the chief regrets of his life that he did not receive a "liberal education." Notwithstanding this lack, however, he was to a greater degree than any townsman of his day a thinker, and might with good reason have been called a Christian freethinker. Although in good standing in the church with which he was connected (Congregational), he refused to be bound by dogmatic utterances of other men, however high they might be in ecclesiastical authority. He reserved for himself the right to be his own interpreter of hidden mysteries, though his uprightness of life and evident honesty of purpose shielded him from the severe criticism of those who held more closely upon the line of commonly-accepted scripture interpretation. He was contemporaneous with Dr. Horace Bushnell, Hartford's noted and much-criticized divine, for whom he had a strong admiration, and of whose writings he was a diligent student. Those of us who can still recall to mind Deacon Watson's gifts as a religious teacher, and his resources in arguing a theological point, cannot but feel that he might have become distinguished as a scholar could he have enjoyed the advantages for study which his mind and heart craved. Politically Deacon Watson was a republican, and represented both New Hartford and Winchester in the general assembly. He was never politically ambitious, however, caring more about being on what he believed to be the right side, and of performing his duties as a citizen in a conscientious and judicious manner, than of being regarded with popular favor. He possessed a keen, Puritanic sense as to the right and wrong of things, which in ante-bellum days led him to become a strong anti-slavery man.

Deacon Watson was born in the western part of New Hartford (Torringford society) in 1800, and died in Winsted March 13, 1876. His widow, a daughter of the late Deacon Elizur Curtis of New Hartford, still survives him (1891), as also do his three daughters — Mrs. Dr. G. B. Miller of Grand Rapids, Mich.; Mrs. Henry Gay of Winsted, and Mrs. Edward R. Beardsley of Hartford.

FRANCIS BROWN, Winsted. (Deceased.)

During the war of the rebellion no resident of Winsted gave evidence of greater regard for her citizen soldiers than did Francis Brown, and his patriotism was of the kind that took firm hold upon his pocketbook as well as his heart. It is still remembered by veterans of the war that when they were starting for "the front" his parting hand-clasp left within theirs generous gifts of money, pressed upon them without ostentation, with the suggestion that it might sometime prove useful. Nor did his sense

FRANCIS BROWN.

of obligation die away the moment peace was restored. The unique memorial tower which to-day is Winsted's most conspicuous feature was made possible by his subscription of $1,000, his gift being supplemented by several thousands more from his generous widow, who still survives him. The story of Mr. Brown's life is full of suggestion and inspiration for young men and boys who aspire to become useful and honored citizens. Told in brief outline it runs as follows: He was born in Hartford, June 30, 1815. At the age of six years his father died, and at eleven he became motherless. He was one of ten children, and was not born "with a golden spoon in his mouth." Not long after the death of his mother he was taken to Norfolk, where he was "bound out" to a relative who was engaged in scythe-making. After a faithful service in that business until about eighteen, he became dissatisfied, having been deprived of schooling and clothing promised him, and decided to "strike out" on his own account. In his passage through Winsted (en route to see his sisters in Hartford, and making the journey on foot, for he started out with but eight cents in his pocket) he called upon Theodore Hinsdale, manager of the Beardsley Scythe Company, hoping to obtain employment. Mr. Hinsdale told the youngster there were no vacant positions there; but, being impressed with the boy's honest face, and his willingness to under-

take any kind of work, he was told that a place would be found for him. The young scythe-maker so grew in the estimation of his employers that at the age of twenty-three he was made foreman of the company, in due time being advanced to the positions of superintendent and president, retiring from the company in 1871, after a service of nearly forty years, having laid aside an ample competence. For several years he received a salary of $3,000 for his services. It should be remembered, however, by all young men who read this sketch that the secret of his successful and honored career was mainly the fact that the welfare of his employers was always his first concern. He did not spend his time clamoring for an eight-hour law; if his services were needed by the company for fifteen hours, they were rendered with cheerfulness. Politically Mr. Brown was a republican, and though never an aspirant for office, he was chosen to represent Winchester in the legislature; on many occasions, however, declining political honors on account of the demands upon his time by his business affairs.

Mr. Brown's death occurred at Saratoga Springs, where he was at the time a temporary visitor, June 1, 1884. His only child, now Mrs. Susan M. B. Perry, survives him, residing in Nichols, Conn.

POSTSCRIPT.

The preparation of the foregoing Sketches was completed and the manuscript placed in the hands of the printer about the first of May. Since that date, until the present completion of the work, the applications for place upon its pages have been so numerous from gentlemen who neglected to respond earlier, and the disappointment occasioned by their necessary denial has been so evident, that the author has been almost compelled in some cases to encourage the hope that a second volume would shortly follow. No final decision favorable to such an undertaking has, however, yet been reached. As the present volume will doubtless come at once under the observation of most persons within the State who have any ambition to appear in a subsequent similar work, this Postscript is introduced here for the purpose of inviting all such to now signify their wishes definitely to the undersigned, with all convenient promptness. If the desire for further biographical work in this line should thus prove as general as many profess to believe it to be, the publication of a second volume would be undertaken without hesitation.

J. A. SPALDING.

Hartford, July, 1891.

9 783337 098315